NAT FOR NOTHING

MARIA SCRIVAN

graphix

An Imprint of

◼ SCHOLASTIC

For the Gremlins
(nice try)

All rights reserved. Published by Graphix, an imprint of Scholastic Inc.,
Publishers since 1920. SCHOLASTIC, GRAPHIX, and associated logos are
trademarks and/or registered trademarks of Scholastic Inc.

The publisher does not have any control over and does not assume any
responsibility for author or third-party websites or their content.

This book is a work of fiction. Names, characters, places, and incidents are
either the product of the author's imagination or are used fictitiously, and any
resemblance to actual persons, living or dead, business establishments,
events, or locales is entirely coincidental.

Library of Congress Control Number: 2021938038

ISBN 978-1-338-71543-9 (hardcover)
ISBN 978-1-338-71542-2 (paperback)

10 9 8 7 6 5 4 3 2 1   23 24 25 26 27

Printed in China 62
First edition, February 2023
Edited by Megan Peace
Book design by Steve Ponzo
Creative Director: Phil Falco
Publisher: David Saylor

CONTENTS

Things	1
Sleep	9
Ex-Best Frenemy	19
Boredom	43
Activities	61
Call It a Draw	65
Art	77
Proposal	91
Gremlins	97
There's No "Us" in "Team"	113
Library	127
Photo Op	141
Advice	149
The Answer	157
Car Wash	167
Talk	173
You Can Do It	181
Presentation	189
Wake Up	199
The Adventures of Supernat and the Comics Caper	213

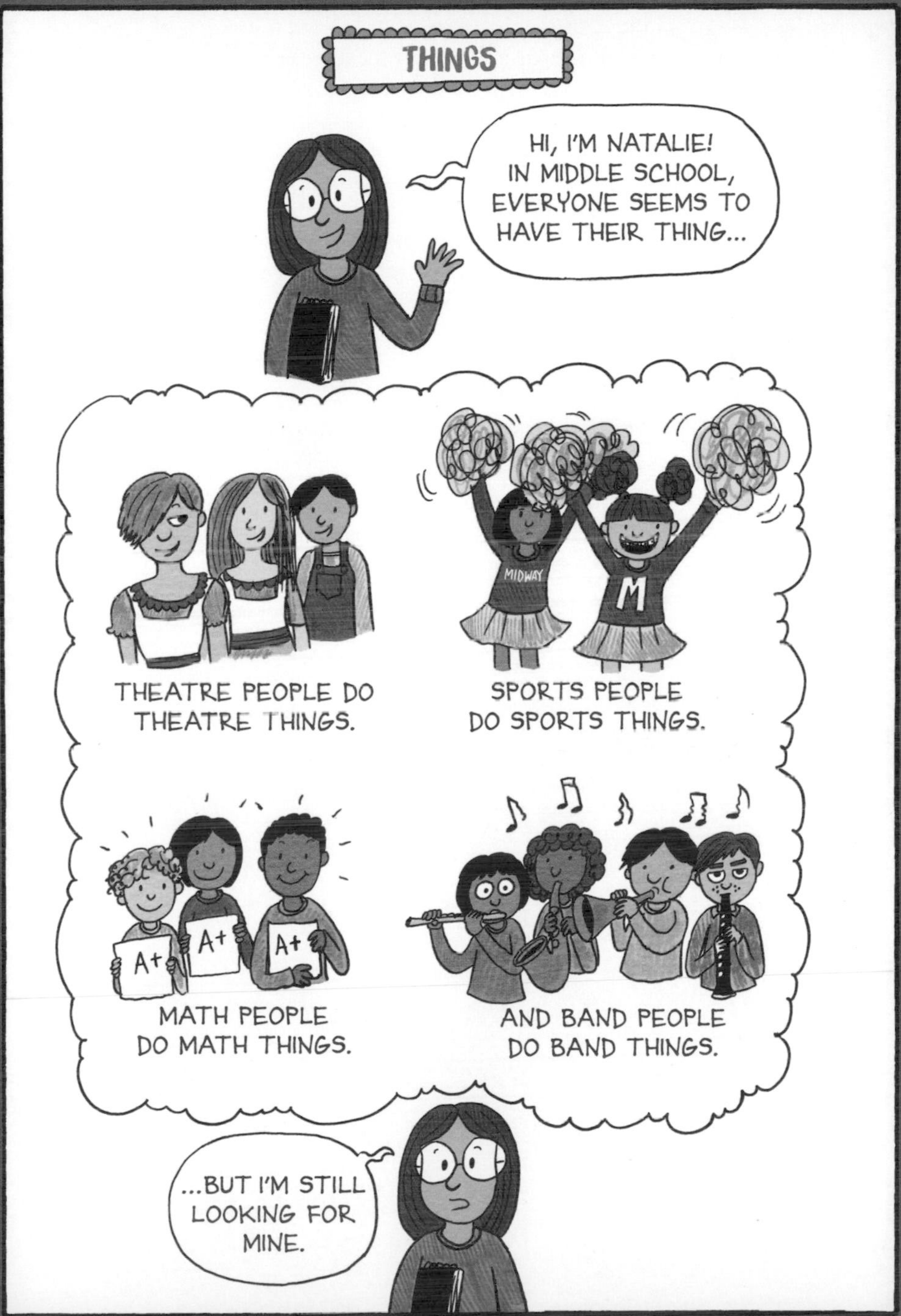
THINGS
HI, I'M NATALIE! IN MIDDLE SCHOOL, EVERYONE SEEMS TO HAVE THEIR THING...
MIDWAY
M
THEATRE PEOPLE DO THEATRE THINGS.
SPORTS PEOPLE DO SPORTS THINGS.
A+
A+
A+
MATH PEOPLE DO MATH THINGS.
AND BAND PEOPLE DO BAND THINGS.
...BUT I'M STILL LOOKING FOR MINE.

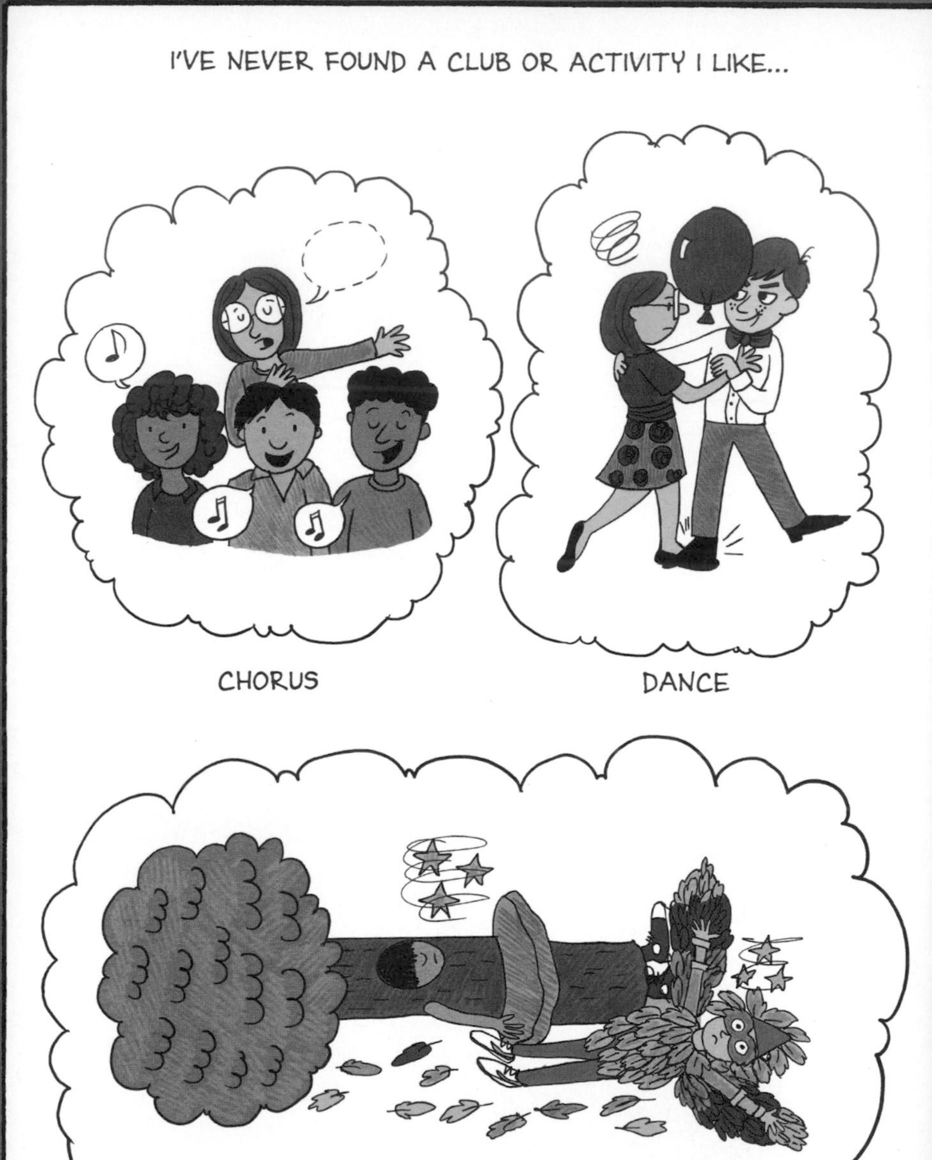
I'VE NEVER FOUND A CLUB OR ACTIVITY I LIKE...
CHORUS
DANCE
THEATRE

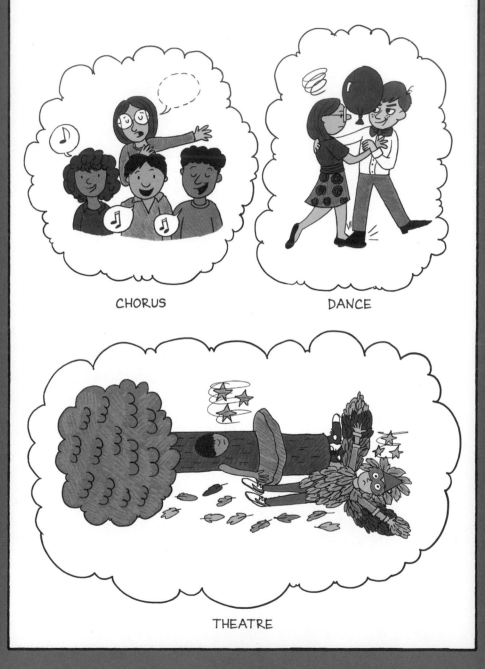

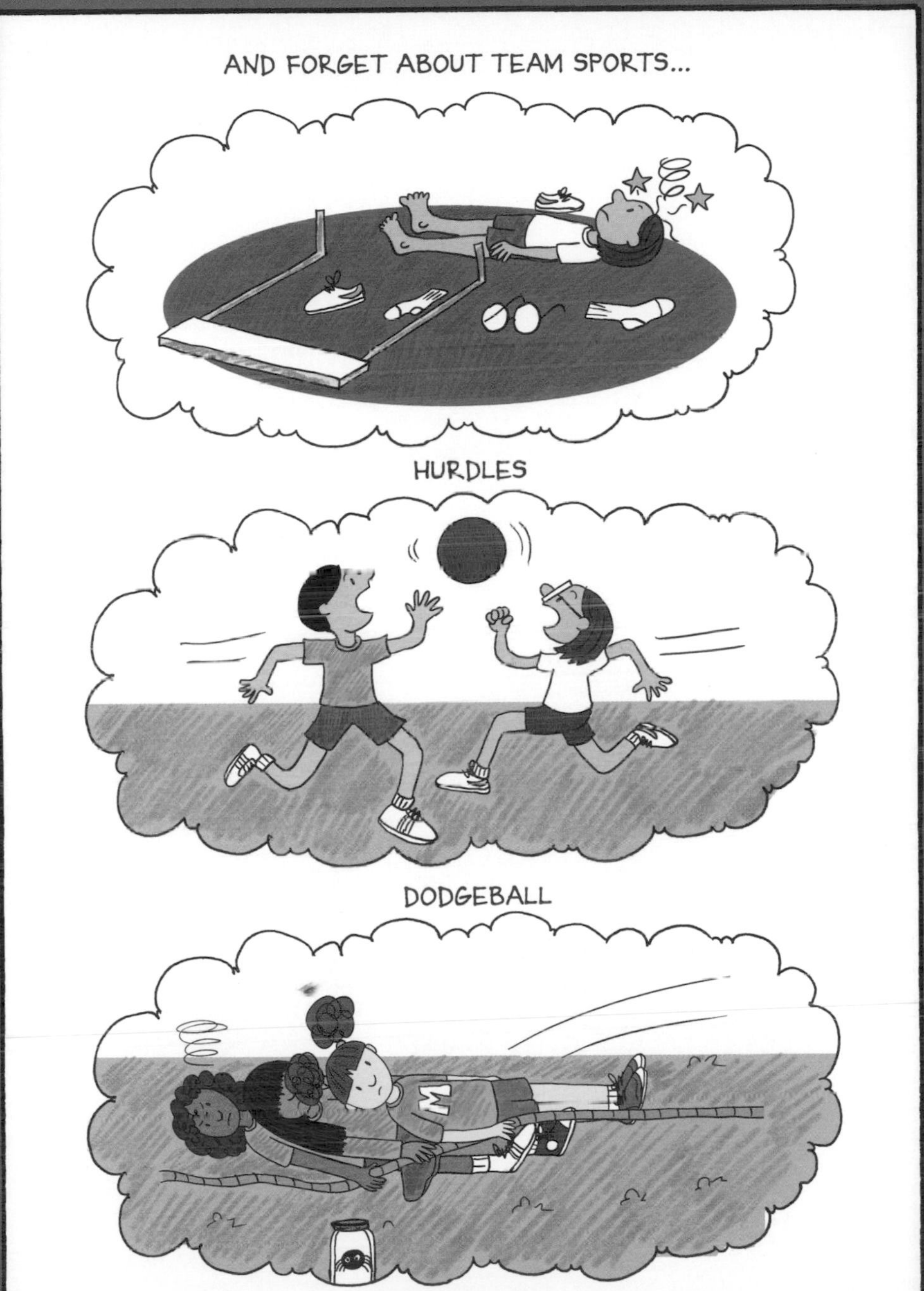
AND FORGET ABOUT TEAM SPORTS...
HURDLES
DODGEBALL
M
TUG-OF-WAR

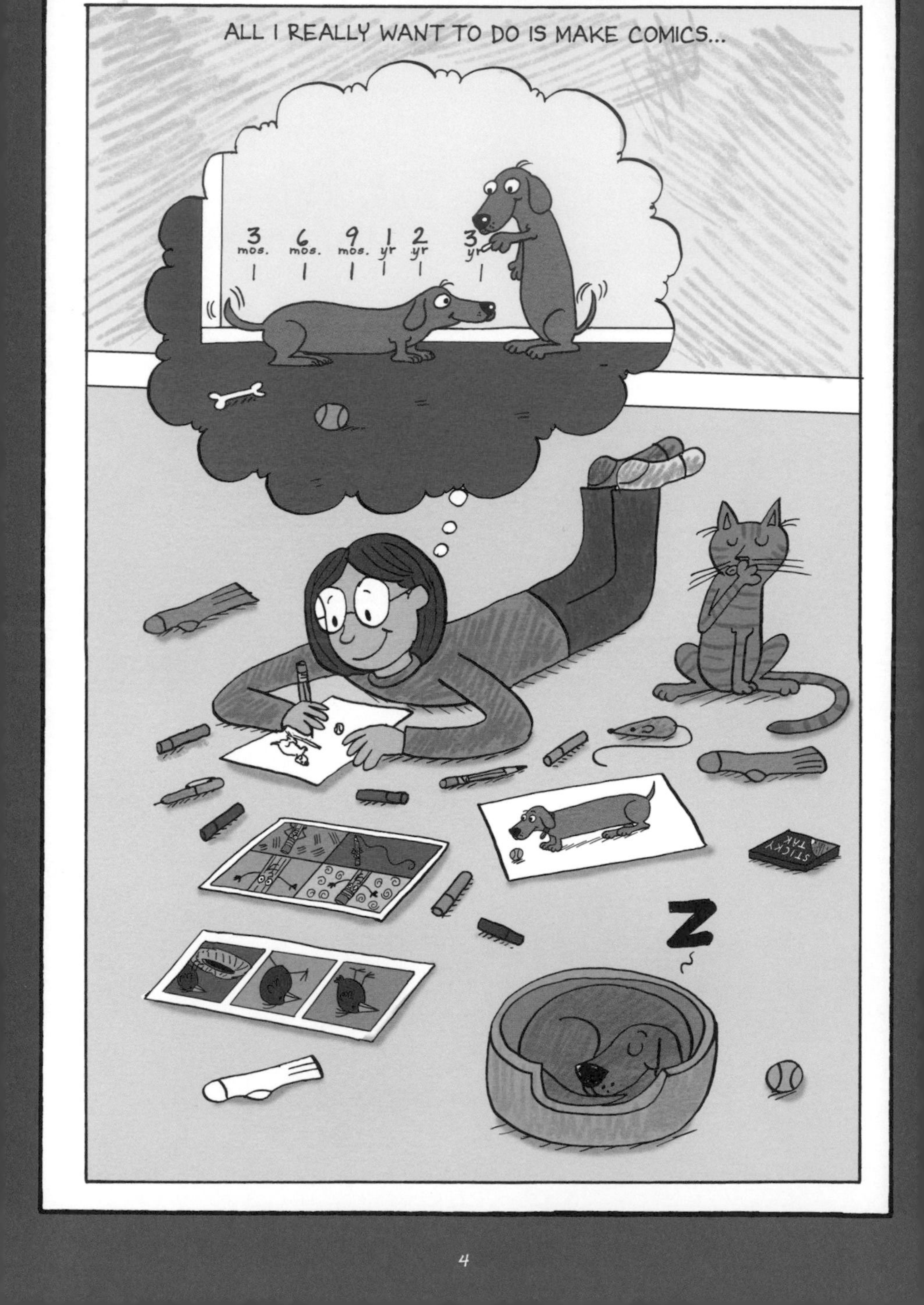
ALL I REALLY WANT TO DO IS MAKE COMICS...
3 mos.
6 mos.
9 mos.
1 yr
2 yr
3 yr
STICKY TAK
Z

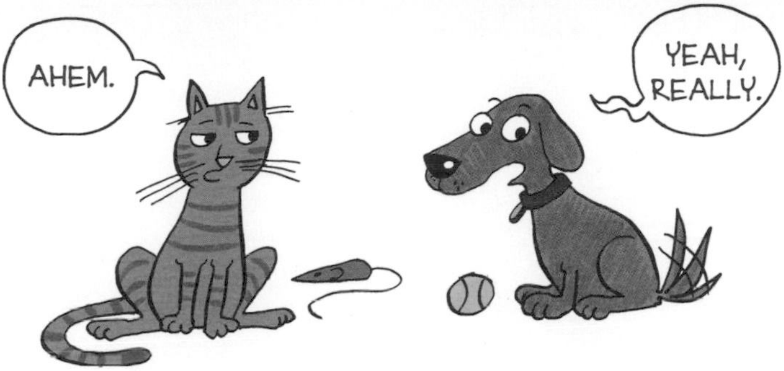
AHEM.
YEAH, REALLY.

...PLAY WITH CAT AND TREAT...

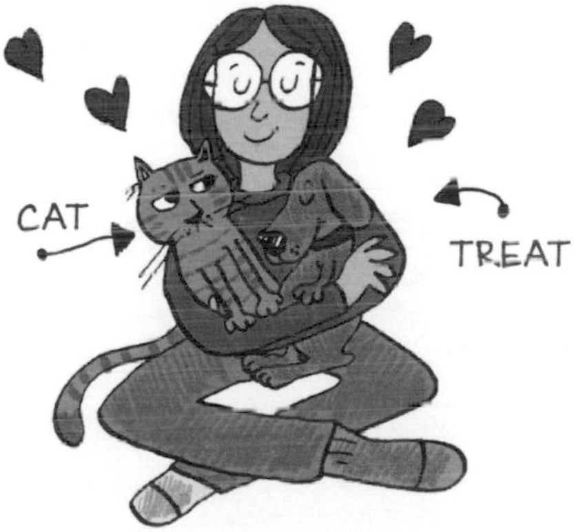
CAT
TREAT

...AND HANG OUT WITH MY FRIENDS.

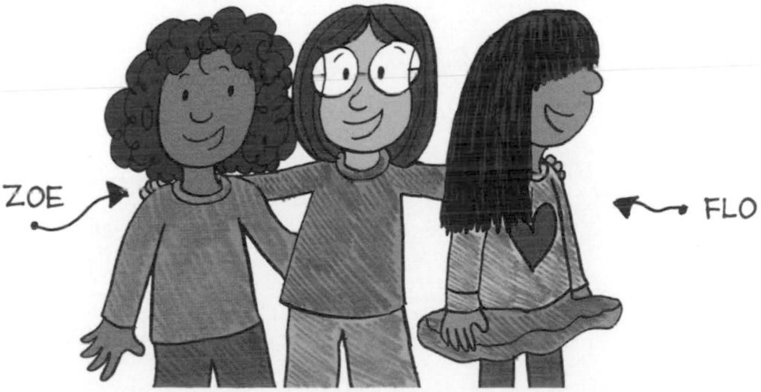
ZOE
FLO

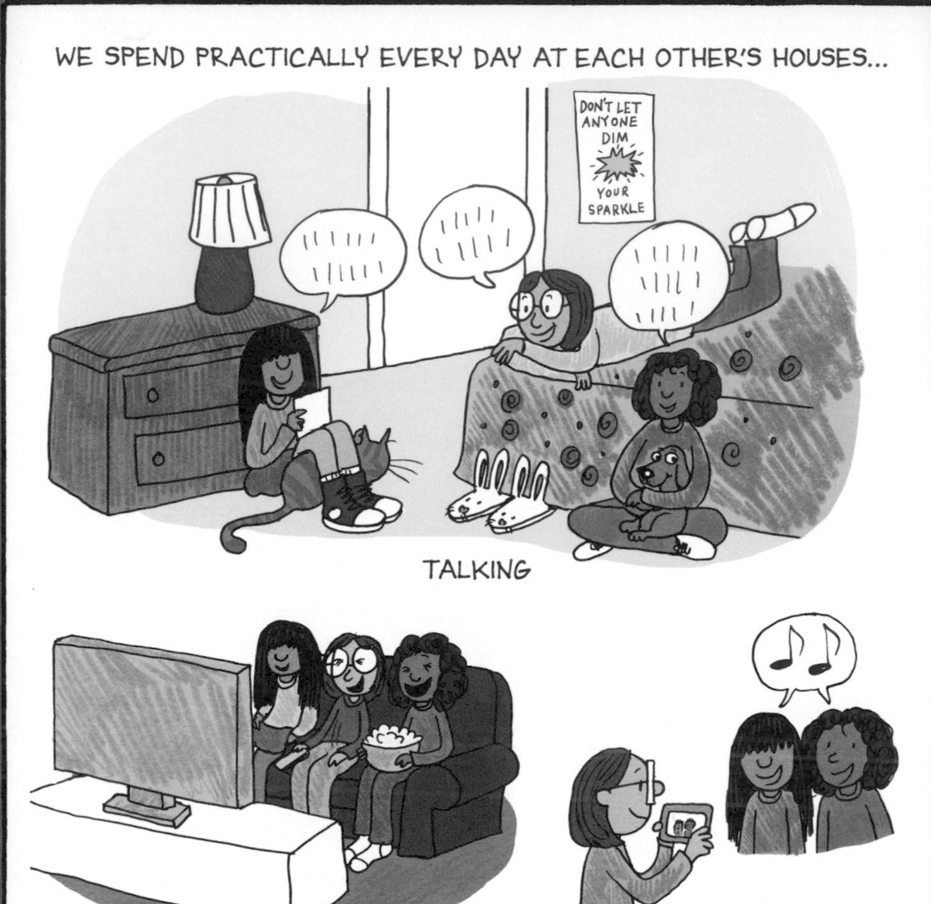
WE SPEND PRACTICALLY EVERY DAY AT EACH OTHER'S HOUSES...
DON'T LET ANYONE DIM YOUR SPARKLE
TALKING
LAUGHING
CREATING
SNACKING

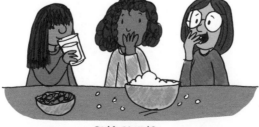

EVEN MY EX-BEST FRIEND AND I ARE GETTING ALONG BETTER.

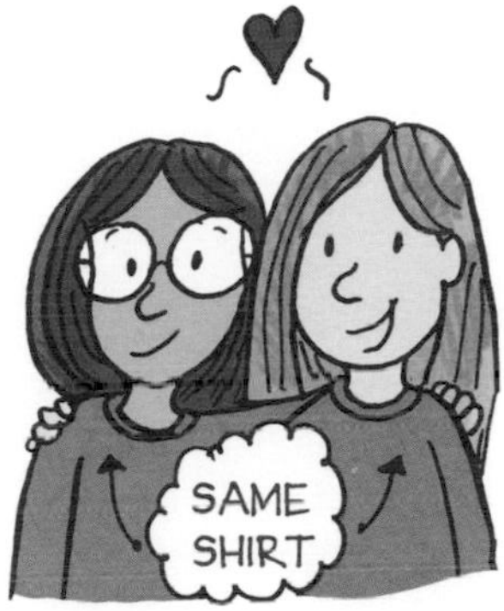
SAME
SHIRT

LILY WAS MY BEST FRIEND

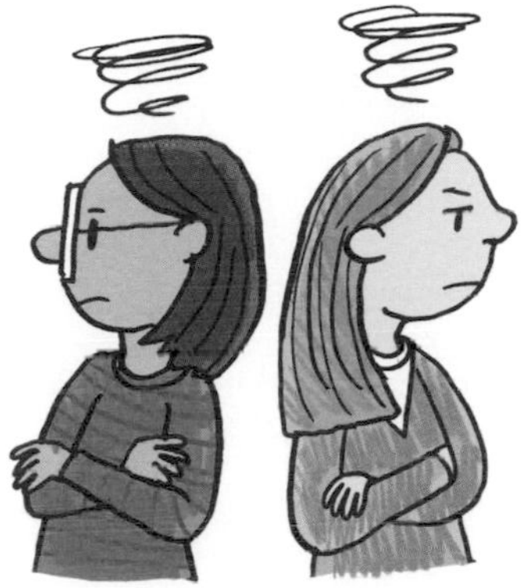

THEN MY EX-BEST FRIEND

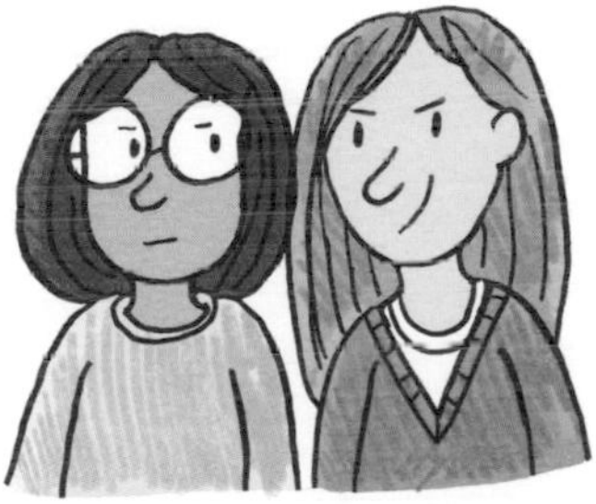

THEN MY FRENEMY

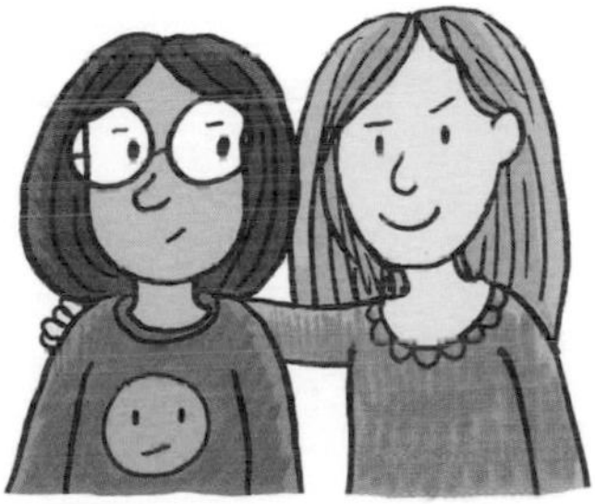

THEN MY BEST FRENEMY

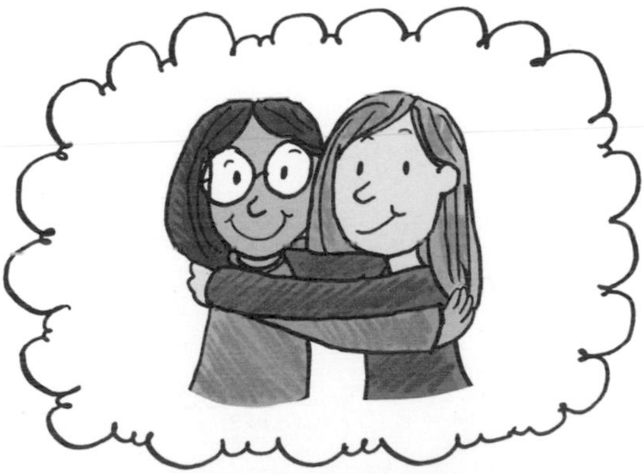

SO I GUESS THAT MAKES HER MY EX-BEST FRENEMY NOW.

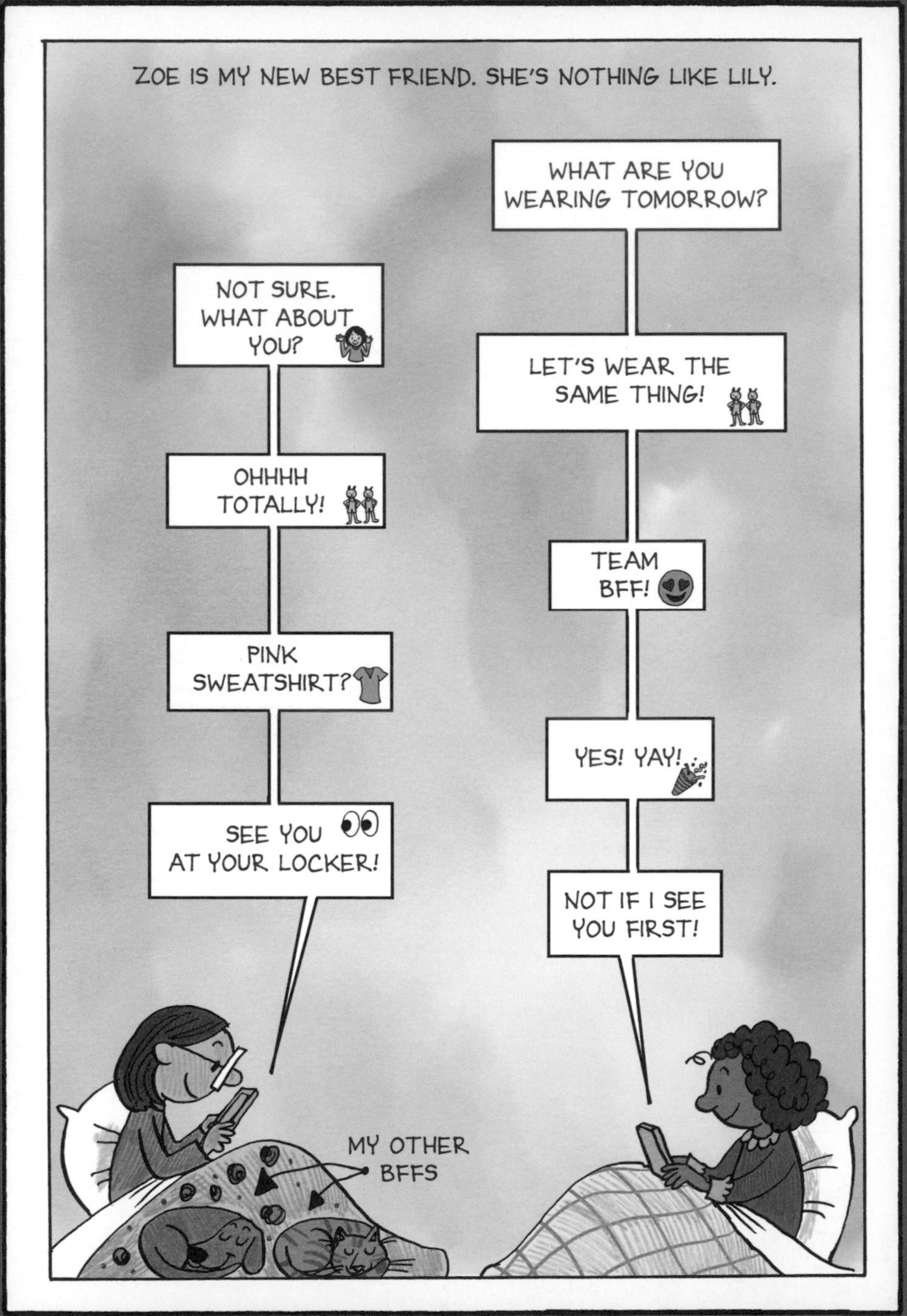
ZOE IS MY NEW BEST FRIEND. SHE'S NOTHING LIKE LILY.
WHAT ARE YOU WEARING TOMORROW?
NOT SURE. WHAT ABOUT YOU?
LET'S WEAR THE SAME THING!
OHHHH TOTALLY!
TEAM BFF!
PINK SWEATSHIRT?
YES! YAY!
SEE YOU AT YOUR LOCKER!
NOT IF I SEE YOU FIRST!
MY OTHER BFFS

CHAPTER 1
SLEEP

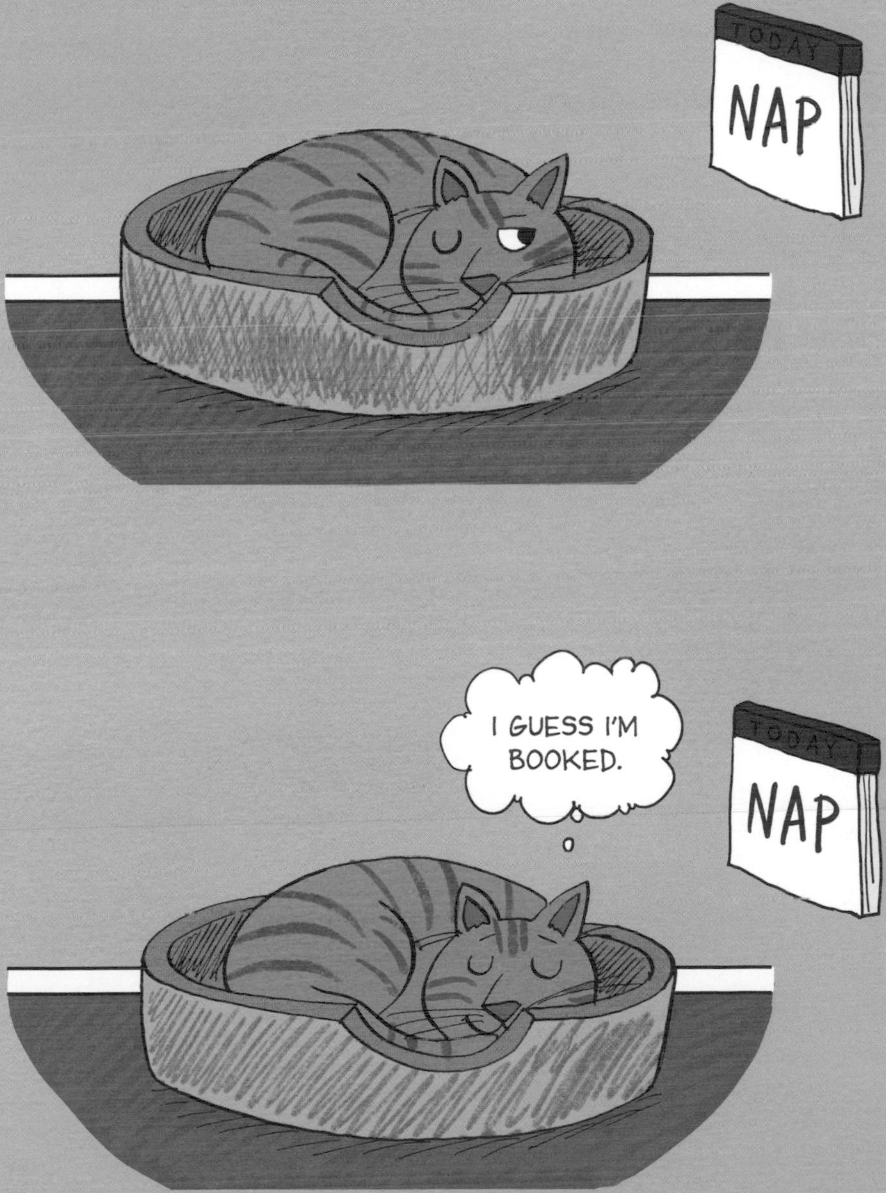
TODAY
NAP
TODAY
NAP
I GUESS I'M BOOKED.

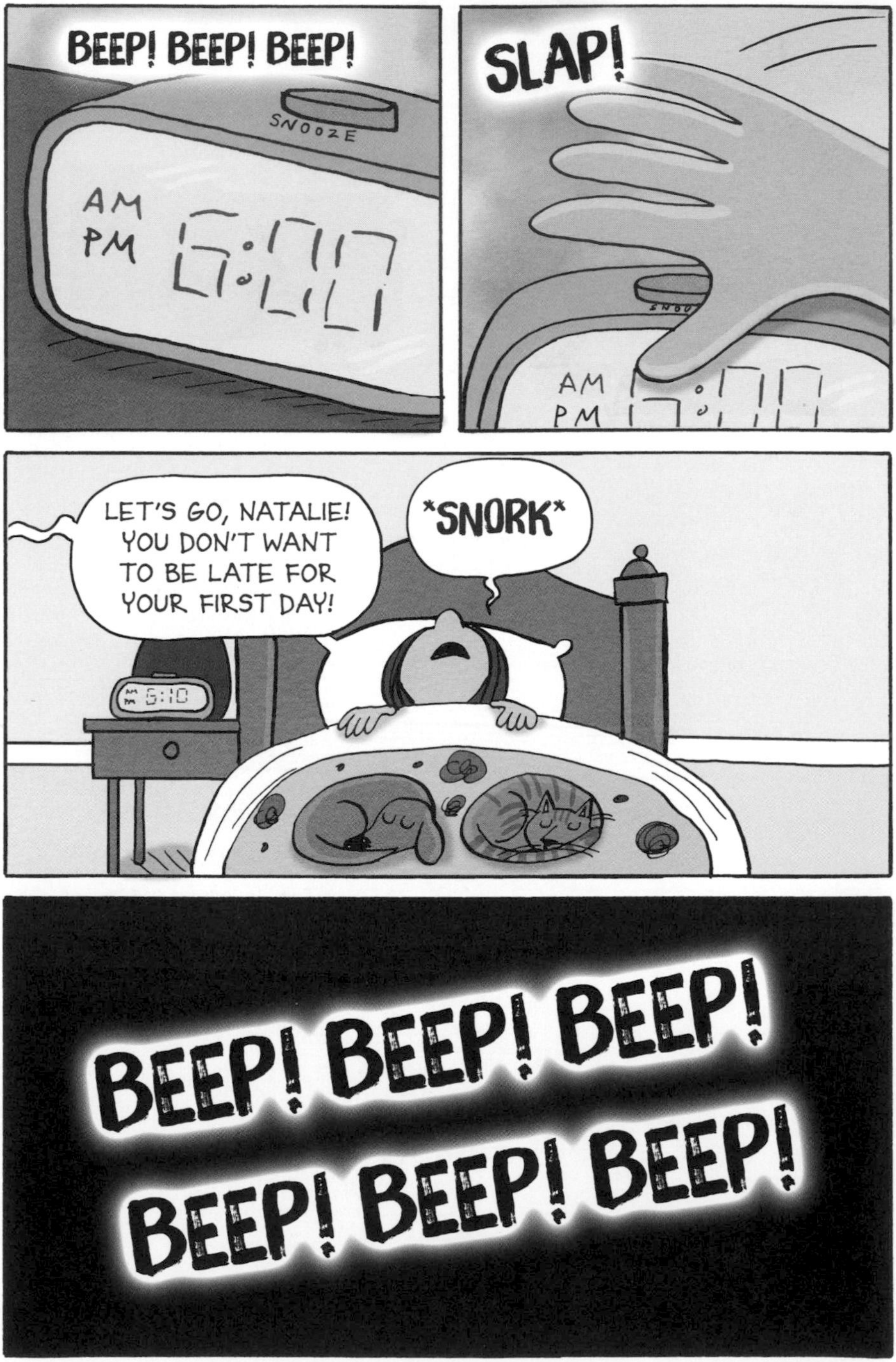
BEEP! BEEP! BEEP!
SNOOZE
AM
PM
6:00
SLAP!
AM
PM
LET'S GO, NATALIE! YOU DON'T WANT TO BE LATE FOR YOUR FIRST DAY!
SNORK
AM
PM
6:10
BEEP! BEEP! BEEP!
BEEP! BEEP! BEEP!

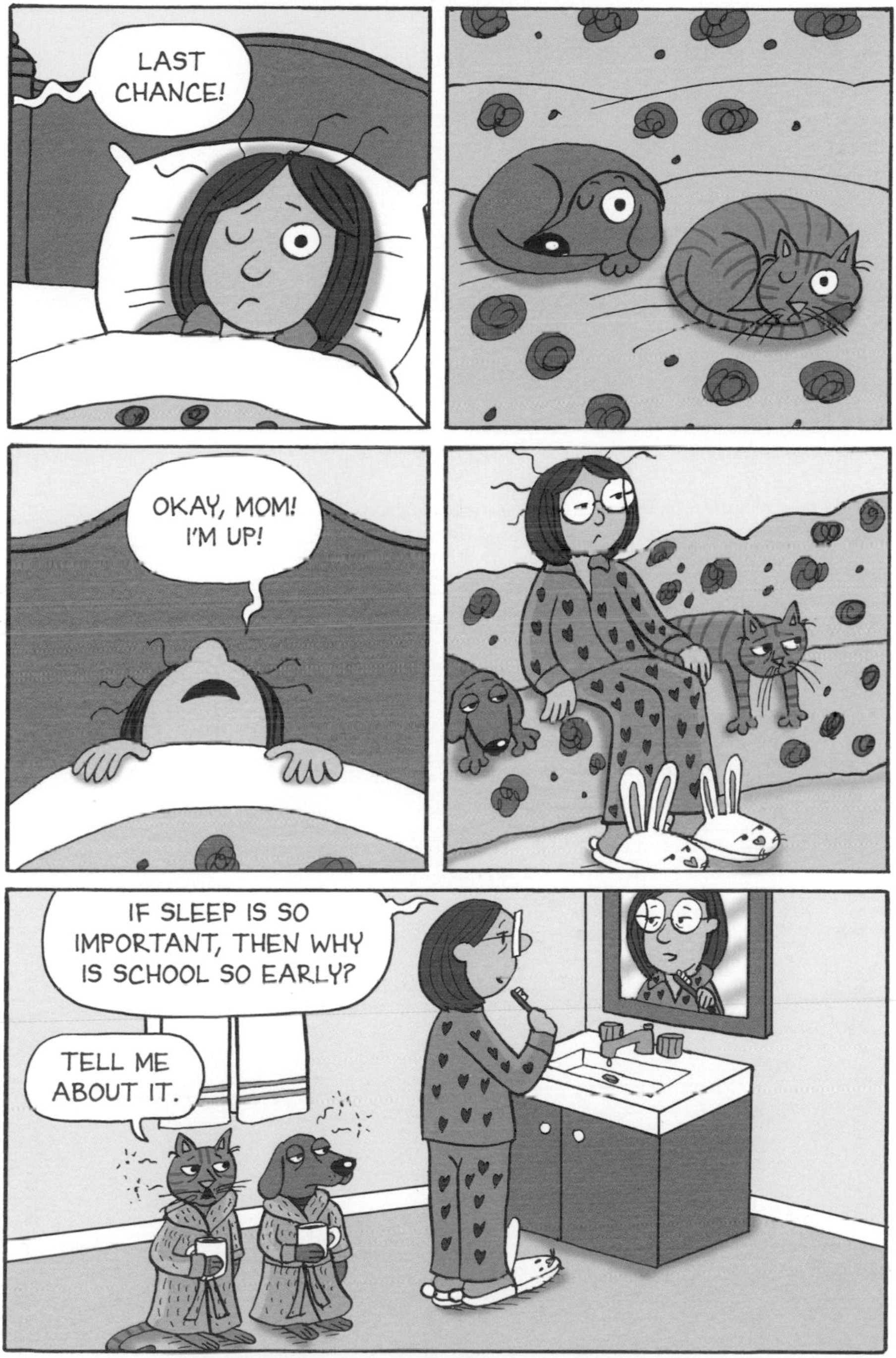
LAST CHANCE!
OKAY, MOM! I'M UP!
IF SLEEP IS SO IMPORTANT, THEN WHY IS SCHOOL SO EARLY?
TELL ME ABOUT IT.

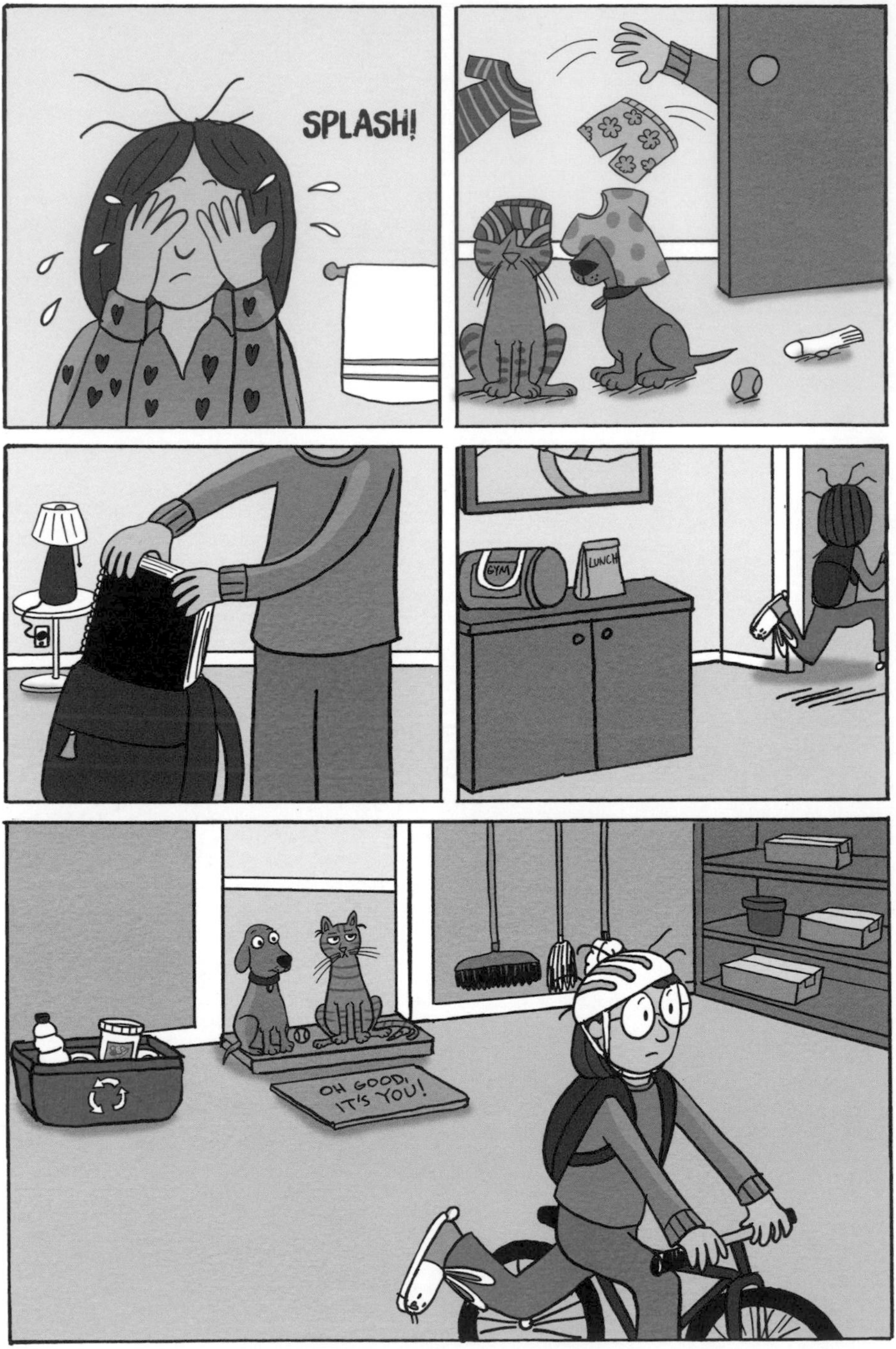
SPLASH!
GYM
LUNCH
OH GOOD, IT'S YOU!

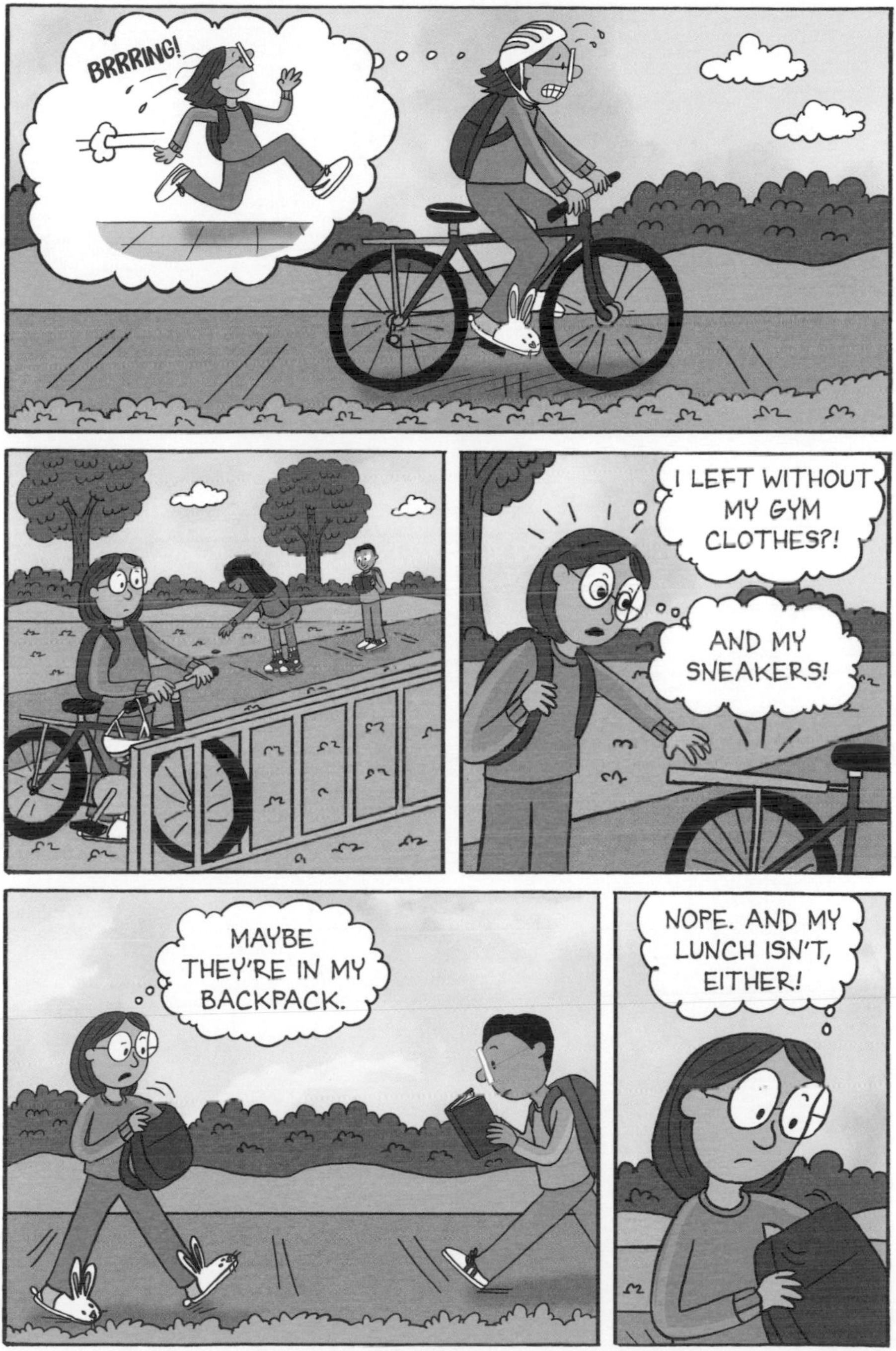
BRRRING!
I LEFT WITHOUT MY GYM CLOTHES?!
AND MY SNEAKERS!
MAYBE THEY'RE IN MY BACKPACK.
NOPE. AND MY LUNCH ISN'T, EITHER!

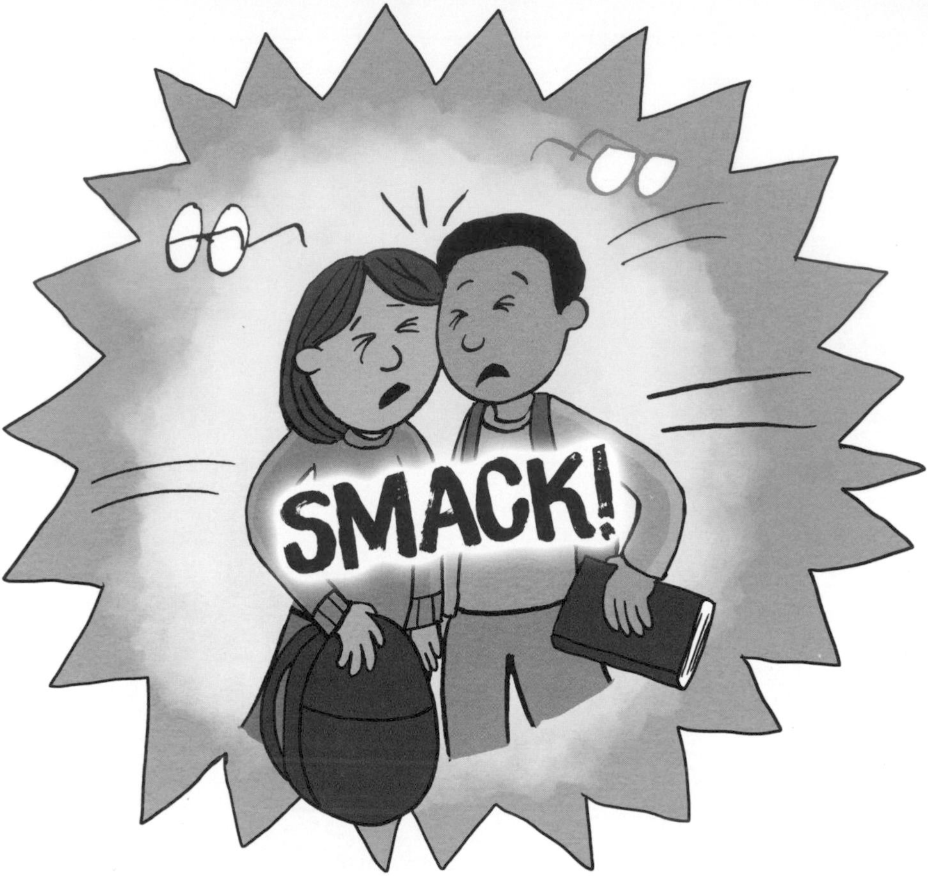
SMACK!

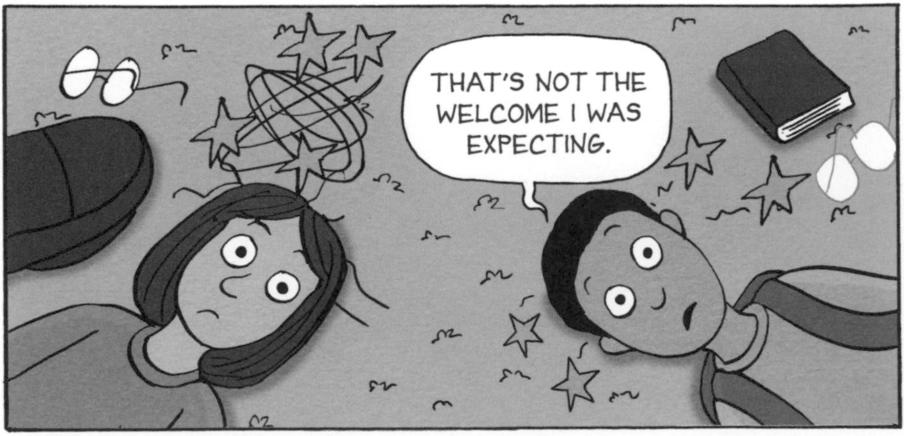
THAT'S NOT THE
WELCOME I WAS
EXPECTING.

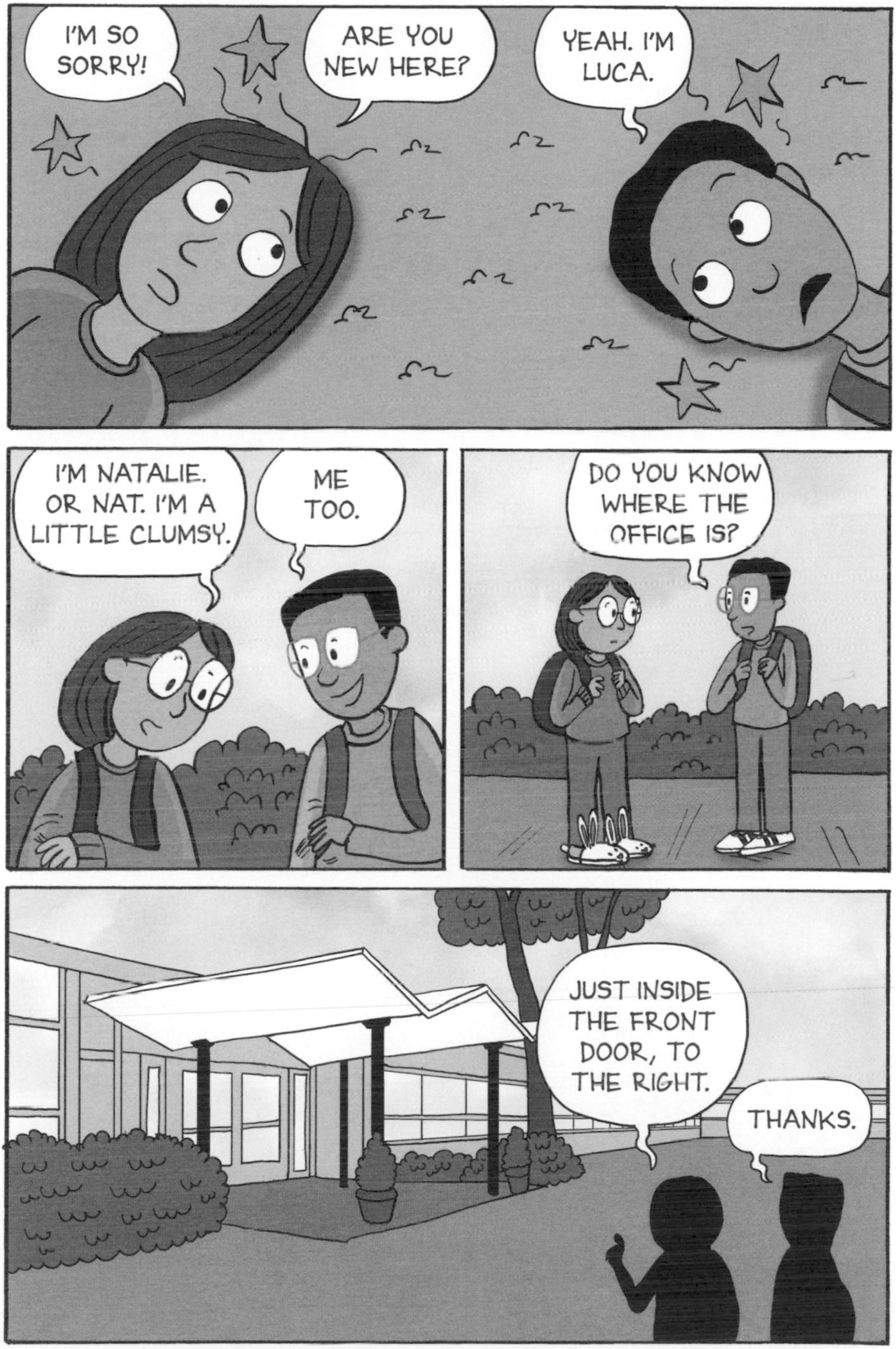
I'M SO SORRY!
ARE YOU NEW HERE?
YEAH. I'M LUCA.
I'M NATALIE. OR NAT. I'M A LITTLE CLUMSY.
ME TOO.
DO YOU KNOW WHERE THE OFFICE IS?
JUST INSIDE THE FRONT DOOR, TO THE RIGHT.
THANKS.

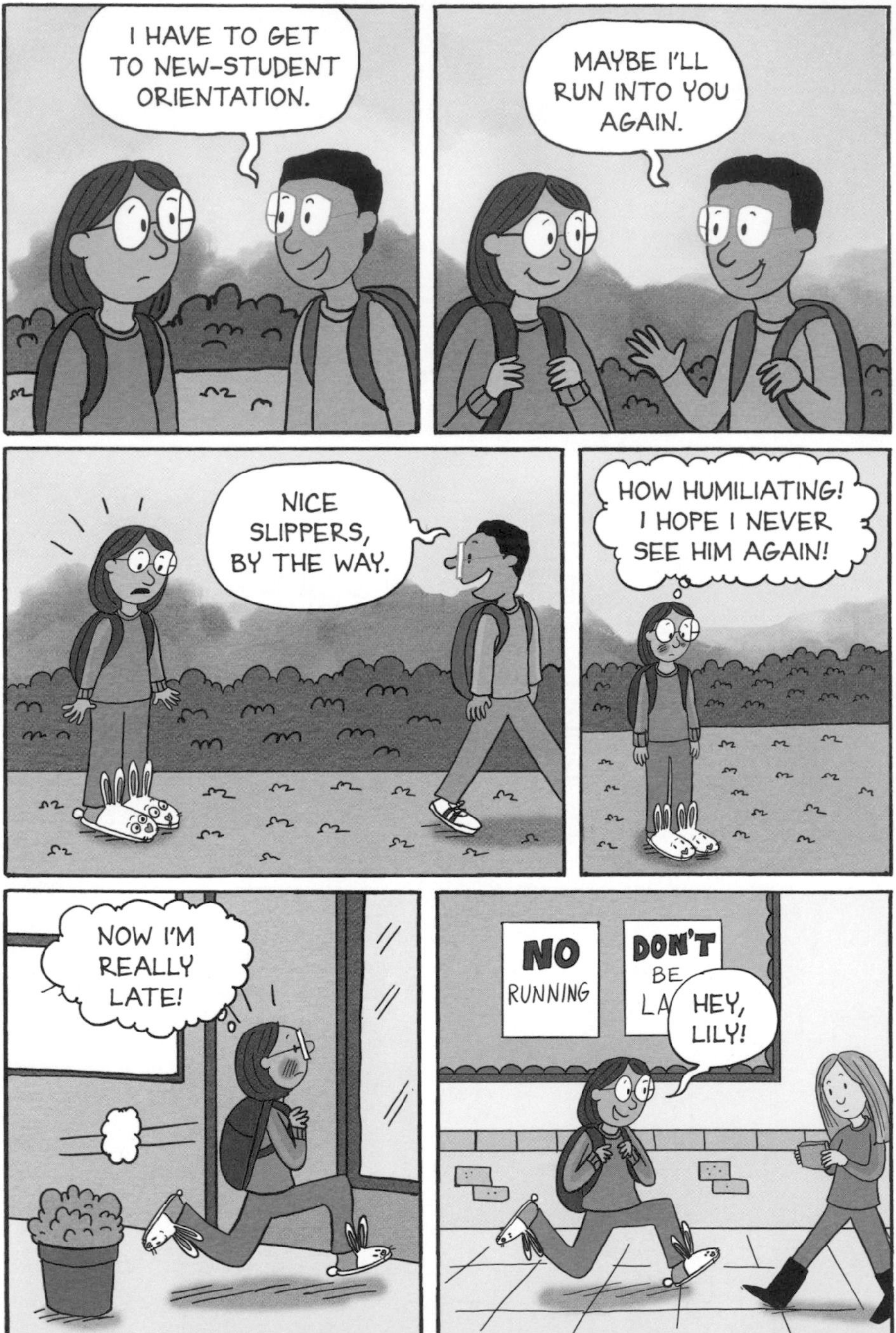
I HAVE TO GET TO NEW-STUDENT ORIENTATION.
MAYBE I'LL RUN INTO YOU AGAIN.
NICE SLIPPERS, BY THE WAY.
HOW HUMILIATING! I HOPE I NEVER SEE HIM AGAIN!
NOW I'M REALLY LATE!
NO RUNNING
DON'T BE LA
HEY, LILY!

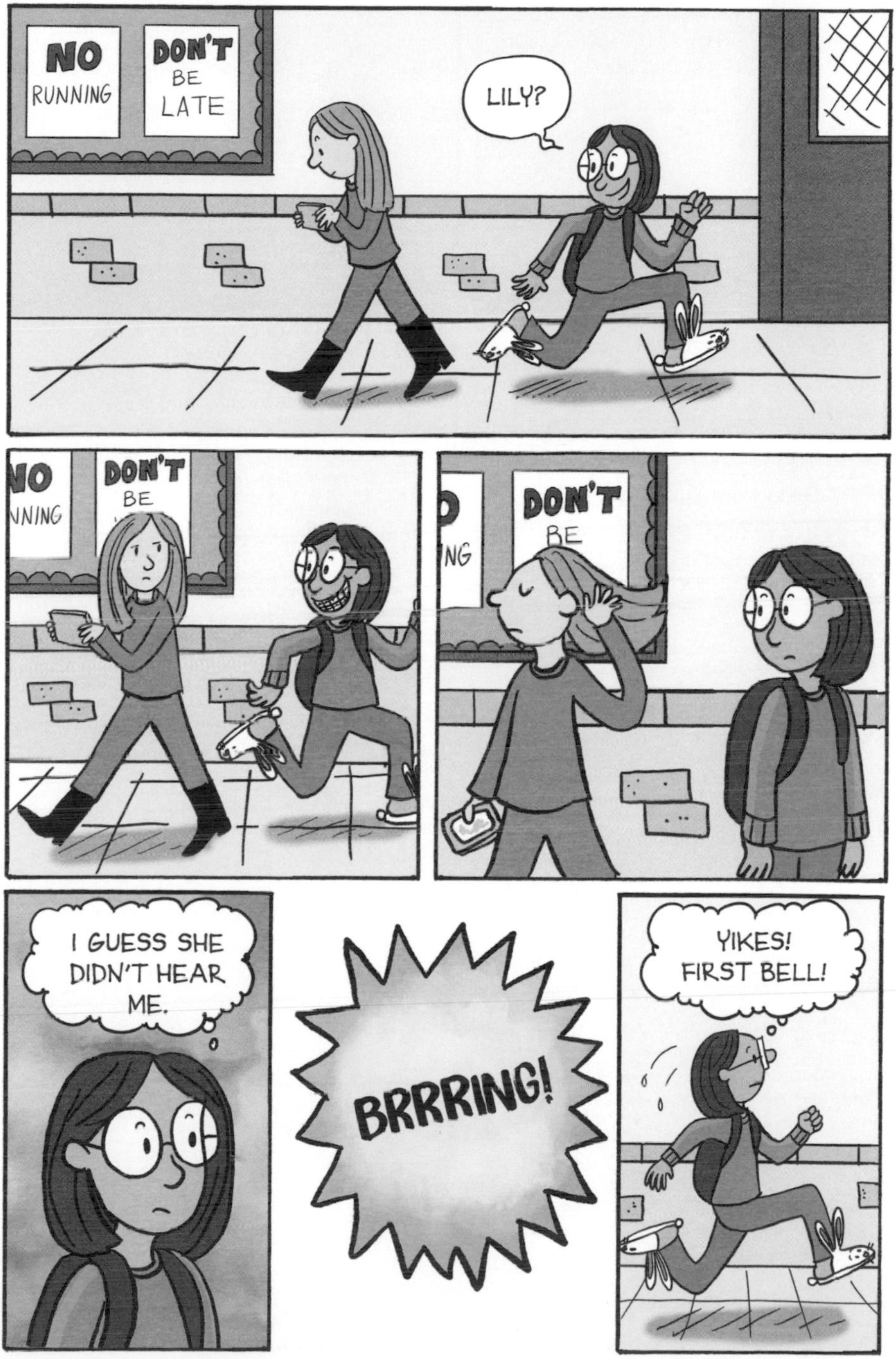
NO RUNNING
DON'T BE LATE
LILY?
I GUESS SHE DIDN'T HEAR ME.
BRRRING!
YIKES! FIRST BELL!

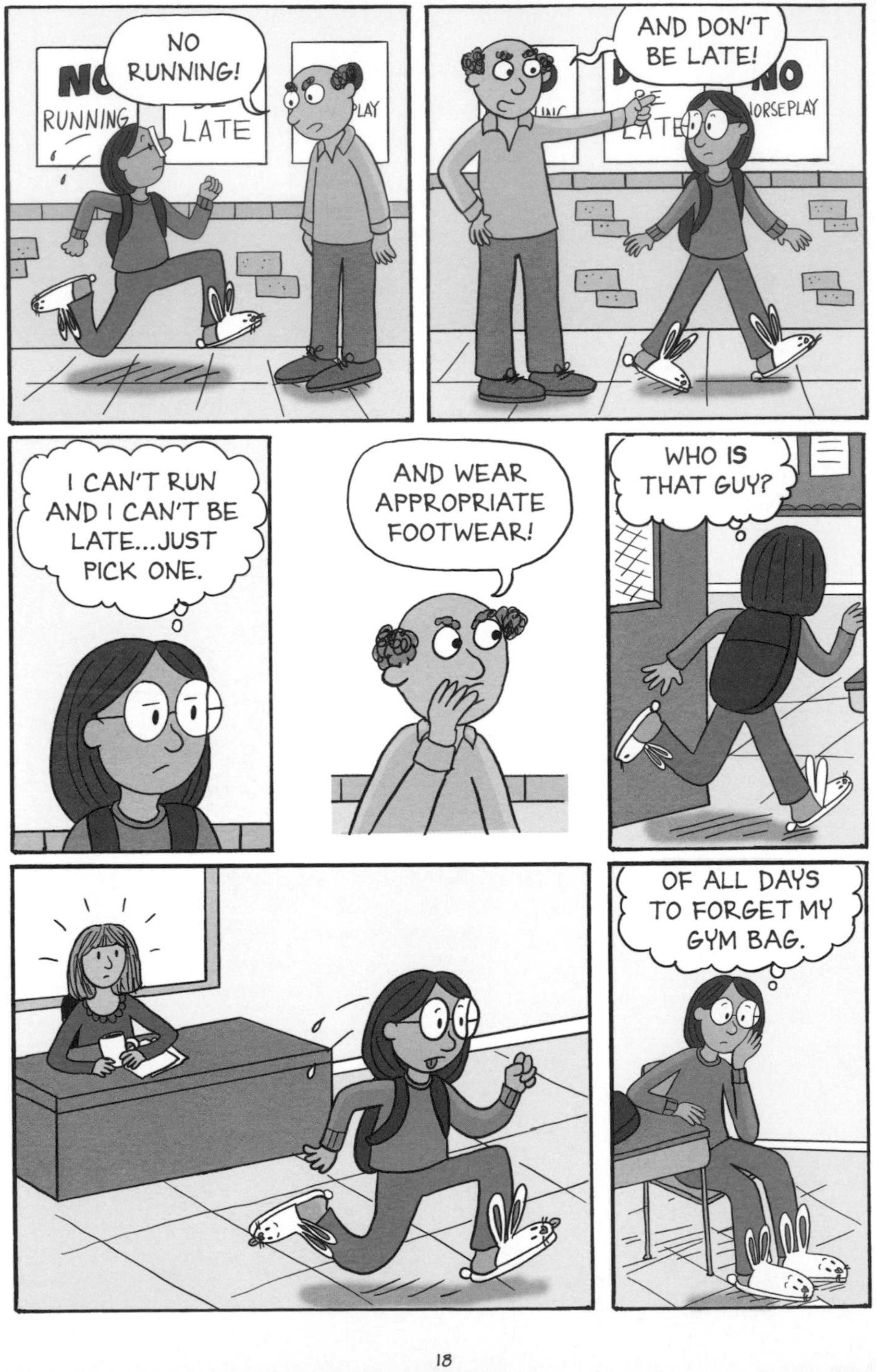
NO
RUNNING
BE
LATE
NO RUNNING!
PLAY
AND DON'T BE LATE!
NO
HORSEPLAY
LATE
I CAN'T RUN AND I CAN'T BE LATE...JUST PICK ONE.
AND WEAR APPROPRIATE FOOTWEAR!
WHO IS THAT GUY?
OF ALL DAYS TO FORGET MY GYM BAG.

CHAPTER 2
EX-BEST FRENEMY

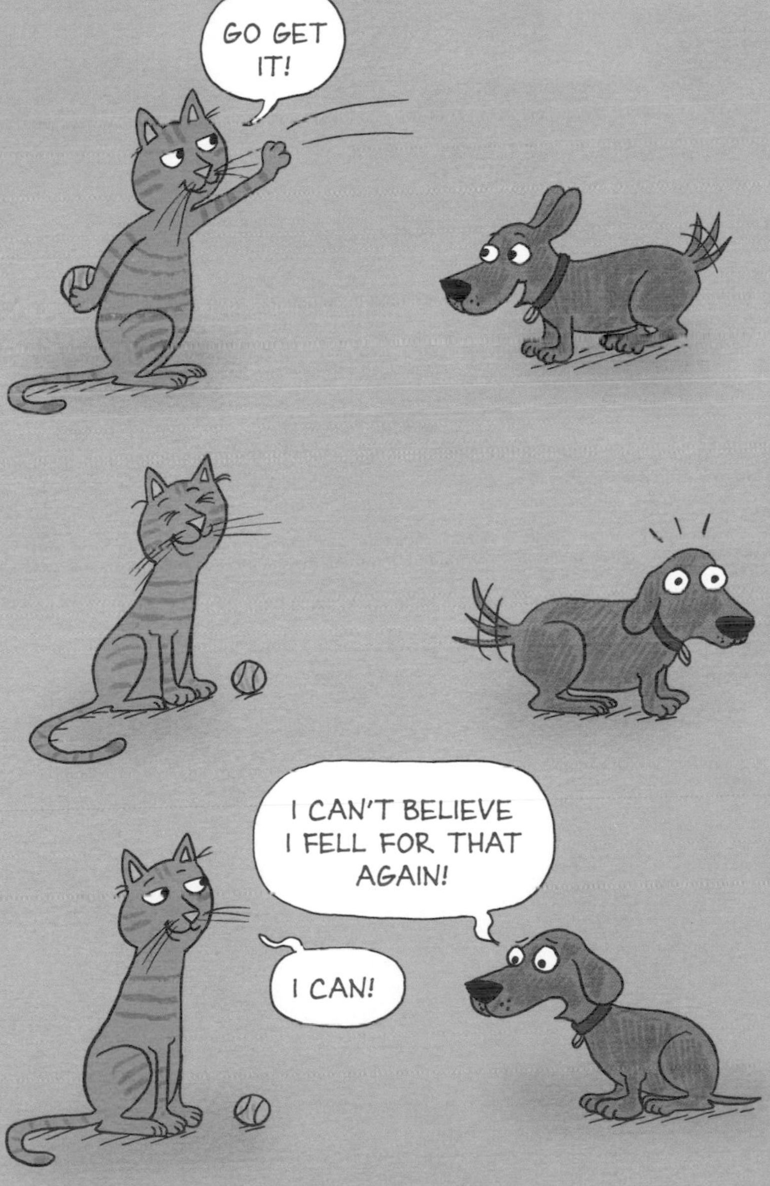
GO GET IT!
I CAN'T BELIEVE I FELL FOR THAT AGAIN!
I CAN!

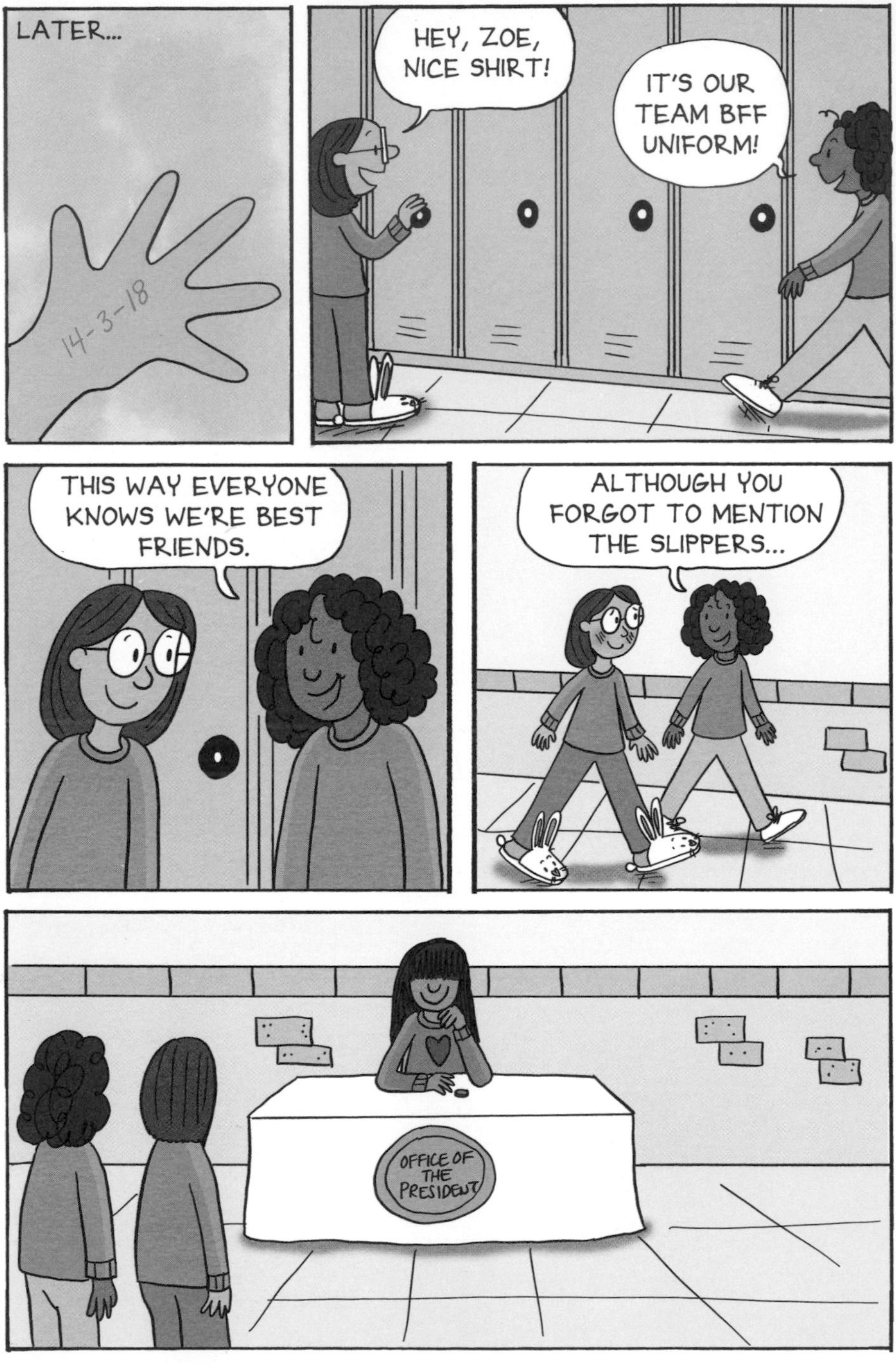
LATER...
14-3-18
HEY, ZOE, NICE SHIRT!
IT'S OUR TEAM BFF UNIFORM!
THIS WAY EVERYONE KNOWS WE'RE BEST FRIENDS.
ALTHOUGH YOU FORGOT TO MENTION THE SLIPPERS...
OFFICE OF THE PRESIDENT

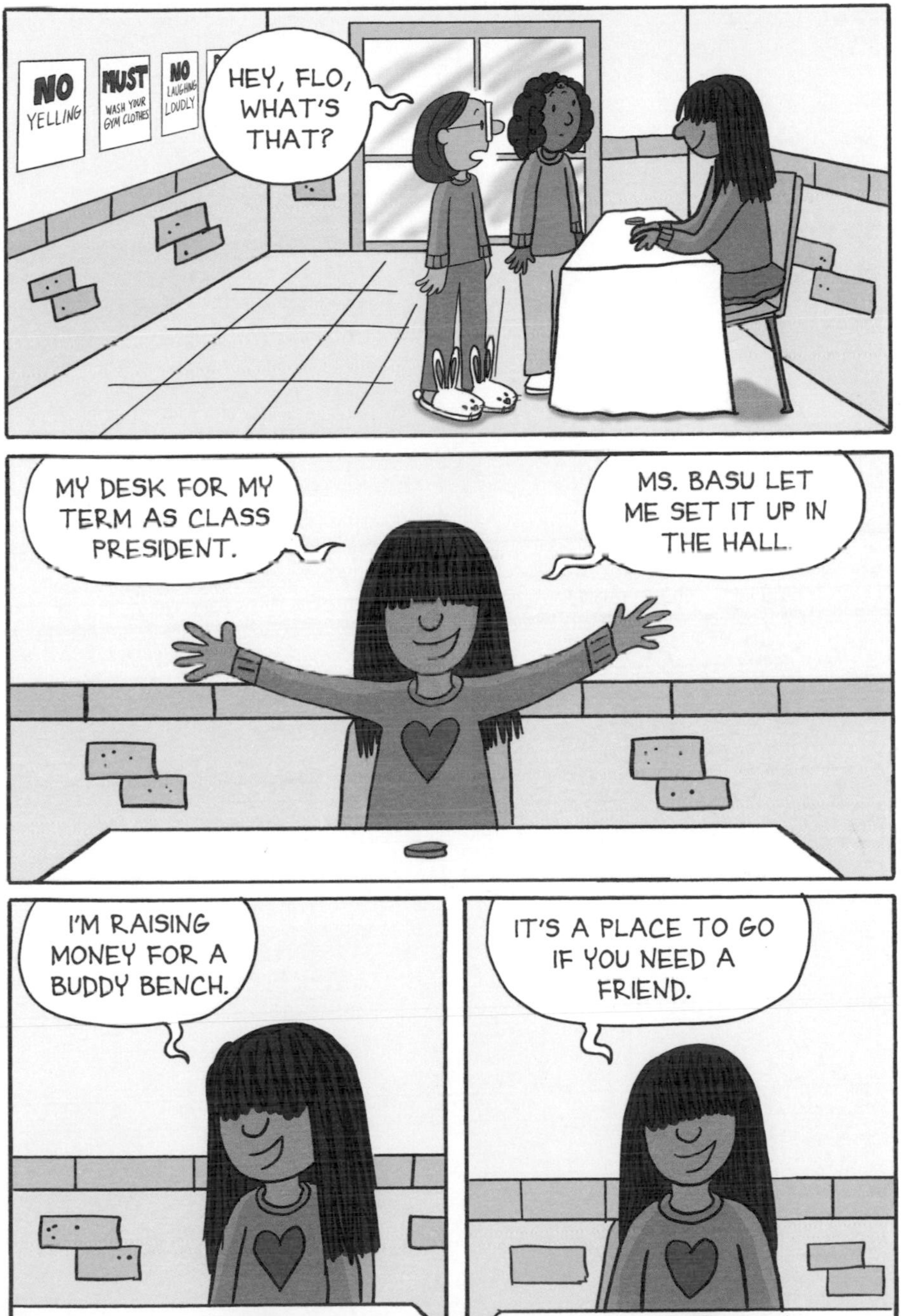
NO YELLING
MUST WASH YOUR GYM CLOTHES
NO LAUGHING LOUDLY
HEY, FLO, WHAT'S THAT?
MY DESK FOR MY TERM AS CLASS PRESIDENT.
MS. BASU LET ME SET IT UP IN THE HALL.
I'M RAISING MONEY FOR A BUDDY BENCH.
IT'S A PLACE TO GO IF YOU NEED A FRIEND.

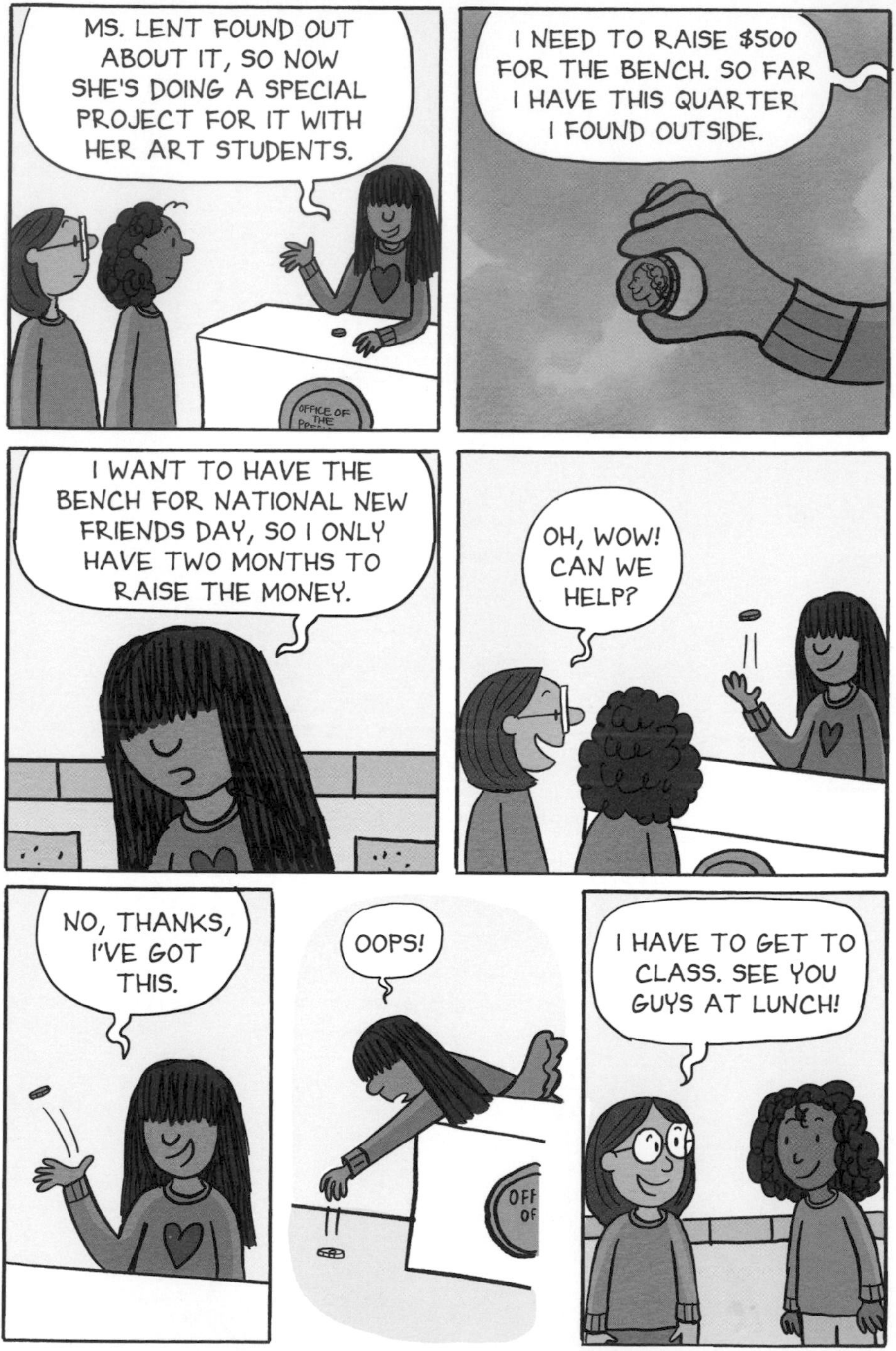
MS. LENT FOUND OUT ABOUT IT, SO NOW SHE'S DOING A SPECIAL PROJECT FOR IT WITH HER ART STUDENTS.
OFFICE OF THE
I NEED TO RAISE $500 FOR THE BENCH. SO FAR I HAVE THIS QUARTER I FOUND OUTSIDE.
I WANT TO HAVE THE BENCH FOR NATIONAL NEW FRIENDS DAY, SO I ONLY HAVE TWO MONTHS TO RAISE THE MONEY.
OH, WOW! CAN WE HELP?
NO, THANKS, I'VE GOT THIS.
OOPS!
I HAVE TO GET TO CLASS. SEE YOU GUYS AT LUNCH!

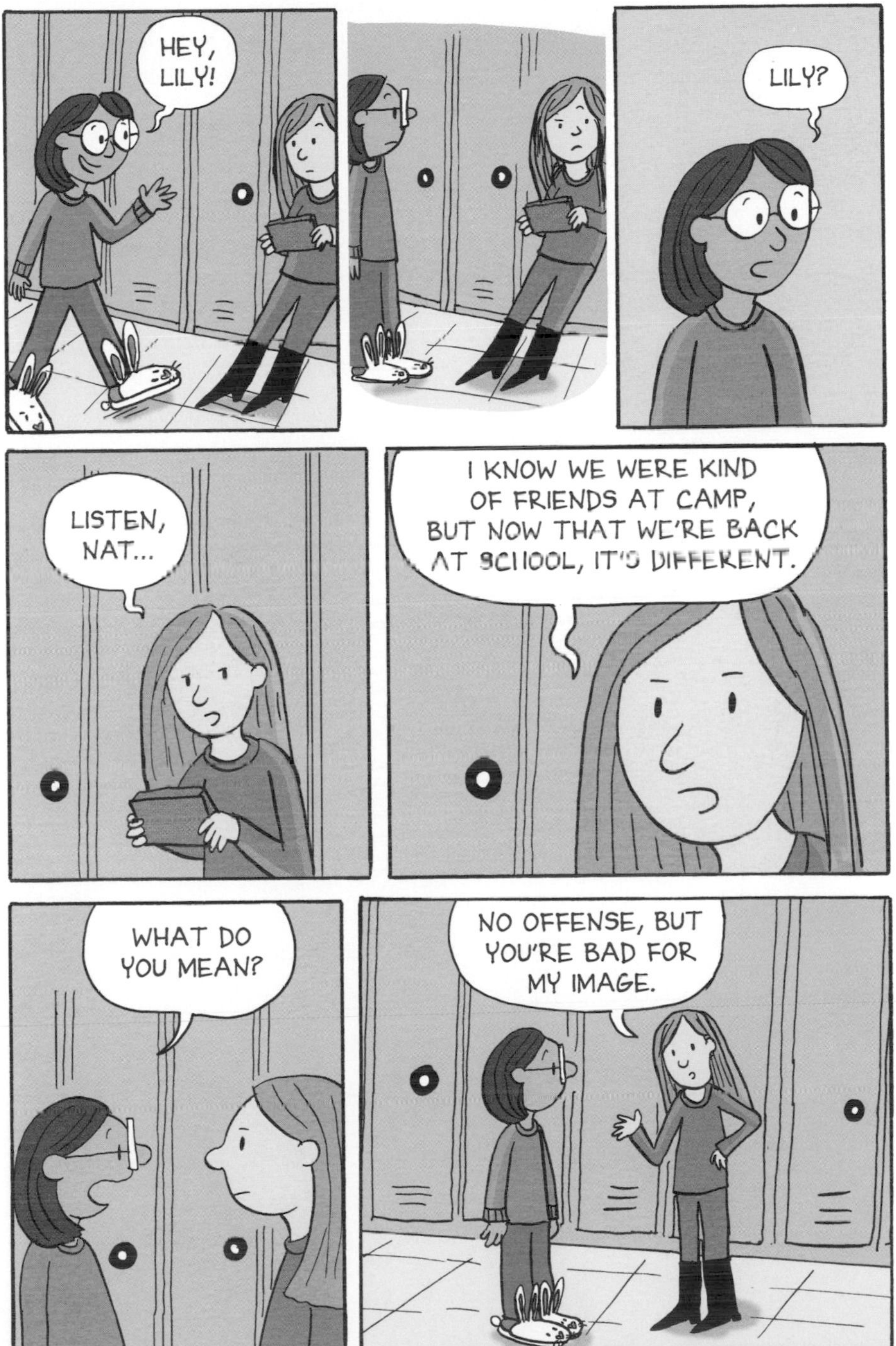
HEY, LILY!
LILY?
LISTEN, NAT...
I KNOW WE WERE KIND OF FRIENDS AT CAMP, BUT NOW THAT WE'RE BACK AT SCHOOL, IT'S DIFFERENT.
WHAT DO YOU MEAN?
NO OFFENSE, BUT YOU'RE BAD FOR MY IMAGE.

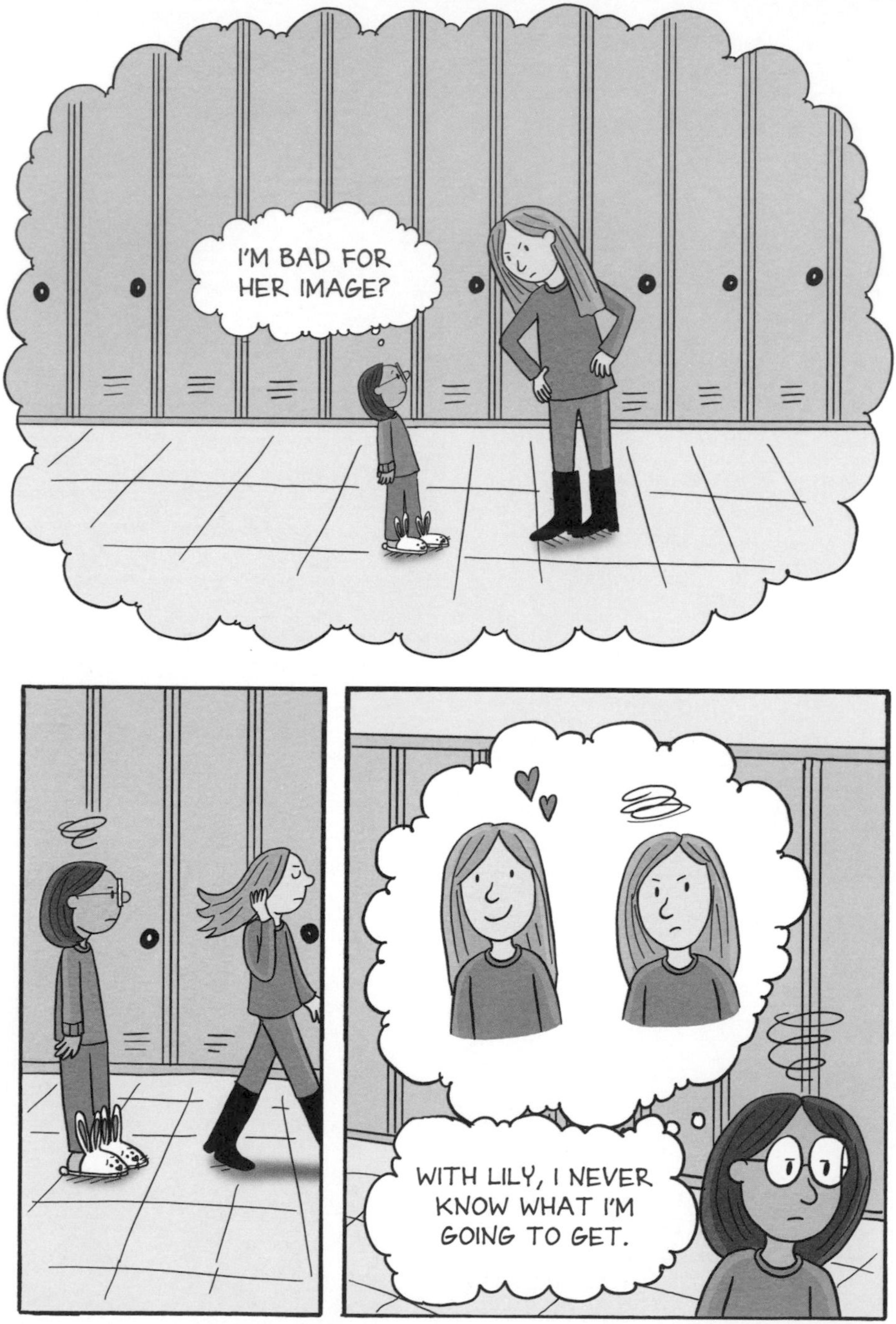
I'M BAD FOR HER IMAGE?
WITH LILY, I NEVER KNOW WHAT I'M GOING TO GET.

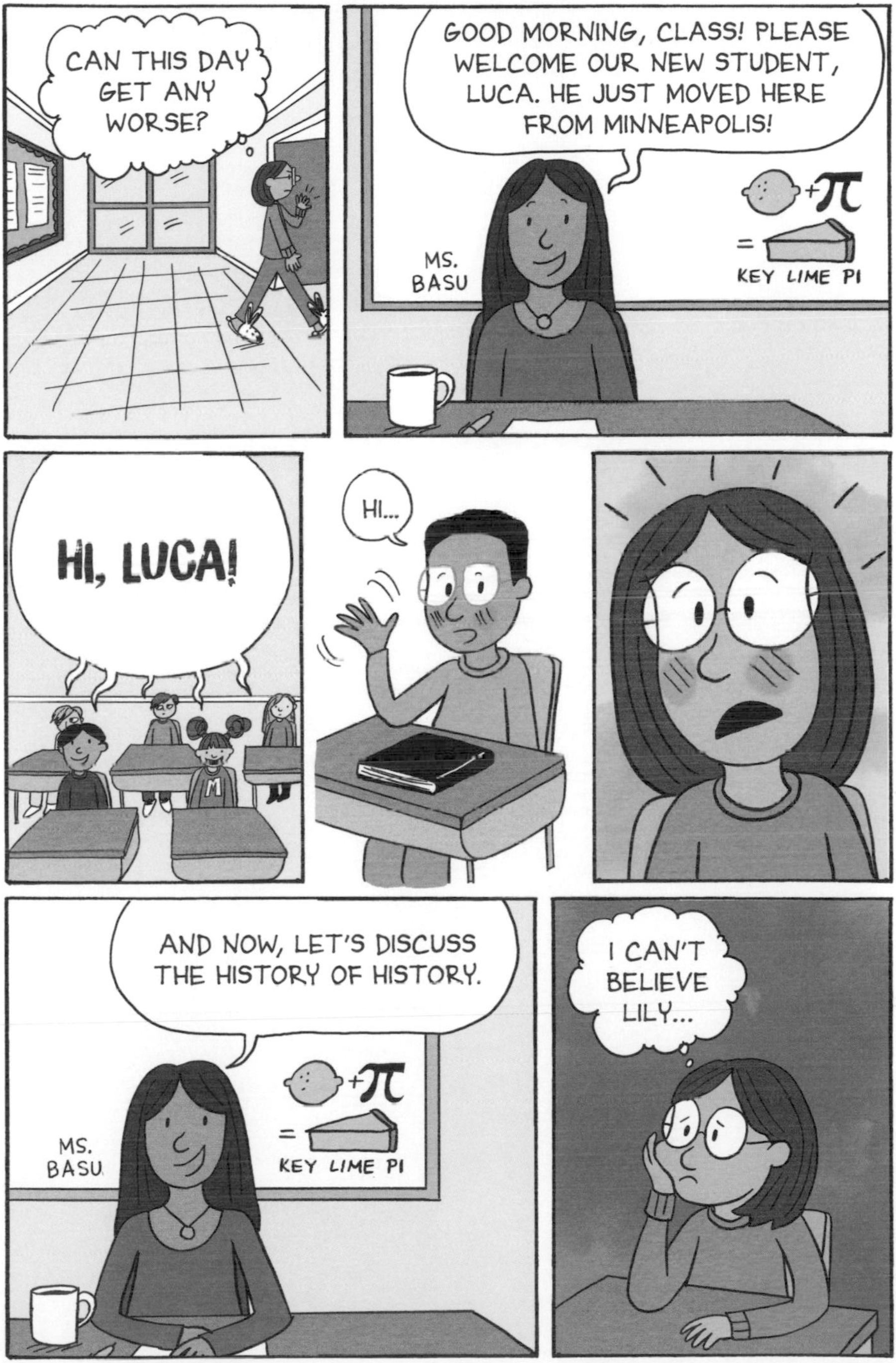
CAN THIS DAY GET ANY WORSE?
GOOD MORNING, CLASS! PLEASE WELCOME OUR NEW STUDENT, LUCA. HE JUST MOVED HERE FROM MINNEAPOLIS!
MS. BASU
= KEY LIME PI
HI, LUCA!
HI...
AND NOW, LET'S DISCUSS THE HISTORY OF HISTORY.
MS. BASU
= KEY LIME PI
I CAN'T BELIEVE LILY...

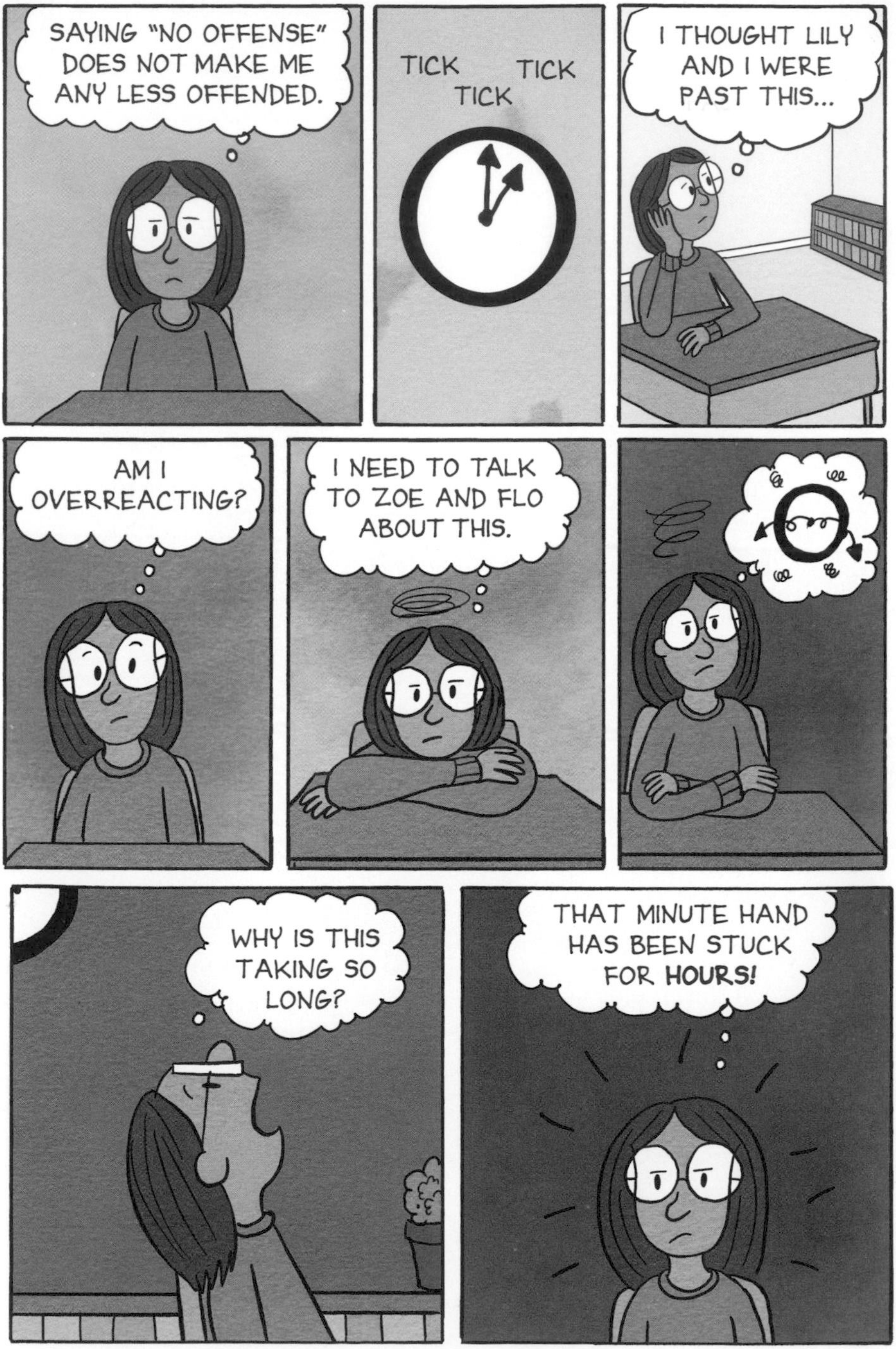
SAYING "NO OFFENSE" DOES NOT MAKE ME ANY LESS OFFENDED.
TICK TICK TICK
I THOUGHT LILY AND I WERE PAST THIS...
AM I OVERREACTING?
I NEED TO TALK TO ZOE AND FLO ABOUT THIS.
WHY IS THIS TAKING SO LONG?
THAT MINUTE HAND HAS BEEN STUCK FOR **HOURS!**

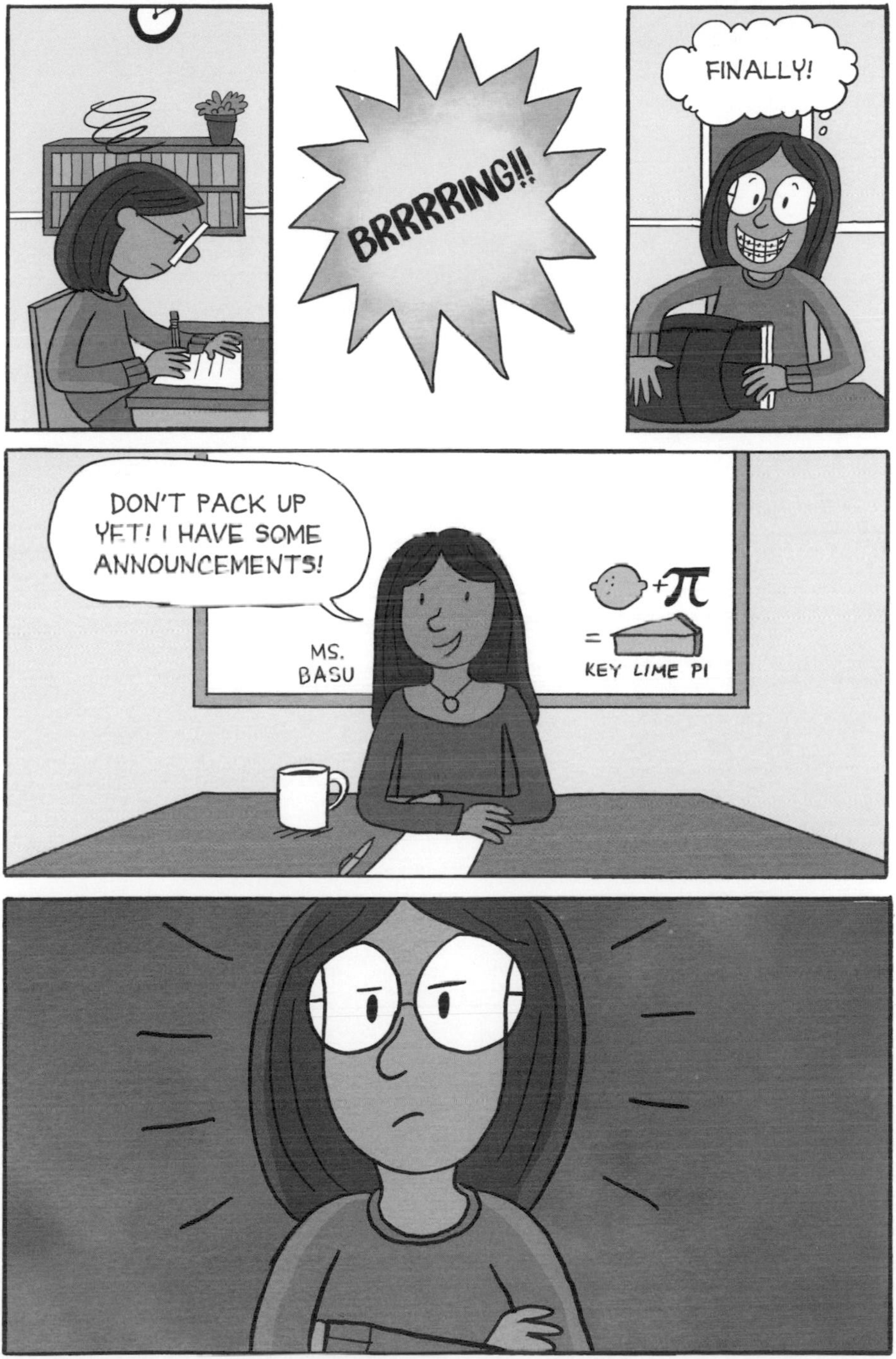
BRRRRING!!
FINALLY!
DON'T PACK UP YET! I HAVE SOME ANNOUNCEMENTS!
MS. BASU
KEY LIME PI

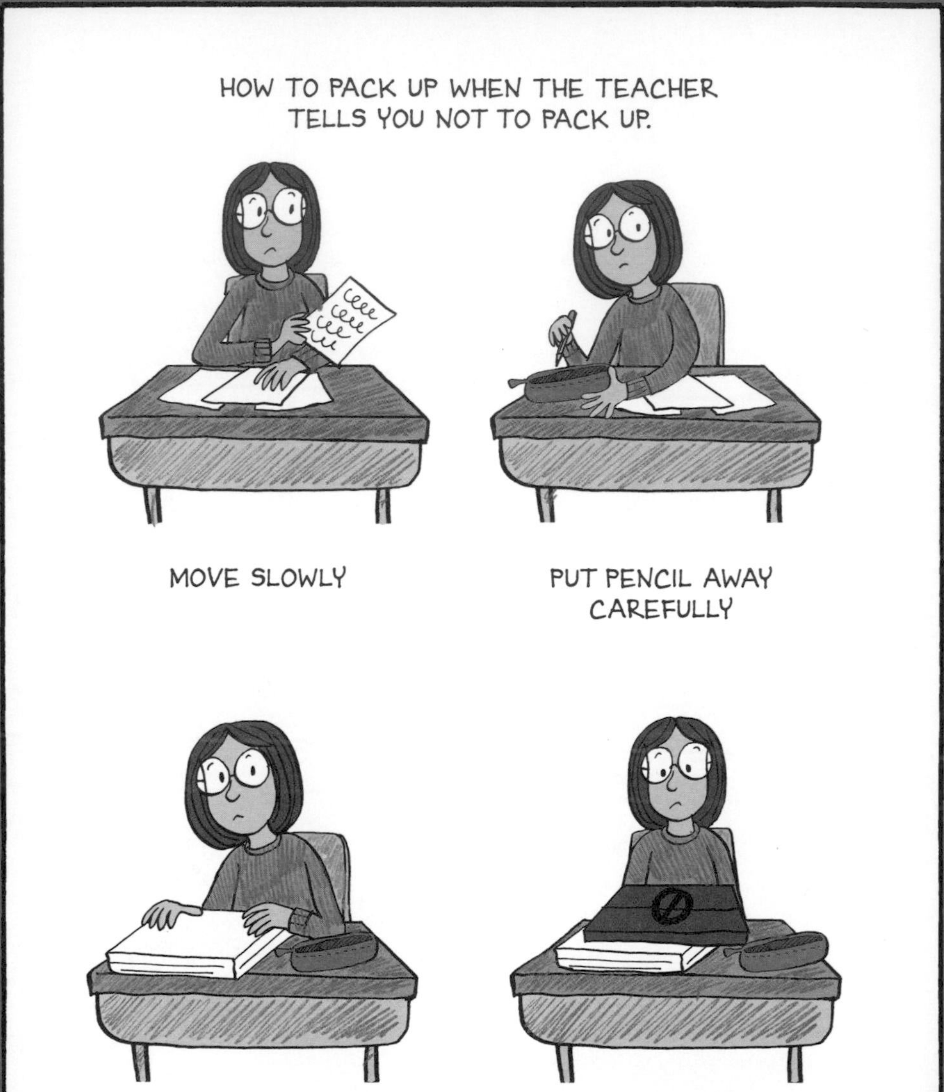
HOW TO PACK UP WHEN THE TEACHER TELLS YOU NOT TO PACK UP.
MOVE SLOWLY
PUT PENCIL AWAY CAREFULLY
STACK UP PAPERS
IF YOUR NOTEBOOK HAS VELCRO, DO NOT OPEN

MAKE A PILE OF
YOUR STUFF

SLIDE STUFF
INTO BACKPACK

MAKE SURE YOUR
SHOES ARE TIED

LEAN TOWARD
THE DOOR

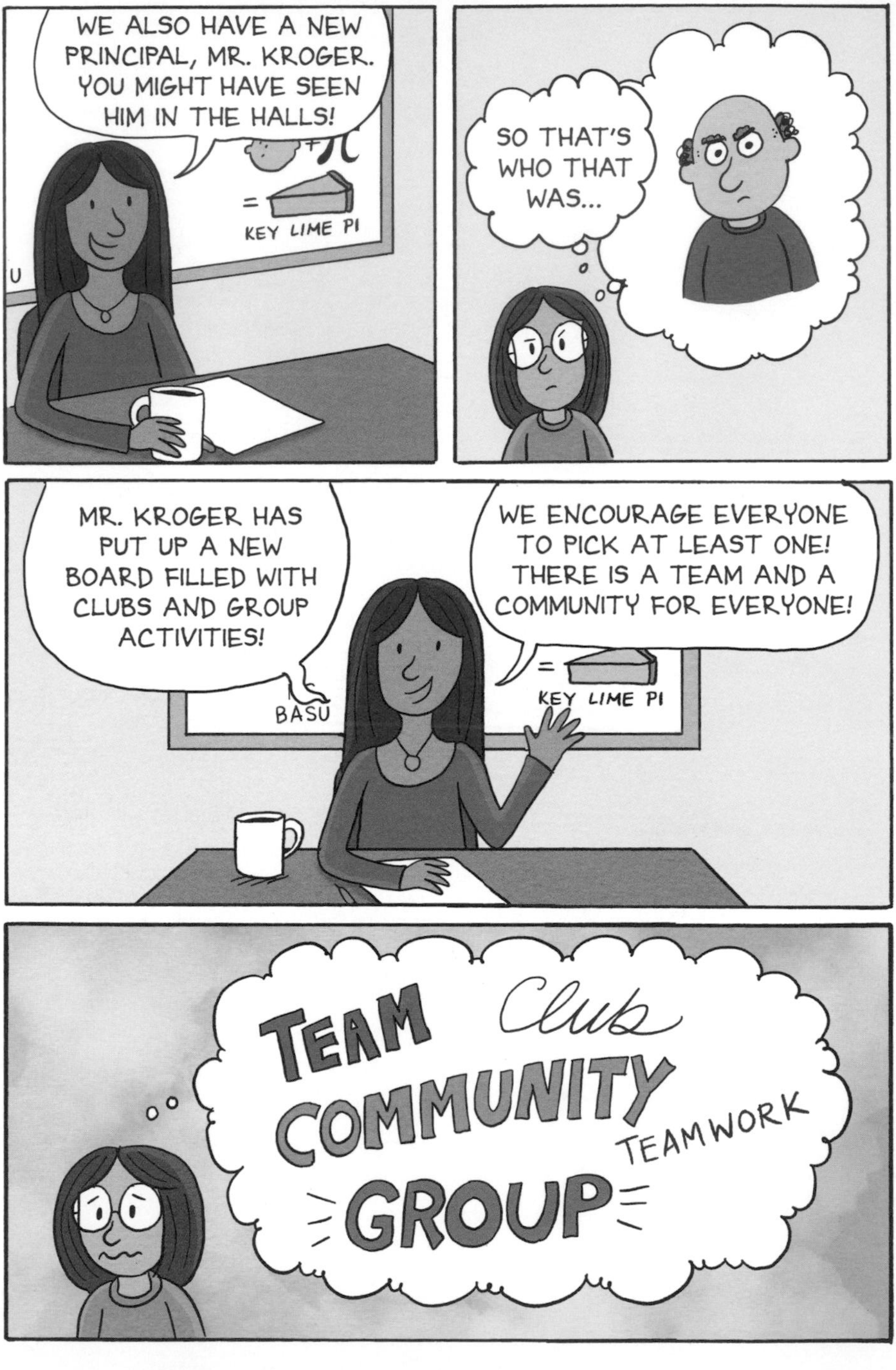
WE ALSO HAVE A NEW PRINCIPAL, MR. KROGER. YOU MIGHT HAVE SEEN HIM IN THE HALLS!
KEY LIME PI
SO THAT'S WHO THAT WAS...
MR. KROGER HAS PUT UP A NEW BOARD FILLED WITH CLUBS AND GROUP ACTIVITIES!
WE ENCOURAGE EVERYONE TO PICK AT LEAST ONE! THERE IS A TEAM AND A COMMUNITY FOR EVERYONE!
BASU
KEY LIME PI
TEAM
Club
COMMUNITY
TEAMWORK
GROUP

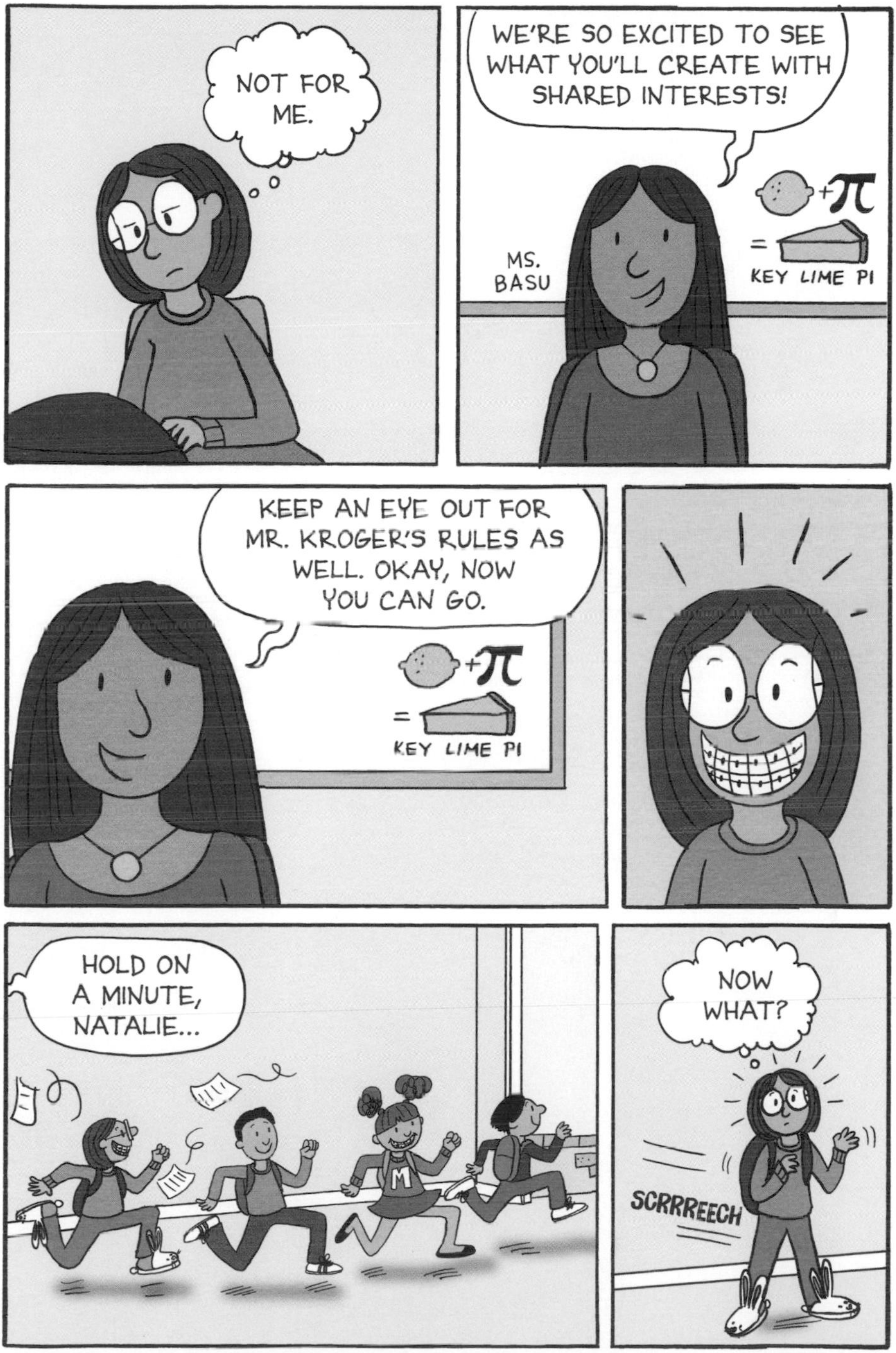
NOT FOR ME.
WE'RE SO EXCITED TO SEE WHAT YOU'LL CREATE WITH SHARED INTERESTS!
MS. BASU
=
KEY LIME PI
KEEP AN EYE OUT FOR MR. KROGER'S RULES AS WELL. OKAY, NOW YOU CAN GO.
=
KEY LIME PI
HOLD ON A MINUTE, NATALIE...
M
NOW WHAT?
SCRRREECH

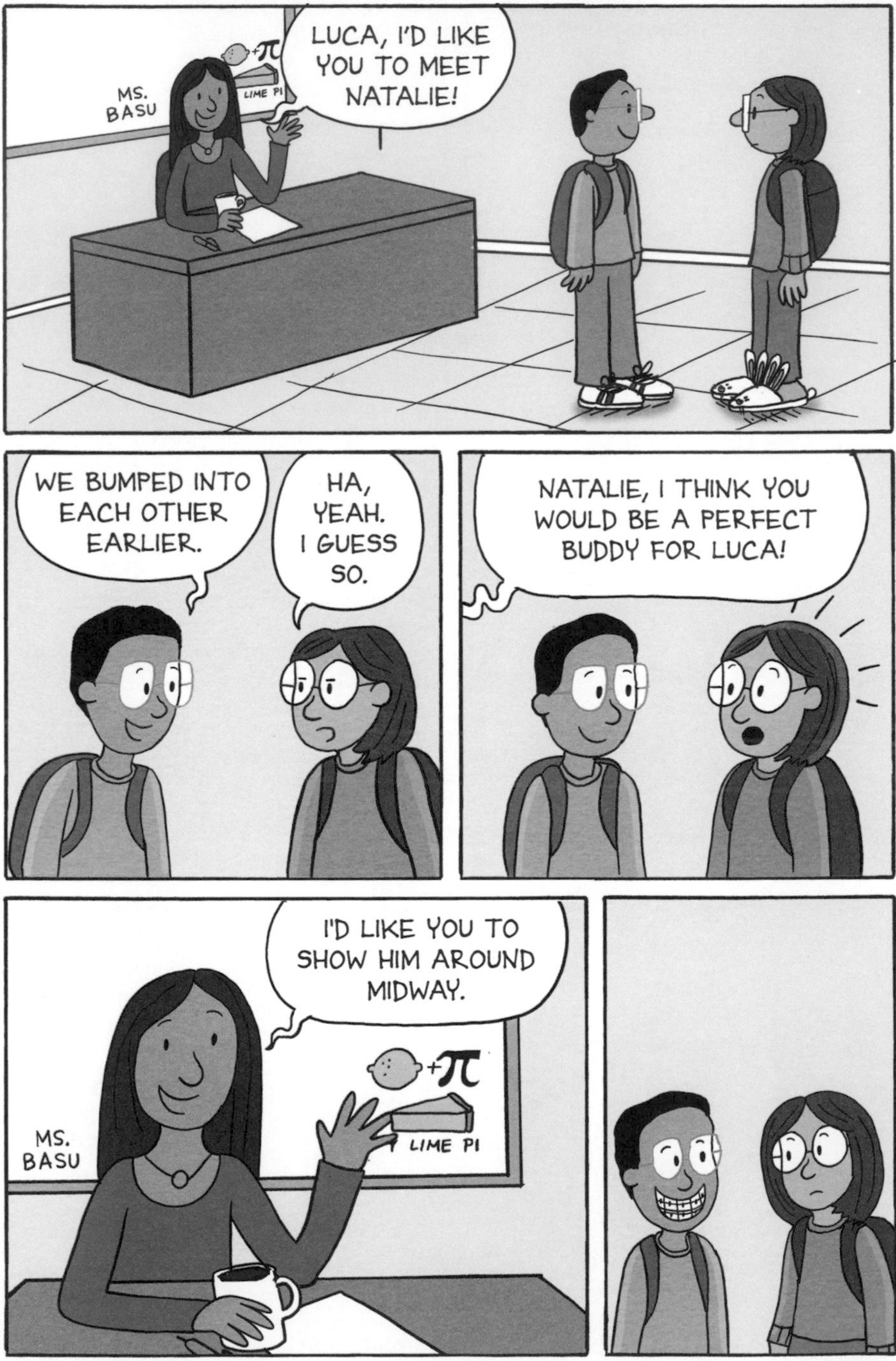
LUCA, I'D LIKE YOU TO MEET NATALIE!
MS. BASU
LIME PI
WE BUMPED INTO EACH OTHER EARLIER.
HA, YEAH. I GUESS SO.
NATALIE, I THINK YOU WOULD BE A PERFECT BUDDY FOR LUCA!
I'D LIKE YOU TO SHOW HIM AROUND MIDWAY.
MS. BASU
LIME PI

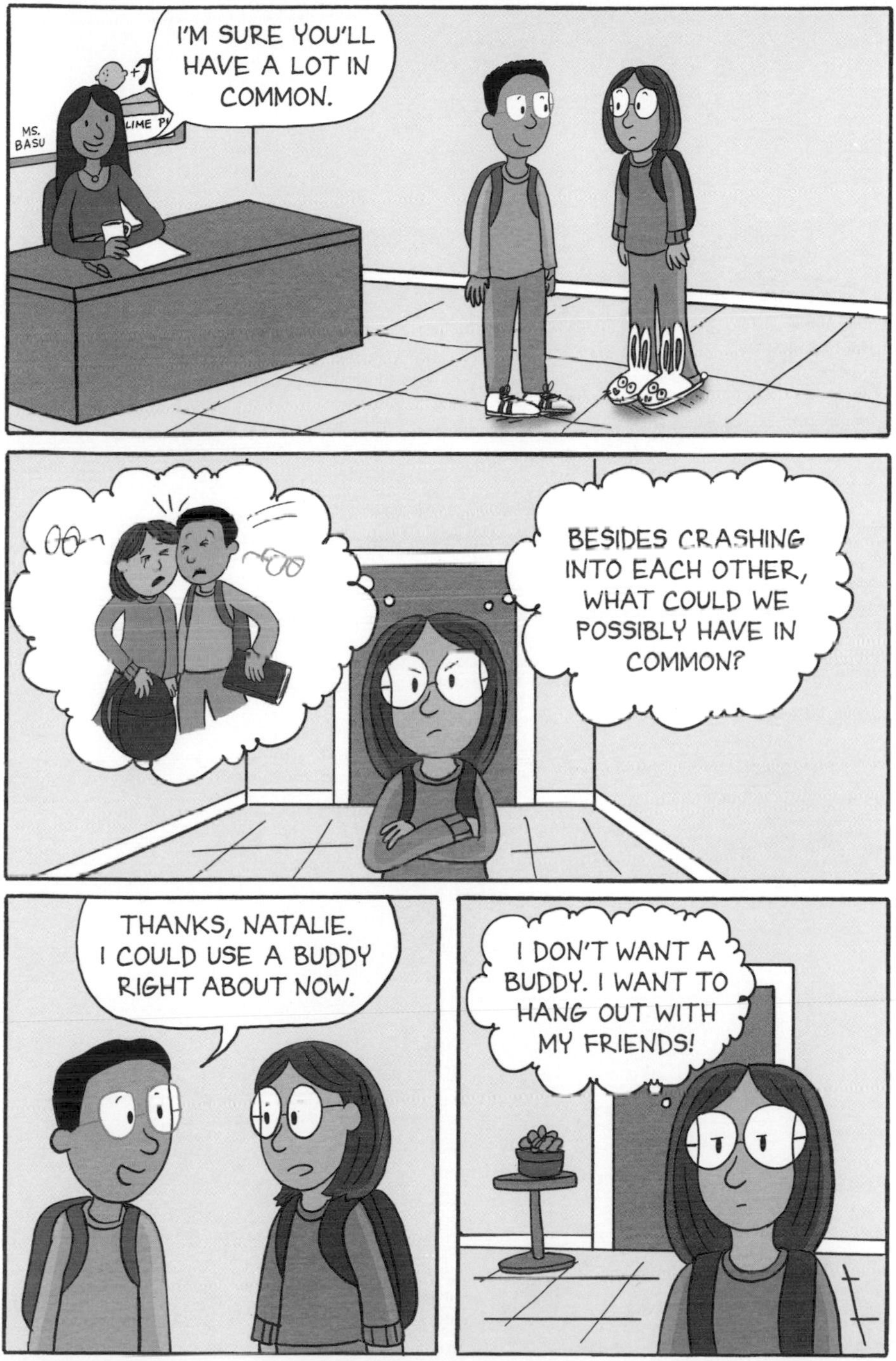
MS. BASU
LIME PI
I'M SURE YOU'LL HAVE A LOT IN COMMON.
BESIDES CRASHING INTO EACH OTHER, WHAT COULD WE POSSIBLY HAVE IN COMMON?
THANKS, NATALIE. I COULD USE A BUDDY RIGHT ABOUT NOW.
I DON'T WANT A BUDDY. I WANT TO HANG OUT WITH MY FRIENDS!

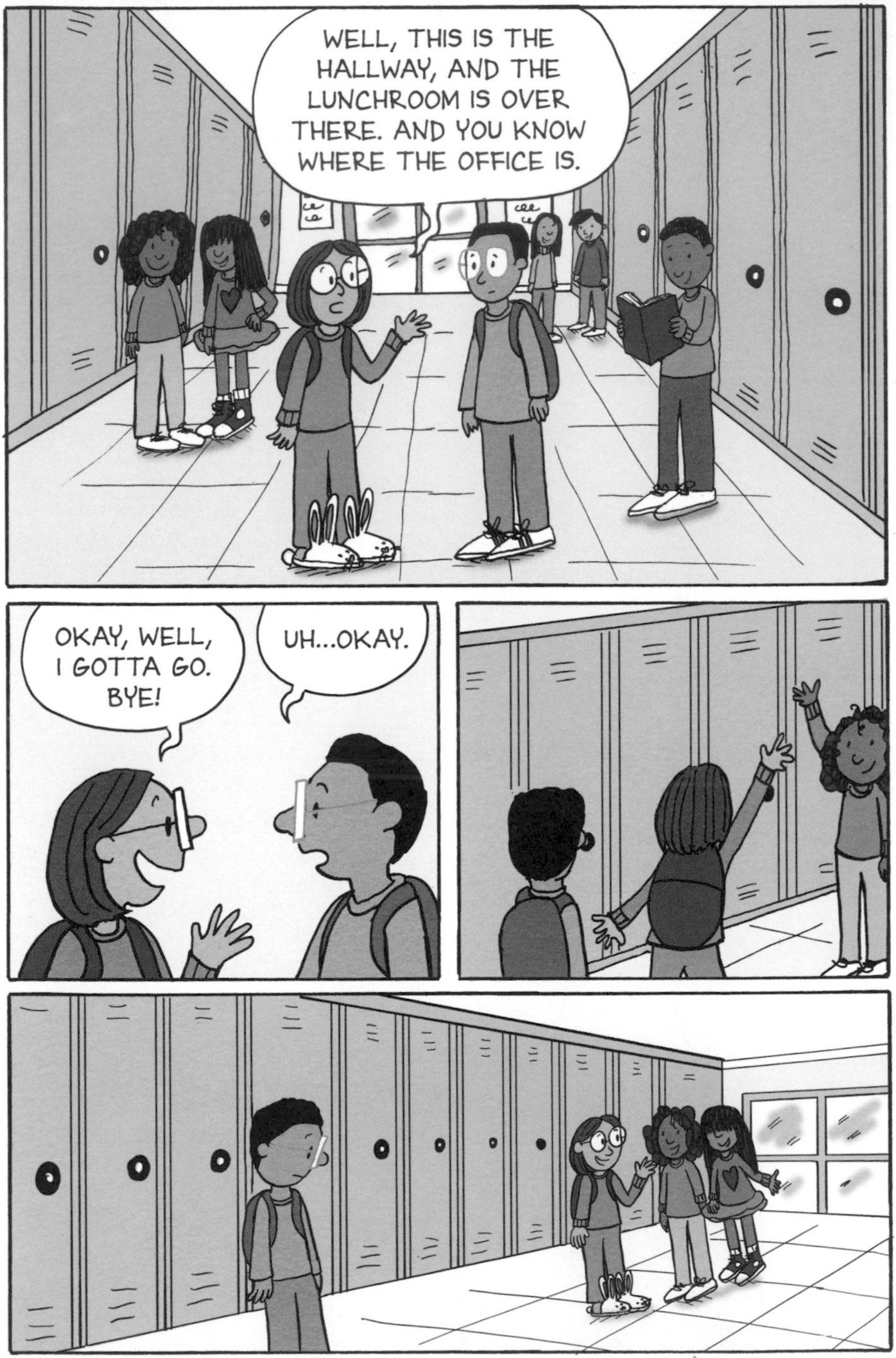
WELL, THIS IS THE HALLWAY, AND THE LUNCHROOM IS OVER THERE. AND YOU KNOW WHERE THE OFFICE IS.
OKAY, WELL, I GOTTA GO. BYE!
UH...OKAY.

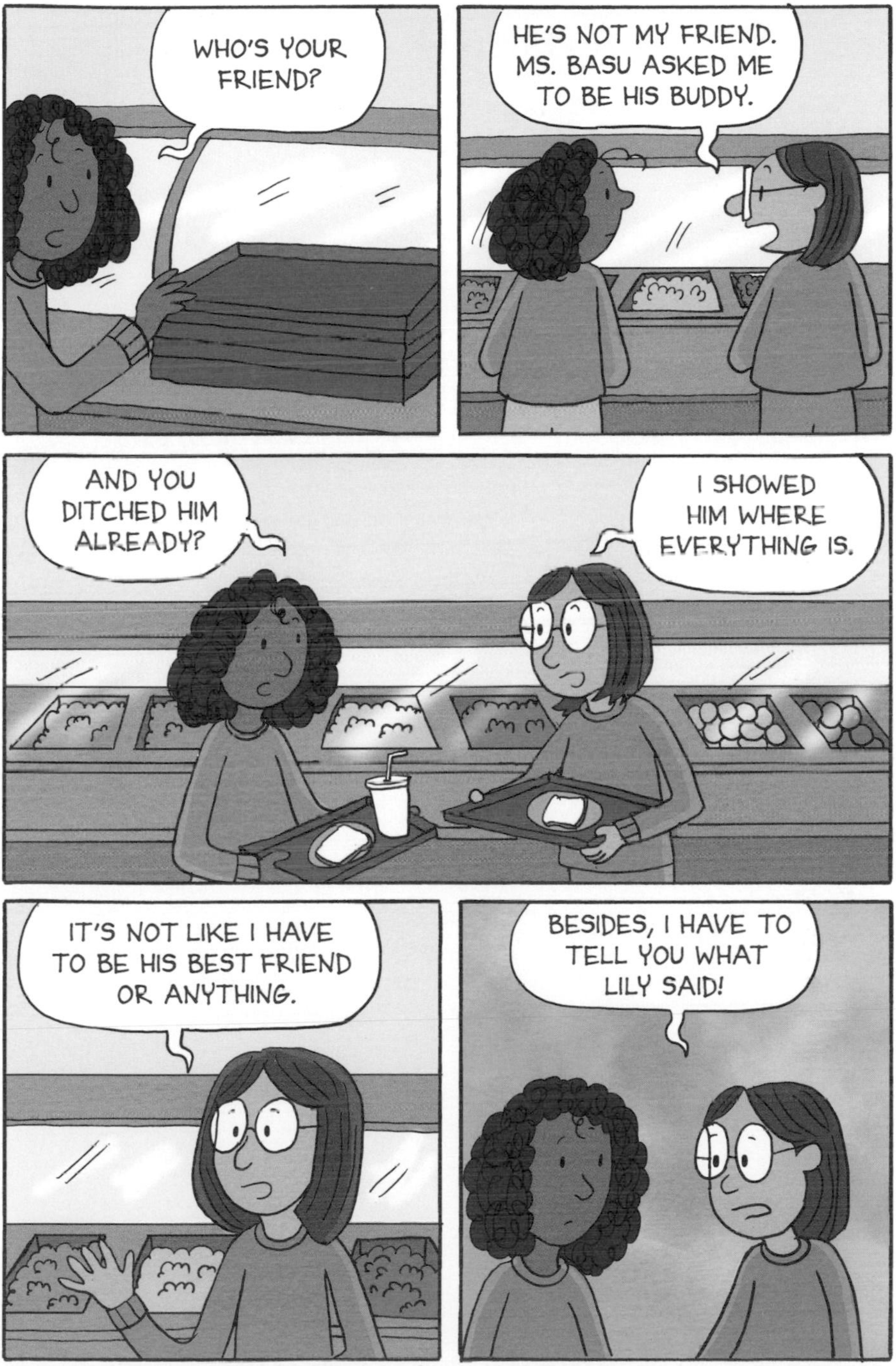
WHO'S YOUR FRIEND?
HE'S NOT MY FRIEND. MS. BASU ASKED ME TO BE HIS BUDDY.
AND YOU DITCHED HIM ALREADY?
I SHOWED HIM WHERE EVERYTHING IS.
IT'S NOT LIKE I HAVE TO BE HIS BEST FRIEND OR ANYTHING.
BESIDES, I HAVE TO TELL YOU WHAT LILY SAID!

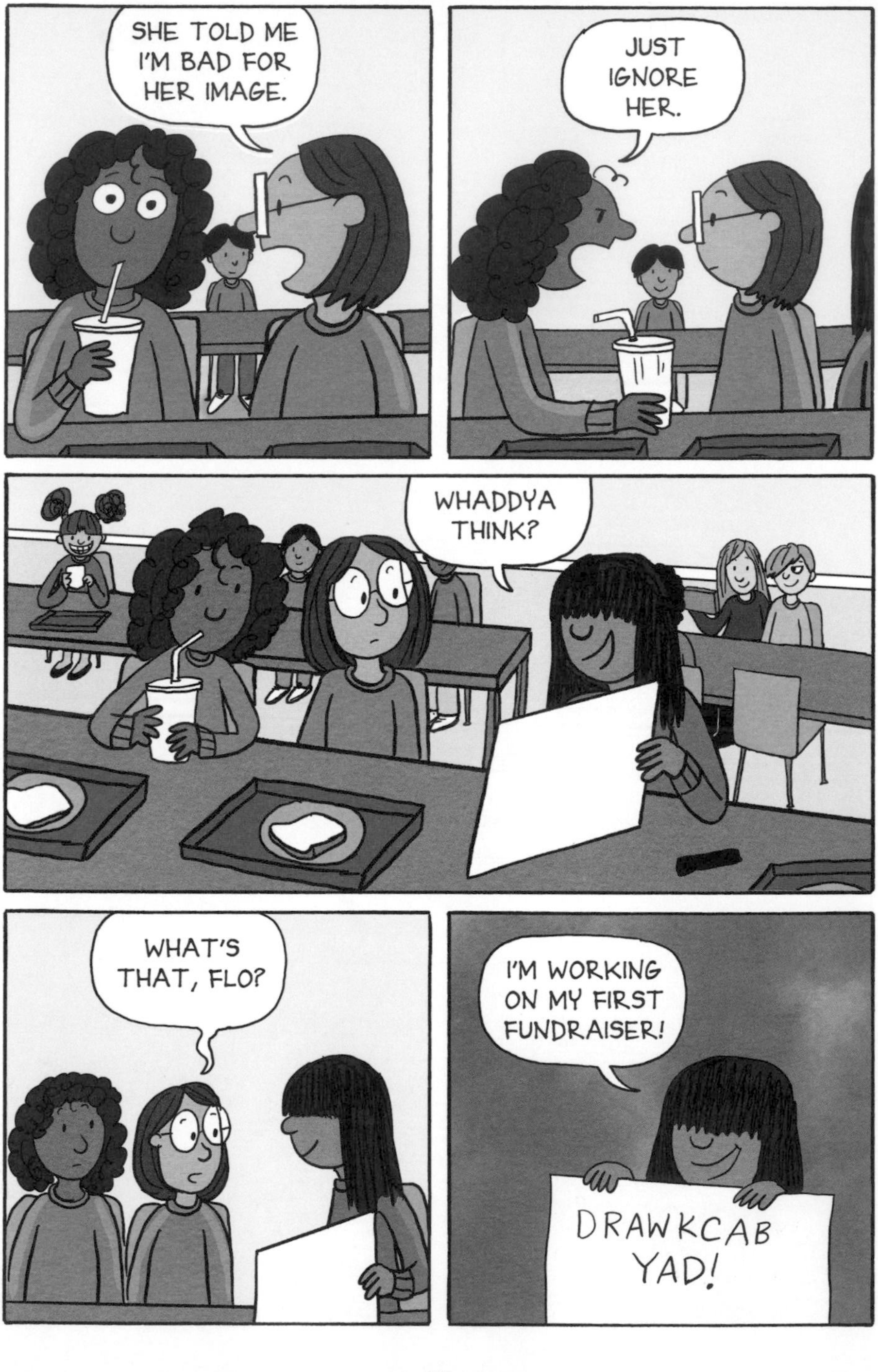
SHE TOLD ME I'M BAD FOR HER IMAGE.
JUST IGNORE HER.
WHADDYA THINK?
WHAT'S THAT, FLO?
I'M WORKING ON MY FIRST FUNDRAISER!
DRAWKCAB YAD!

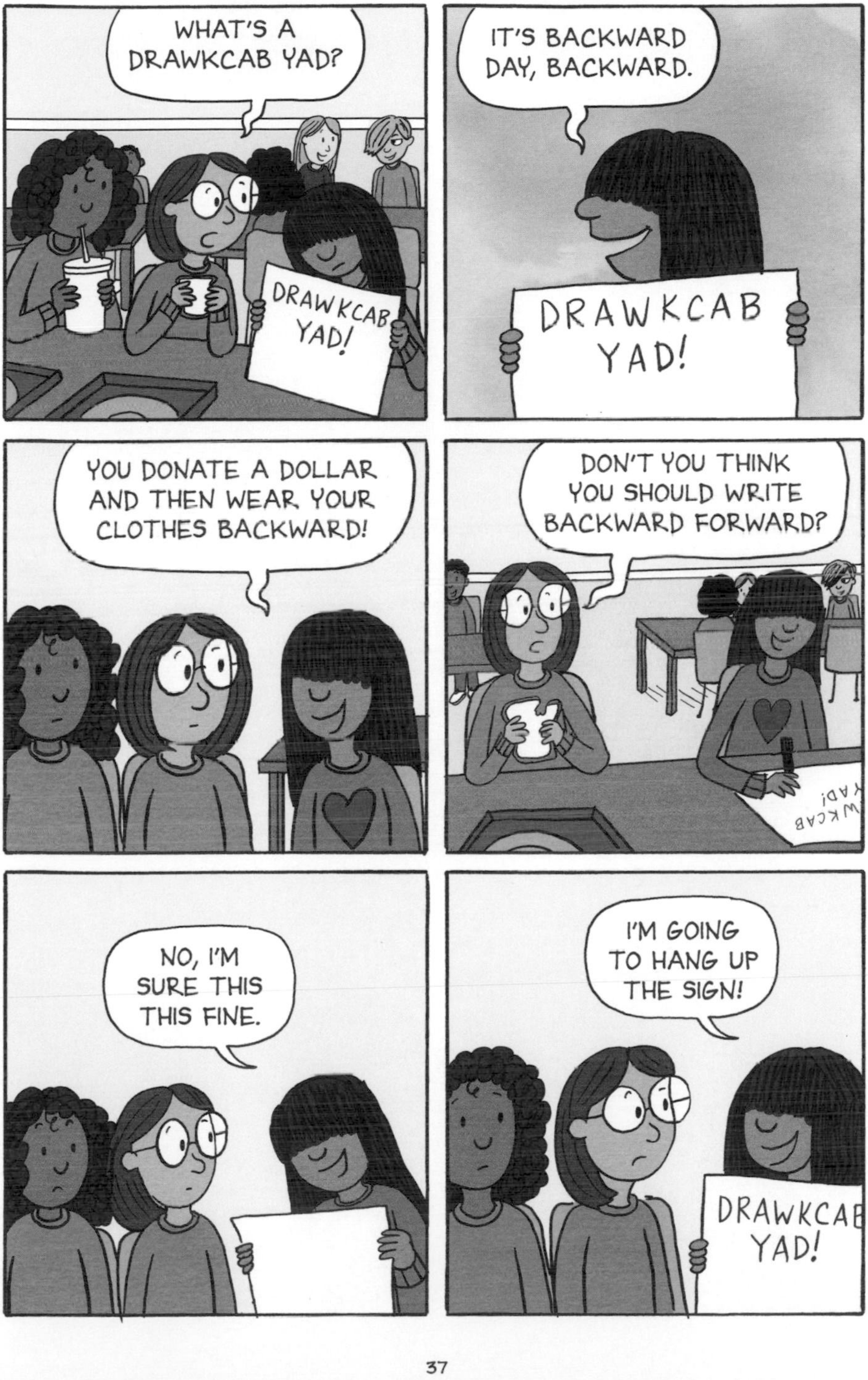
WHAT'S A DRAWKCAB YAD?
DRAWKCAB YAD!
IT'S BACKWARD DAY, BACKWARD.
DRAWKCAB YAD!
YOU DONATE A DOLLAR AND THEN WEAR YOUR CLOTHES BACKWARD!
DON'T YOU THINK YOU SHOULD WRITE BACKWARD FORWARD?
NO, I'M SURE THIS THIS FINE.
I'M GOING TO HANG UP THE SIGN!
DRAWKCAB YAD!

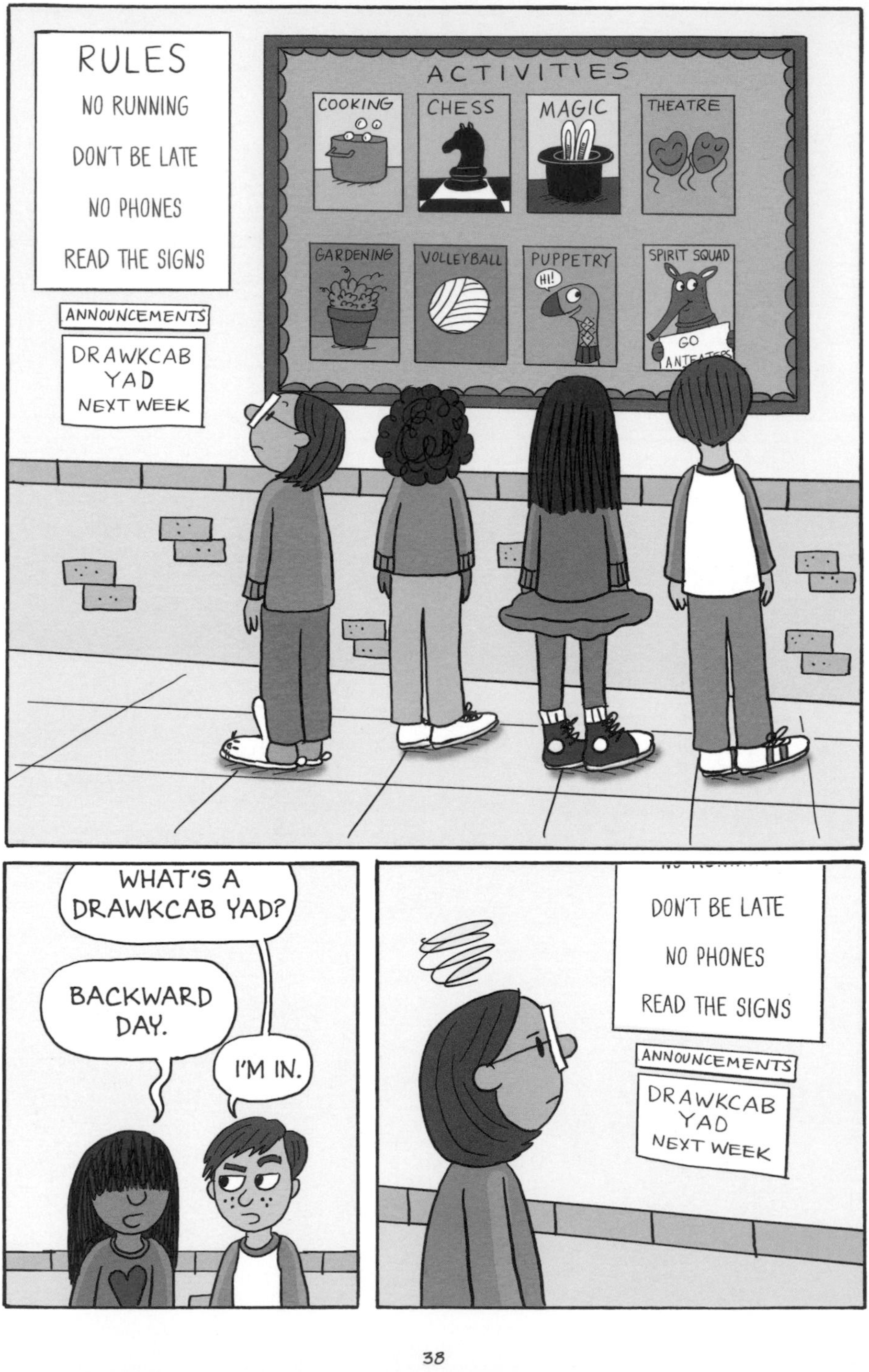
RULES
NO RUNNING
DON'T BE LATE
NO PHONES
READ THE SIGNS
ANNOUNCEMENTS
DRAWKCAB YAD NEXT WEEK
ACTIVITIES
COOKING
CHESS
MAGIC
THEATRE
GARDENING
VOLLEYBALL
PUPPETRY
HI!
SPIRIT SQUAD
GO
WHAT'S A DRAWKCAB YAD?
BACKWARD DAY.
I'M IN.
DON'T BE LATE
NO PHONES
READ THE SIGNS
ANNOUNCEMENTS
DRAWKCAB YAD NEXT WEEK

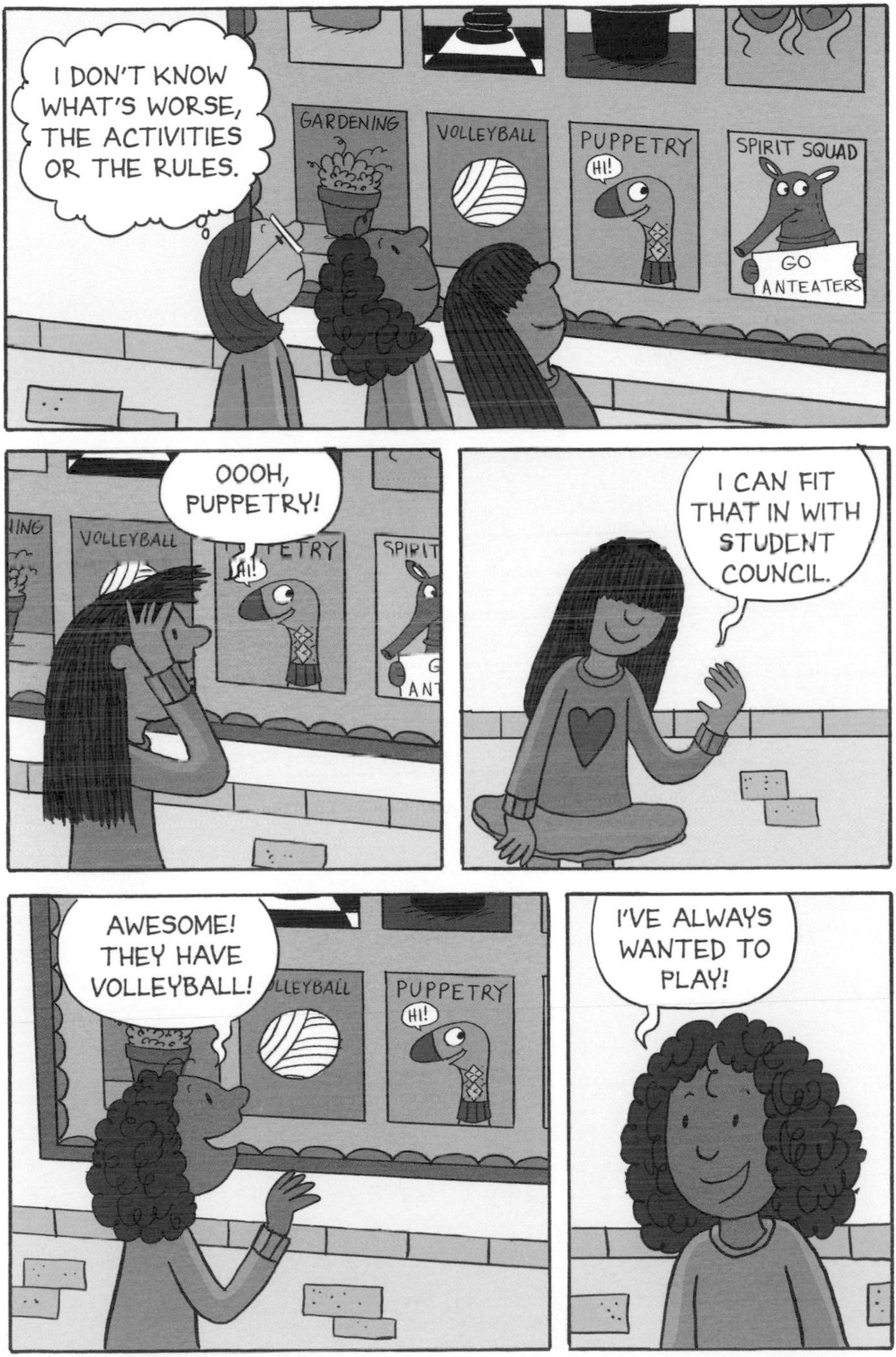
I DON'T KNOW WHAT'S WORSE, THE ACTIVITIES OR THE RULES.
GARDENING
VOLLEYBALL
PUPPETRY
HI!
SPIRIT SQUAD
GO ANTEATERS
OOOH, PUPPETRY!
I CAN FIT THAT IN WITH STUDENT COUNCIL.
AWESOME! THEY HAVE VOLLEYBALL!
I'VE ALWAYS WANTED TO PLAY!

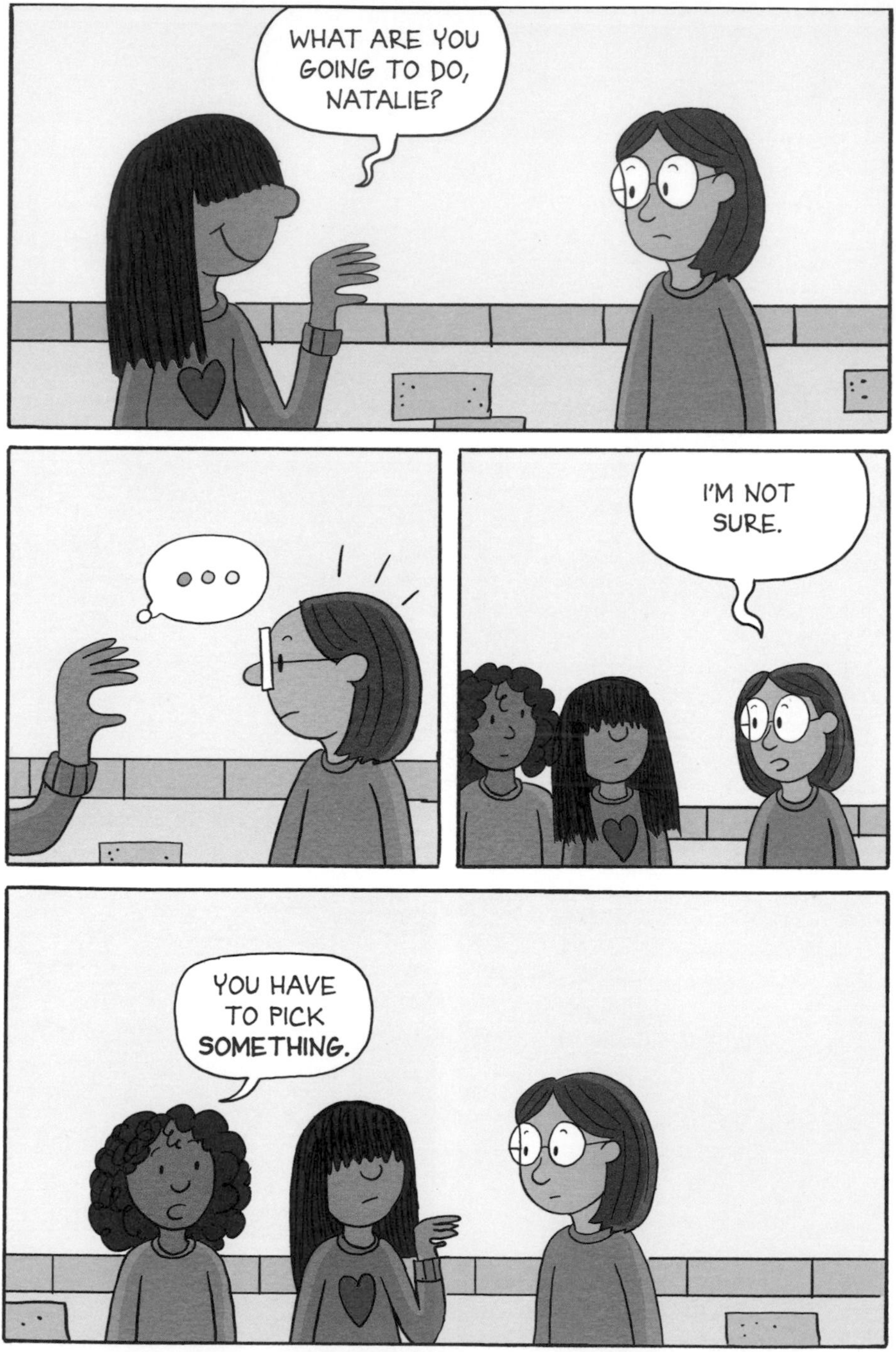
WHAT ARE YOU GOING TO DO, NATALIE?
...
I'M NOT SURE.
YOU HAVE TO PICK SOMETHING.

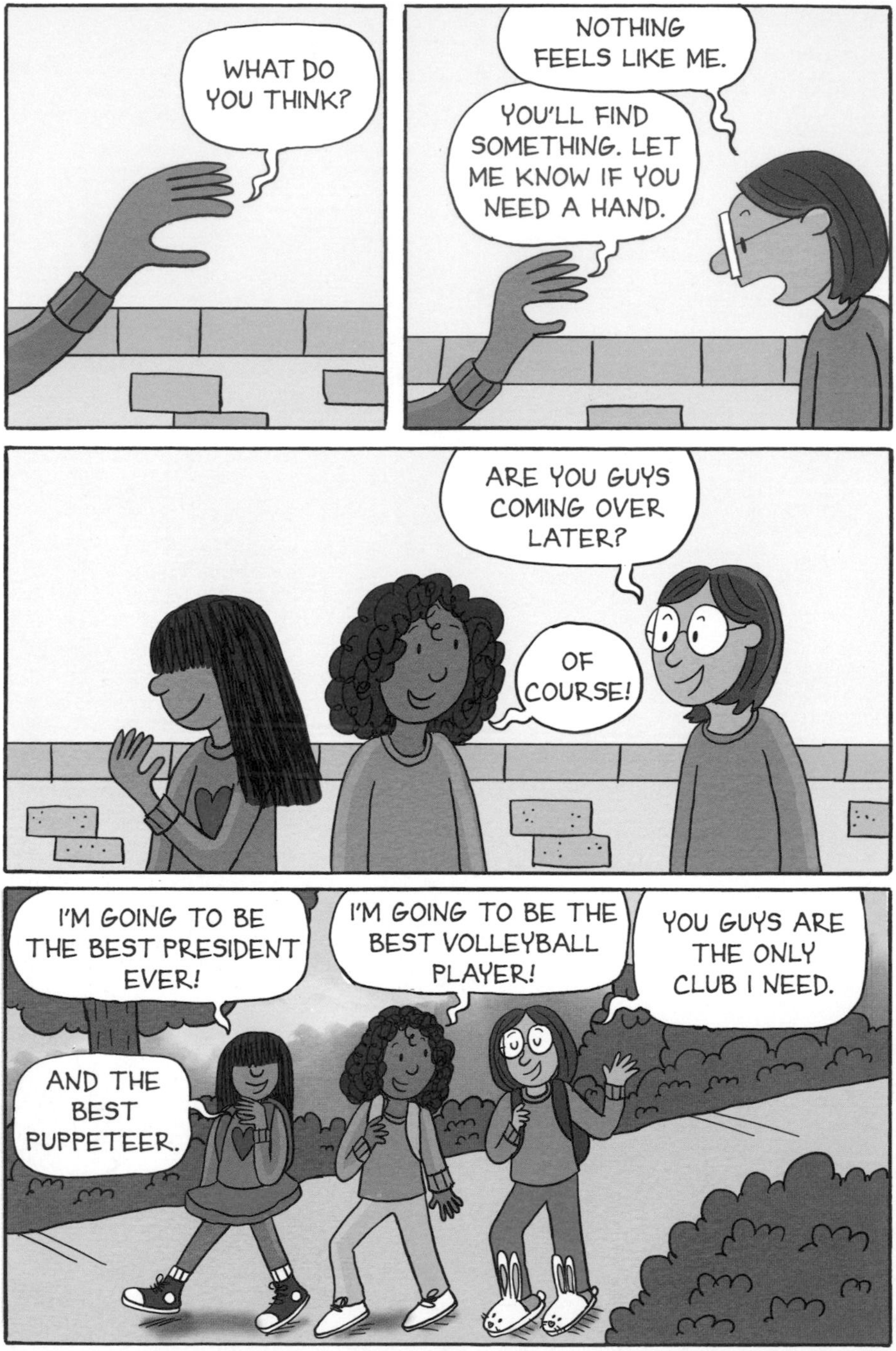
WHAT DO YOU THINK?
NOTHING FEELS LIKE ME.
YOU'LL FIND SOMETHING. LET ME KNOW IF YOU NEED A HAND.
ARE YOU GUYS COMING OVER LATER?
OF COURSE!
I'M GOING TO BE THE BEST PRESIDENT EVER!
AND THE BEST PUPPETEER.
I'M GOING TO BE THE BEST VOLLEYBALL PLAYER!
YOU GUYS ARE THE ONLY CLUB I NEED.

CHAPTER 3
BOREDOM

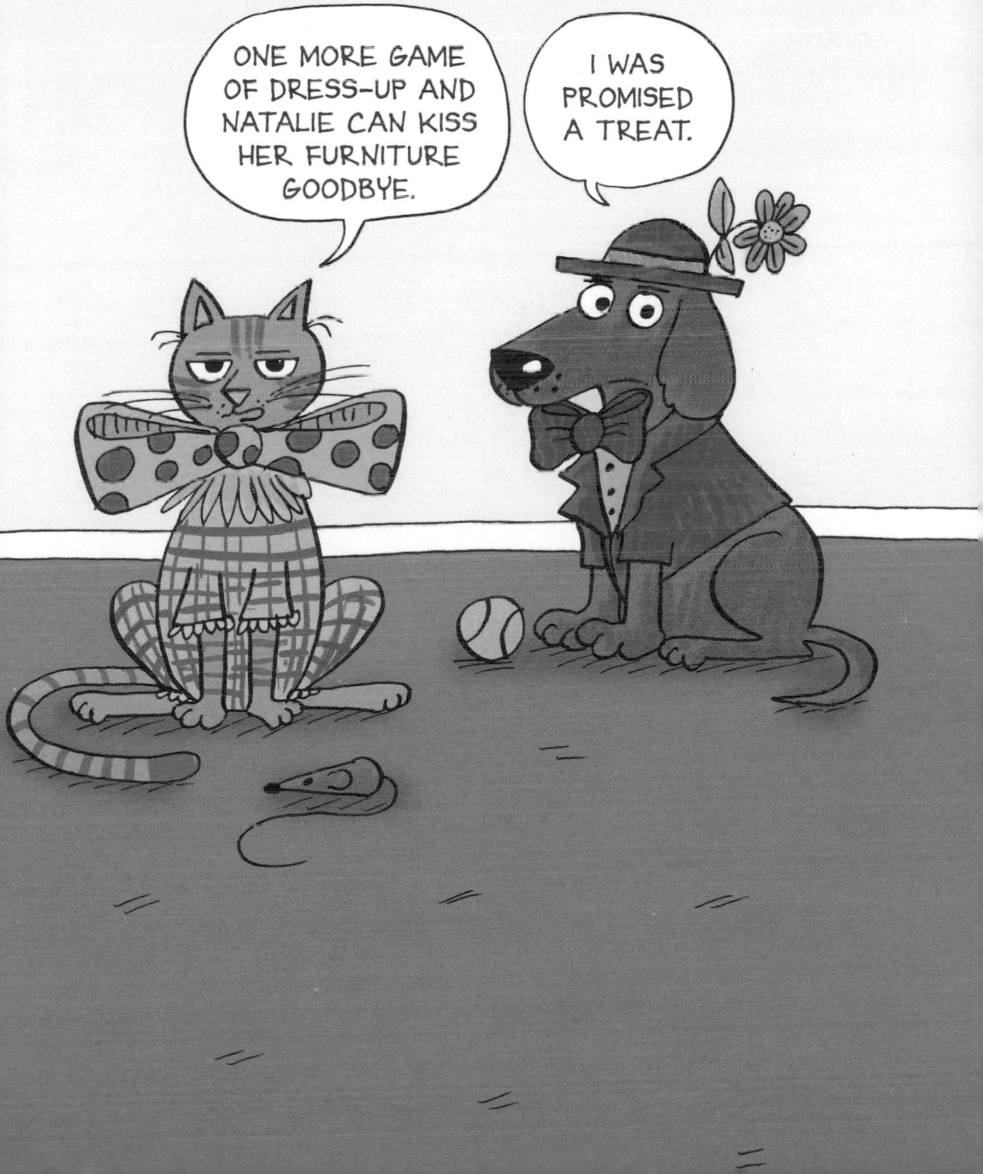

ONE MORE GAME OF DRESS-UP AND NATALIE CAN KISS HER FURNITURE GOODBYE.
I WAS PROMISED A TREAT.

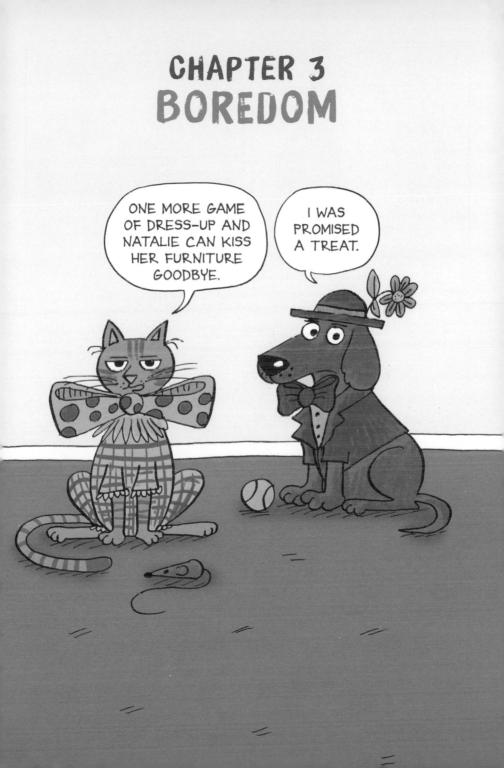

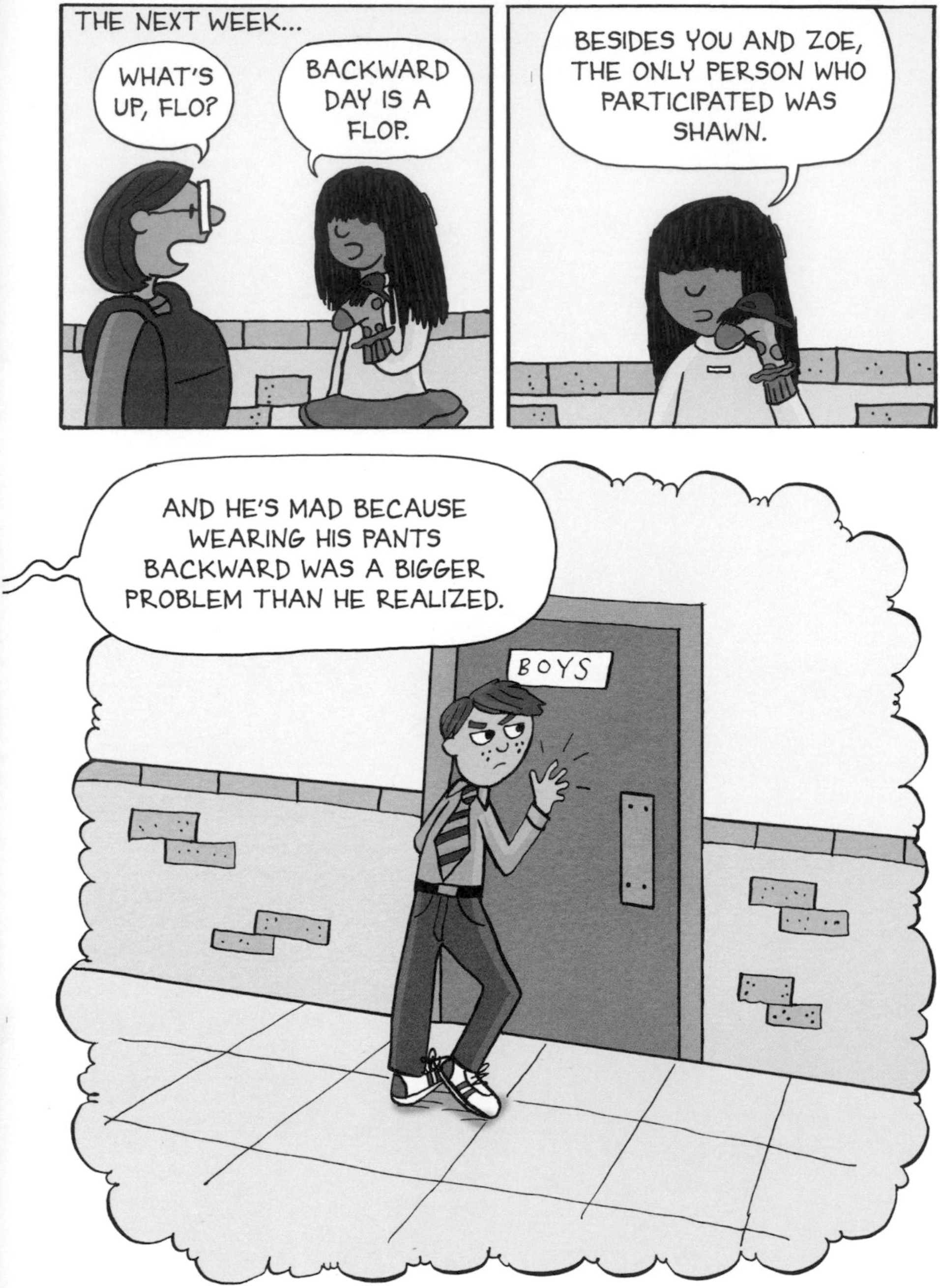
THE NEXT WEEK...
WHAT'S UP, FLO?
BACKWARD DAY IS A FLOP.
BESIDES YOU AND ZOE, THE ONLY PERSON WHO PARTICIPATED WAS SHAWN.
AND HE'S MAD BECAUSE WEARING HIS PANTS BACKWARD WAS A BIGGER PROBLEM THAN HE REALIZED.
BOYS

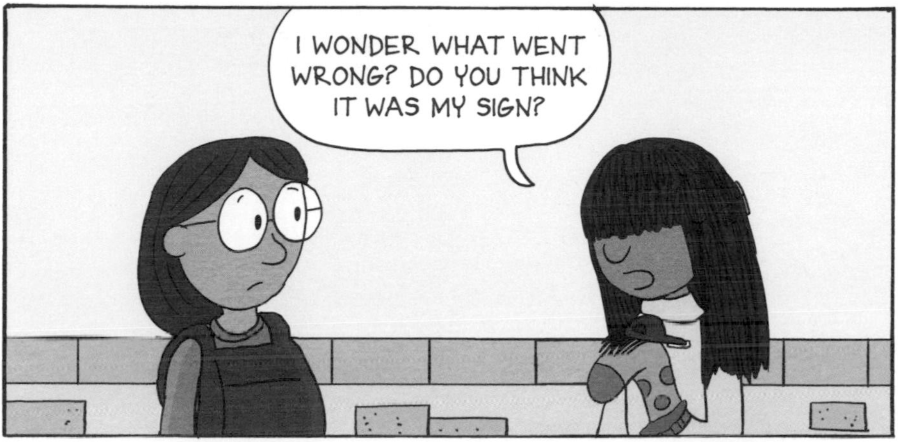
I WONDER WHAT WENT WRONG? DO YOU THINK IT WAS MY SIGN?

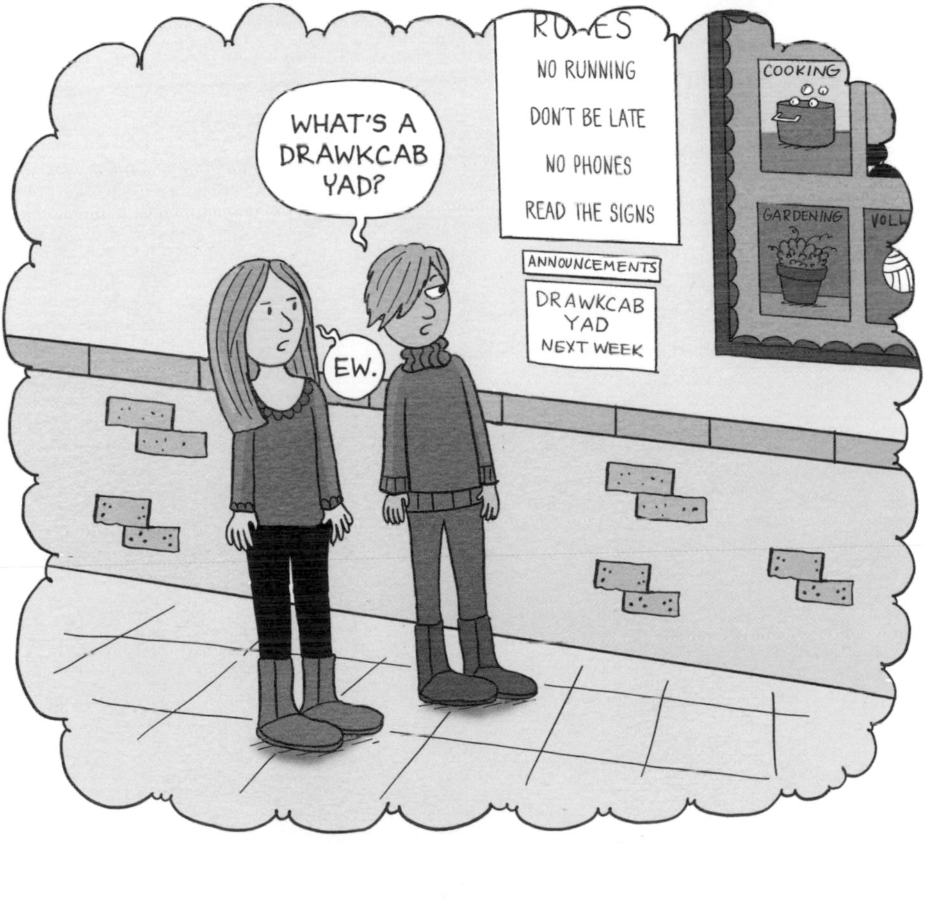
RU ES
NO RUNNING
DON'T BE LATE
NO PHONES
READ THE SIGNS
COOKING
GARDENING
VOLL
ANNOUNCEMENTS
DRAWKCAB YAD NEXT WEEK
WHAT'S A DRAWKCAB YAD?
EW.

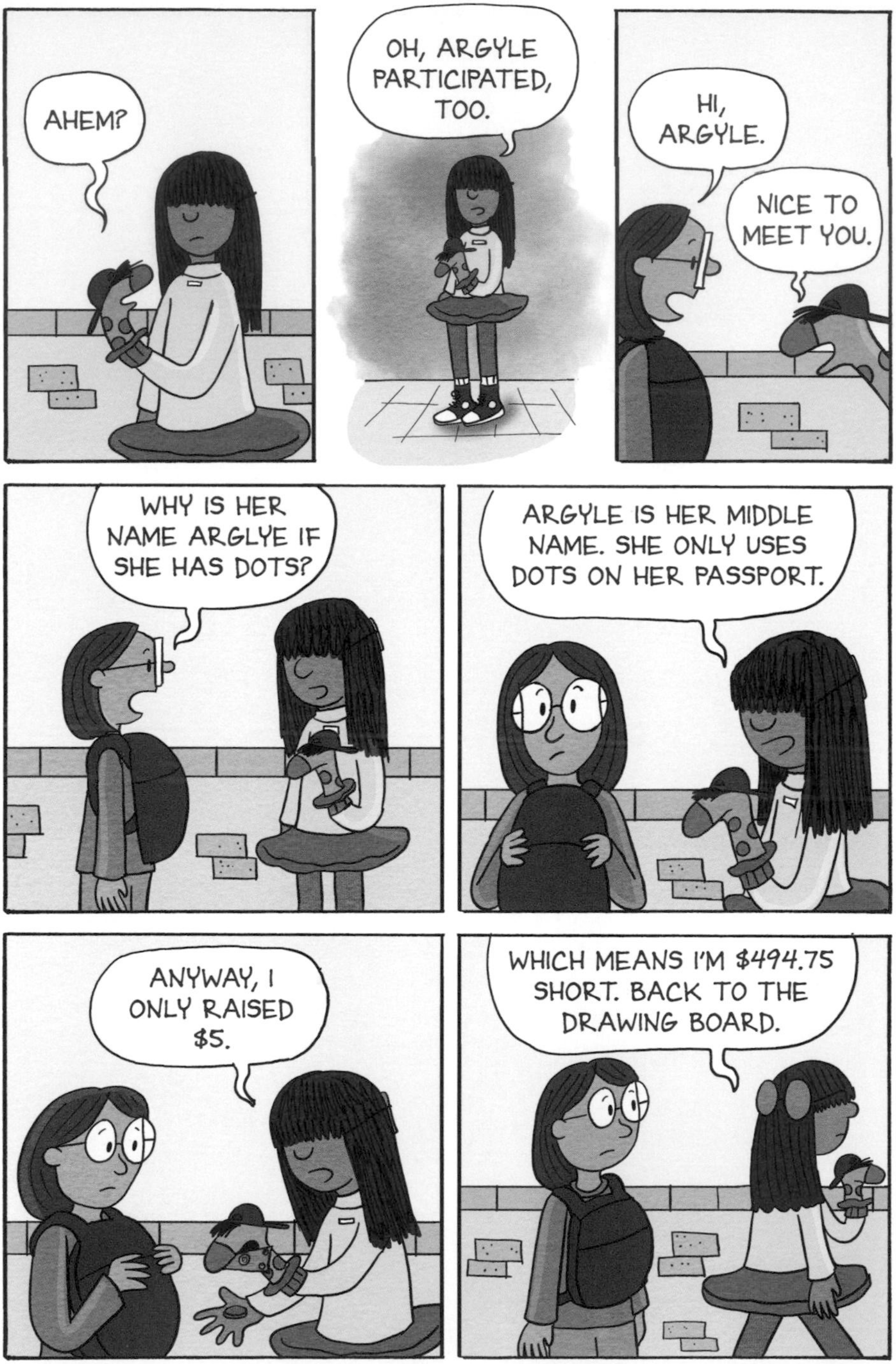
AHEM?
OH, ARGYLE PARTICIPATED, TOO.
HI, ARGYLE.
NICE TO MEET YOU.
WHY IS HER NAME ARGLYE IF SHE HAS DOTS?
ARGYLE IS HER MIDDLE NAME. SHE ONLY USES DOTS ON HER PASSPORT.
ANYWAY, I ONLY RAISED $5.
WHICH MEANS I'M $494.75 SHORT. BACK TO THE DRAWING BOARD.

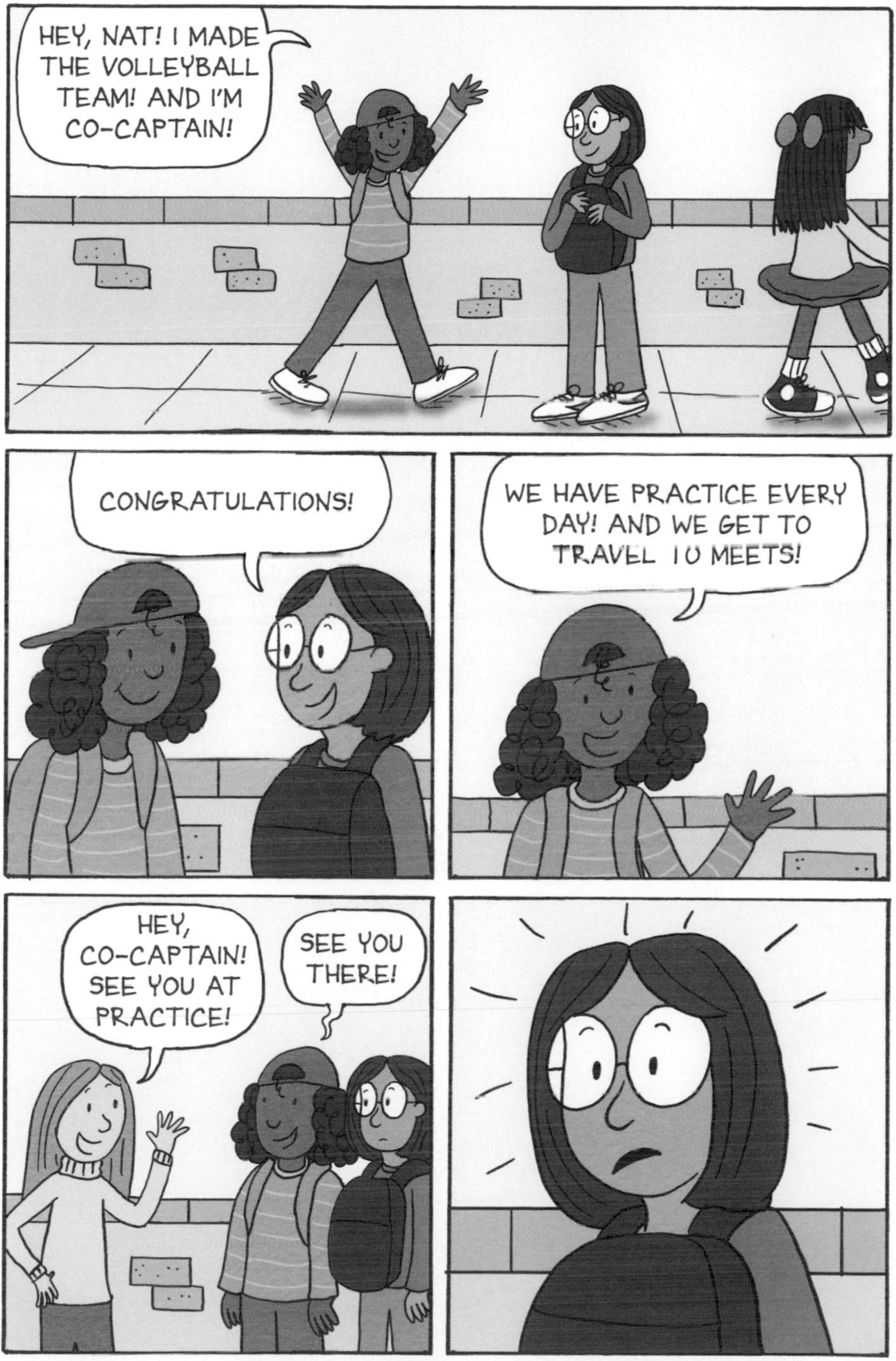
HEY, NAT! I MADE THE VOLLEYBALL TEAM! AND I'M CO-CAPTAIN!
CONGRATULATIONS!
WE HAVE PRACTICE EVERY DAY! AND WE GET TO TRAVEL TO MEETS!
HEY, CO-CAPTAIN! SEE YOU AT PRACTICE!
SEE YOU THERE!

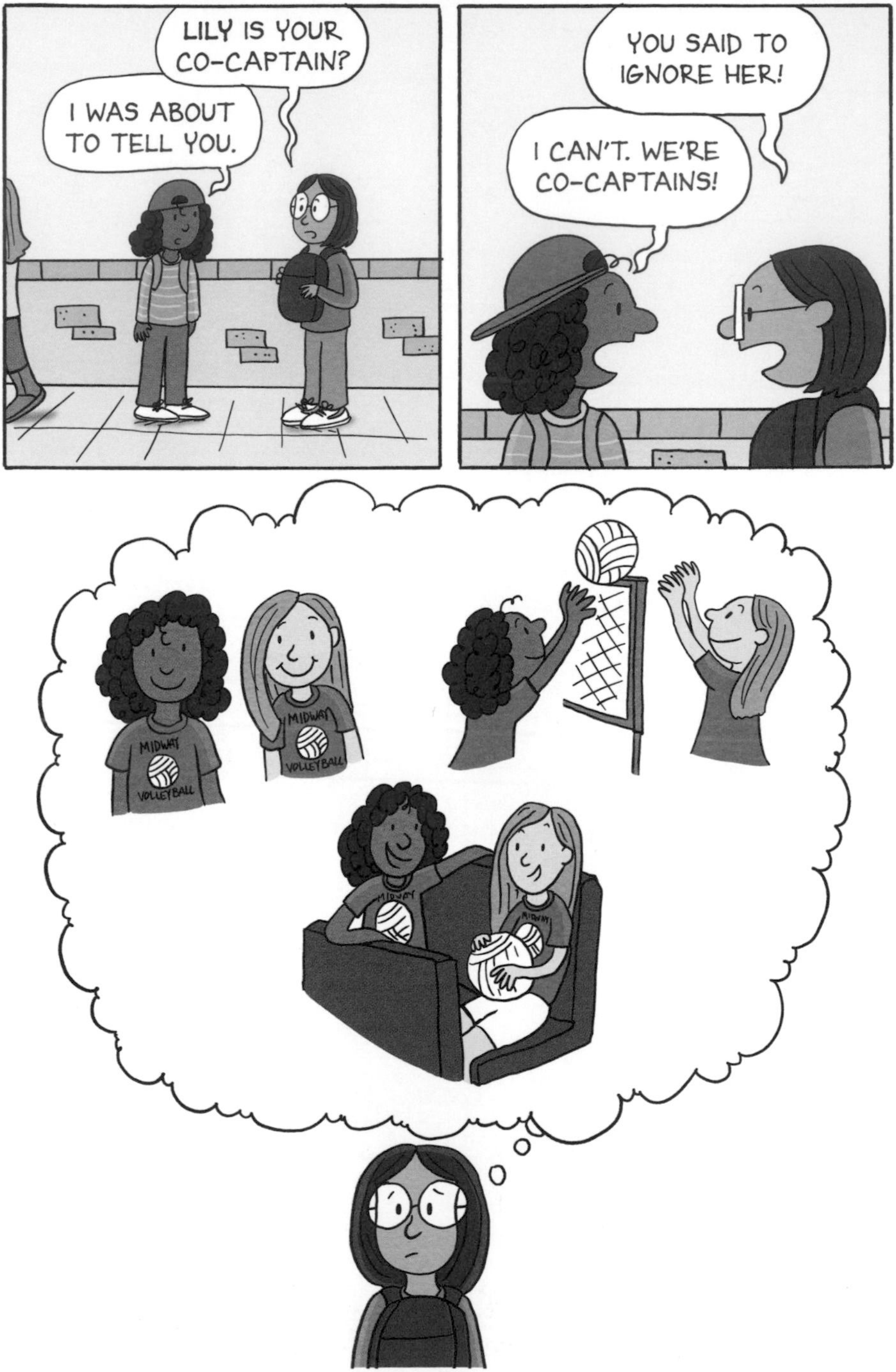
I WAS ABOUT TO TELL YOU.
LILY IS YOUR CO-CAPTAIN?
YOU SAID TO IGNORE HER!
I CAN'T. WE'RE CO-CAPTAINS!
MIDWAY VOLLEYBALL
MIDWAY VOLLEYBALL
MIDWAY
MIDWAY

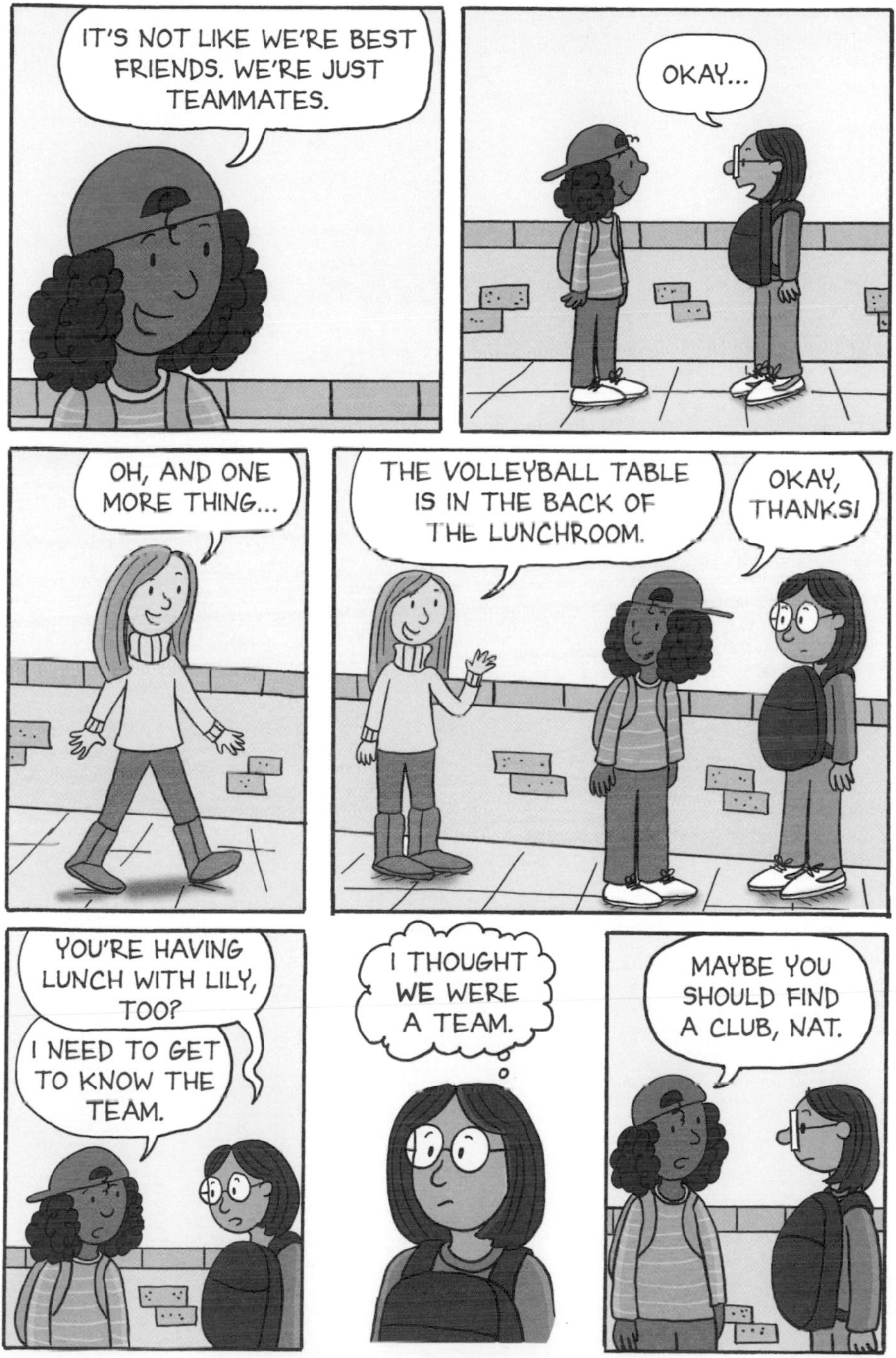
IT'S NOT LIKE WE'RE BEST FRIENDS. WE'RE JUST TEAMMATES.
OKAY...
OH, AND ONE MORE THING...
THE VOLLEYBALL TABLE IS IN THE BACK OF THE LUNCHROOM.
OKAY, THANKS!
YOU'RE HAVING LUNCH WITH LILY, TOO?
I NEED TO GET TO KNOW THE TEAM.
I THOUGHT WE WERE A TEAM.
MAYBE YOU SHOULD FIND A CLUB, NAT.

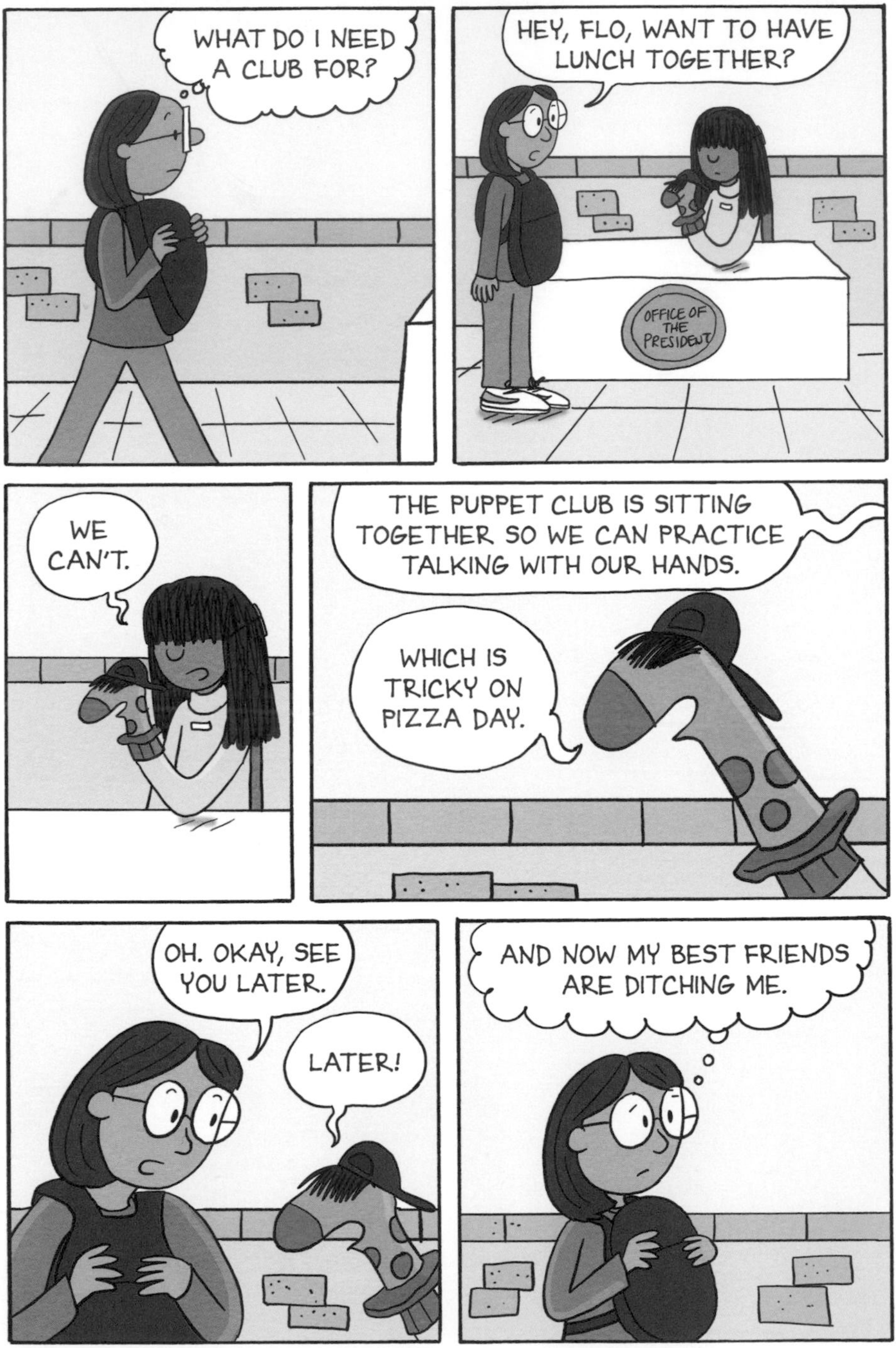
WHAT DO I NEED A CLUB FOR?
HEY, FLO, WANT TO HAVE LUNCH TOGETHER?
OFFICE OF THE PRESIDENT
WE CAN'T.
THE PUPPET CLUB IS SITTING TOGETHER SO WE CAN PRACTICE TALKING WITH OUR HANDS.
WHICH IS TRICKY ON PIZZA DAY.
OH. OKAY, SEE YOU LATER.
LATER!
AND NOW MY BEST FRIENDS ARE DITCHING ME.

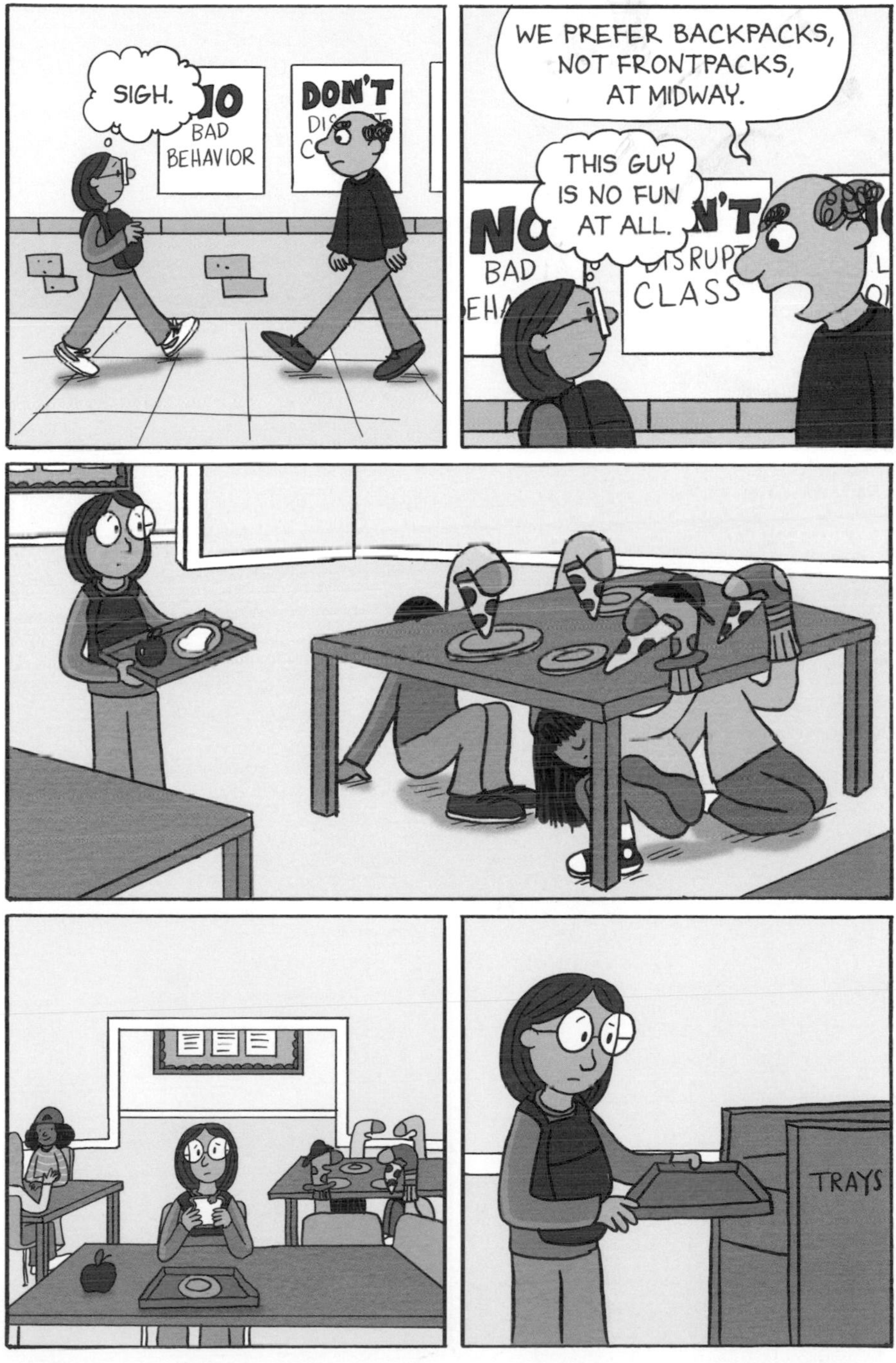
SIGH.
NO BAD BEHAVIOR
DON'T
WE PREFER BACKPACKS, NOT FRONTPACKS, AT MIDWAY.
THIS GUY IS NO FUN AT ALL.
BAD
DISRUPT CLASS
TRAYS

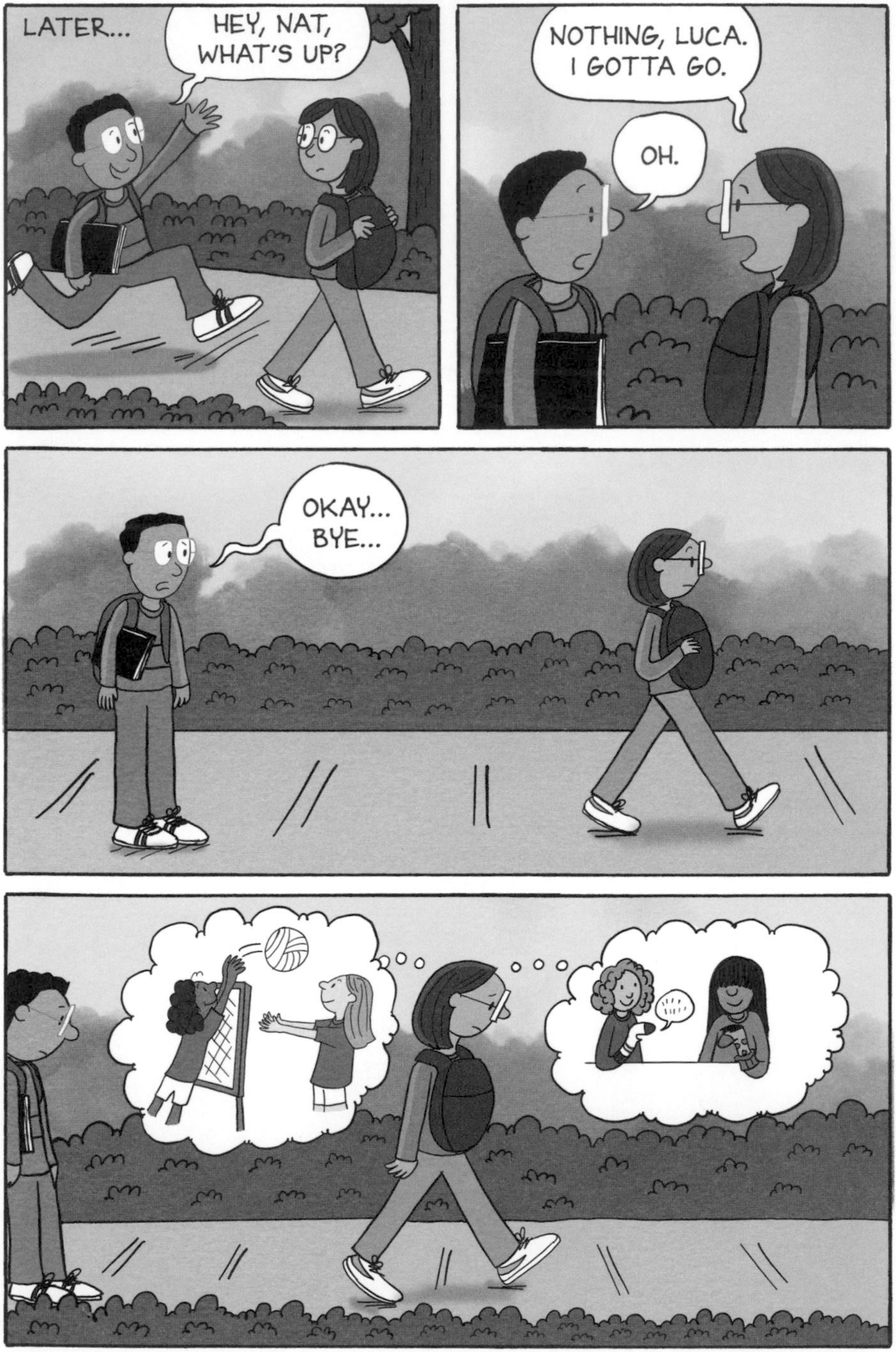
LATER...
HEY, NAT, WHAT'S UP?
NOTHING, LUCA. I GOTTA GO.
OH.
OKAY... BYE...

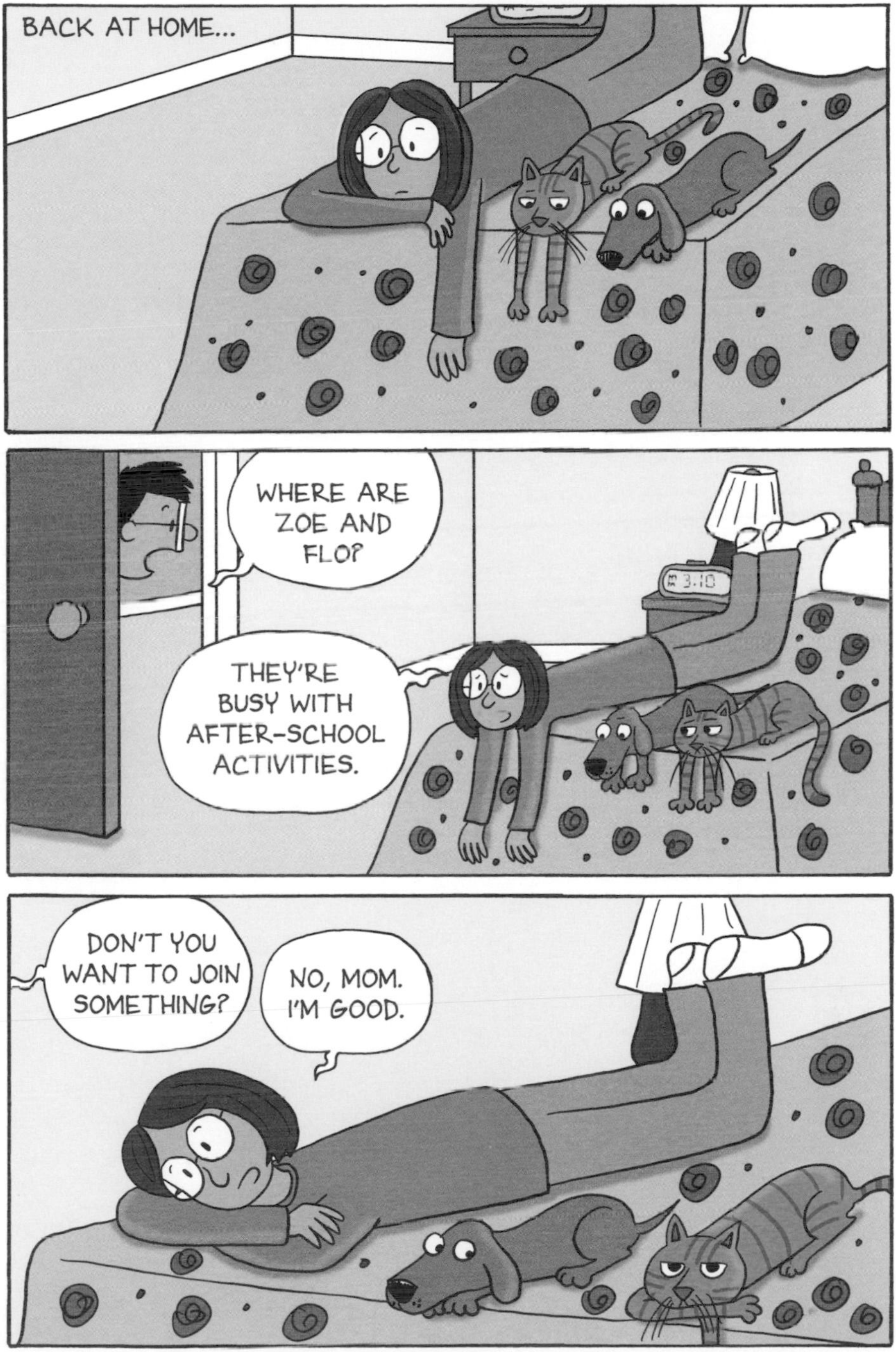
BACK AT HOME...
WHERE ARE ZOE AND FLO?
THEY'RE BUSY WITH AFTER-SCHOOL ACTIVITIES.
DON'T YOU WANT TO JOIN SOMETHING?
NO, MOM. I'M GOOD.

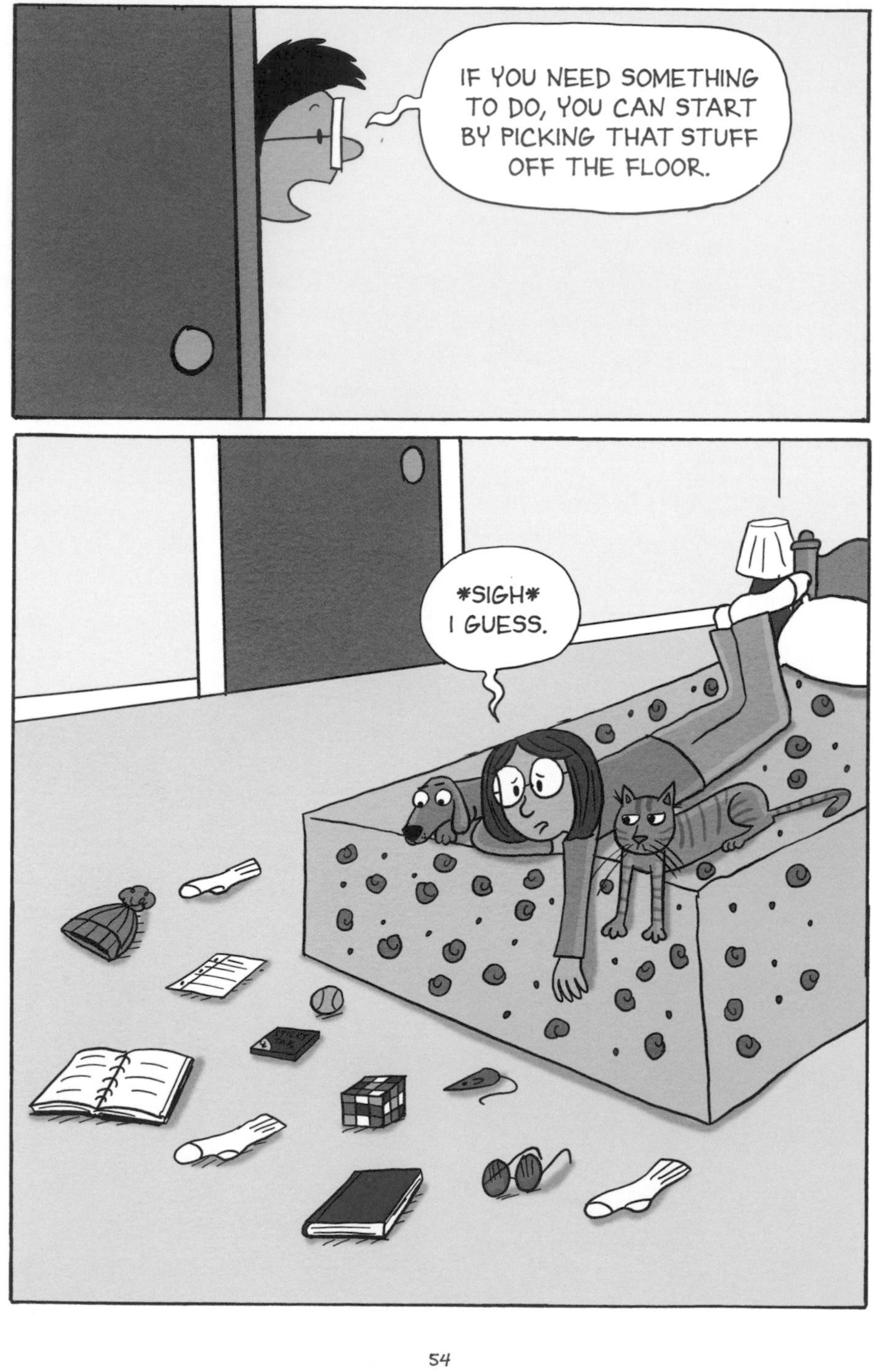
IF YOU NEED SOMETHING TO DO, YOU CAN START BY PICKING THAT STUFF OFF THE FLOOR.
SIGH I GUESS.

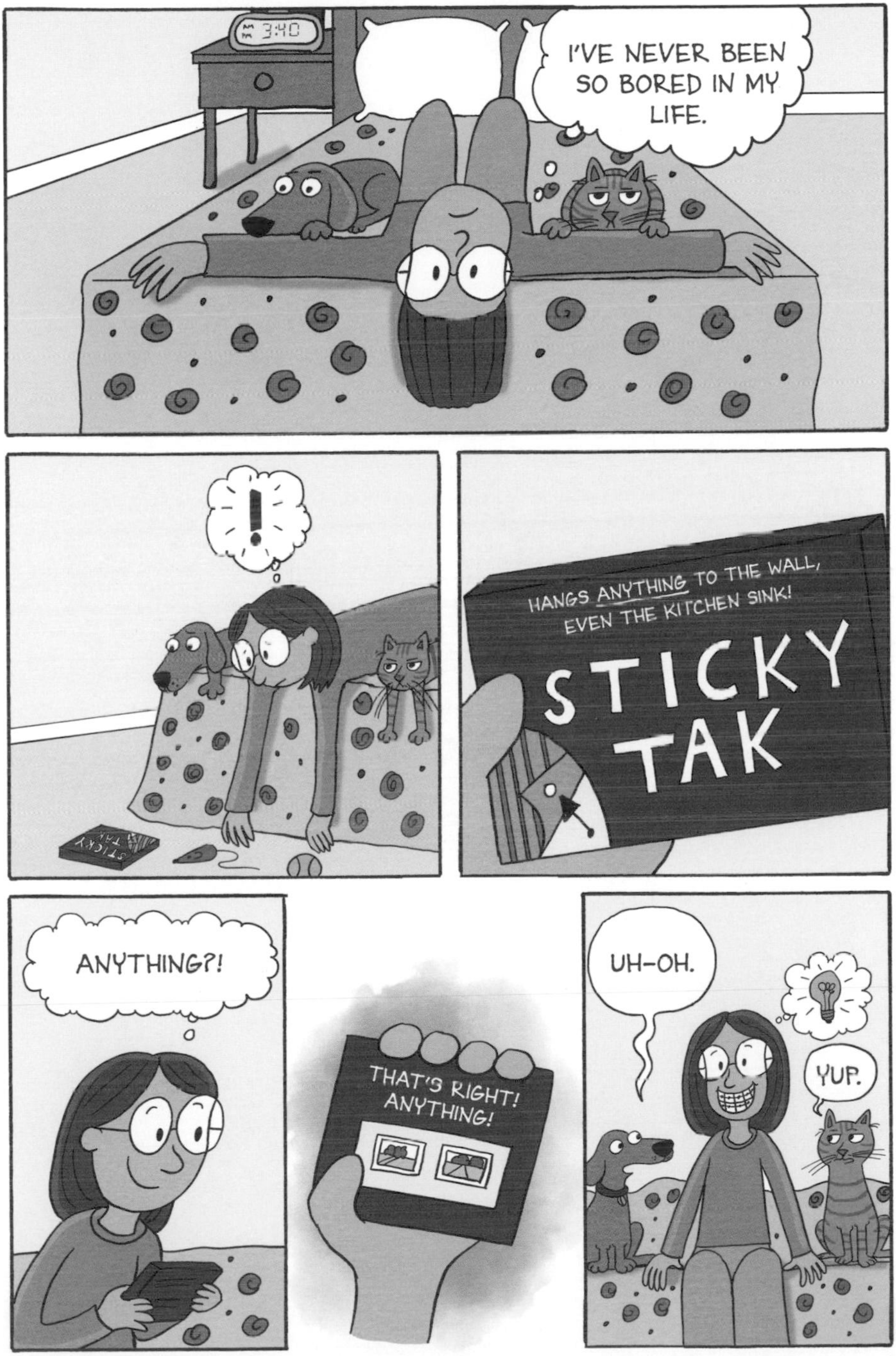
3:40
I'VE NEVER BEEN SO BORED IN MY LIFE.
!
HANGS ANYTHING TO THE WALL, EVEN THE KITCHEN SINK!
STICKY TAK
ANYTHING?!
THAT'S RIGHT! ANYTHING!
UH-OH.
YUP.

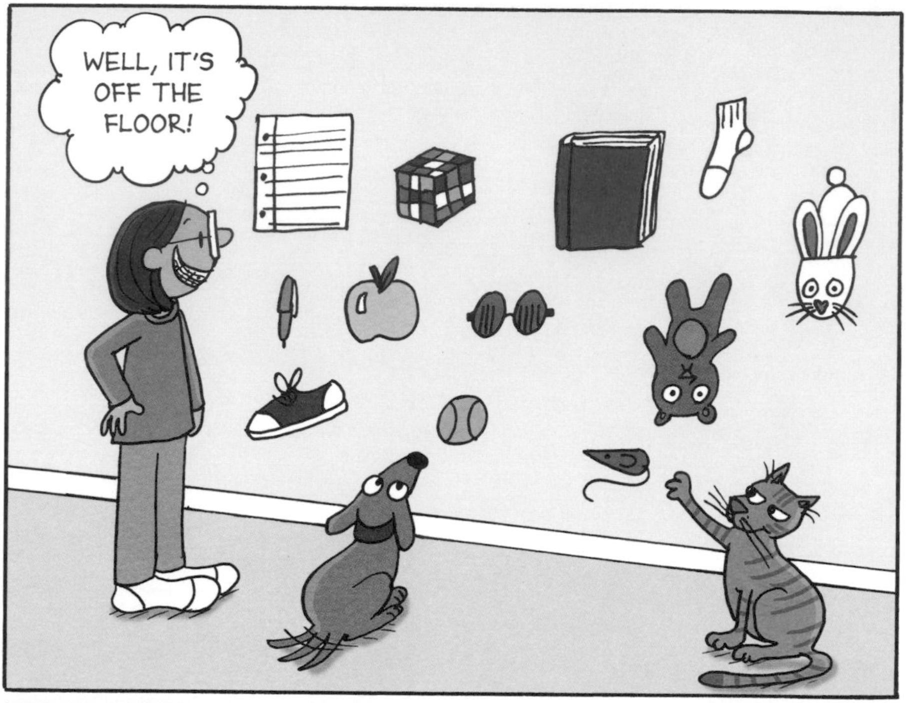
WELL, IT'S OFF THE FLOOR!

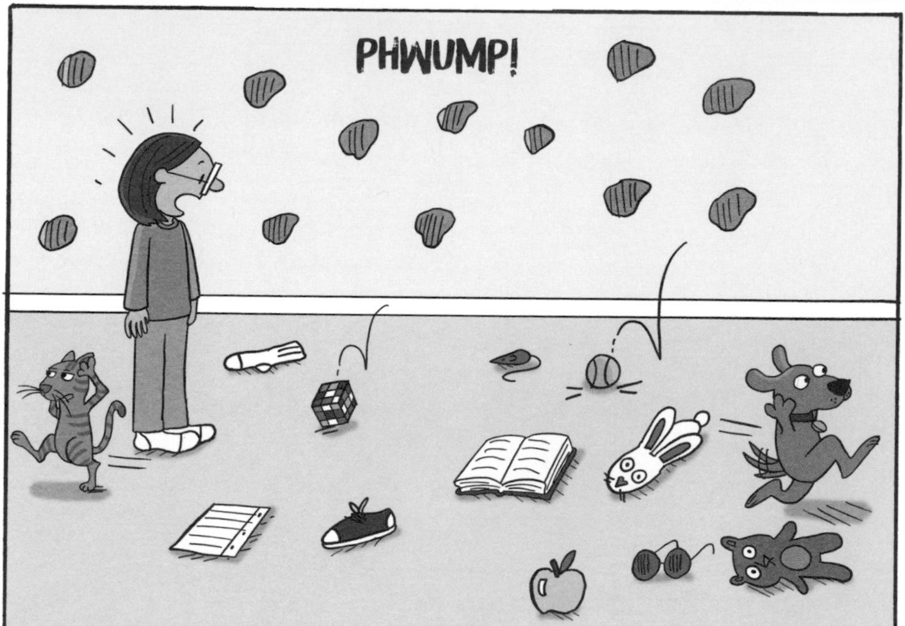
PHWUMP!

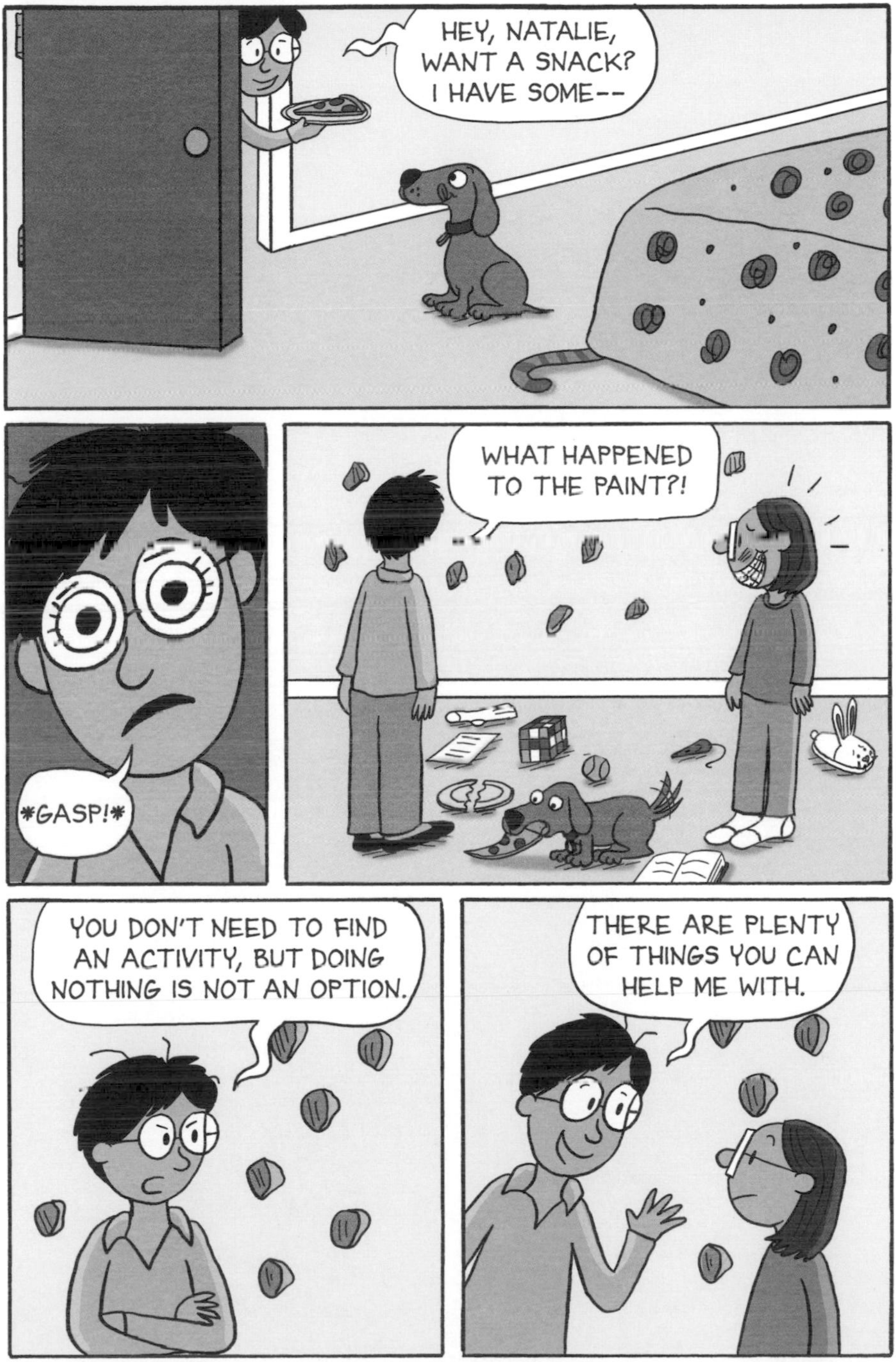
HEY, NATALIE,
WANT A SNACK?
I HAVE SOME--
GASP!
WHAT HAPPENED
TO THE PAINT?!
YOU DON'T NEED TO FIND
AN ACTIVITY, BUT DOING
NOTHING IS NOT AN OPTION.
THERE ARE PLENTY
OF THINGS YOU CAN
HELP ME WITH.

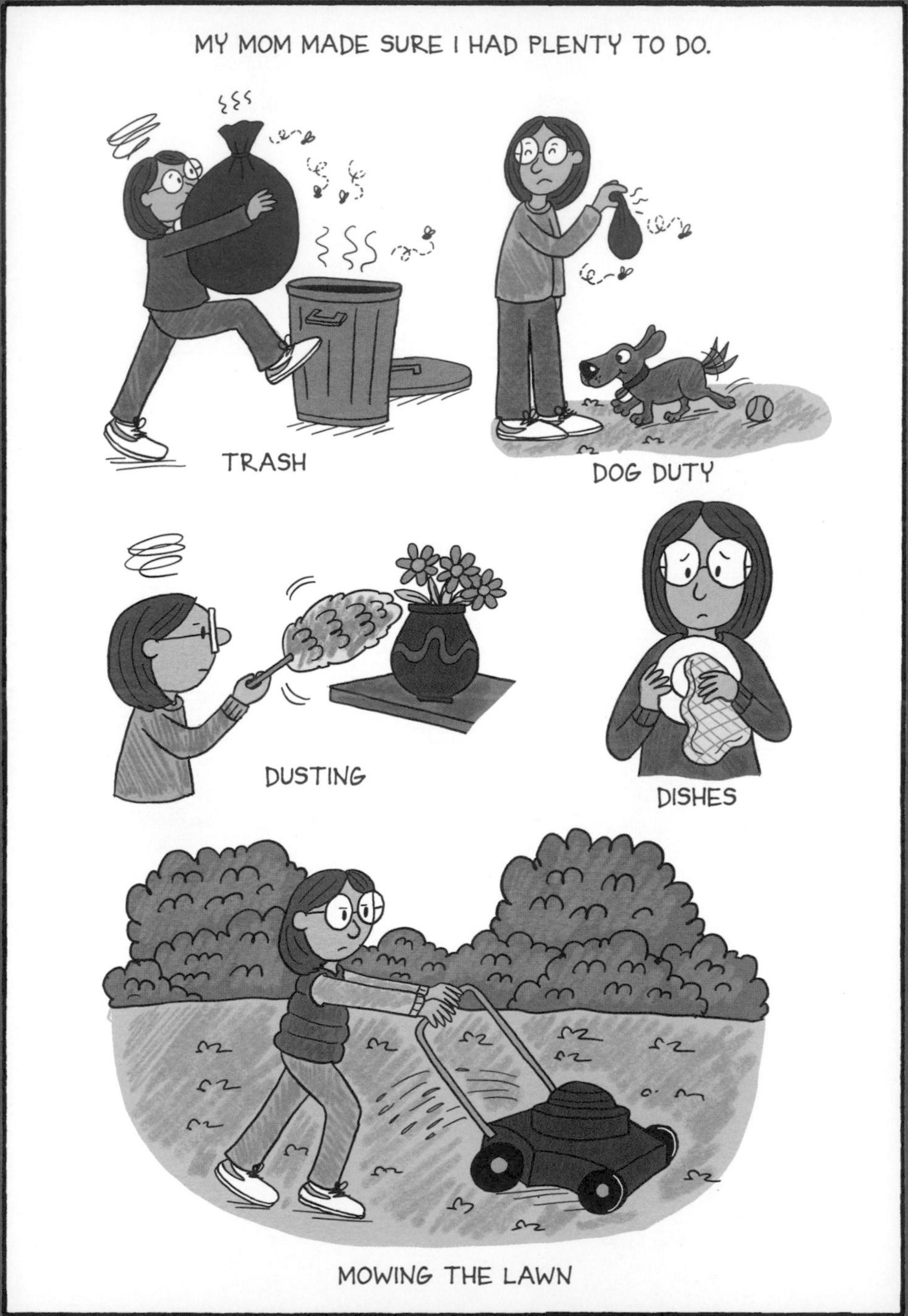
MY MOM MADE SURE I HAD PLENTY TO DO.
TRASH
DOG DUTY
DUSTING
DISHES
MOWING THE LAWN

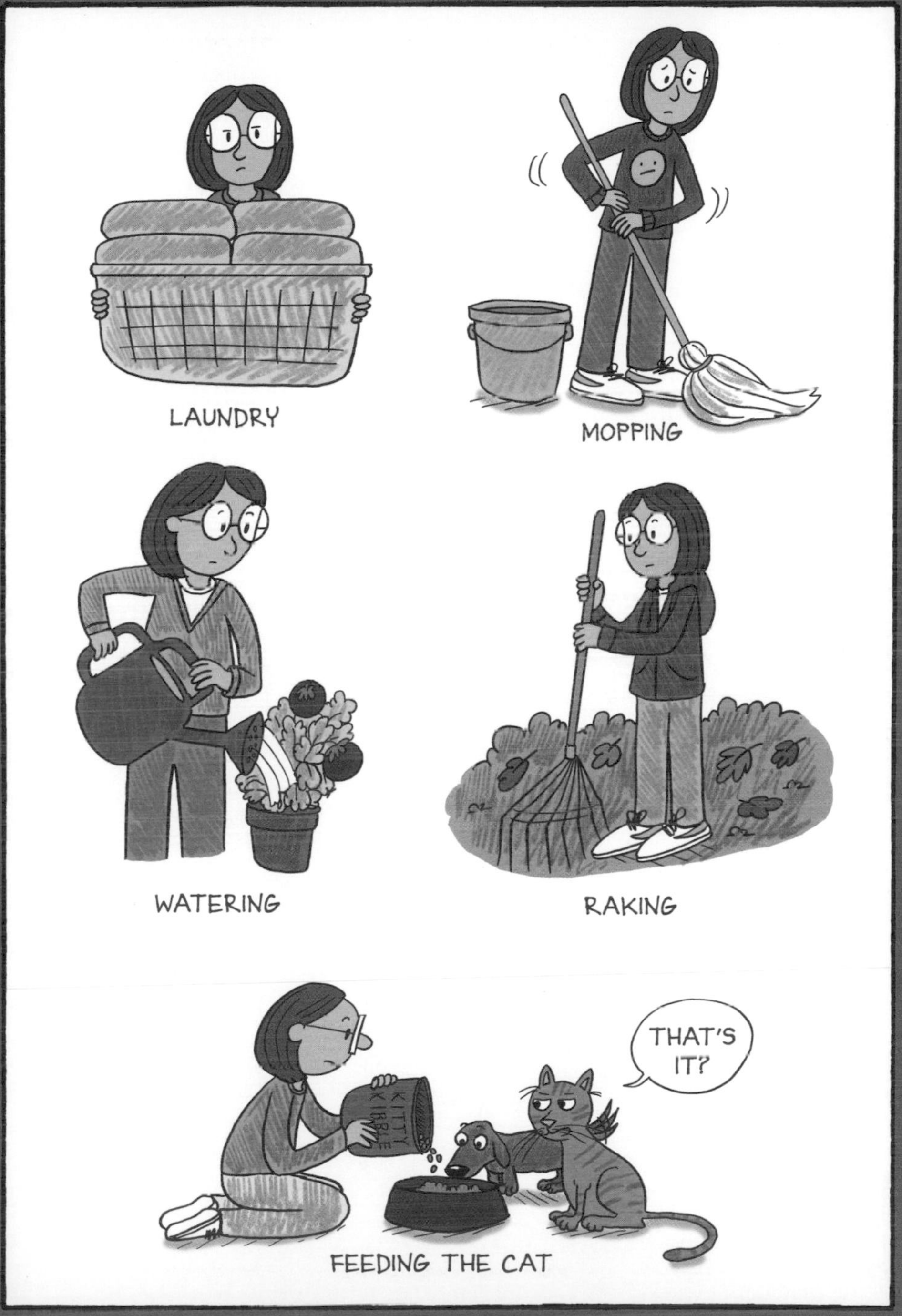
LAUNDRY
MOPPING
WATERING
RAKING
KITTY KIBBLE
THAT'S IT?
FEEDING THE CAT

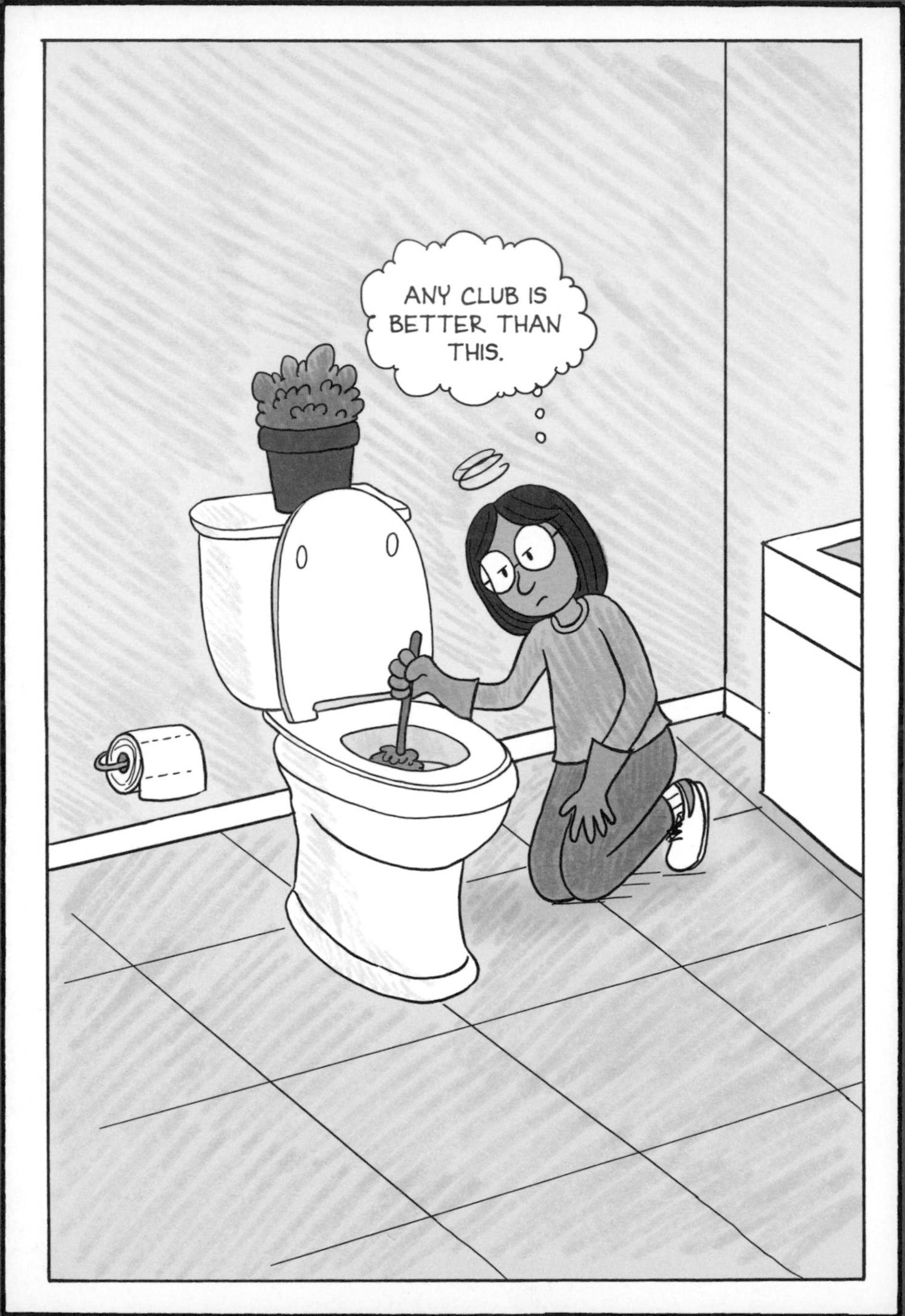
ANY CLUB IS BETTER THAN THIS.

CHAPTER 4
ACTIVITIES

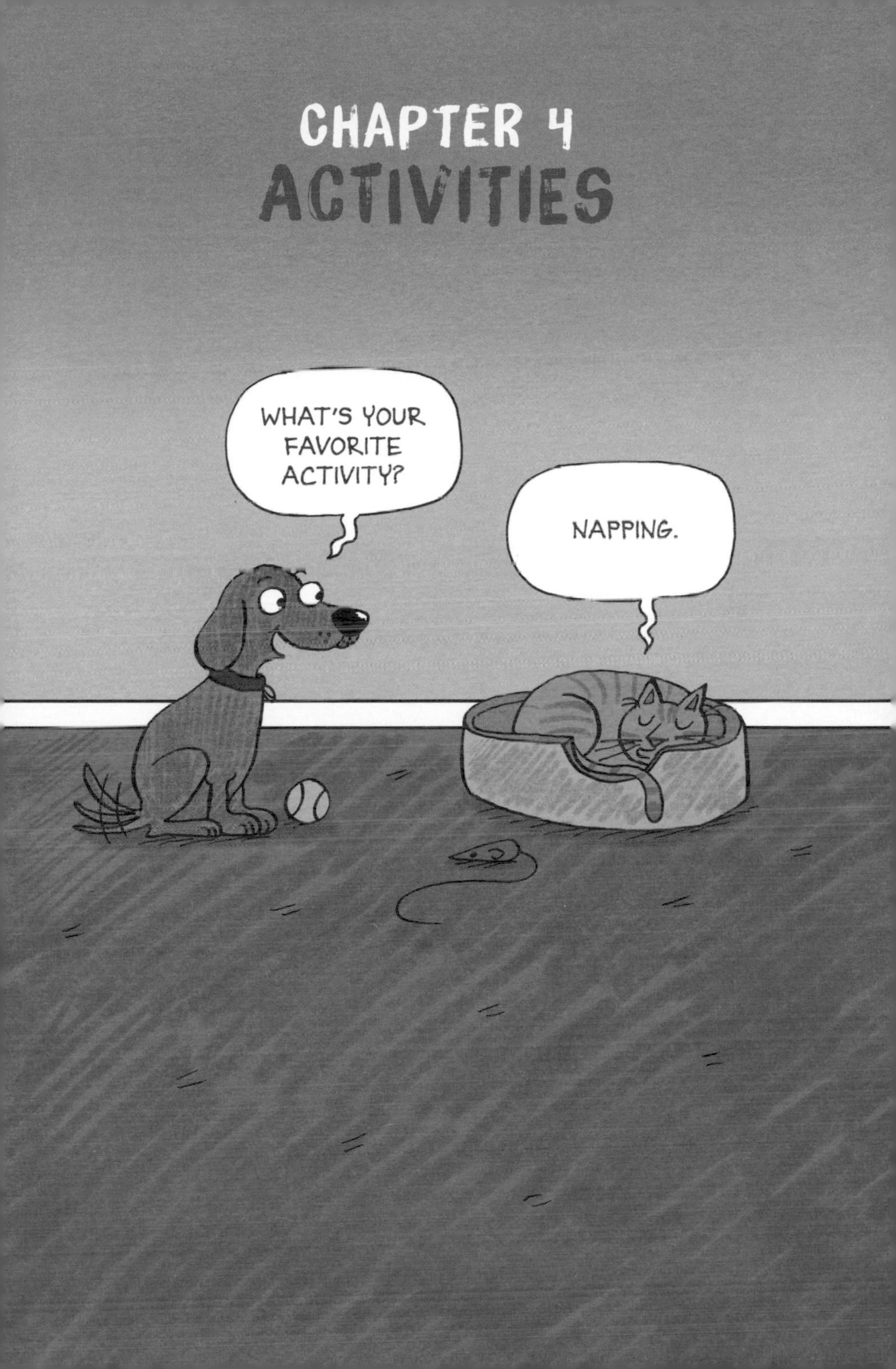
WHAT'S YOUR FAVORITE ACTIVITY?
NAPPING.

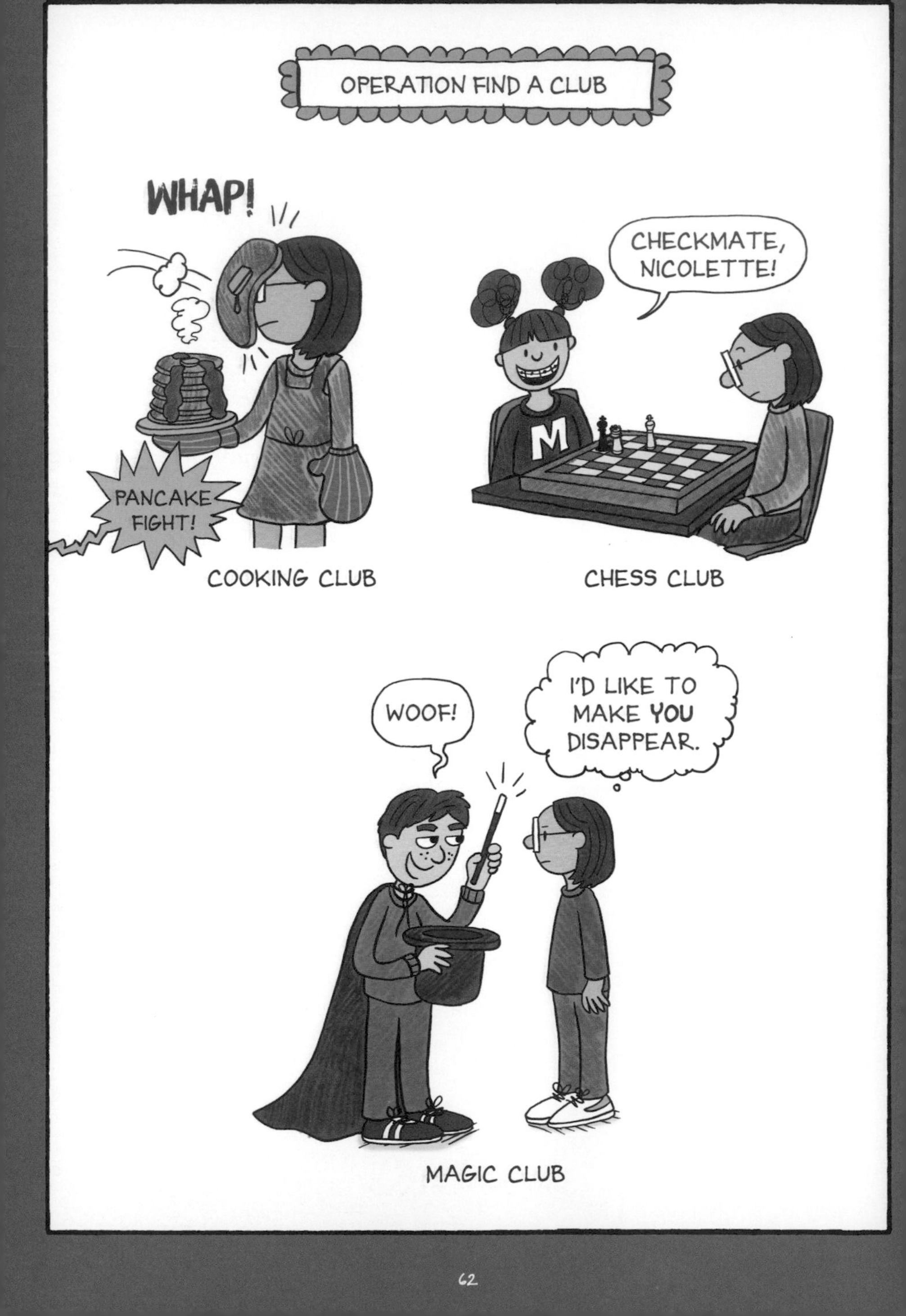
OPERATION FIND A CLUB
WHAP!
PANCAKE FIGHT!
COOKING CLUB
CHECKMATE, NICOLETTE!
M
CHESS CLUB
WOOF!
I'D LIKE TO MAKE **YOU** DISAPPEAR.
MAGIC CLUB

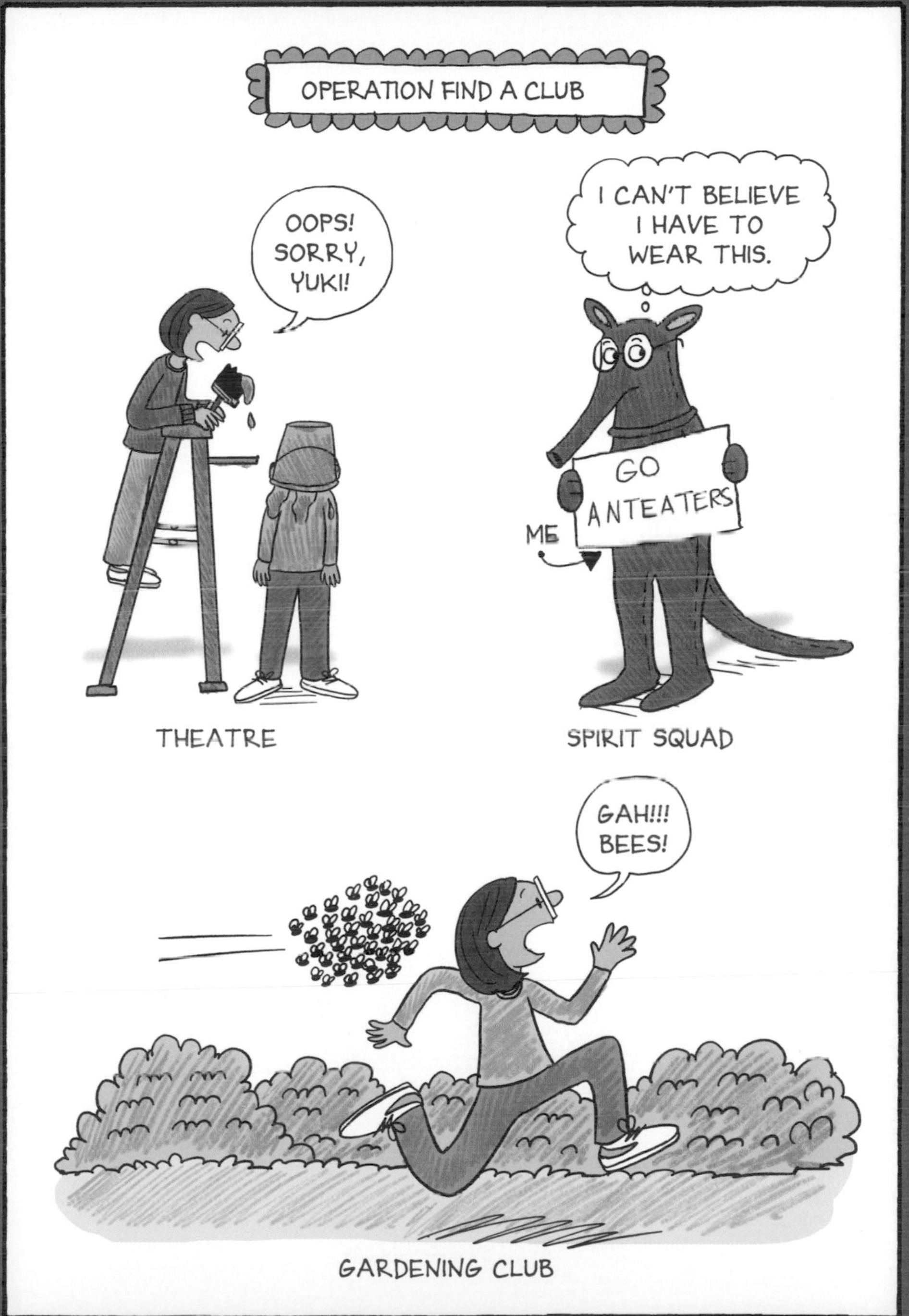
OPERATION FIND A CLUB
OOPS! SORRY, YUKI!
THEATRE
I CAN'T BELIEVE I HAVE TO WEAR THIS.
GO ANTEATERS
ME
SPIRIT SQUAD
GAH!!! BEES!
GARDENING CLUB

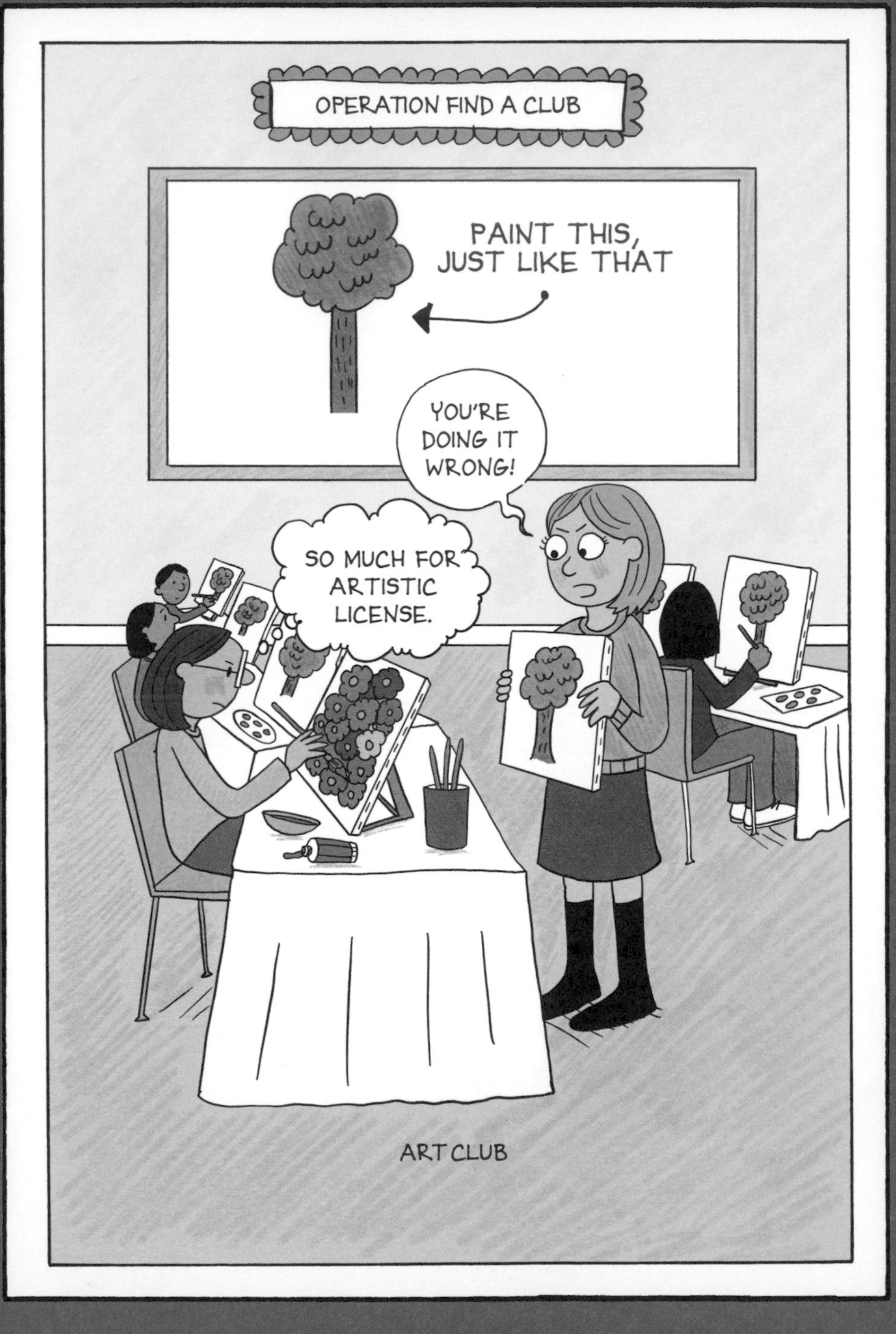
OPERATION FIND A CLUB
PAINT THIS, JUST LIKE THAT
YOU'RE DOING IT WRONG!
SO MUCH FOR ARTISTIC LICENSE.
ART CLUB

CHAPTER 5
CALL IT A DRAW

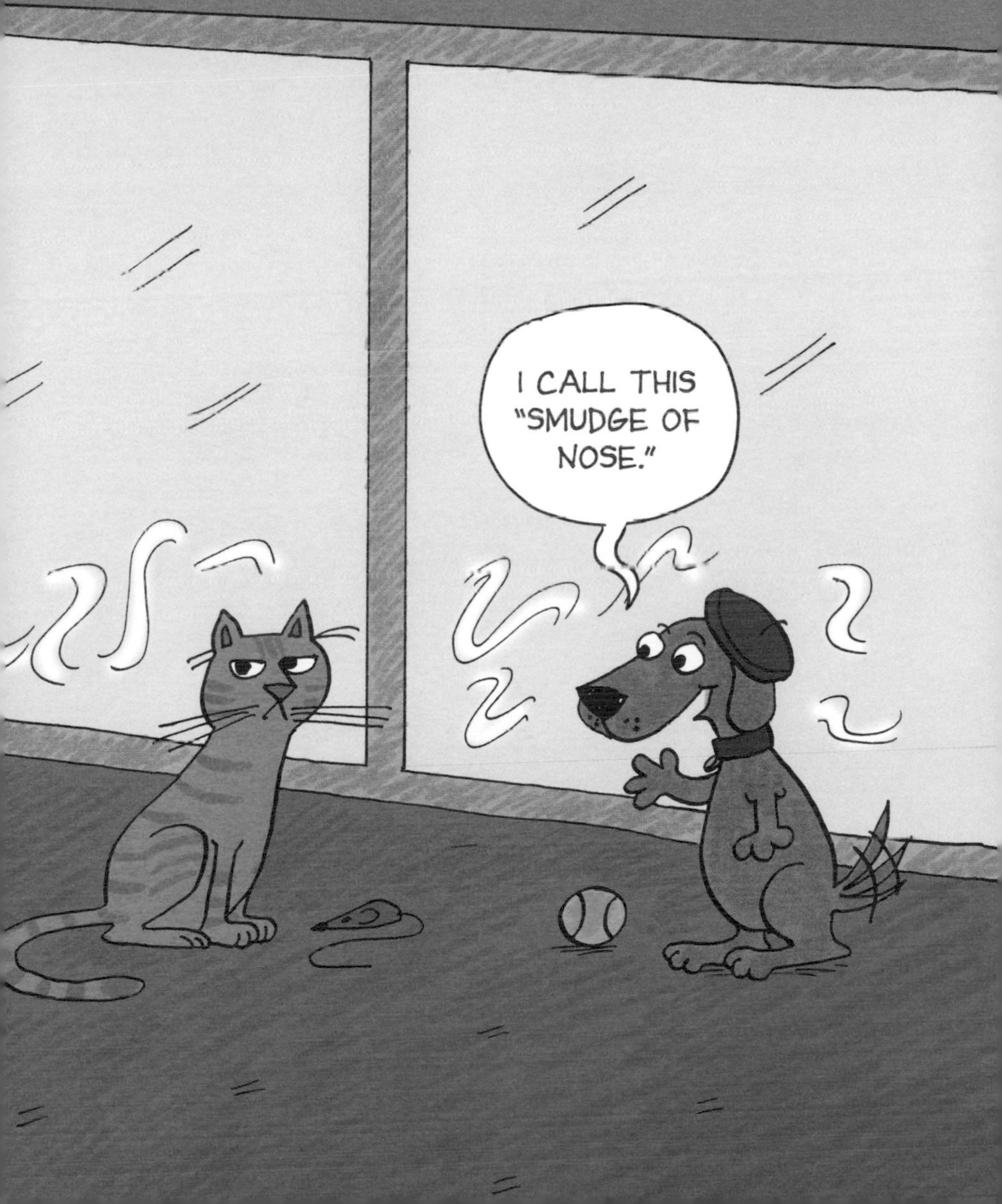
I CALL THIS "SMUDGE OF NOSE."

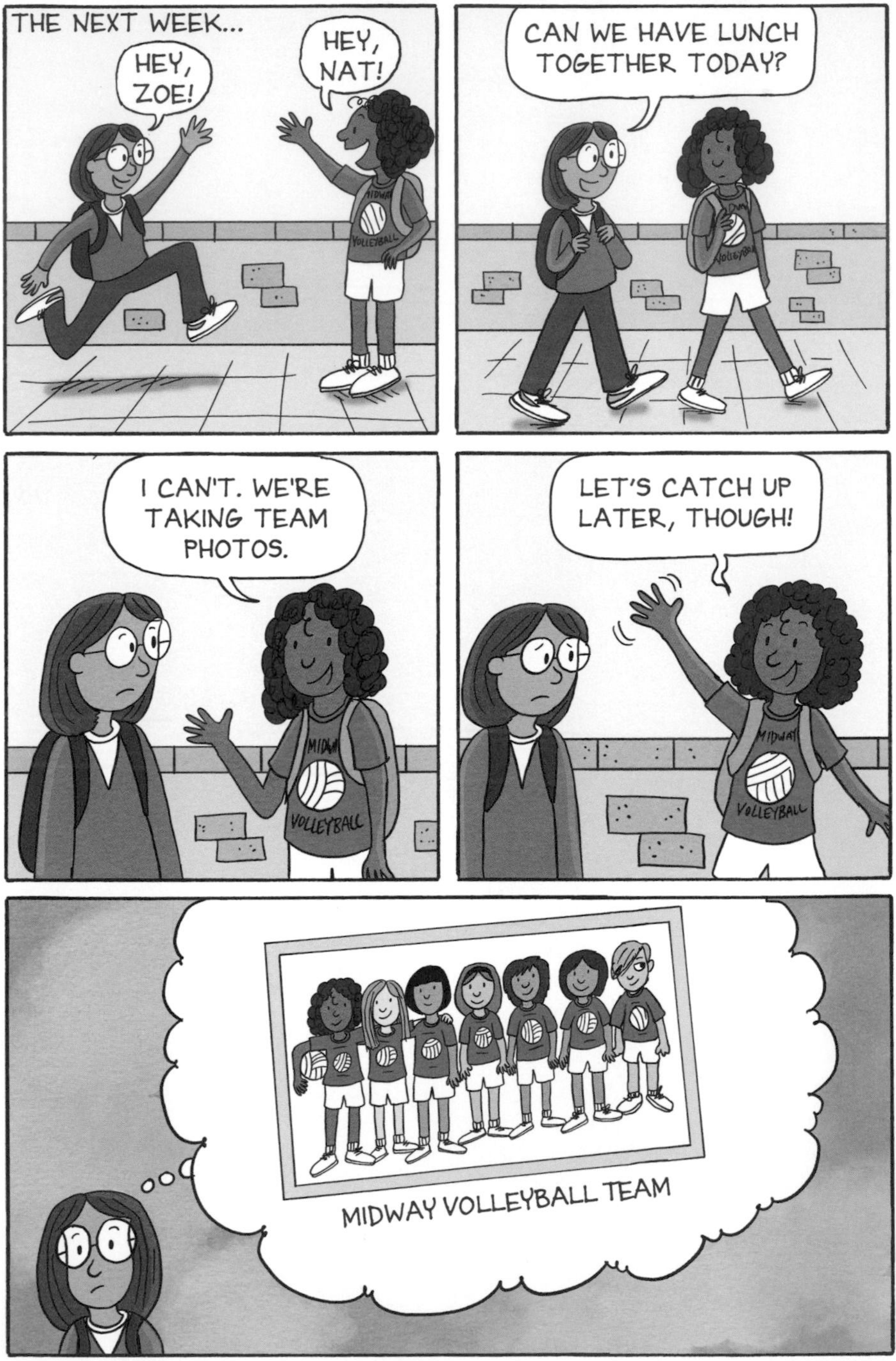
THE NEXT WEEK...
HEY, ZOE!
HEY, NAT!
CAN WE HAVE LUNCH TOGETHER TODAY?
I CAN'T. WE'RE TAKING TEAM PHOTOS.
LET'S CATCH UP LATER, THOUGH!
MIDWAY VOLLEYBALL TEAM

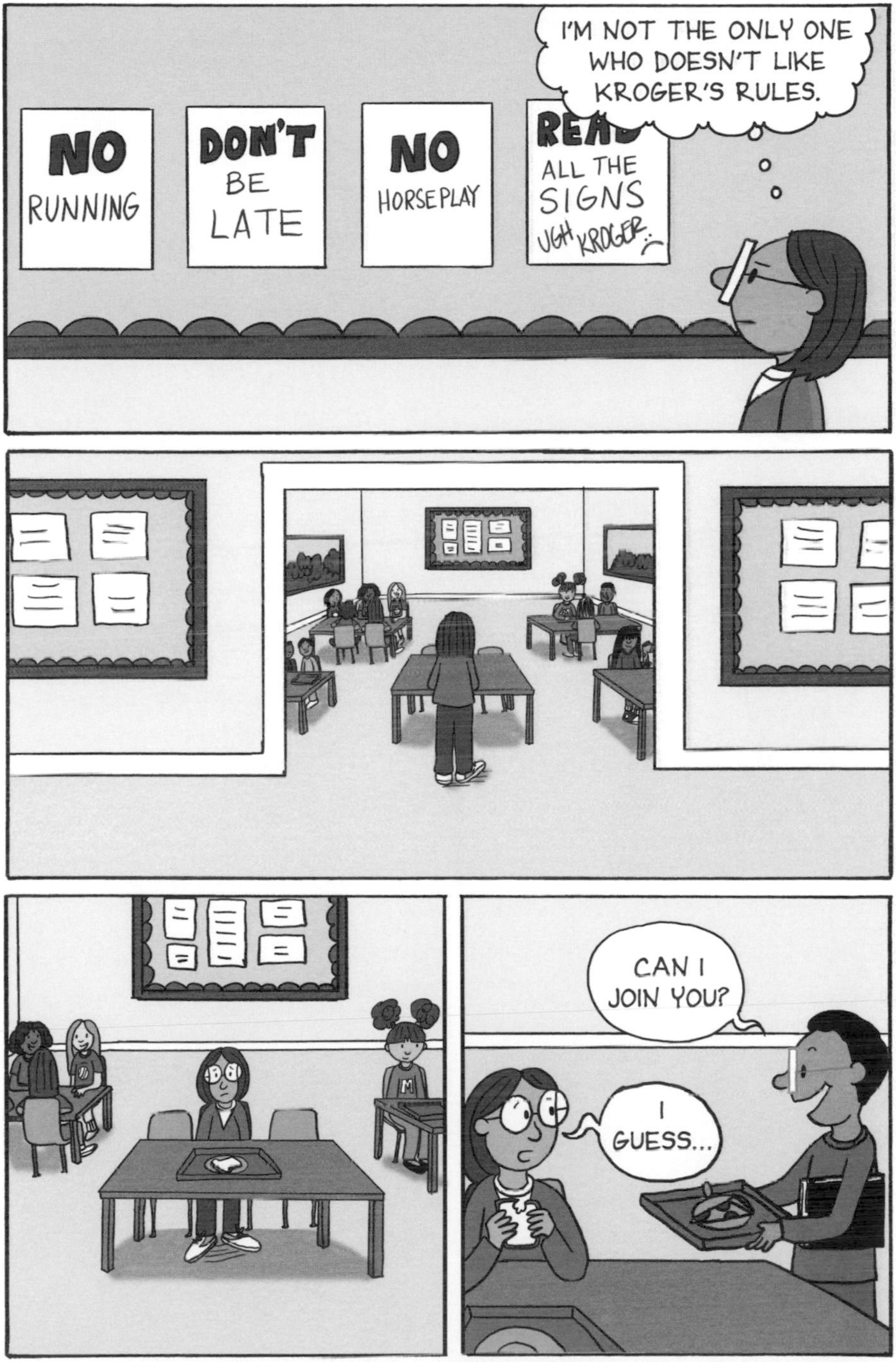
I'M NOT THE ONLY ONE WHO DOESN'T LIKE KROGER'S RULES.
NO RUNNING
DON'T BE LATE
NO HORSEPLAY
READ ALL THE SIGNS
UGH KROGER
CAN I JOIN YOU?
I GUESS...

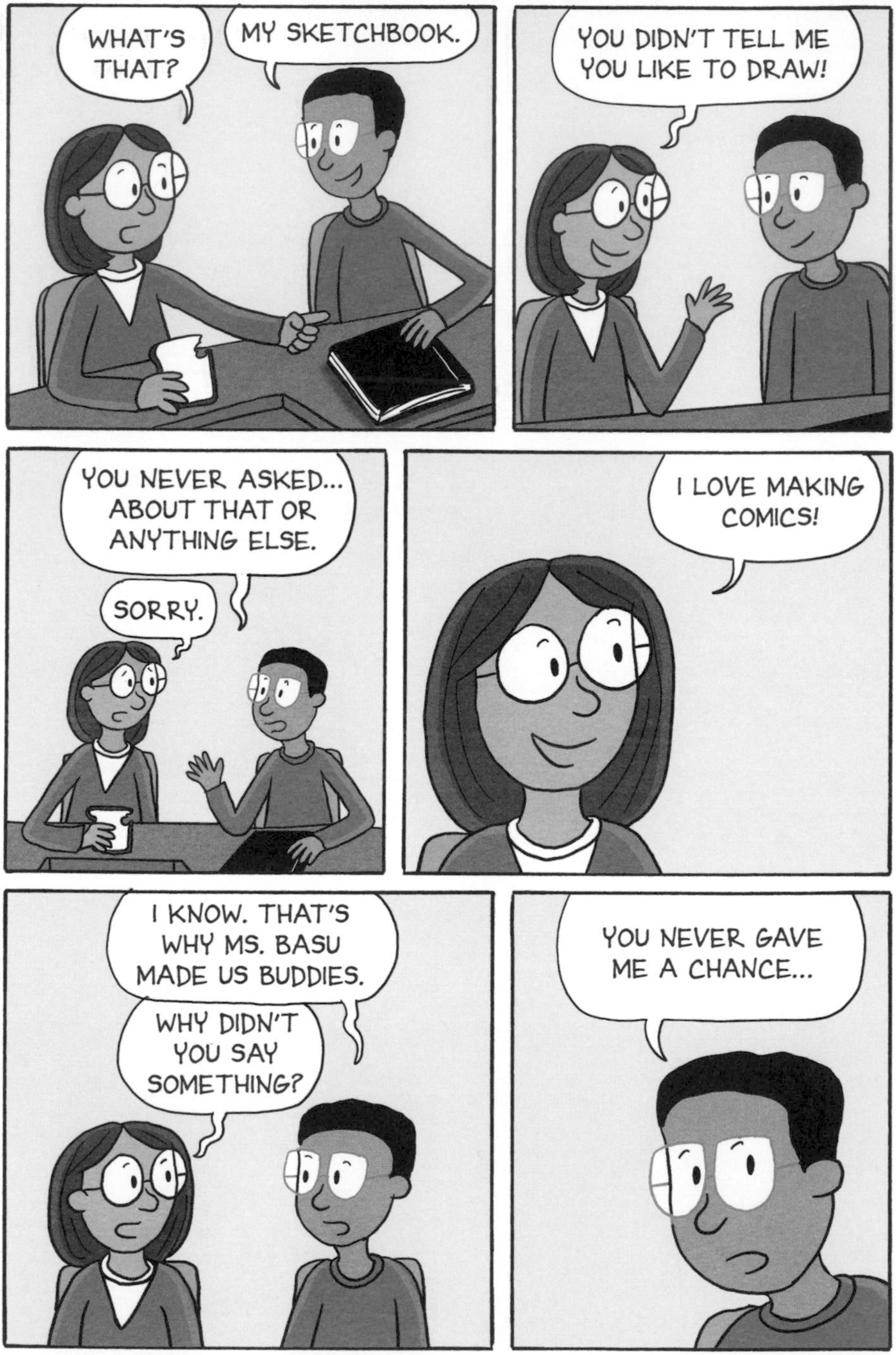
WHAT'S THAT?
MY SKETCHBOOK.
YOU DIDN'T TELL ME YOU LIKE TO DRAW!
YOU NEVER ASKED... ABOUT THAT OR ANYTHING ELSE.
SORRY.
I LOVE MAKING COMICS!
I KNOW. THAT'S WHY MS. BASU MADE US BUDDIES.
WHY DIDN'T YOU SAY SOMETHING?
YOU NEVER GAVE ME A CHANCE...

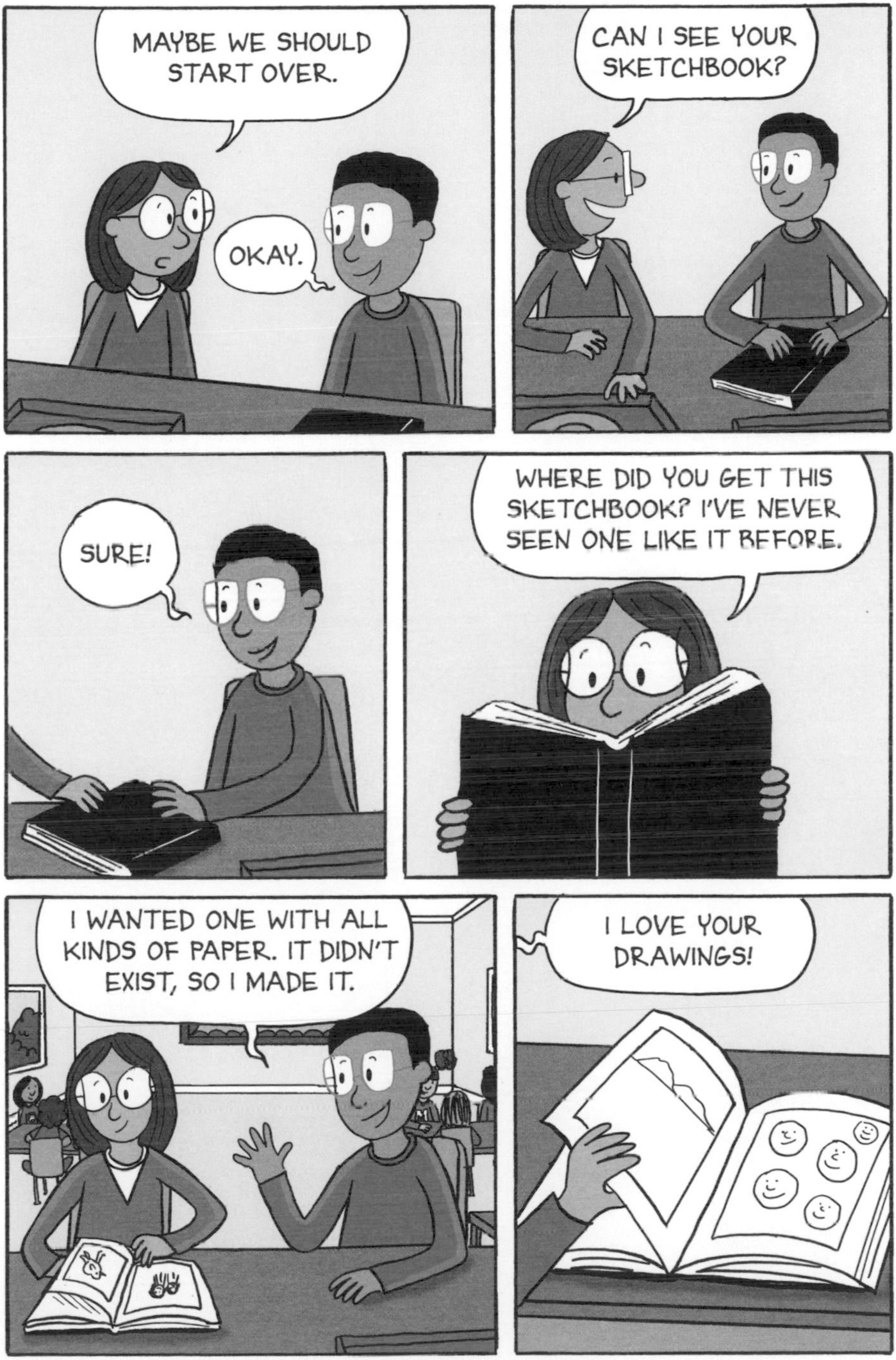
MAYBE WE SHOULD START OVER.
OKAY.
CAN I SEE YOUR SKETCHBOOK?
SURE!
WHERE DID YOU GET THIS SKETCHBOOK? I'VE NEVER SEEN ONE LIKE IT BEFORE.
I WANTED ONE WITH ALL KINDS OF PAPER. IT DIDN'T EXIST, SO I MADE IT.
I LOVE YOUR DRAWINGS!

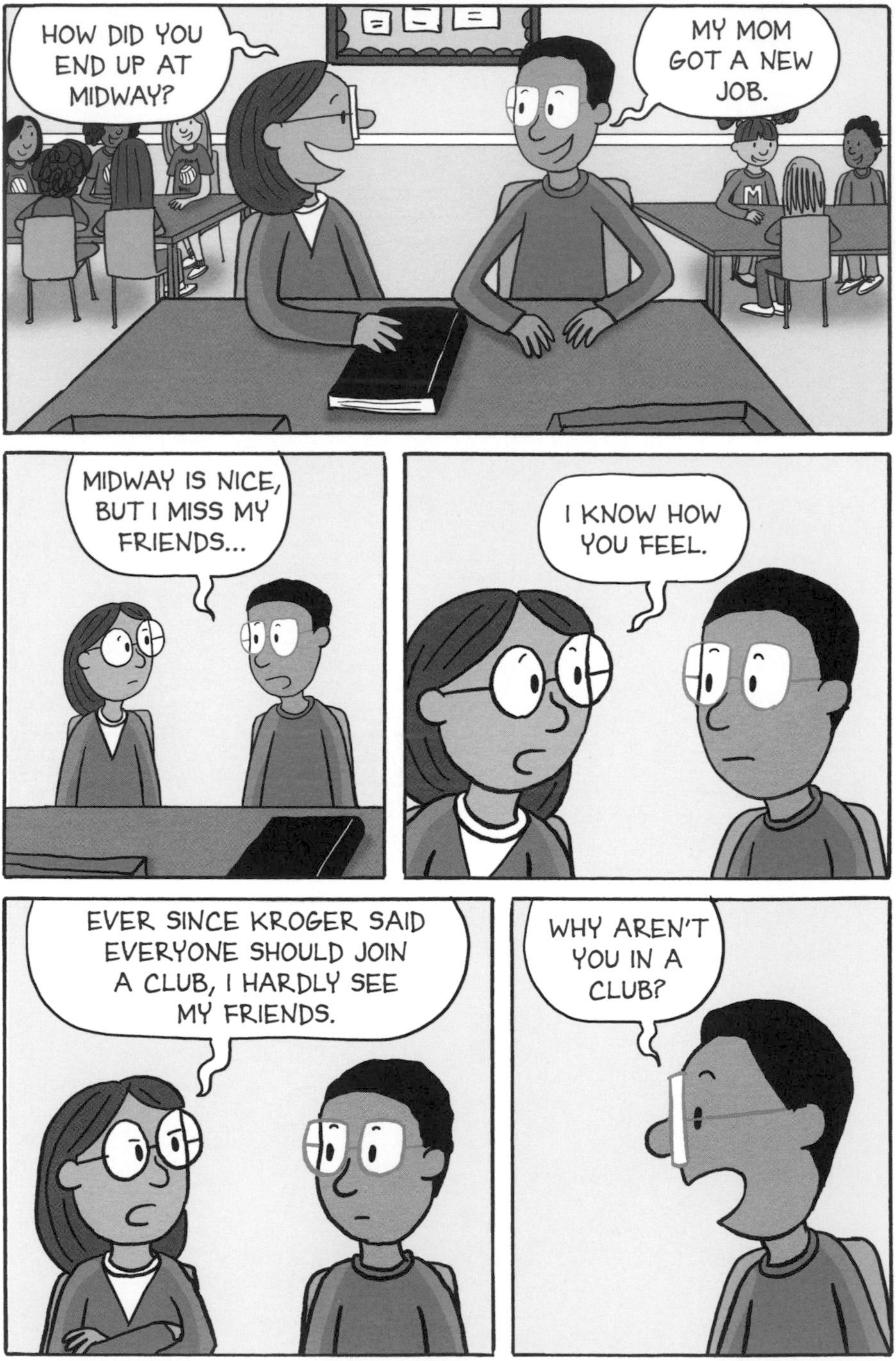
HOW DID YOU END UP AT MIDWAY?
MY MOM GOT A NEW JOB.
MIDWAY IS NICE, BUT I MISS MY FRIENDS...
I KNOW HOW YOU FEEL.
EVER SINCE KROGER SAID EVERYONE SHOULD JOIN A CLUB, I HARDLY SEE MY FRIENDS.
WHY AREN'T YOU IN A CLUB?

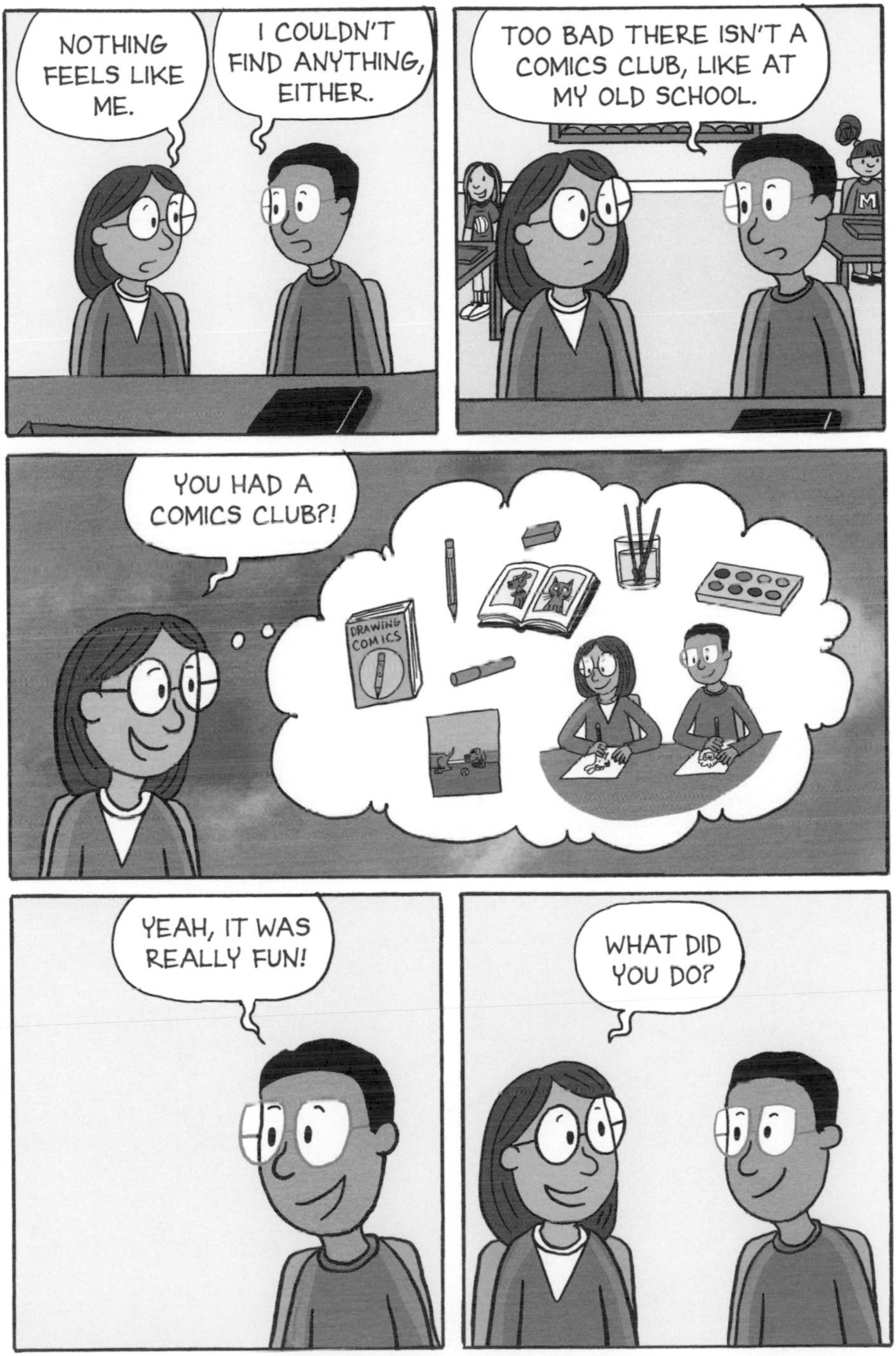
NOTHING FEELS LIKE ME.
I COULDN'T FIND ANYTHING, EITHER.
TOO BAD THERE ISN'T A COMICS CLUB, LIKE AT MY OLD SCHOOL.
YOU HAD A COMICS CLUB?!
DRAWING COMICS
YEAH, IT WAS REALLY FUN!
WHAT DID YOU DO?

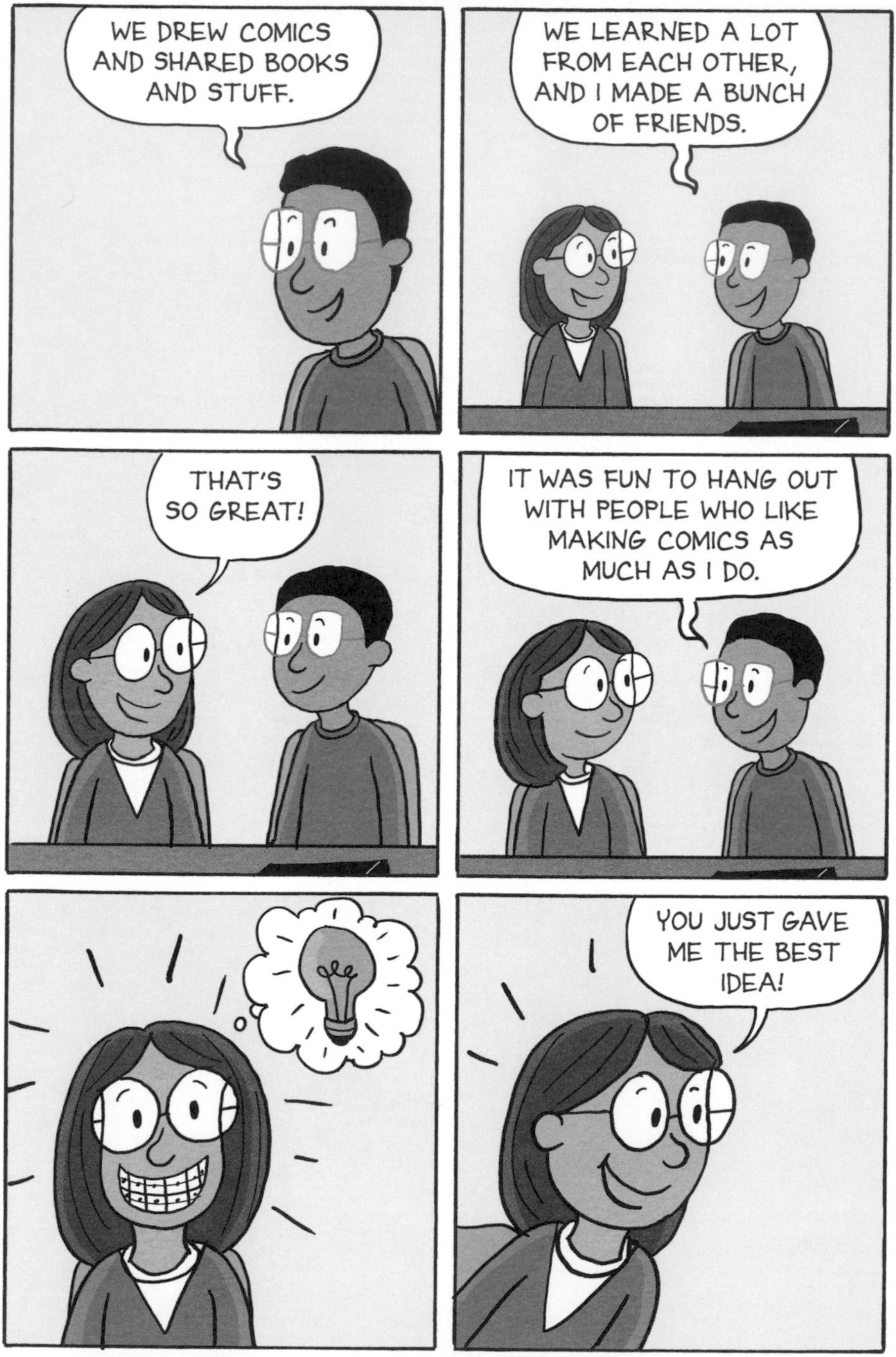
WE DREW COMICS AND SHARED BOOKS AND STUFF.
WE LEARNED A LOT FROM EACH OTHER, AND I MADE A BUNCH OF FRIENDS.
THAT'S SO GREAT!
IT WAS FUN TO HANG OUT WITH PEOPLE WHO LIKE MAKING COMICS AS MUCH AS I DO.
YOU JUST GAVE ME THE BEST IDEA!

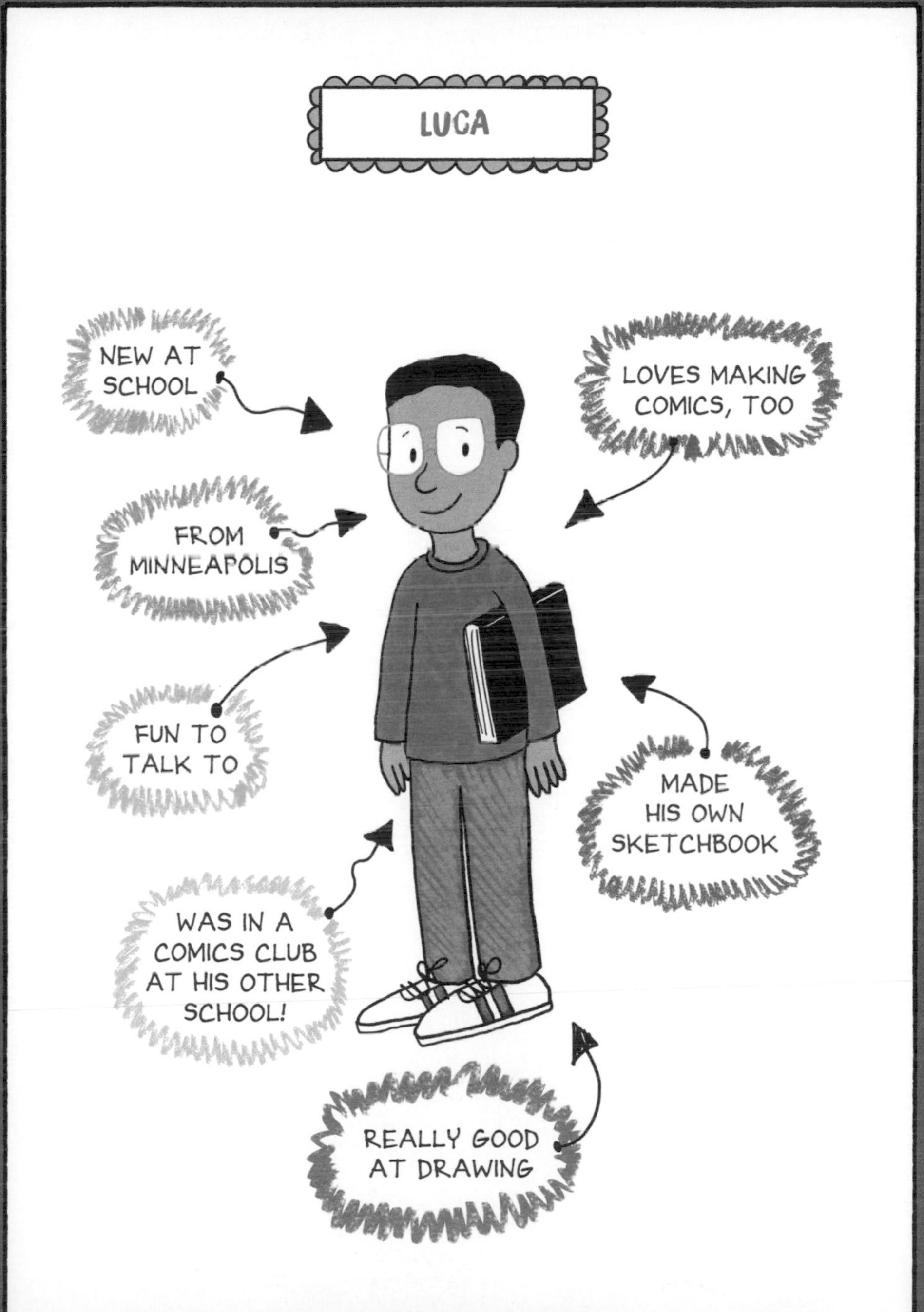
LUCA
NEW AT SCHOOL
FROM MINNEAPOLIS
FUN TO TALK TO
WAS IN A COMICS CLUB AT HIS OTHER SCHOOL!
LOVES MAKING COMICS, TOO
MADE HIS OWN SKETCHBOOK
REALLY GOOD AT DRAWING

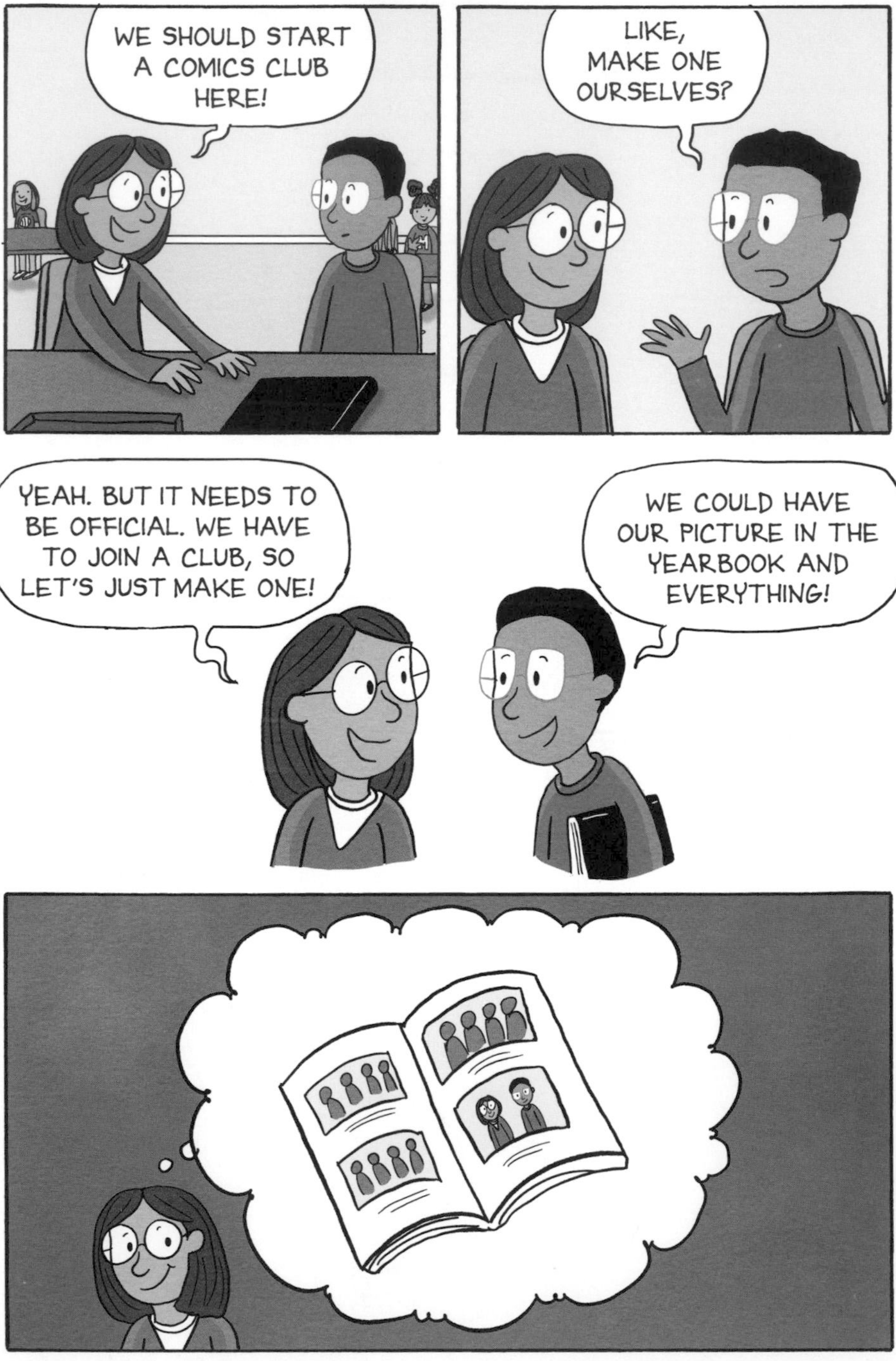
WE SHOULD START A COMICS CLUB HERE!
LIKE, MAKE ONE OURSELVES?
YEAH. BUT IT NEEDS TO BE OFFICIAL. WE HAVE TO JOIN A CLUB, SO LET'S JUST MAKE ONE!
WE COULD HAVE OUR PICTURE IN THE YEARBOOK AND EVERYTHING!

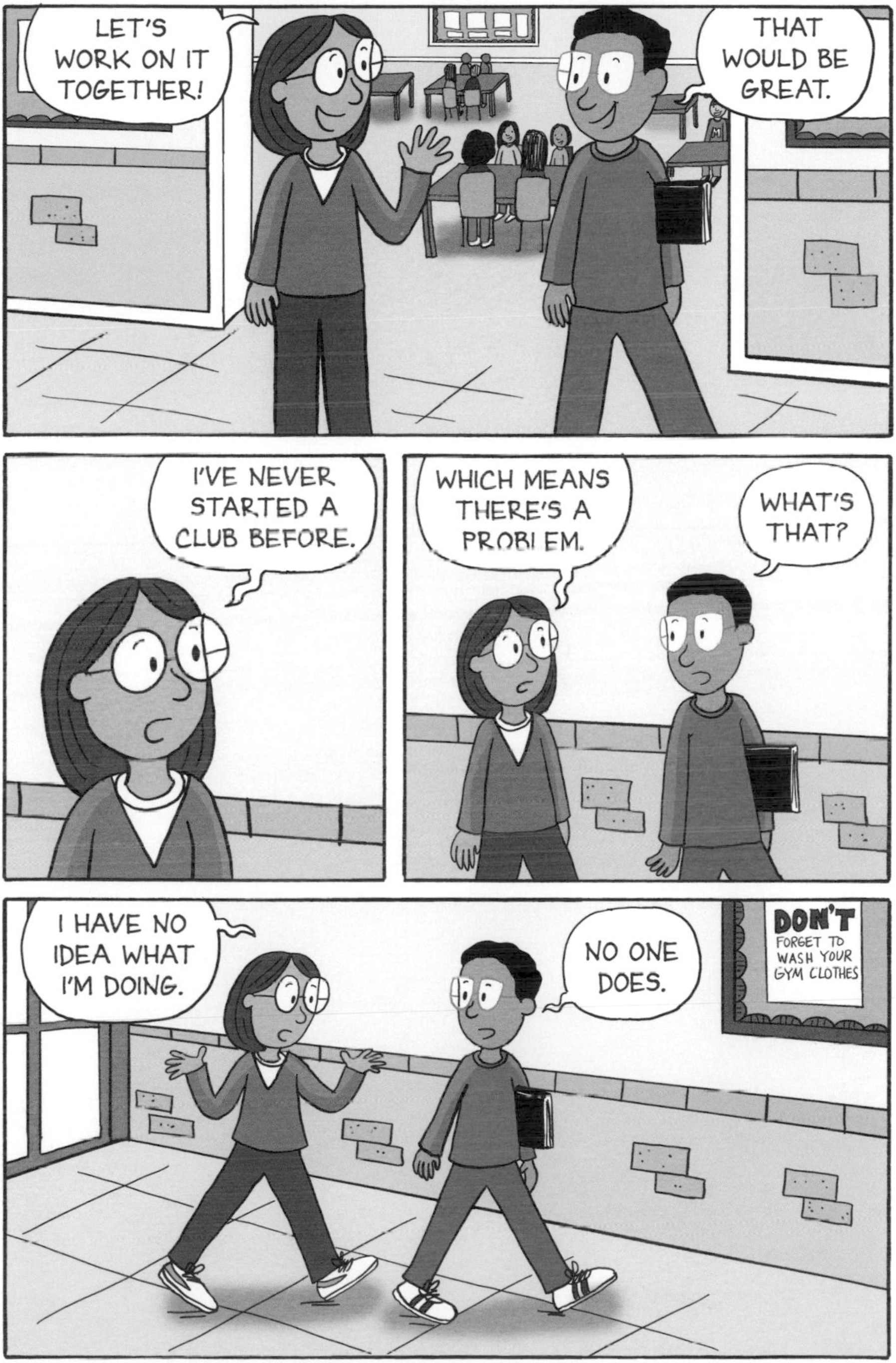
LET'S WORK ON IT TOGETHER!
THAT WOULD BE GREAT.
I'VE NEVER STARTED A CLUB BEFORE.
WHICH MEANS THERE'S A PROBLEM.
WHAT'S THAT?
I HAVE NO IDEA WHAT I'M DOING.
NO ONE DOES.
DON'T FORGET TO WASH YOUR GYM CLOTHES

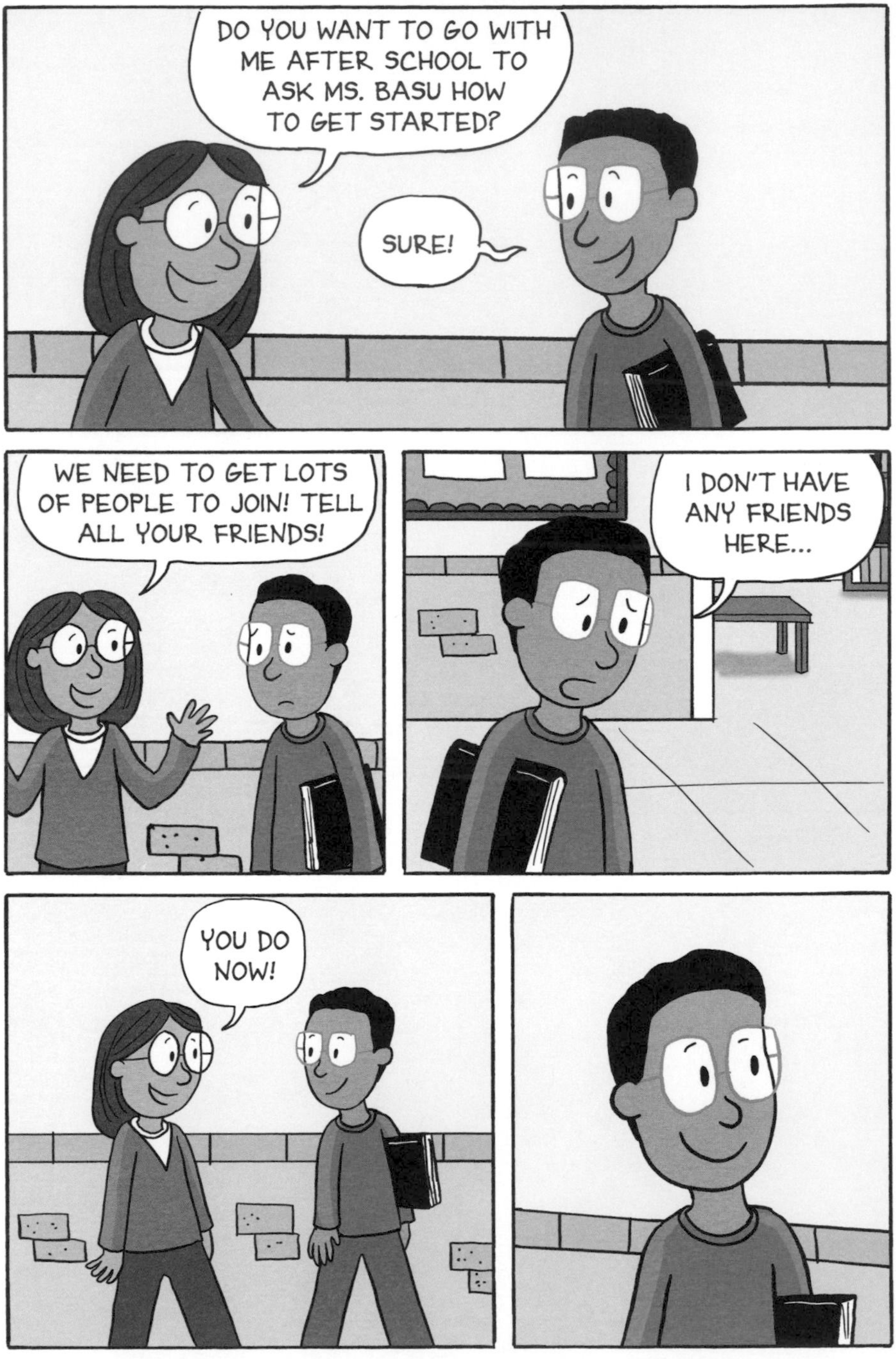
DO YOU WANT TO GO WITH ME AFTER SCHOOL TO ASK MS. BASU HOW TO GET STARTED?
SURE!
WE NEED TO GET LOTS OF PEOPLE TO JOIN! TELL ALL YOUR FRIENDS!
I DON'T HAVE ANY FRIENDS HERE...
YOU DO NOW!

CHAPTER 6

ART

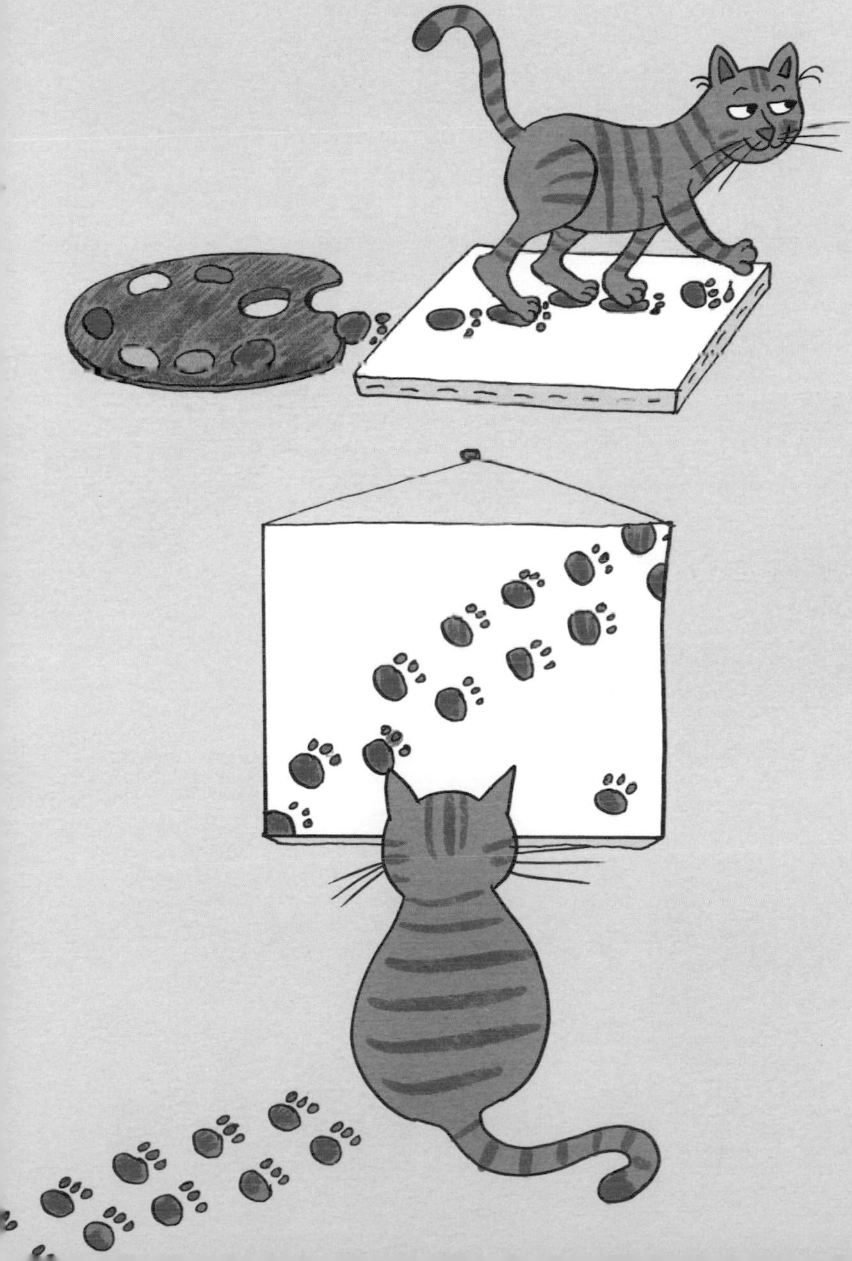

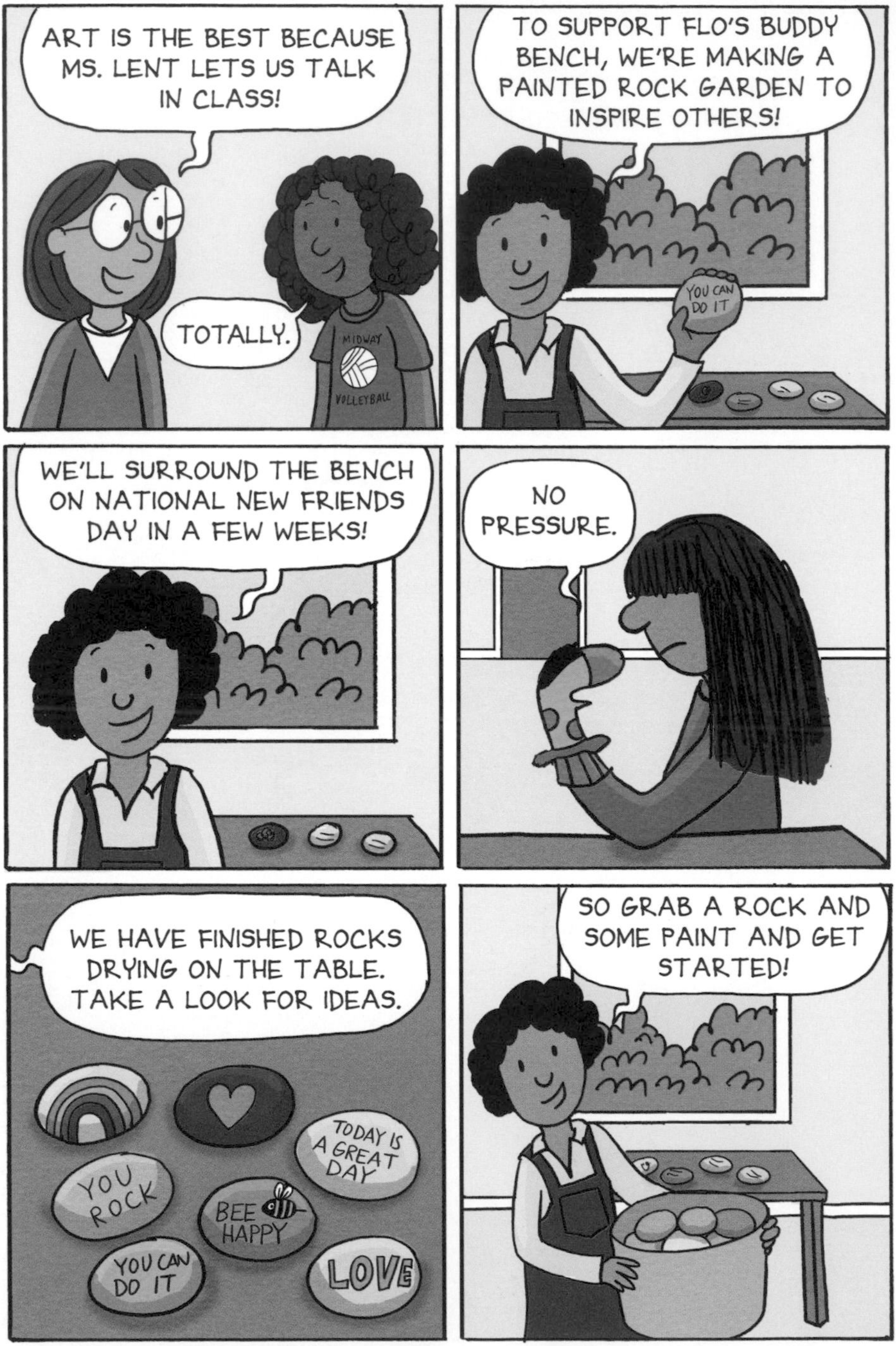
ART IS THE BEST BECAUSE MS. LENT LETS US TALK IN CLASS!
TOTALLY.
MIDWAY VOLLEYBALL
TO SUPPORT FLO'S BUDDY BENCH, WE'RE MAKING A PAINTED ROCK GARDEN TO INSPIRE OTHERS!
YOU CAN DO IT
WE'LL SURROUND THE BENCH ON NATIONAL NEW FRIENDS DAY IN A FEW WEEKS!
NO PRESSURE.
WE HAVE FINISHED ROCKS DRYING ON THE TABLE. TAKE A LOOK FOR IDEAS.
TODAY IS A GREAT DAY
YOU ROCK
BEE HAPPY
YOU CAN DO IT
LOVE
SO GRAB A ROCK AND SOME PAINT AND GET STARTED!

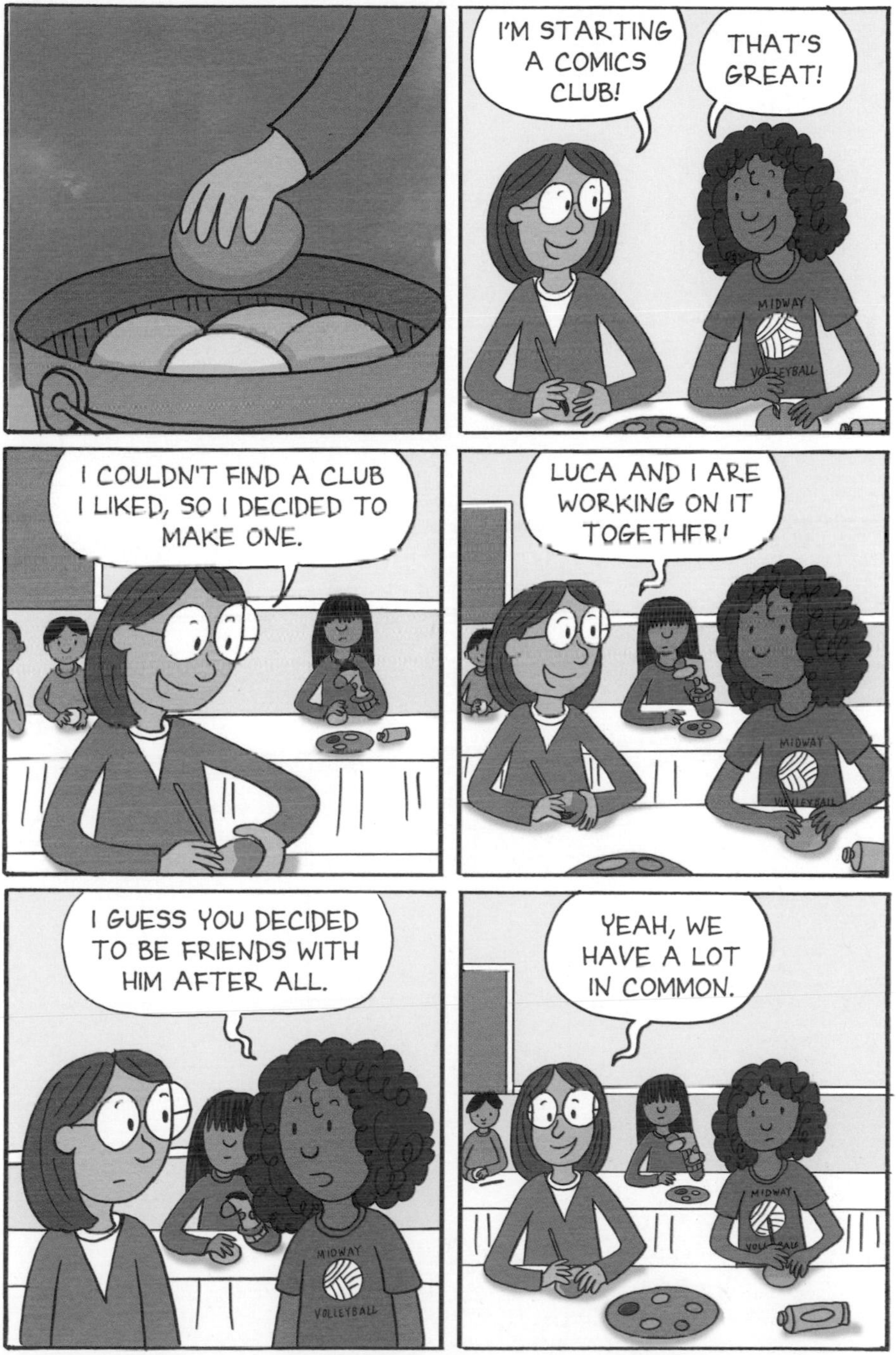
I'M STARTING A COMICS CLUB!
THAT'S GREAT!
I COULDN'T FIND A CLUB I LIKED, SO I DECIDED TO MAKE ONE.
LUCA AND I ARE WORKING ON IT TOGETHER!
I GUESS YOU DECIDED TO BE FRIENDS WITH HIM AFTER ALL.
YEAH, WE HAVE A LOT IN COMMON.

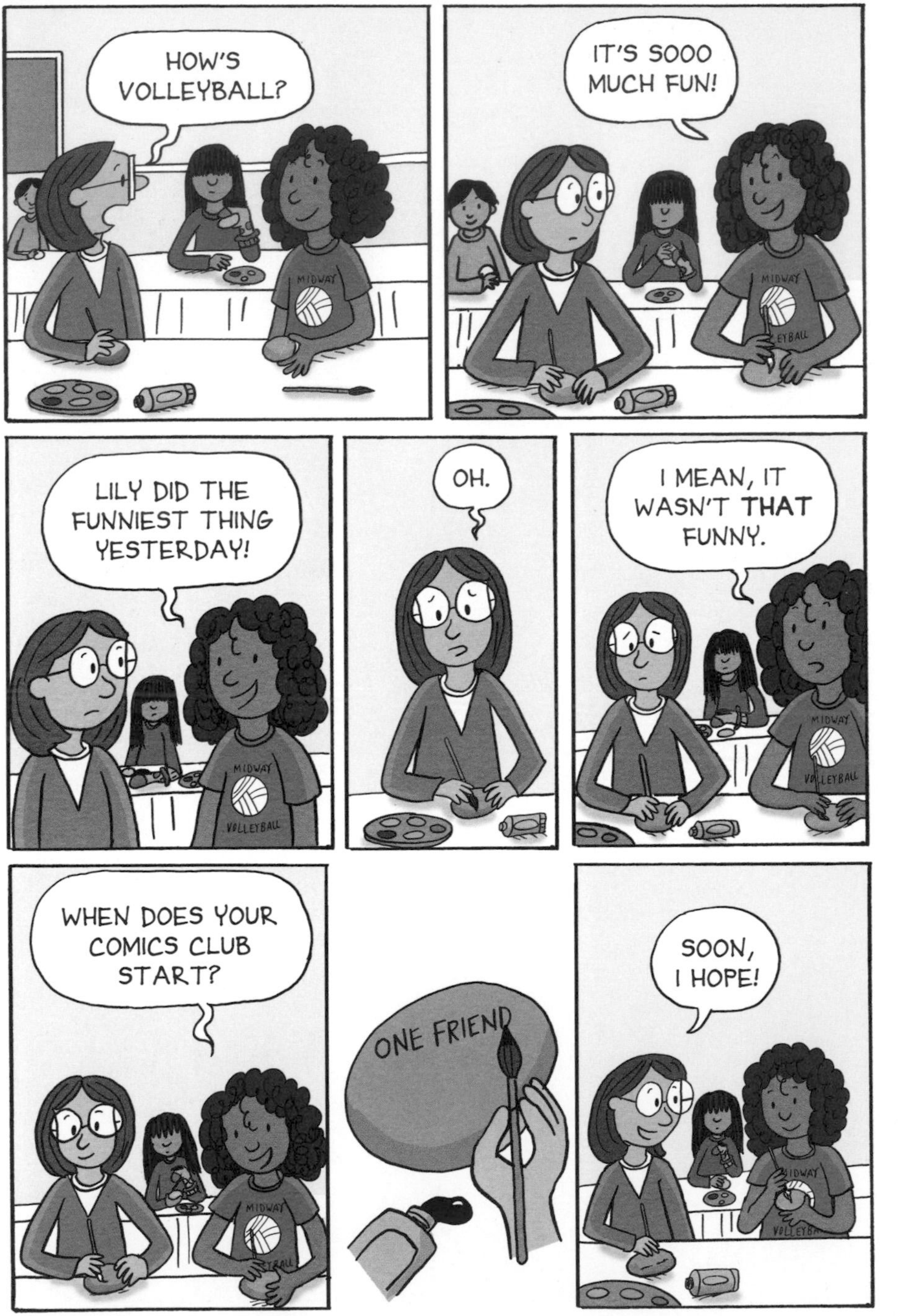
HOW'S VOLLEYBALL?
MIDWAY
IT'S SOOO MUCH FUN!
MIDWAY
LILY DID THE FUNNIEST THING YESTERDAY!
MIDWAY
VOLLEYBALL
OH.
I MEAN, IT WASN'T **THAT** FUNNY.
MIDWAY
WHEN DOES YOUR COMICS CLUB START?
MIDWAY
ONE FRIEND
SOON, I HOPE!

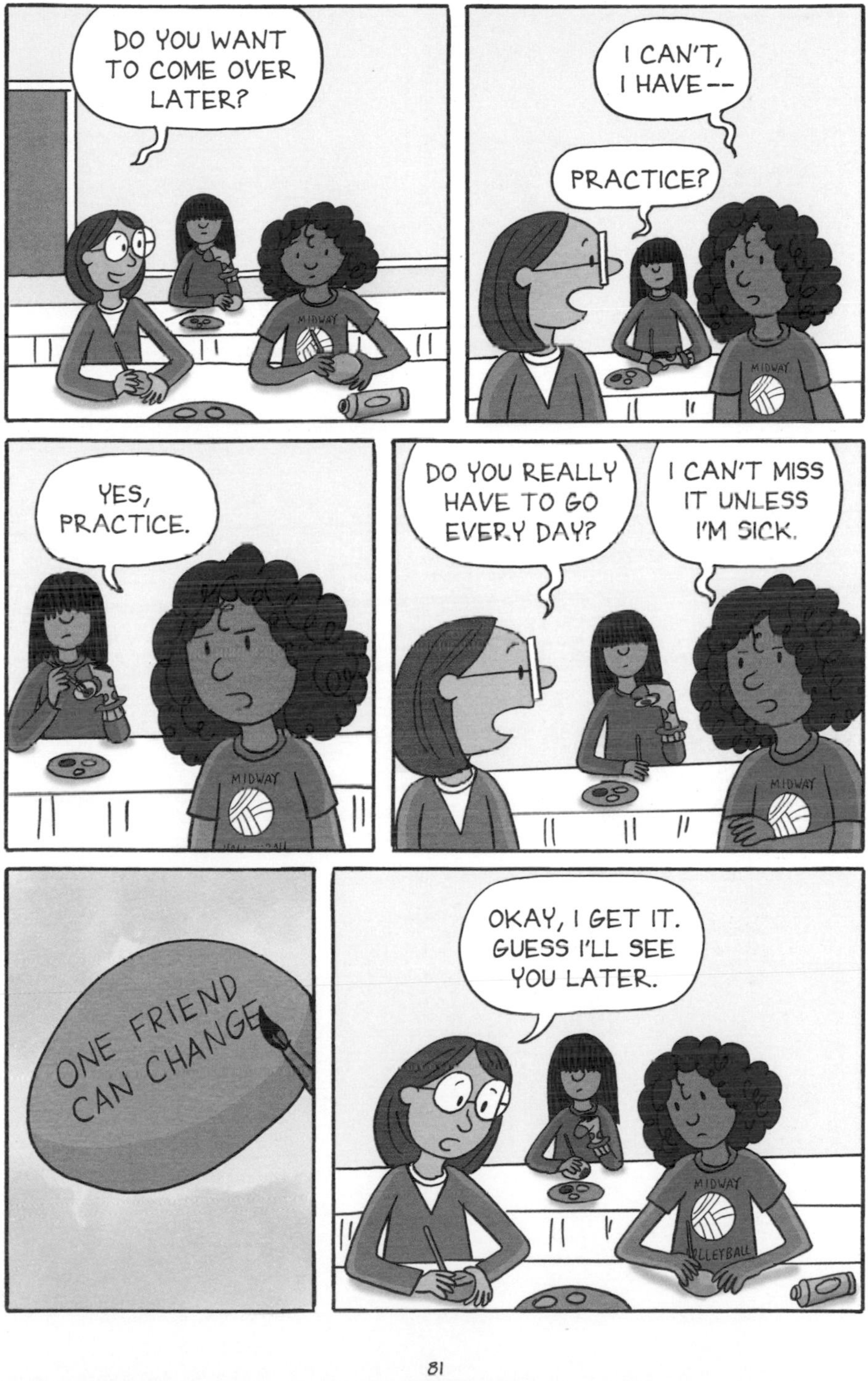
DO YOU WANT TO COME OVER LATER?
I CAN'T, I HAVE--
PRACTICE?
YES, PRACTICE.
DO YOU REALLY HAVE TO GO EVERY DAY?
I CAN'T MISS IT UNLESS I'M SICK.
ONE FRIEND CAN CHANGE
OKAY, I GET IT. GUESS I'LL SEE YOU LATER.

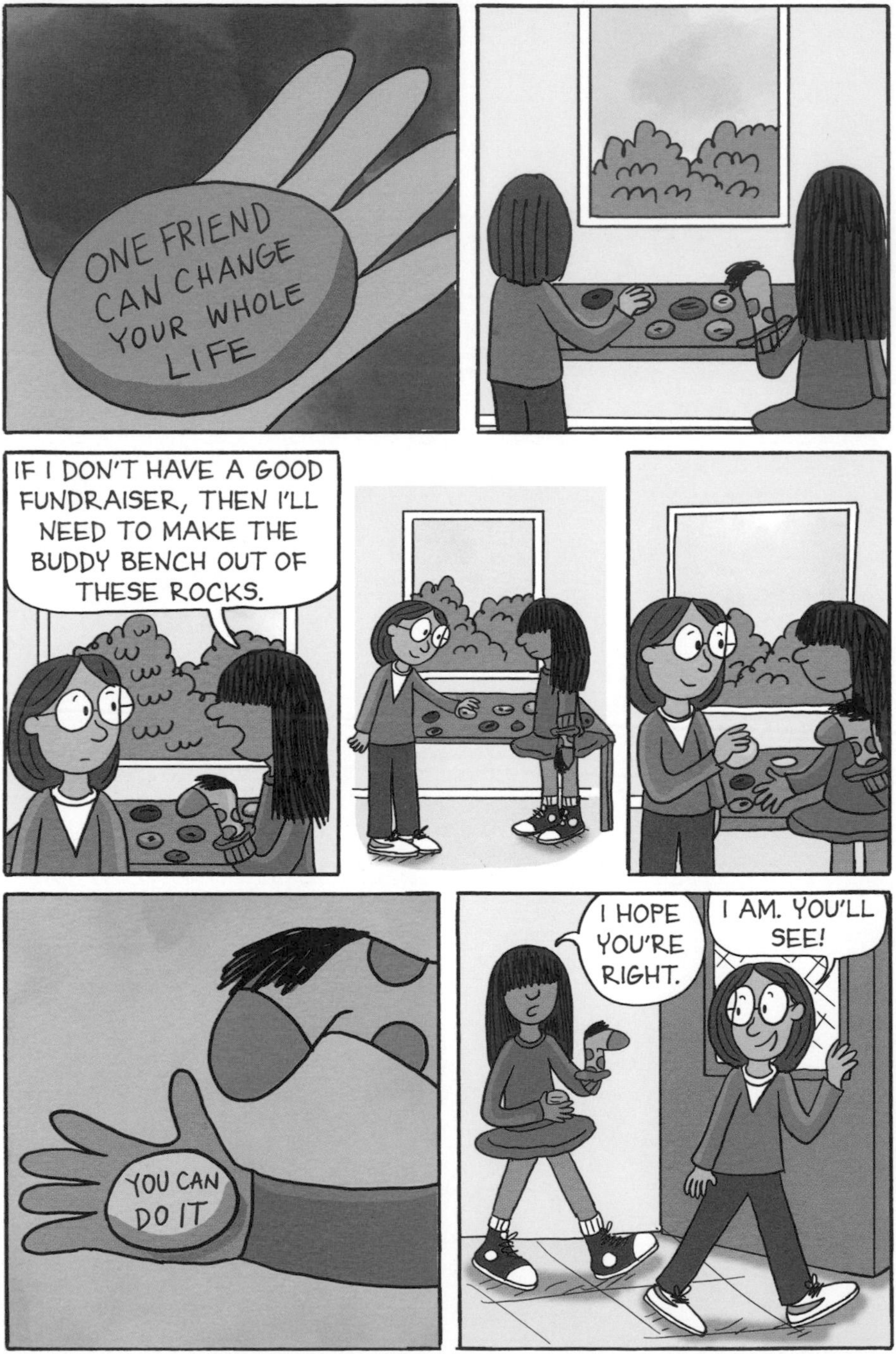
ONE FRIEND CAN CHANGE YOUR WHOLE LIFE
IF I DON'T HAVE A GOOD FUNDRAISER, THEN I'LL NEED TO MAKE THE BUDDY BENCH OUT OF THESE ROCKS.
YOU CAN DO IT
I HOPE YOU'RE RIGHT.
I AM. YOU'LL SEE!

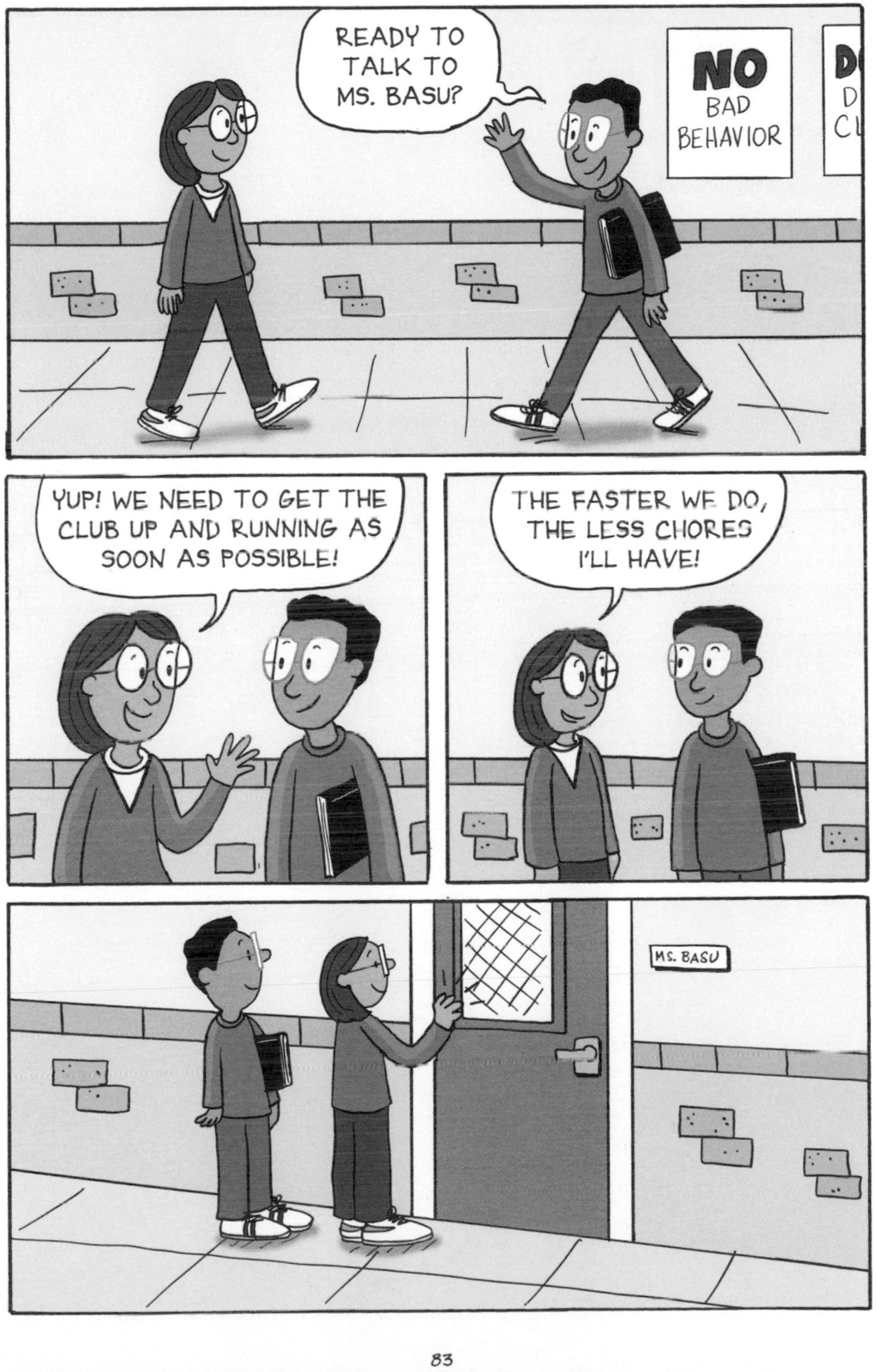
READY TO TALK TO MS. BASU?
NO BAD BEHAVIOR
YUP! WE NEED TO GET THE CLUB UP AND RUNNING AS SOON AS POSSIBLE!
THE FASTER WE DO, THE LESS CHORES I'LL HAVE!
MS. BASU

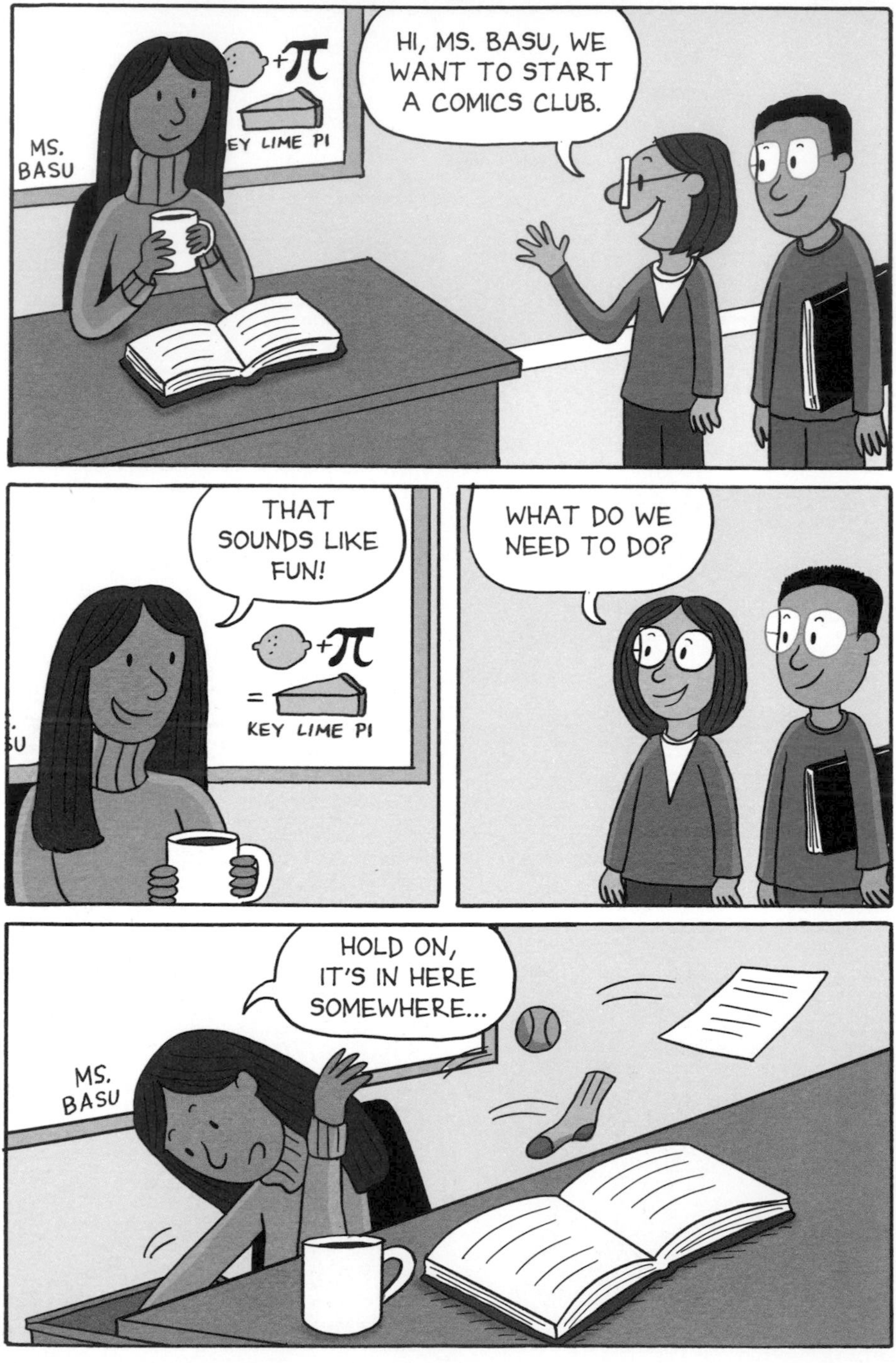
HI, MS. BASU, WE WANT TO START A COMICS CLUB.
MS. BASU
EY LIME PI
THAT SOUNDS LIKE FUN!
KEY LIME PI
WHAT DO WE NEED TO DO?
HOLD ON, IT'S IN HERE SOMEWHERE...
MS. BASU

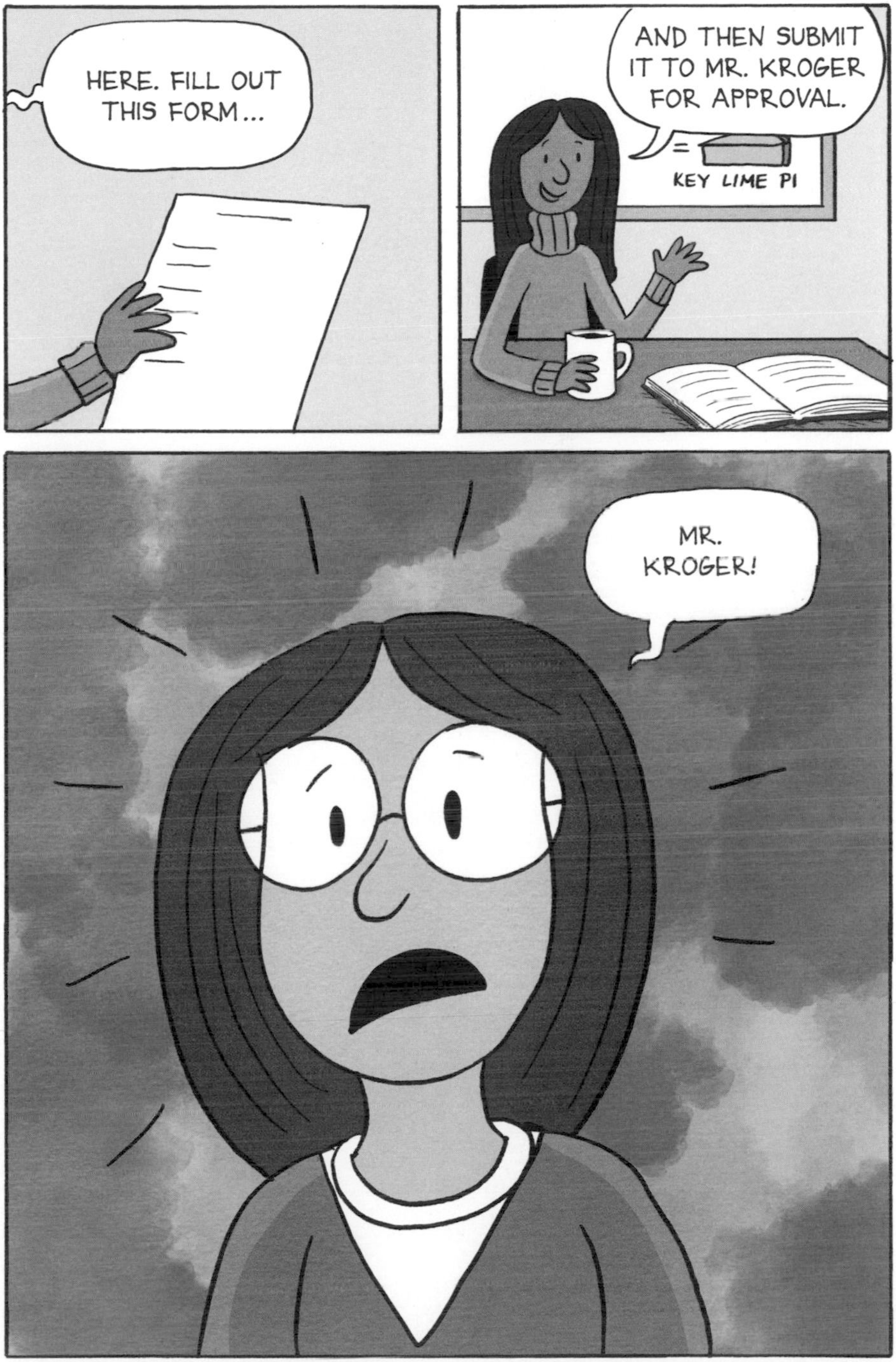
HERE. FILL OUT THIS FORM...
AND THEN SUBMIT IT TO MR. KROGER FOR APPROVAL.
KEY LIME PI
MR. KROGER!

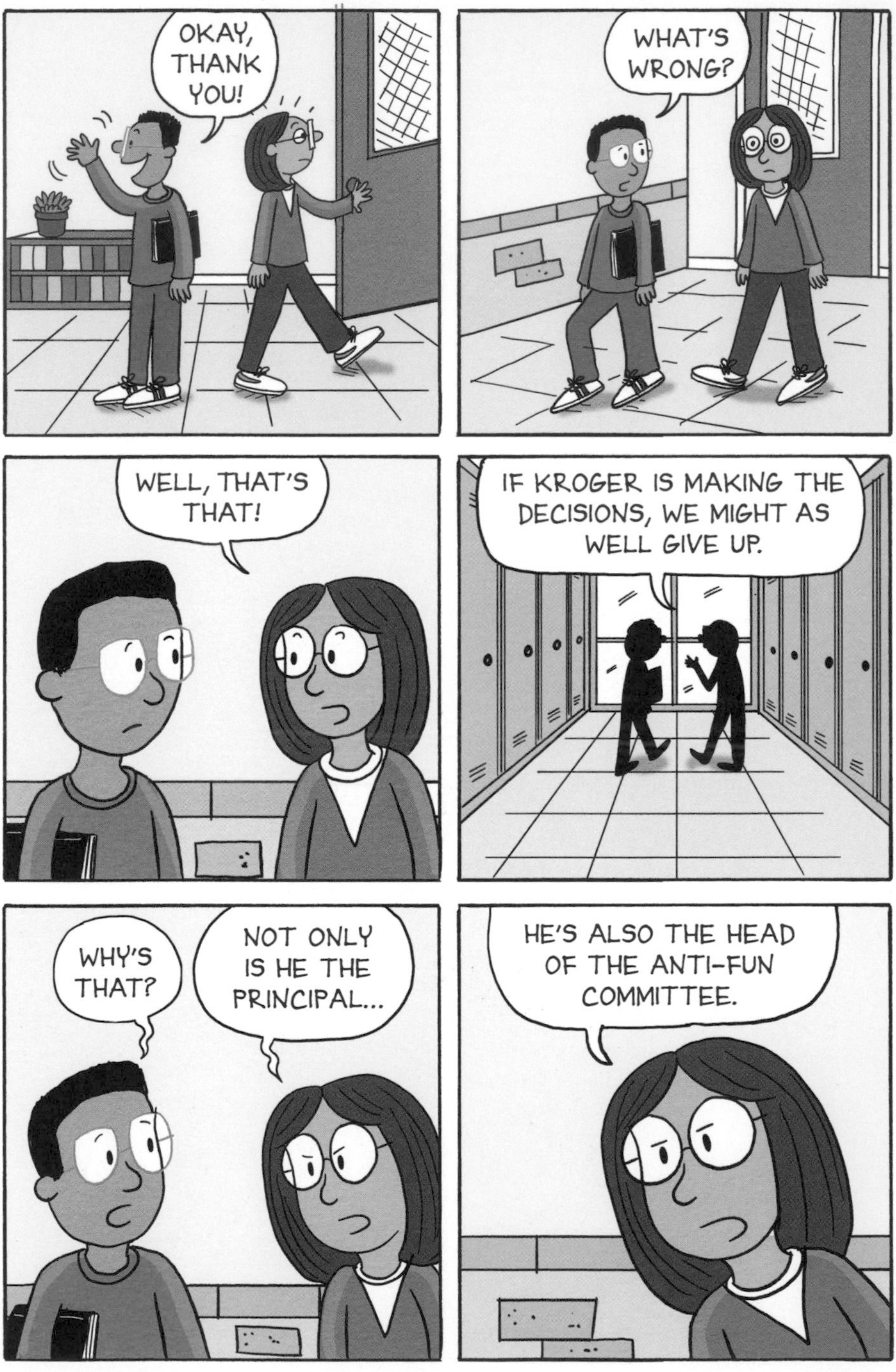
OKAY, THANK YOU!
WHAT'S WRONG?
WELL, THAT'S THAT!
IF KROGER IS MAKING THE DECISIONS, WE MIGHT AS WELL GIVE UP.
WHY'S THAT?
NOT ONLY IS HE THE PRINCIPAL...
HE'S ALSO THE HEAD OF THE ANTI-FUN COMMITTEE.

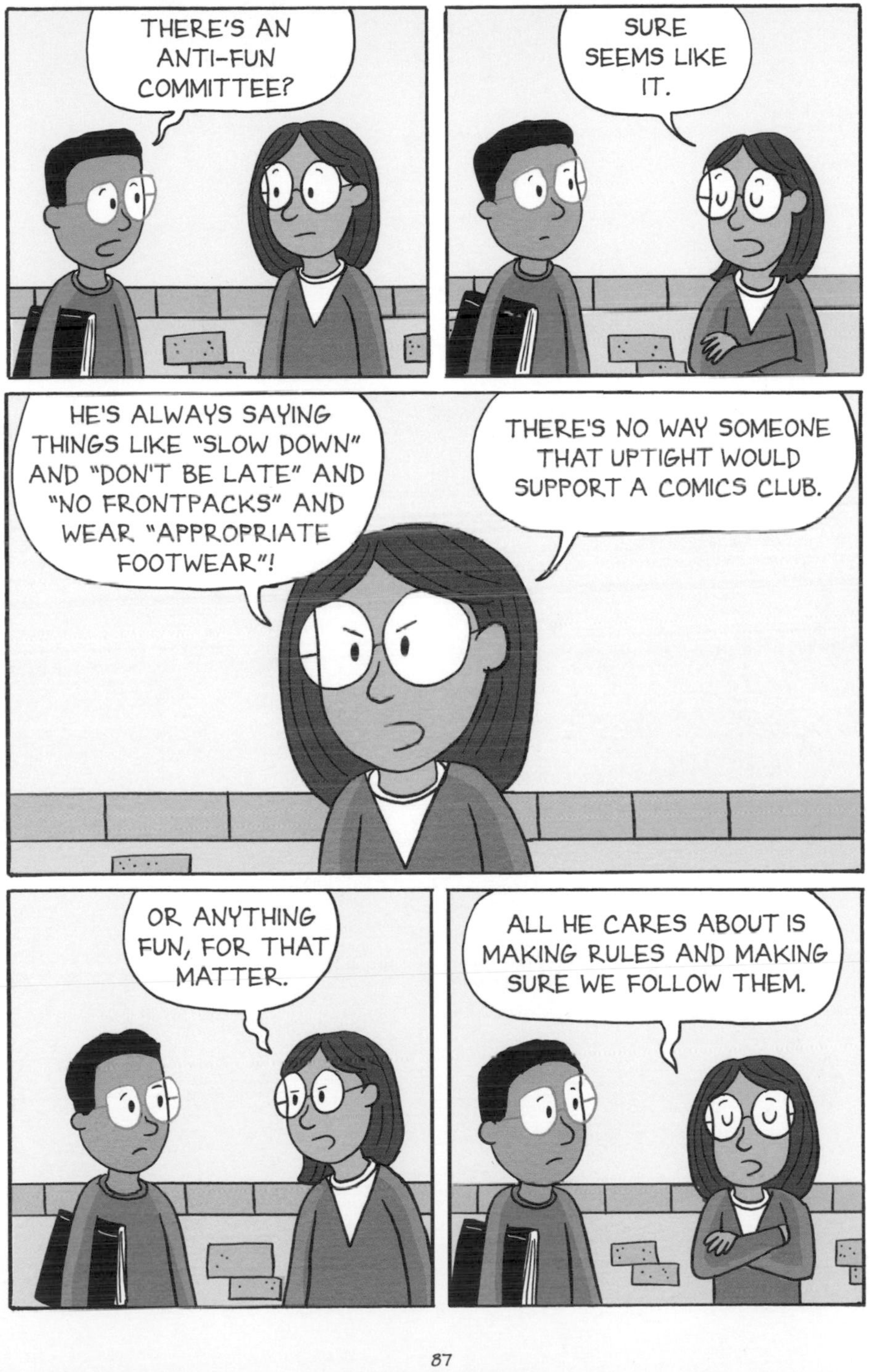

THERE'S AN ANTI-FUN COMMITTEE?
SURE SEEMS LIKE IT.
HE'S ALWAYS SAYING THINGS LIKE "SLOW DOWN" AND "DON'T BE LATE" AND "NO FRONTPACKS" AND WEAR "APPROPRIATE FOOTWEAR"!
THERE'S NO WAY SOMEONE THAT UPTIGHT WOULD SUPPORT A COMICS CLUB.
OR ANYTHING FUN, FOR THAT MATTER.
ALL HE CARES ABOUT IS MAKING RULES AND MAKING SURE WE FOLLOW THEM.

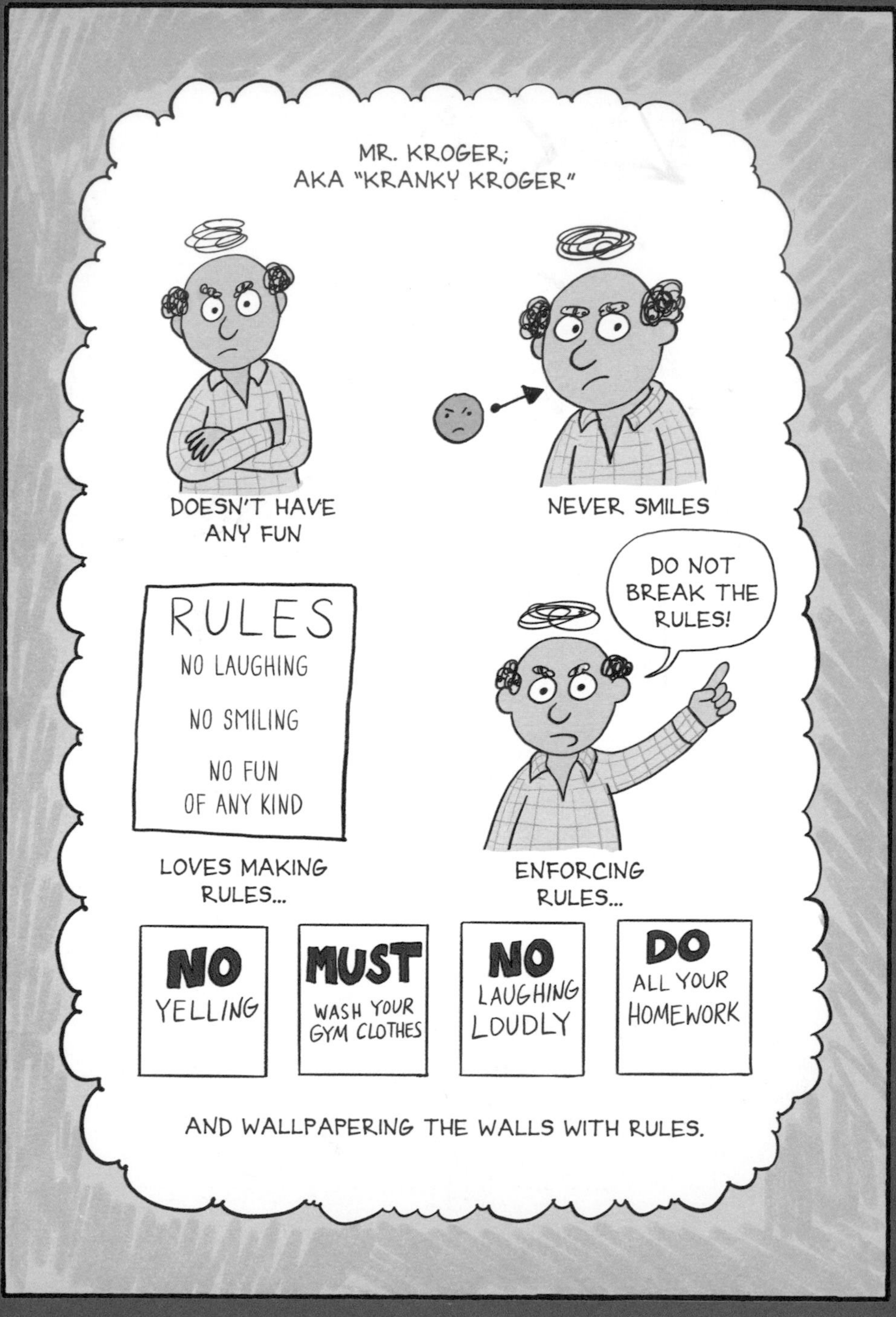
MR. KROGER;
AKA "KRANKY KROGER"
DOESN'T HAVE
ANY FUN
NEVER SMILES
RULES
NO LAUGHING
NO SMILING
NO FUN
OF ANY KIND
LOVES MAKING
RULES...
DO NOT
BREAK THE
RULES!
ENFORCING
RULES...
NO
YELLING
MUST
WASH YOUR
GYM CLOTHES
NO
LAUGHING
LOUDLY
DO
ALL YOUR
HOMEWORK
AND WALLPAPERING THE WALLS WITH RULES.

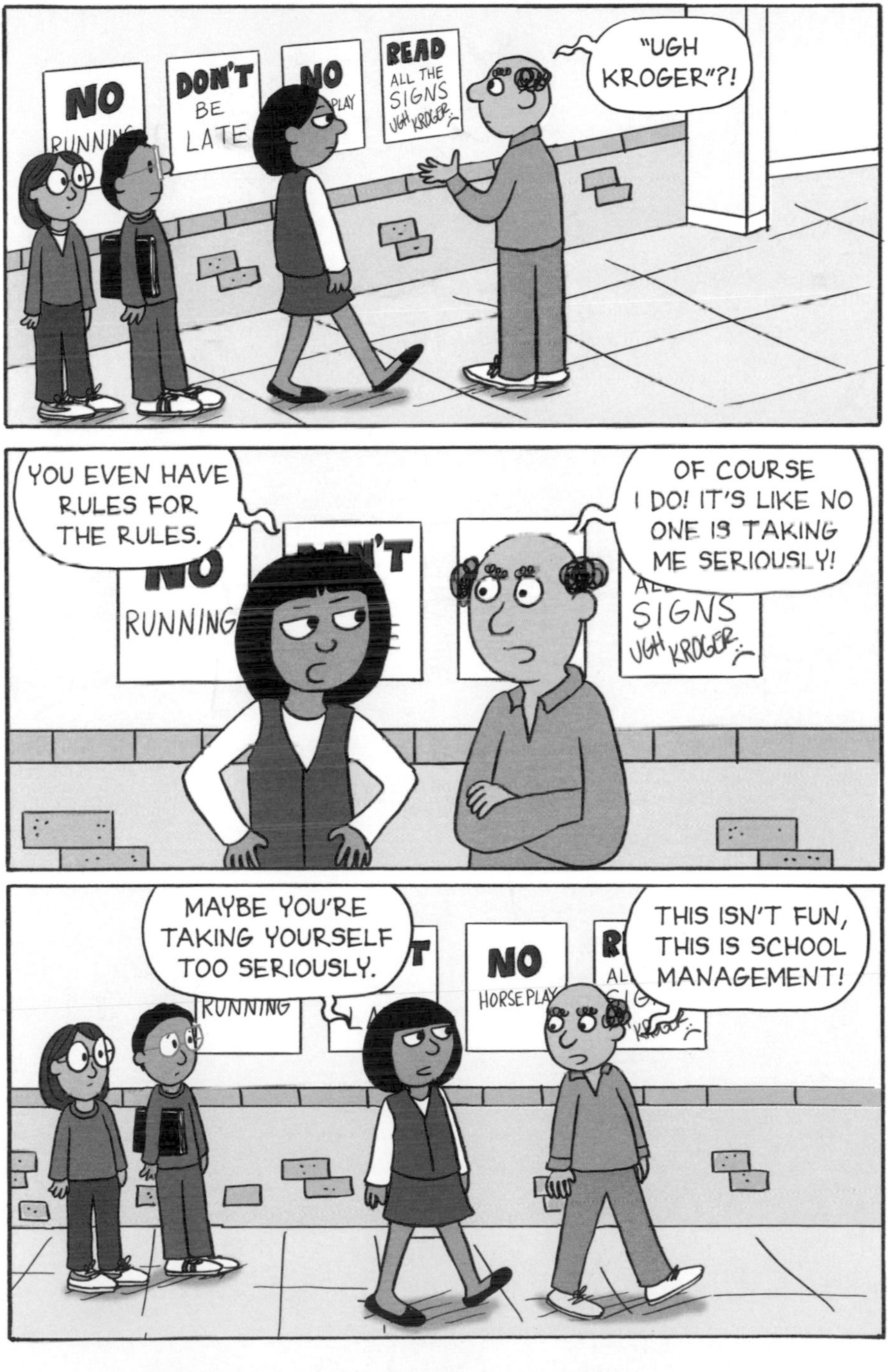
NO RUNNING
DON'T BE LATE
READ ALL THE SIGNS
UGH KROGER
"UGH KROGER"?!
YOU EVEN HAVE RULES FOR THE RULES.
OF COURSE I DO! IT'S LIKE NO ONE IS TAKING ME SERIOUSLY!
MAYBE YOU'RE TAKING YOURSELF TOO SERIOUSLY.
NO HORSEPLAY
THIS ISN'T FUN, THIS IS SCHOOL MANAGEMENT!

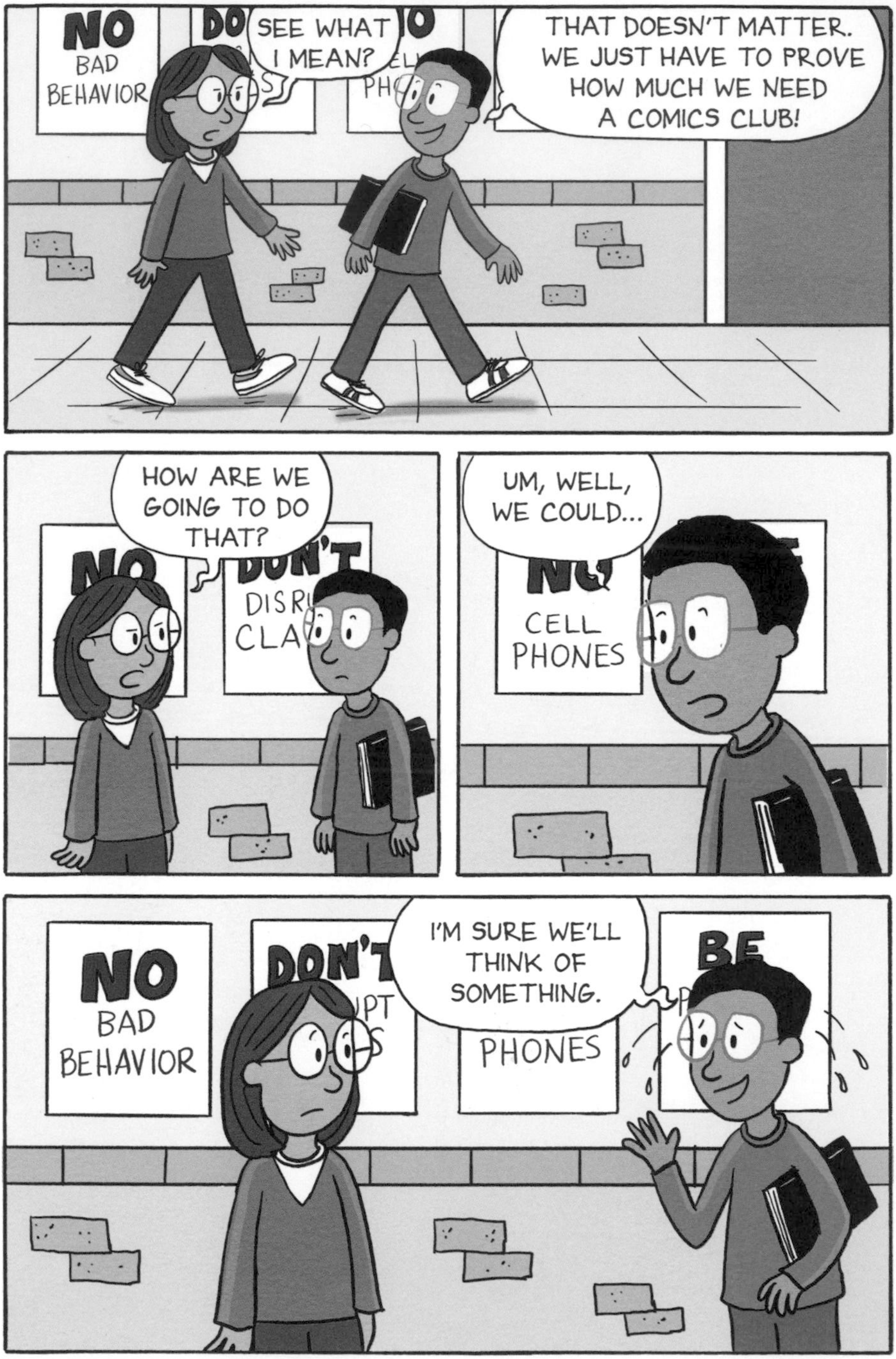
NO
BAD BEHAVIOR
SEE WHAT I MEAN?
THAT DOESN'T MATTER. WE JUST HAVE TO PROVE HOW MUCH WE NEED A COMICS CLUB!
HOW ARE WE GOING TO DO THAT?
UM, WELL, WE COULD...
CELL PHONES
NO
BAD BEHAVIOR
I'M SURE WE'LL THINK OF SOMETHING.
PHONES
BE

CHAPTER 7
PROPOSAL

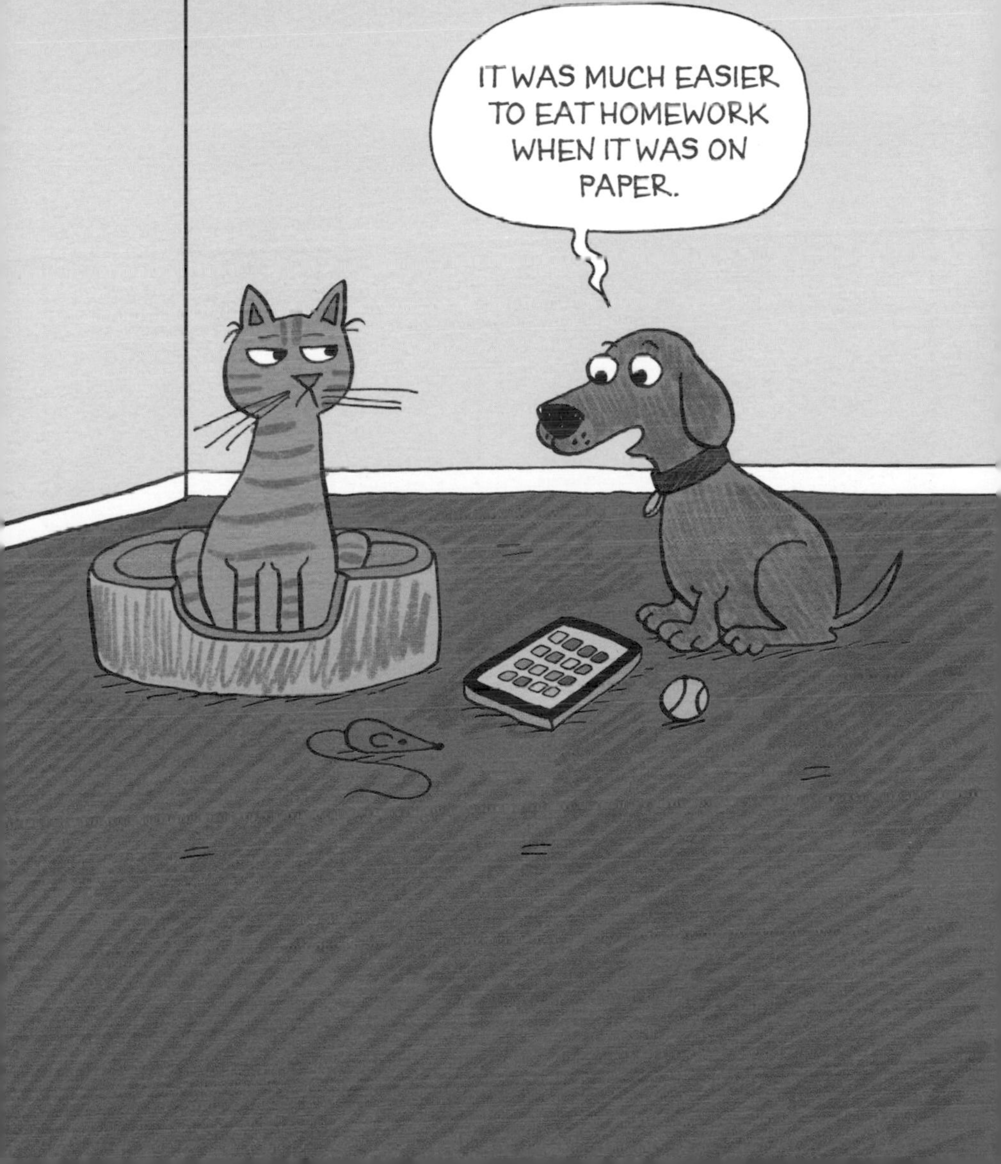
IT WAS MUCH EASIER TO EAT HOMEWORK WHEN IT WAS ON PAPER.

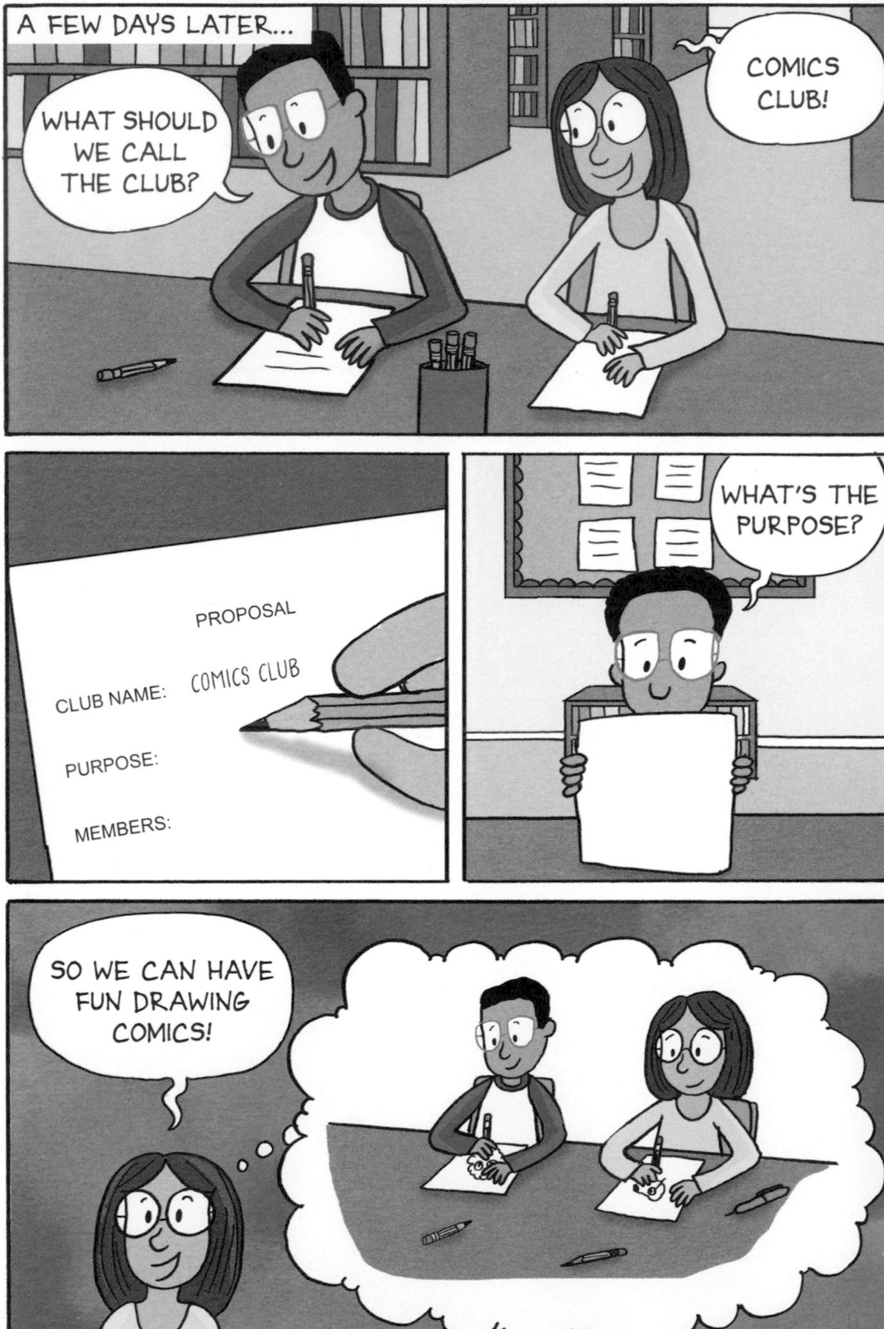
A FEW DAYS LATER...
WHAT SHOULD WE CALL THE CLUB?
COMICS CLUB!
PROPOSAL
CLUB NAME: COMICS CLUB
PURPOSE:
MEMBERS:
WHAT'S THE PURPOSE?
SO WE CAN HAVE FUN DRAWING COMICS!

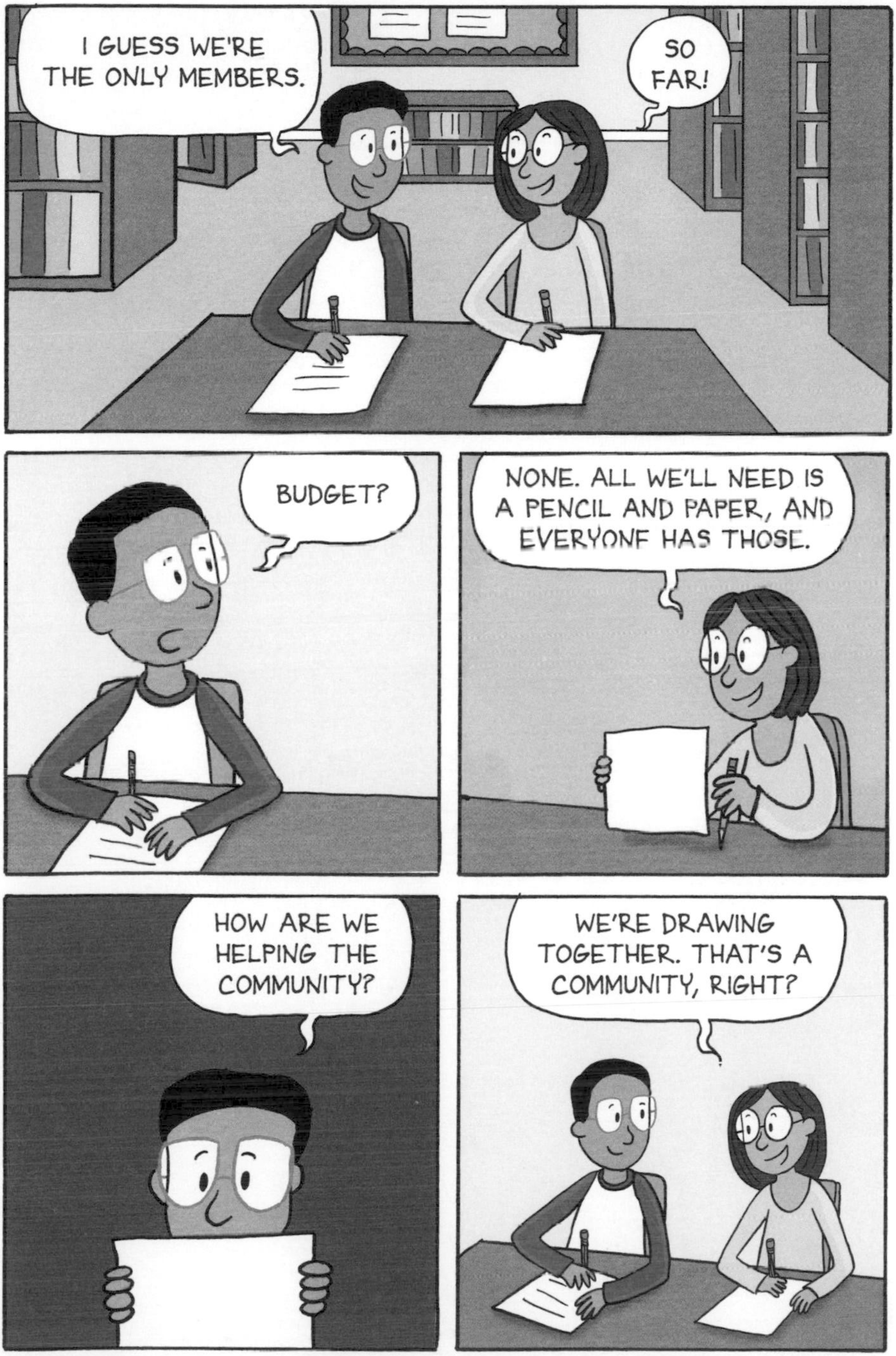
I GUESS WE'RE THE ONLY MEMBERS.
SO FAR!
BUDGET?
NONE. ALL WE'LL NEED IS A PENCIL AND PAPER, AND EVERYONE HAS THOSE.
HOW ARE WE HELPING THE COMMUNITY?
WE'RE DRAWING TOGETHER. THAT'S A COMMUNITY, RIGHT?

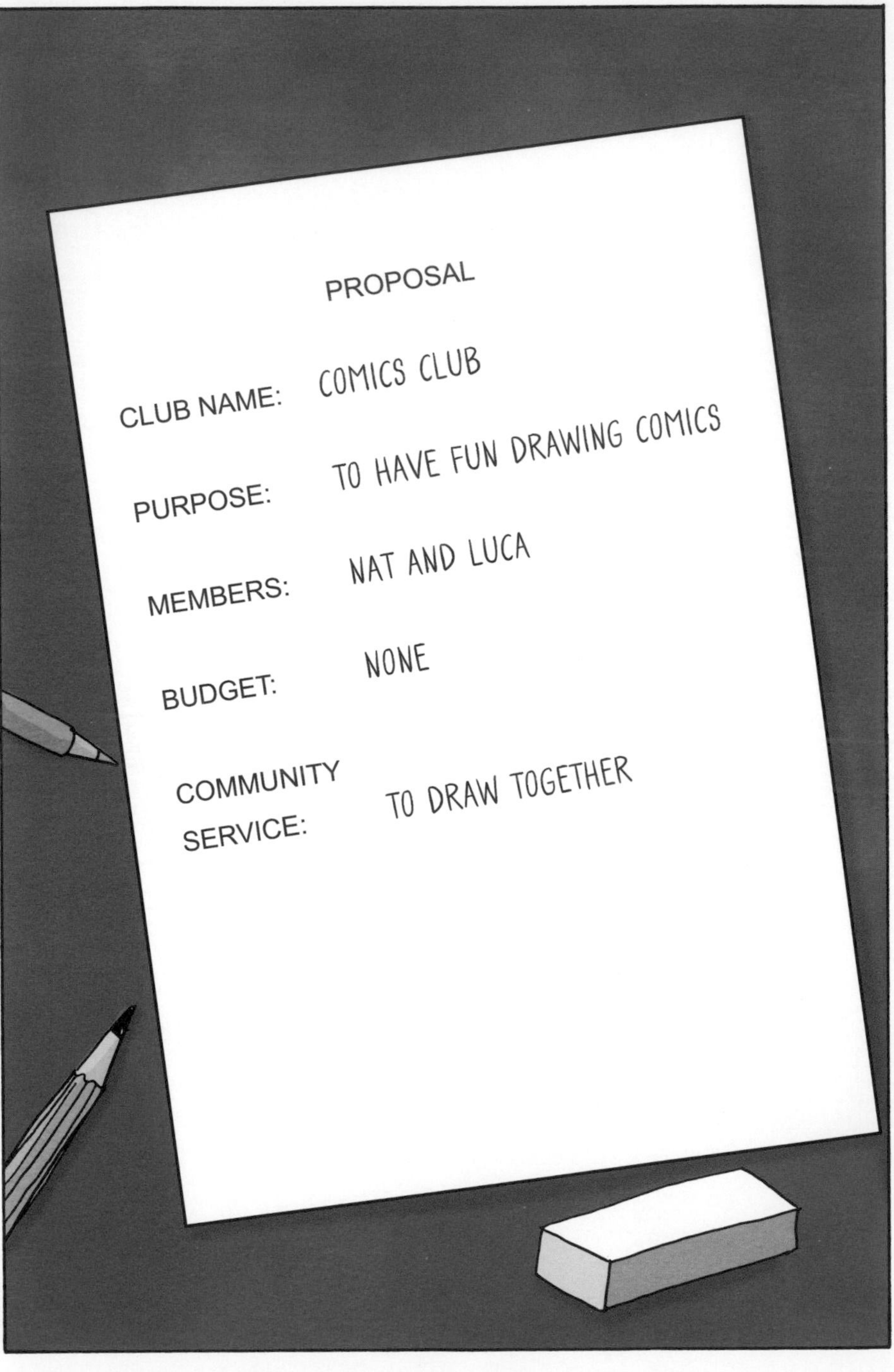
PROPOSAL
CLUB NAME: COMICS CLUB
PURPOSE: TO HAVE FUN DRAWING COMICS
MEMBERS: NAT AND LUCA
BUDGET: NONE
COMMUNITY SERVICE: TO DRAW TOGETHER

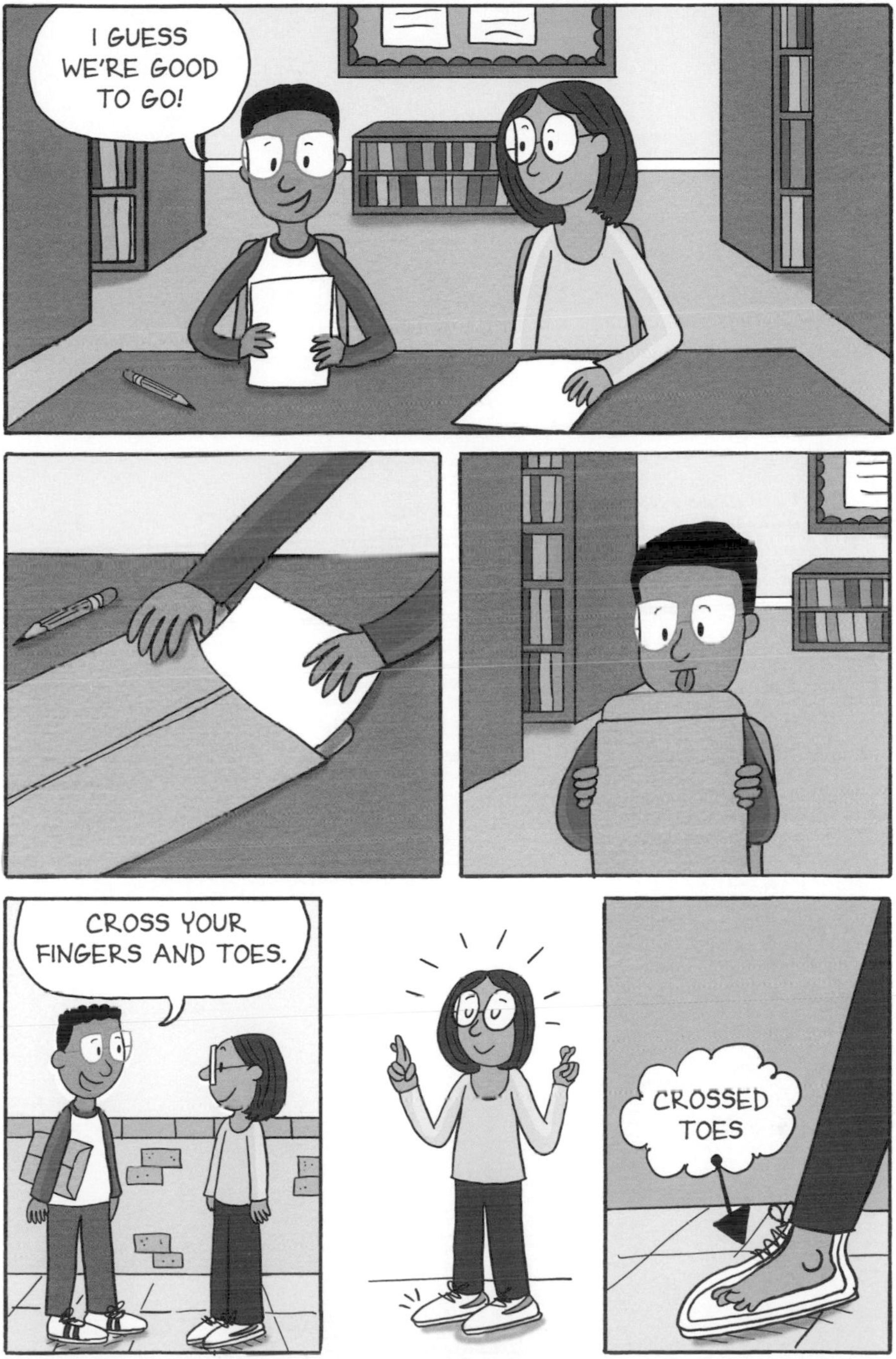
I GUESS WE'RE GOOD TO GO!
CROSS YOUR FINGERS AND TOES.
CROSSED TOES

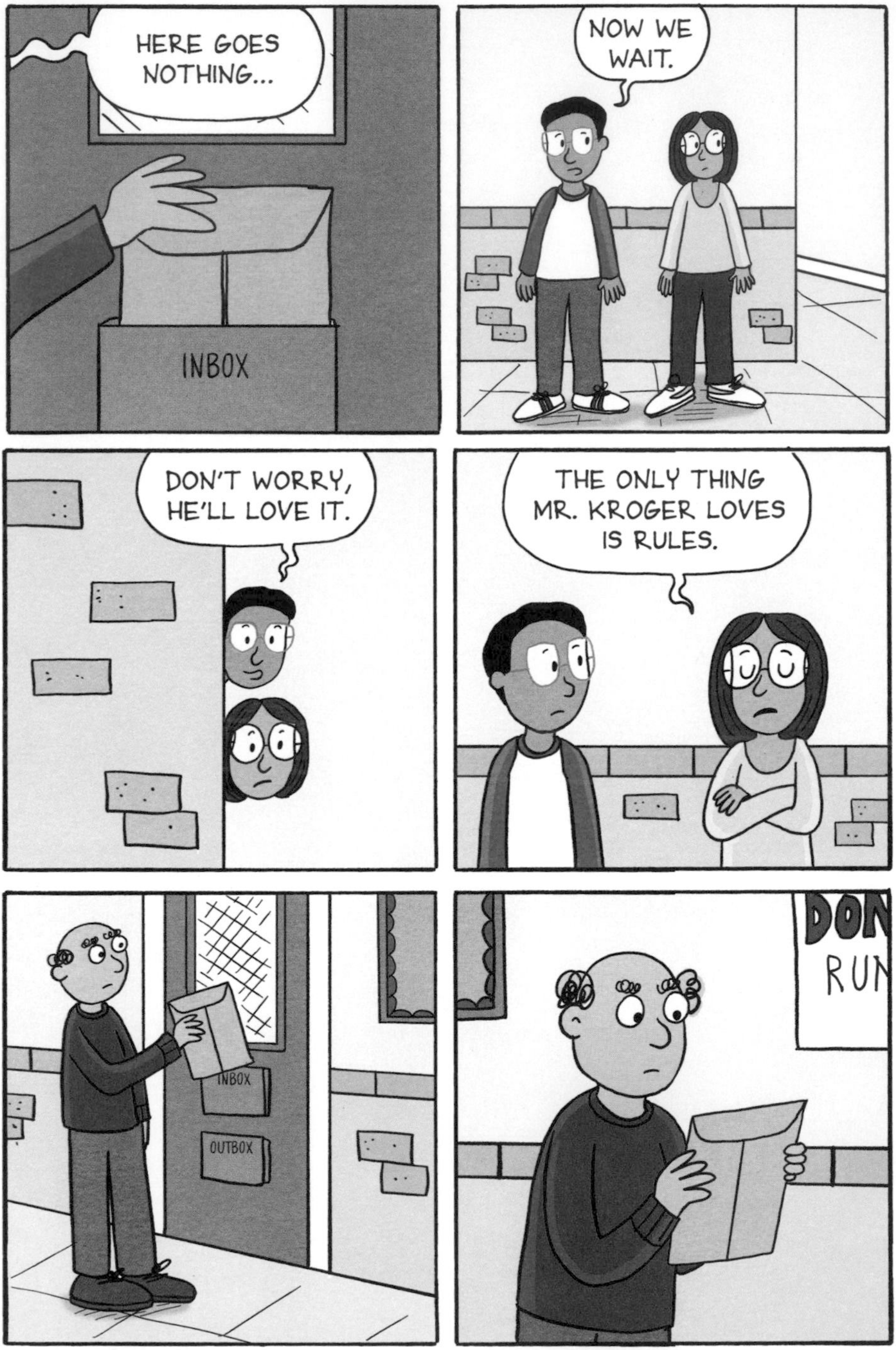
HERE GOES NOTHING...
INBOX
NOW WE WAIT.
DON'T WORRY, HE'LL LOVE IT.
THE ONLY THING MR. KROGER LOVES IS RULES.
INBOX
OUTBOX
DON
RUN

CHAPTER 8
GREMLINS

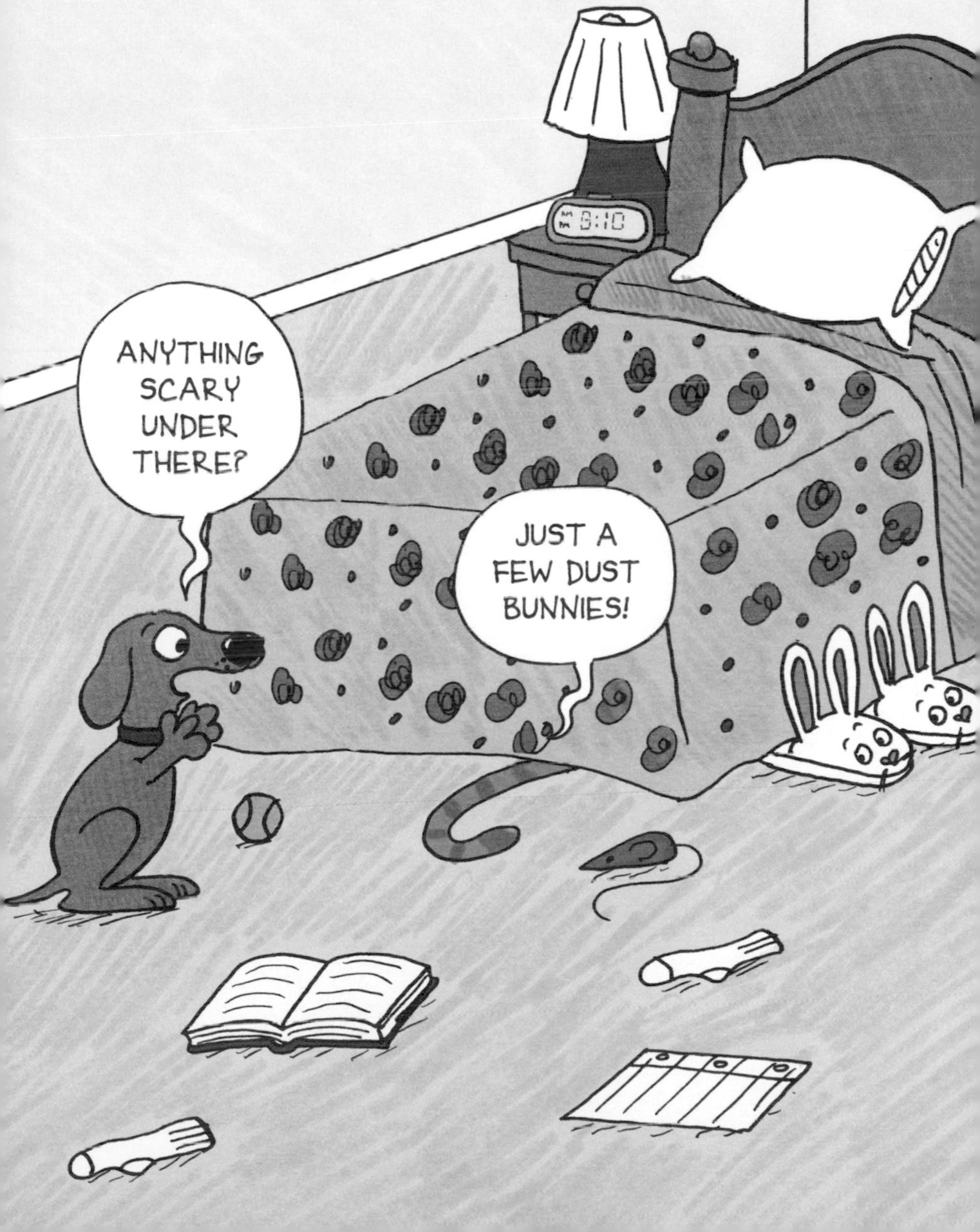
ANYTHING SCARY UNDER THERE?
JUST A FEW DUST BUNNIES!

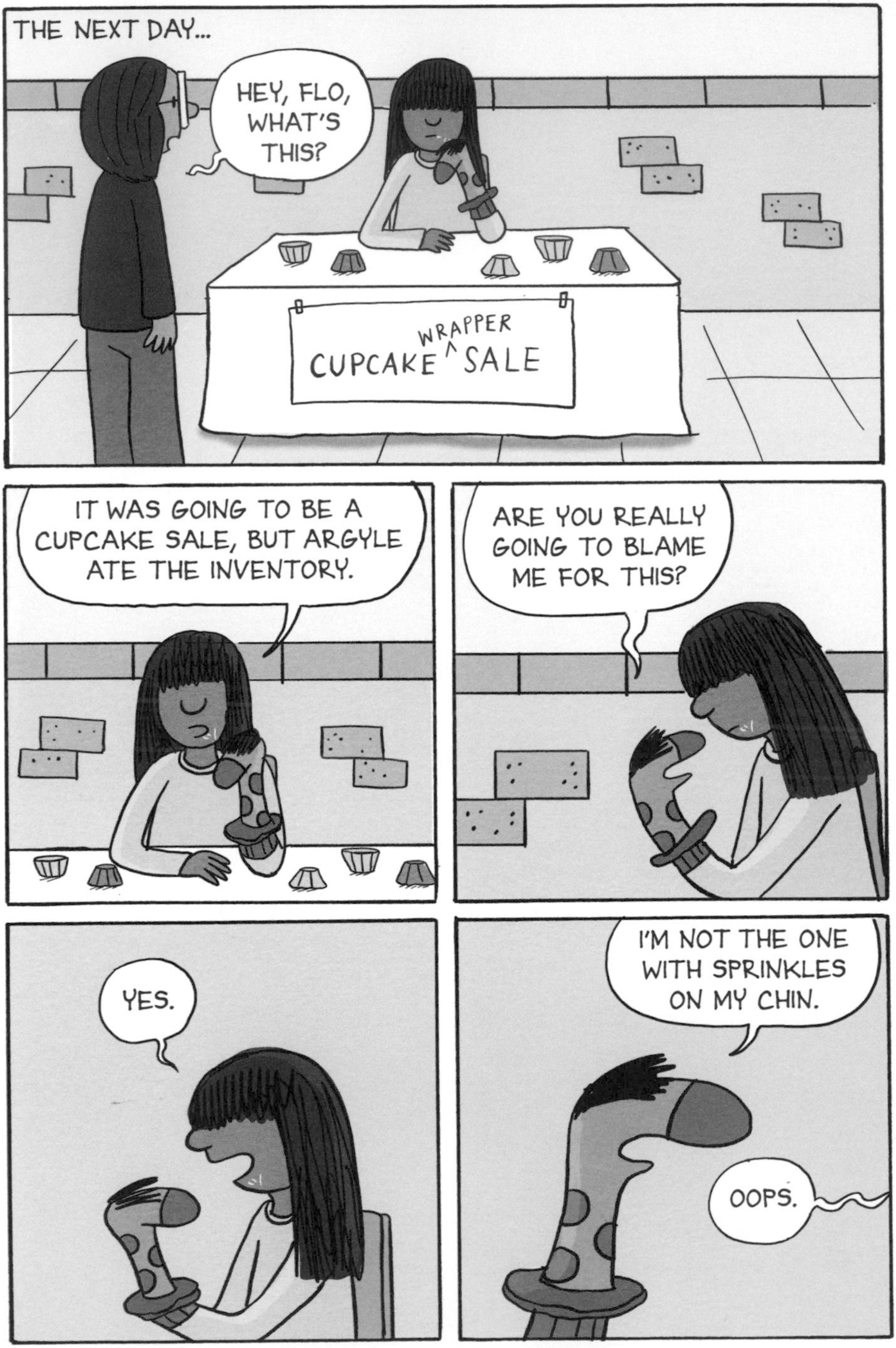
THE NEXT DAY...
HEY, FLO, WHAT'S THIS?
CUPCAKE WRAPPER SALE
IT WAS GOING TO BE A CUPCAKE SALE, BUT ARGYLE ATE THE INVENTORY.
ARE YOU REALLY GOING TO BLAME ME FOR THIS?
YES.
I'M NOT THE ONE WITH SPRINKLES ON MY CHIN.
OOPS.

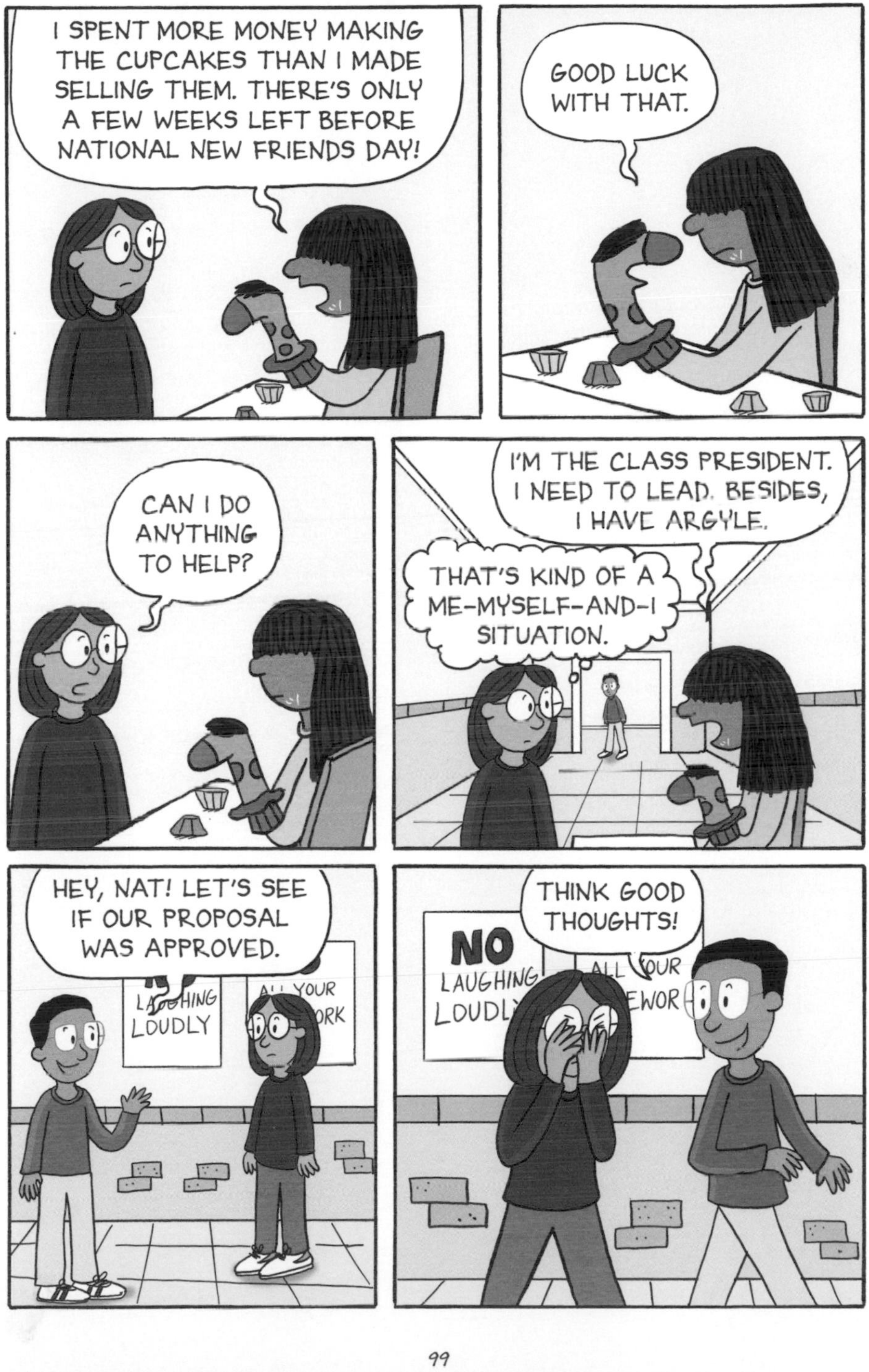
I SPENT MORE MONEY MAKING THE CUPCAKES THAN I MADE SELLING THEM. THERE'S ONLY A FEW WEEKS LEFT BEFORE NATIONAL NEW FRIENDS DAY!
GOOD LUCK WITH THAT.
CAN I DO ANYTHING TO HELP?
I'M THE CLASS PRESIDENT. I NEED TO LEAD. BESIDES, I HAVE ARGYLE.
THAT'S KIND OF A ME-MYSELF-AND-I SITUATION.
HEY, NAT! LET'S SEE IF OUR PROPOSAL WAS APPROVED.
THINK GOOD THOUGHTS!
NO
LAUGHING

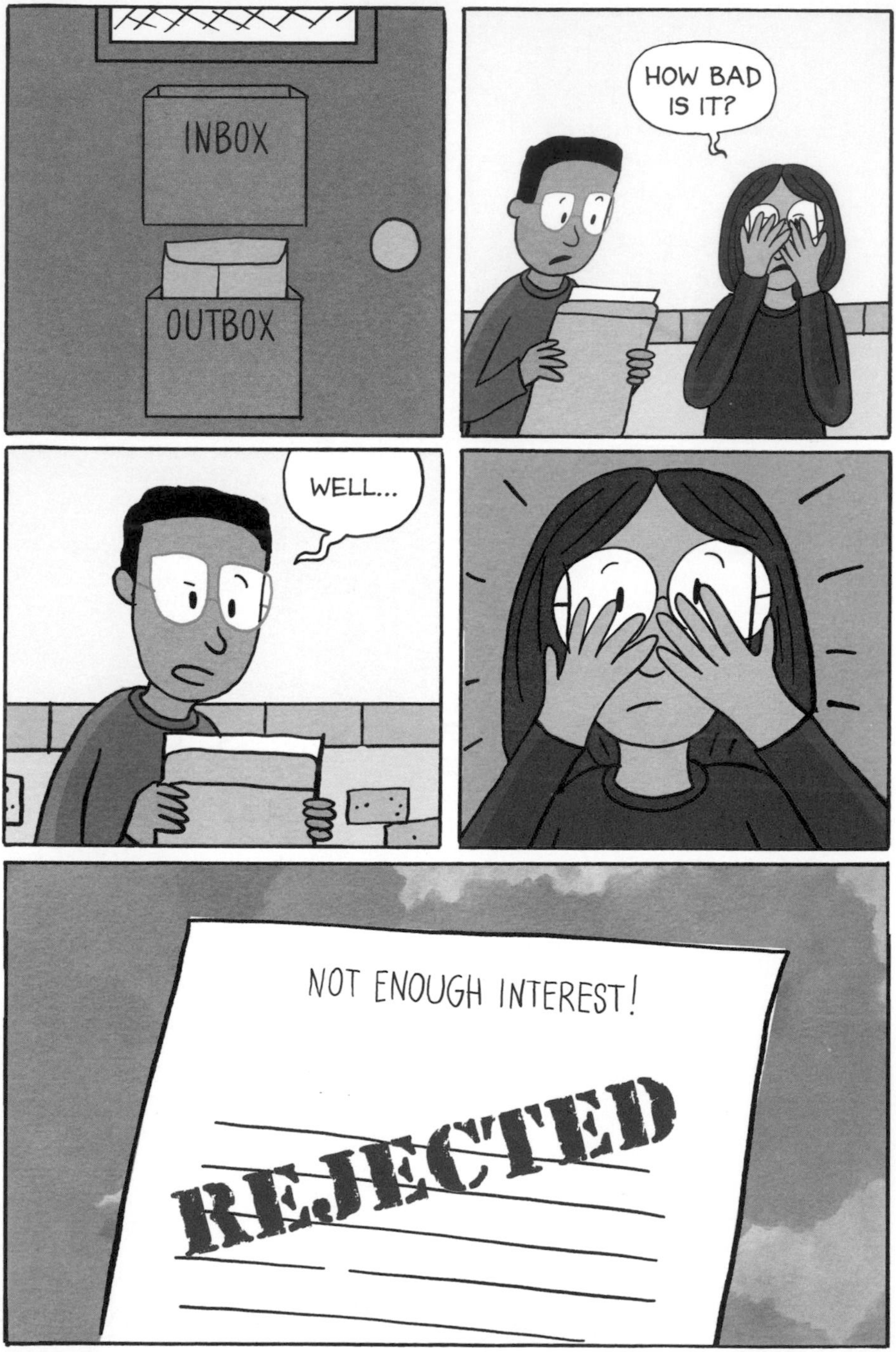
INBOX
OUTBOX
HOW BAD IS IT?
WELL...
NOT ENOUGH INTEREST!
REJECTED

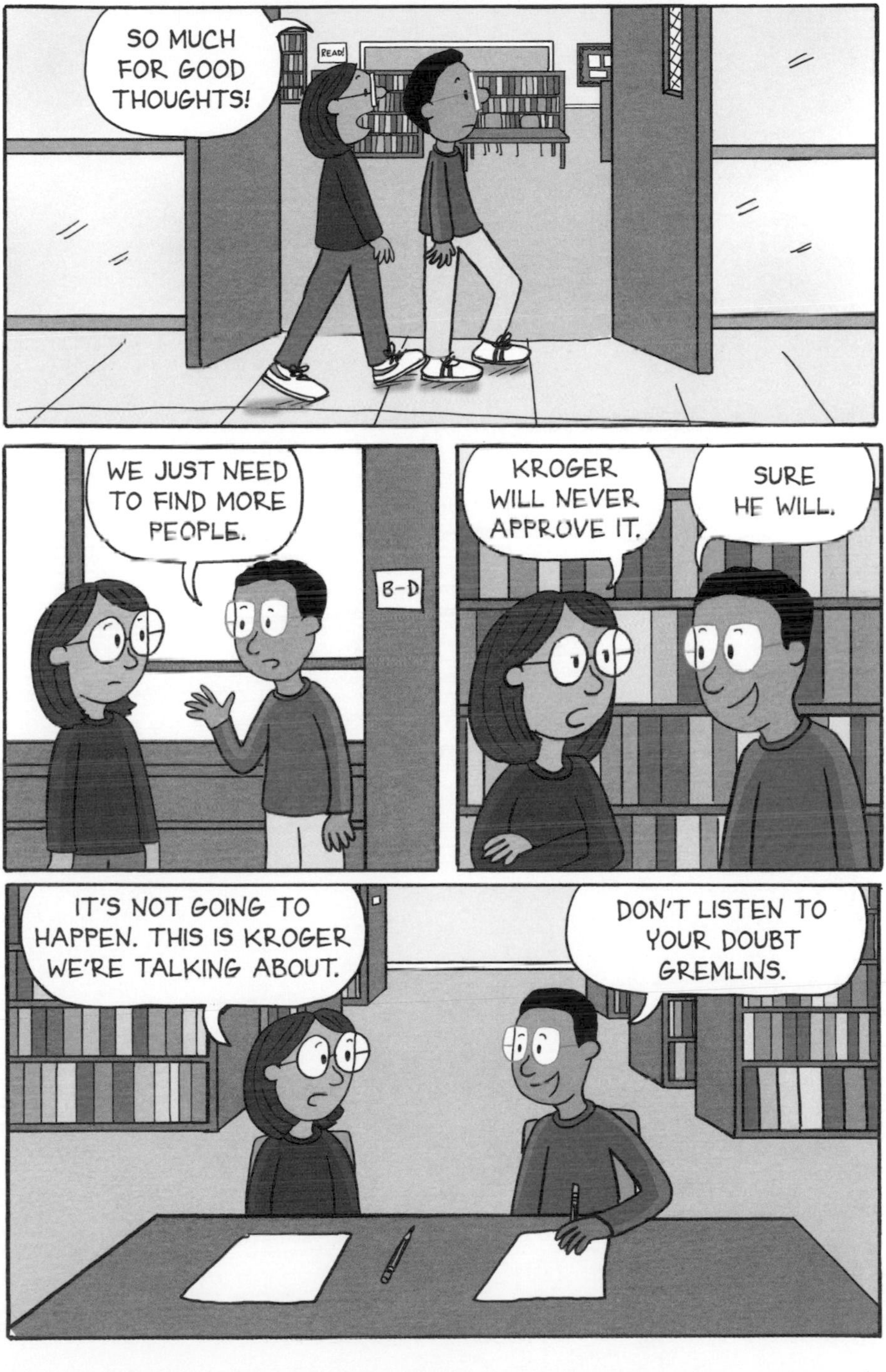
SO MUCH FOR GOOD THOUGHTS!
READ!
WE JUST NEED TO FIND MORE PEOPLE.
B–D
KROGER WILL NEVER APPROVE IT.
SURE HE WILL.
IT'S NOT GOING TO HAPPEN. THIS IS KROGER WE'RE TALKING ABOUT.
DON'T LISTEN TO YOUR DOUBT GREMLINS.

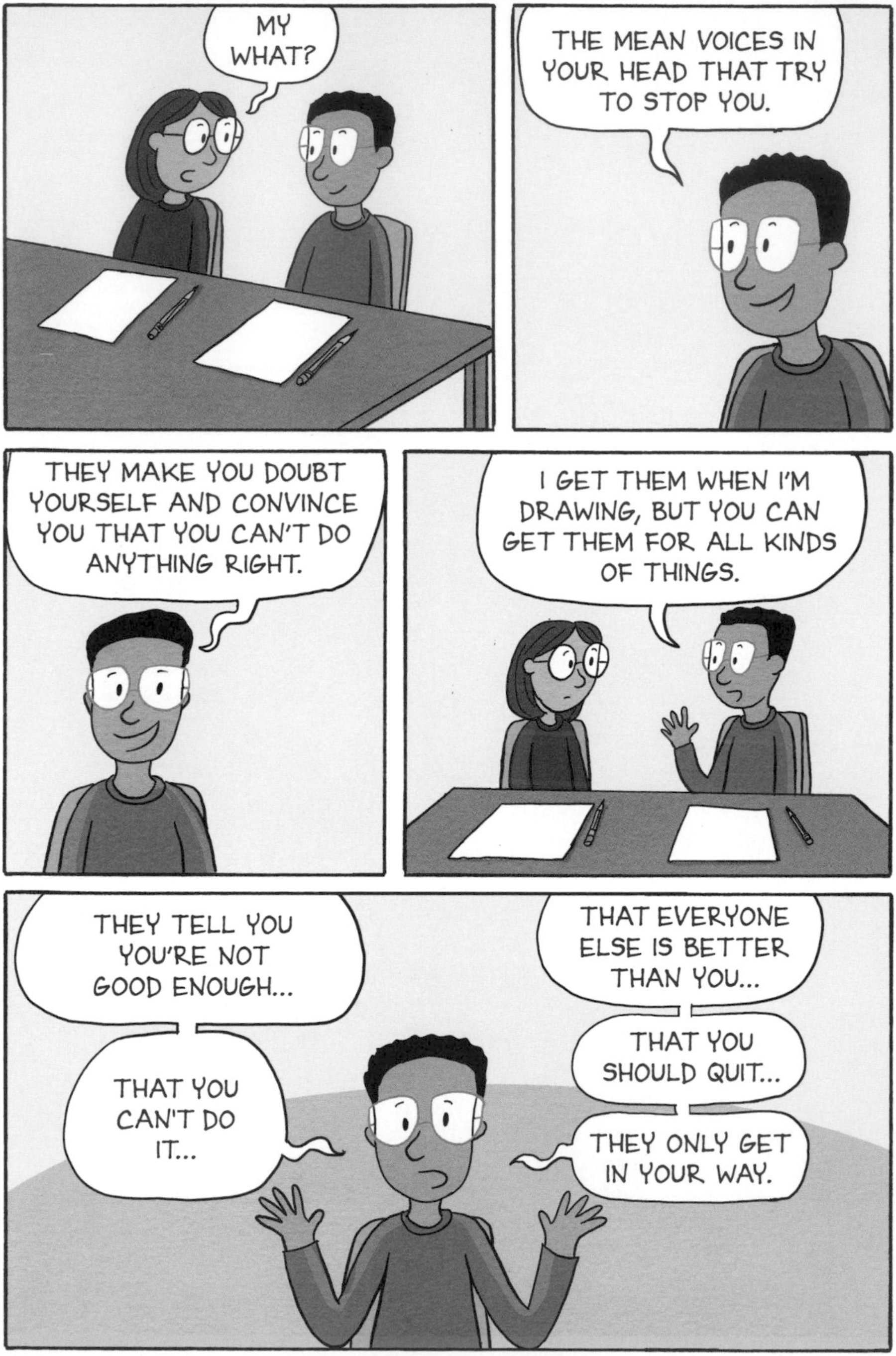
MY WHAT?
THE MEAN VOICES IN YOUR HEAD THAT TRY TO STOP YOU.
THEY MAKE YOU DOUBT YOURSELF AND CONVINCE YOU THAT YOU CAN'T DO ANYTHING RIGHT.
I GET THEM WHEN I'M DRAWING, BUT YOU CAN GET THEM FOR ALL KINDS OF THINGS.
THEY TELL YOU YOU'RE NOT GOOD ENOUGH...
THAT YOU CAN'T DO IT...
THAT EVERYONE ELSE IS BETTER THAN YOU...
THAT YOU SHOULD QUIT...
THEY ONLY GET IN YOUR WAY.

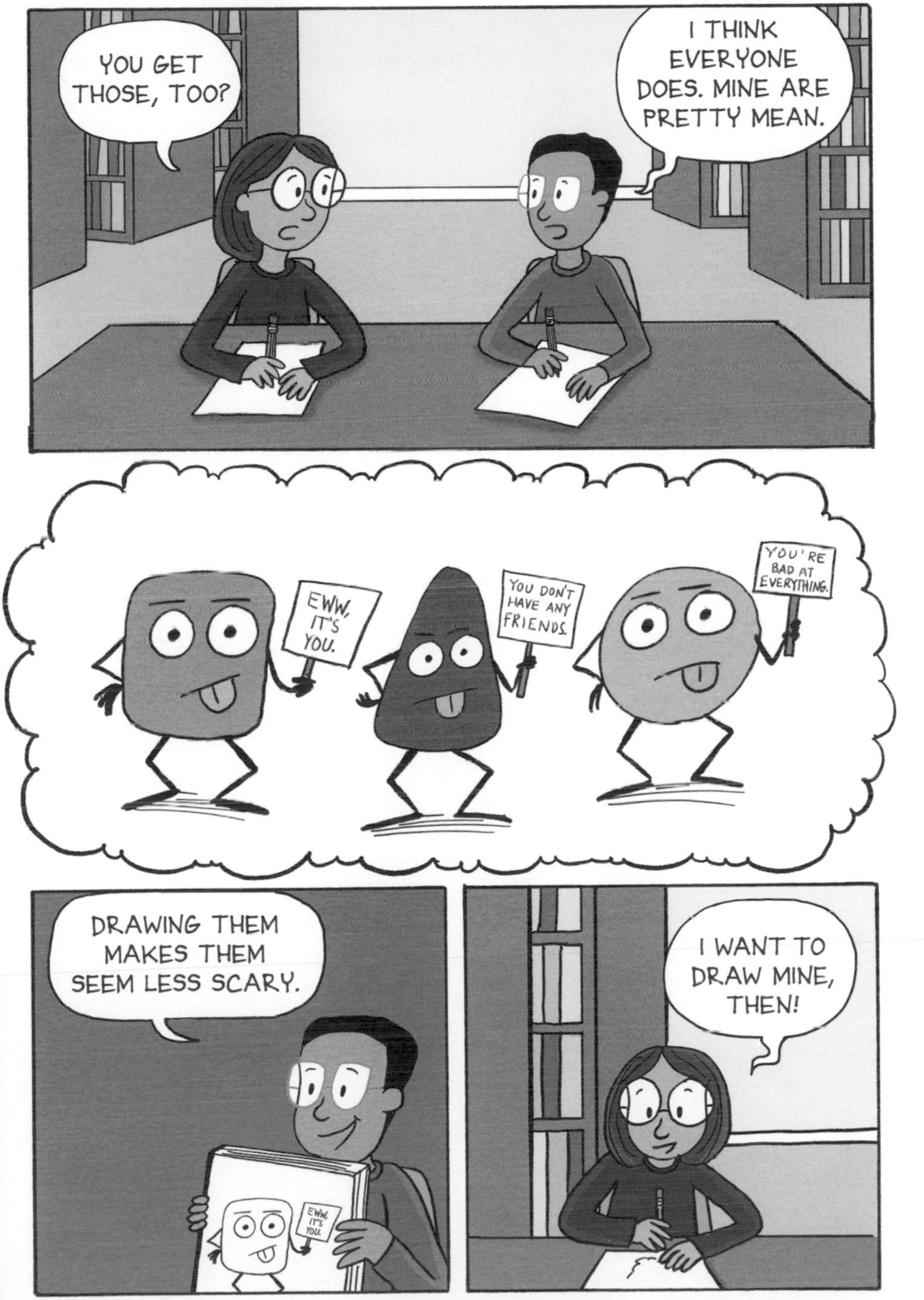
YOU GET THOSE, TOO?
I THINK EVERYONE DOES. MINE ARE PRETTY MEAN.
EWW, IT'S YOU.
YOU DON'T HAVE ANY FRIENDS.
YOU'RE BAD AT EVERYTHING.
DRAWING THEM MAKES THEM SEEM LESS SCARY.
EWW, IT'S YOU.
I WANT TO DRAW MINE, THEN!

DOUBT GREMLINS

YOU STINK!
YOU'RE THE WORST
YOU CAN'T DO IT!

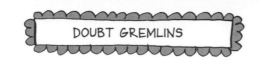

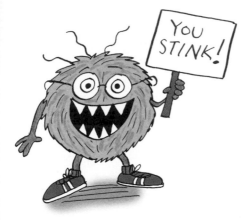

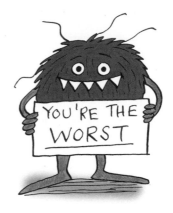

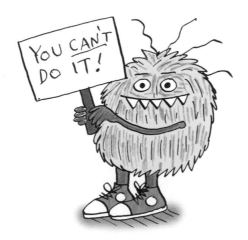

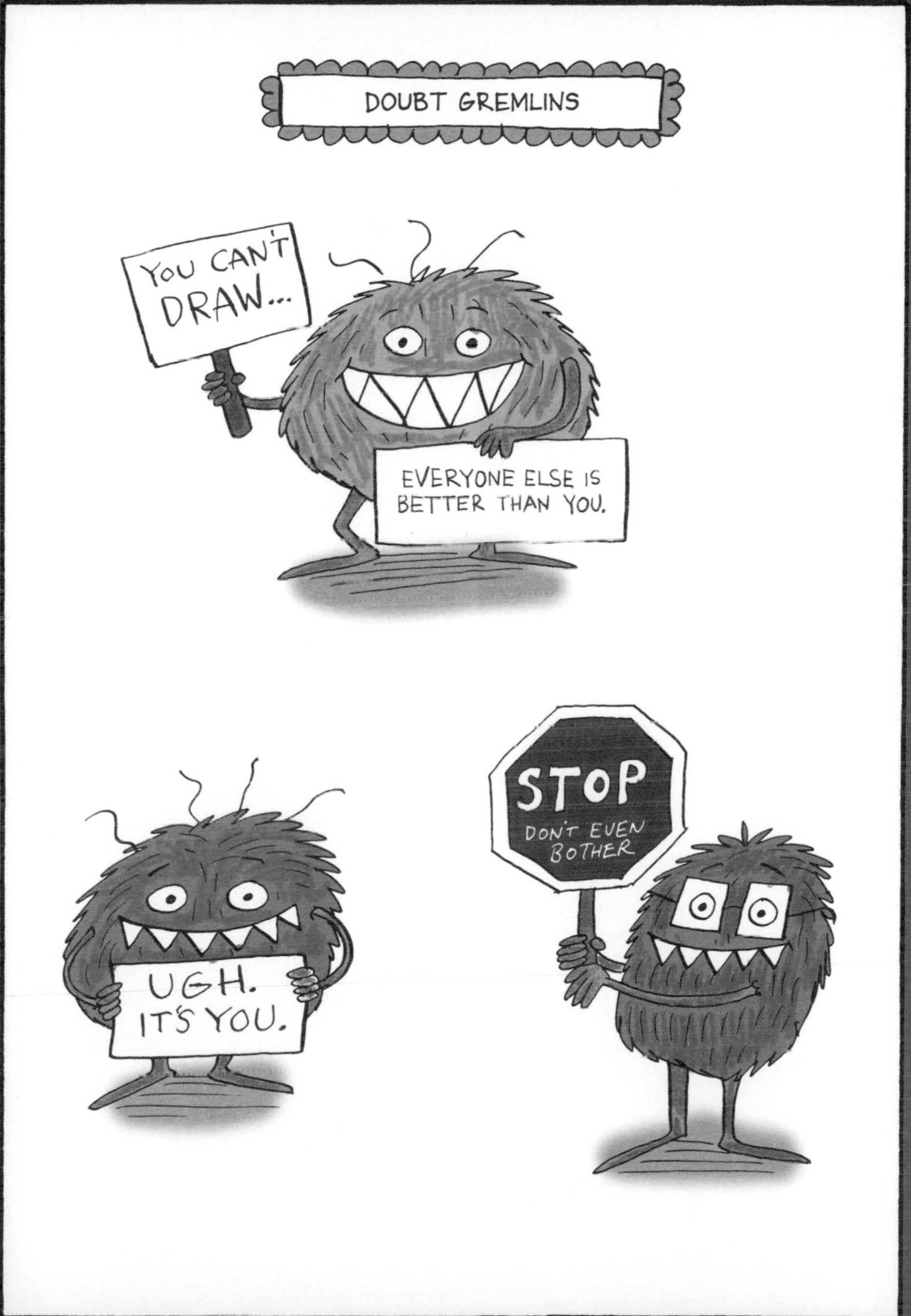
DOUBT GREMLINS
YOU CAN'T DRAW...
EVERYONE ELSE IS BETTER THAN YOU.
UGH. IT'S YOU.
STOP
DON'T EVEN BOTHER

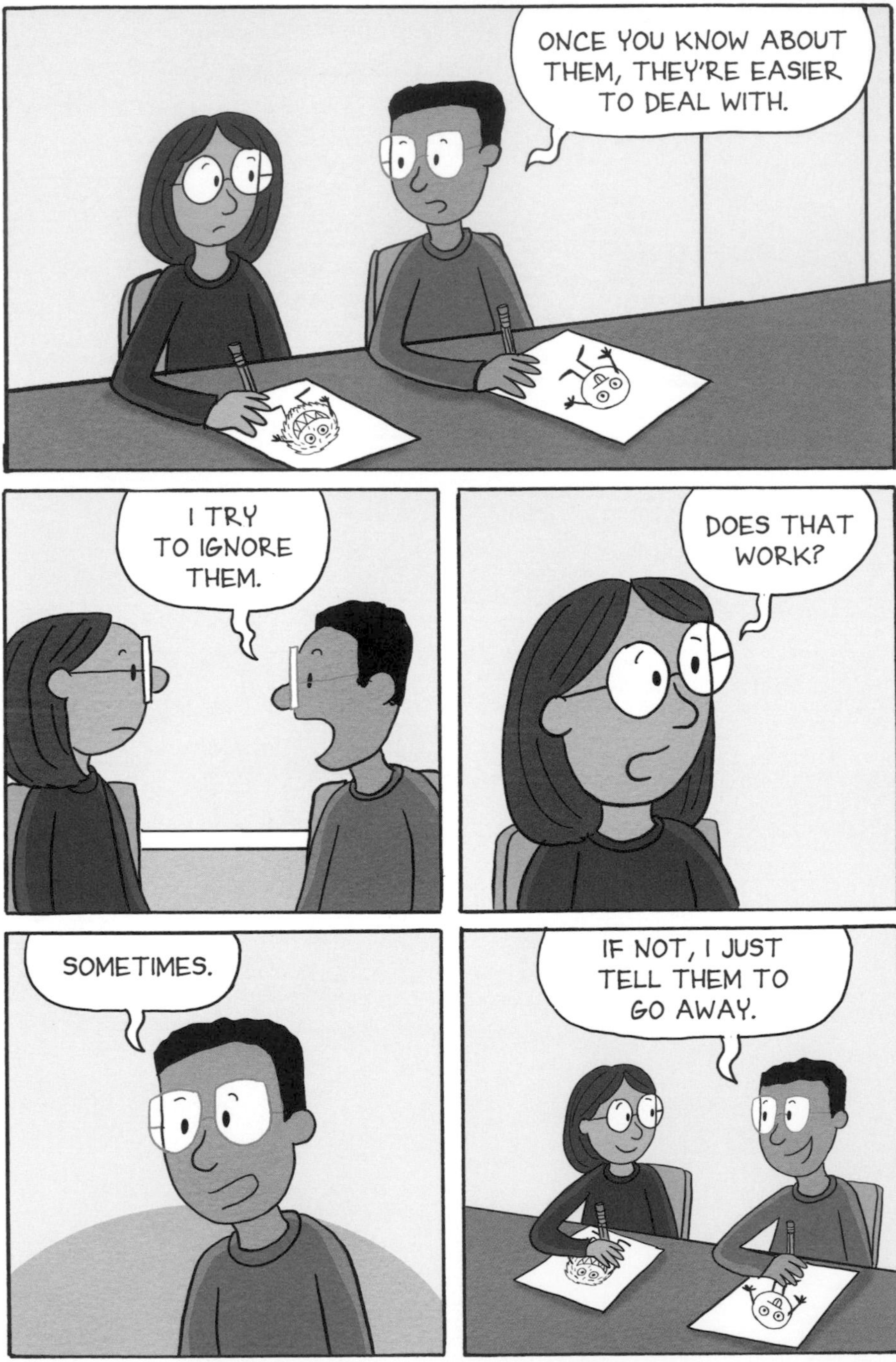
ONCE YOU KNOW ABOUT THEM, THEY'RE EASIER TO DEAL WITH.
I TRY TO IGNORE THEM.
DOES THAT WORK?
SOMETIMES.
IF NOT, I JUST TELL THEM TO GO AWAY.

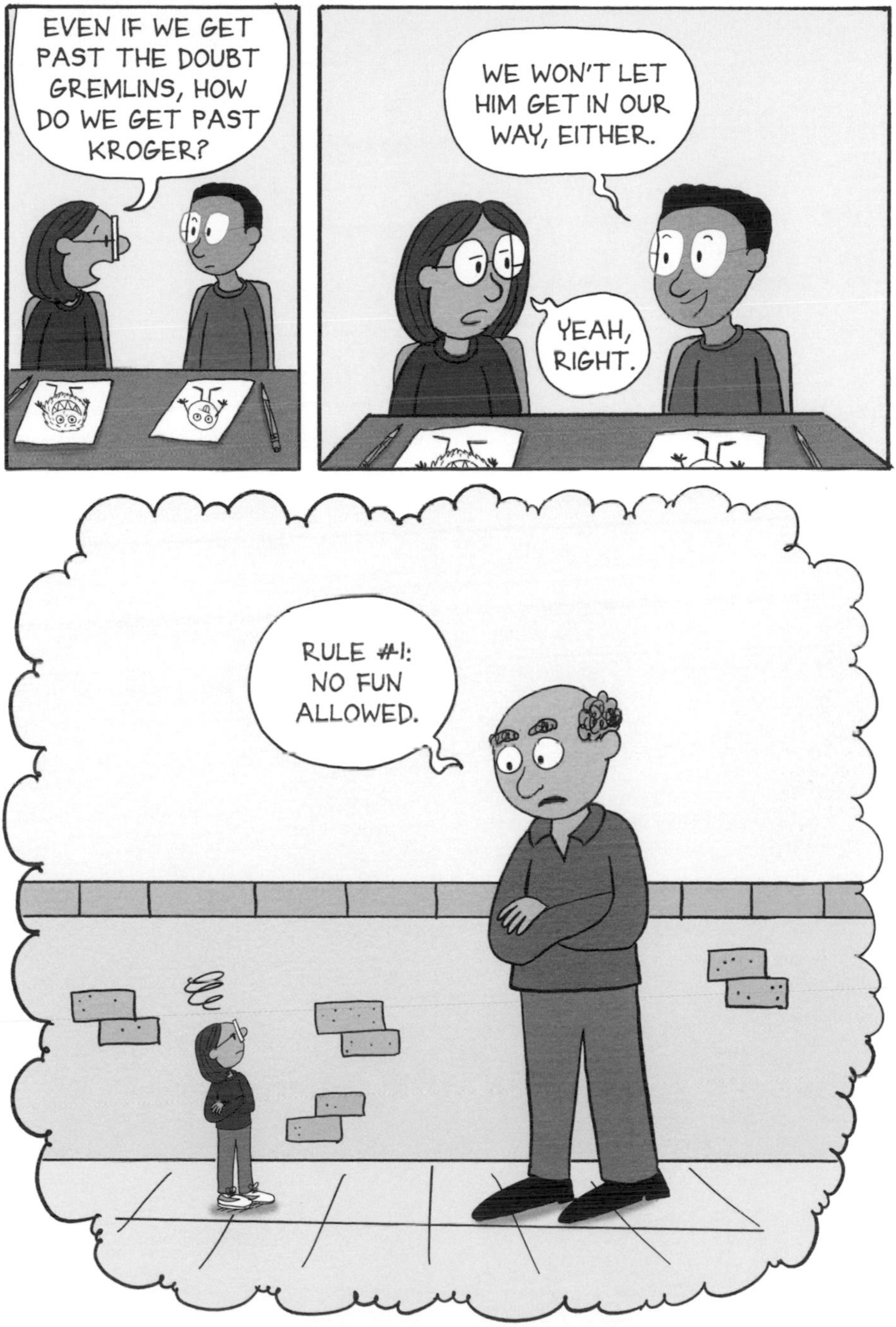
EVEN IF WE GET PAST THE DOUBT GREMLINS, HOW DO WE GET PAST KROGER?
WE WON'T LET HIM GET IN OUR WAY, EITHER.
YEAH, RIGHT.
RULE #1: NO FUN ALLOWED.

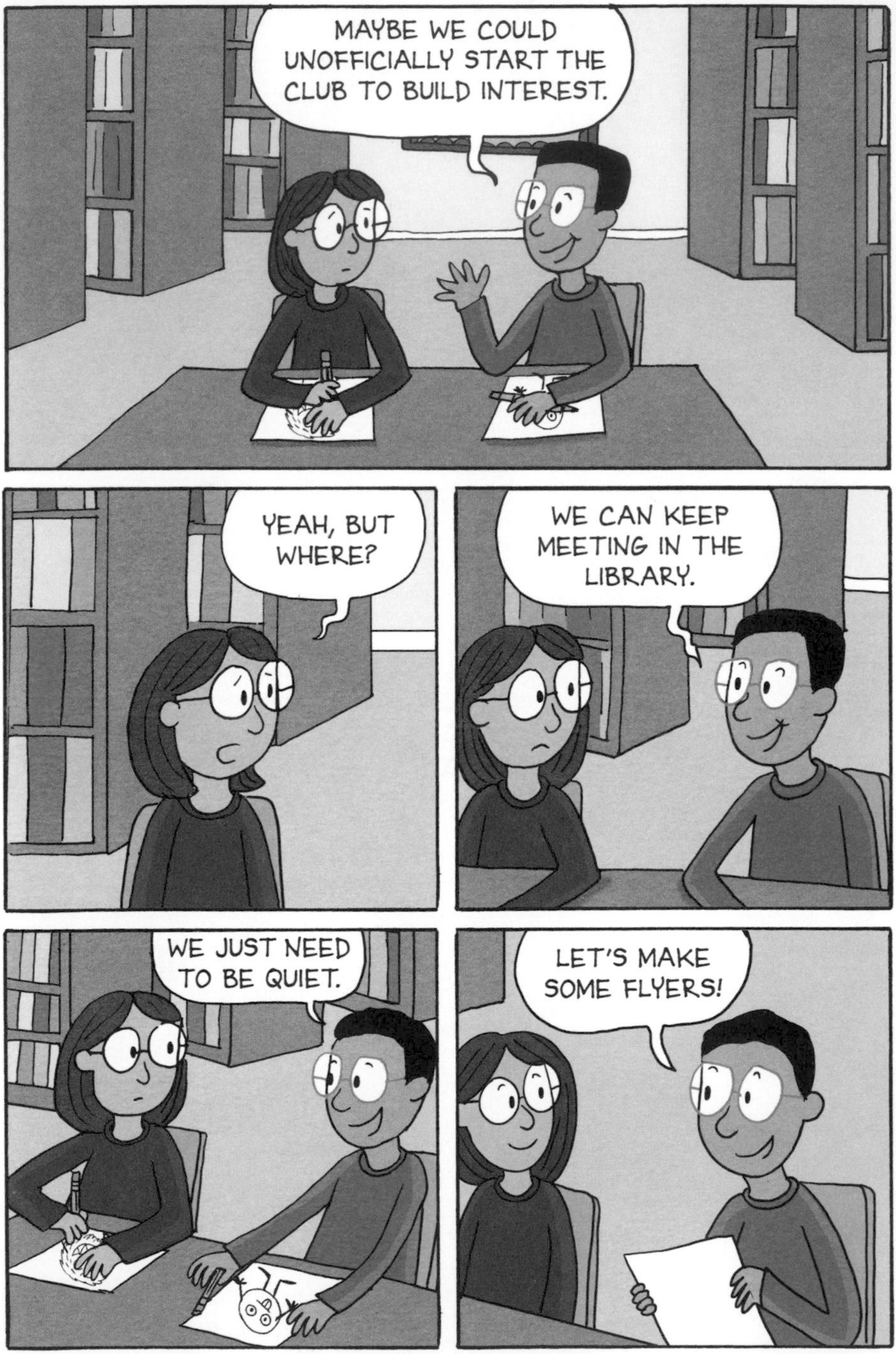
MAYBE WE COULD UNOFFICIALLY START THE CLUB TO BUILD INTEREST.
YEAH, BUT WHERE?
WE CAN KEEP MEETING IN THE LIBRARY.
WE JUST NEED TO BE QUIET.
LET'S MAKE SOME FLYERS!

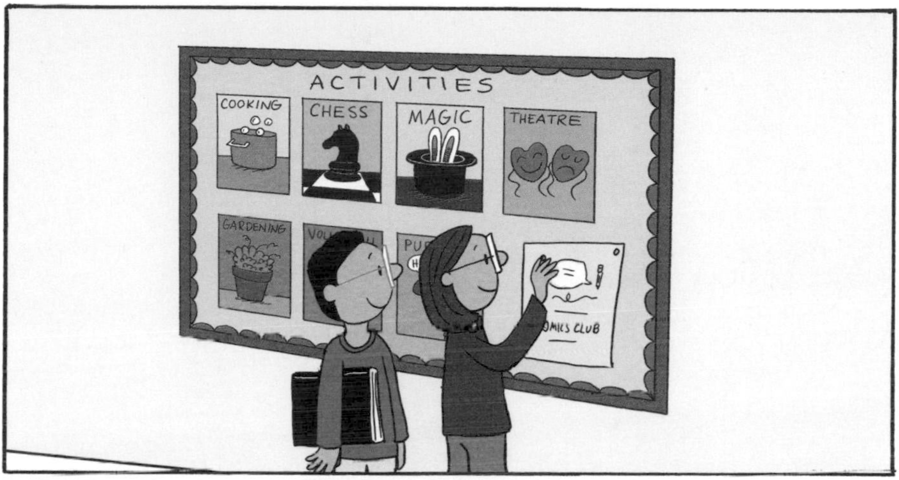
ACTIVITIES
COOKING
CHESS
MAGIC
THEATRE
GARDENING

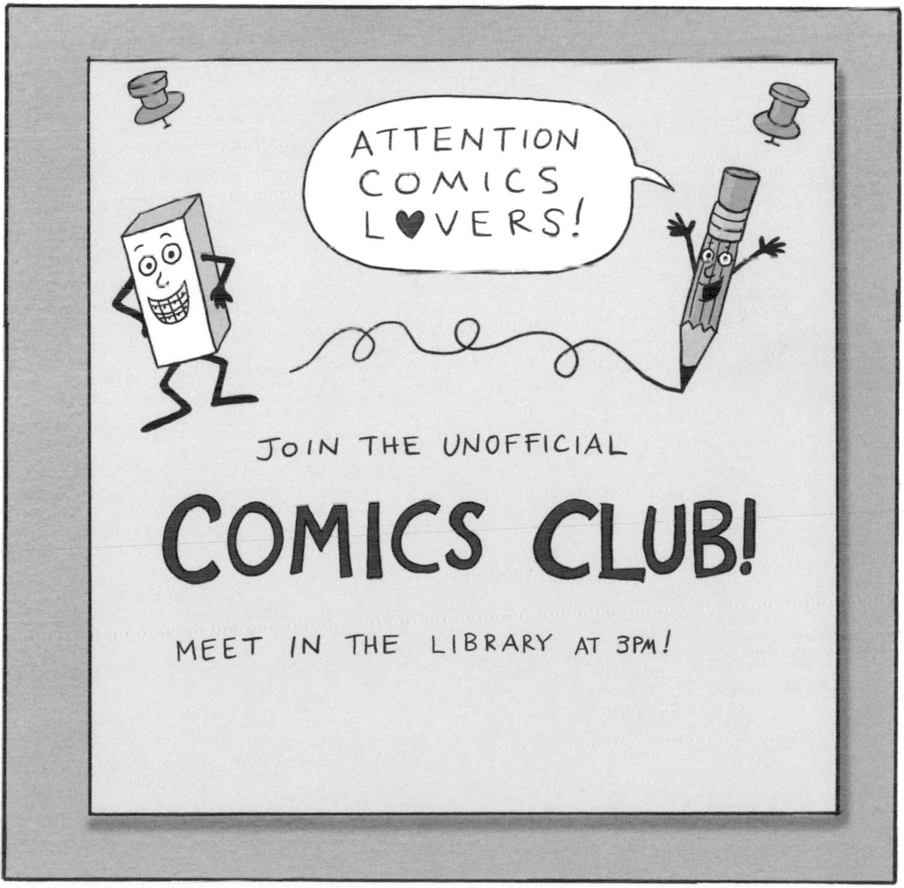
ATTENTION COMICS L♥VERS!
JOIN THE UNOFFICIAL
COMICS CLUB!
MEET IN THE LIBRARY AT 3PM!

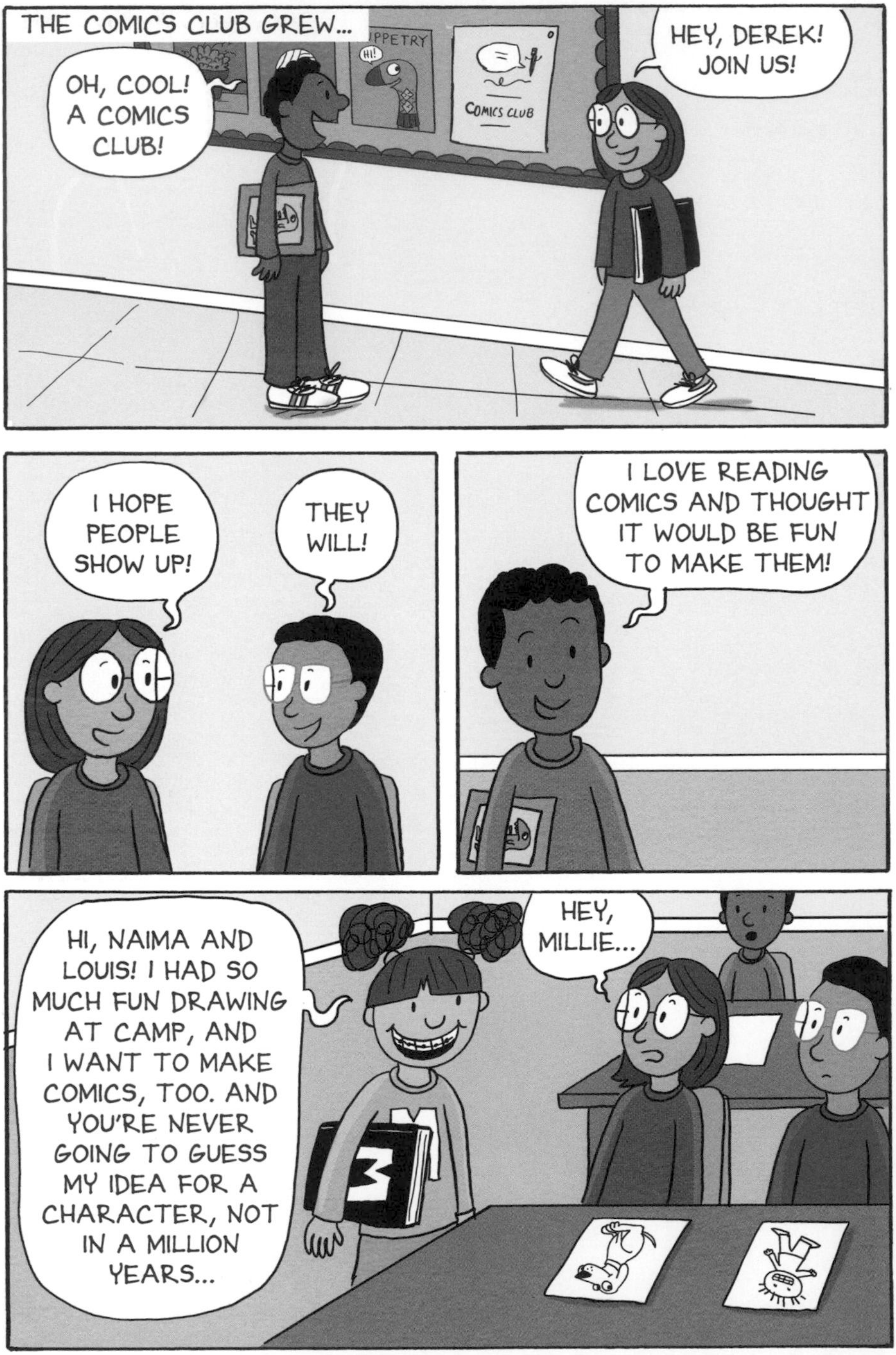
THE COMICS CLUB GREW...
OH, COOL! A COMICS CLUB!
HEY, DEREK! JOIN US!
UPPETRY
HI!
COMICS CLUB
I HOPE PEOPLE SHOW UP!
THEY WILL!
I LOVE READING COMICS AND THOUGHT IT WOULD BE FUN TO MAKE THEM!
HI, NAIMA AND LOUIS! I HAD SO MUCH FUN DRAWING AT CAMP, AND I WANT TO MAKE COMICS, TOO. AND YOU'RE NEVER GOING TO GUESS MY IDEA FOR A CHARACTER, NOT IN A MILLION YEARS...
HEY, MILLIE...

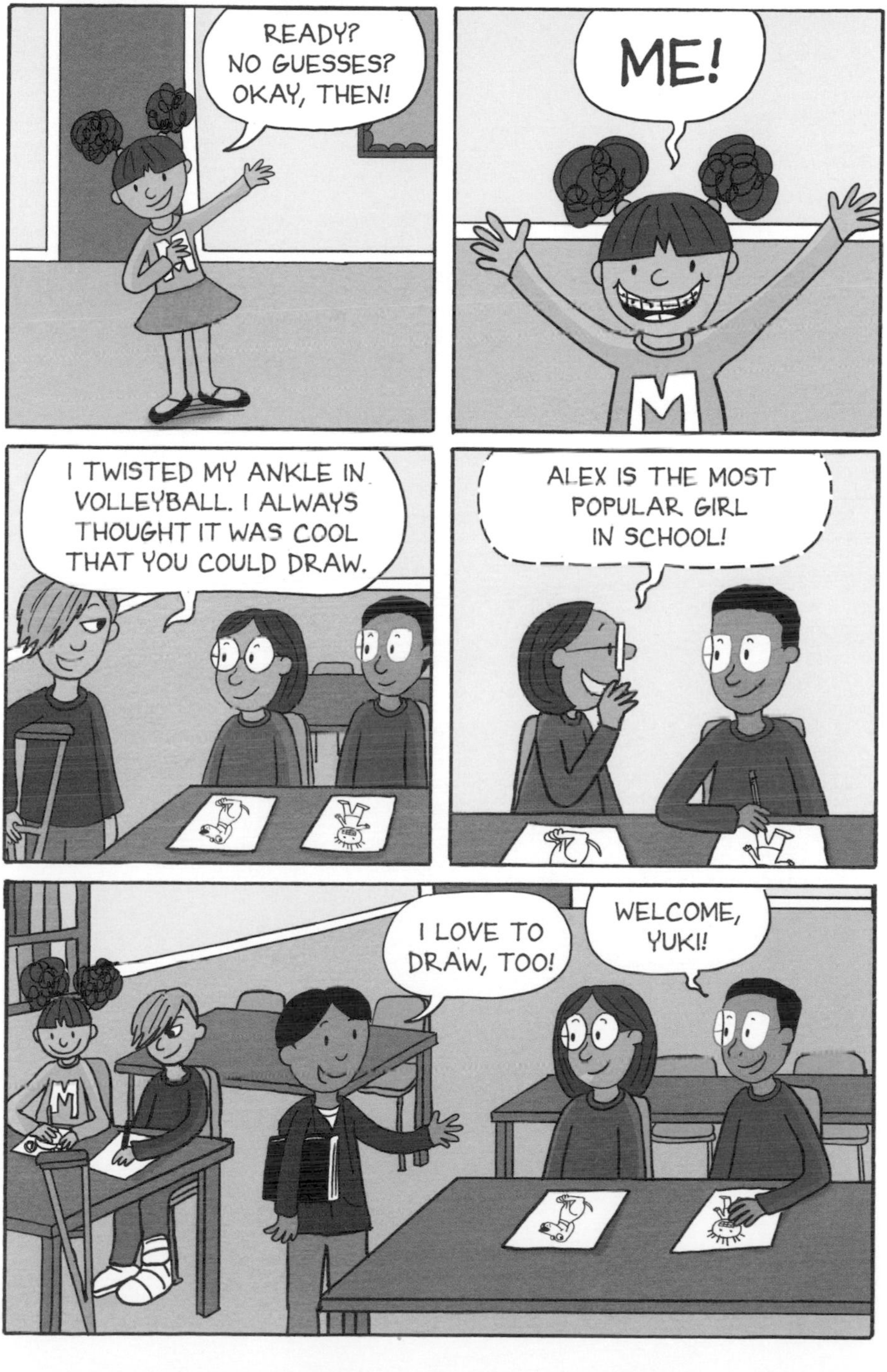
READY? NO GUESSES? OKAY, THEN!
ME!
I TWISTED MY ANKLE IN VOLLEYBALL. I ALWAYS THOUGHT IT WAS COOL THAT YOU COULD DRAW.
ALEX IS THE MOST POPULAR GIRL IN SCHOOL!
I LOVE TO DRAW, TOO!
WELCOME, YUKI!

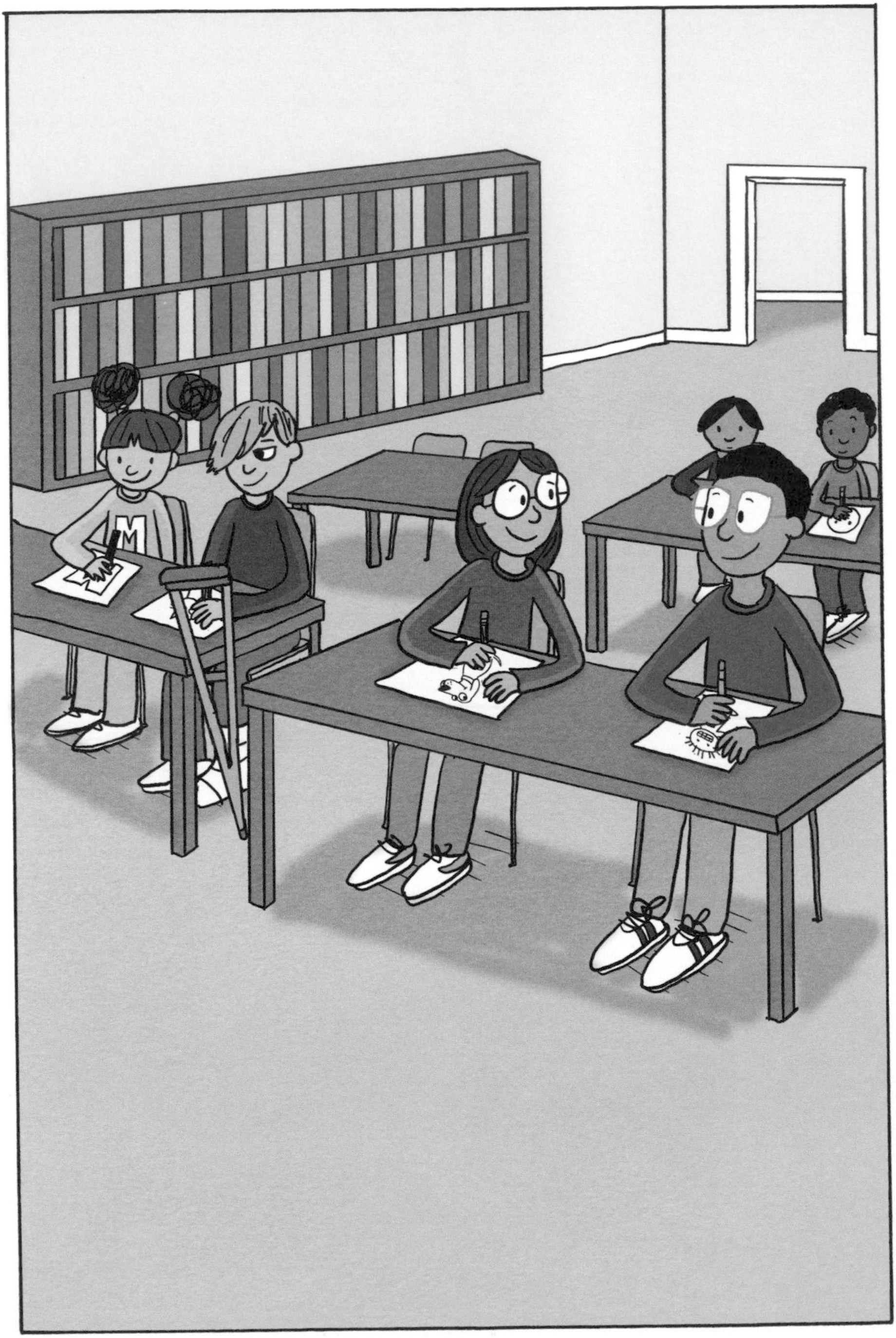

CHAPTER 9
THERE'S NO "US" IN "TEAM"

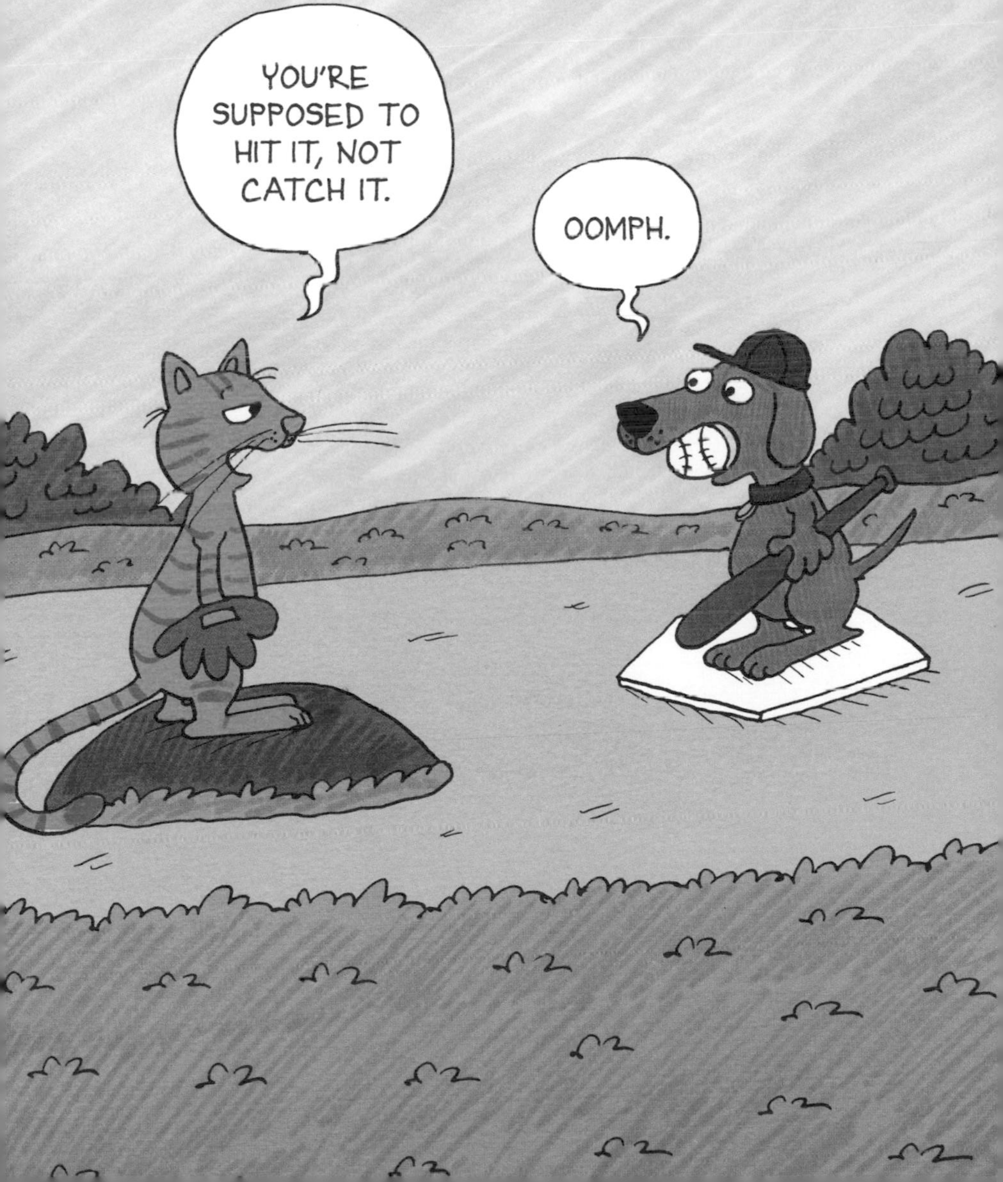
YOU'RE SUPPOSED TO HIT IT, NOT CATCH IT.
OOMPH.

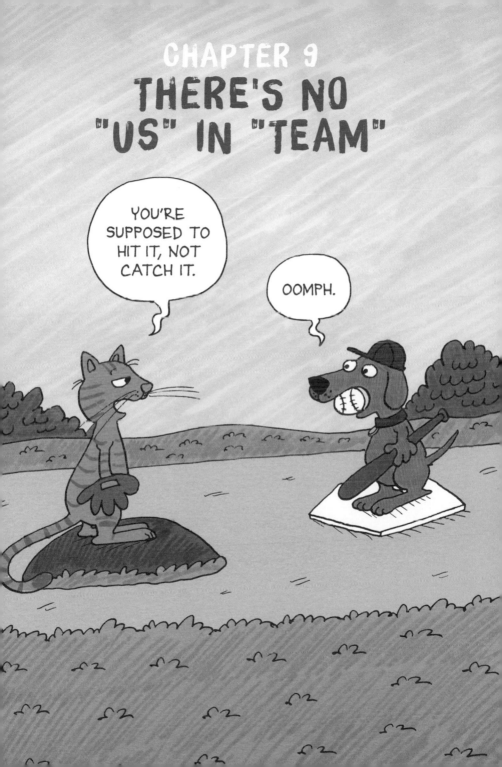

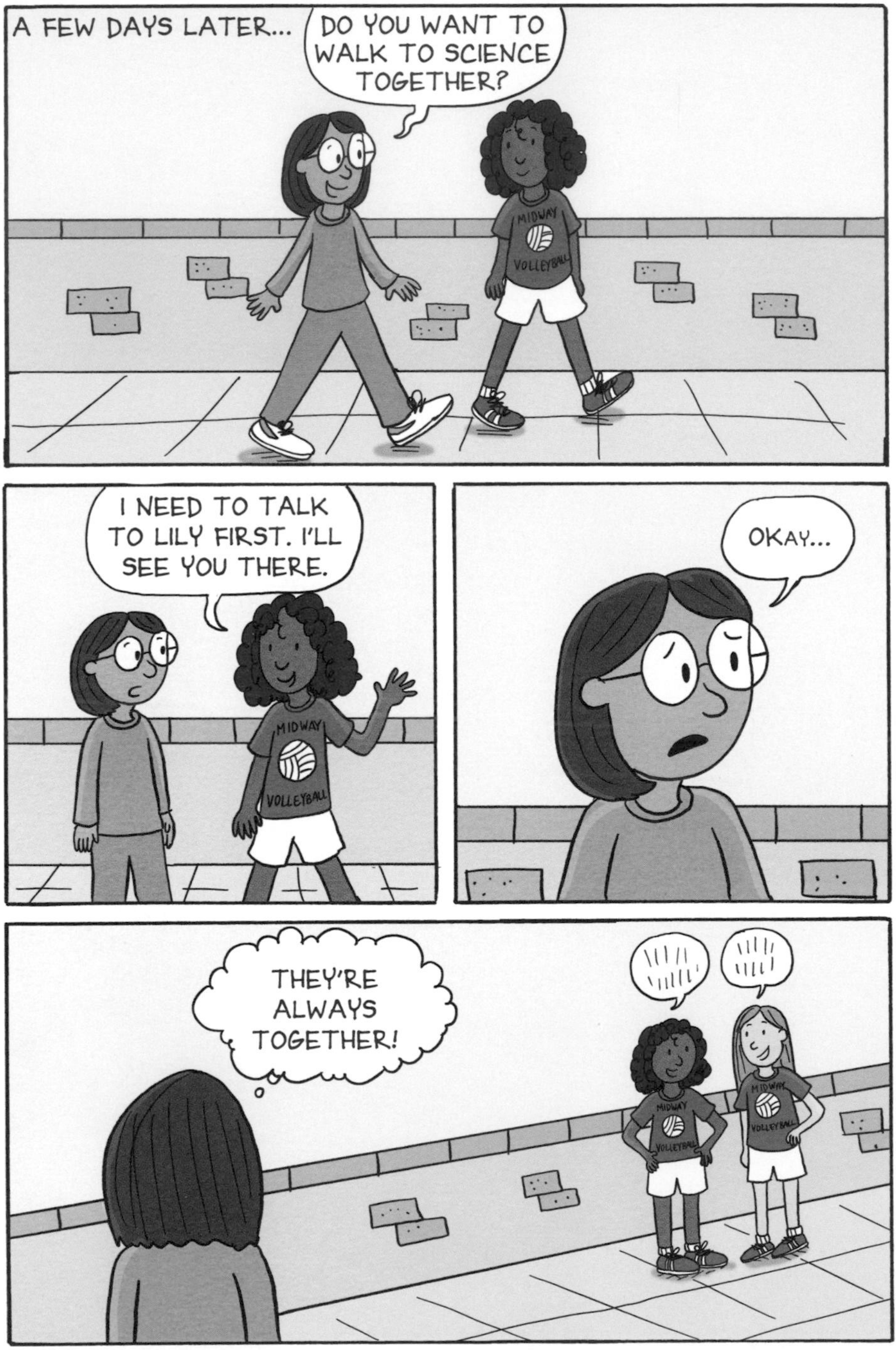
A FEW DAYS LATER...
DO YOU WANT TO WALK TO SCIENCE TOGETHER?
MIDWAY VOLLEYBALL
I NEED TO TALK TO LILY FIRST. I'LL SEE YOU THERE.
MIDWAY VOLLEYBALL
OKAY...
THEY'RE ALWAYS TOGETHER!
MIDWAY VOLLEYBALL
MIDWAY VOLLEYBALL

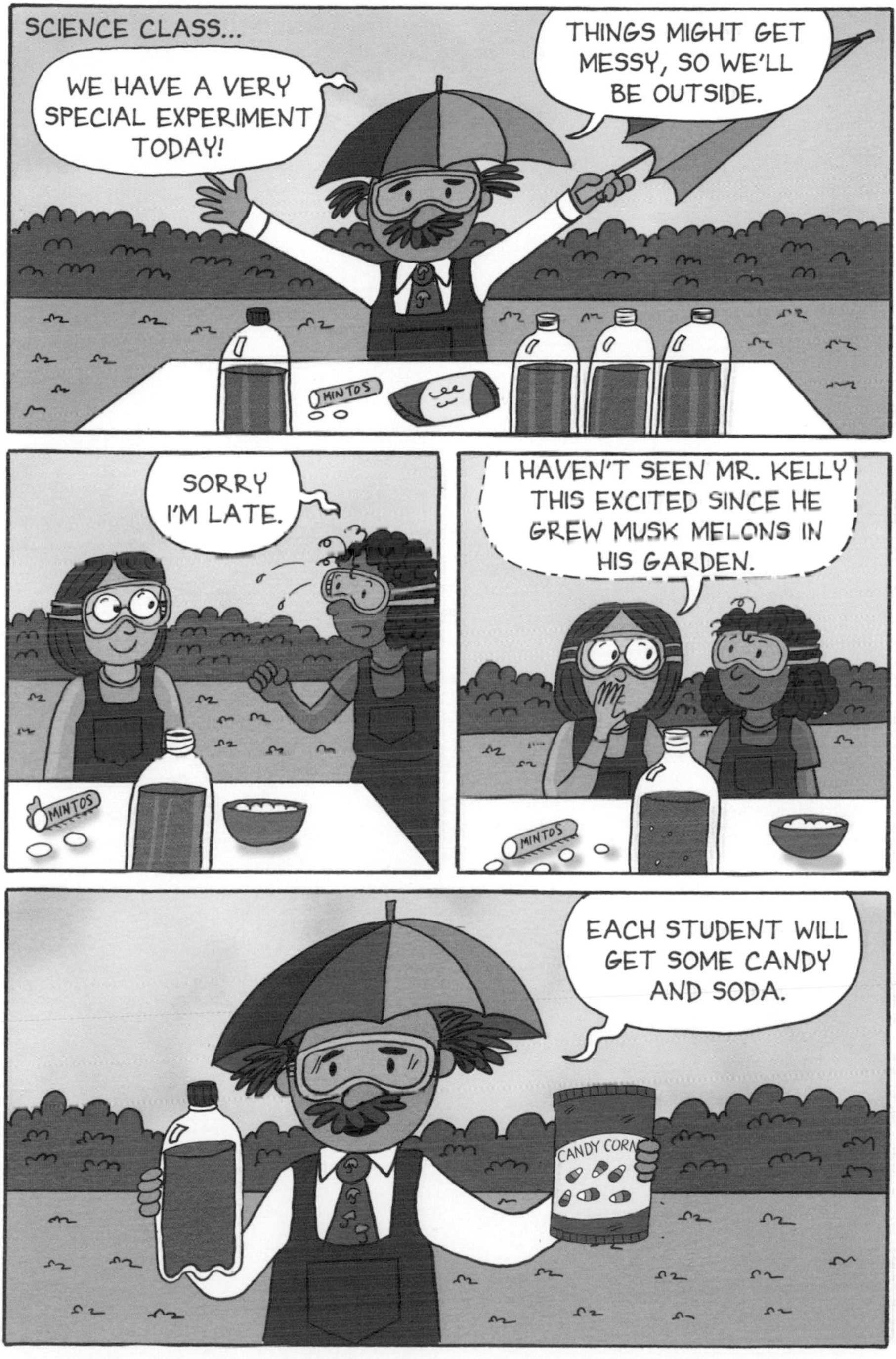
SCIENCE CLASS...
WE HAVE A VERY SPECIAL EXPERIMENT TODAY!
THINGS MIGHT GET MESSY, SO WE'LL BE OUTSIDE.
MINTOS
SORRY I'M LATE.
MINTOS
I HAVEN'T SEEN MR. KELLY THIS EXCITED SINCE HE GREW MUSK MELONS IN HIS GARDEN.
MINTOS
EACH STUDENT WILL GET SOME CANDY AND SODA.
CANDY CORN

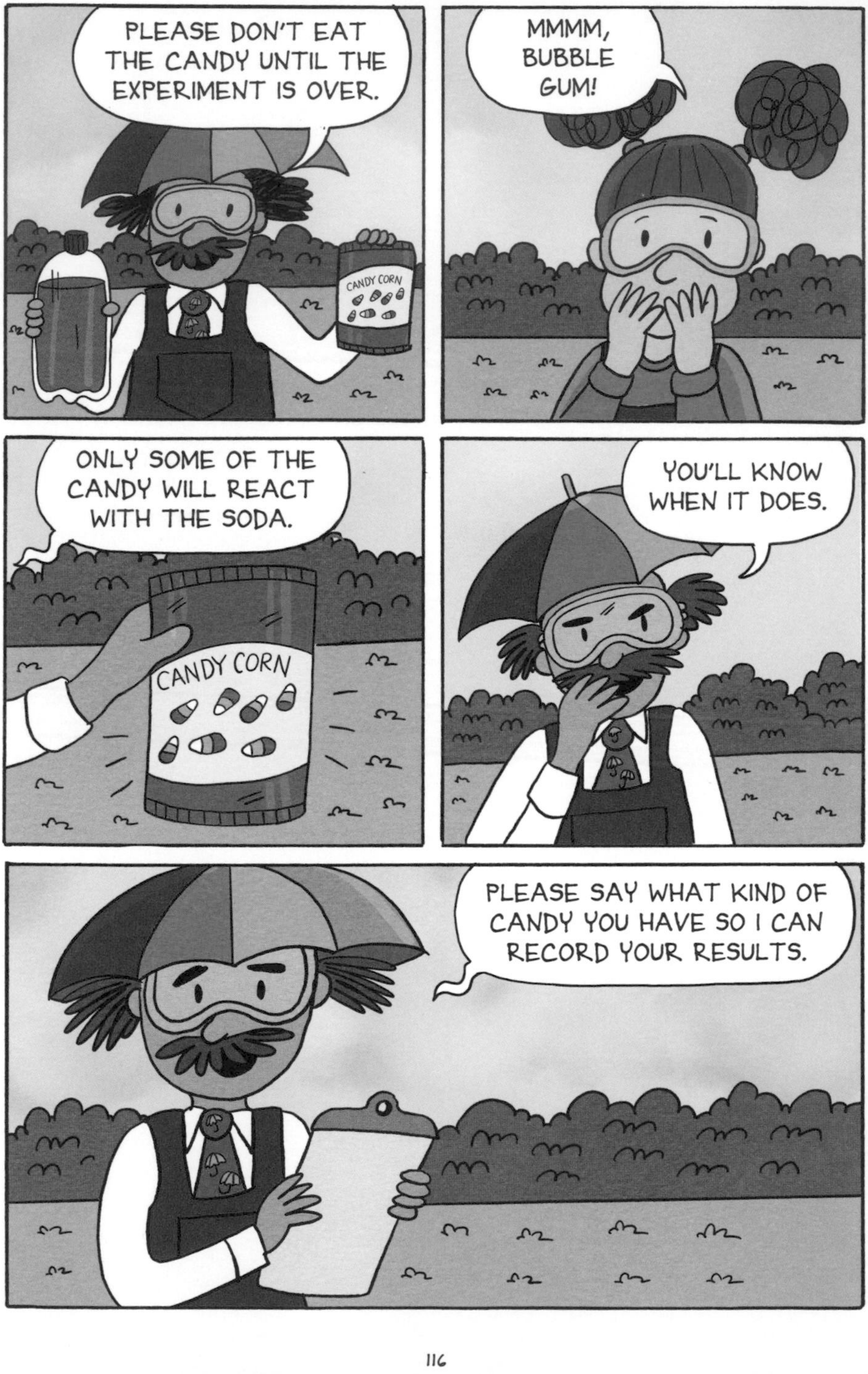
PLEASE DON'T EAT THE CANDY UNTIL THE EXPERIMENT IS OVER.
CANDY CORN
MMMM, BUBBLE GUM!
ONLY SOME OF THE CANDY WILL REACT WITH THE SODA.
CANDY CORN
YOU'LL KNOW WHEN IT DOES.
PLEASE SAY WHAT KIND OF CANDY YOU HAVE SO I CAN RECORD YOUR RESULTS.

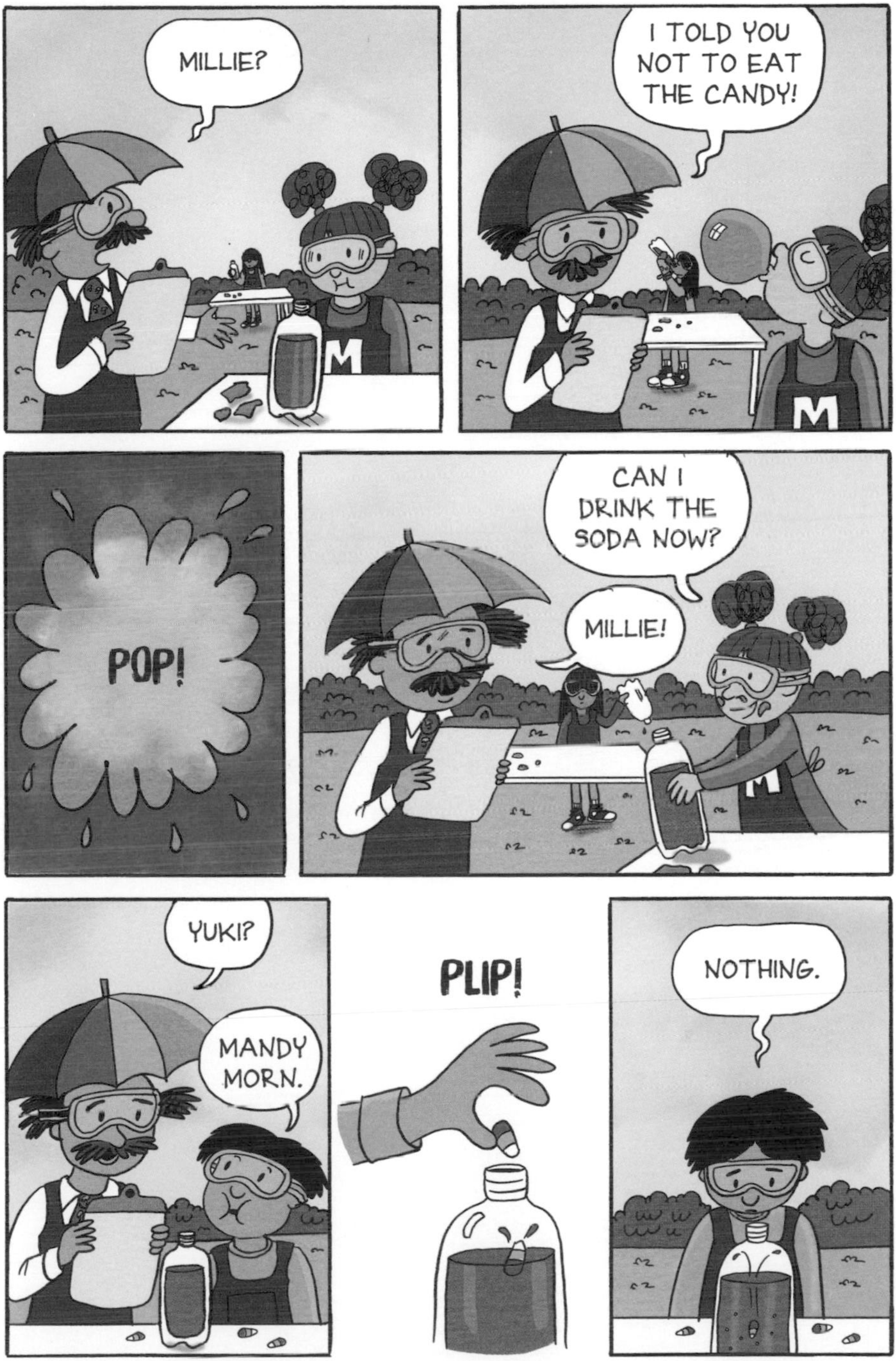
MILLIE?
I TOLD YOU NOT TO EAT THE CANDY!
POP!
CAN I DRINK THE SODA NOW?
MILLIE!
YUKI?
MANDY MORN.
PLIP!
NOTHING.

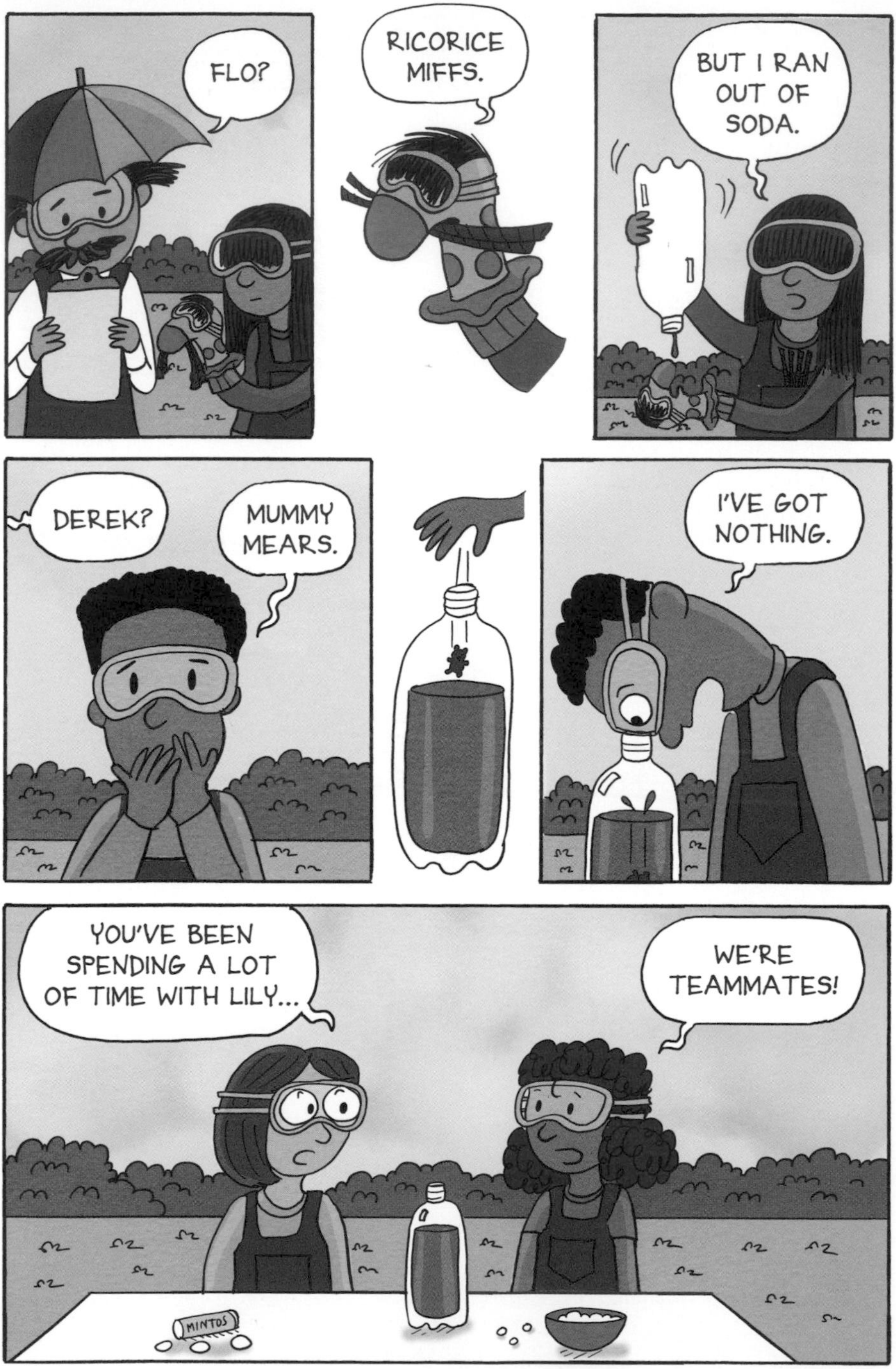
FLO?
RICORICE MIFFS.
BUT I RAN OUT OF SODA.
DEREK?
MUMMY MEARS.
I'VE GOT NOTHING.
YOU'VE BEEN SPENDING A LOT OF TIME WITH LILY...
WE'RE TEAMMATES!
MINTOS

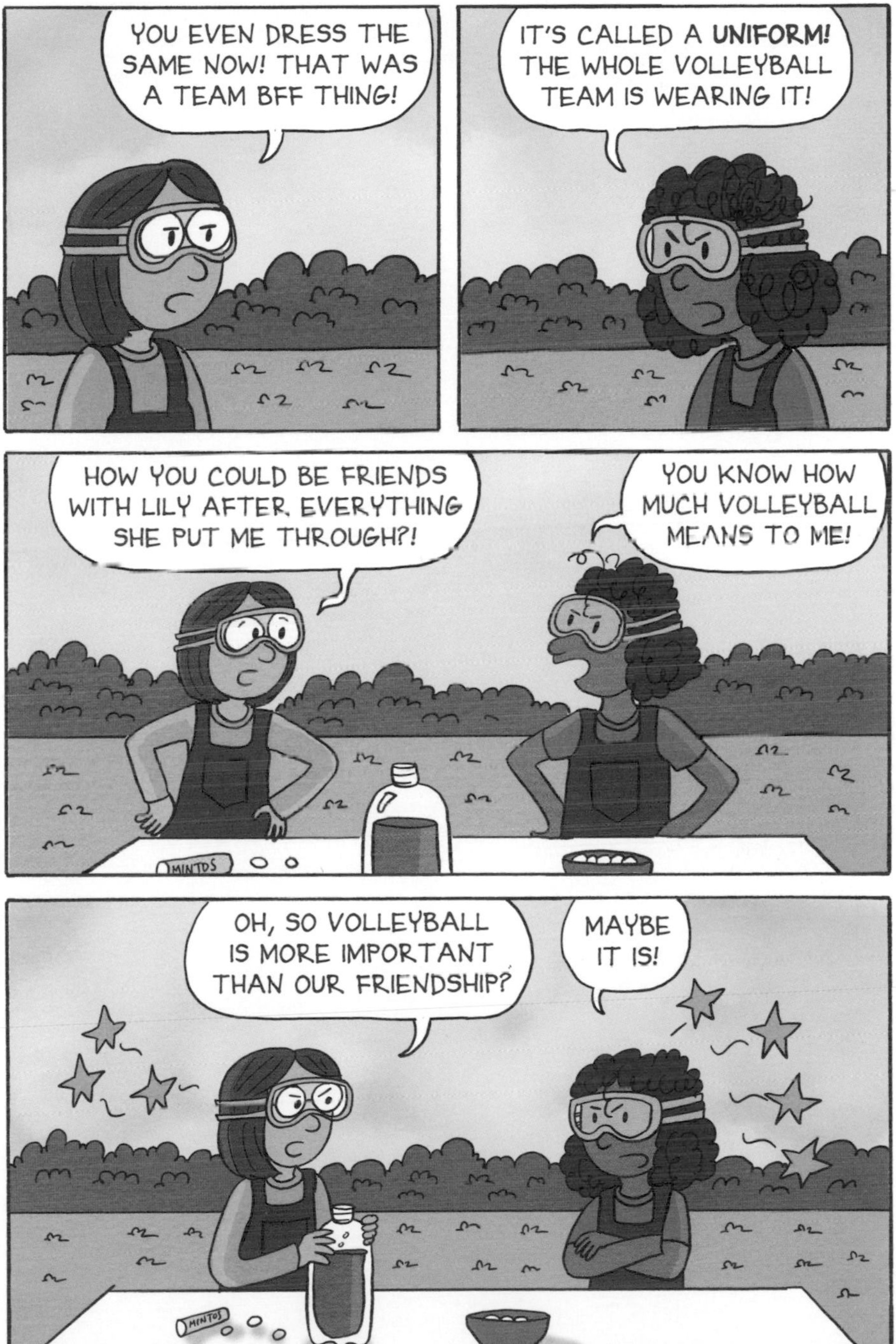
YOU EVEN DRESS THE SAME NOW! THAT WAS A TEAM BFF THING!
IT'S CALLED A **UNIFORM!** THE WHOLE VOLLEYBALL TEAM IS WEARING IT!
HOW YOU COULD BE FRIENDS WITH LILY AFTER EVERYTHING SHE PUT ME THROUGH?!
YOU KNOW HOW MUCH VOLLEYBALL MEANS TO ME!
MINTOS
OH, SO VOLLEYBALL IS MORE IMPORTANT THAN OUR FRIENDSHIP?
MAYBE IT IS!
MINTOS

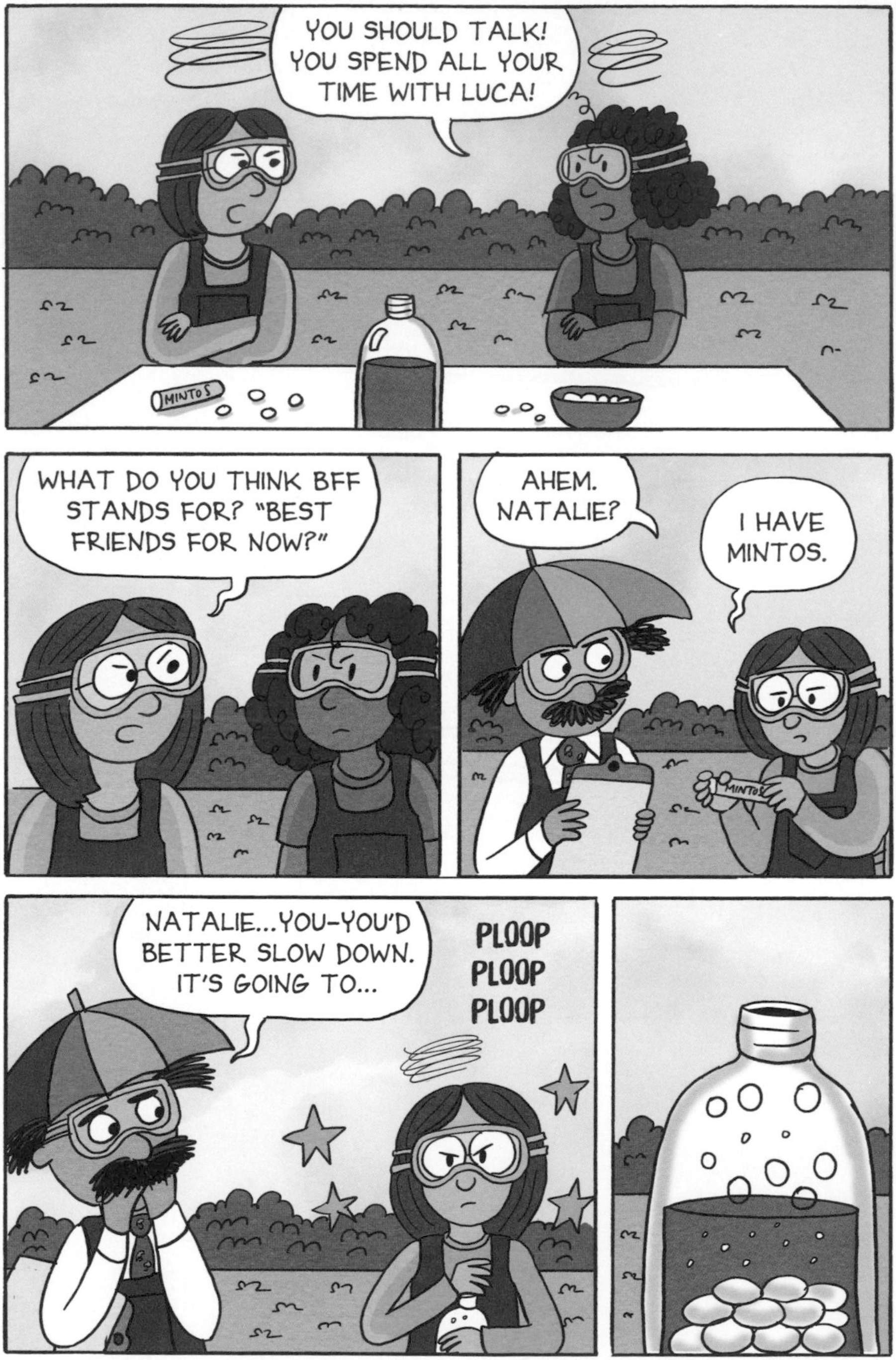
YOU SHOULD TALK! YOU SPEND ALL YOUR TIME WITH LUCA!
MINTOS
WHAT DO YOU THINK BFF STANDS FOR? "BEST FRIENDS FOR NOW?"
AHEM. NATALIE?
I HAVE MINTOS.
MINTOS
NATALIE...YOU-YOU'D BETTER SLOW DOWN. IT'S GOING TO...
PLOOP
PLOOP
PLOOP

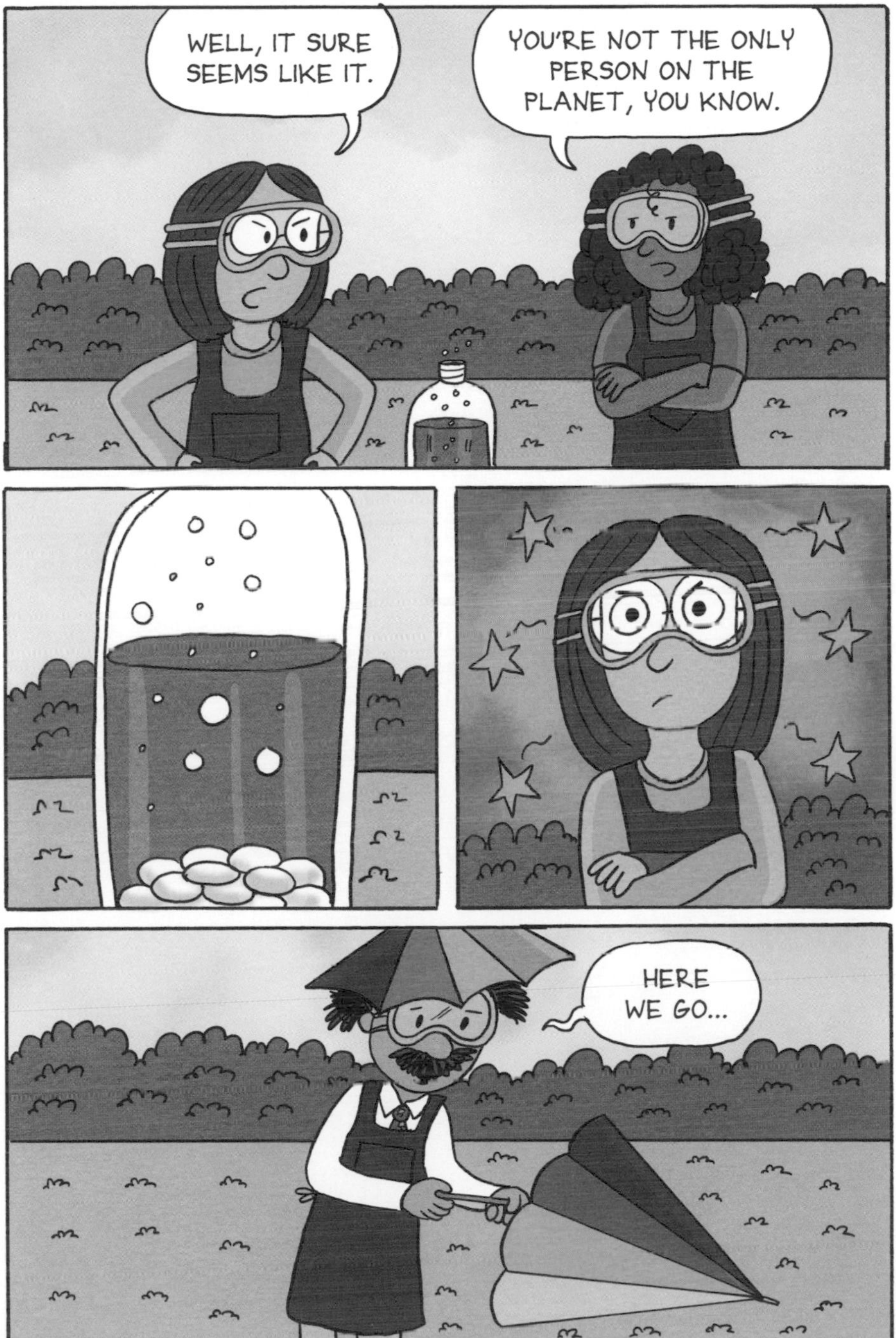
WELL, IT SURE SEEMS LIKE IT.
YOU'RE NOT THE ONLY PERSON ON THE PLANET, YOU KNOW.
HERE WE GO...

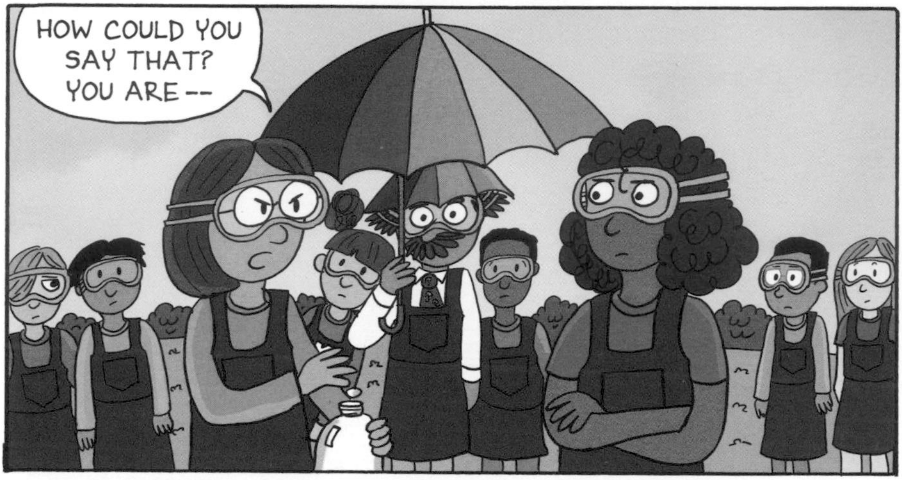
HOW COULD YOU SAY THAT? YOU ARE--

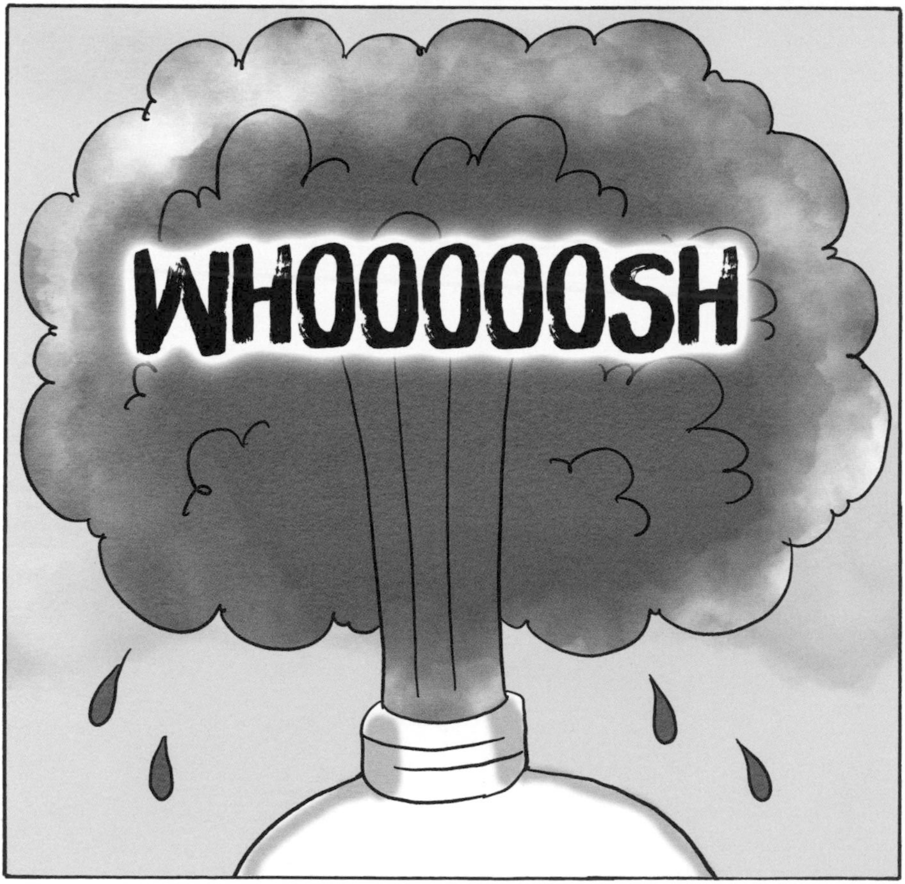
WHOOOOOOSH

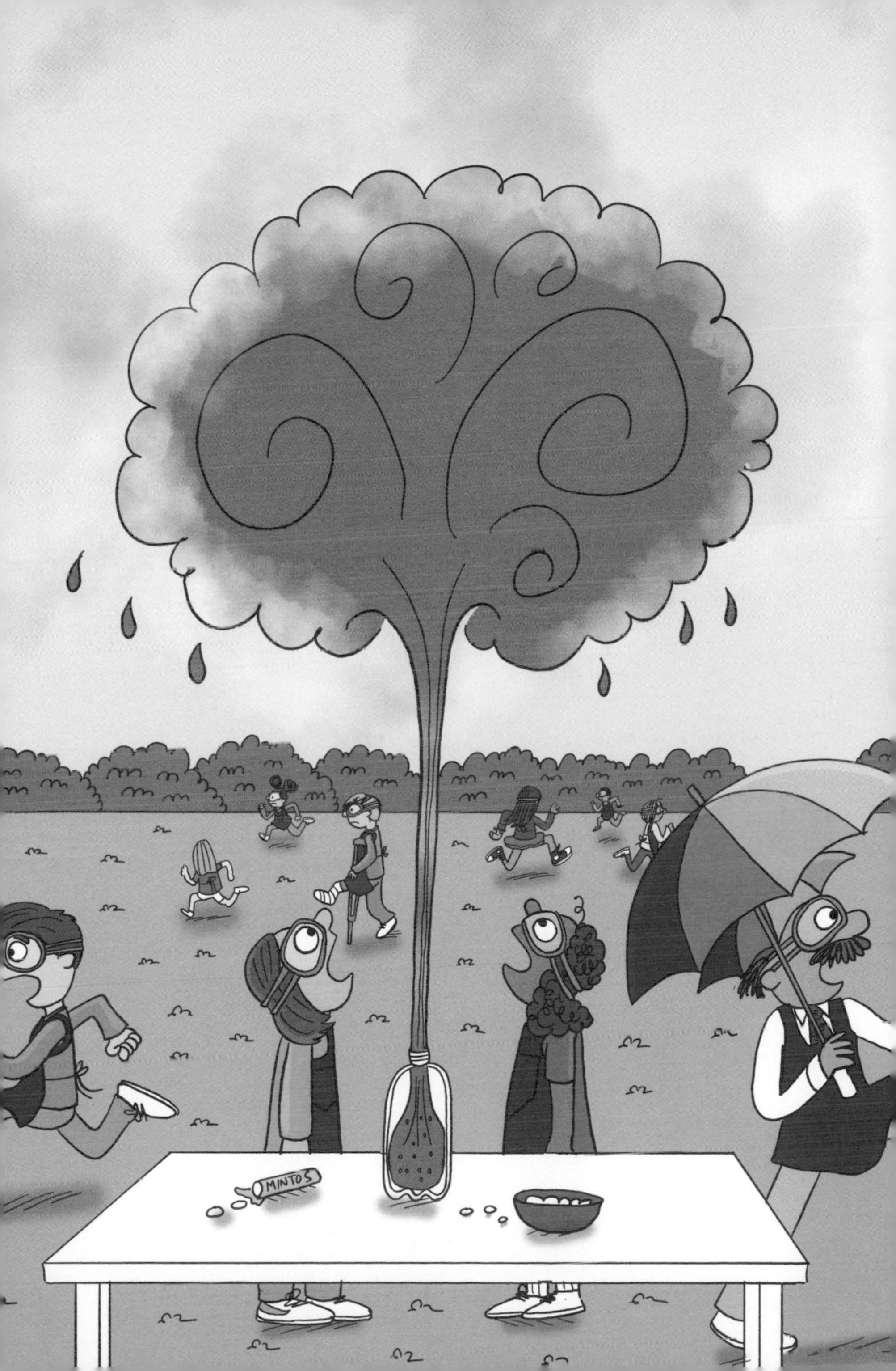
MINTOS

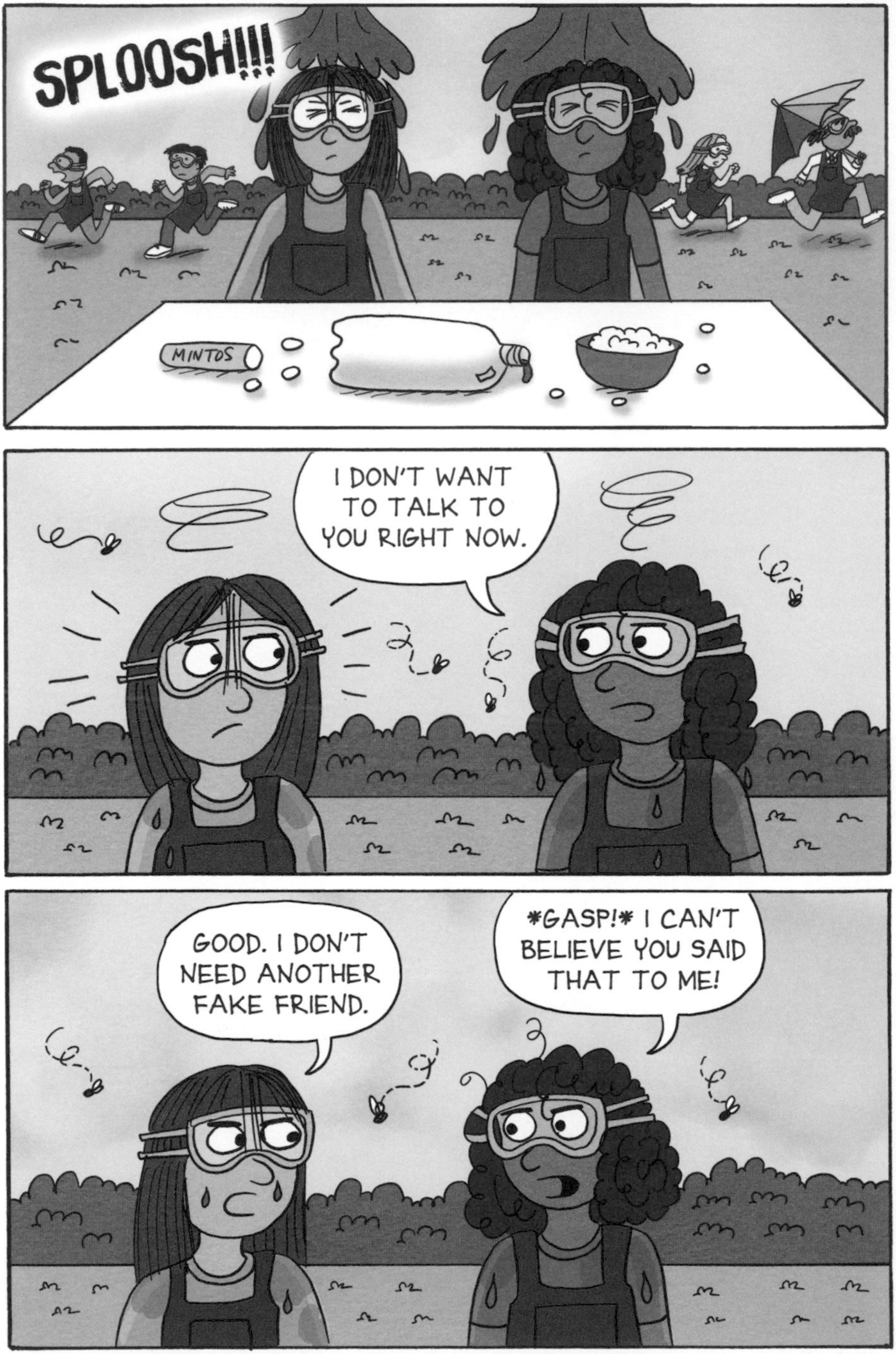
SPLOOSH!!!
MINTOS
I DON'T WANT TO TALK TO YOU RIGHT NOW.
GOOD. I DON'T NEED ANOTHER FAKE FRIEND.
GASP! I CAN'T BELIEVE YOU SAID THAT TO ME!

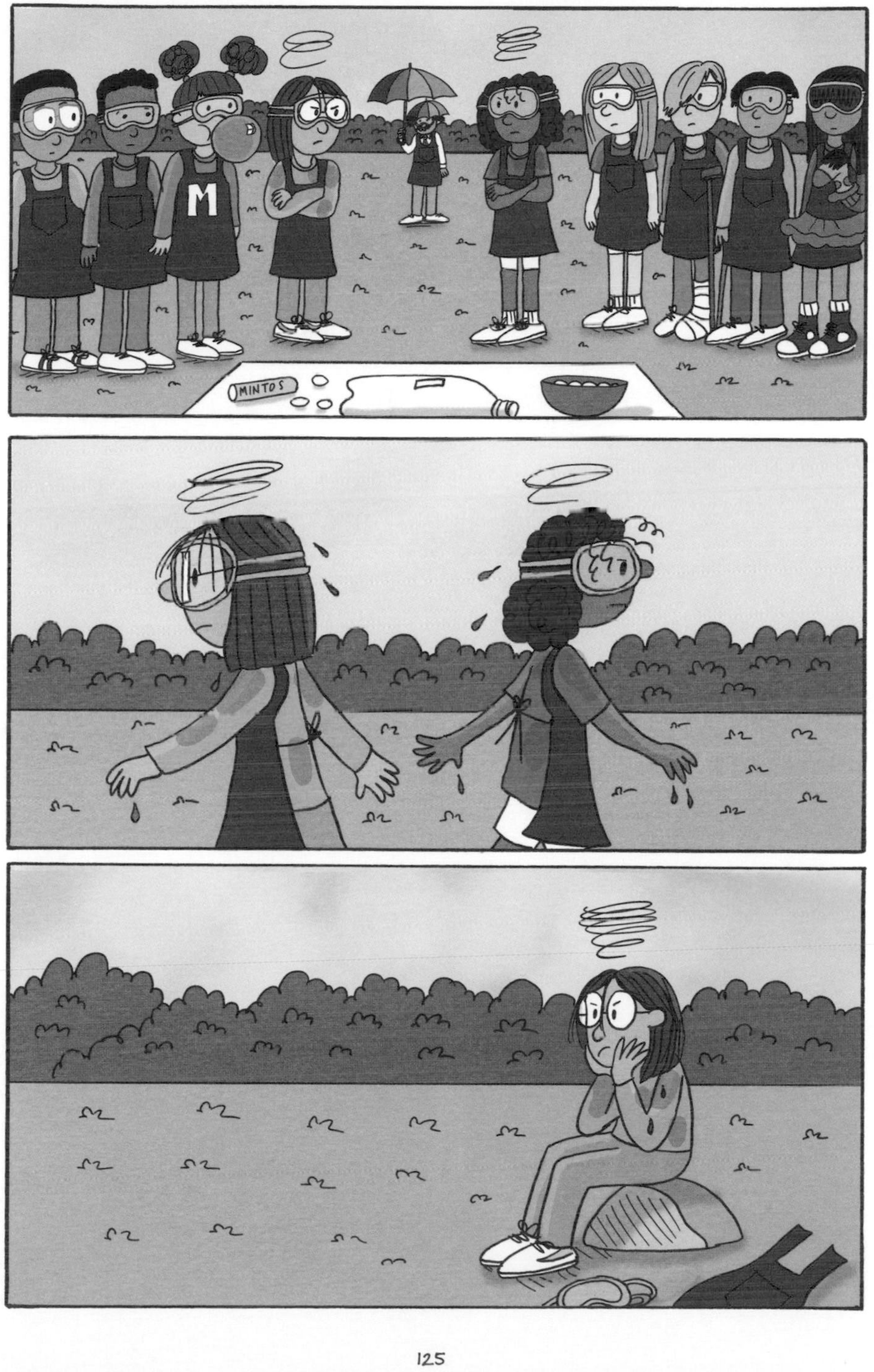
MINTOS

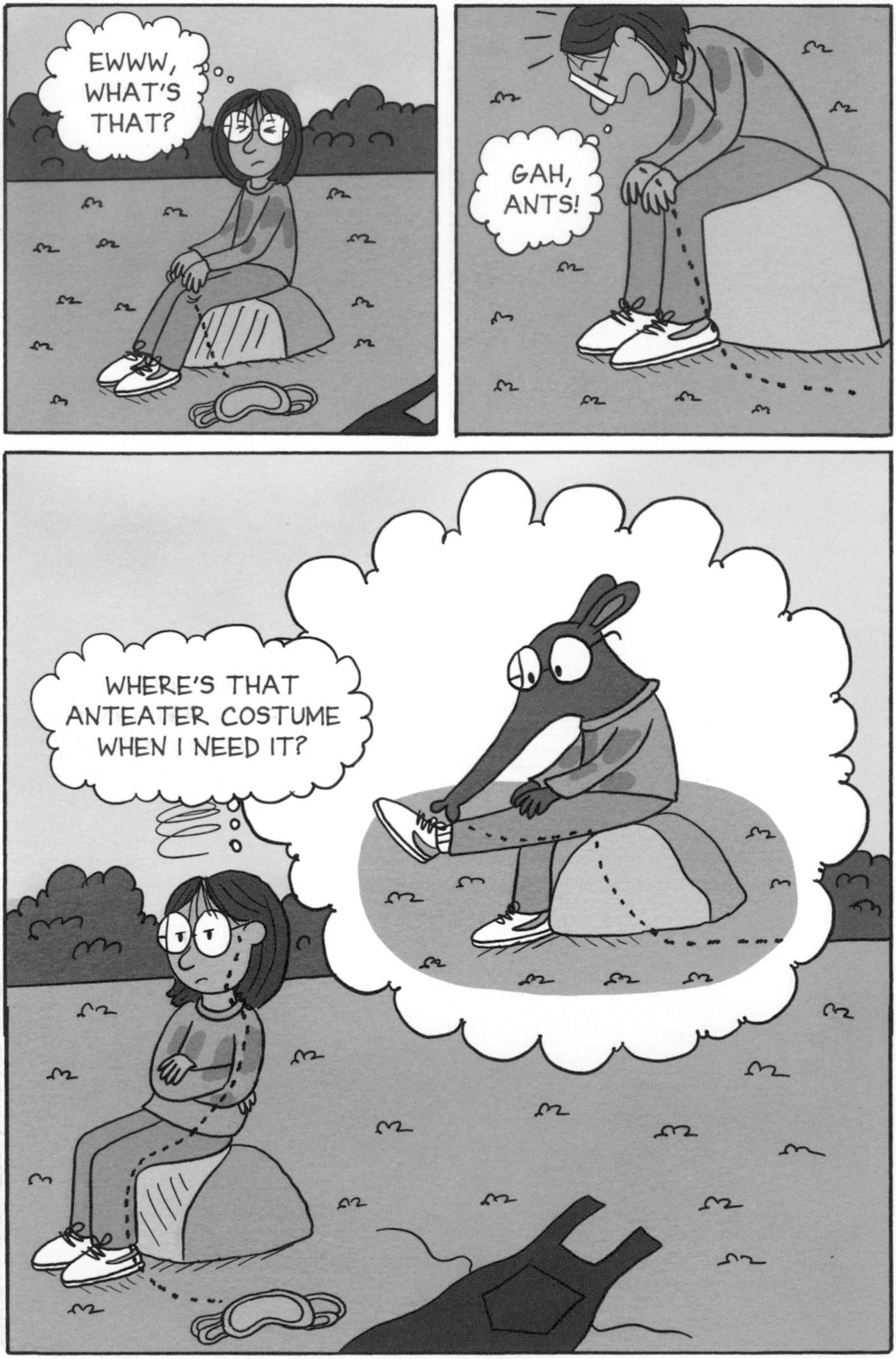
EWWW, WHAT'S THAT?
GAH, ANTS!
WHERE'S THAT ANTEATER COSTUME WHEN I NEED IT?

CHAPTER 10
LIBRARY

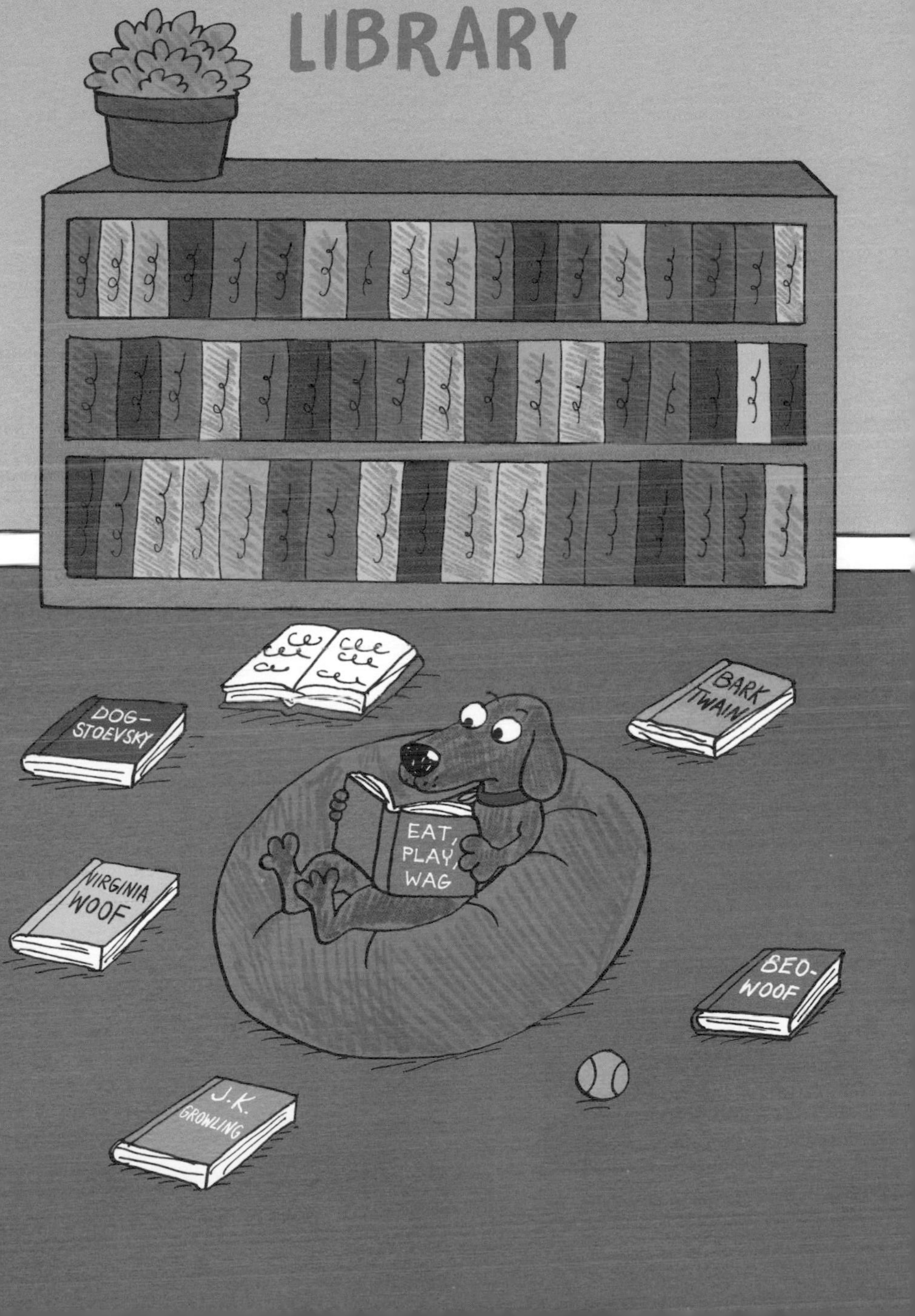
DOG-
STOEVSKY
BARK
TWAIN
EAT,
PLAY,
WAG
VIRGINIA
WOOF
BEO-
WOOF
J.K.
GROWLING

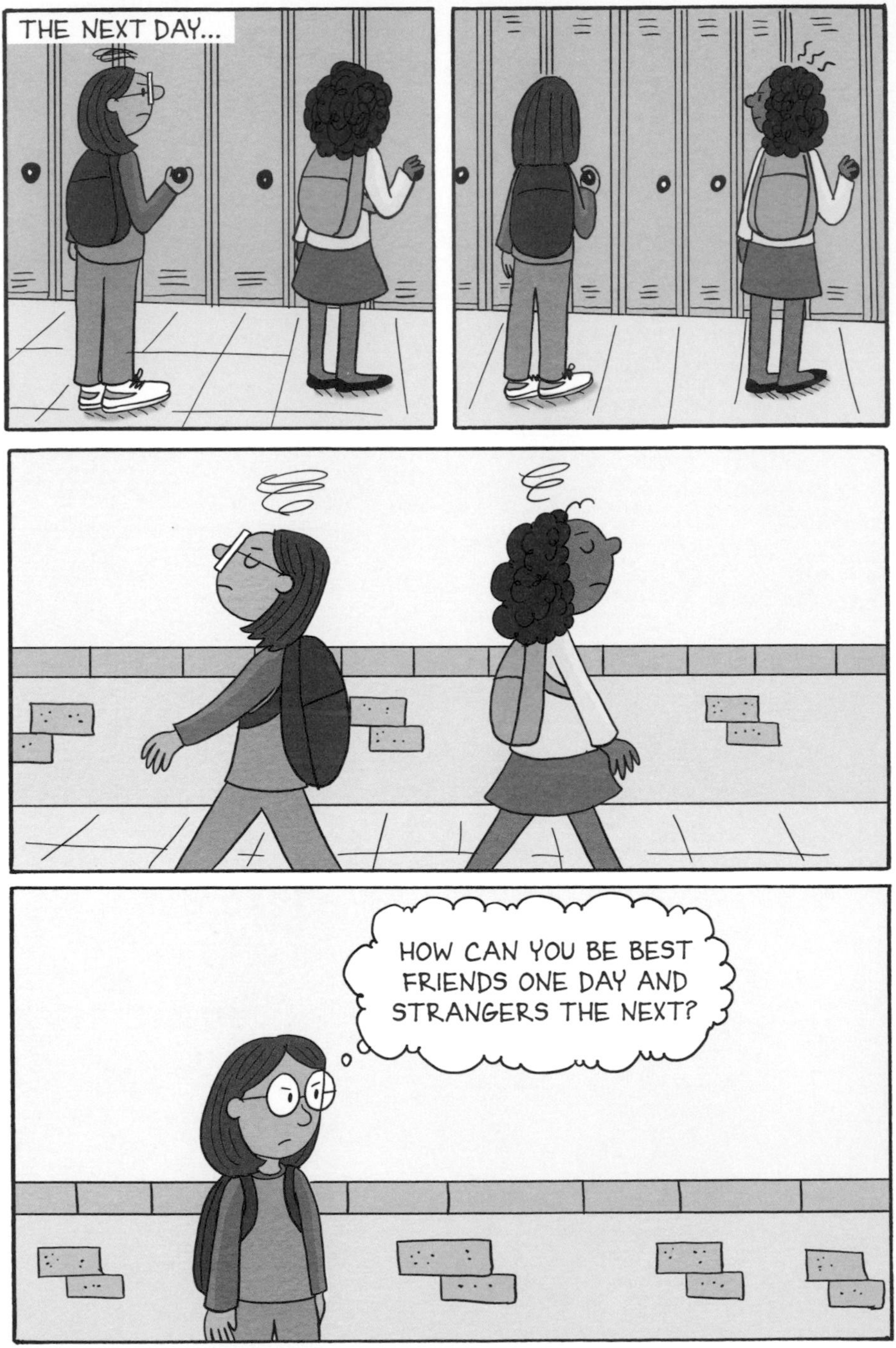
THE NEXT DAY...
HOW CAN YOU BE BEST FRIENDS ONE DAY AND STRANGERS THE NEXT?

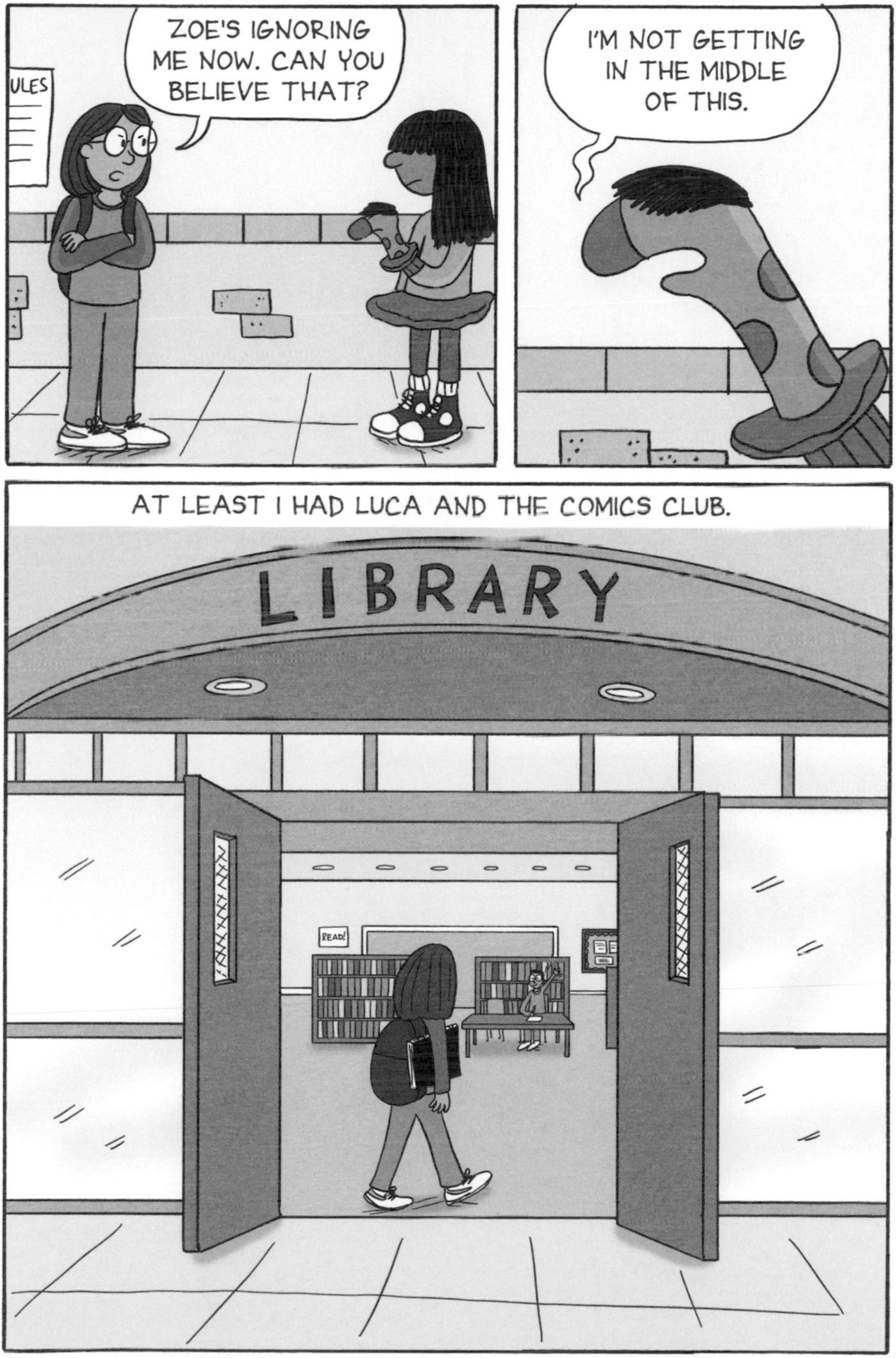
ULES
ZOE'S IGNORING ME NOW. CAN YOU BELIEVE THAT?
I'M NOT GETTING IN THE MIDDLE OF THIS.
AT LEAST I HAD LUCA AND THE COMICS CLUB.
LIBRARY
READ!

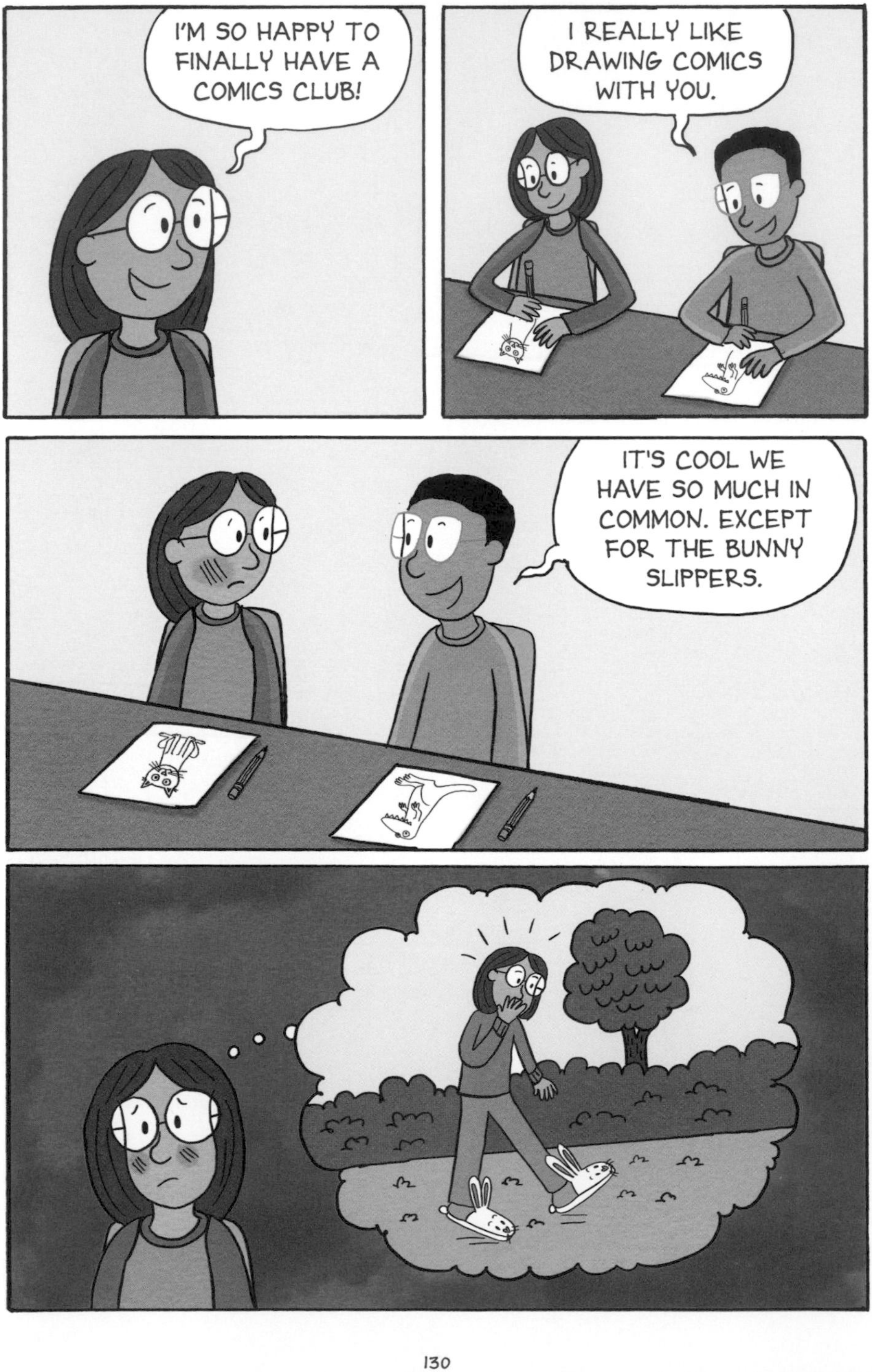
I'M SO HAPPY TO FINALLY HAVE A COMICS CLUB!
I REALLY LIKE DRAWING COMICS WITH YOU.
IT'S COOL WE HAVE SO MUCH IN COMMON. EXCEPT FOR THE BUNNY SLIPPERS.

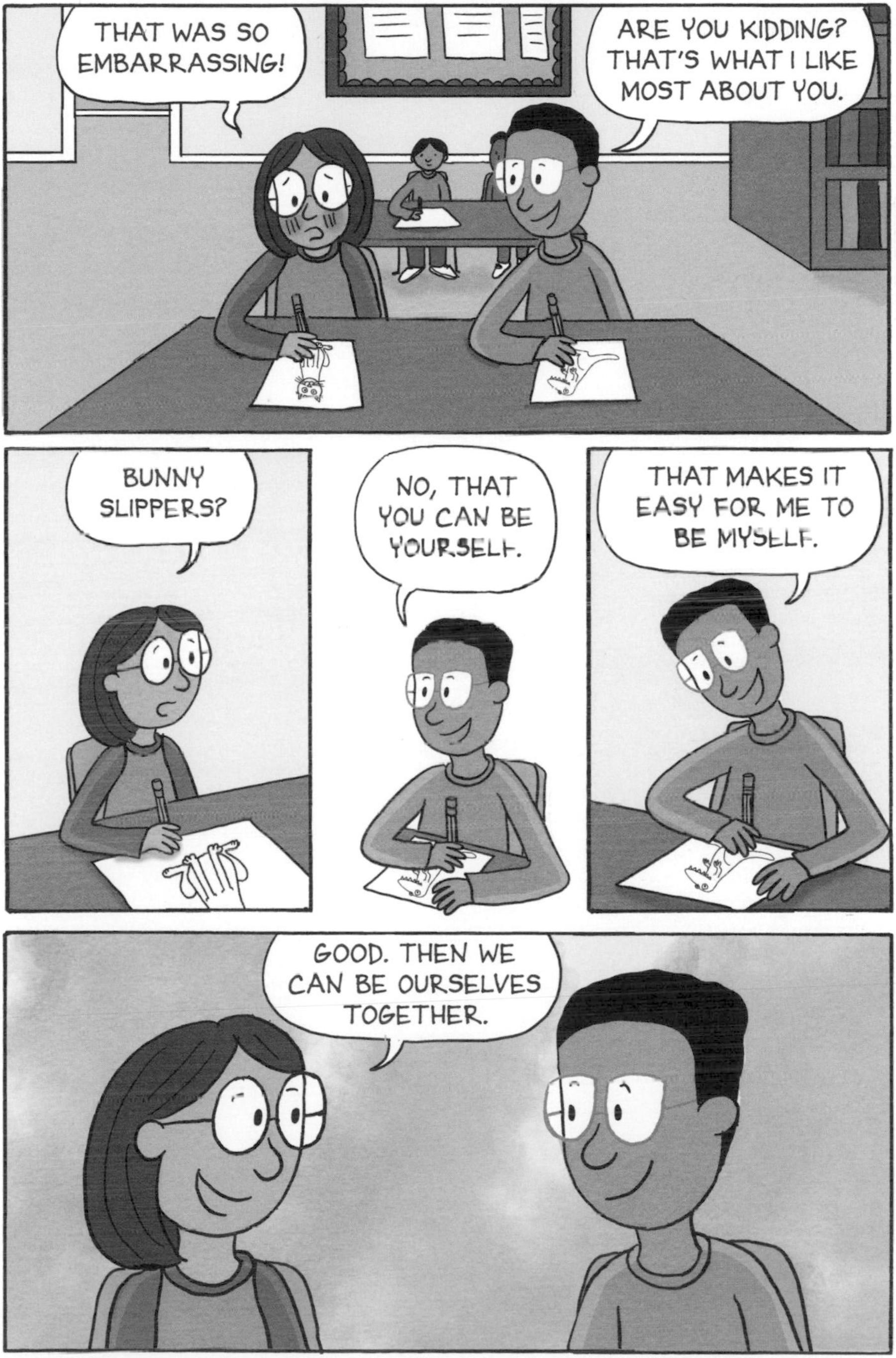
THAT WAS SO EMBARRASSING!
ARE YOU KIDDING? THAT'S WHAT I LIKE MOST ABOUT YOU.
BUNNY SLIPPERS?
NO, THAT YOU CAN BE YOURSELF.
THAT MAKES IT EASY FOR ME TO BE MYSELF.
GOOD. THEN WE CAN BE OURSELVES TOGETHER.

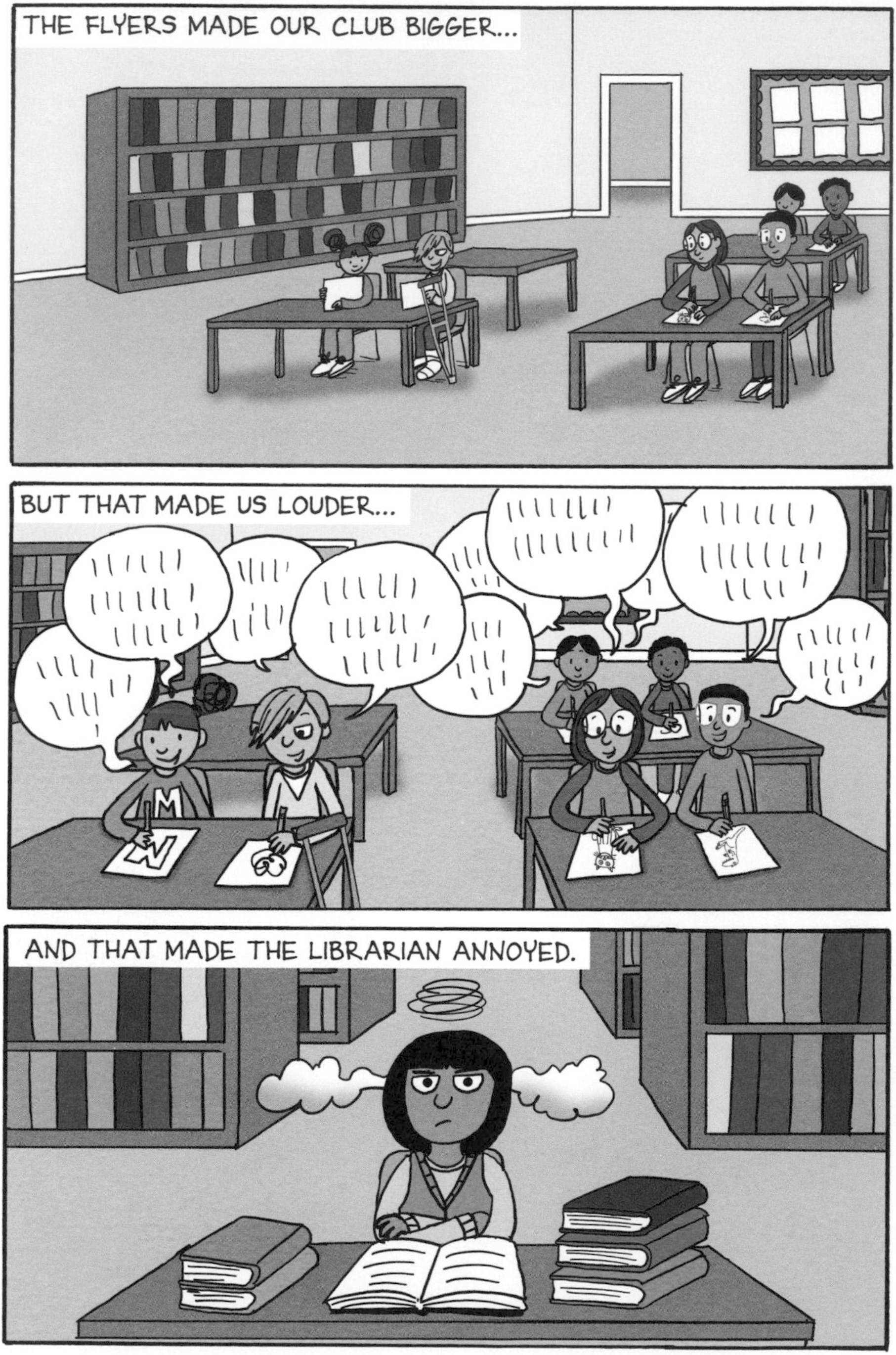
THE FLYERS MADE OUR CLUB BIGGER...
BUT THAT MADE US LOUDER...
M
AND THAT MADE THE LIBRARIAN ANNOYED.

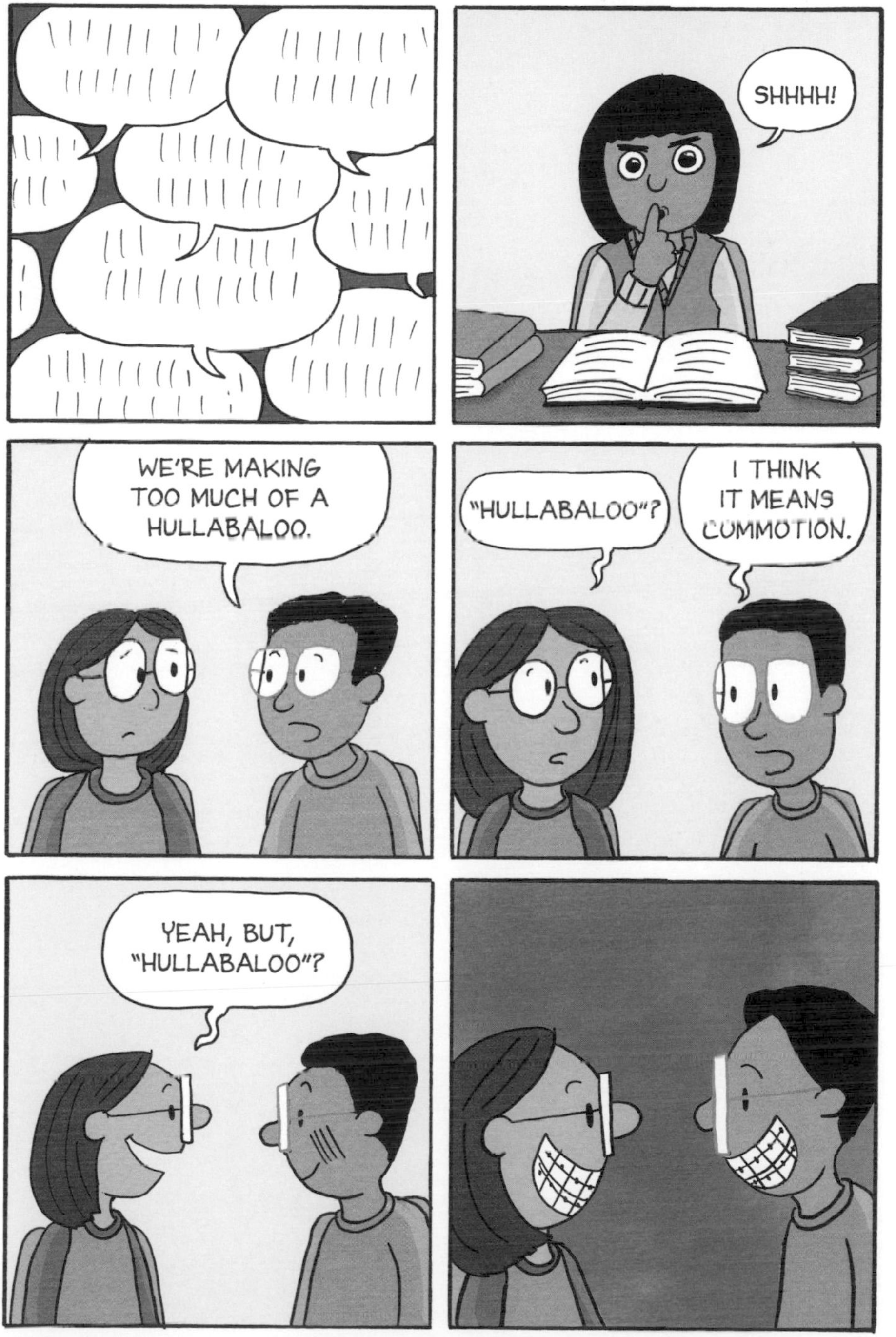
SHHHH!
WE'RE MAKING TOO MUCH OF A HULLABALOO.
"HULLABALOO"?
I THINK IT MEANS COMMOTION.
YEAH, BUT, "HULLABALOO"?

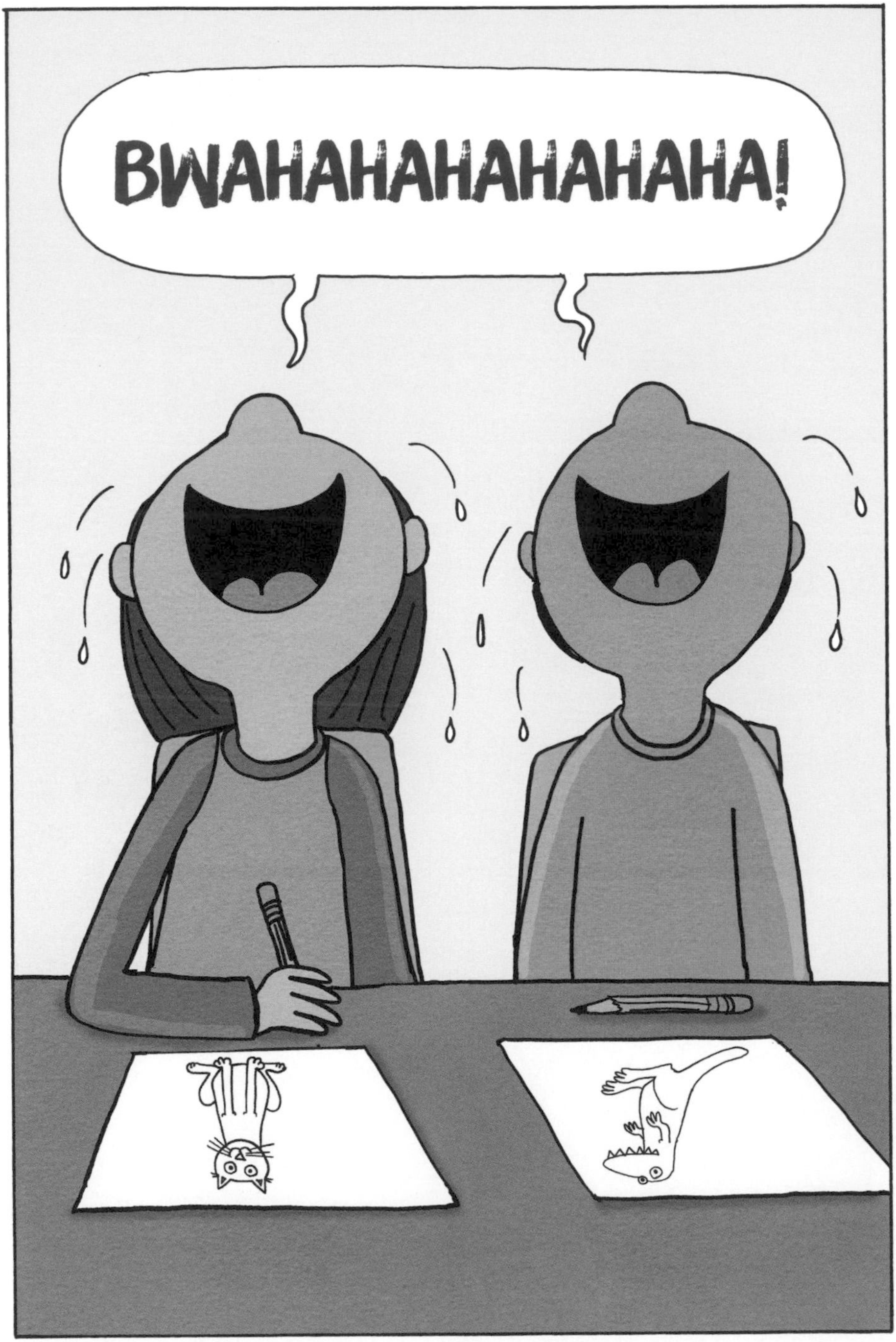
BWAHAHAHAHAHAHAHA!

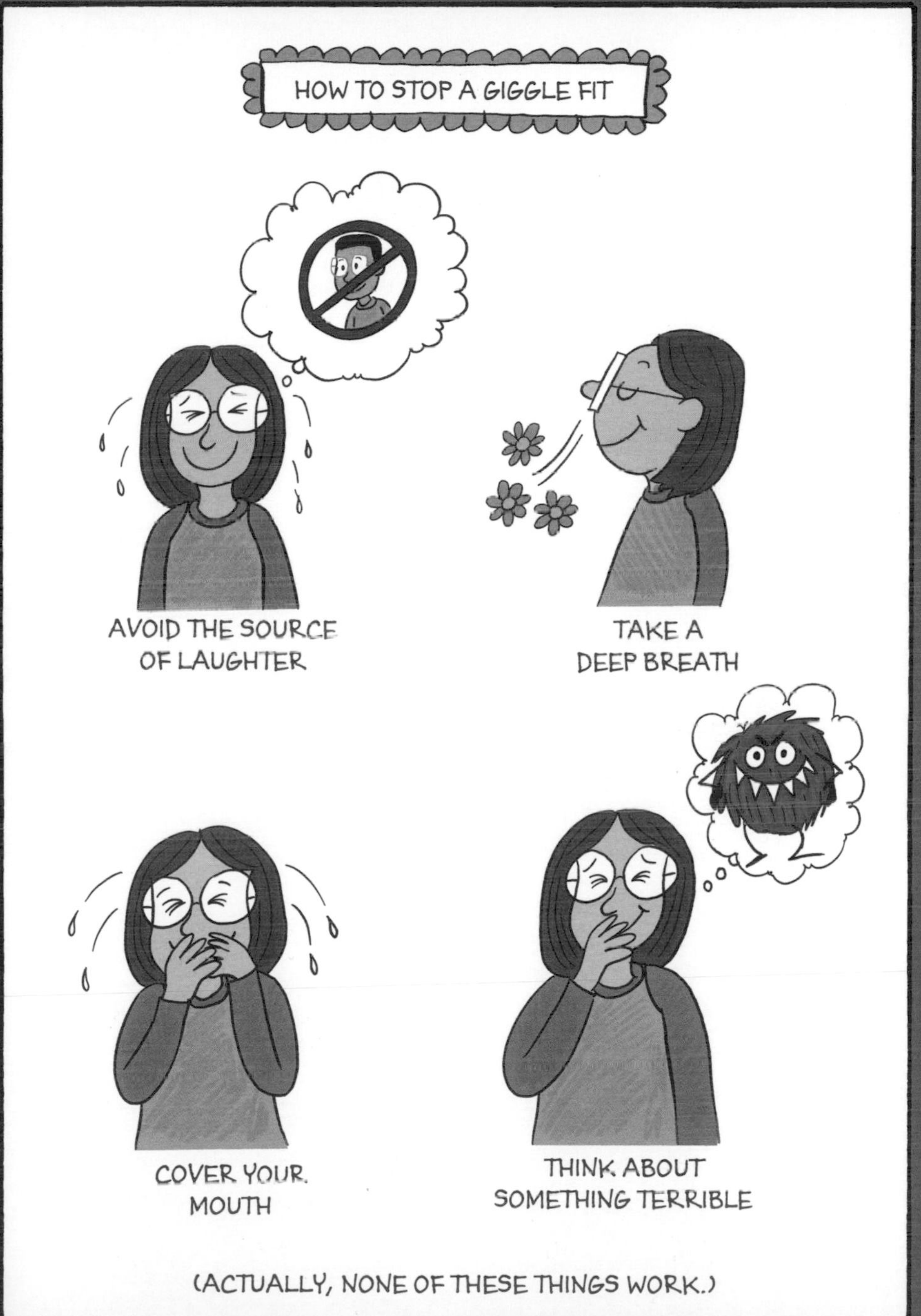
HOW TO STOP A GIGGLE FIT
AVOID THE SOURCE OF LAUGHTER
TAKE A DEEP BREATH
COVER YOUR MOUTH
THINK ABOUT SOMETHING TERRIBLE
(ACTUALLY, NONE OF THESE THINGS WORK.)

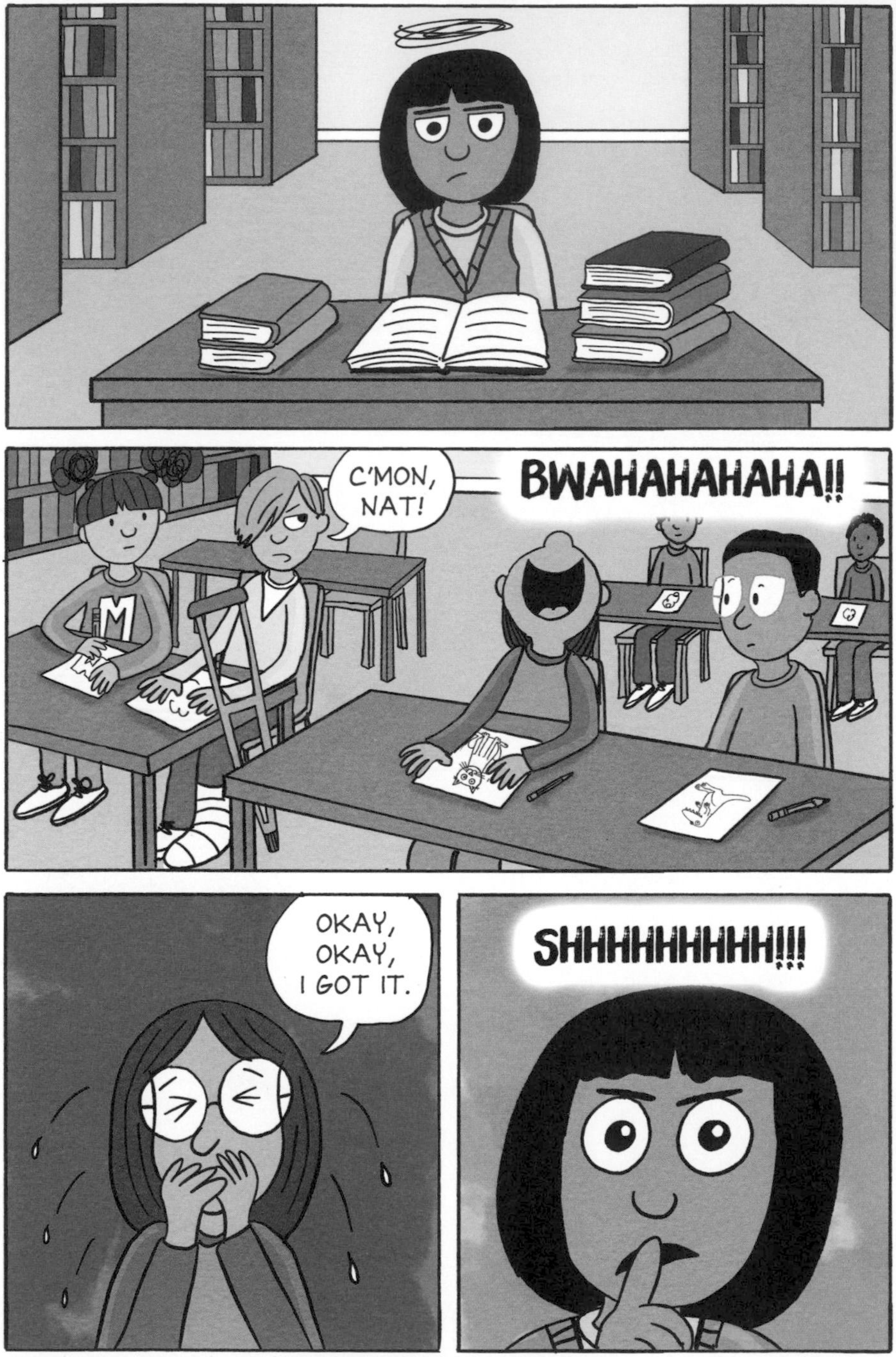
C'MON, NAT!
BWAHAHAHAHA!!
OKAY, OKAY, I GOT IT.
SHHHHHHHHH!!!

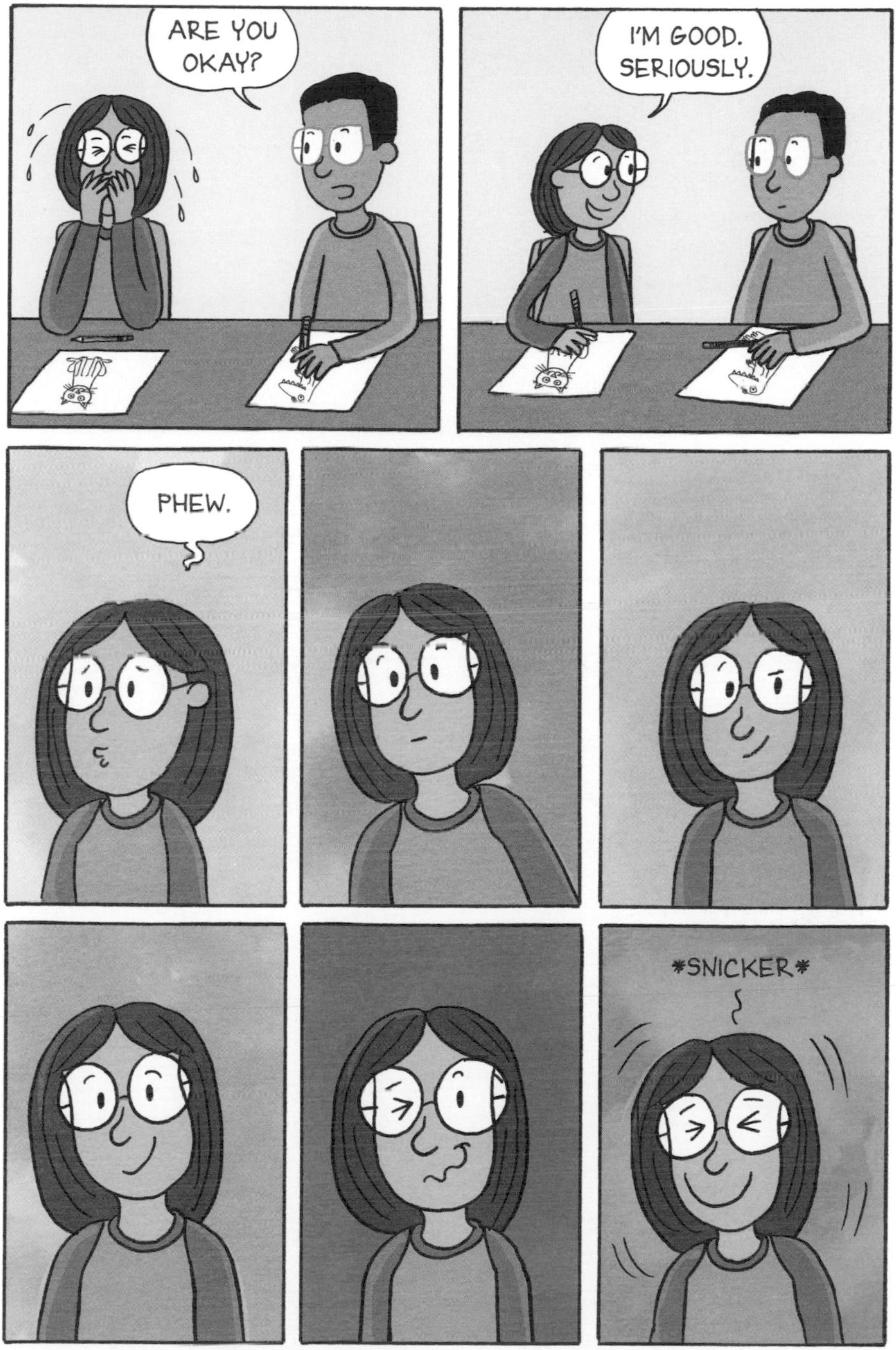
ARE YOU OKAY?
I'M GOOD. SERIOUSLY.
PHEW.
SNICKER

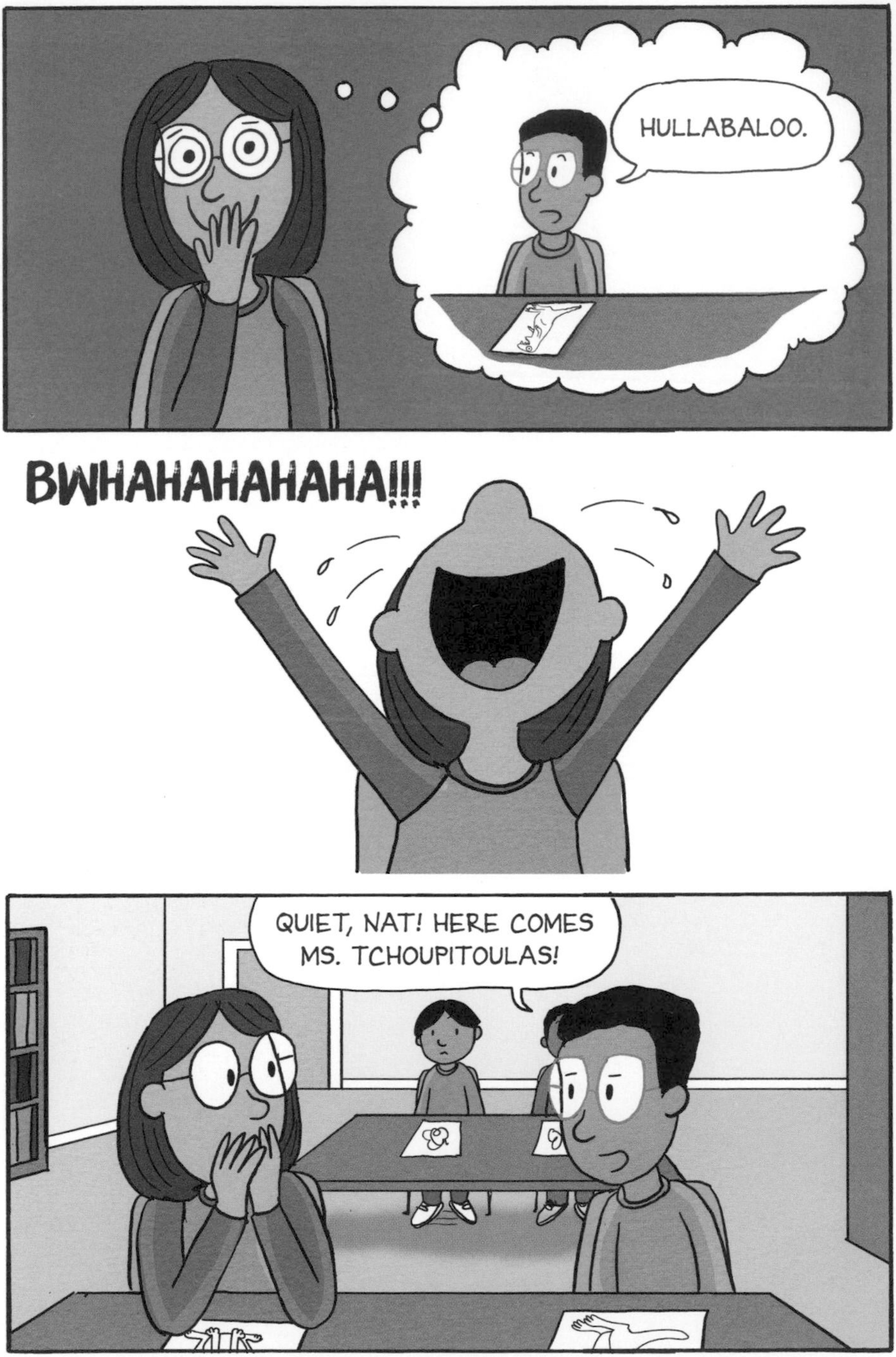
HULLABALOO.
BWHAHAHAHAHA!!!
QUIET, NAT! HERE COMES MS. TCHOUPITOULAS!

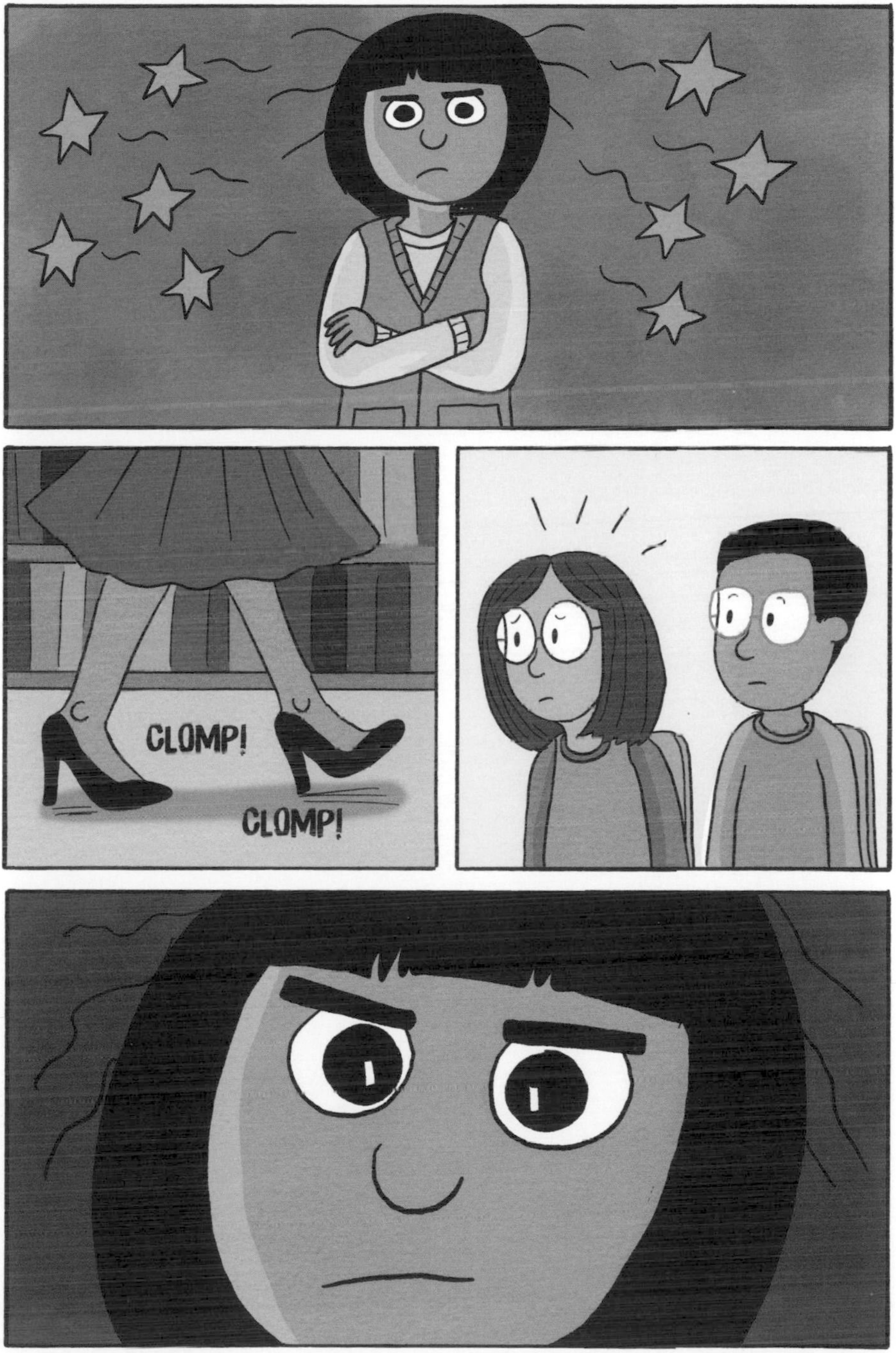
CLOMP!
CLOMP!

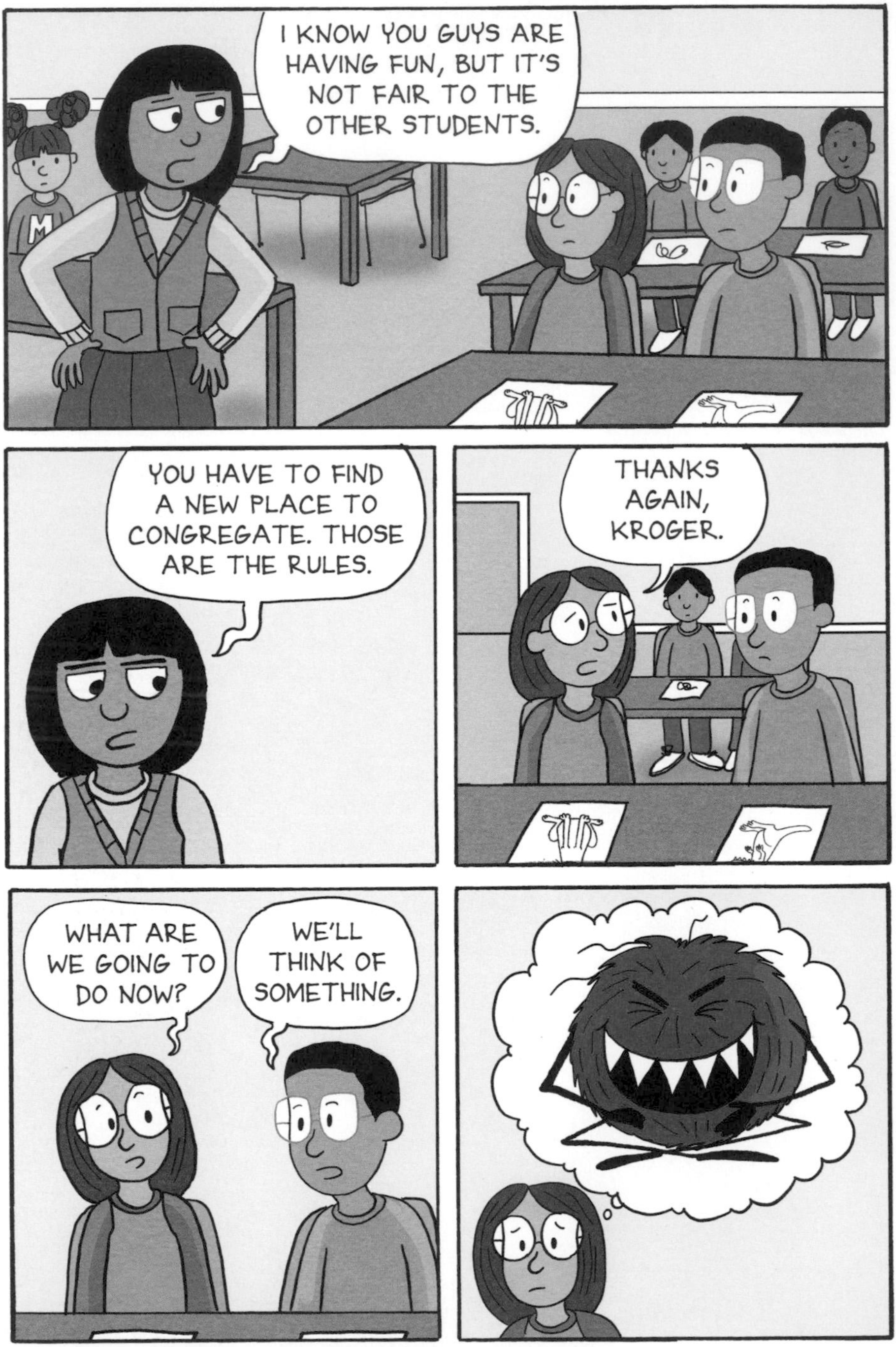
I KNOW YOU GUYS ARE HAVING FUN, BUT IT'S NOT FAIR TO THE OTHER STUDENTS.
YOU HAVE TO FIND A NEW PLACE TO CONGREGATE. THOSE ARE THE RULES.
THANKS AGAIN, KROGER.
WHAT ARE WE GOING TO DO NOW?
WE'LL THINK OF SOMETHING.

CHAPTER 11
PHOTO OP

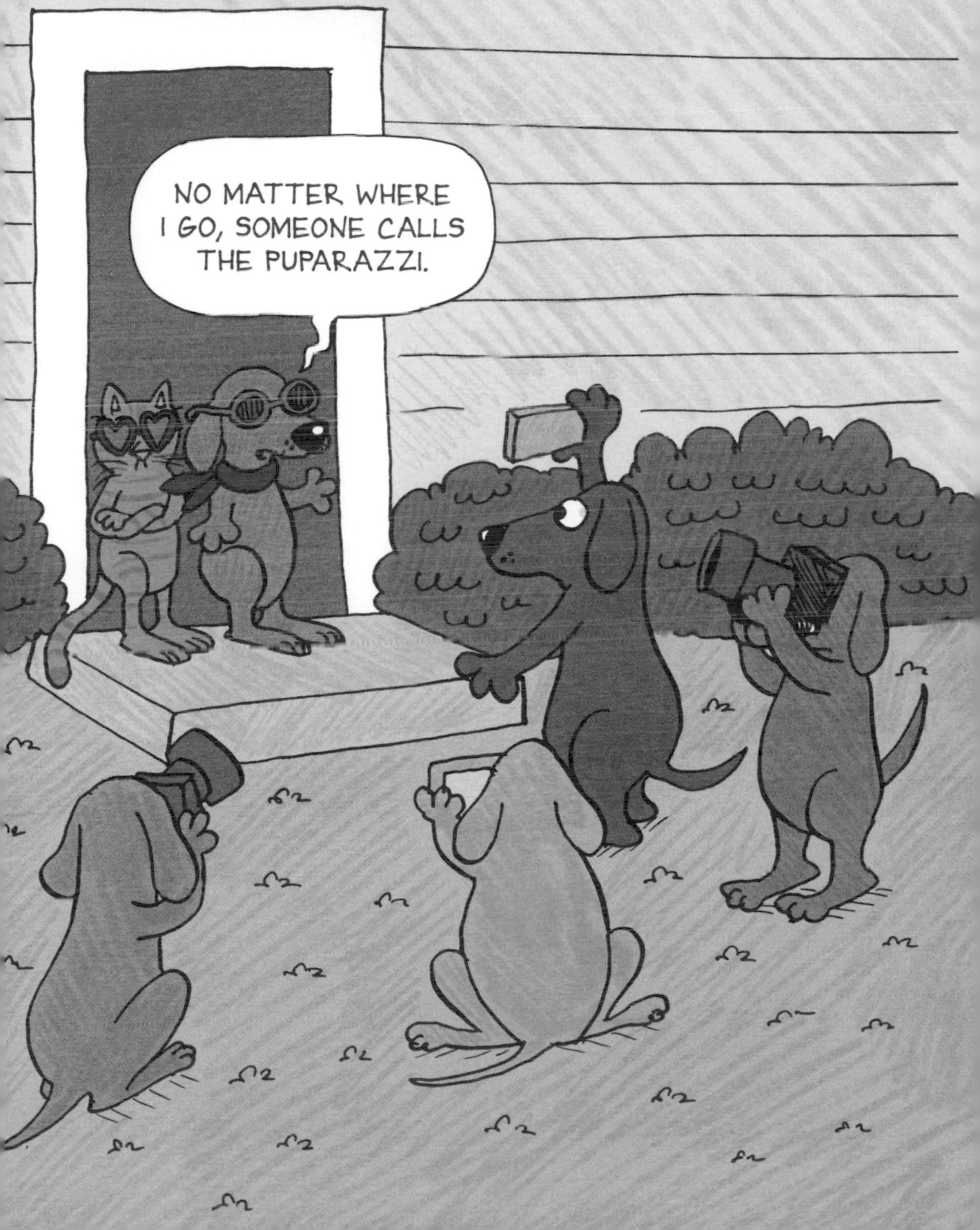
NO MATTER WHERE I GO, SOMEONE CALLS THE PUPARAZZI.

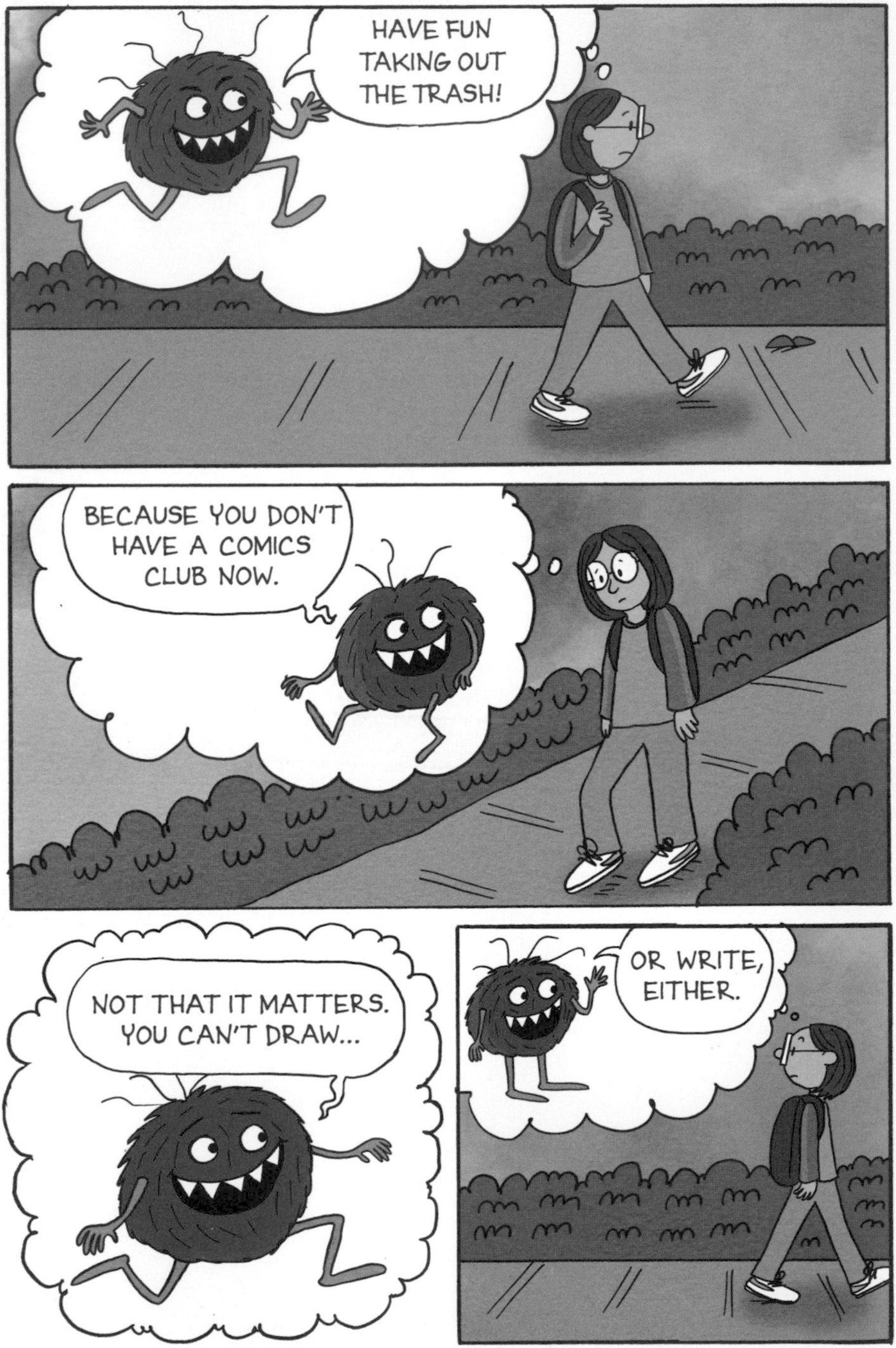
HAVE FUN TAKING OUT THE TRASH!
BECAUSE YOU DON'T HAVE A COMICS CLUB NOW.
NOT THAT IT MATTERS. YOU CAN'T DRAW...
OR WRITE, EITHER.

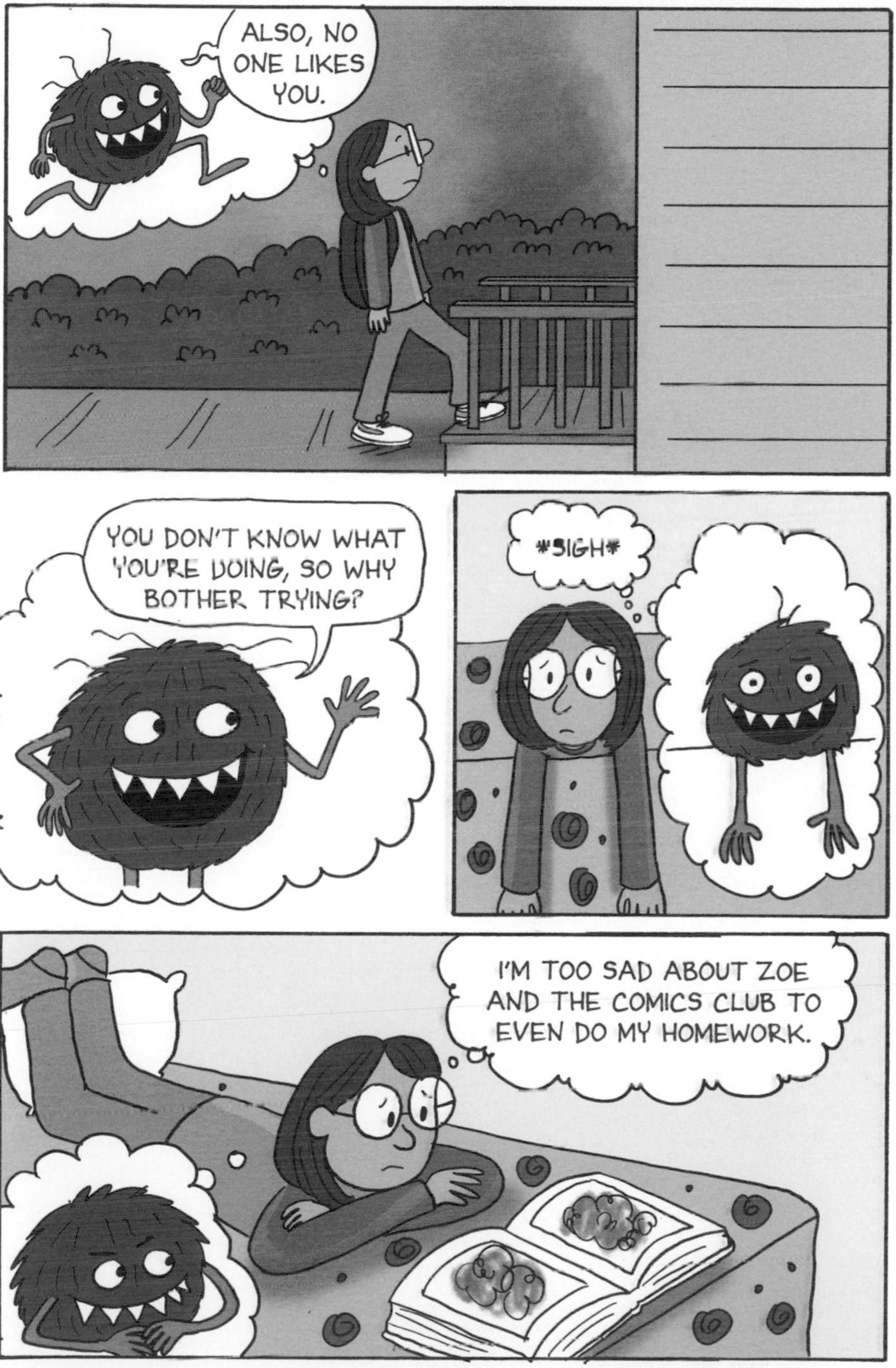
ALSO, NO ONE LIKES YOU.
YOU DON'T KNOW WHAT YOU'RE DOING, SO WHY BOTHER TRYING?
SIGH
I'M TOO SAD ABOUT ZOE AND THE COMICS CLUB TO EVEN DO MY HOMEWORK.

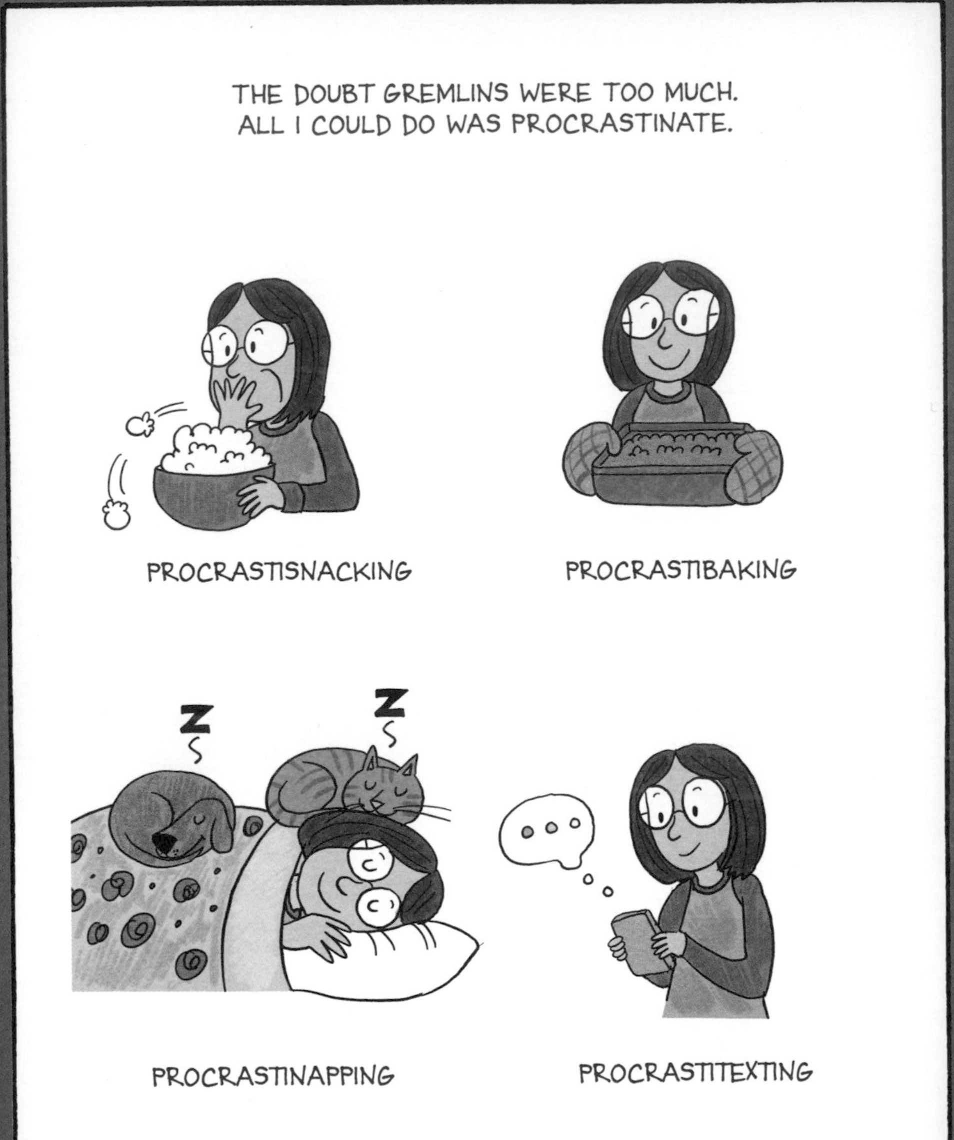
THE DOUBT GREMLINS WERE TOO MUCH.
ALL I COULD DO WAS PROCRASTINATE.
PROCRASTISNACKING
PROCRASTIBAKING
Z
Z
PROCRASTINAPPING
PROCRASTITEXTING

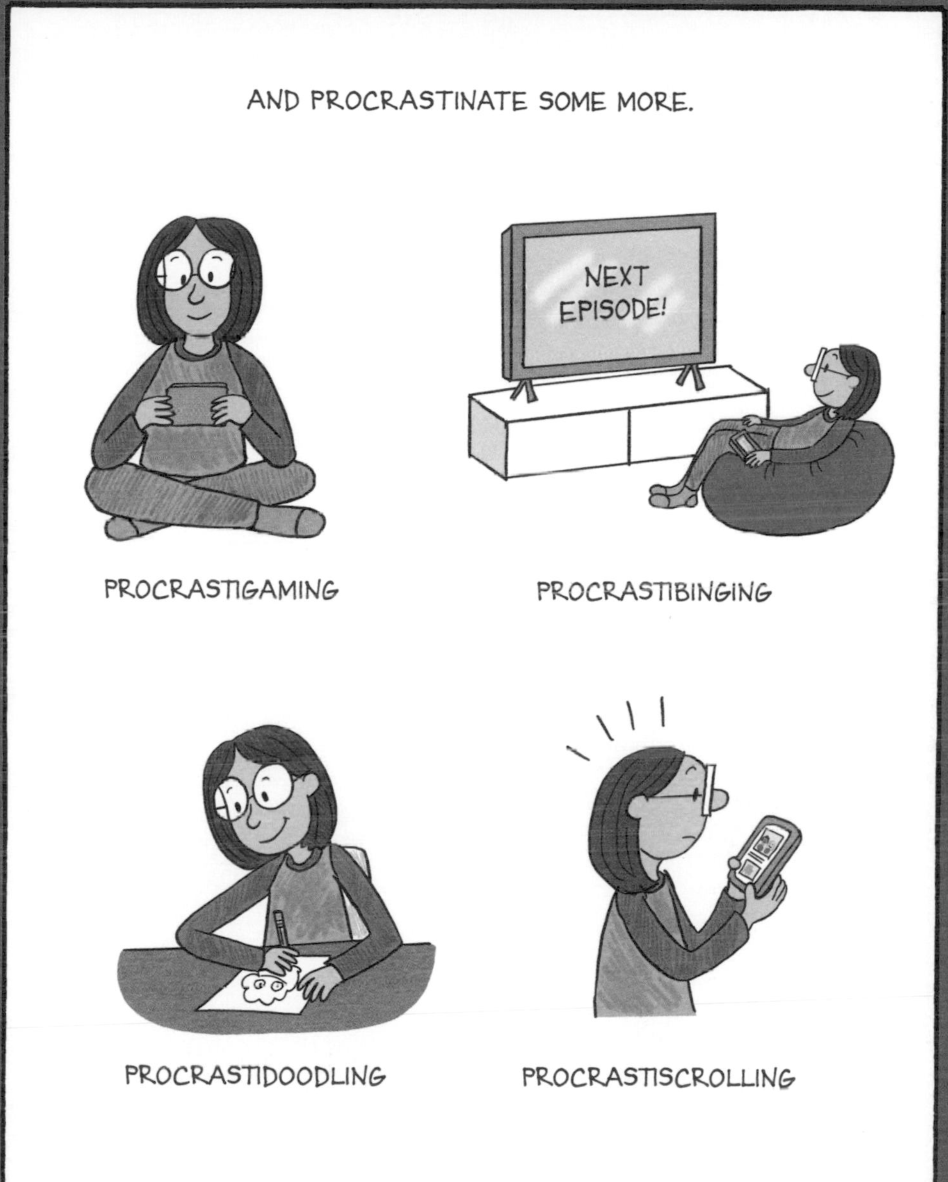
AND PROCRASTINATE SOME MORE.
PROCRASTIGAMING
NEXT EPISODE!
PROCRASTIBINGING
PROCRASTIDOODLING
PROCRASTISCROLLING

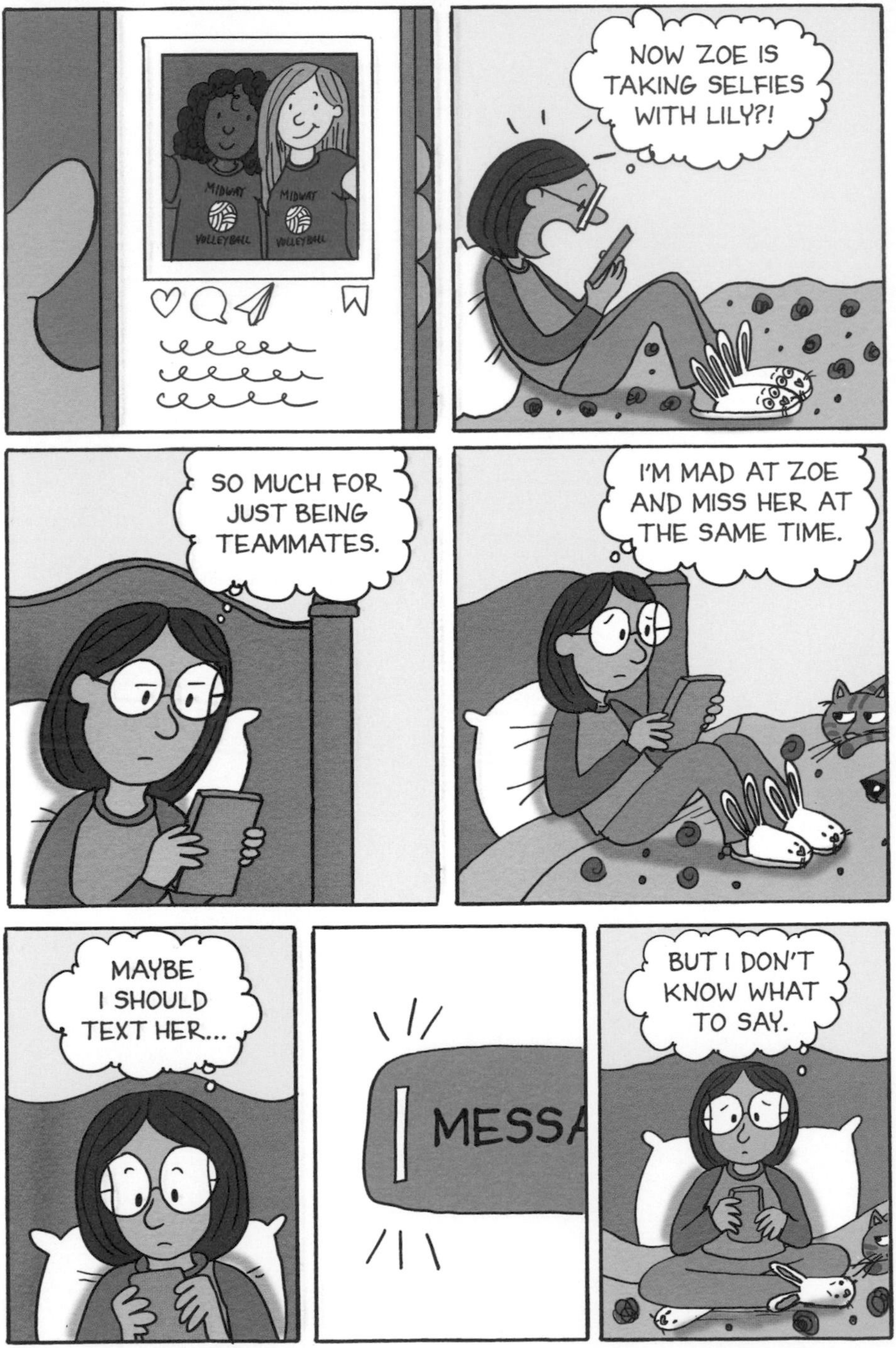
MIDWAY VOLLEYBALL
MIDWAY VOLLEYBALL
NOW ZOE IS TAKING SELFIES WITH LILY?!
SO MUCH FOR JUST BEING TEAMMATES.
I'M MAD AT ZOE AND MISS HER AT THE SAME TIME.
MAYBE I SHOULD TEXT HER...
MESSA
BUT I DON'T KNOW WHAT TO SAY.

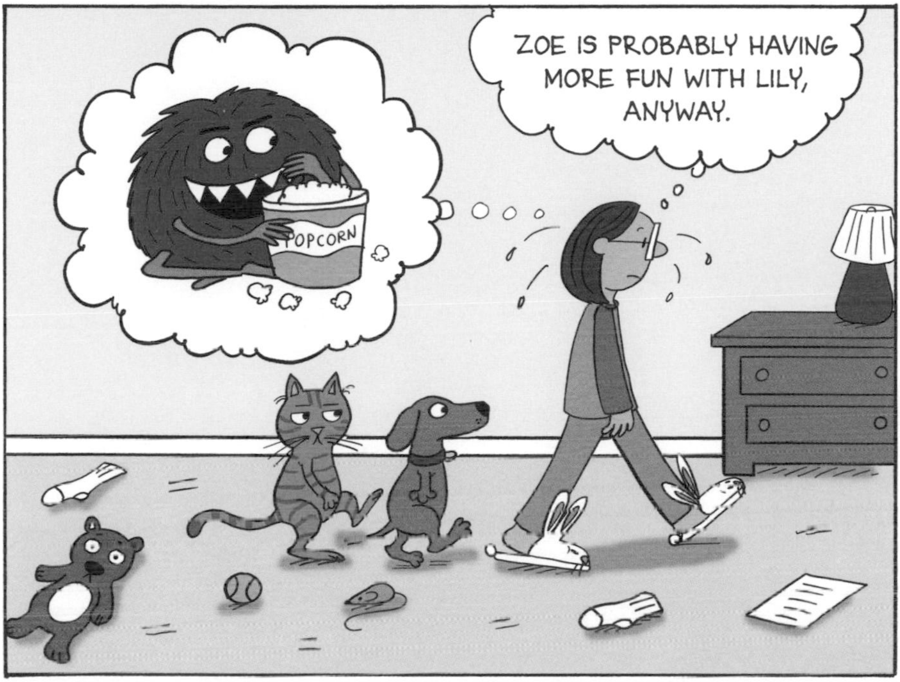
POPCORN
ZOE IS PROBABLY HAVING MORE FUN WITH LILY, ANYWAY.

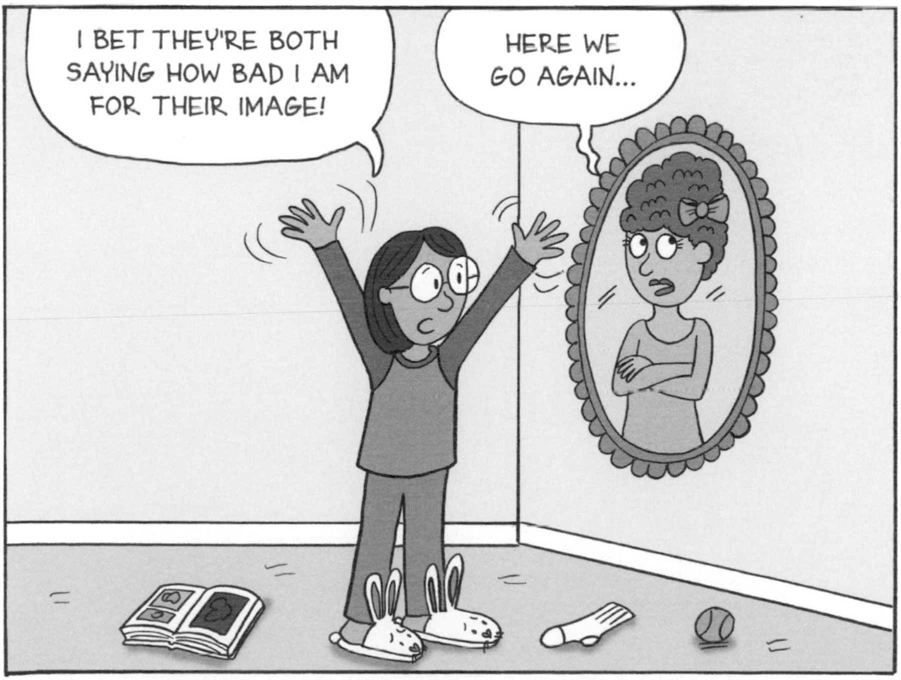
I BET THEY'RE BOTH SAYING HOW BAD I AM FOR THEIR IMAGE!
HERE WE GO AGAIN...

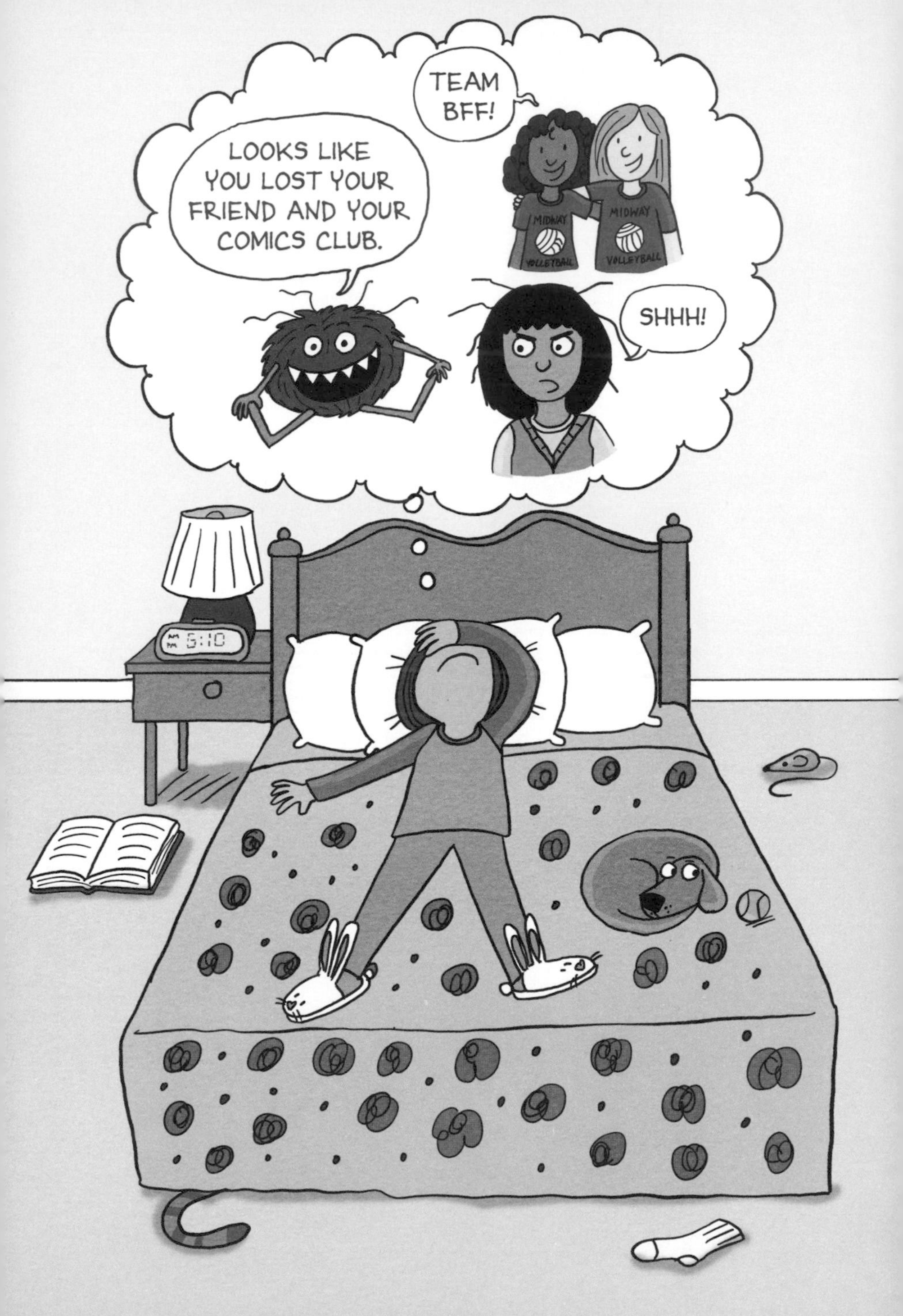
TEAM BFF!
LOOKS LIKE YOU LOST YOUR FRIEND AND YOUR COMICS CLUB.
MIDWAY VOLLEYBALL
MIDWAY VOLLEYBALL
SHHH!
5:10

CHAPTER 12
ADVICE

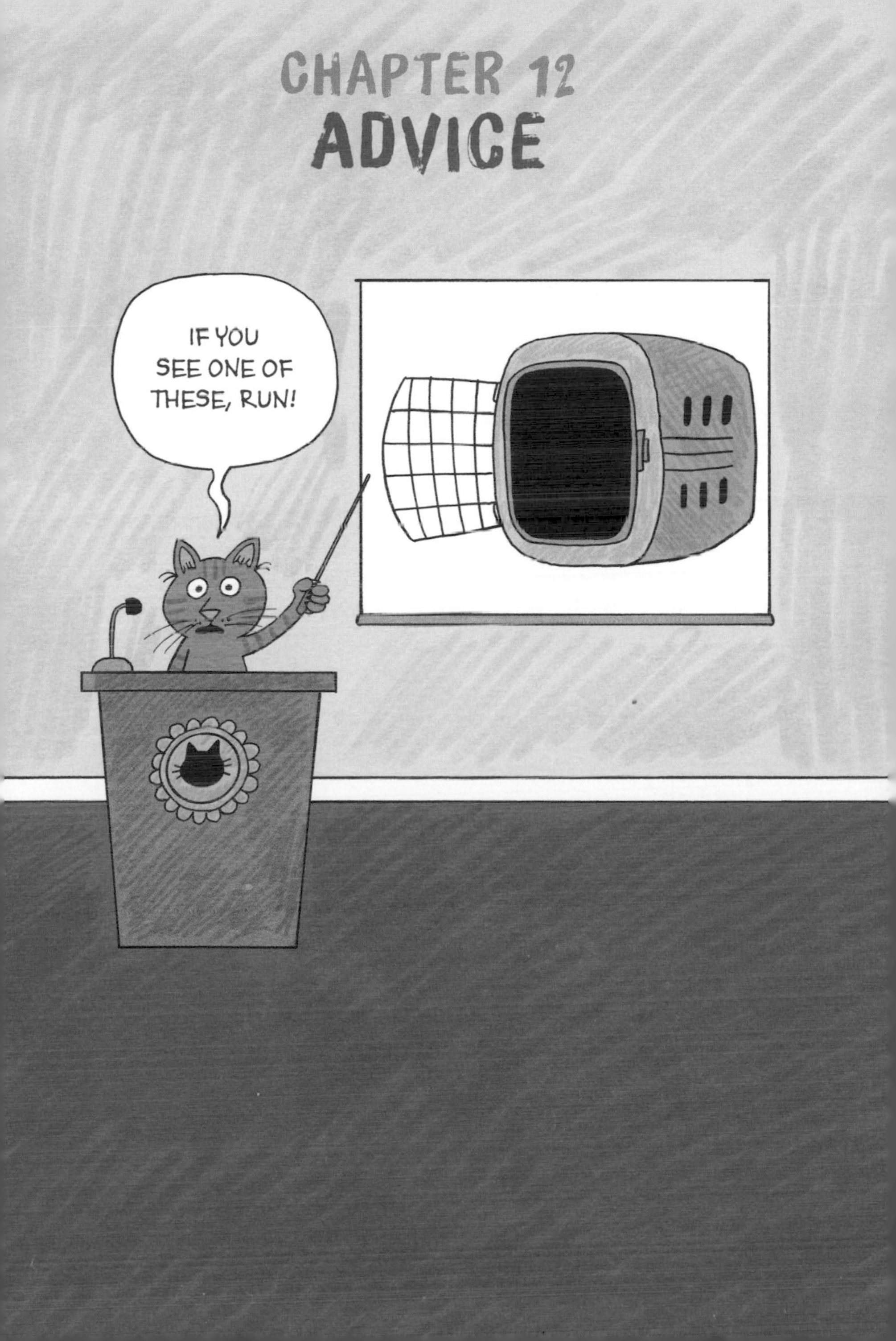
IF YOU SEE ONE OF THESE, RUN!

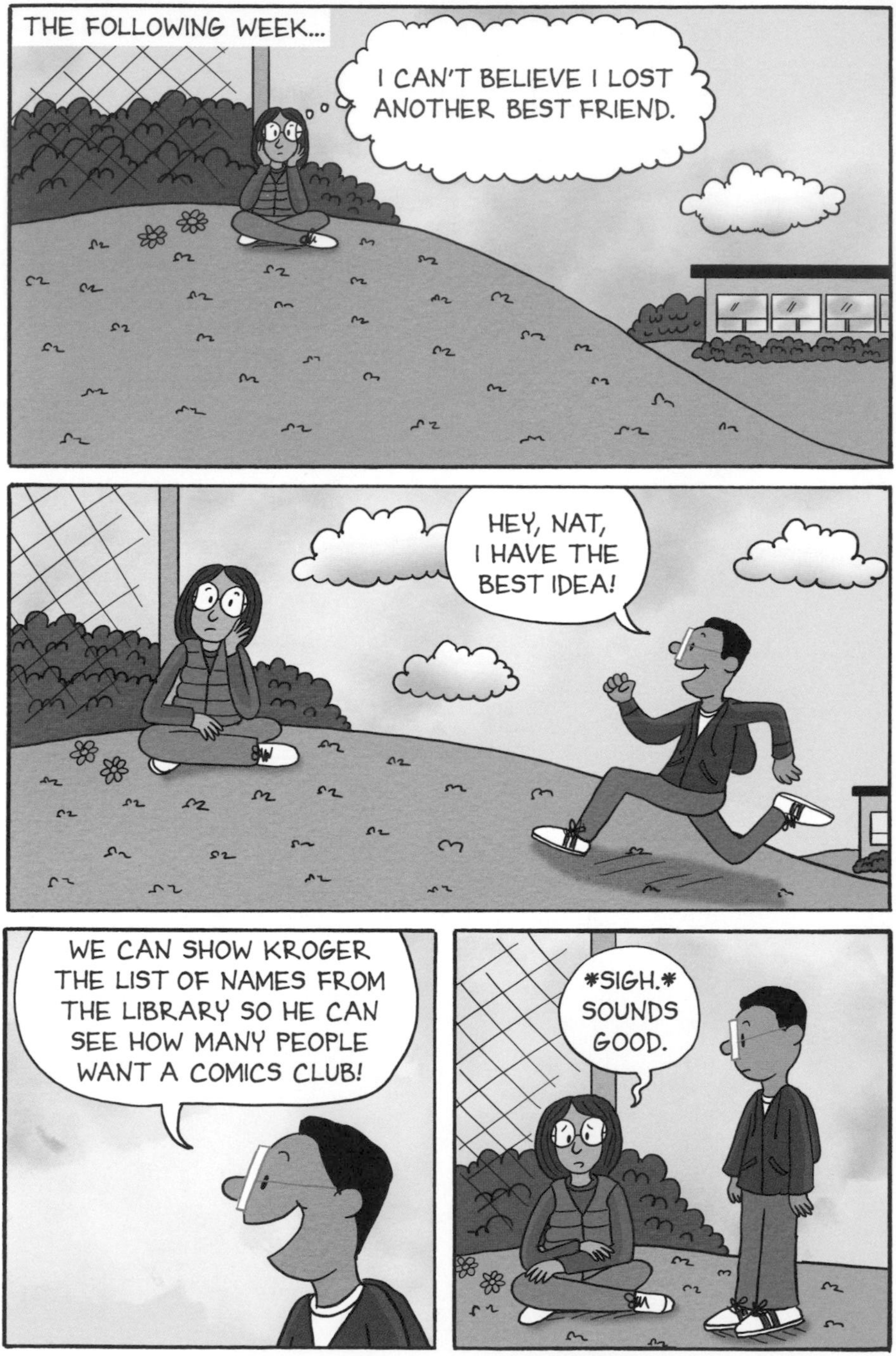
THE FOLLOWING WEEK...
I CAN'T BELIEVE I LOST ANOTHER BEST FRIEND.
HEY, NAT, I HAVE THE BEST IDEA!
WE CAN SHOW KROGER THE LIST OF NAMES FROM THE LIBRARY SO HE CAN SEE HOW MANY PEOPLE WANT A COMICS CLUB!
SIGH. SOUNDS GOOD.

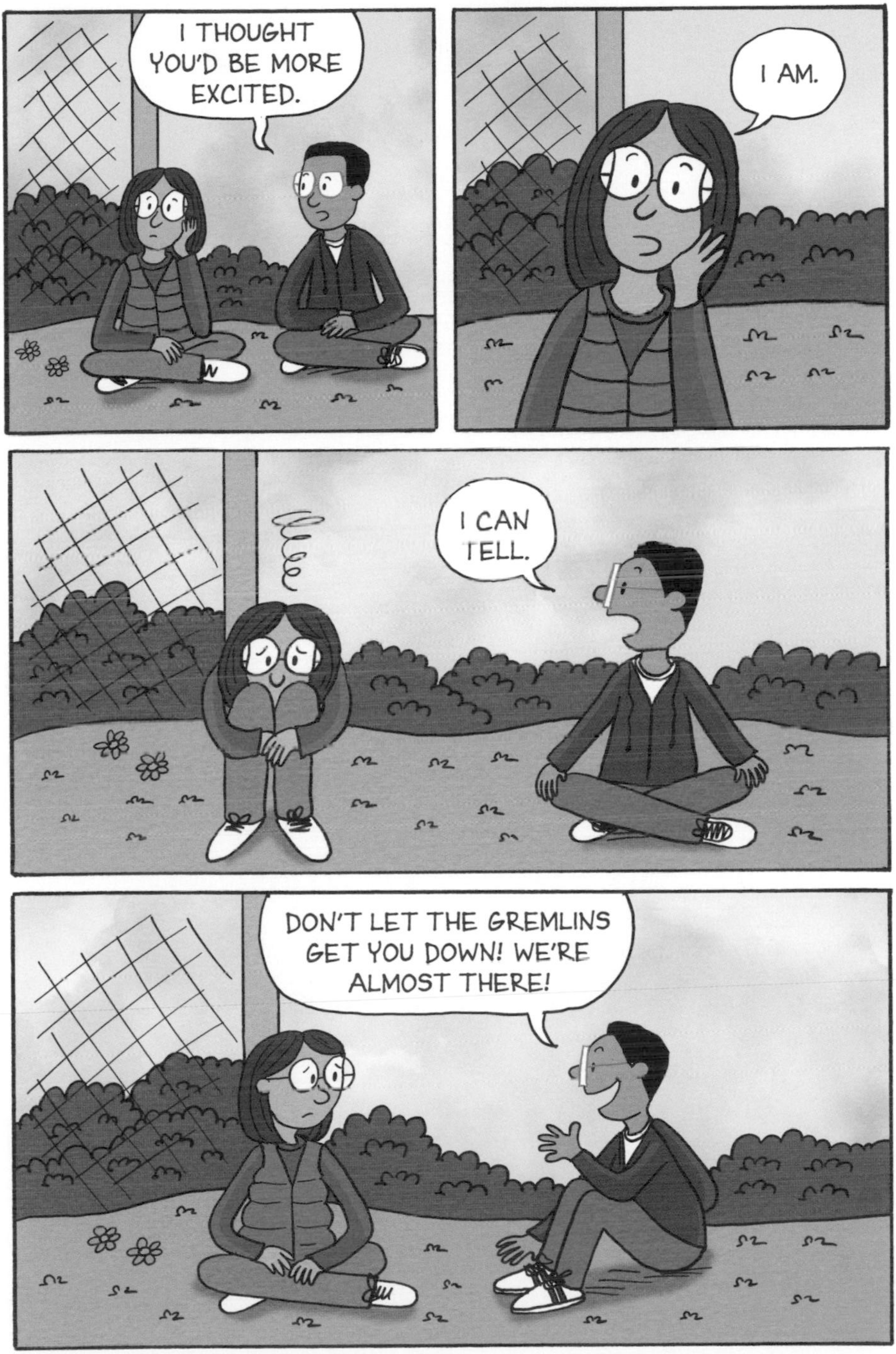
I THOUGHT YOU'D BE MORE EXCITED.
I AM.
I CAN TELL.
DON'T LET THE GREMLINS GET YOU DOWN! WE'RE ALMOST THERE!

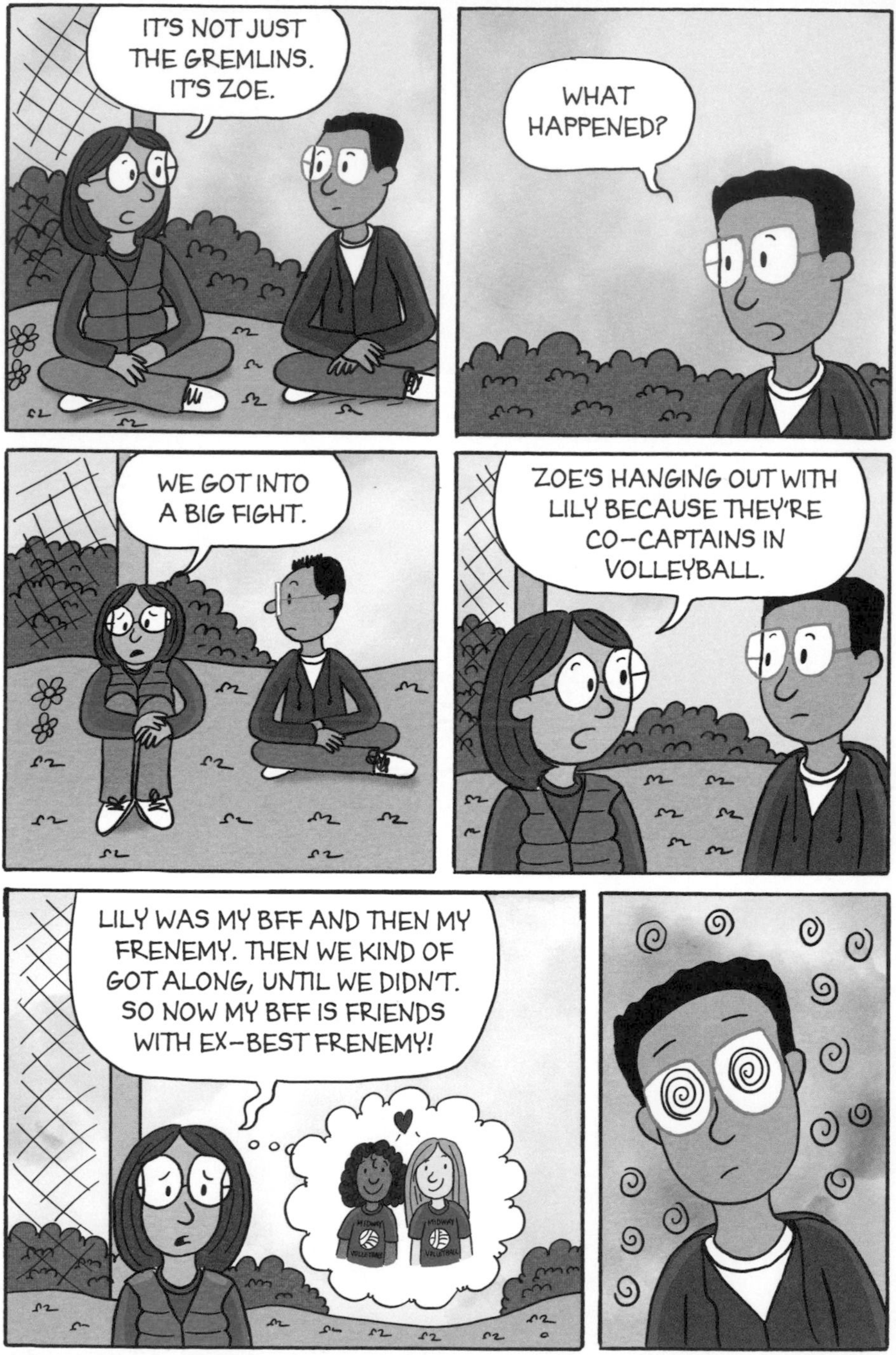
IT'S NOT JUST THE GREMLINS. IT'S ZOE.
WHAT HAPPENED?
WE GOT INTO A BIG FIGHT.
ZOE'S HANGING OUT WITH LILY BECAUSE THEY'RE CO-CAPTAINS IN VOLLEYBALL.
LILY WAS MY BFF AND THEN MY FRENEMY. THEN WE KIND OF GOT ALONG, UNTIL WE DIDN'T. SO NOW MY BFF IS FRIENDS WITH EX-BEST FRENEMY!

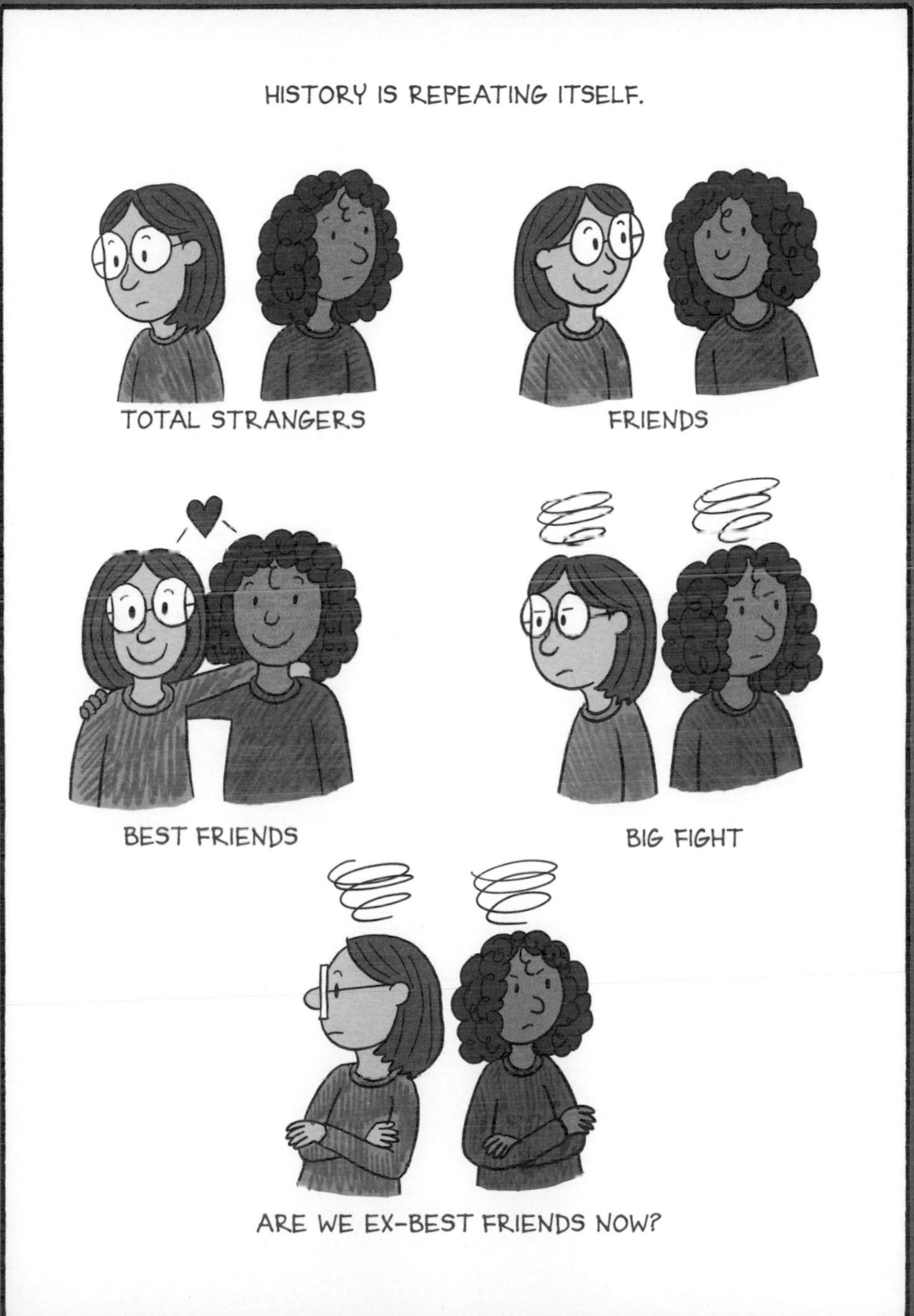
HISTORY IS REPEATING ITSELF.
TOTAL STRANGERS
FRIENDS
BEST FRIENDS
BIG FIGHT
ARE WE EX-BEST FRIENDS NOW?

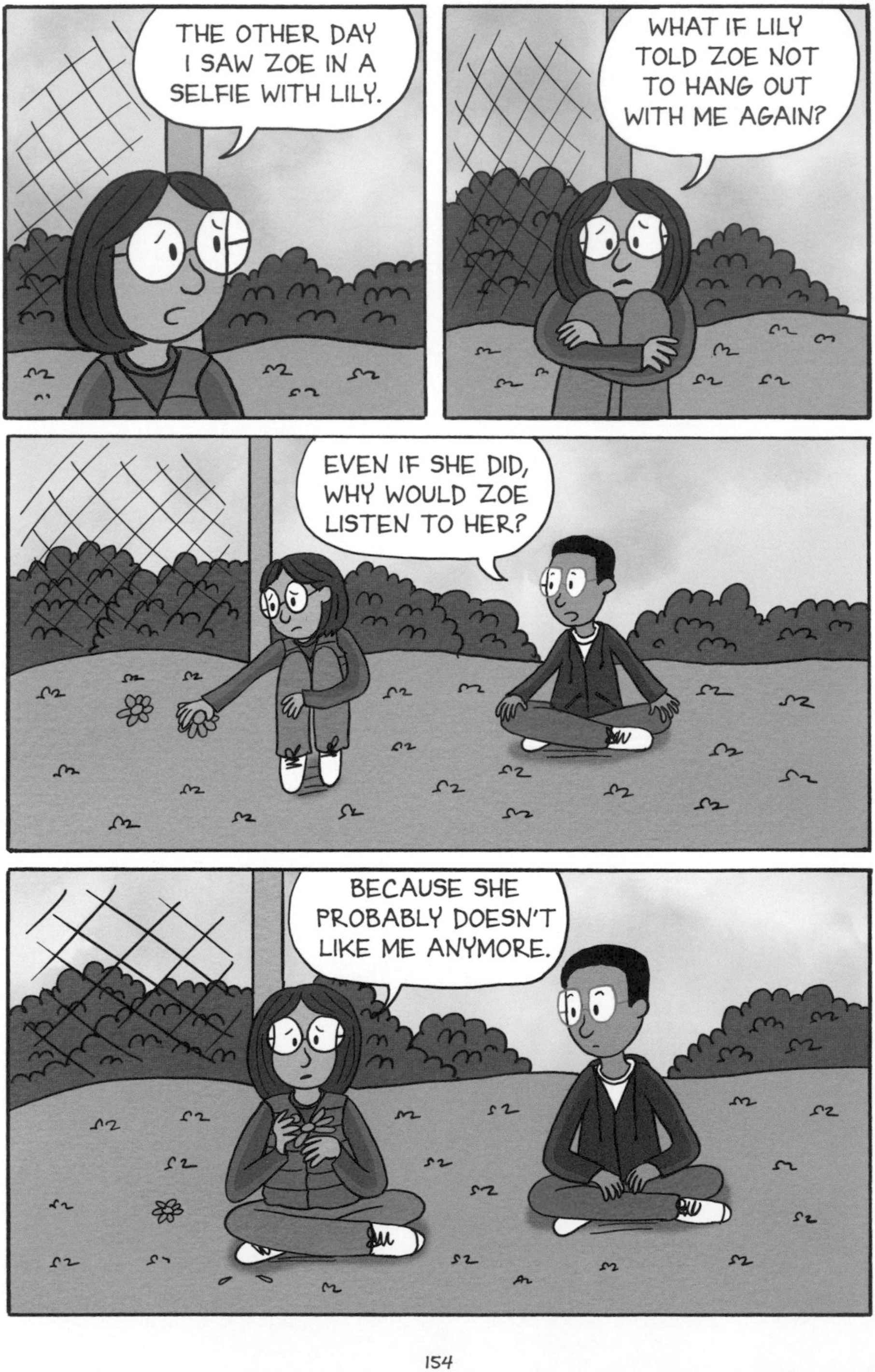
THE OTHER DAY I SAW ZOE IN A SELFIE WITH LILY.
WHAT IF LILY TOLD ZOE NOT TO HANG OUT WITH ME AGAIN?
EVEN IF SHE DID, WHY WOULD ZOE LISTEN TO HER?
BECAUSE SHE PROBABLY DOESN'T LIKE ME ANYMORE.

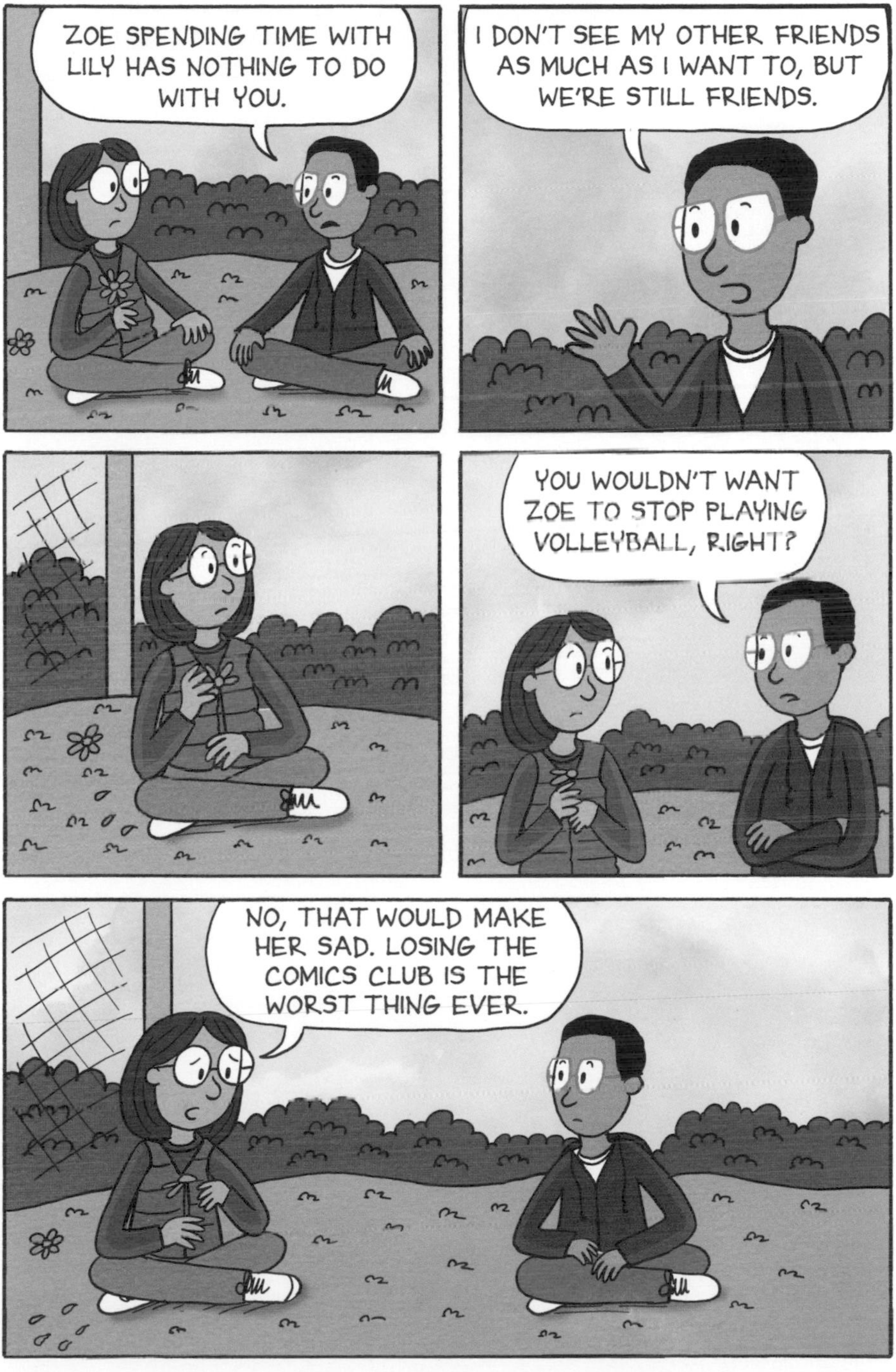
ZOE SPENDING TIME WITH LILY HAS NOTHING TO DO WITH YOU.
I DON'T SEE MY OTHER FRIENDS AS MUCH AS I WANT TO, BUT WE'RE STILL FRIENDS.
YOU WOULDN'T WANT ZOE TO STOP PLAYING VOLLEYBALL, RIGHT?
NO, THAT WOULD MAKE HER SAD. LOSING THE COMICS CLUB IS THE WORST THING EVER.

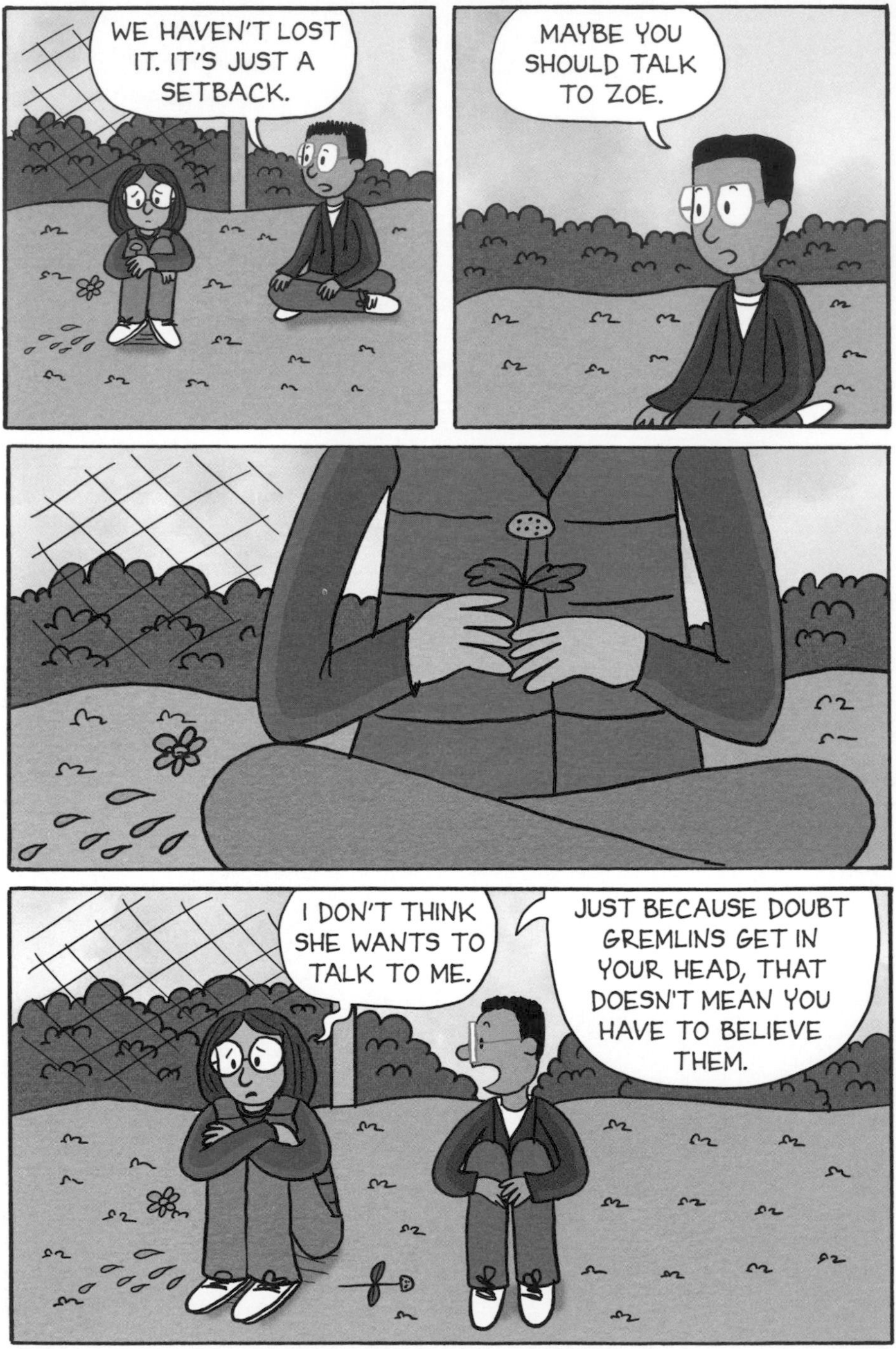
WE HAVEN'T LOST IT. IT'S JUST A SETBACK.
MAYBE YOU SHOULD TALK TO ZOE.
I DON'T THINK SHE WANTS TO TALK TO ME.
JUST BECAUSE DOUBT GREMLINS GET IN YOUR HEAD, THAT DOESN'T MEAN YOU HAVE TO BELIEVE THEM.

CHAPTER 13
THE ANSWER

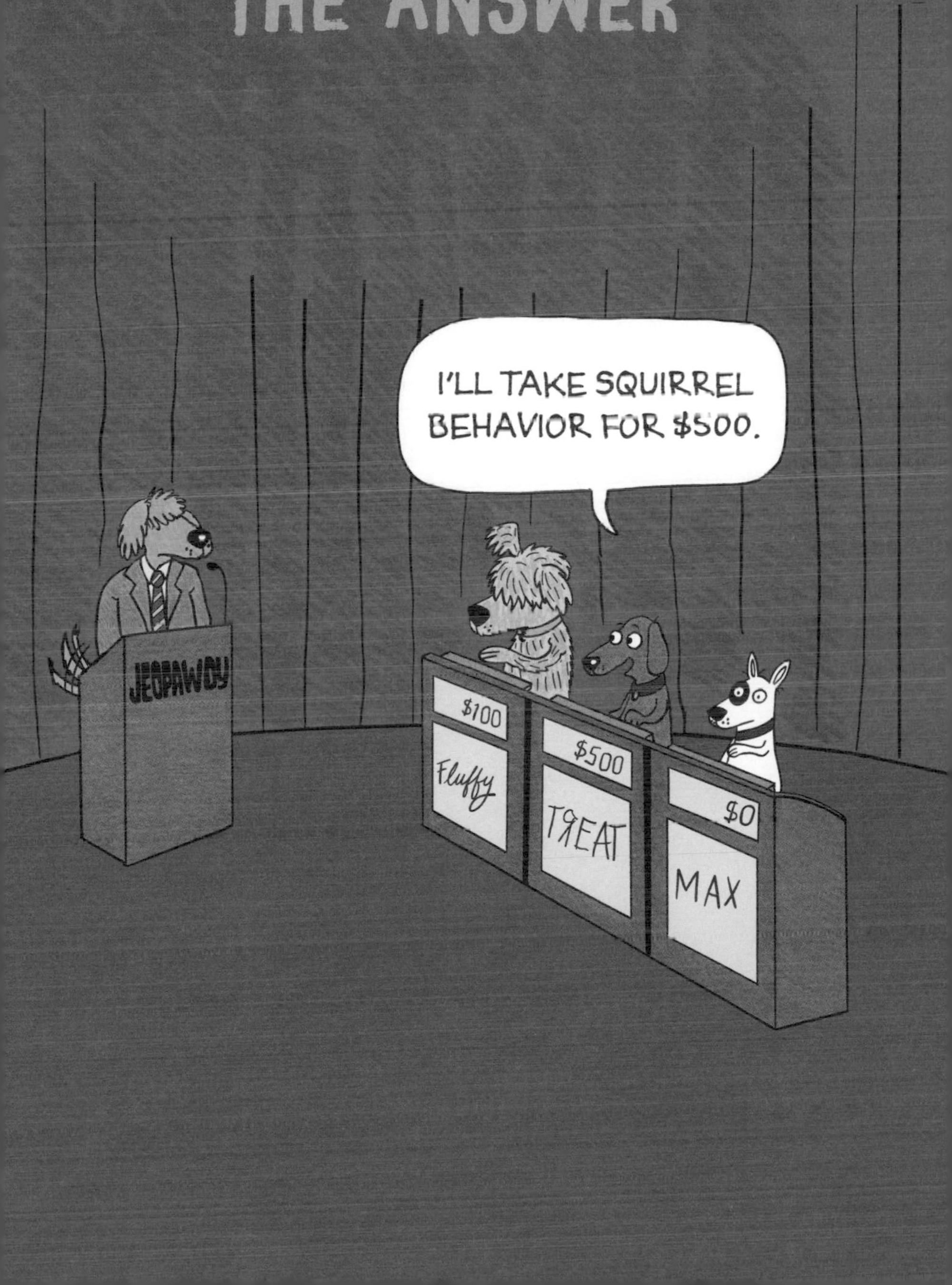

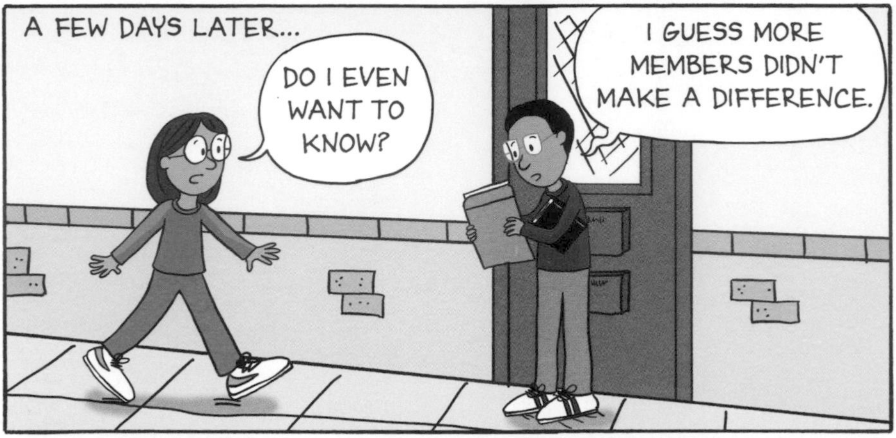
A FEW DAYS LATER...
DO I EVEN WANT TO KNOW?
I GUESS MORE MEMBERS DIDN'T MAKE A DIFFERENCE.

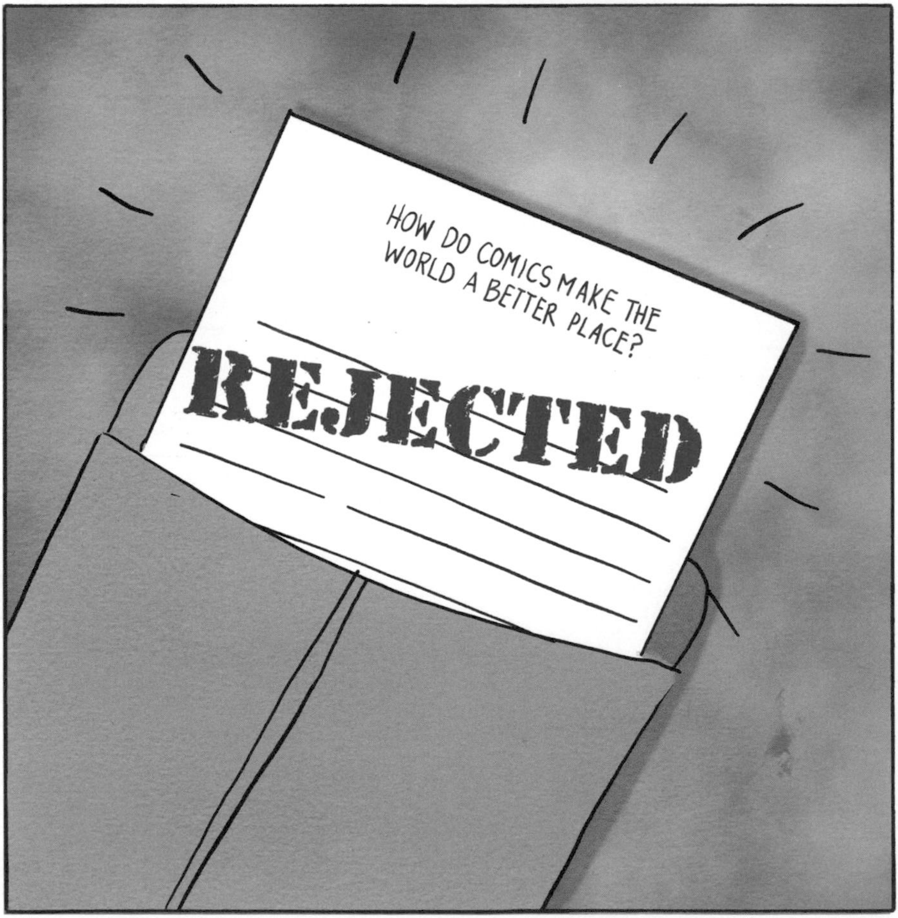
HOW DO COMICS MAKE THE WORLD A BETTER PLACE?
REJECTED

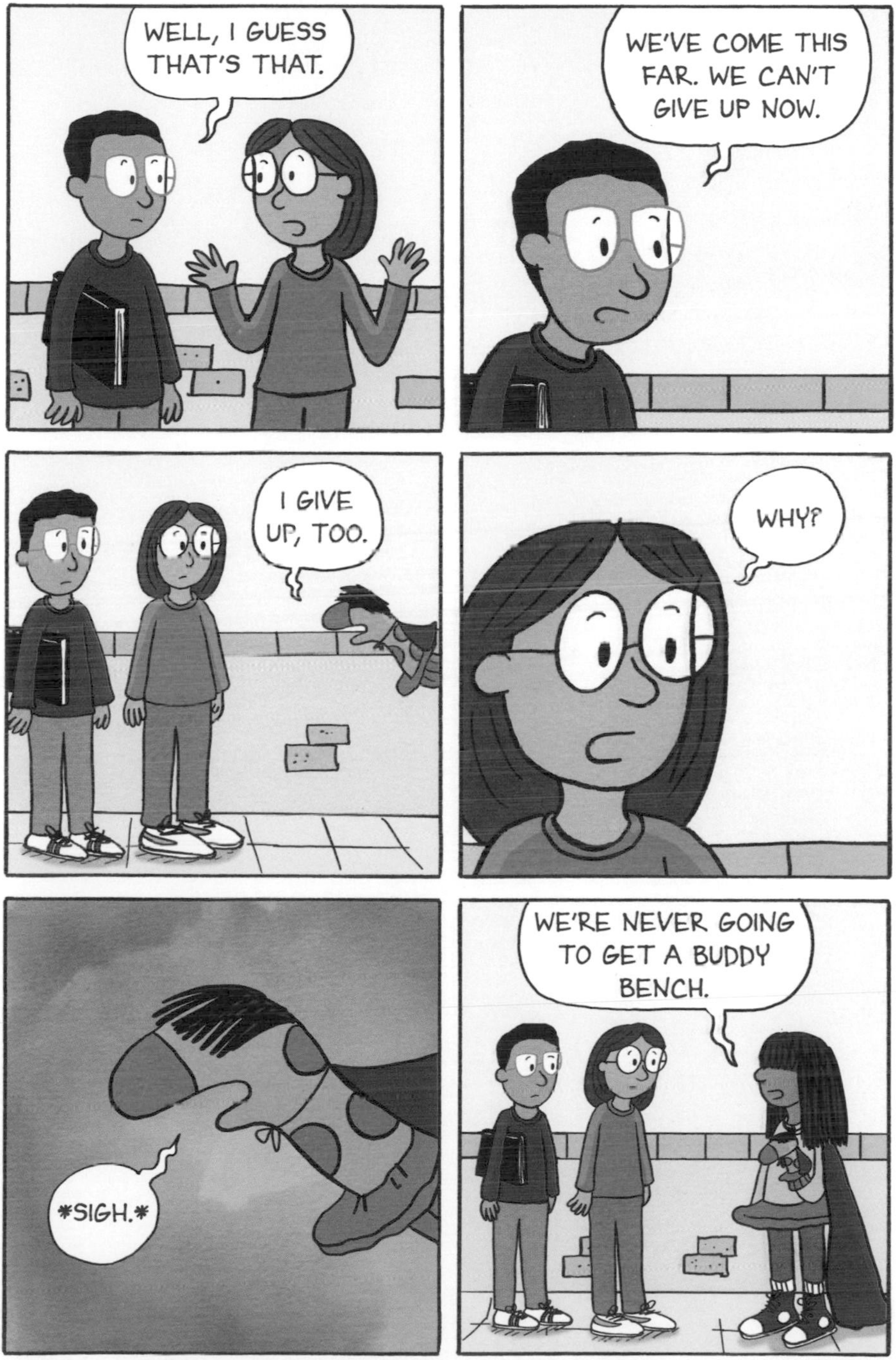
WELL, I GUESS THAT'S THAT.
WE'VE COME THIS FAR. WE CAN'T GIVE UP NOW.
I GIVE UP, TOO.
WHY?
SIGH.
WE'RE NEVER GOING TO GET A BUDDY BENCH.

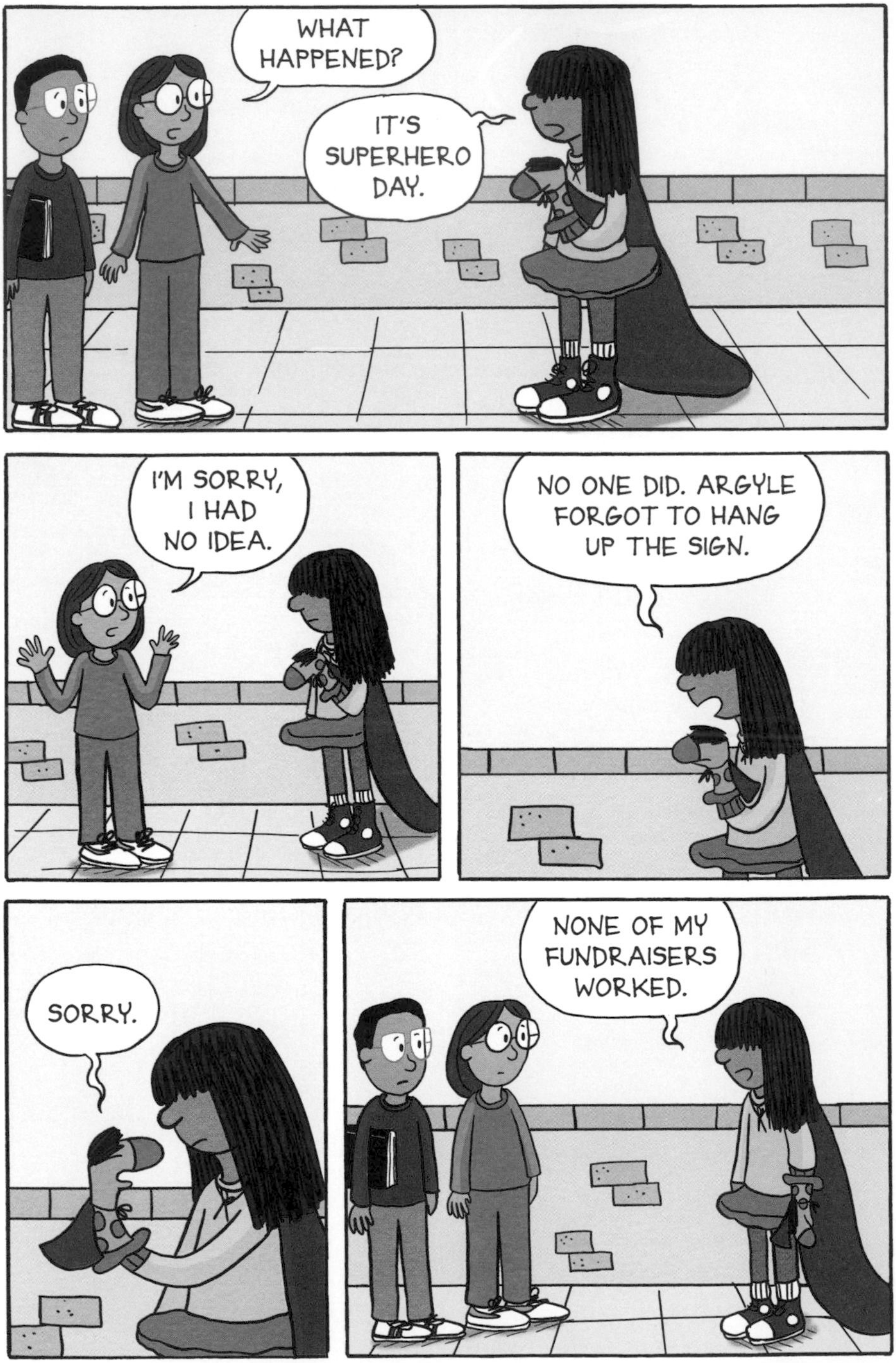
WHAT HAPPENED?
IT'S SUPERHERO DAY.
I'M SORRY, I HAD NO IDEA.
NO ONE DID. ARGYLE FORGOT TO HANG UP THE SIGN.
SORRY.
NONE OF MY FUNDRAISERS WORKED.

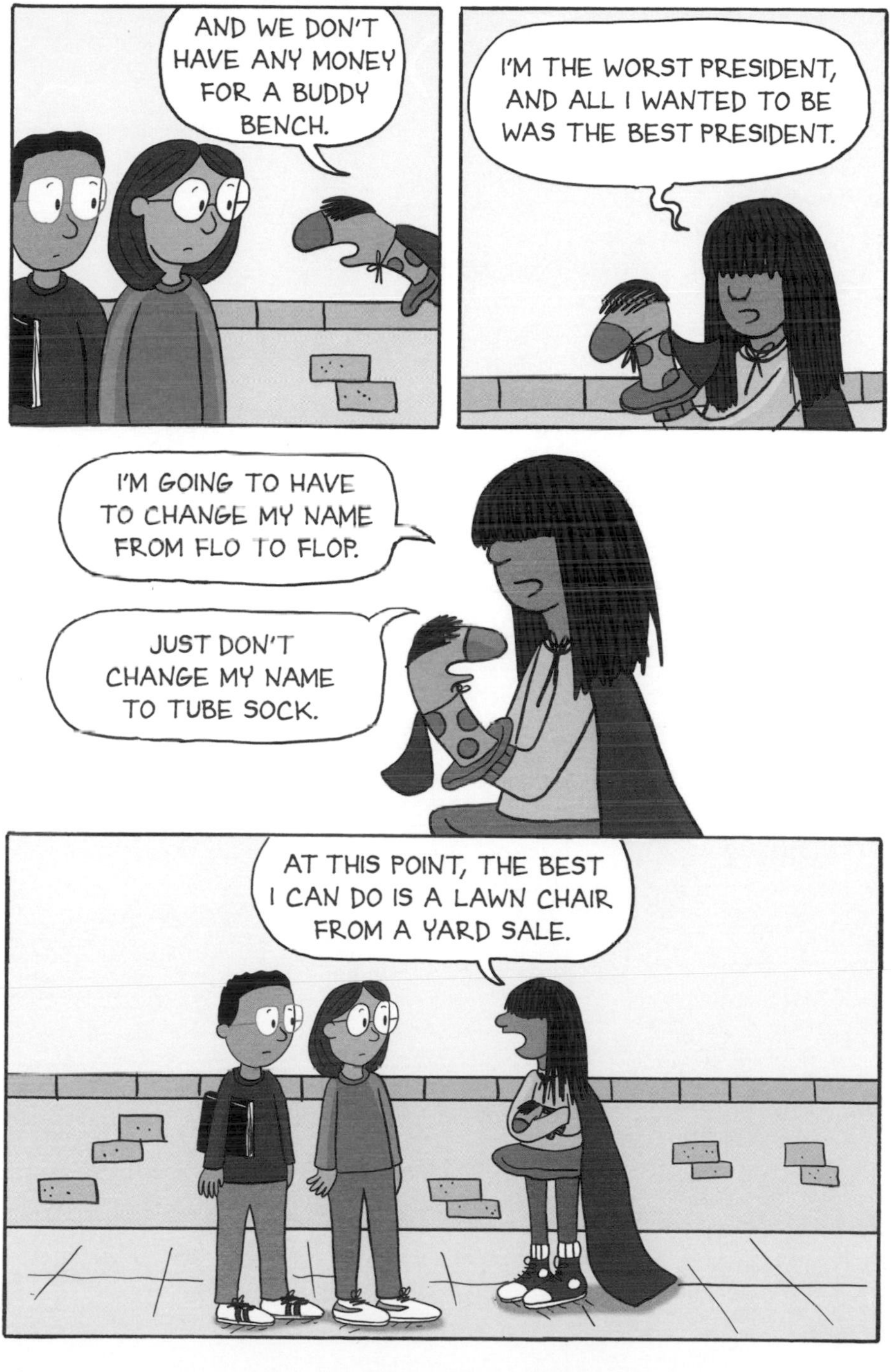
AND WE DON'T HAVE ANY MONEY FOR A BUDDY BENCH.
I'M THE WORST PRESIDENT, AND ALL I WANTED TO BE WAS THE BEST PRESIDENT.
I'M GOING TO HAVE TO CHANGE MY NAME FROM FLO TO FLOP.
JUST DON'T CHANGE MY NAME TO TUBE SOCK.
AT THIS POINT, THE BEST I CAN DO IS A LAWN CHAIR FROM A YARD SALE.

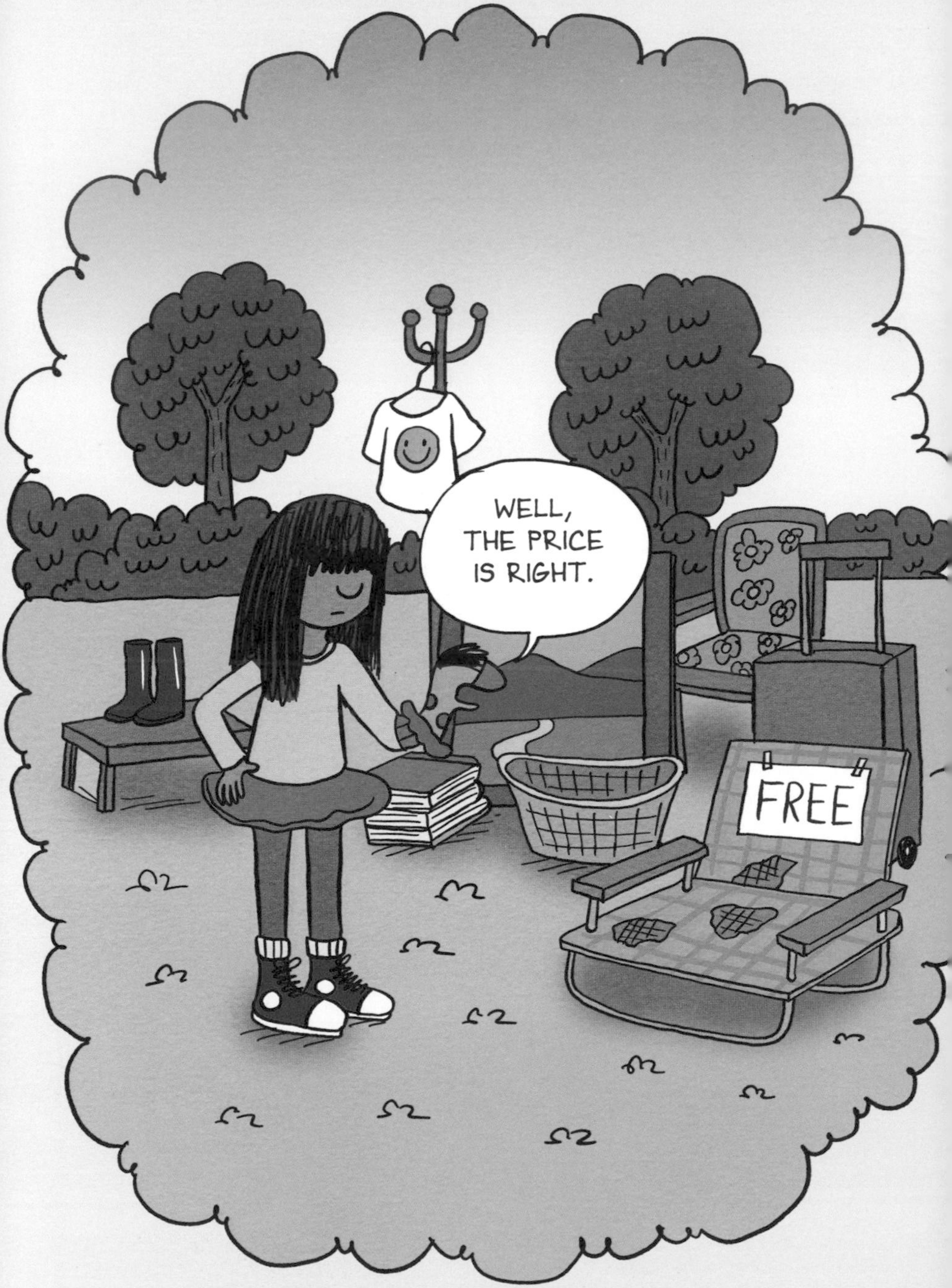
WELL, THE PRICE IS RIGHT.
FREE

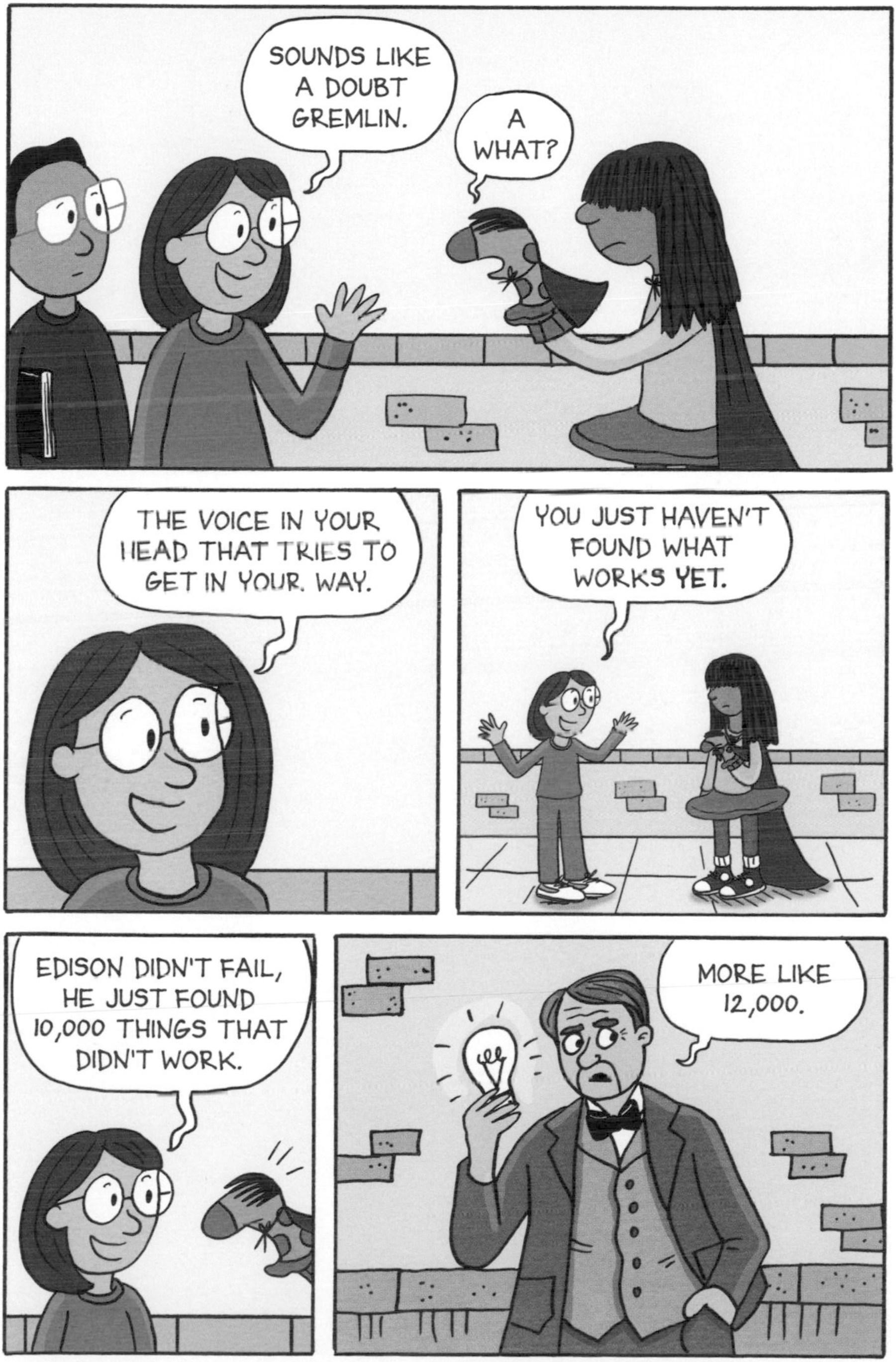
SOUNDS LIKE A DOUBT GREMLIN.
A WHAT?
THE VOICE IN YOUR HEAD THAT TRIES TO GET IN YOUR WAY.
YOU JUST HAVEN'T FOUND WHAT WORKS YET.
EDISON DIDN'T FAIL, HE JUST FOUND 10,000 THINGS THAT DIDN'T WORK.
MORE LIKE 12,000.

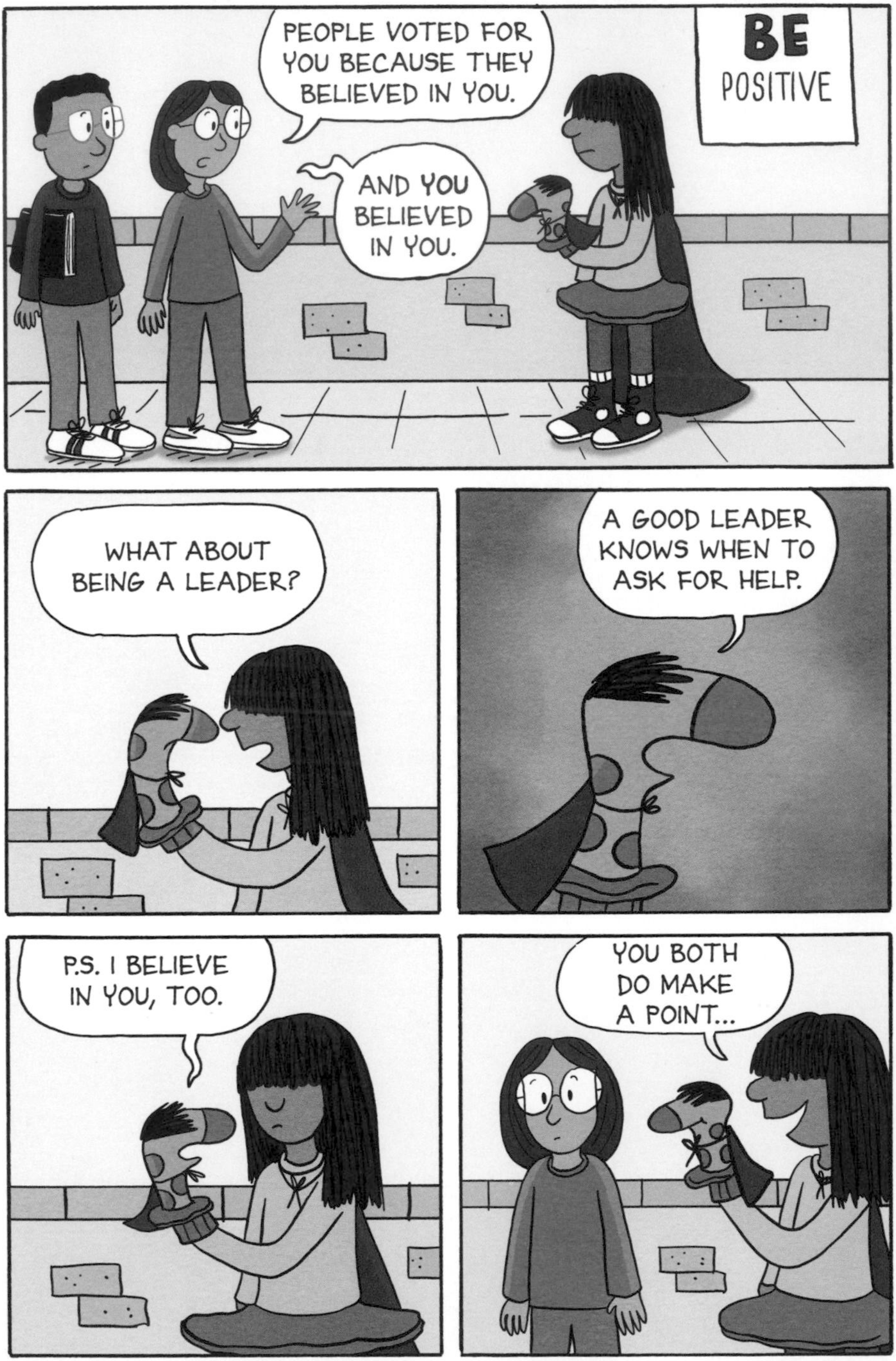
PEOPLE VOTED FOR YOU BECAUSE THEY BELIEVED IN YOU.
BE POSITIVE
AND YOU BELIEVED IN YOU.
WHAT ABOUT BEING A LEADER?
A GOOD LEADER KNOWS WHEN TO ASK FOR HELP.
P.S. I BELIEVE IN YOU, TOO.
YOU BOTH DO MAKE A POINT...

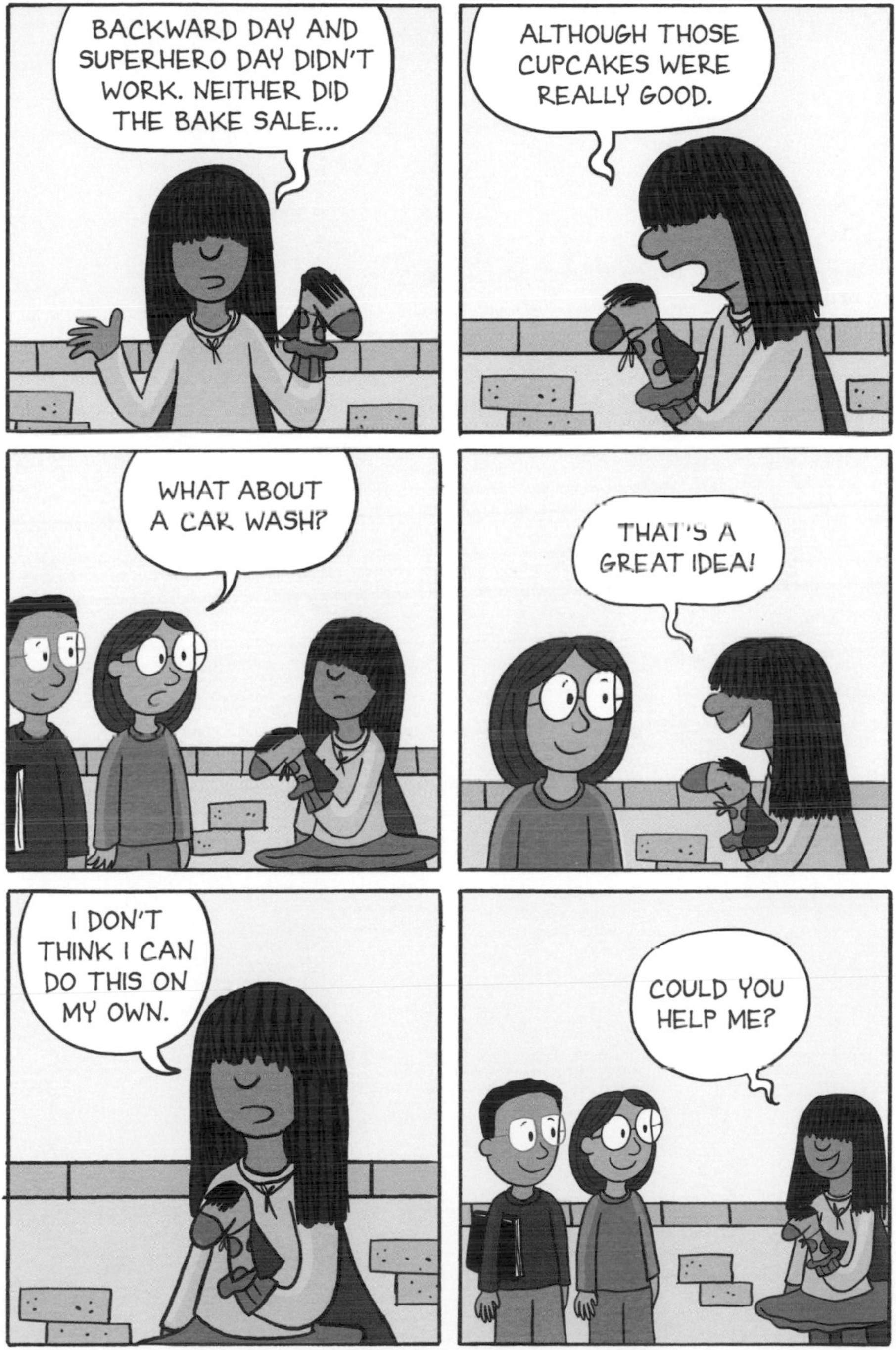
BACKWARD DAY AND SUPERHERO DAY DIDN'T WORK. NEITHER DID THE BAKE SALE...
ALTHOUGH THOSE CUPCAKES WERE REALLY GOOD.
WHAT ABOUT A CAR WASH?
THAT'S A GREAT IDEA!
I DON'T THINK I CAN DO THIS ON MY OWN.
COULD YOU HELP ME?

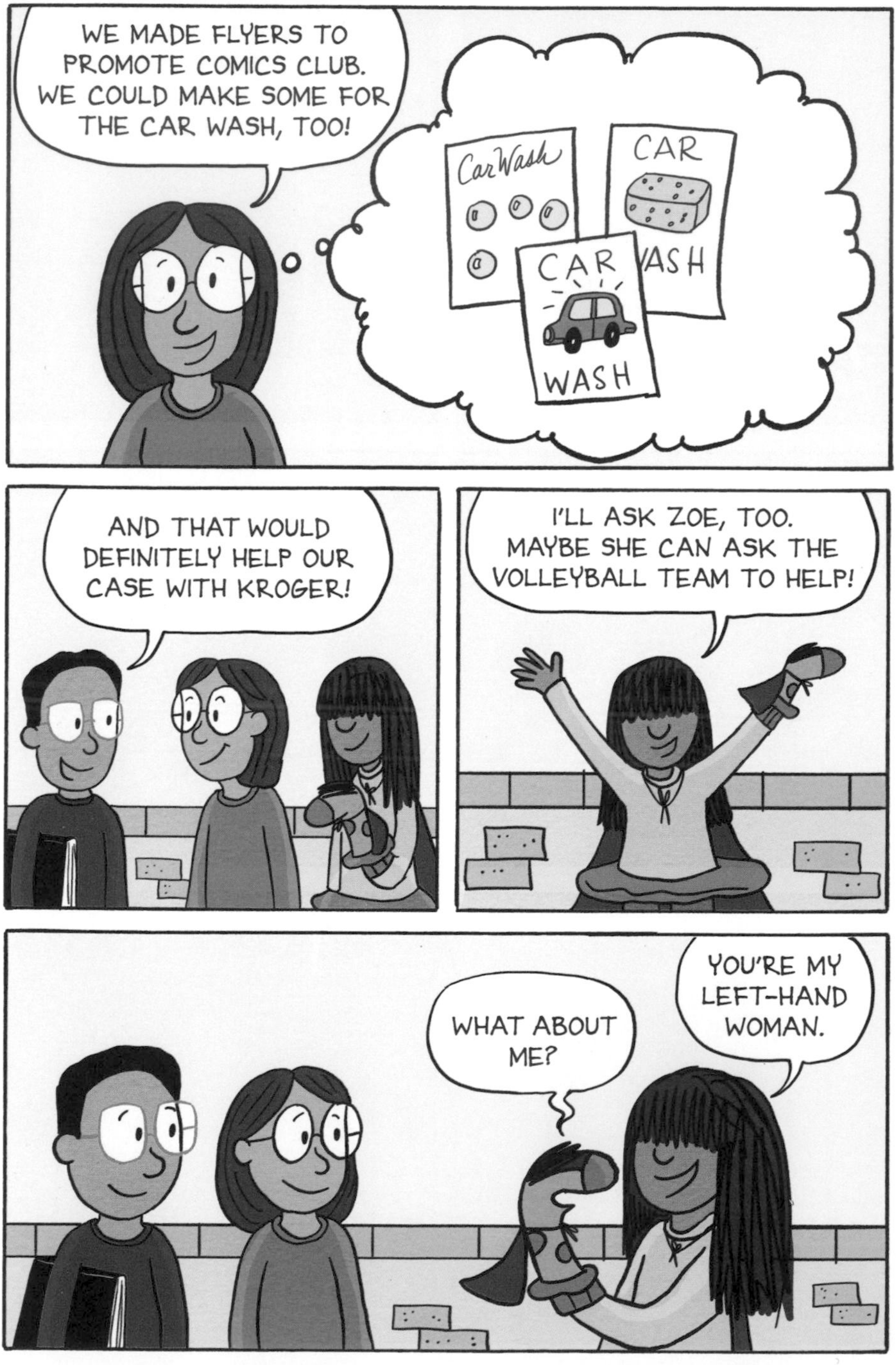
WE MADE FLYERS TO PROMOTE COMICS CLUB. WE COULD MAKE SOME FOR THE CAR WASH, TOO!
Car Wash
CAR WASH
CAR WASH
AND THAT WOULD DEFINITELY HELP OUR CASE WITH KROGER!
I'LL ASK ZOE, TOO. MAYBE SHE CAN ASK THE VOLLEYBALL TEAM TO HELP!
WHAT ABOUT ME?
YOU'RE MY LEFT-HAND WOMAN.

CHAPTER 14
CAR WASH

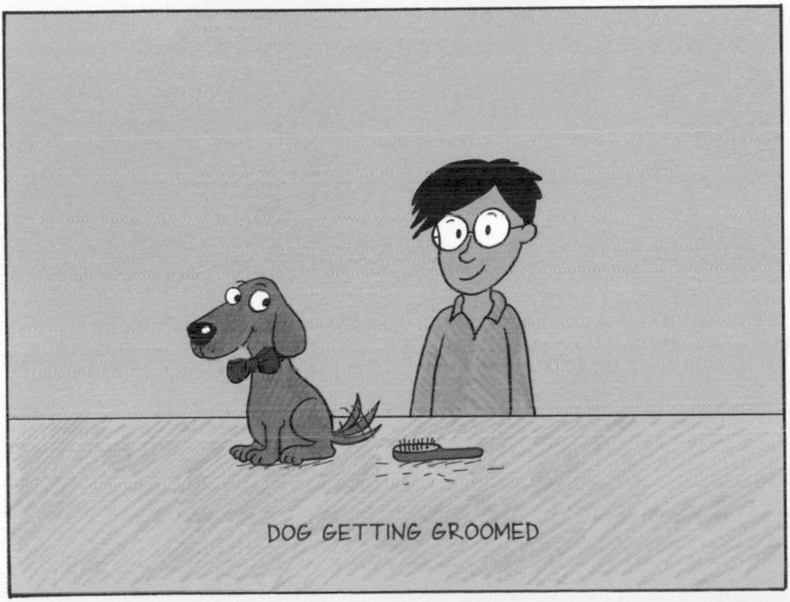
DOG GETTING GROOMED

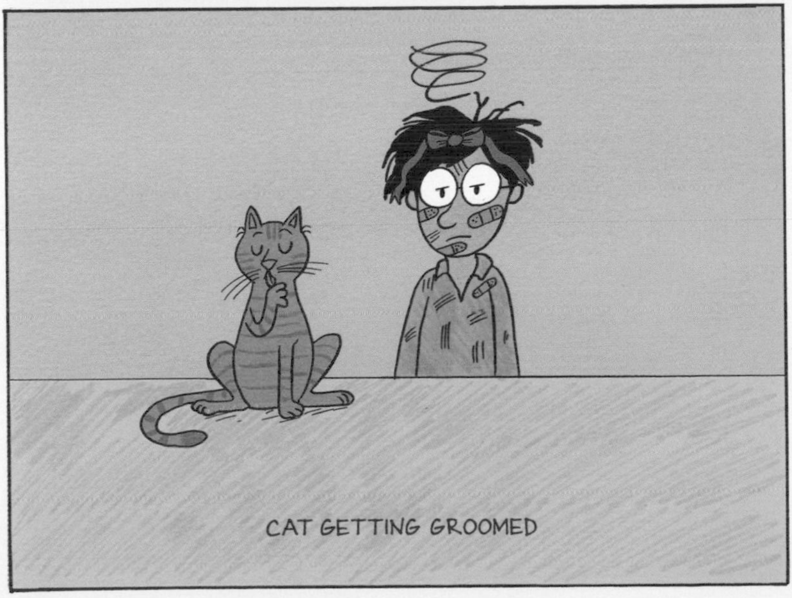
CAT GETTING GROOMED

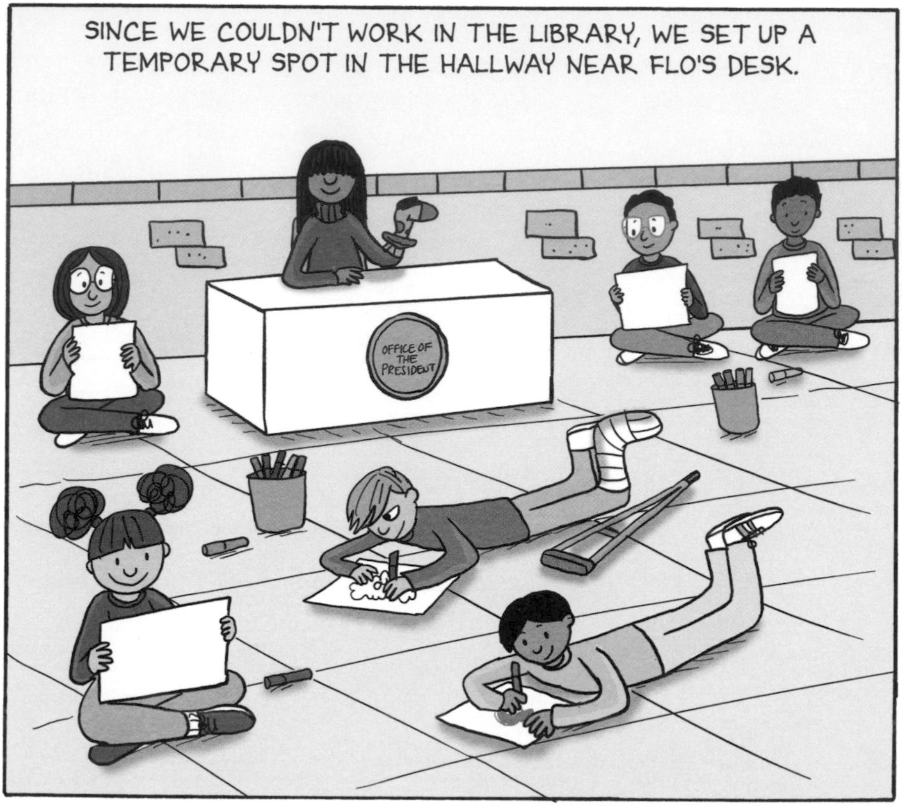
SINCE WE COULDN'T WORK IN THE LIBRARY, WE SET UP A TEMPORARY SPOT IN THE HALLWAY NEAR FLO'S DESK.
OFFICE OF THE PRESIDENT

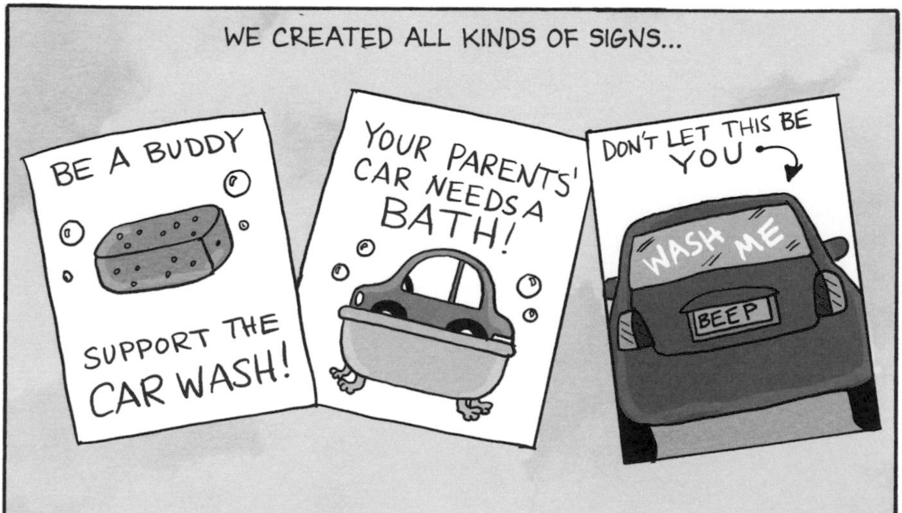
WE CREATED ALL KINDS OF SIGNS...
BE A BUDDY
SUPPORT THE CAR WASH!
YOUR PARENTS' CAR NEEDS A BATH!
DON'T LET THIS BE YOU
WASH ME
BEEP

AND HUNG THEM UP ALL OVER SCHOOL.

CAR WASH!
MONDAY AT MIDWAY!
CAR WASH!
RULES
NO RUNNING
DON'T BE LATE
NO HORSEPLAY
CAR WASH
CAR WASH!

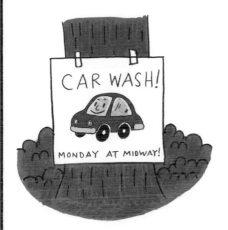

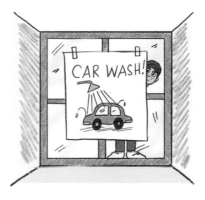

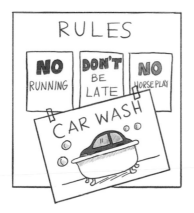

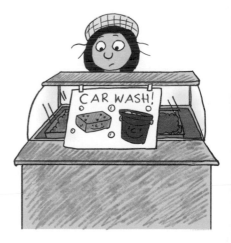

WHEN WE FINALLY HELD THE CAR WASH,
THE LINE WENT AROUND THE BLOCK.

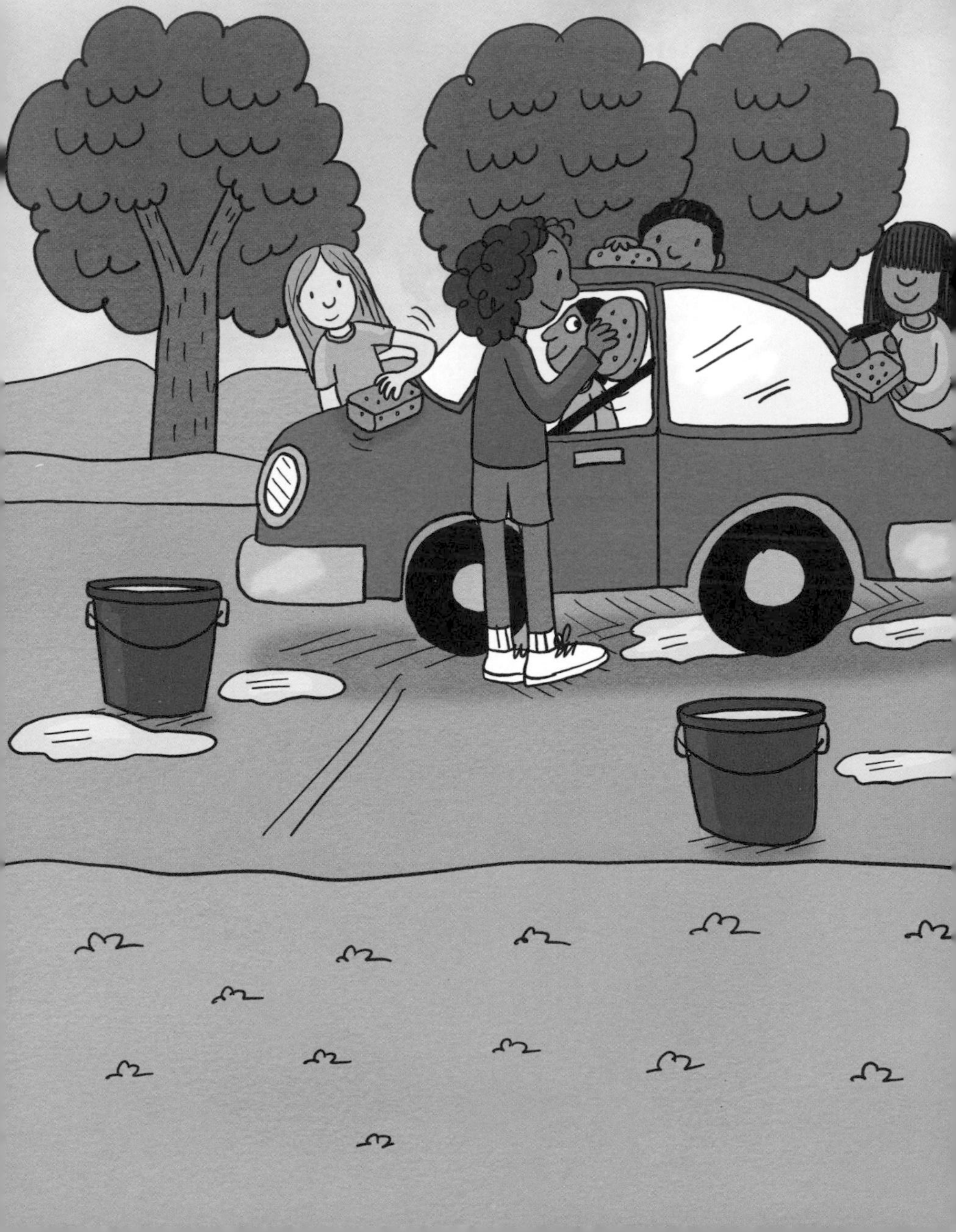

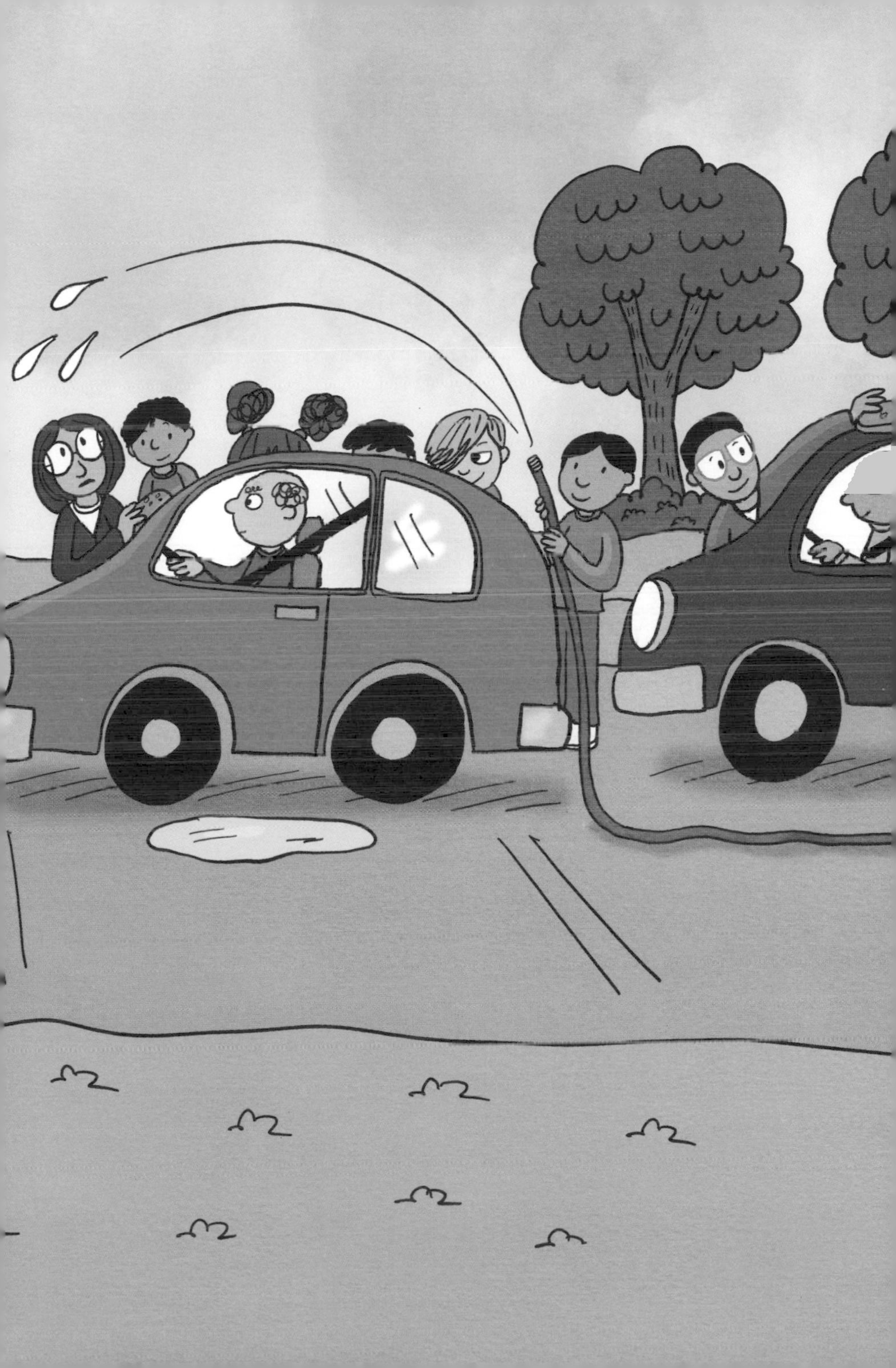

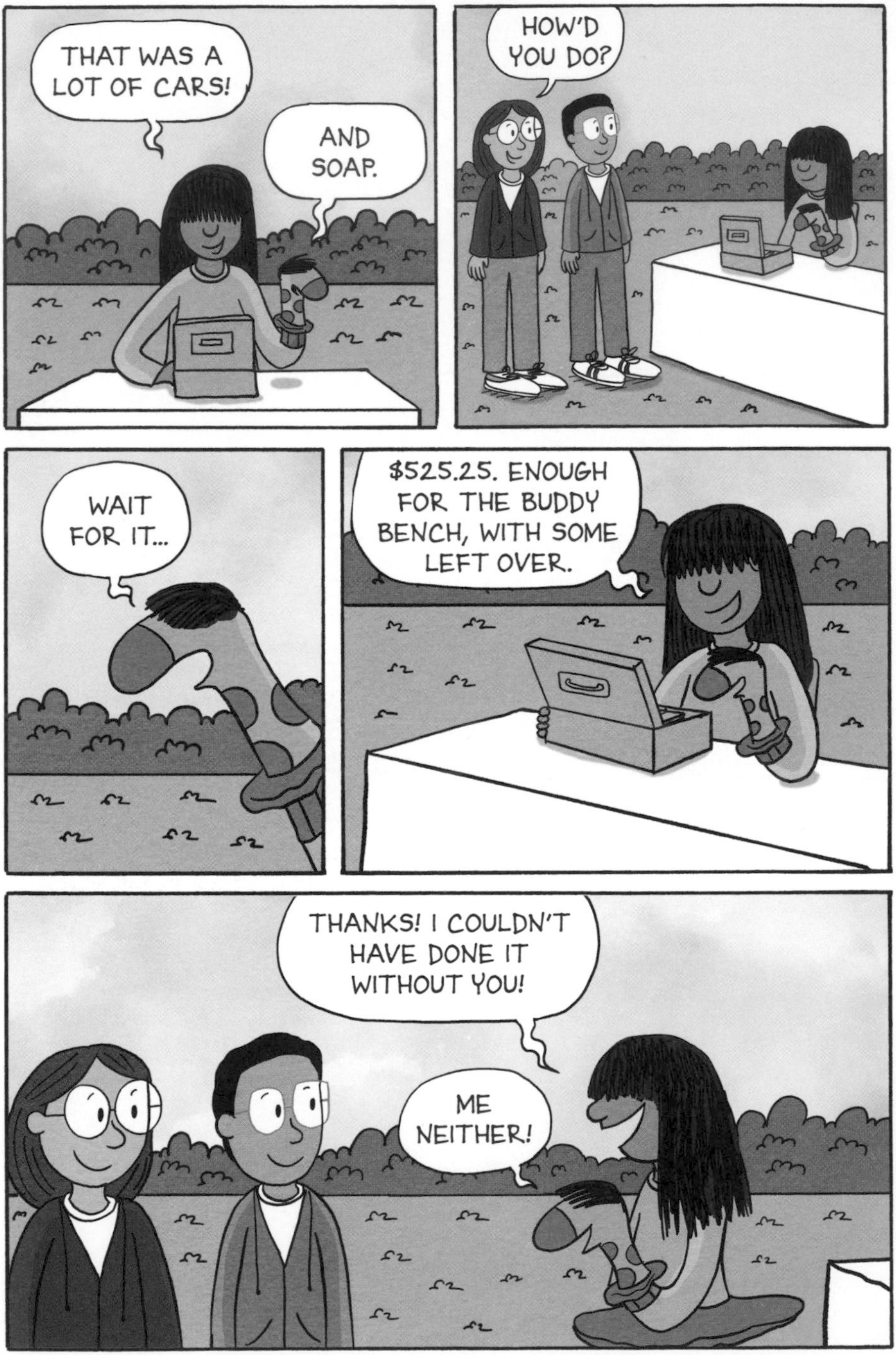

THAT WAS A LOT OF CARS!
AND SOAP.
HOW'D YOU DO?
WAIT FOR IT...
$525.25. ENOUGH FOR THE BUDDY BENCH, WITH SOME LEFT OVER.
THANKS! I COULDN'T HAVE DONE IT WITHOUT YOU!
ME NEITHER!

CHAPTER 15
TALK

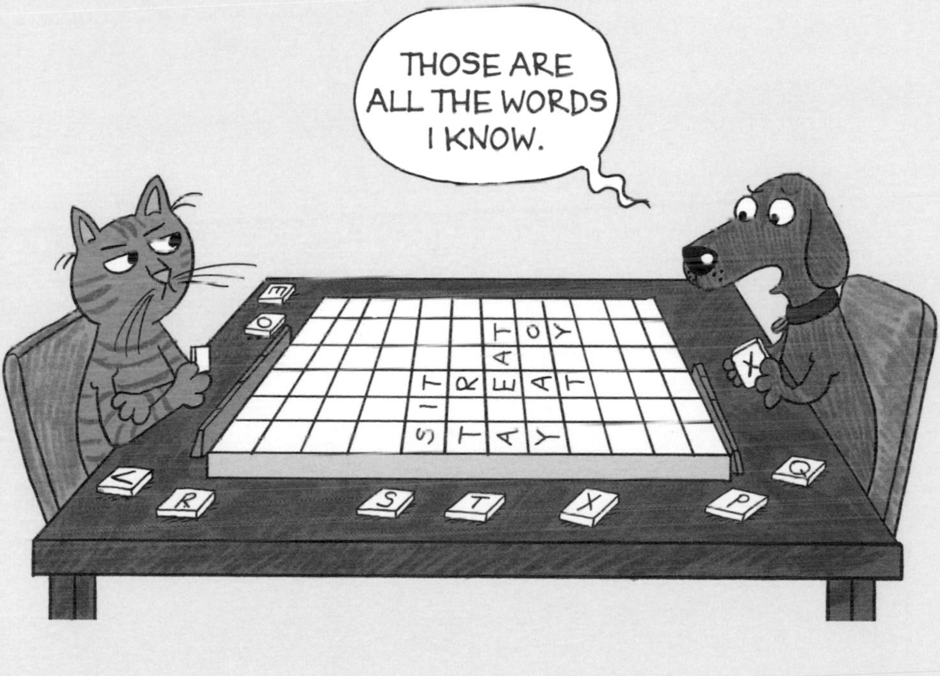
THOSE ARE ALL THE WORDS I KNOW.

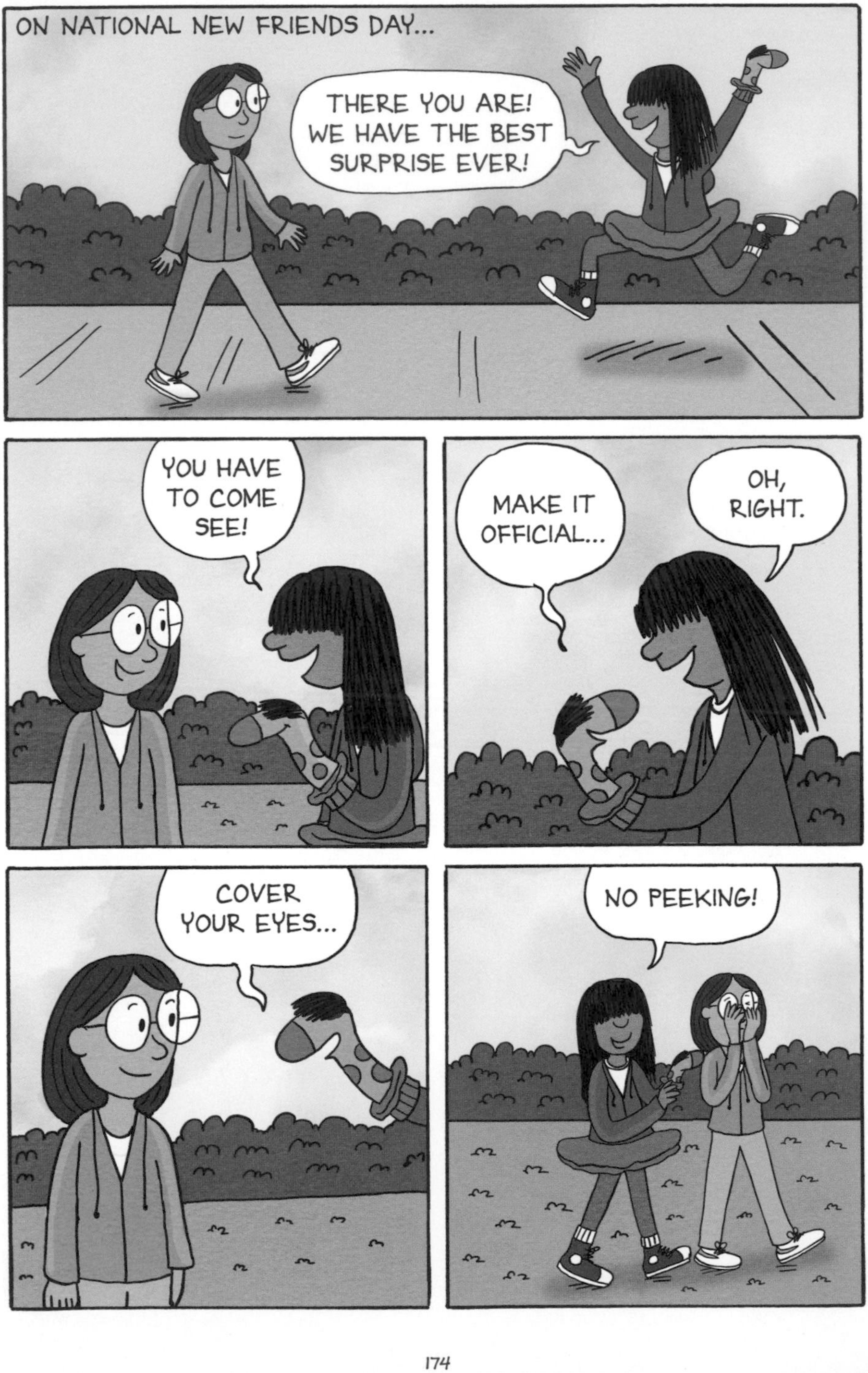
ON NATIONAL NEW FRIENDS DAY...
THERE YOU ARE! WE HAVE THE BEST SURPRISE EVER!
YOU HAVE TO COME SEE!
MAKE IT OFFICIAL...
OH, RIGHT.
COVER YOUR EYES...
NO PEEKING!

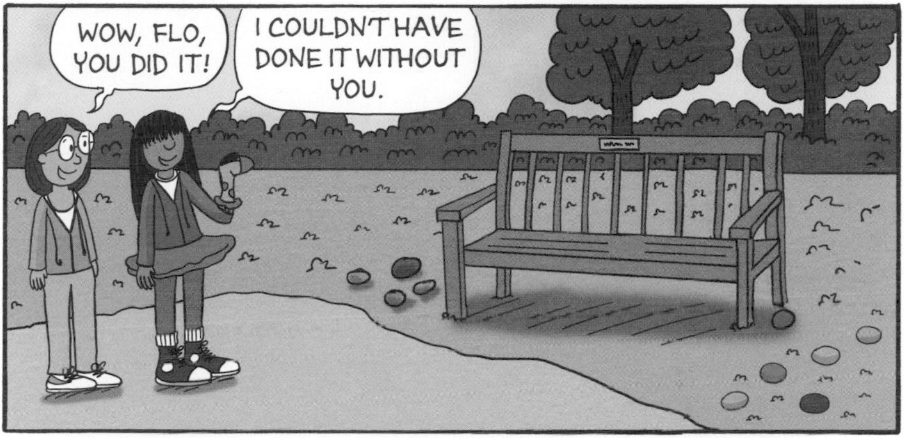
WOW, FLO, YOU DID IT!
I COULDN'T HAVE DONE IT WITHOUT YOU.

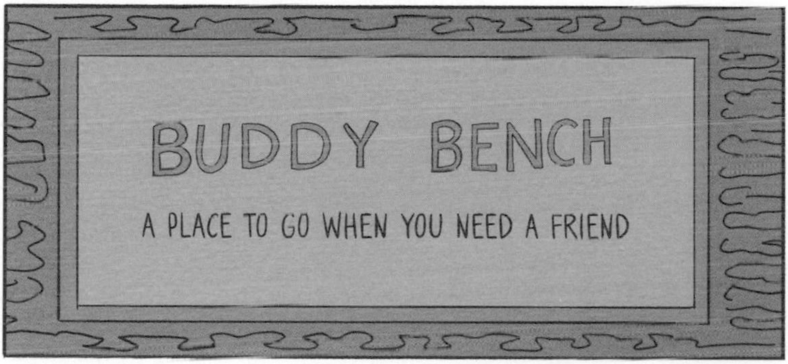
BUDDY BENCH
A PLACE TO GO WHEN YOU NEED A FRIEND

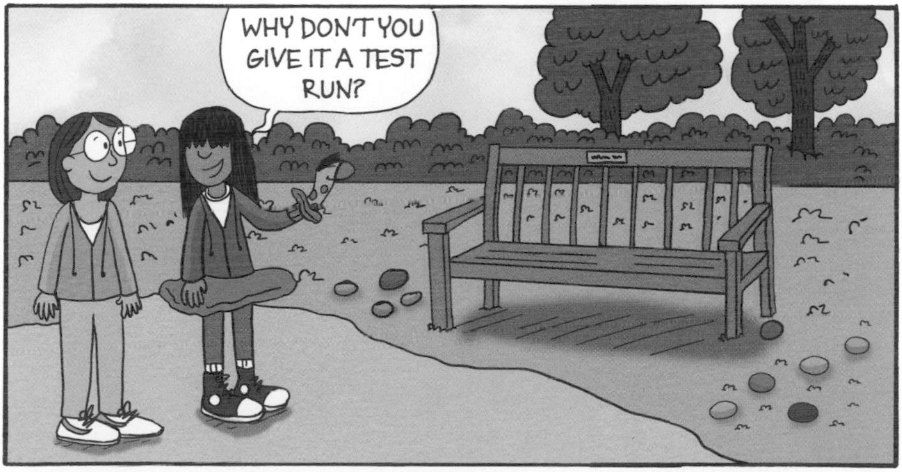
WHY DON'T YOU GIVE IT A TEST RUN?

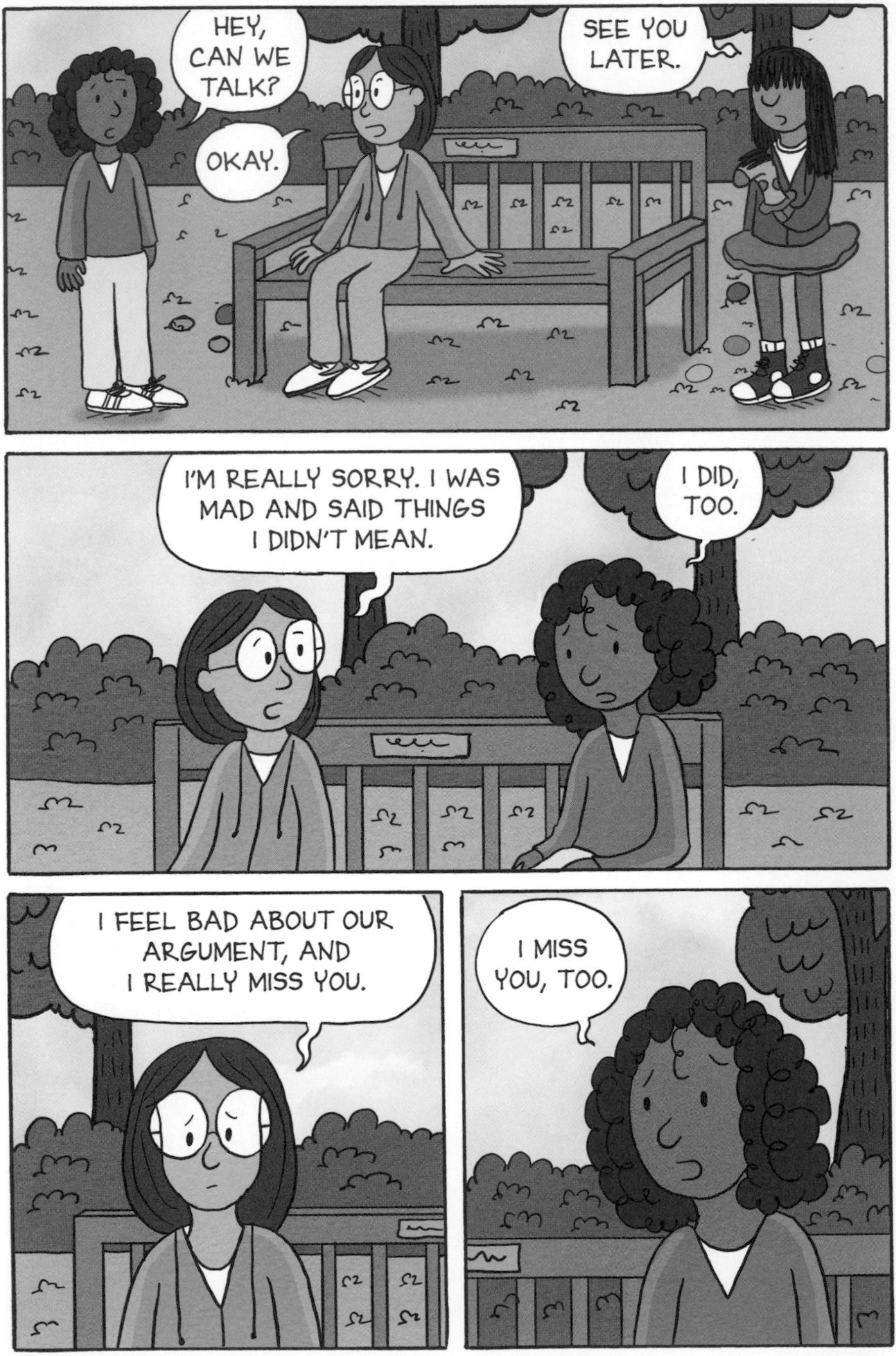

HEY, CAN WE TALK?
OKAY.
SEE YOU LATER.
I'M REALLY SORRY. I WAS MAD AND SAID THINGS I DIDN'T MEAN.
I DID, TOO.
I FEEL BAD ABOUT OUR ARGUMENT, AND I REALLY MISS YOU.
I MISS YOU, TOO.

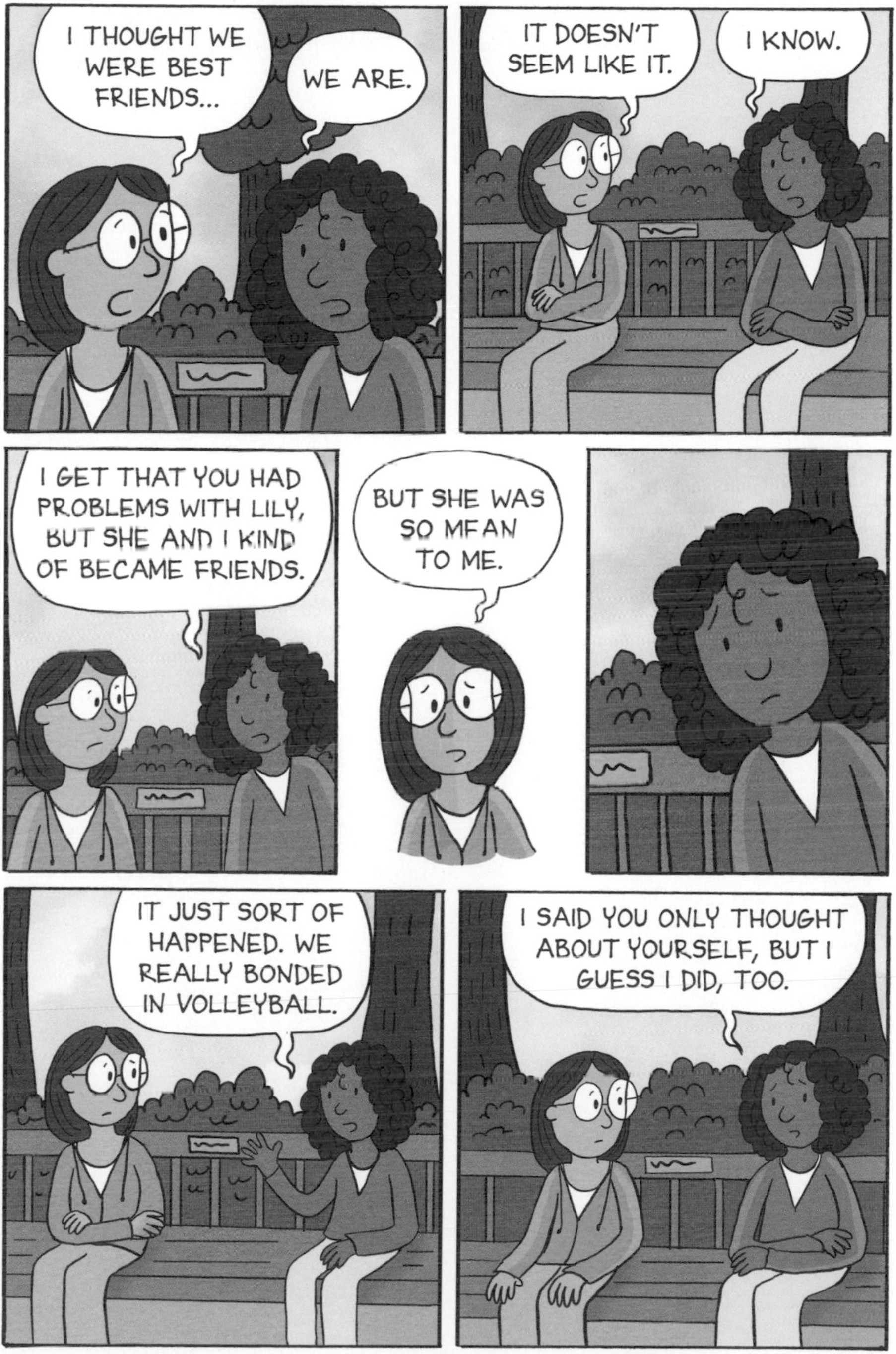
I THOUGHT WE WERE BEST FRIENDS...
WE ARE.
IT DOESN'T SEEM LIKE IT.
I KNOW.
I GET THAT YOU HAD PROBLEMS WITH LILY, BUT SHE AND I KIND OF BECAME FRIENDS.
BUT SHE WAS SO MEAN TO ME.
IT JUST SORT OF HAPPENED. WE REALLY BONDED IN VOLLEYBALL.
I SAID YOU ONLY THOUGHT ABOUT YOURSELF, BUT I GUESS I DID, TOO.

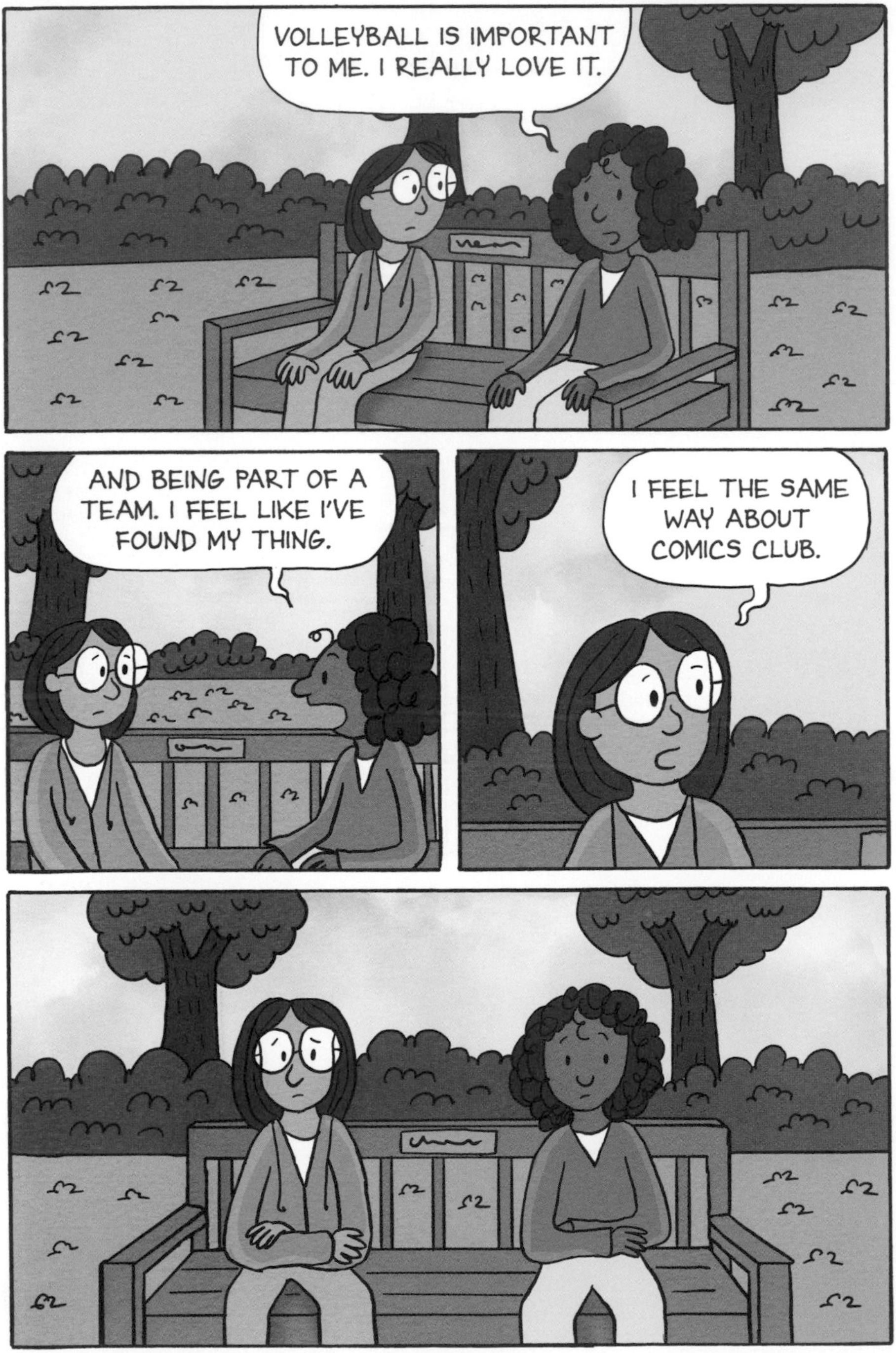
VOLLEYBALL IS IMPORTANT TO ME. I REALLY LOVE IT.
AND BEING PART OF A TEAM. I FEEL LIKE I'VE FOUND MY THING.
I FEEL THE SAME WAY ABOUT COMICS CLUB.

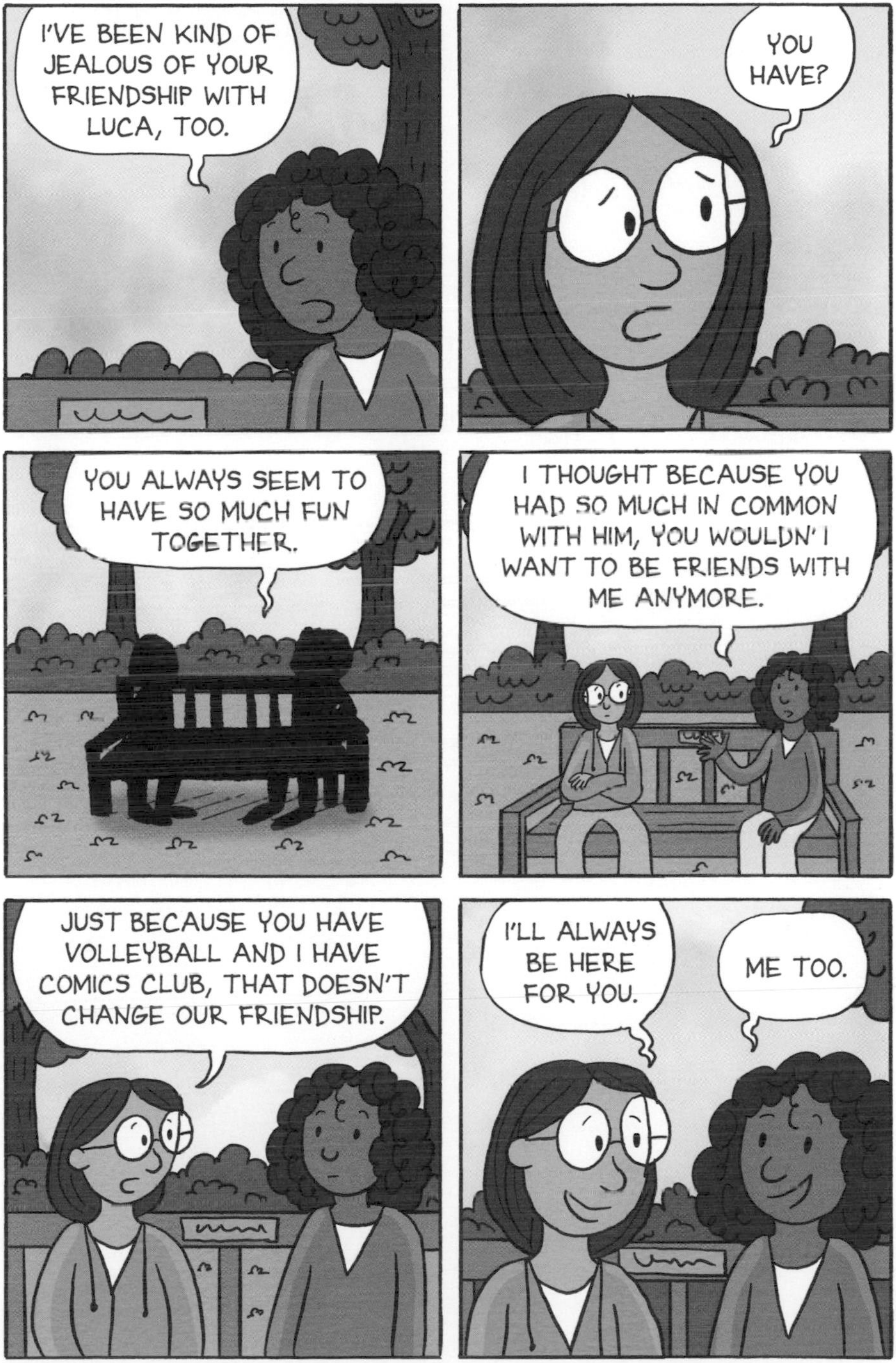
I'VE BEEN KIND OF JEALOUS OF YOUR FRIENDSHIP WITH LUCA, TOO.
YOU HAVE?
YOU ALWAYS SEEM TO HAVE SO MUCH FUN TOGETHER.
I THOUGHT BECAUSE YOU HAD SO MUCH IN COMMON WITH HIM, YOU WOULDN'T WANT TO BE FRIENDS WITH ME ANYMORE.
JUST BECAUSE YOU HAVE VOLLEYBALL AND I HAVE COMICS CLUB, THAT DOESN'T CHANGE OUR FRIENDSHIP.
I'LL ALWAYS BE HERE FOR YOU.
ME TOO.

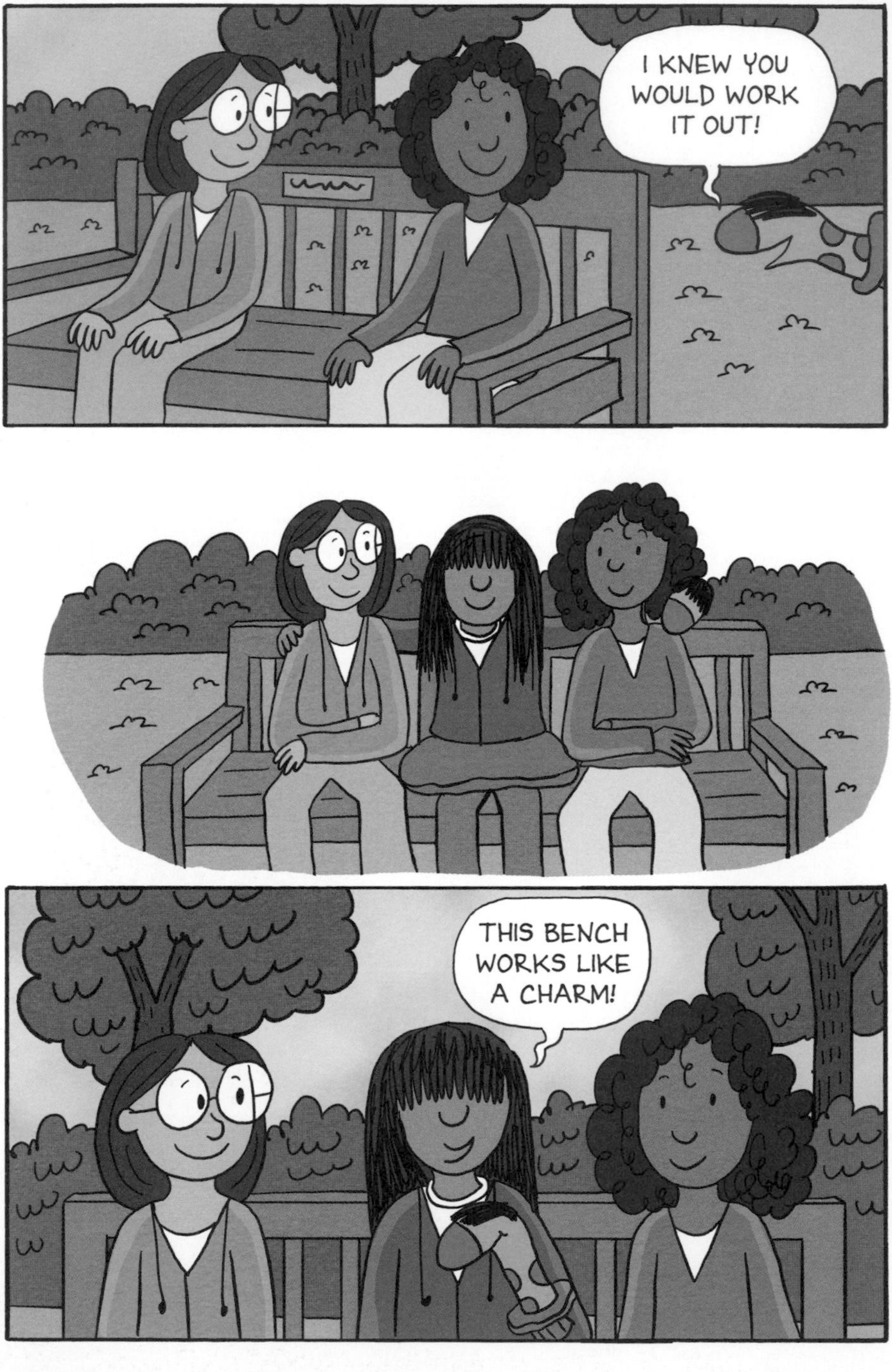
I KNEW YOU WOULD WORK IT OUT!
THIS BENCH WORKS LIKE A CHARM!

CHAPTER 16
YOU CAN DO IT

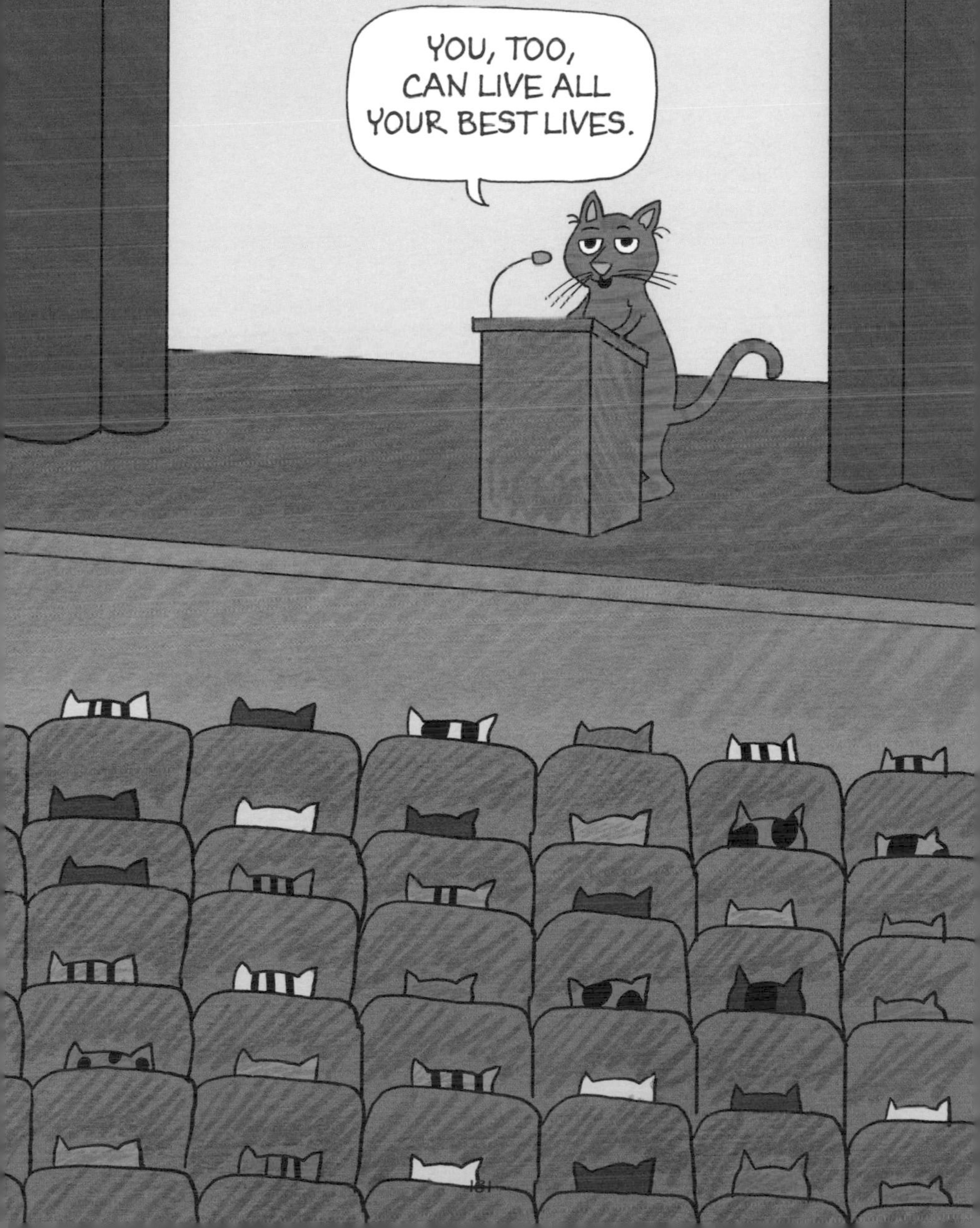
YOU, TOO, CAN LIVE ALL YOUR BEST LIVES.

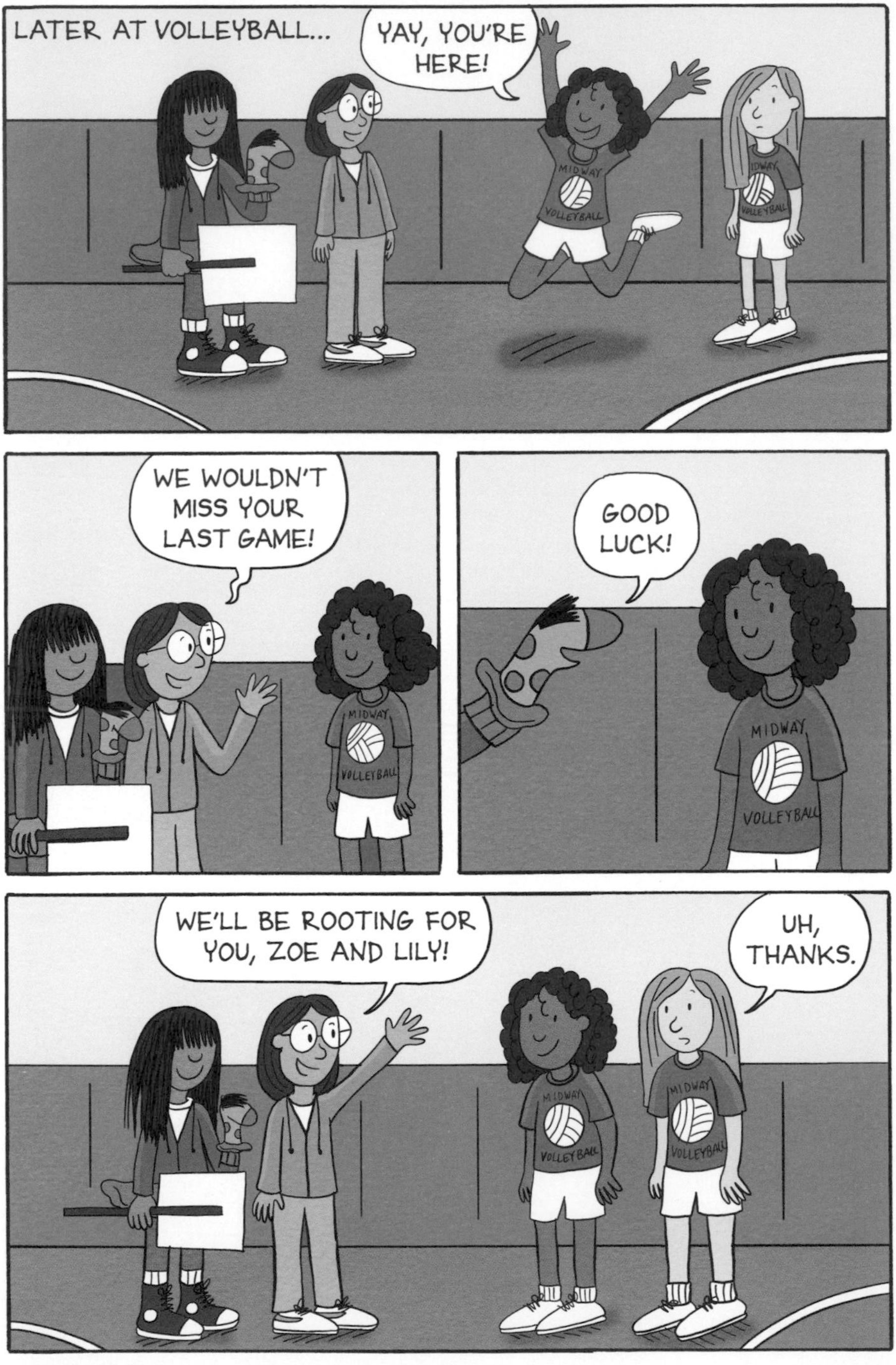
LATER AT VOLLEYBALL...
YAY, YOU'RE HERE!
MIDWAY VOLLEYBALL
MIDWAY VOLLEYBALL
WE WOULDN'T MISS YOUR LAST GAME!
MIDWAY VOLLEYBALL
GOOD LUCK!
MIDWAY VOLLEYBALL
WE'LL BE ROOTING FOR YOU, ZOE AND LILY!
UH, THANKS.
MIDWAY VOLLEYBALL
MIDWAY VOLLEYBALL

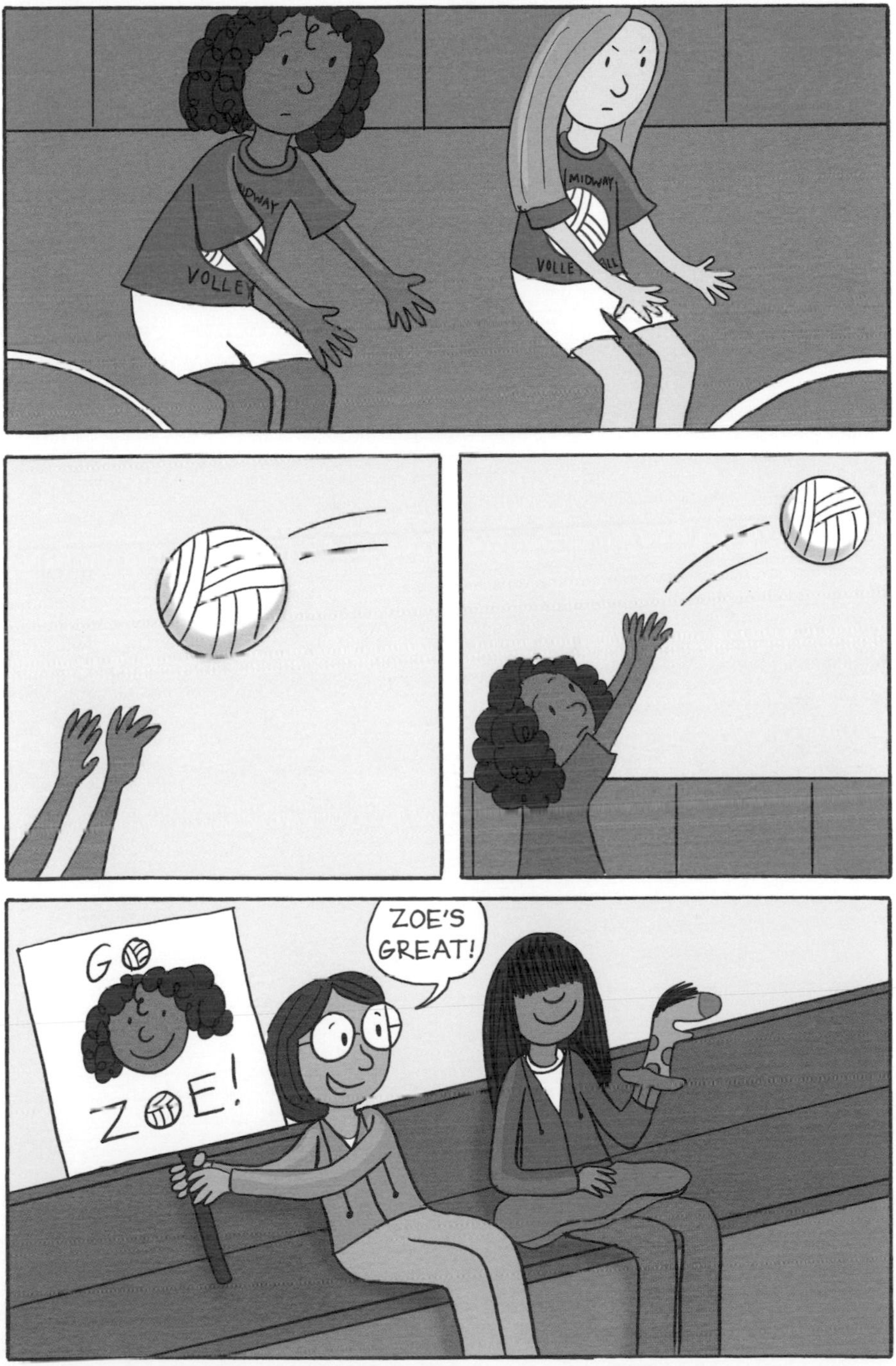
MIDWAY
VOLLEY
MIDWAY
VOLLEY
GO
ZOE!
ZOE'S GREAT!

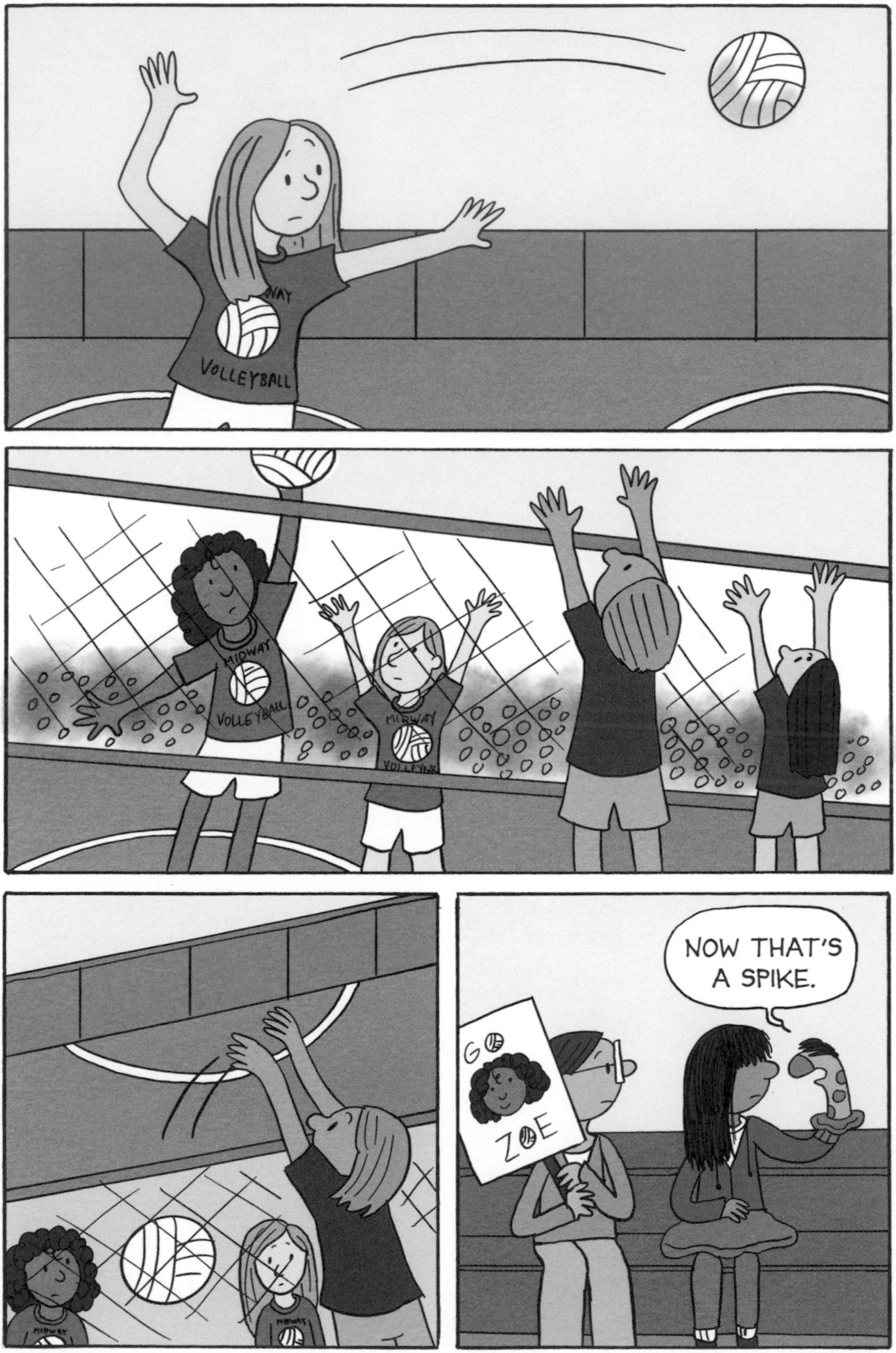
MIDWAY
VOLLEYBALL
MIDWAY
VOLLEYBALL
MIDWAY
NOW THAT'S A SPIKE.
GO
ZOE

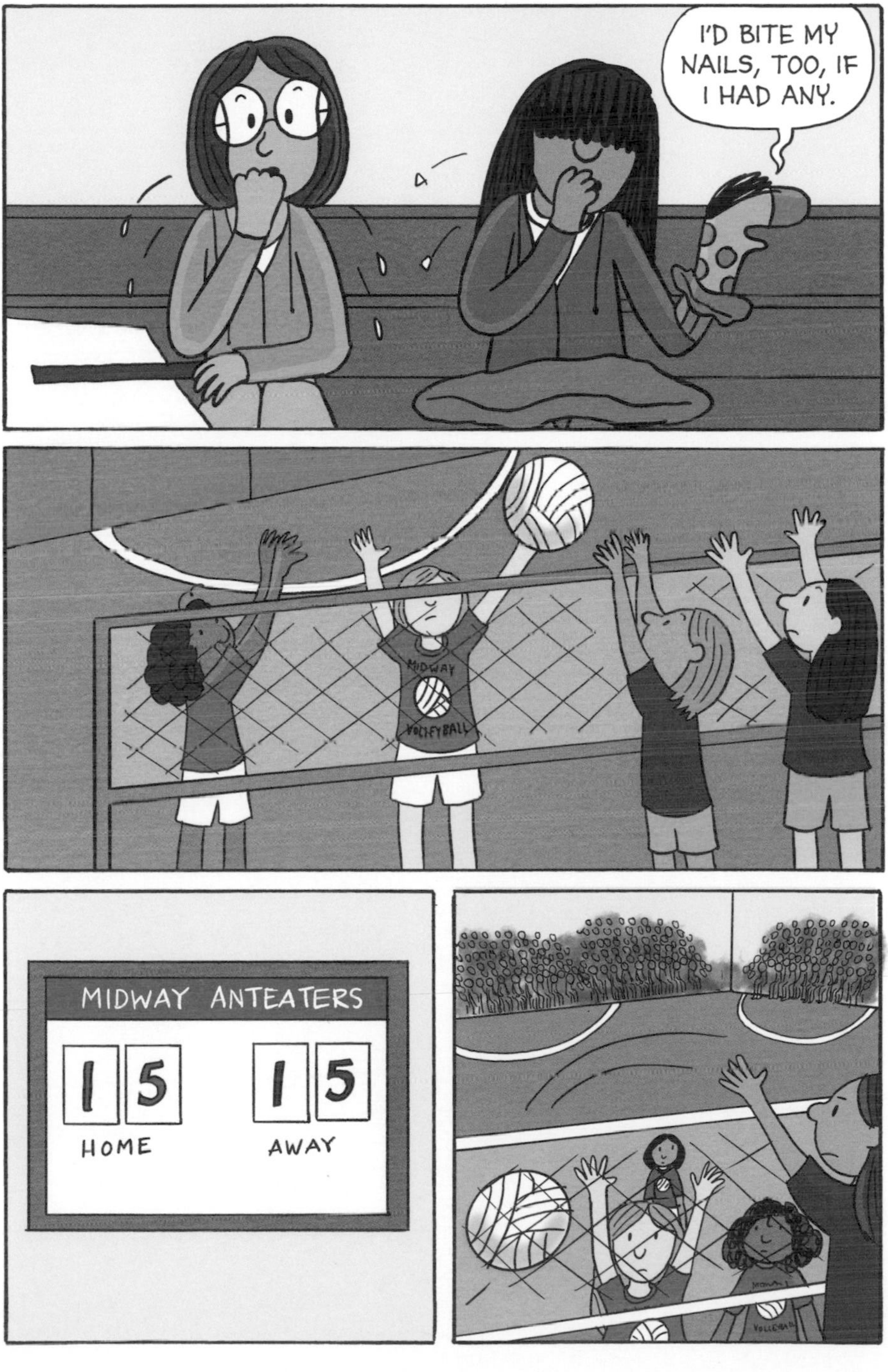
I'D BITE MY NAILS, TOO, IF I HAD ANY.
MIDWAY VOLLEYBALL
MIDWAY ANTEATERS
15
15
HOME
AWAY

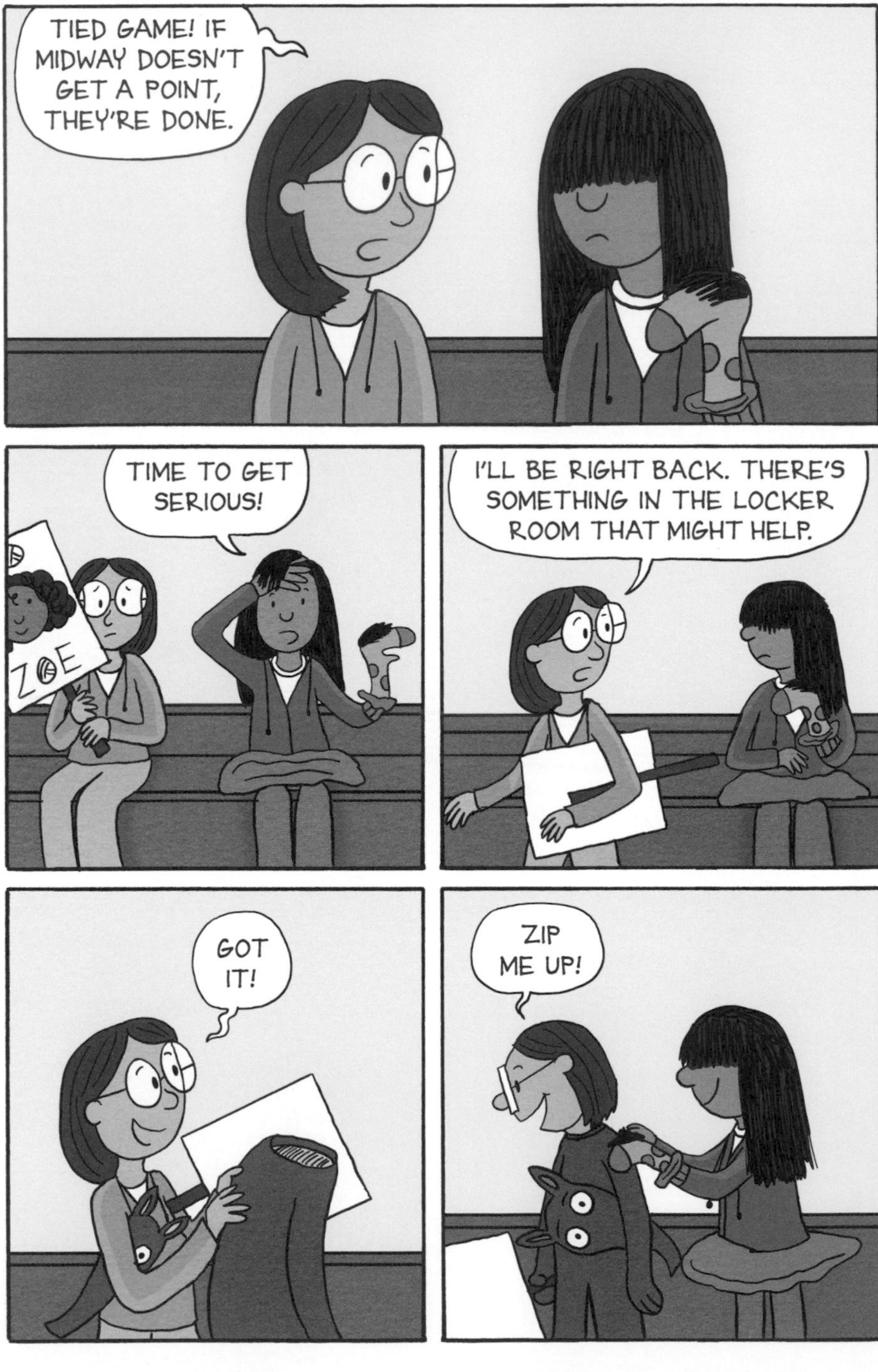
TIED GAME! IF MIDWAY DOESN'T GET A POINT, THEY'RE DONE.
TIME TO GET SERIOUS!
ZOE
I'LL BE RIGHT BACK. THERE'S SOMETHING IN THE LOCKER ROOM THAT MIGHT HELP.
GOT IT!
ZIP ME UP!

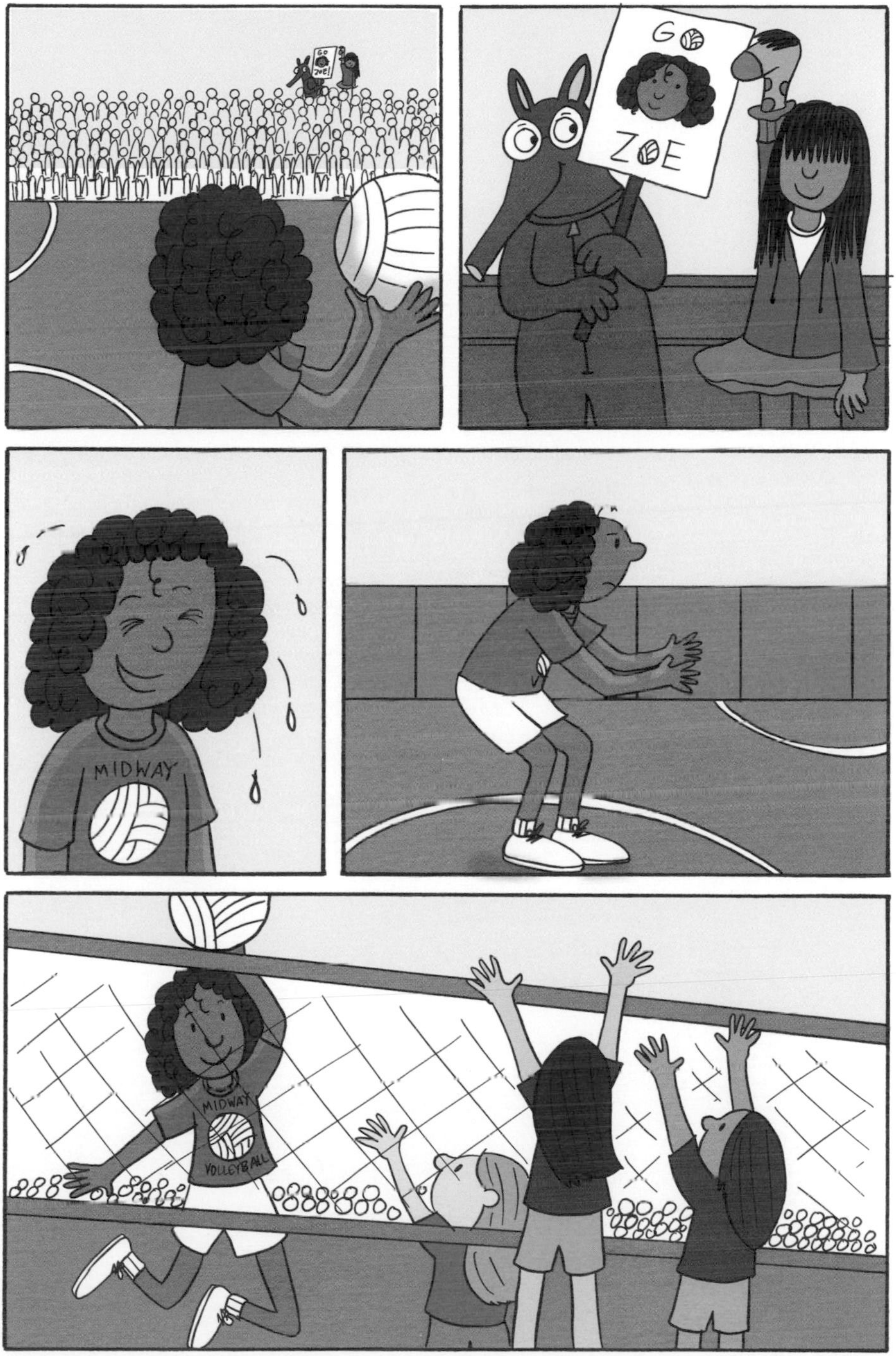
GO ZOE
MIDWAY
MIDWAY VOLLEYBALL

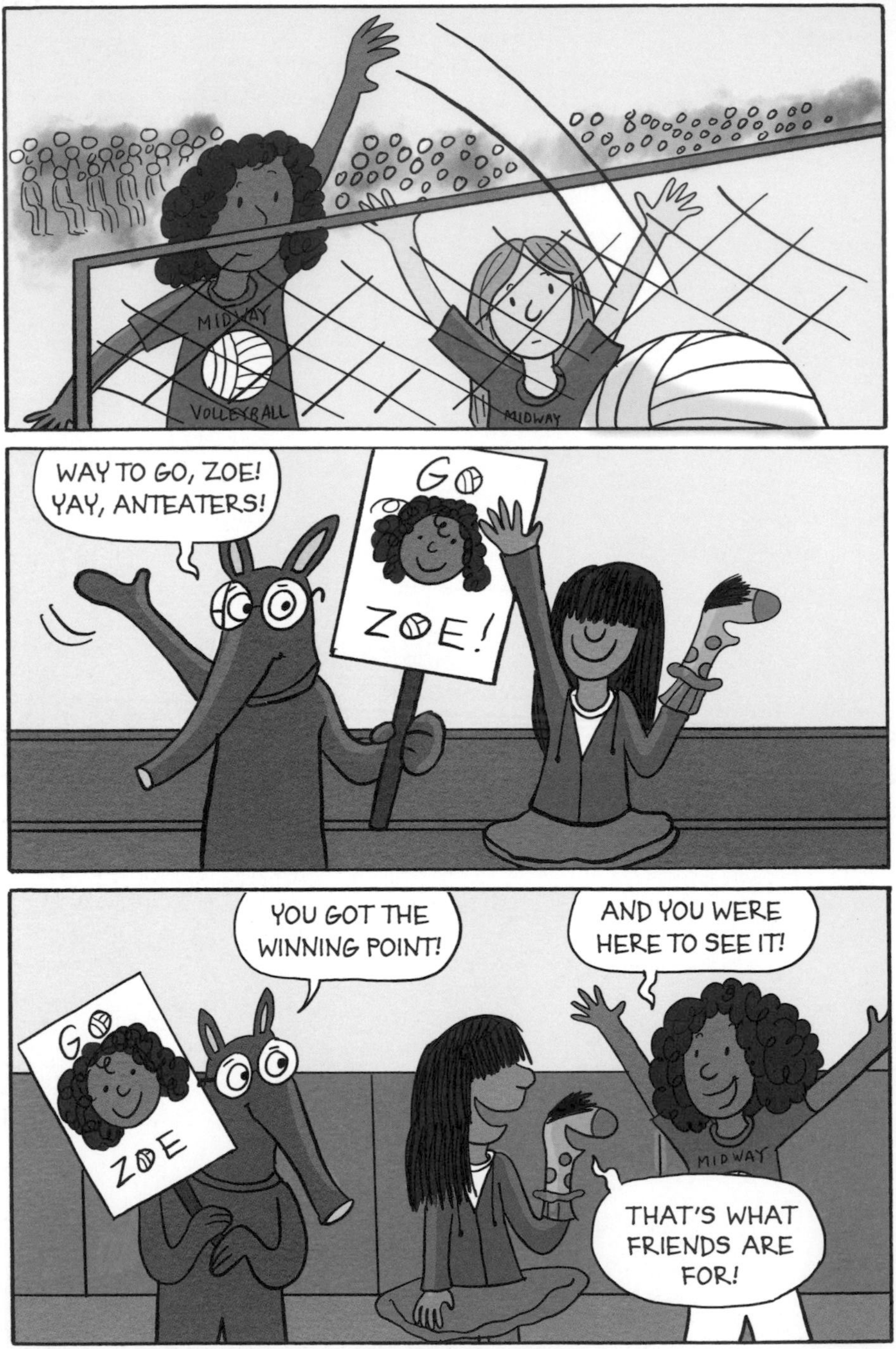
MIDWAY
VOLLEYBALL
MIDWAY
WAY TO GO, ZOE! YAY, ANTEATERS!
GO ZOE!
YOU GOT THE WINNING POINT!
AND YOU WERE HERE TO SEE IT!
GO ZOE
MIDWAY
THAT'S WHAT FRIENDS ARE FOR!

CHAPTER 17
PRESENTATION

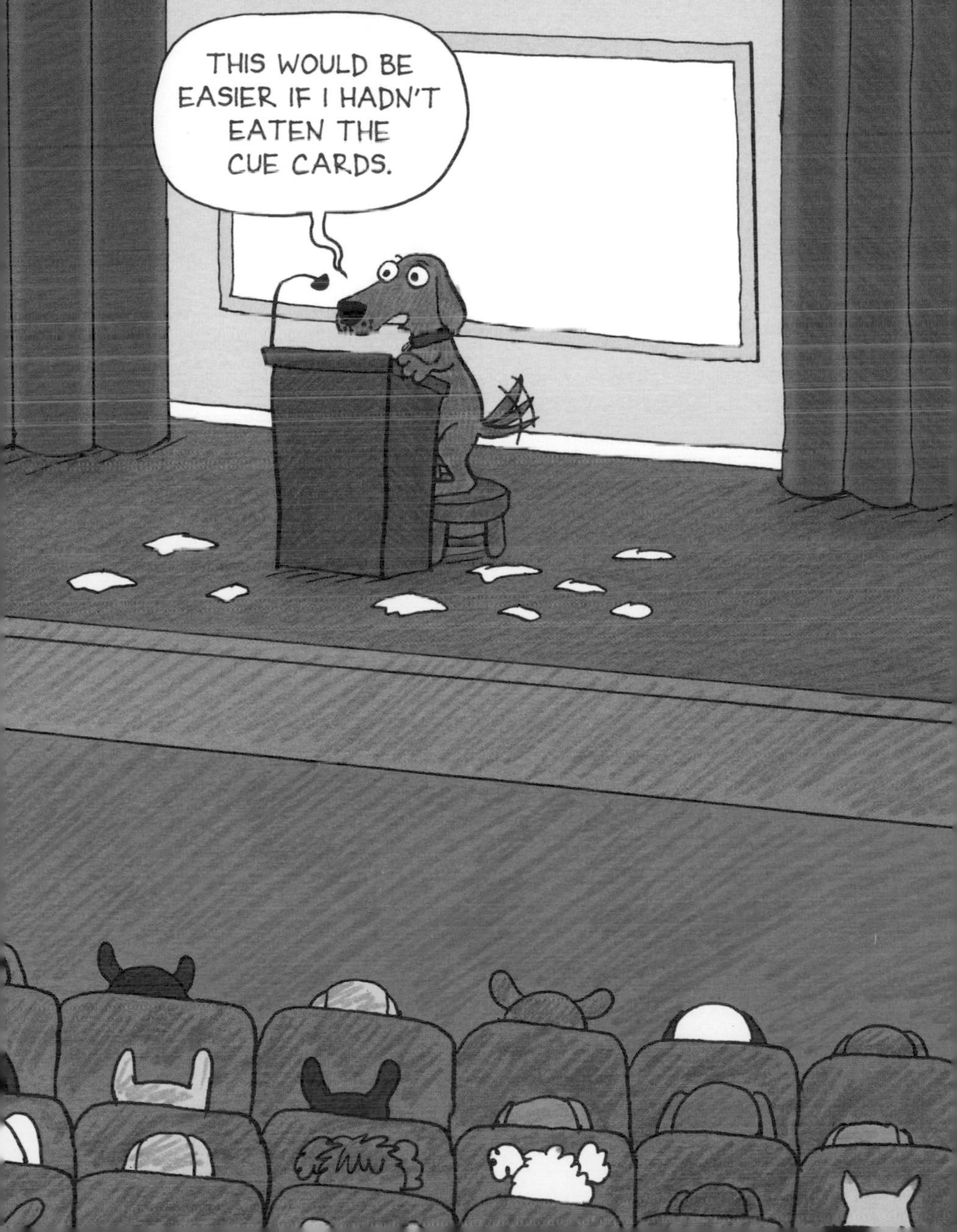
THIS WOULD BE EASIER IF I HADN'T EATEN THE CUE CARDS.

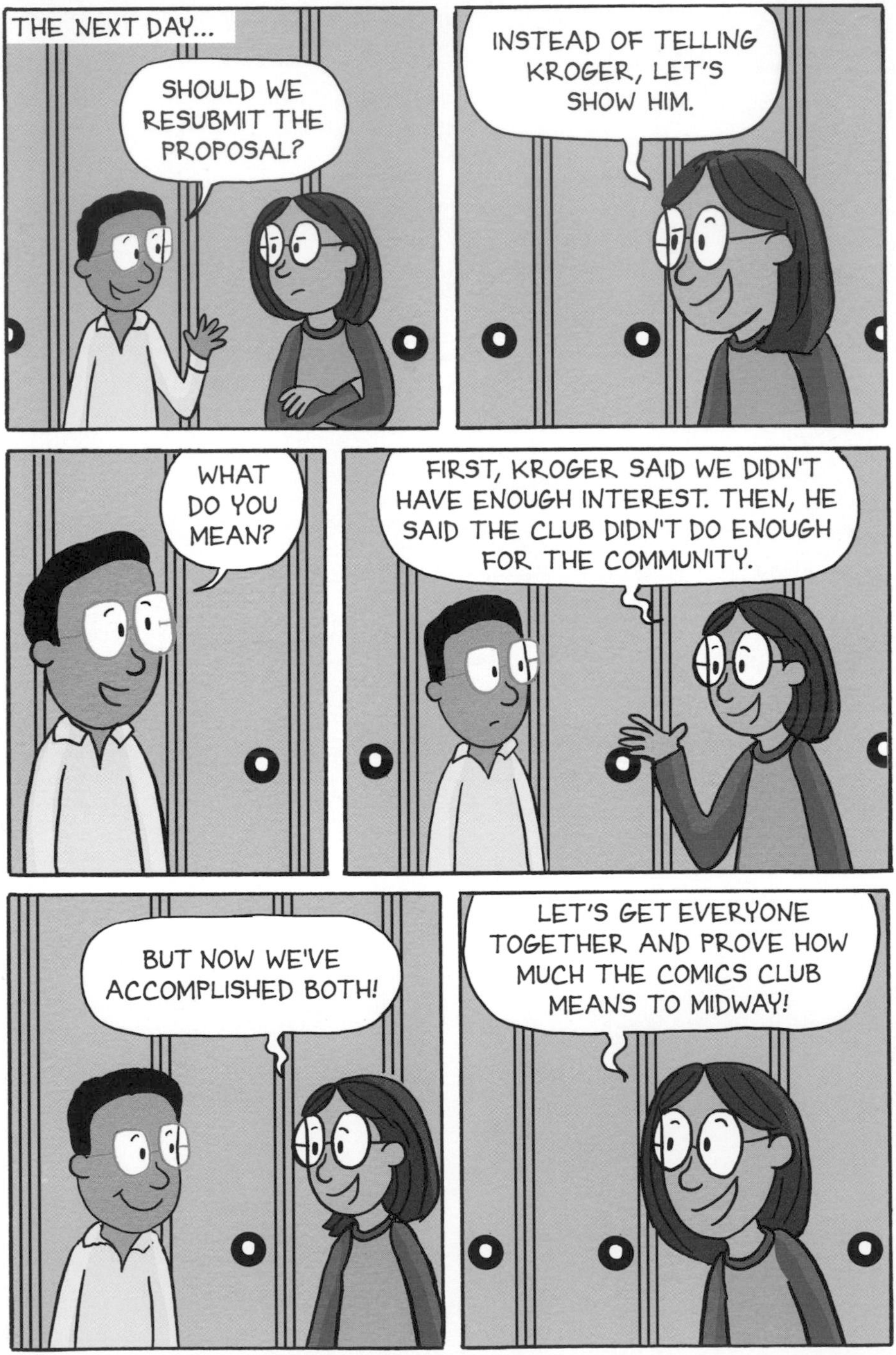
THE NEXT DAY...
SHOULD WE RESUBMIT THE PROPOSAL?
INSTEAD OF TELLING KROGER, LET'S SHOW HIM.
WHAT DO YOU MEAN?
FIRST, KROGER SAID WE DIDN'T HAVE ENOUGH INTEREST. THEN, HE SAID THE CLUB DIDN'T DO ENOUGH FOR THE COMMUNITY.
BUT NOW WE'VE ACCOMPLISHED BOTH!
LET'S GET EVERYONE TOGETHER AND PROVE HOW MUCH THE COMICS CLUB MEANS TO MIDWAY!

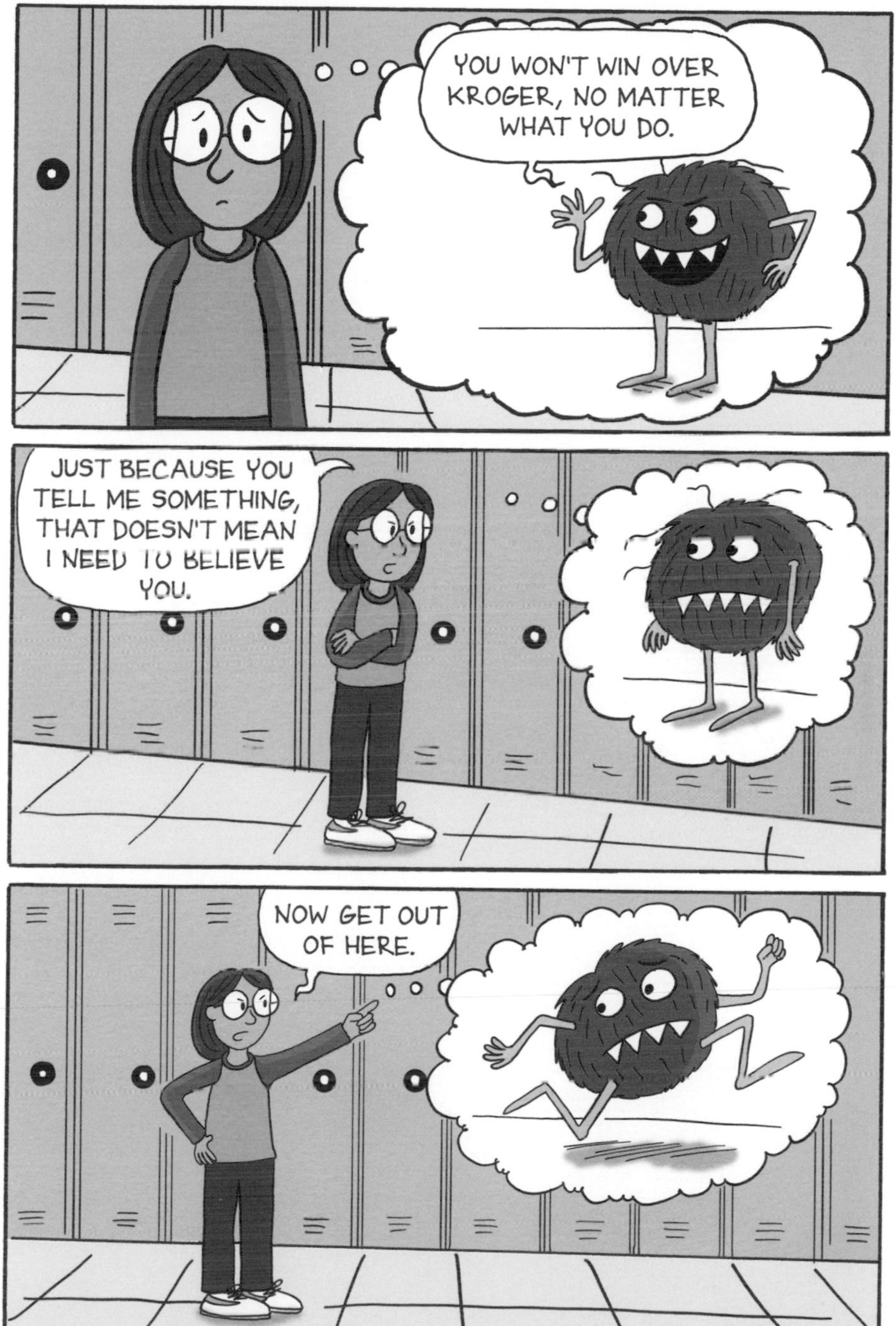
YOU WON'T WIN OVER KROGER, NO MATTER WHAT YOU DO.
JUST BECAUSE YOU TELL ME SOMETHING, THAT DOESN'T MEAN I NEED TO BELIEVE YOU.
NOW GET OUT OF HERE.

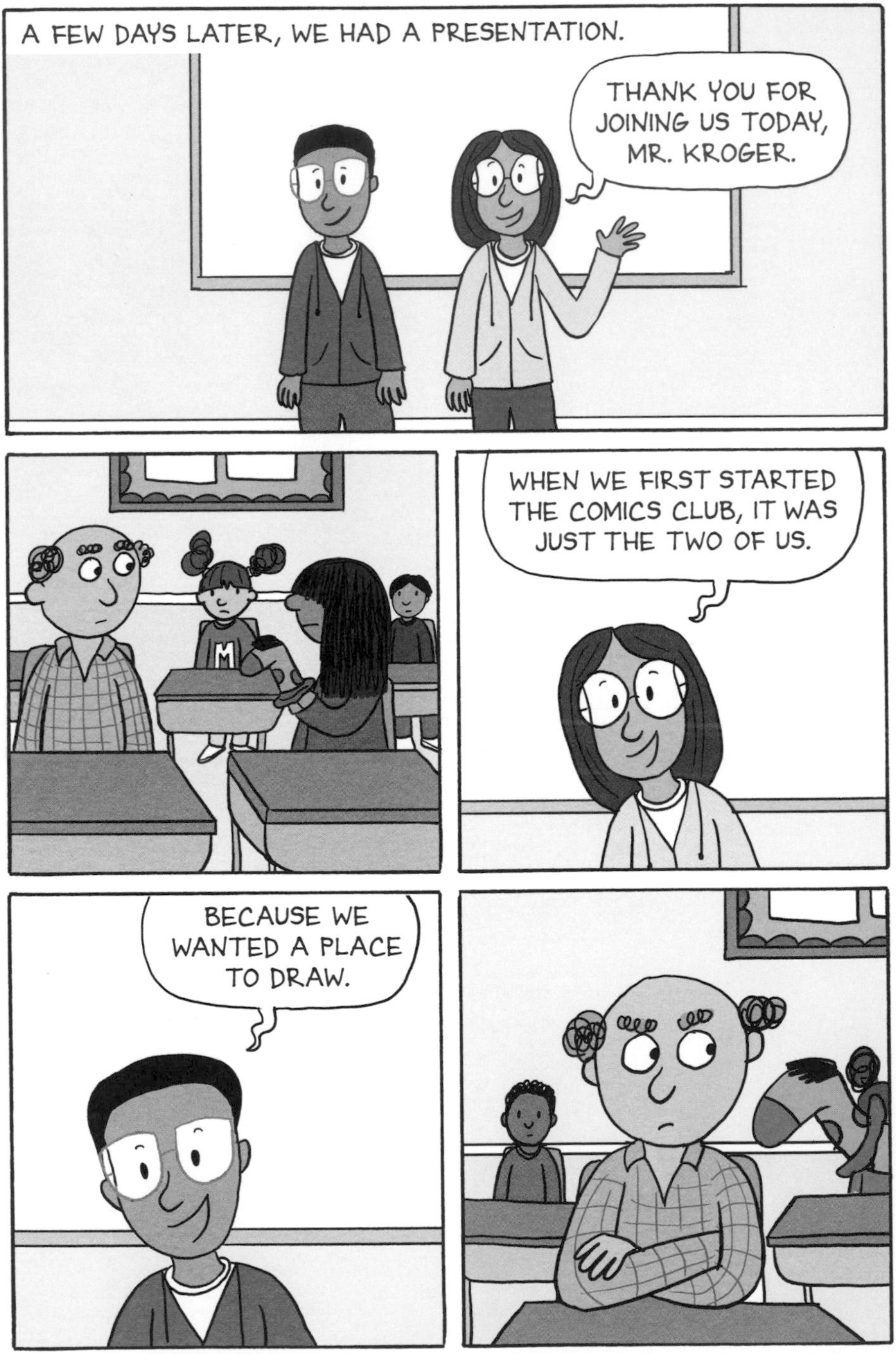
A FEW DAYS LATER, WE HAD A PRESENTATION.
THANK YOU FOR JOINING US TODAY, MR. KROGER.
WHEN WE FIRST STARTED THE COMICS CLUB, IT WAS JUST THE TWO OF US.
BECAUSE WE WANTED A PLACE TO DRAW.

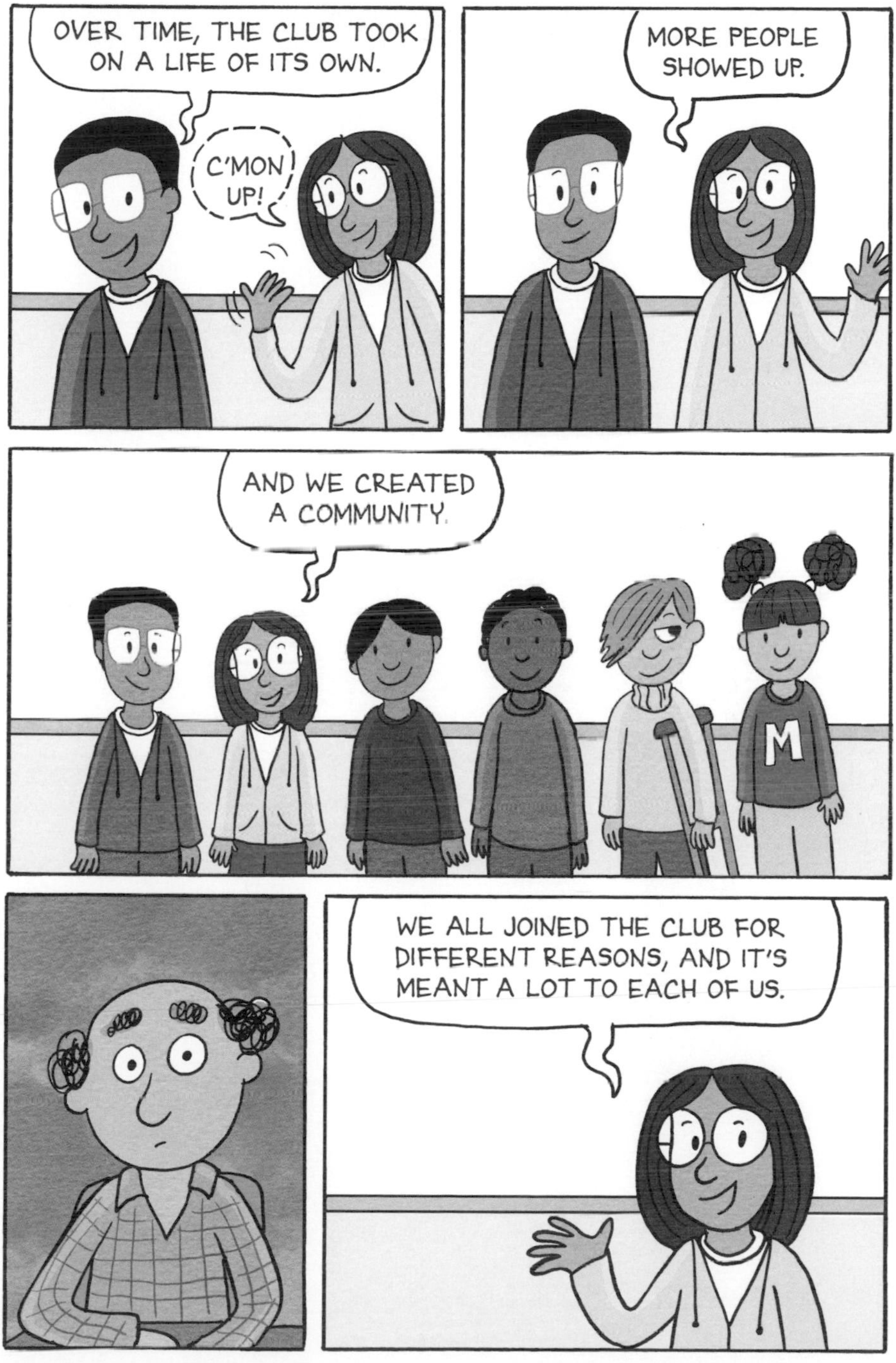
OVER TIME, THE CLUB TOOK ON A LIFE OF ITS OWN.
C'MON UP!
MORE PEOPLE SHOWED UP.
AND WE CREATED A COMMUNITY.
M
WE ALL JOINED THE CLUB FOR DIFFERENT REASONS, AND IT'S MEANT A LOT TO EACH OF US.

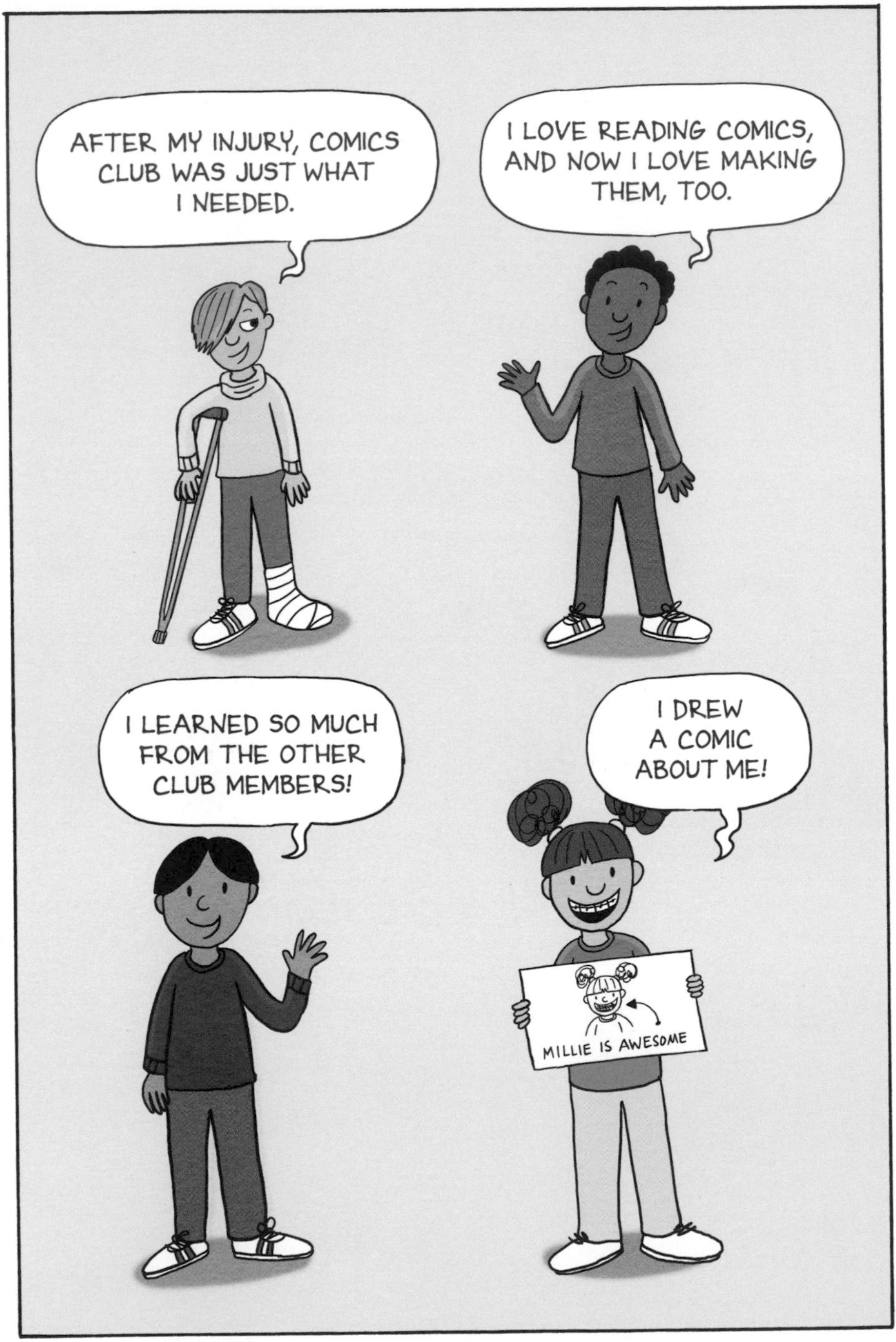
AFTER MY INJURY, COMICS CLUB WAS JUST WHAT I NEEDED.
I LOVE READING COMICS, AND NOW I LOVE MAKING THEM, TOO.
I LEARNED SO MUCH FROM THE OTHER CLUB MEMBERS!
I DREW A COMIC ABOUT ME!
MILLIE IS AWESOME

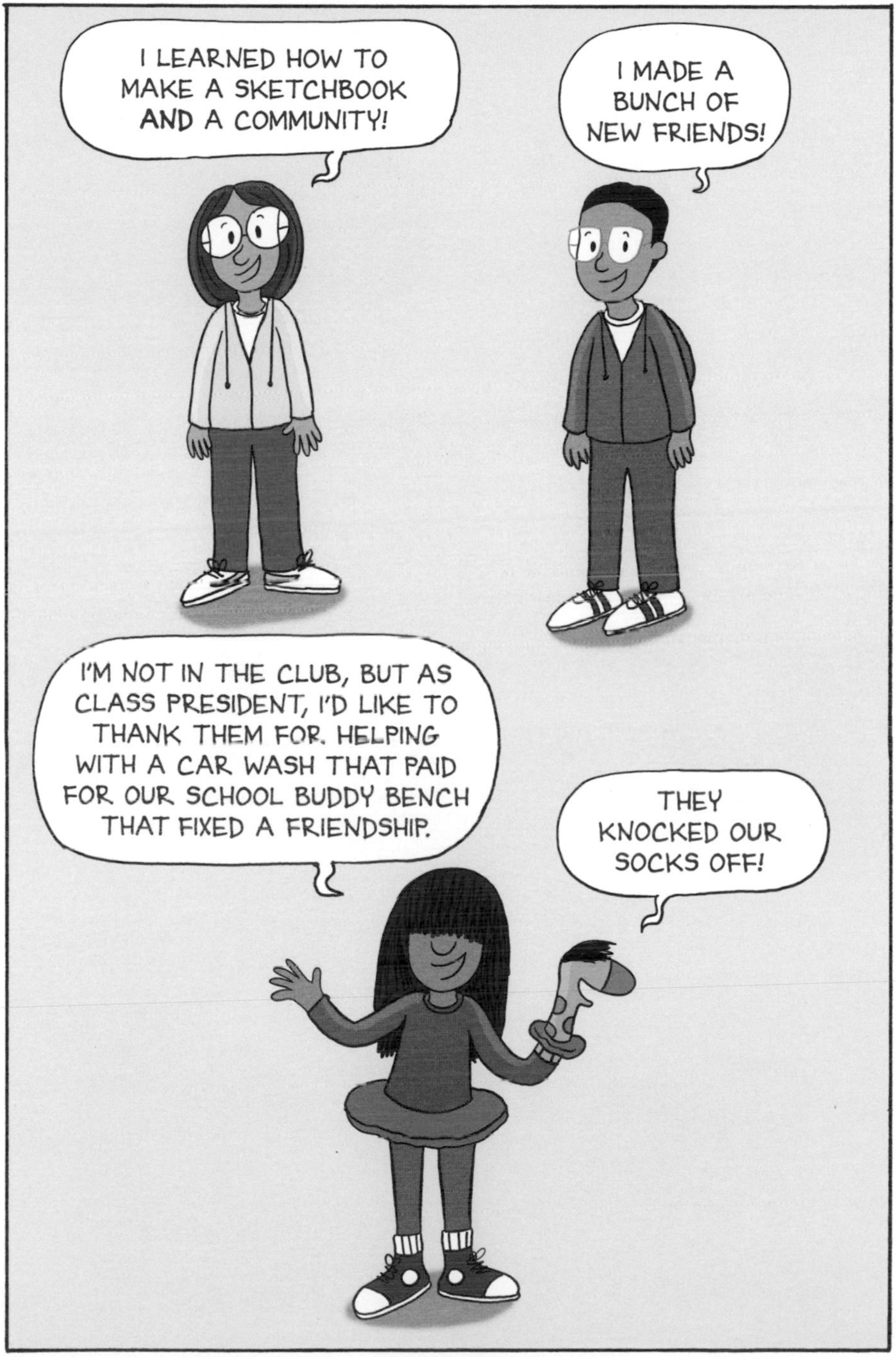
I LEARNED HOW TO MAKE A SKETCHBOOK AND A COMMUNITY!
I MADE A BUNCH OF NEW FRIENDS!
I'M NOT IN THE CLUB, BUT AS CLASS PRESIDENT, I'D LIKE TO THANK THEM FOR HELPING WITH A CAR WASH THAT PAID FOR OUR SCHOOL BUDDY BENCH THAT FIXED A FRIENDSHIP.
THEY KNOCKED OUR SOCKS OFF!

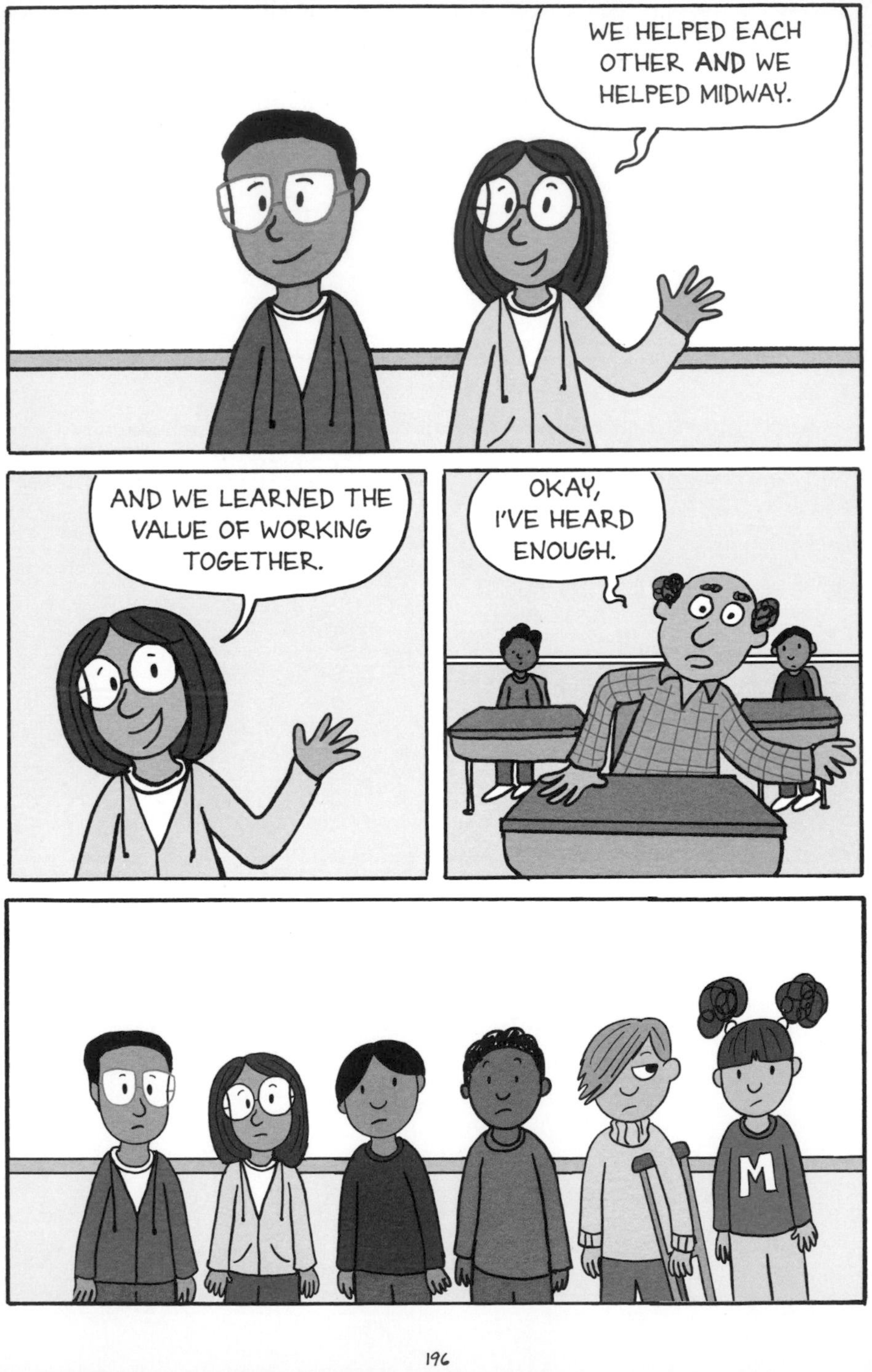
WE HELPED EACH OTHER AND WE HELPED MIDWAY.
AND WE LEARNED THE VALUE OF WORKING TOGETHER.
OKAY, I'VE HEARD ENOUGH.
M

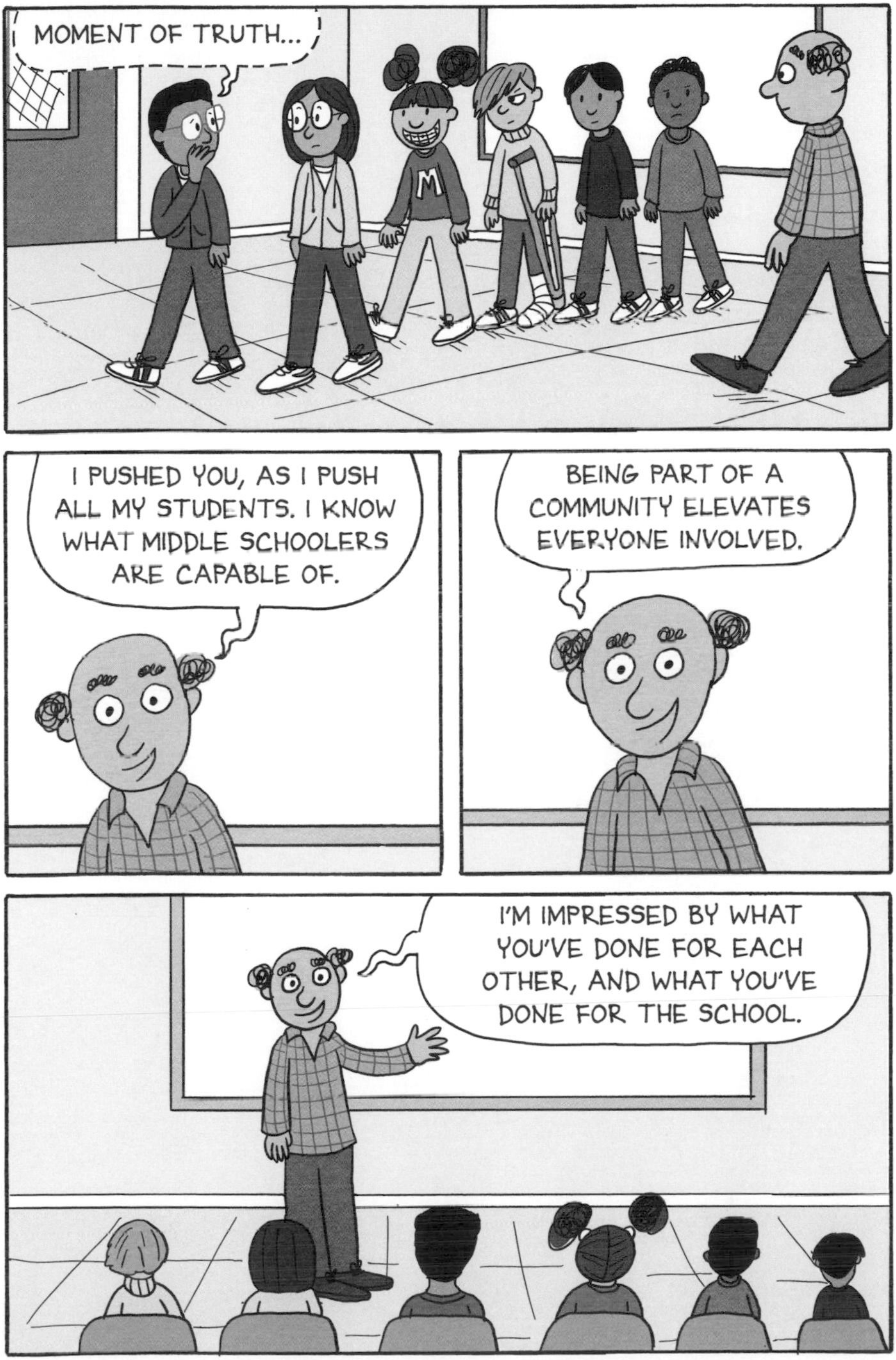
MOMENT OF TRUTH...
I PUSHED YOU, AS I PUSH ALL MY STUDENTS. I KNOW WHAT MIDDLE SCHOOLERS ARE CAPABLE OF.
BEING PART OF A COMMUNITY ELEVATES EVERYONE INVOLVED.
I'M IMPRESSED BY WHAT YOU'VE DONE FOR EACH OTHER, AND WHAT YOU'VE DONE FOR THE SCHOOL.

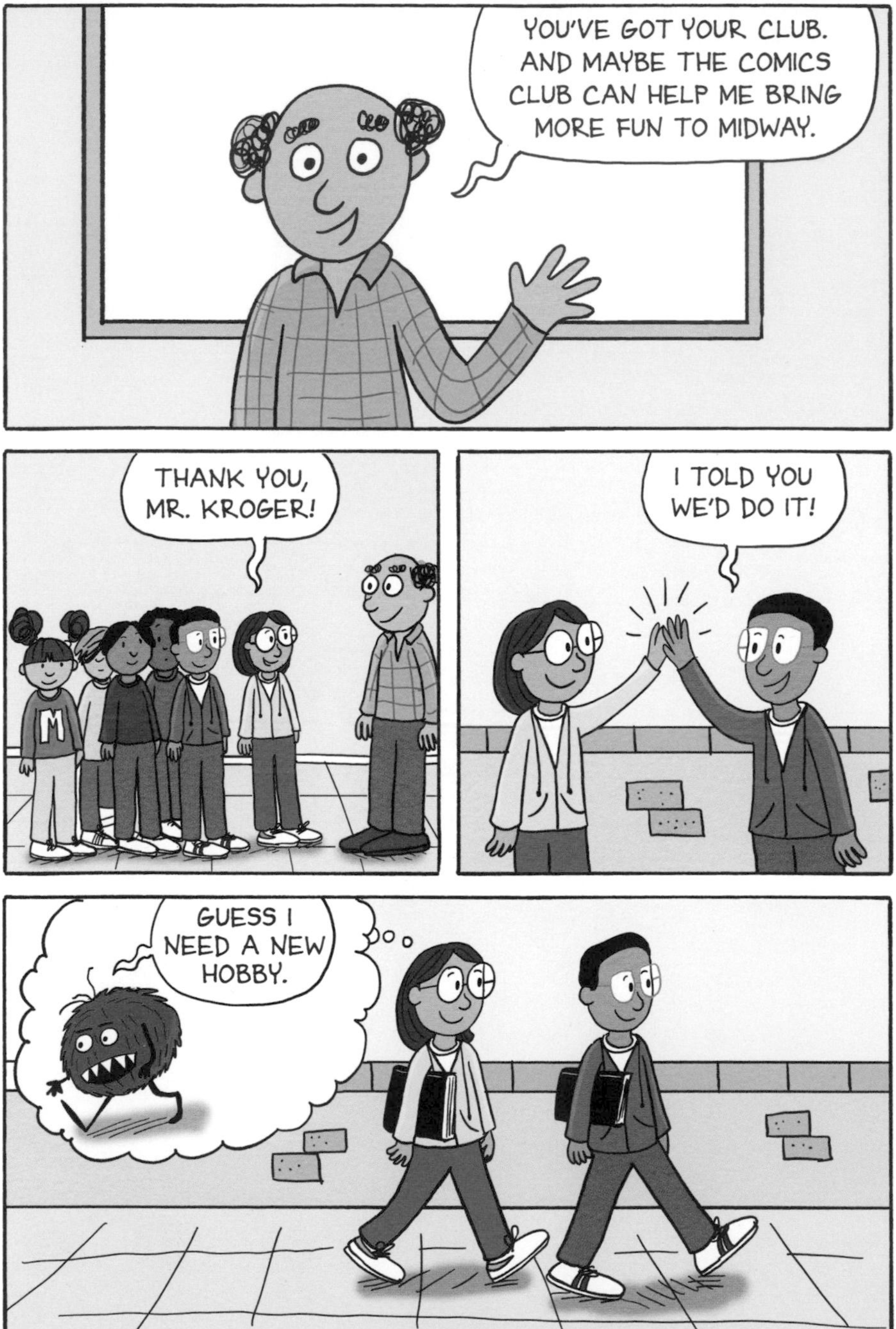
YOU'VE GOT YOUR CLUB. AND MAYBE THE COMICS CLUB CAN HELP ME BRING MORE FUN TO MIDWAY.
THANK YOU, MR. KROGER!
I TOLD YOU WE'D DO IT!
GUESS I NEED A NEW HOBBY.

CHAPTER 18
WAKE UP

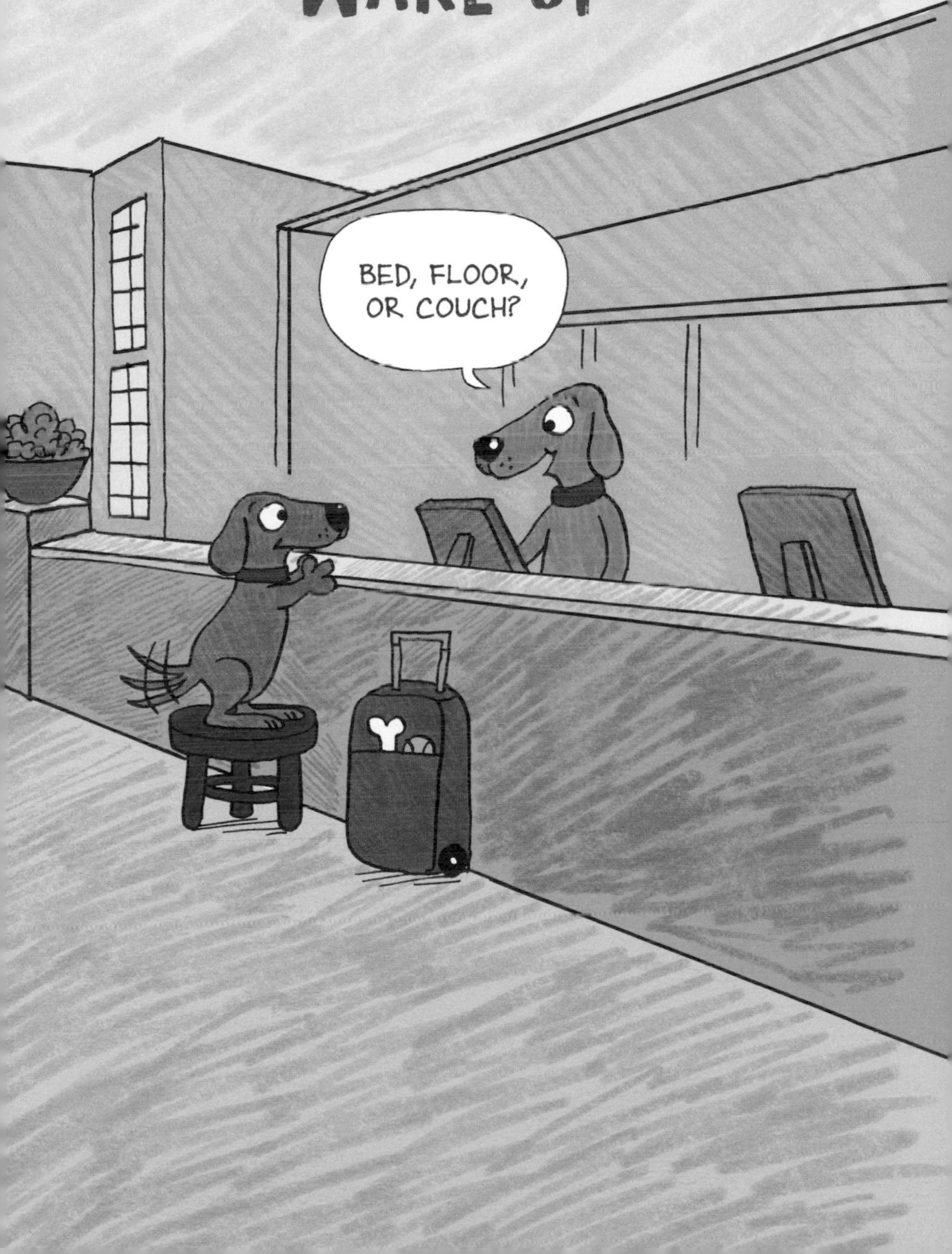
BED, FLOOR,
OR COUCH?

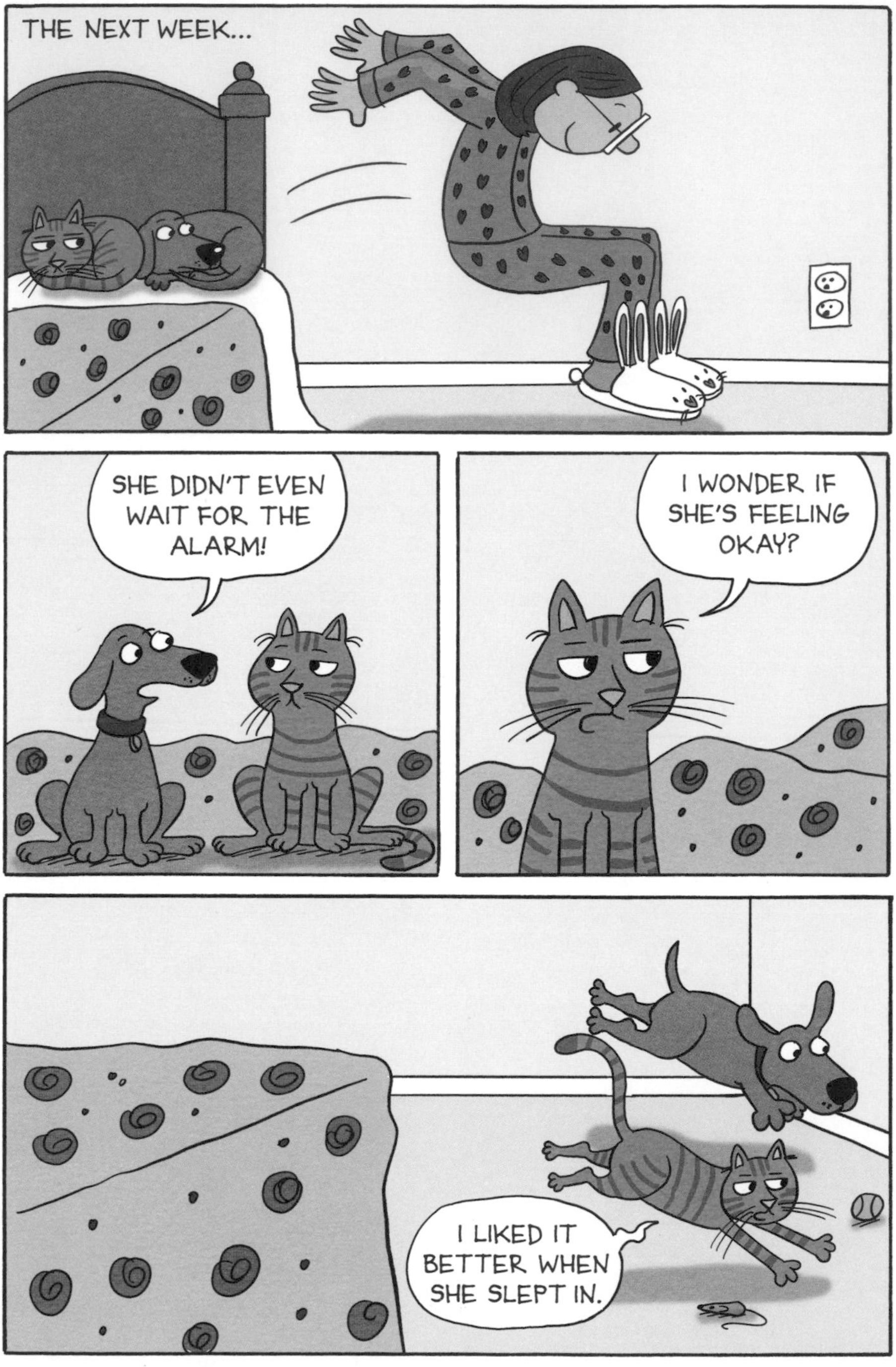
THE NEXT WEEK...
SHE DIDN'T EVEN WAIT FOR THE ALARM!
I WONDER IF SHE'S FEELING OKAY?
I LIKED IT BETTER WHEN SHE SLEPT IN.

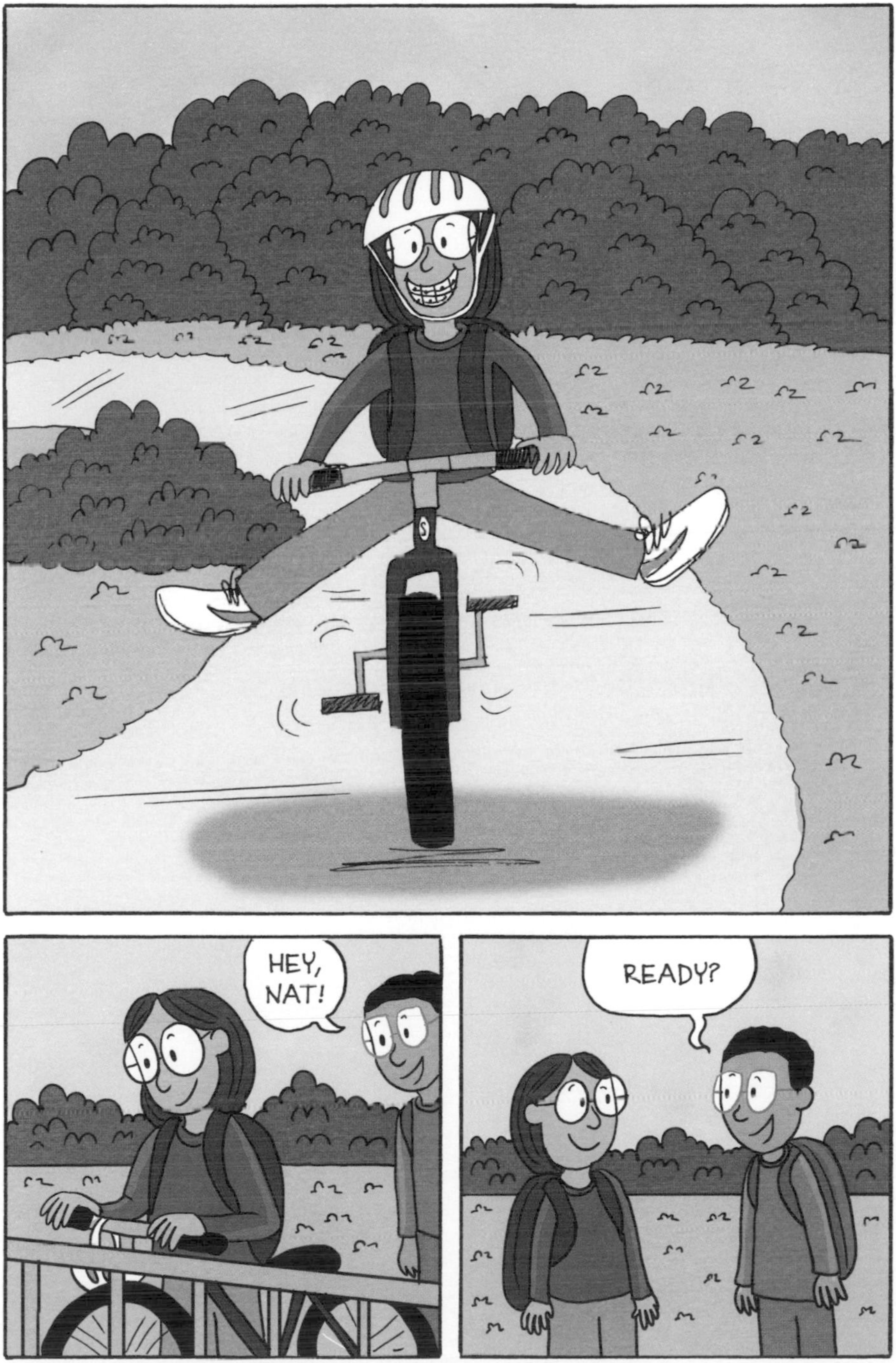
HEY, NAT!
READY?

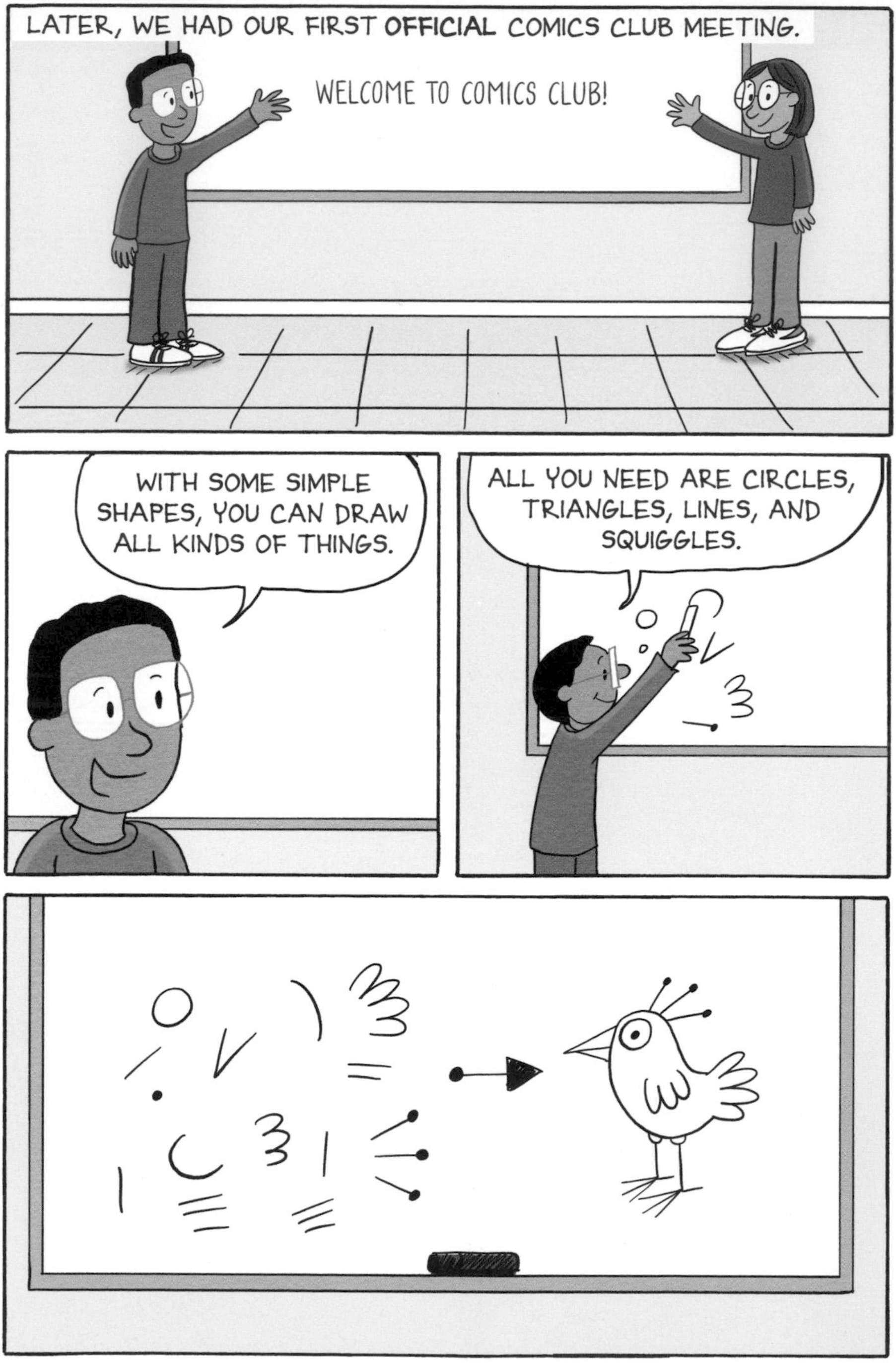
LATER, WE HAD OUR FIRST OFFICIAL COMICS CLUB MEETING.
WELCOME TO COMICS CLUB!
WITH SOME SIMPLE SHAPES, YOU CAN DRAW ALL KINDS OF THINGS.
ALL YOU NEED ARE CIRCLES, TRIANGLES, LINES, AND SQUIGGLES.

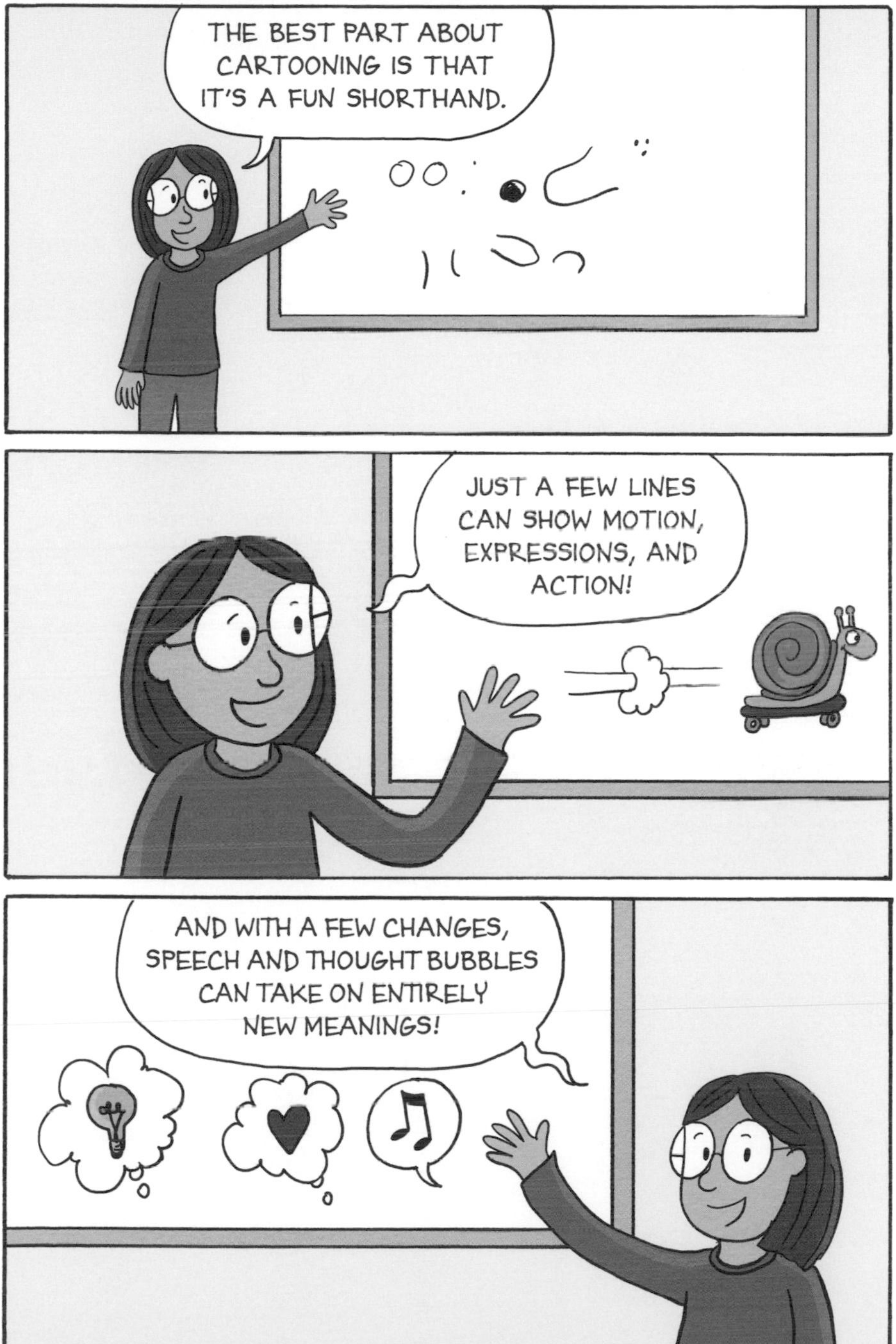
THE BEST PART ABOUT CARTOONING IS THAT IT'S A FUN SHORTHAND.
JUST A FEW LINES CAN SHOW MOTION, EXPRESSIONS, AND ACTION!
AND WITH A FEW CHANGES, SPEECH AND THOUGHT BUBBLES CAN TAKE ON ENTIRELY NEW MEANINGS!

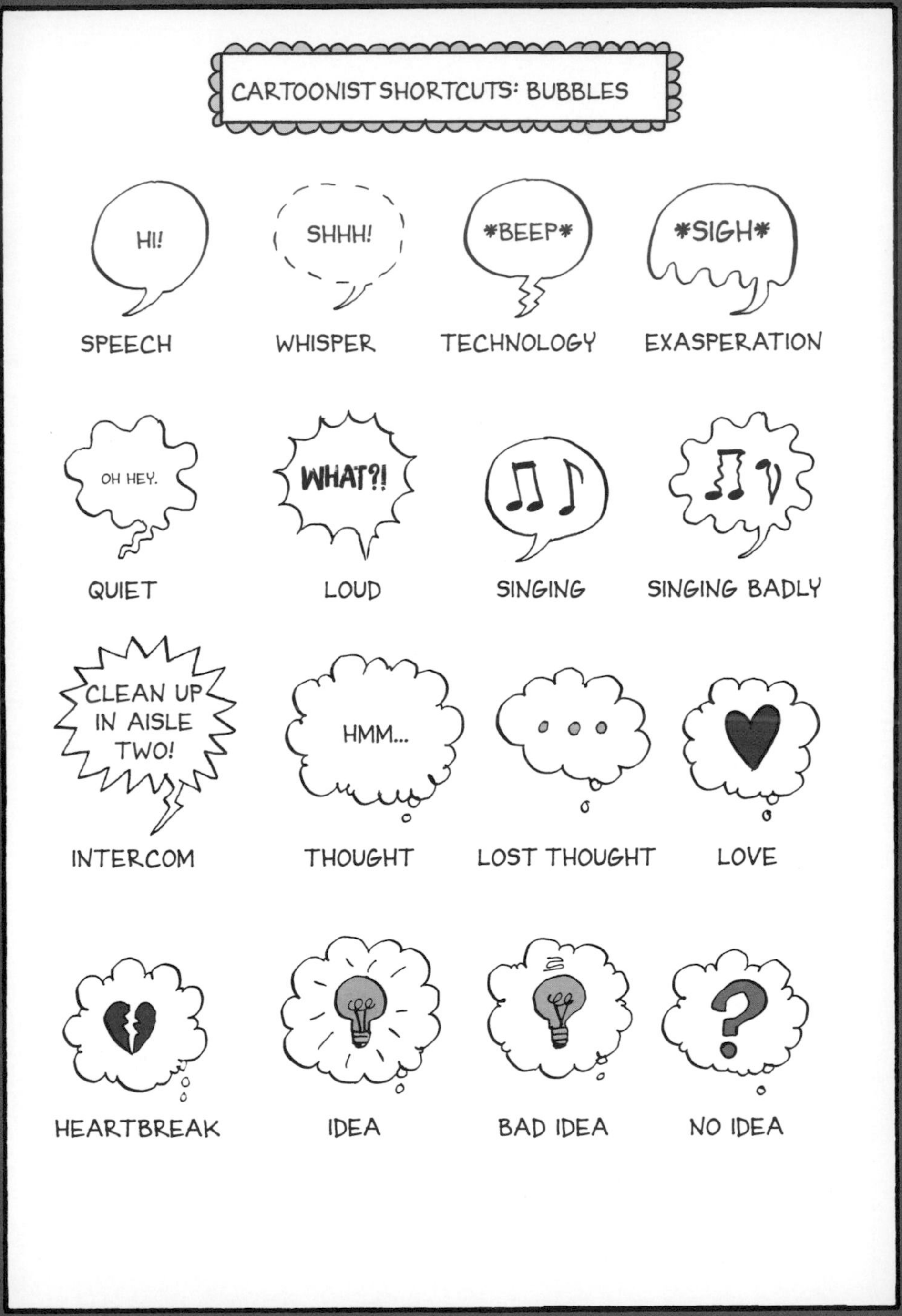
CARTOONIST SHORTCUTS: BUBBLES
HI!
SPEECH
SHHH!
WHISPER
BEEP
TECHNOLOGY
SIGH
EXASPERATION
OH HEY.
QUIET
WHAT?!
LOUD
SINGING
SINGING BADLY
CLEAN UP IN AISLE TWO!
INTERCOM
HMM...
THOUGHT
LOST THOUGHT
LOVE
HEARTBREAK
IDEA
BAD IDEA
NO IDEA

CARTOONIST SHORTCUTS: ACTIONS

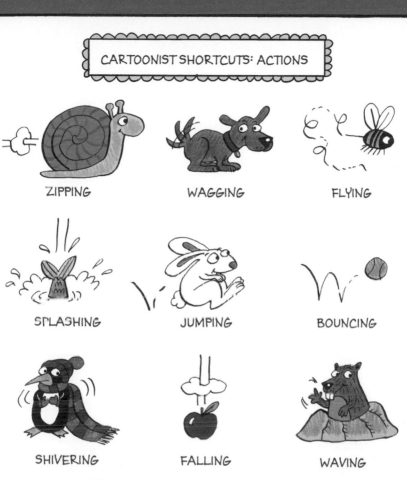

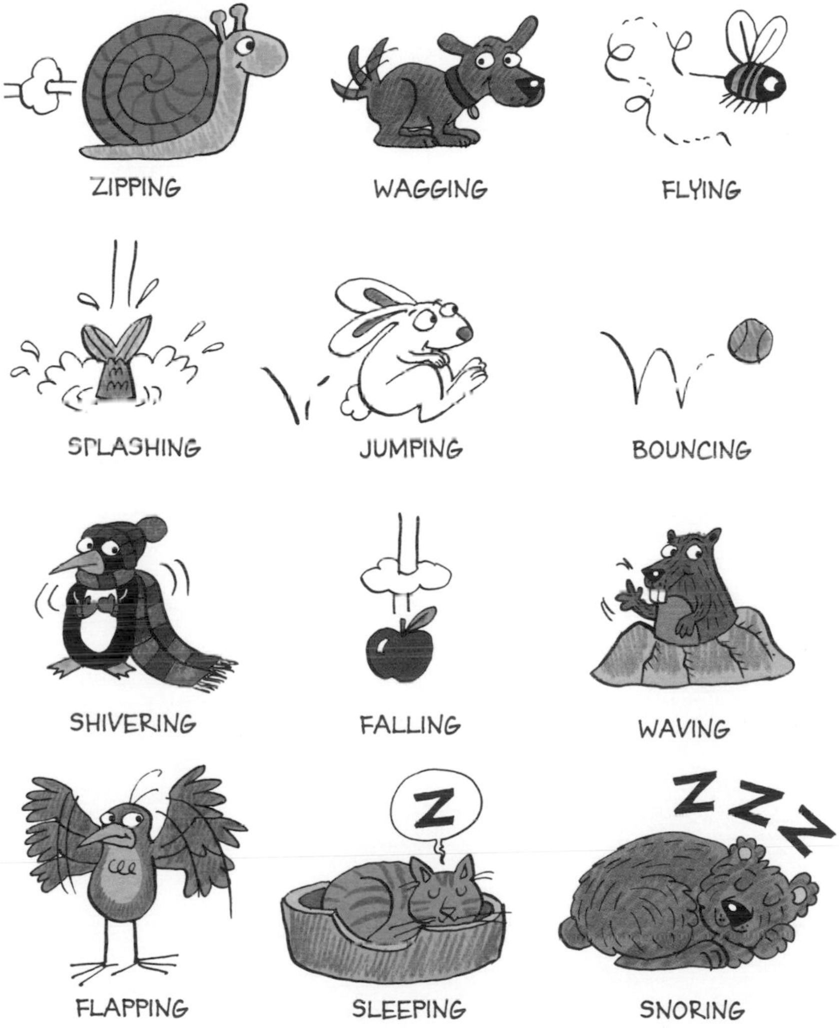
ZIPPING
WAGGING
FLYING
SPLASHING
JUMPING
BOUNCING
SHIVERING
FALLING
WAVING
Z
ZZZ
FLAPPING
SLEEPING
SNORING

EXPRESSIONS

HAPPY

REALLY HAPPY

CONFUSED

ANGRY

IN LOVE

HEARTBROKEN

EMBARRASSED

ANNOYED

SAD

EXPRESSIONS

EXHAUSTED

SWEATING

SHEEPISH

BAFFLED

SLEEPY

SLEEPING

PROUD

CONFIDENT

LAUGHING

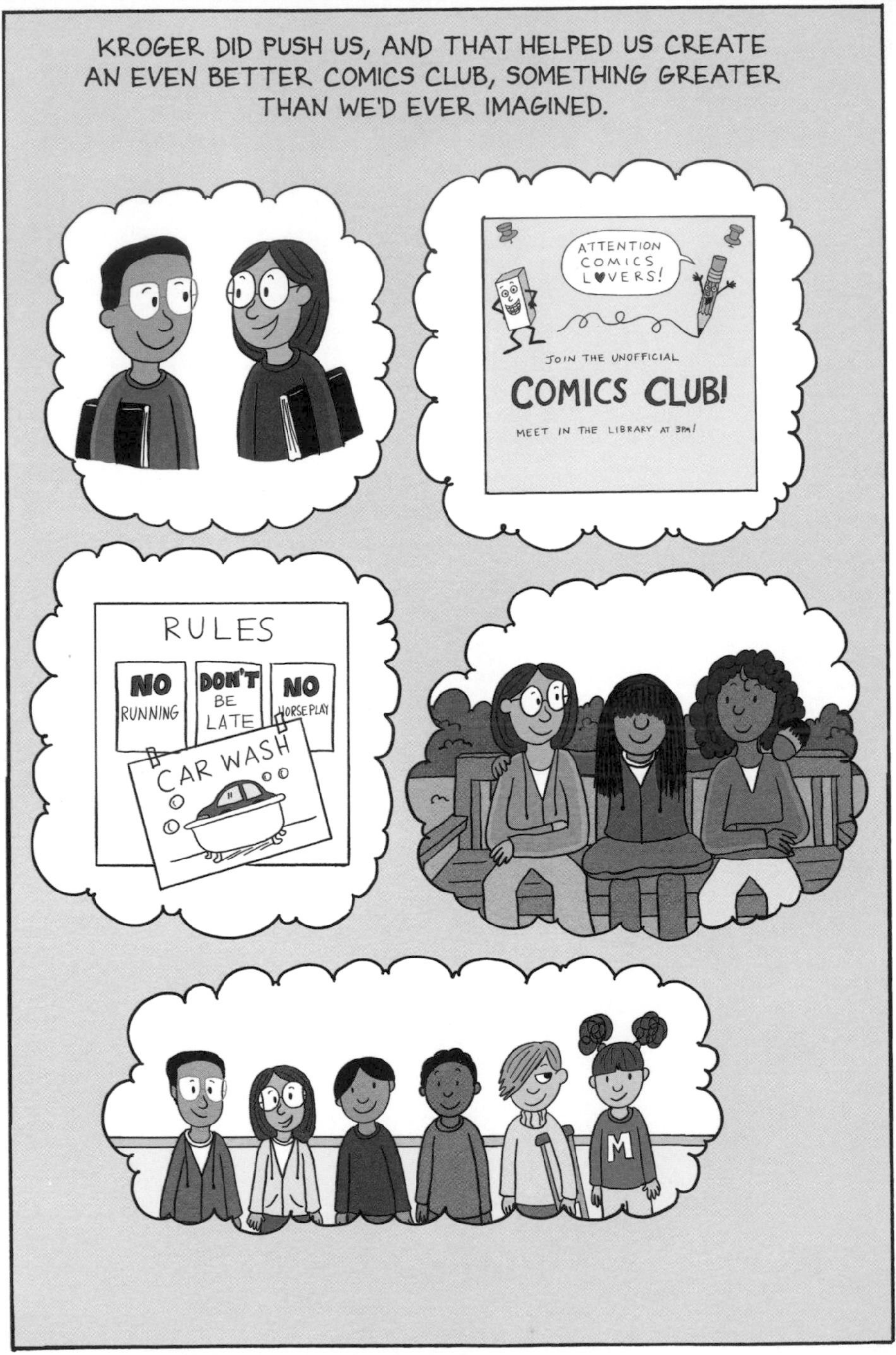
KROGER DID PUSH US, AND THAT HELPED US CREATE AN EVEN BETTER COMICS CLUB, SOMETHING GREATER THAN WE'D EVER IMAGINED.
ATTENTION COMICS LOVERS!
JOIN THE UNOFFICIAL
COMICS CLUB!
MEET IN THE LIBRARY AT 3PM!
RULES
NO RUNNING
DON'T BE LATE
NO HORSEPLAY
CAR WASH
M

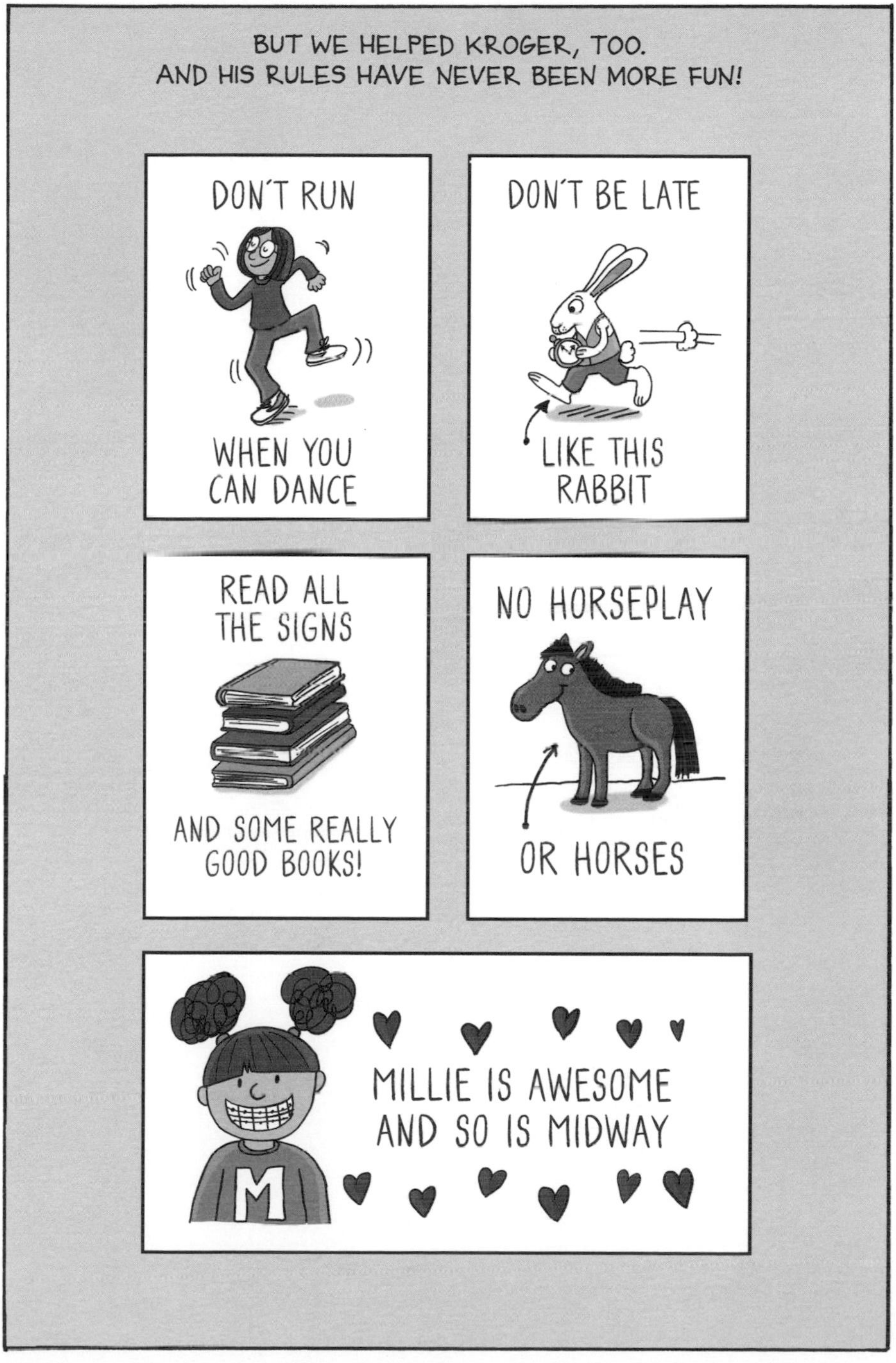
BUT WE HELPED KROGER, TOO.
AND HIS RULES HAVE NEVER BEEN MORE FUN!
DON'T RUN
WHEN YOU CAN DANCE
DON'T BE LATE
LIKE THIS RABBIT
READ ALL THE SIGNS
AND SOME REALLY GOOD BOOKS!
NO HORSEPLAY
OR HORSES
M
MILLIE IS AWESOME AND SO IS MIDWAY

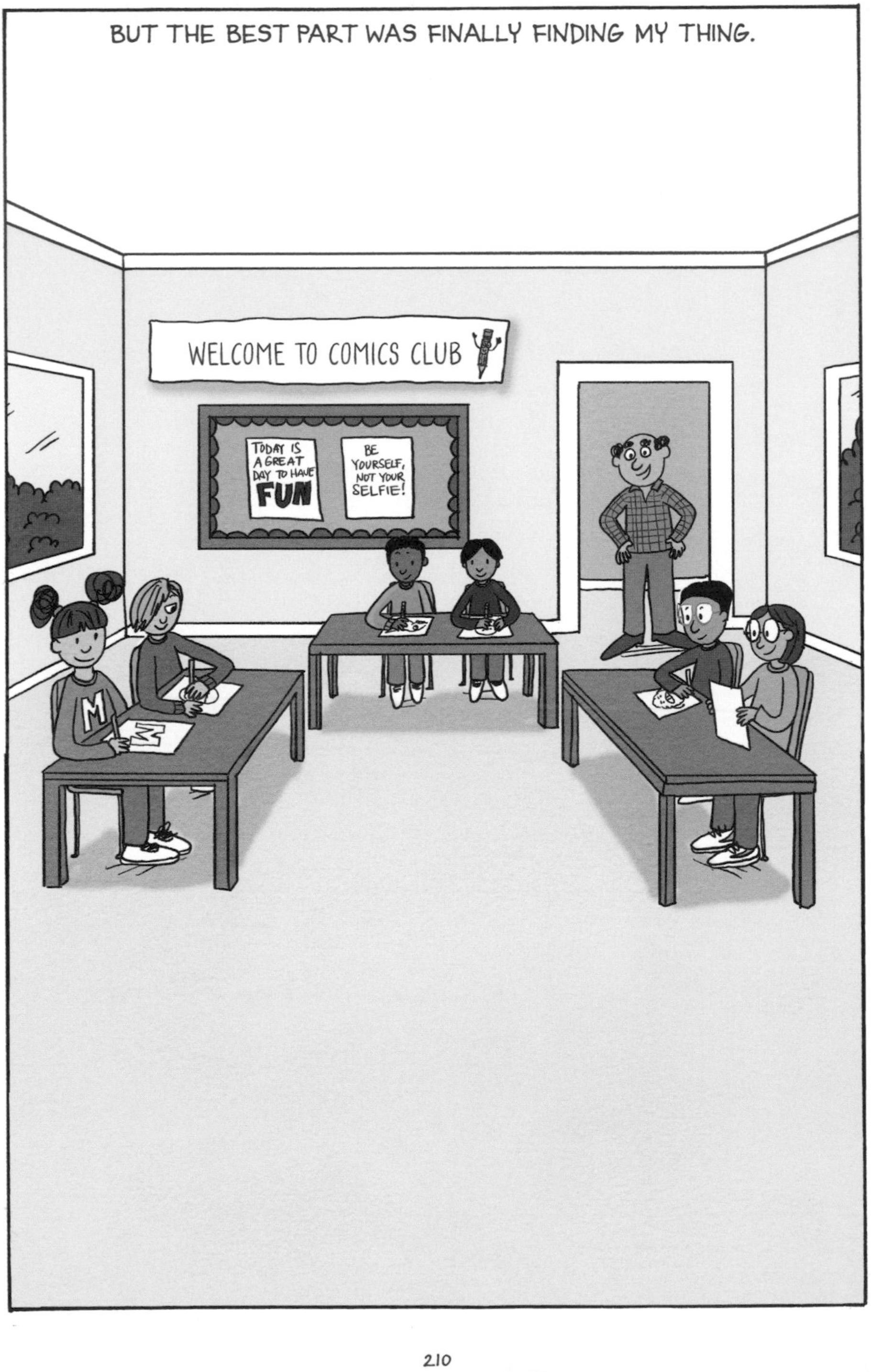
BUT THE BEST PART WAS FINALLY FINDING MY THING.
WELCOME TO COMICS CLUB
TODAY IS A GREAT DAY TO HAVE FUN
BE YOURSELF, NOT YOUR SELFIE!
M

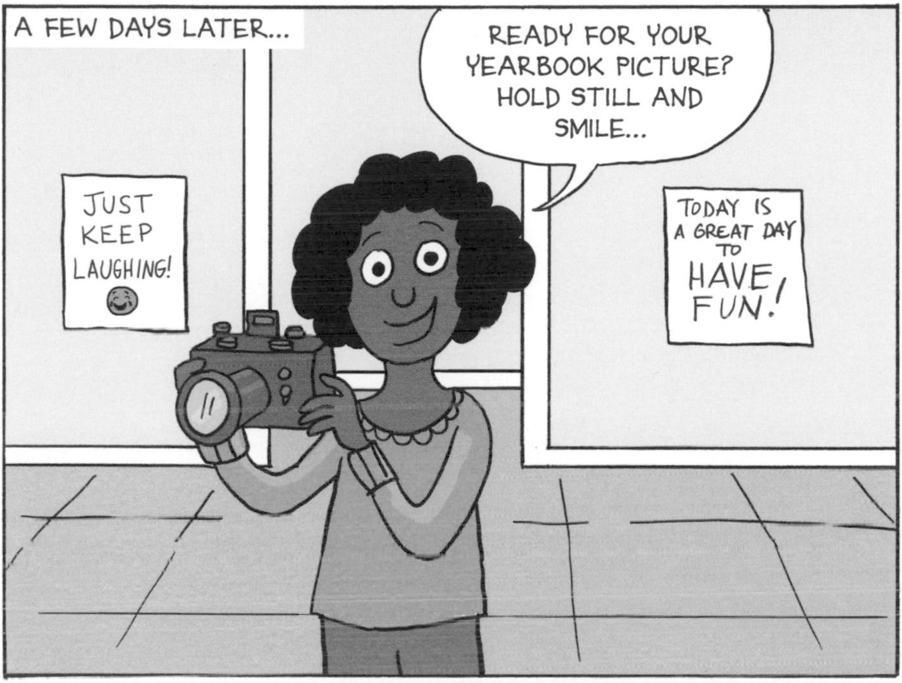
A FEW DAYS LATER...
READY FOR YOUR YEARBOOK PICTURE? HOLD STILL AND SMILE...
JUST KEEP LAUGHING!
TODAY IS A GREAT DAY TO HAVE FUN!

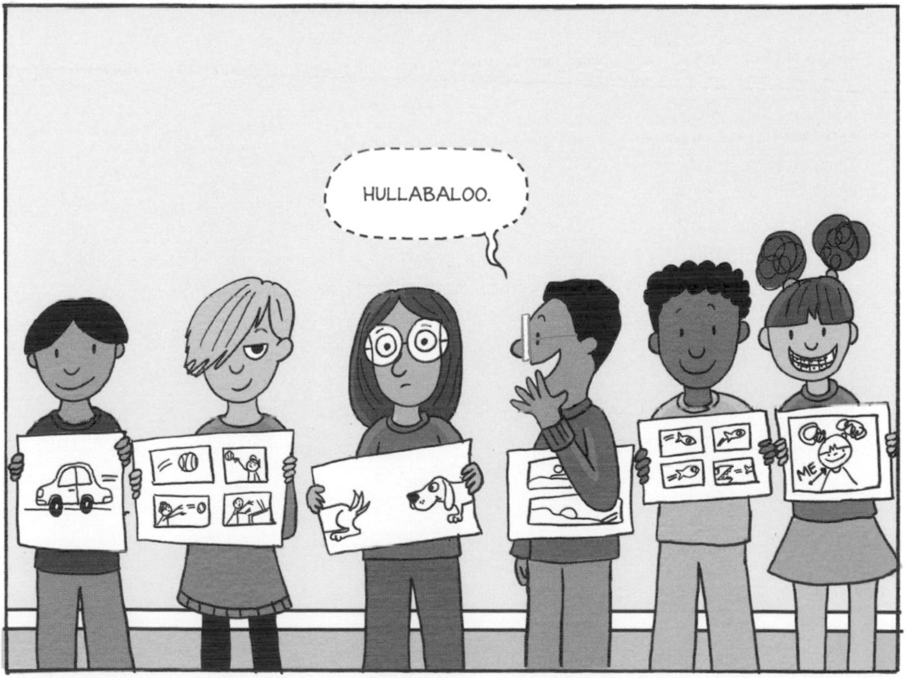
HULLABALOO.
ME

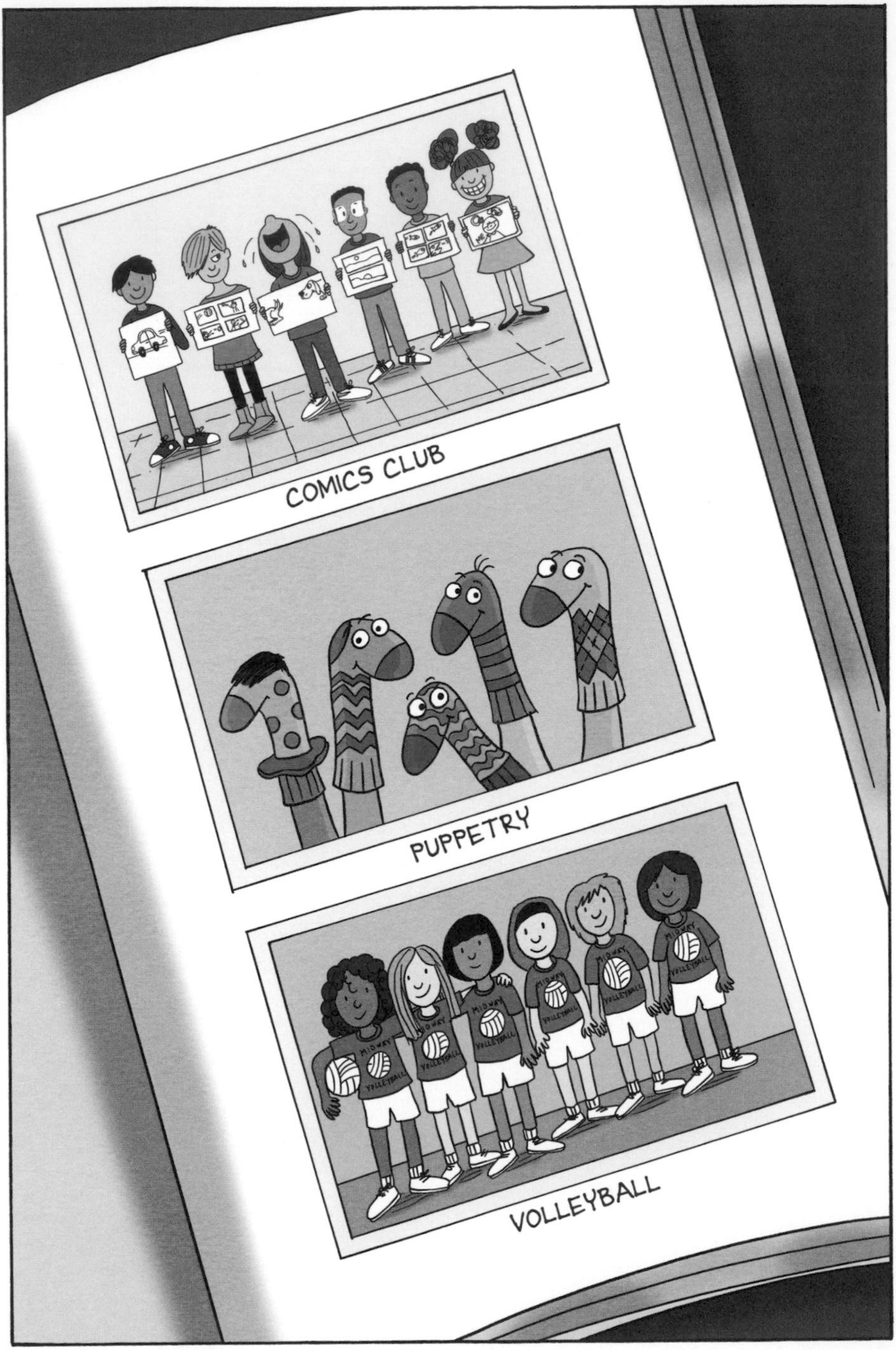
COMICS CLUB
PUPPETRY
VOLLEYBALL

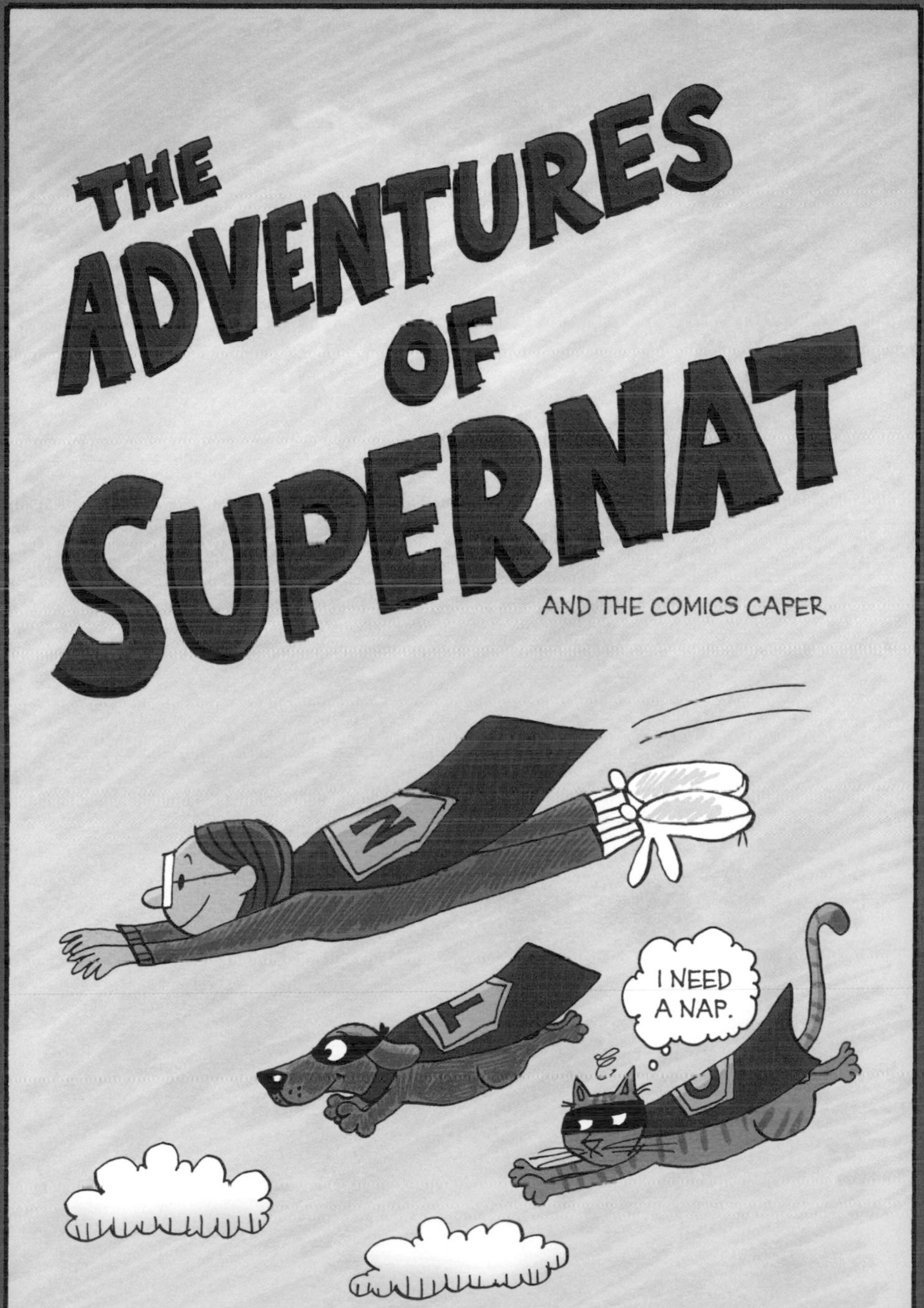
THE ADVENTURES OF SUPERNAT
AND THE COMICS CAPER
I NEED A NAP.

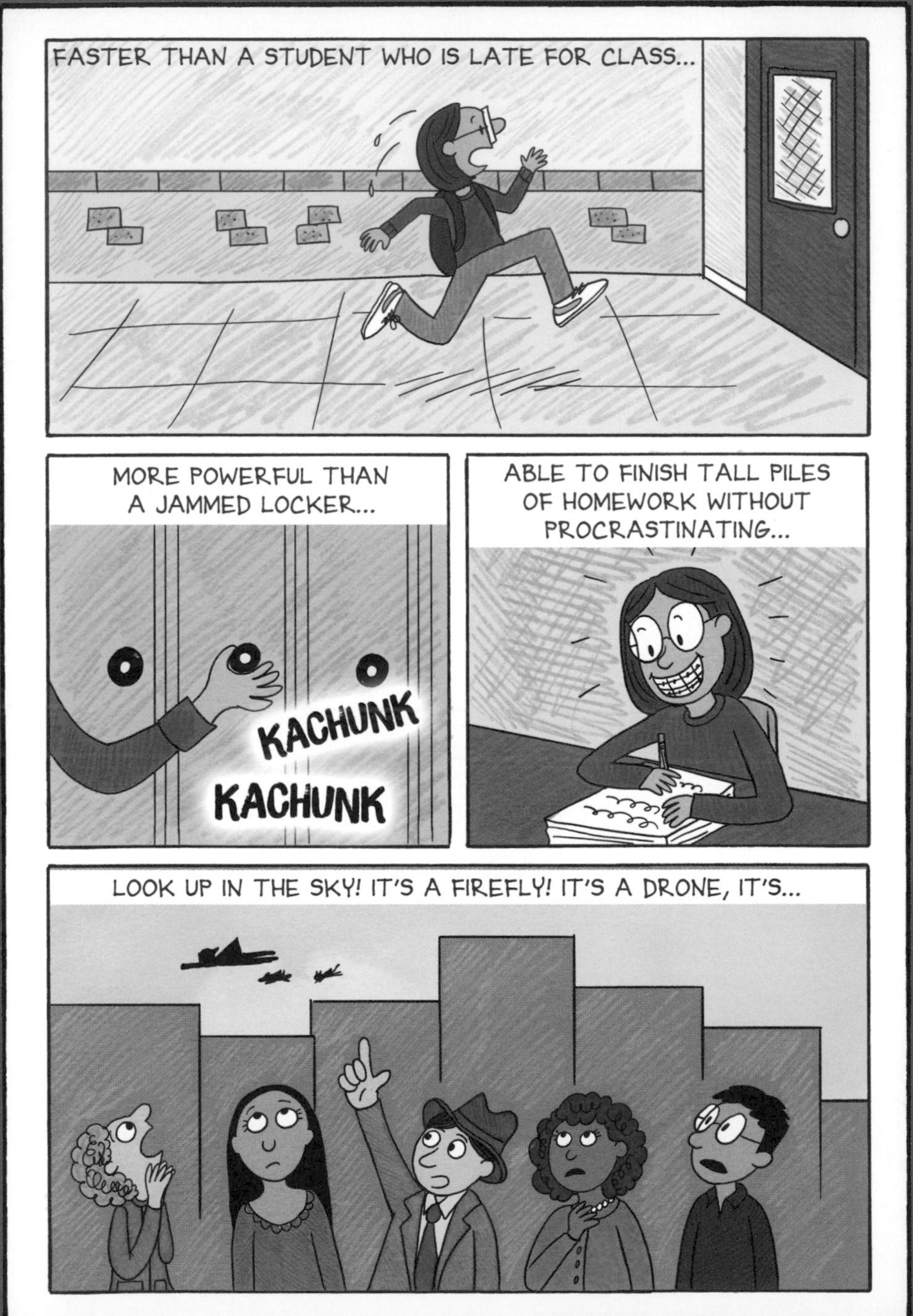
FASTER THAN A STUDENT WHO IS LATE FOR CLASS...
MORE POWERFUL THAN A JAMMED LOCKER...
KACHUNK
KACHUNK
ABLE TO FINISH TALL PILES OF HOMEWORK WITHOUT PROCRASTINATING...
LOOK UP IN THE SKY! IT'S A FIREFLY! IT'S A DRONE, IT'S...

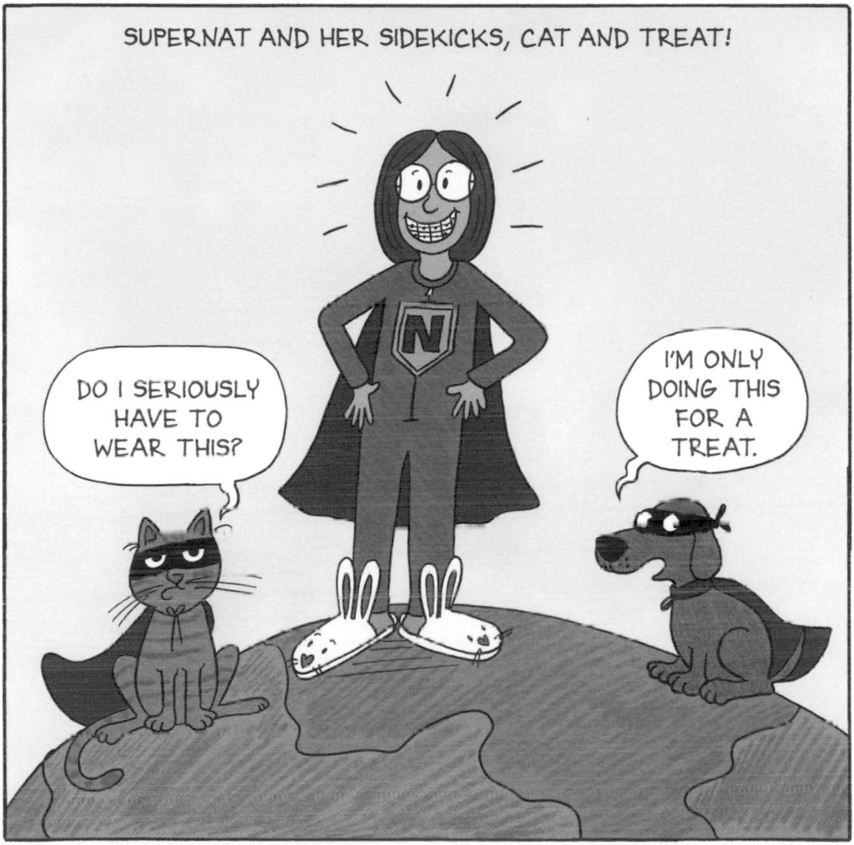
SUPERNAT AND HER SIDEKICKS, CAT AND TREAT!
DO I SERIOUSLY HAVE TO WEAR THIS?
I'M ONLY DOING THIS FOR A TREAT.

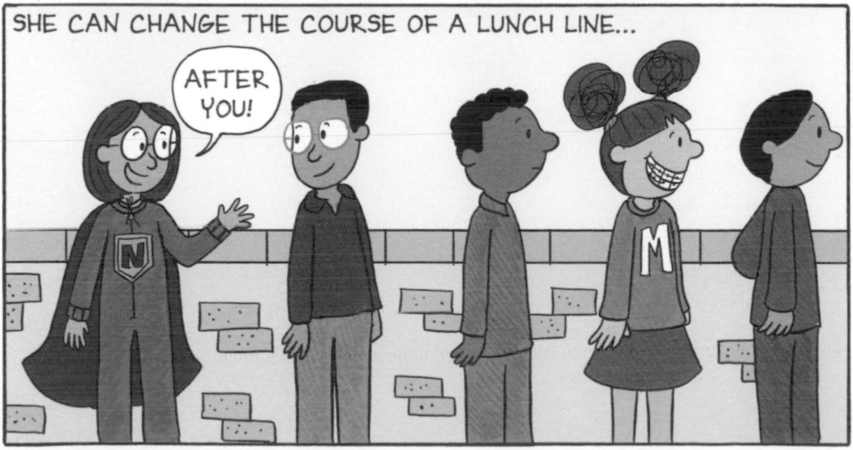
SHE CAN CHANGE THE COURSE OF A LUNCH LINE...
AFTER YOU!

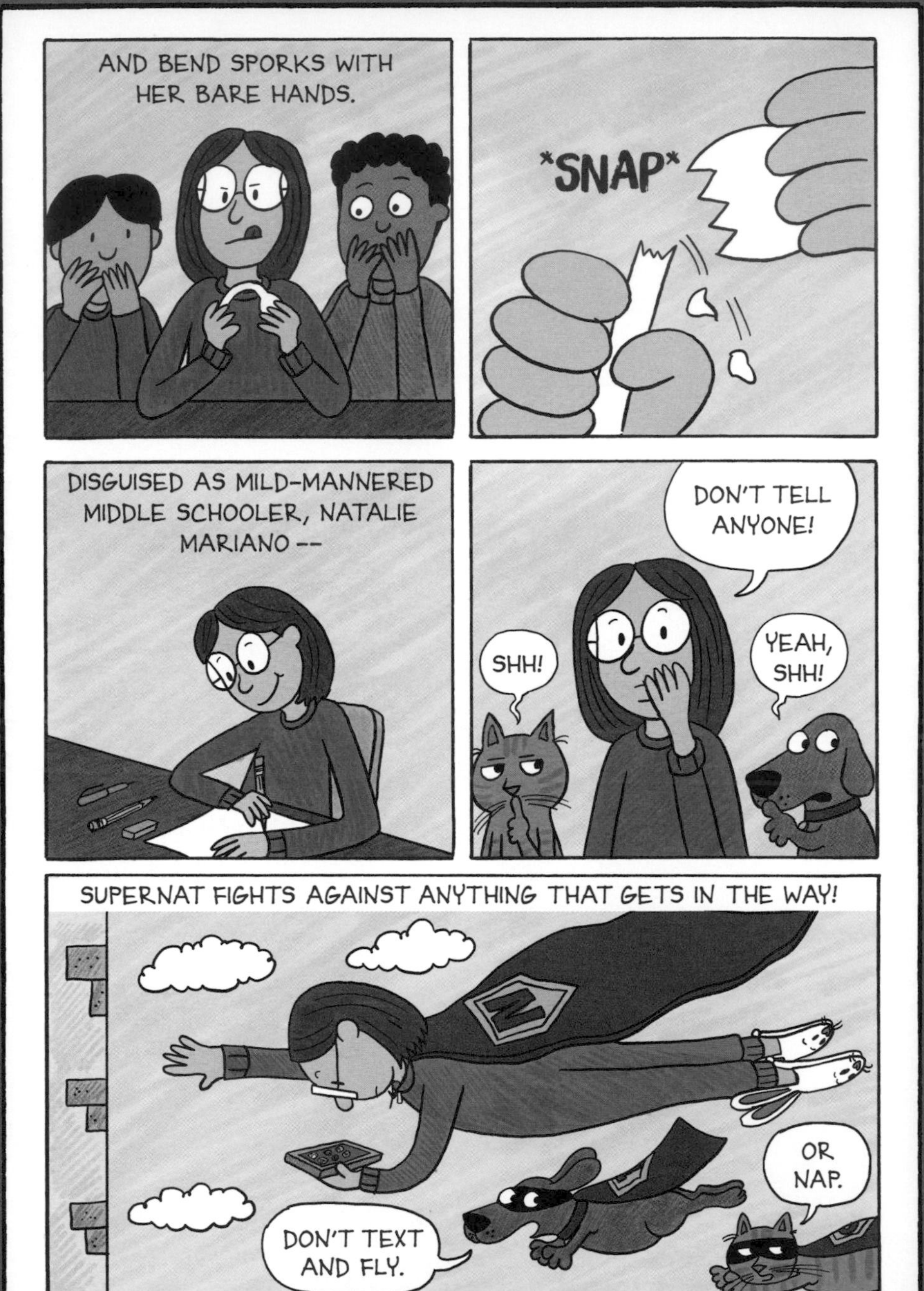
AND BEND SPORKS WITH HER BARE HANDS.
SNAP
DISGUISED AS MILD-MANNERED MIDDLE SCHOOLER, NATALIE MARIANO --
DON'T TELL ANYONE!
SHH!
YEAH, SHH!
SUPERNAT FIGHTS AGAINST ANYTHING THAT GETS IN THE WAY!
DON'T TEXT AND FLY.
OR NAP.

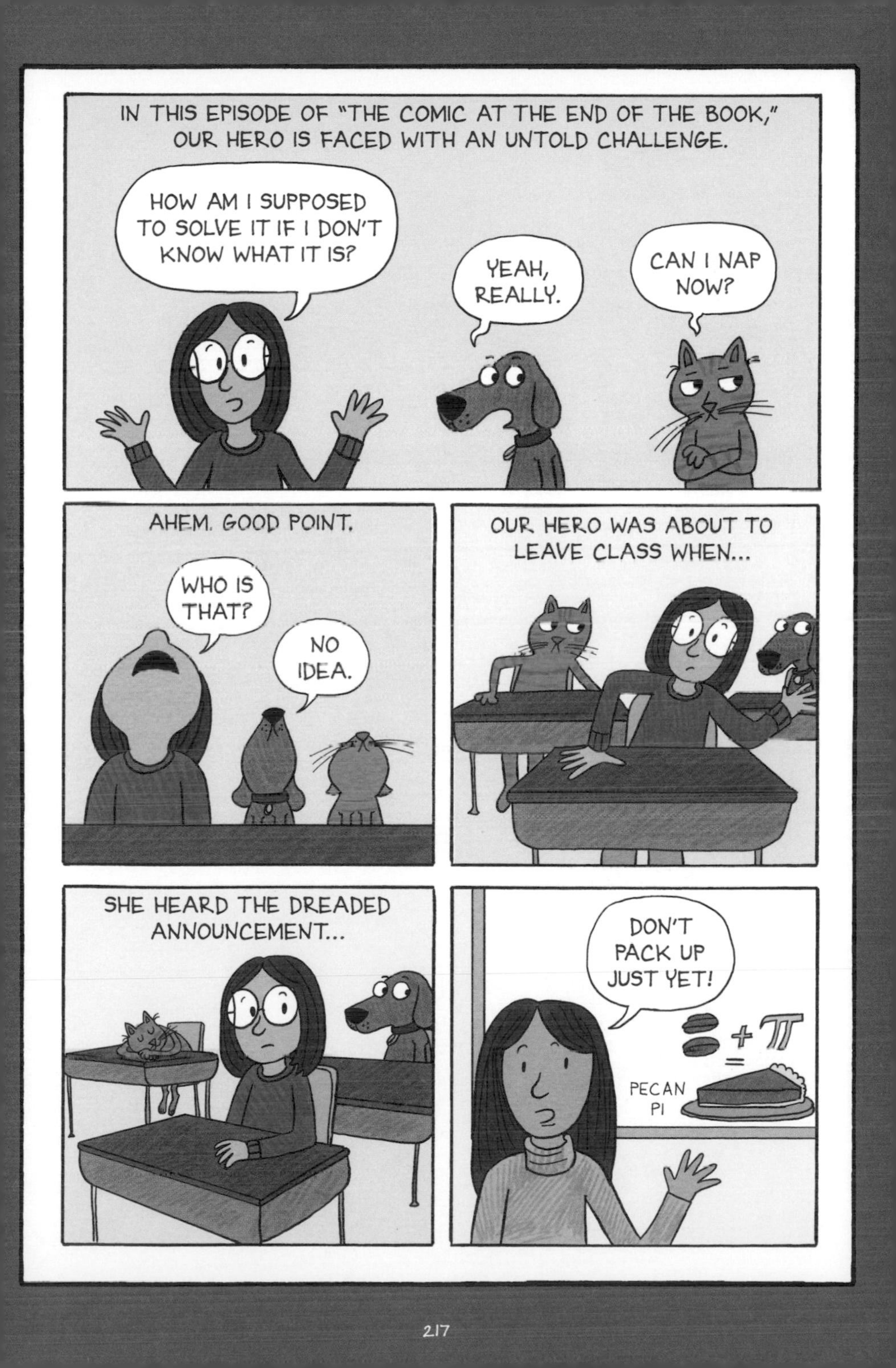
IN THIS EPISODE OF "THE COMIC AT THE END OF THE BOOK," OUR HERO IS FACED WITH AN UNTOLD CHALLENGE.
HOW AM I SUPPOSED TO SOLVE IT IF I DON'T KNOW WHAT IT IS?
YEAH, REALLY.
CAN I NAP NOW?
AHEM. GOOD POINT.
WHO IS THAT?
NO IDEA.
OUR HERO WAS ABOUT TO LEAVE CLASS WHEN...
SHE HEARD THE DREADED ANNOUNCEMENT...
DON'T PACK UP JUST YET!
PECAN PI

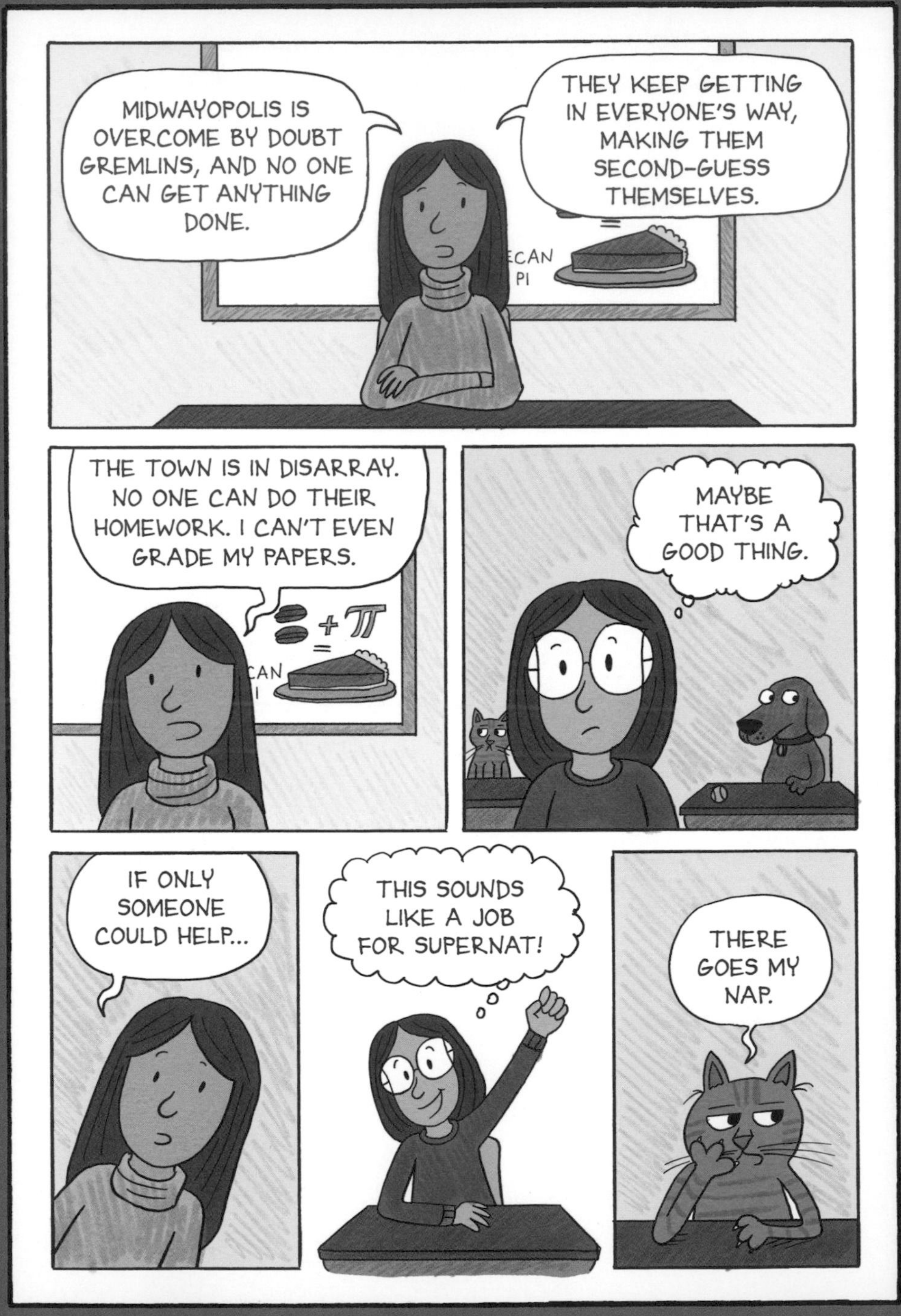
MIDWAYOPOLIS IS OVERCOME BY DOUBT GREMLINS, AND NO ONE CAN GET ANYTHING DONE.
THEY KEEP GETTING IN EVERYONE'S WAY, MAKING THEM SECOND-GUESS THEMSELVES.
ECAN PI
THE TOWN IS IN DISARRAY. NO ONE CAN DO THEIR HOMEWORK. I CAN'T EVEN GRADE MY PAPERS.
MAYBE THAT'S A GOOD THING.
IF ONLY SOMEONE COULD HELP...
THIS SOUNDS LIKE A JOB FOR SUPERNAT!
THERE GOES MY NAP.

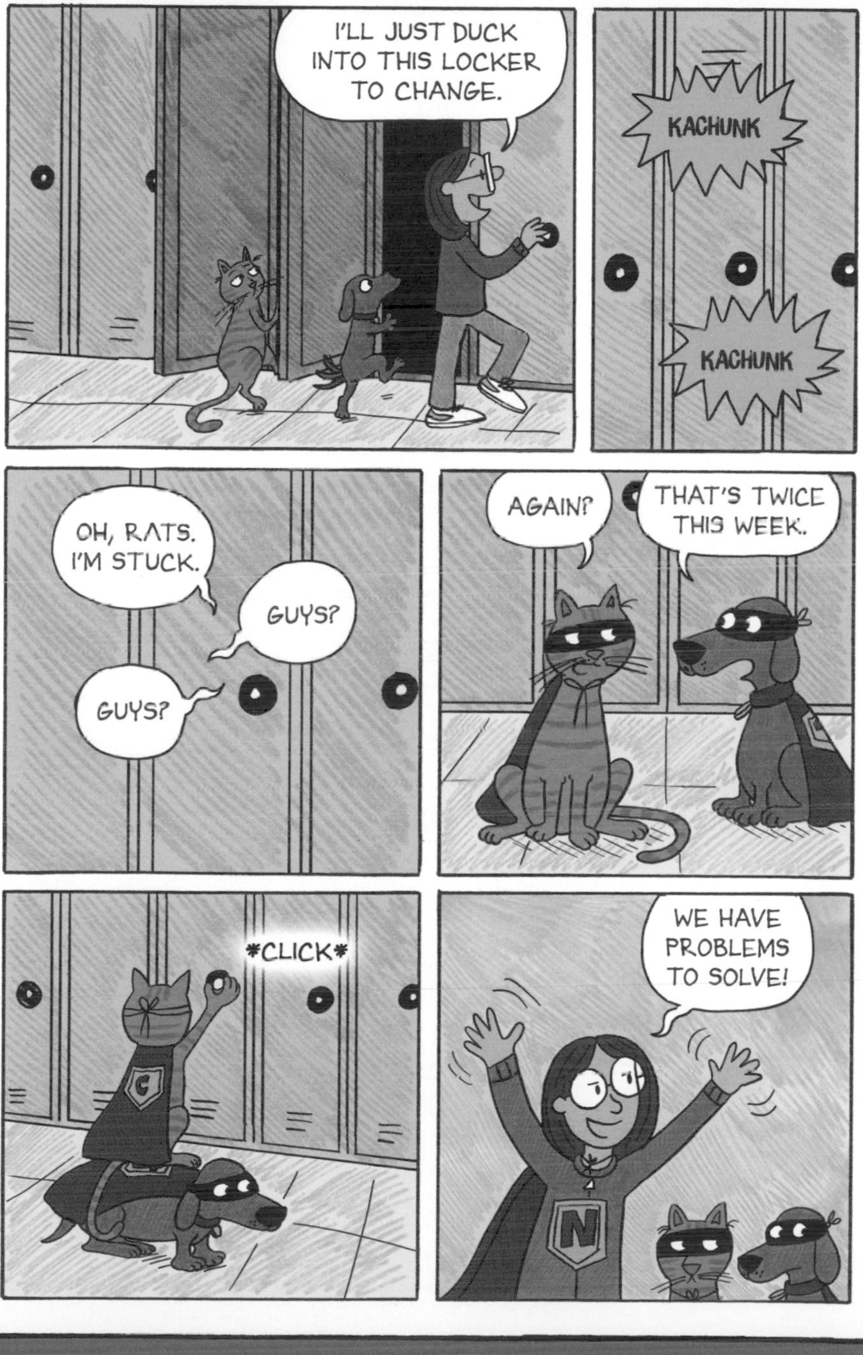
I'LL JUST DUCK INTO THIS LOCKER TO CHANGE.
KACHUNK
KACHUNK
OH, RATS. I'M STUCK.
GUYS?
GUYS?
AGAIN?
THAT'S TWICE THIS WEEK.
CLICK
WE HAVE PROBLEMS TO SOLVE!

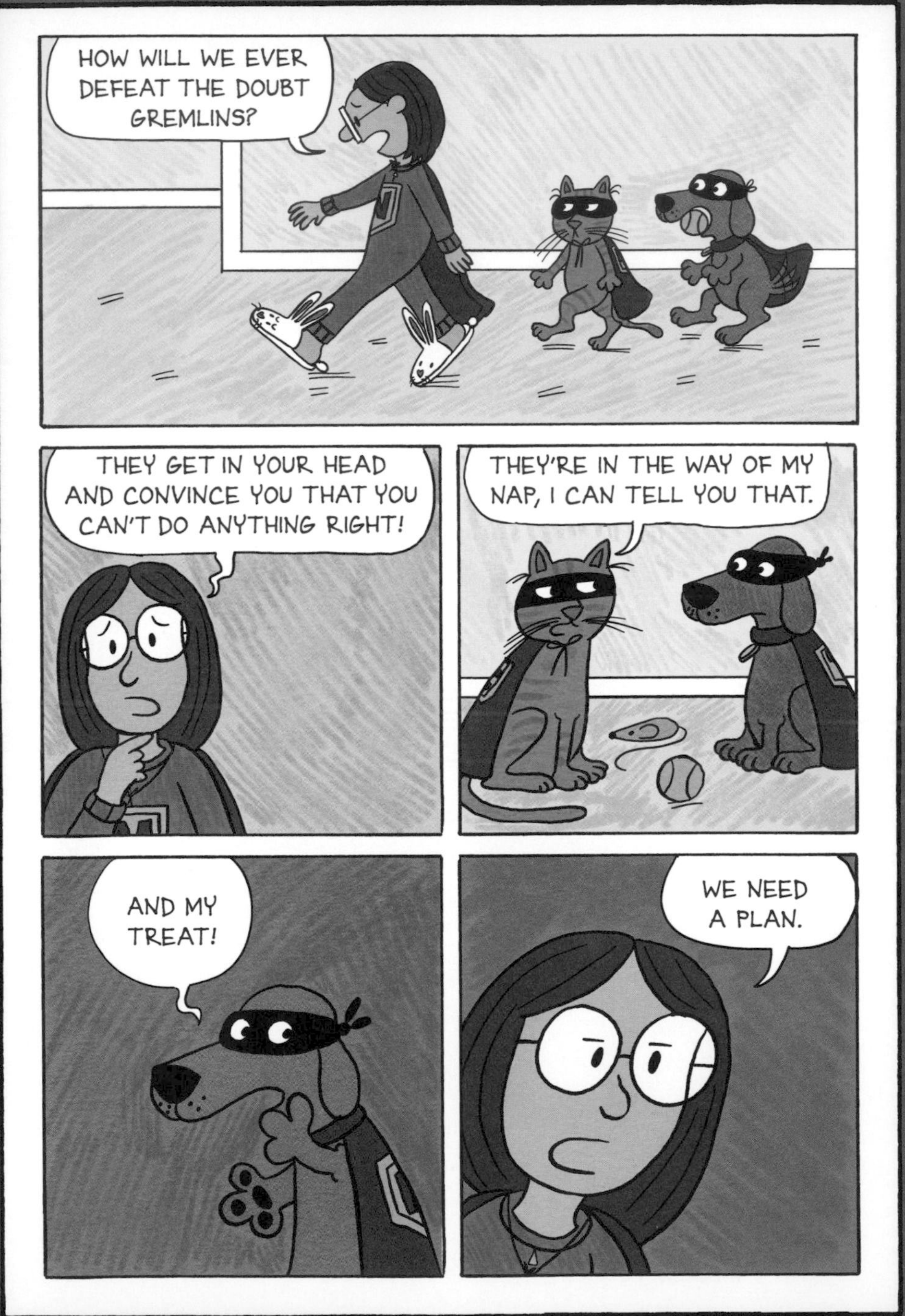
HOW WILL WE EVER DEFEAT THE DOUBT GREMLINS?
THEY GET IN YOUR HEAD AND CONVINCE YOU THAT YOU CAN'T DO ANYTHING RIGHT!
THEY'RE IN THE WAY OF MY NAP, I CAN TELL YOU THAT.
AND MY TREAT!
WE NEED A PLAN.

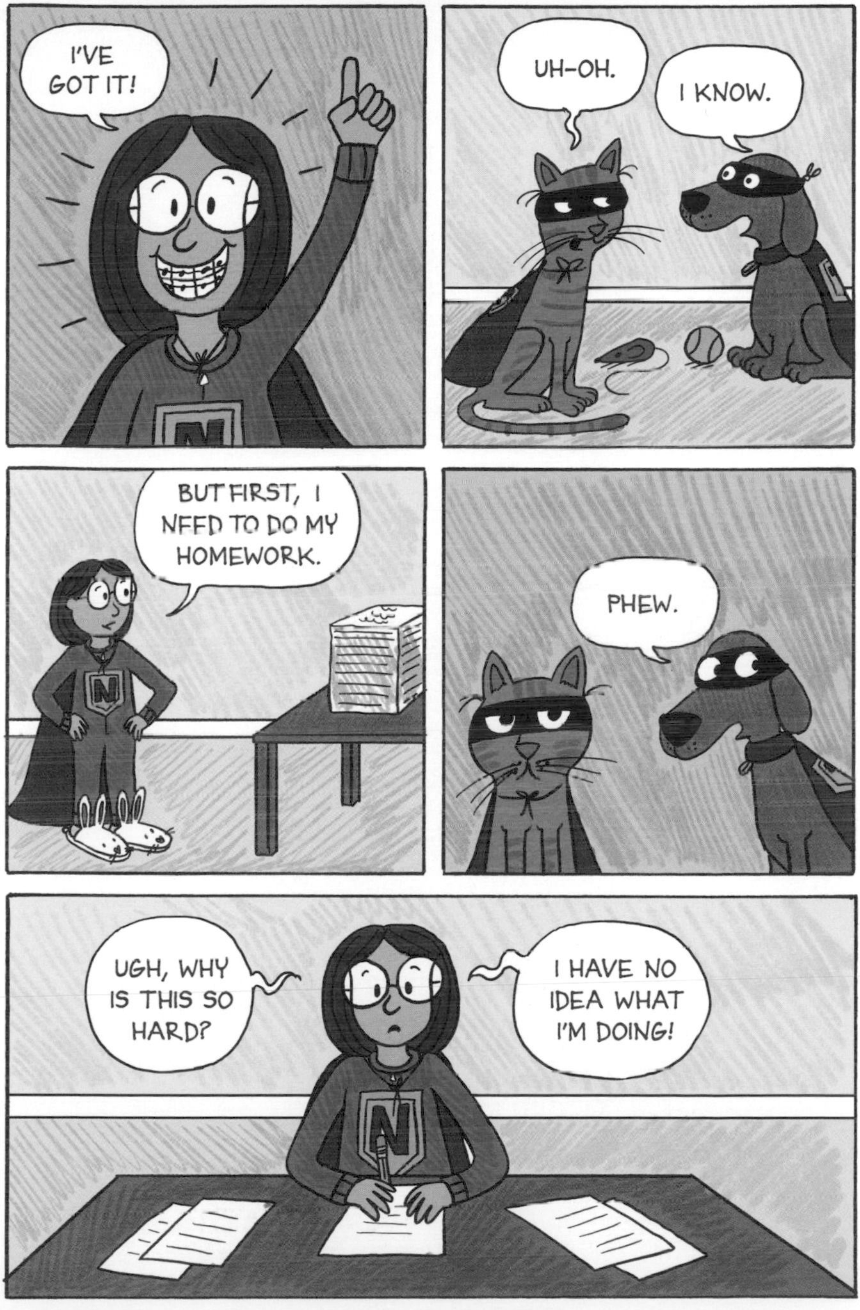
I'VE GOT IT!
UH-OH.
I KNOW.
BUT FIRST, I NEED TO DO MY HOMEWORK.
PHEW.
UGH, WHY IS THIS SO HARD?
I HAVE NO IDEA WHAT I'M DOING!

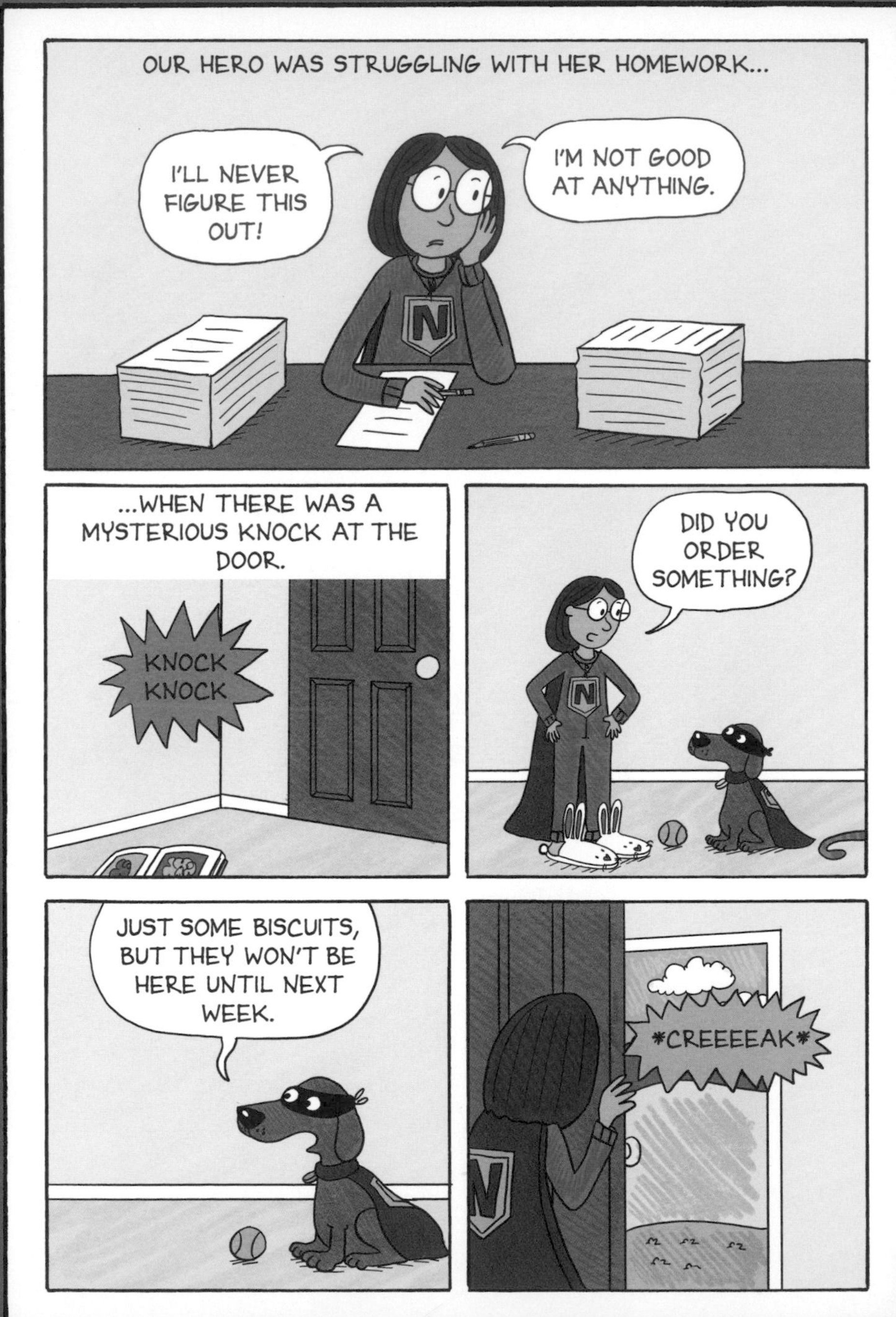
OUR HERO WAS STRUGGLING WITH HER HOMEWORK...
I'LL NEVER FIGURE THIS OUT!
I'M NOT GOOD AT ANYTHING.
...WHEN THERE WAS A MYSTERIOUS KNOCK AT THE DOOR.
KNOCK KNOCK
DID YOU ORDER SOMETHING?
JUST SOME BISCUITS, BUT THEY WON'T BE HERE UNTIL NEXT WEEK.
CREEEEAK

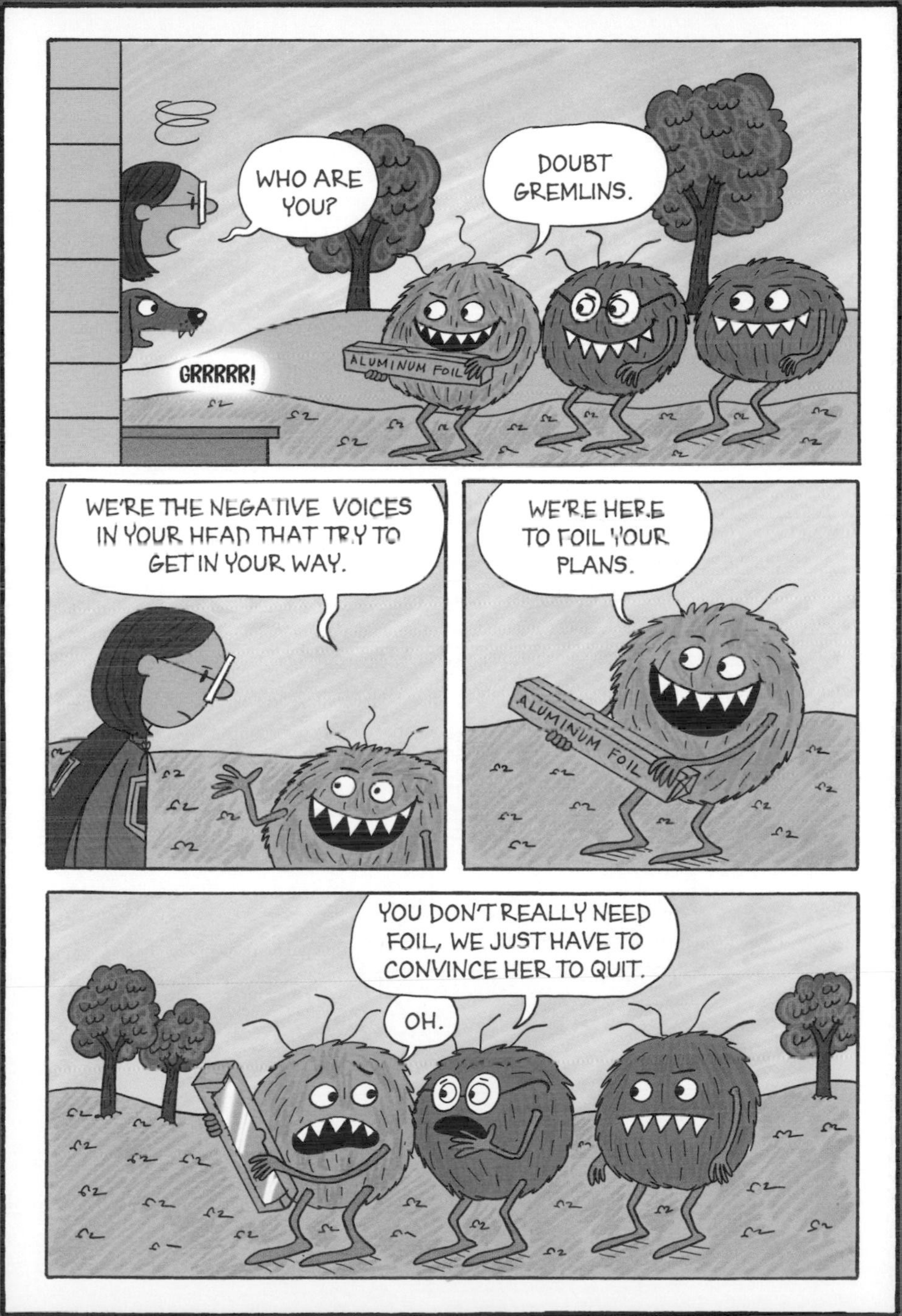
WHO ARE YOU?
DOUBT GREMLINS.
GRRRRR!
ALUMINUM FOIL
WE'RE THE NEGATIVE VOICES IN YOUR HEAD THAT TRY TO GET IN YOUR WAY.
WE'RE HERE TO FOIL YOUR PLANS.
ALUMINUM FOIL
YOU DON'T REALLY NEED FOIL, WE JUST HAVE TO CONVINCE HER TO QUIT.
OH.

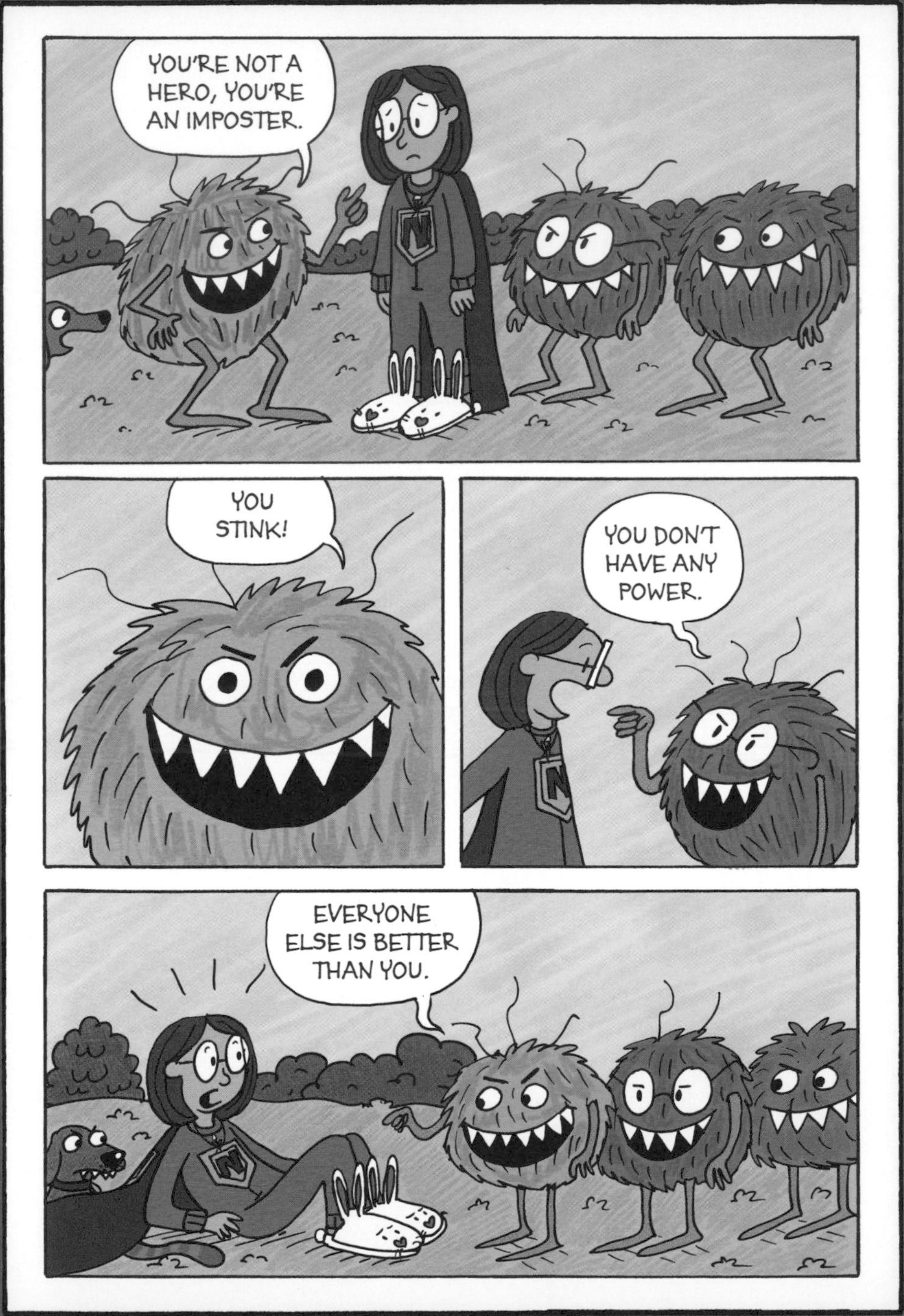
YOU'RE NOT A HERO, YOU'RE AN IMPOSTER.
YOU STINK!
YOU DON'T HAVE ANY POWER.
EVERYONE ELSE IS BETTER THAN YOU.

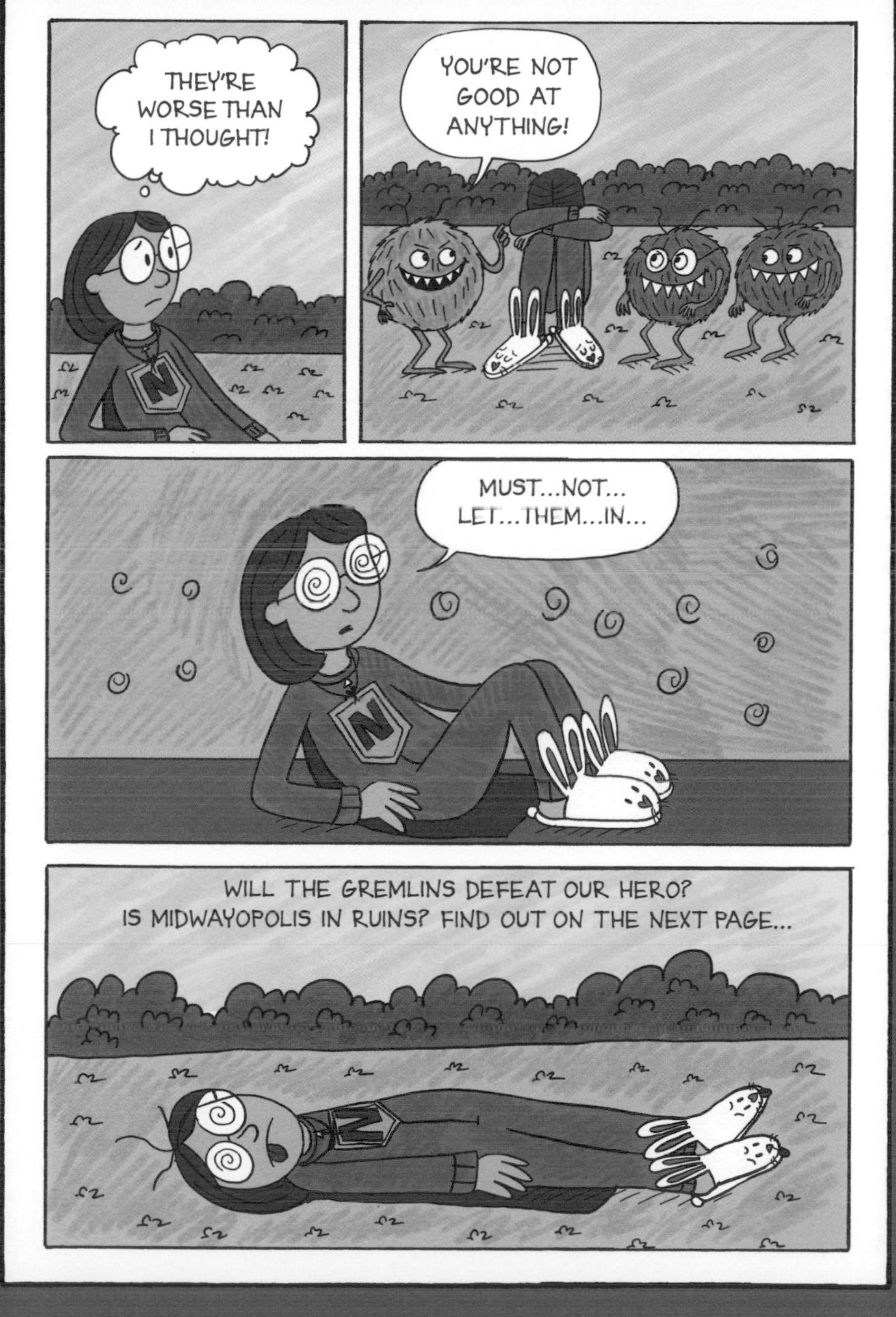
THEY'RE WORSE THAN I THOUGHT!
YOU'RE NOT GOOD AT ANYTHING!
MUST...NOT... LET...THEM...IN...
WILL THE GREMLINS DEFEAT OUR HERO? IS MIDWAYOPOLIS IN RUINS? FIND OUT ON THE NEXT PAGE...

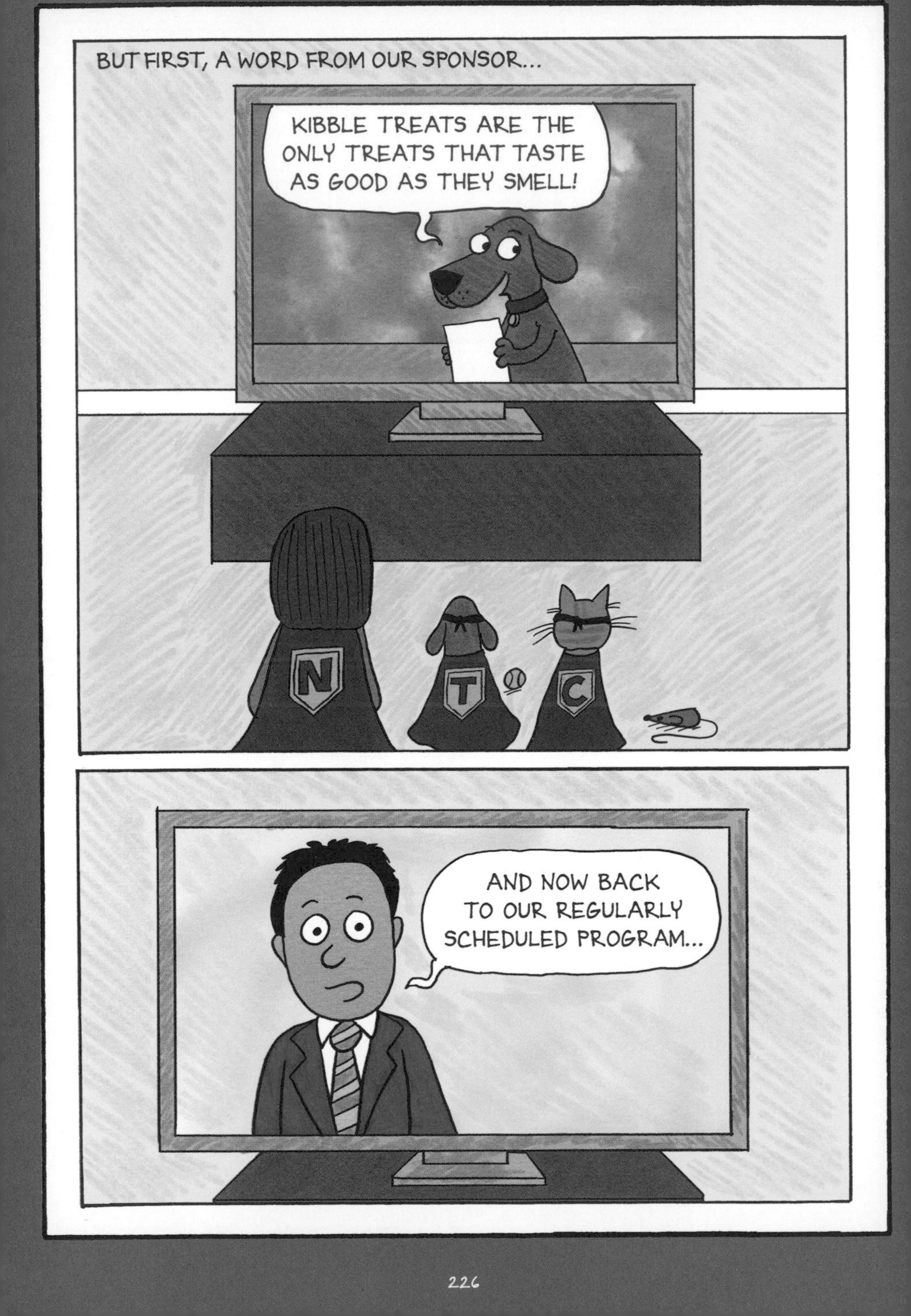
BUT FIRST, A WORD FROM OUR SPONSOR...
KIBBLE TREATS ARE THE ONLY TREATS THAT TASTE AS GOOD AS THEY SMELL!
N
T
C
AND NOW BACK TO OUR REGULARLY SCHEDULED PROGRAM...

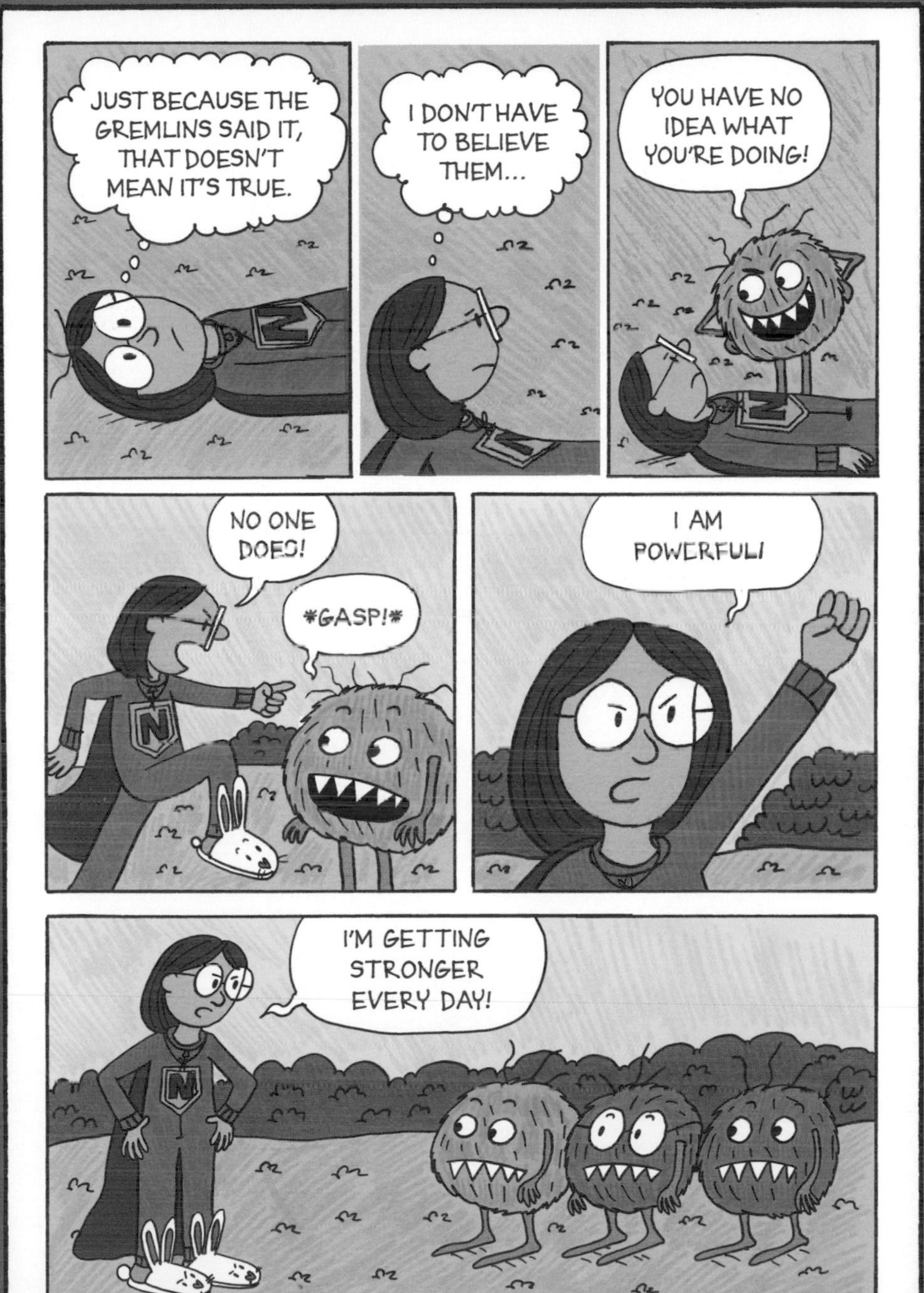
JUST BECAUSE THE GREMLINS SAID IT, THAT DOESN'T MEAN IT'S TRUE.
I DON'T HAVE TO BELIEVE THEM...
YOU HAVE NO IDEA WHAT YOU'RE DOING!
NO ONE DOES!
GASP!
I AM POWERFUL!
I'M GETTING STRONGER EVERY DAY!

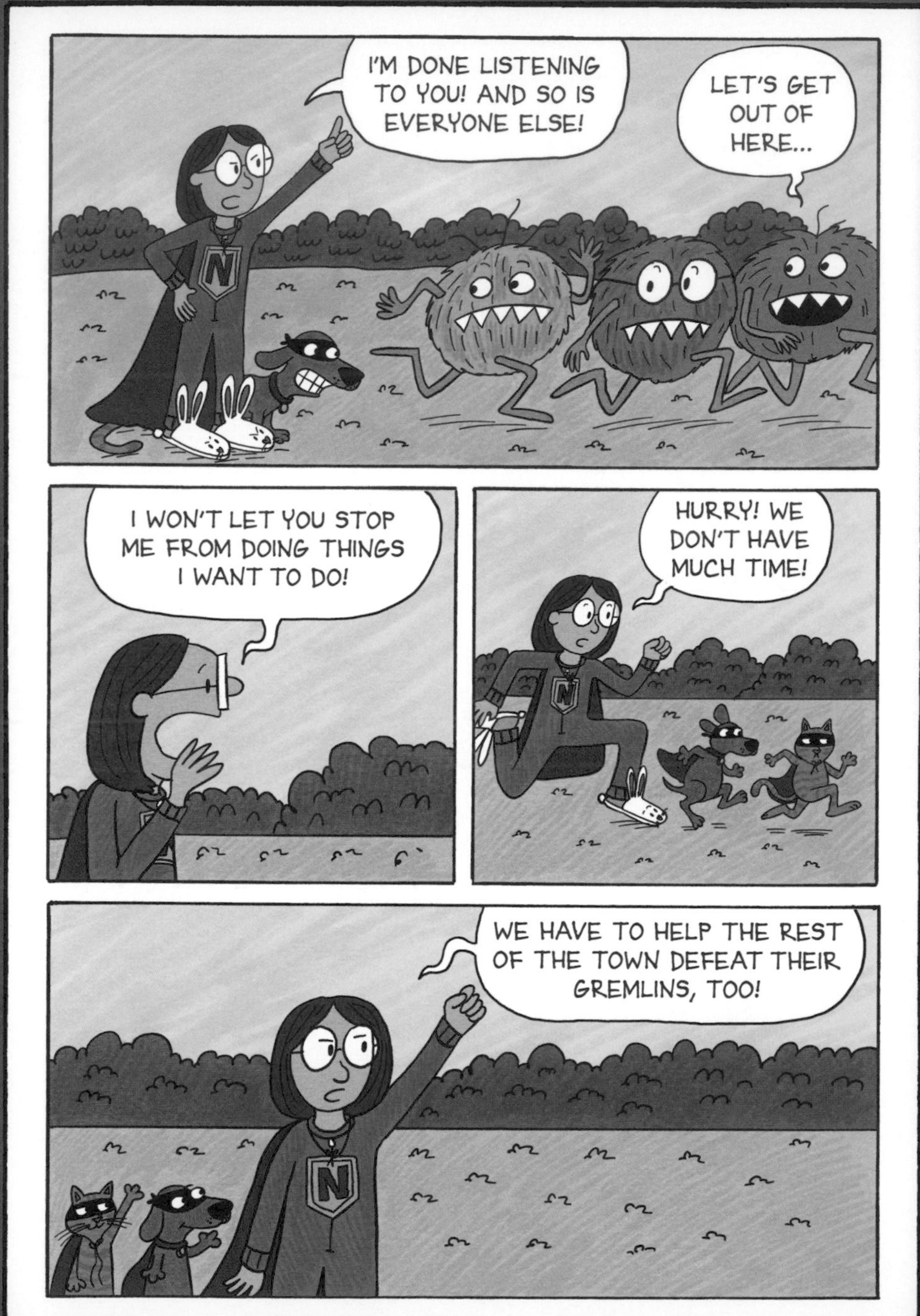
I'M DONE LISTENING TO YOU! AND SO IS EVERYONE ELSE!
LET'S GET OUT OF HERE...
I WON'T LET YOU STOP ME FROM DOING THINGS I WANT TO DO!
HURRY! WE DON'T HAVE MUCH TIME!
WE HAVE TO HELP THE REST OF THE TOWN DEFEAT THEIR GREMLINS, TOO!

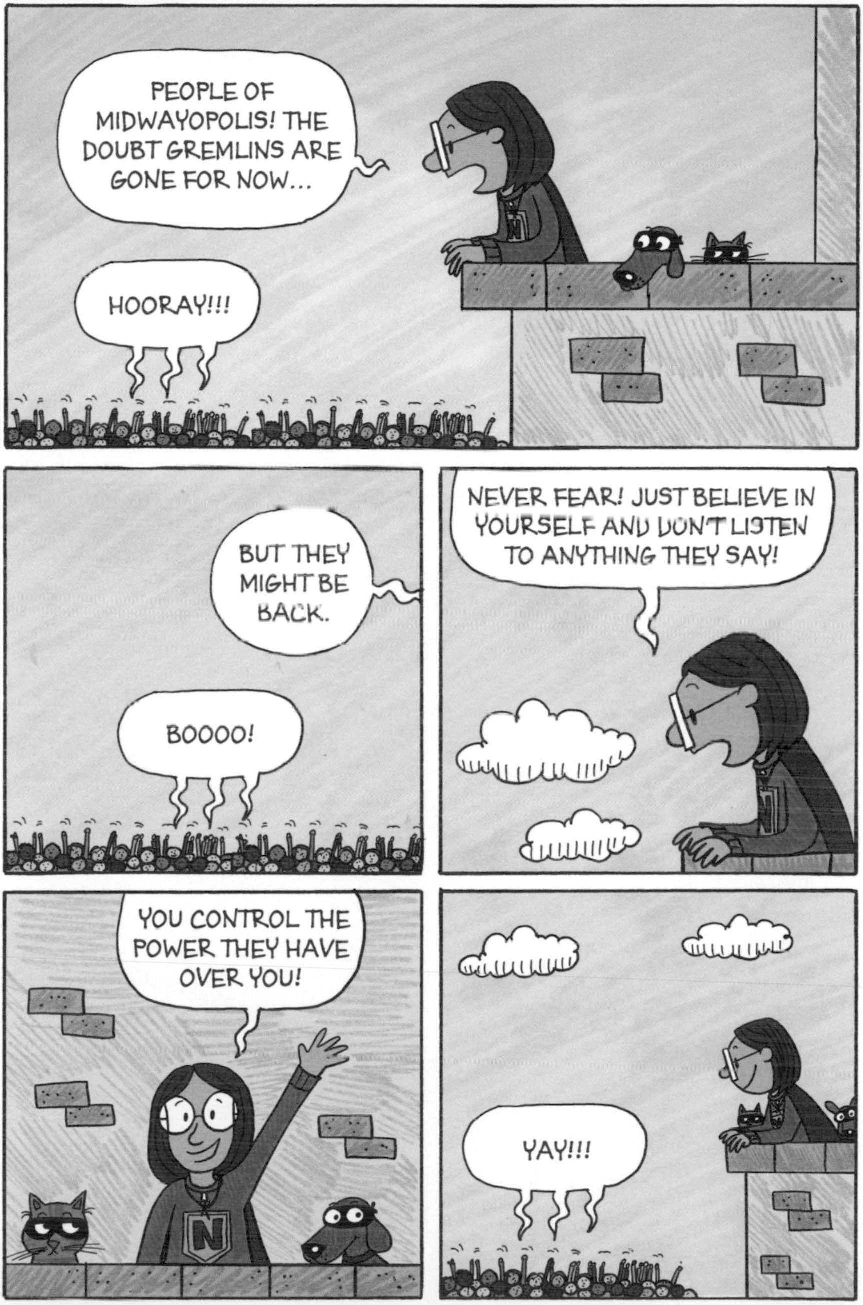
PEOPLE OF MIDWAYOPOLIS! THE DOUBT GREMLINS ARE GONE FOR NOW...
HOORAY!!!
BUT THEY MIGHT BE BACK.
BOOOO!
NEVER FEAR! JUST BELIEVE IN YOURSELF AND DON'T LISTEN TO ANYTHING THEY SAY!
YOU CONTROL THE POWER THEY HAVE OVER YOU!
YAY!!!

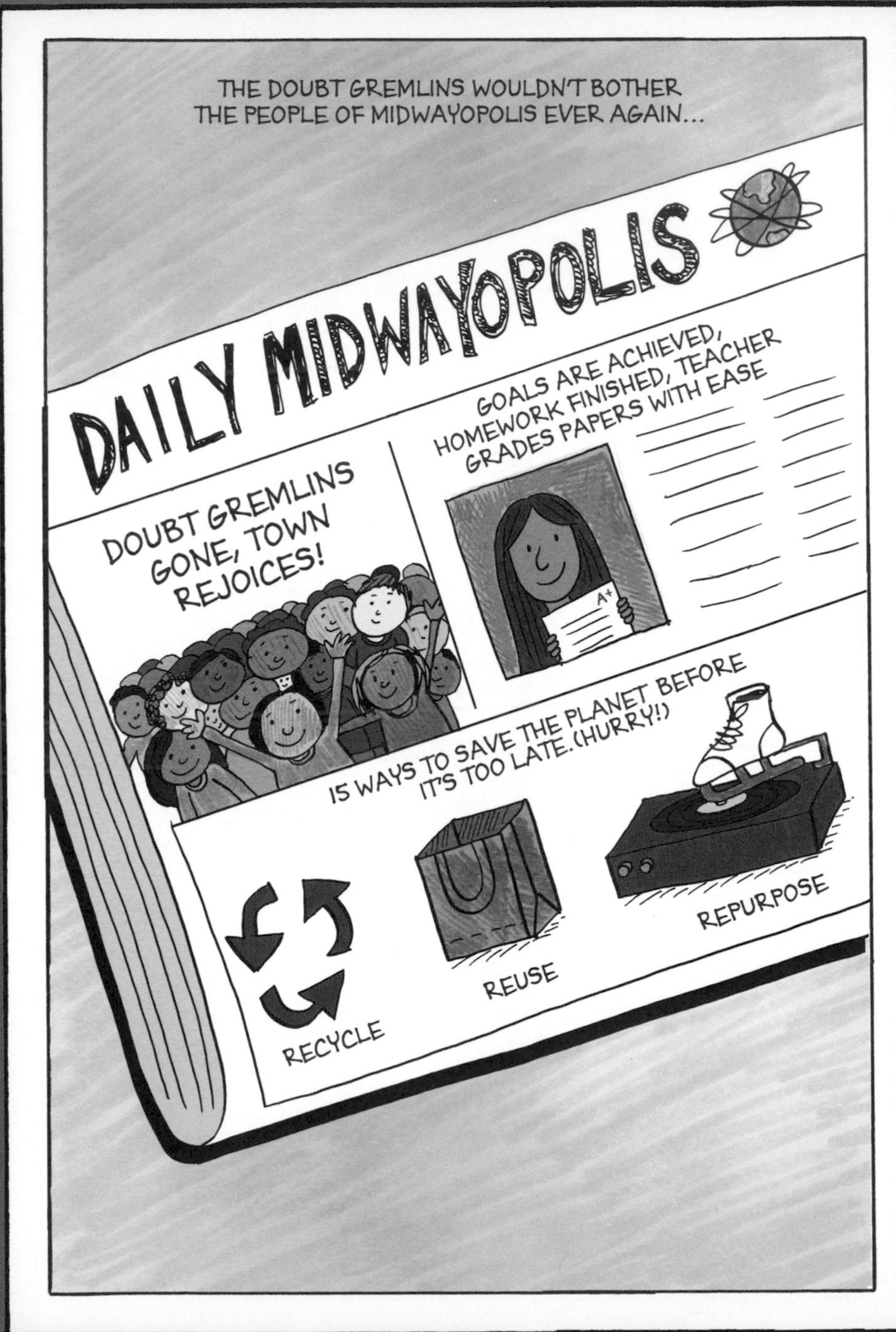
THE DOUBT GREMLINS WOULDN'T BOTHER THE PEOPLE OF MIDWAYOPOLIS EVER AGAIN...
DAILY MIDWAYOPOLIS
GOALS ARE ACHIEVED, HOMEWORK FINISHED, TEACHER GRADES PAPERS WITH EASE
DOUBT GREMLINS GONE, TOWN REJOICES!
A+
15 WAYS TO SAVE THE PLANET BEFORE IT'S TOO LATE. (HURRY!)
RECYCLE
REUSE
REPURPOSE

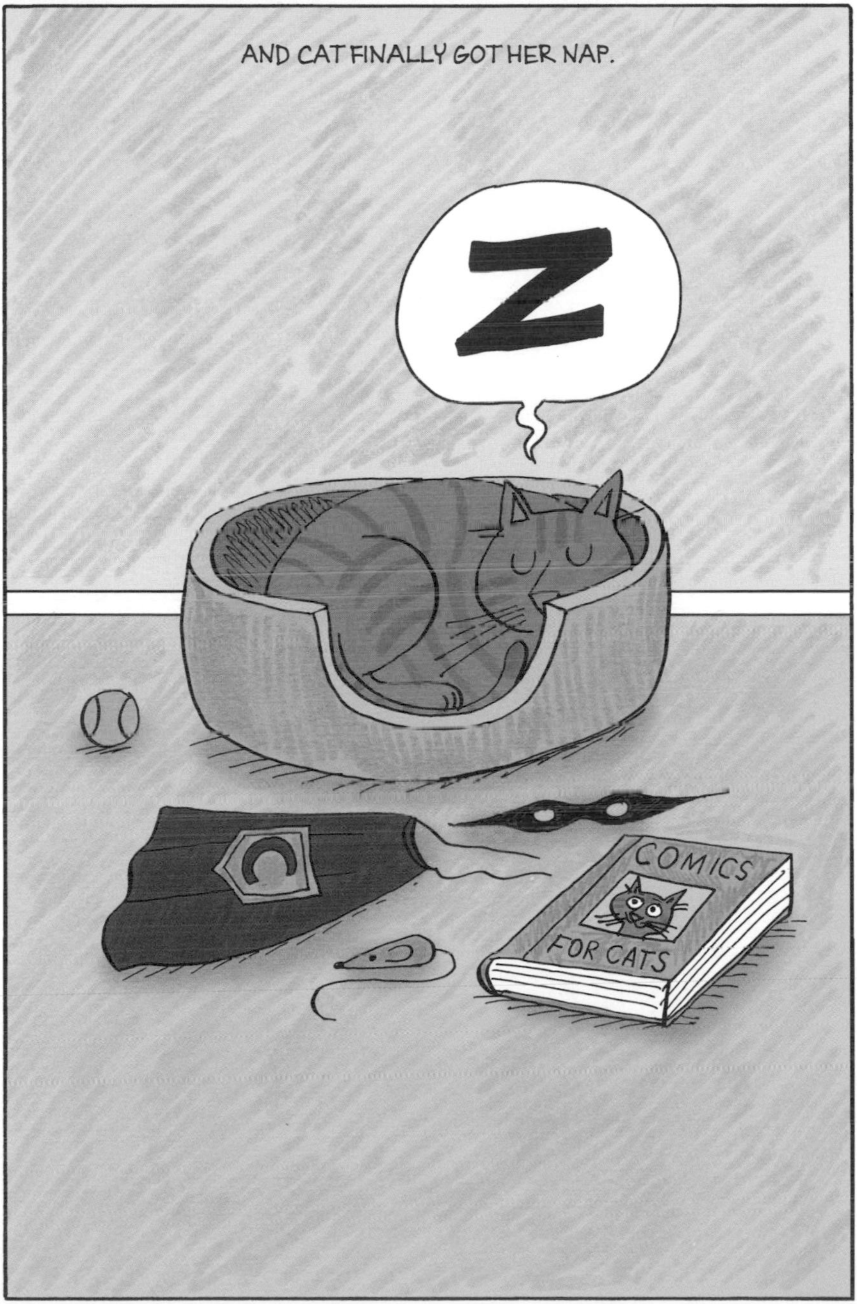
AND CAT FINALLY GOT HER NAP.
Z
COMICS
FOR CATS

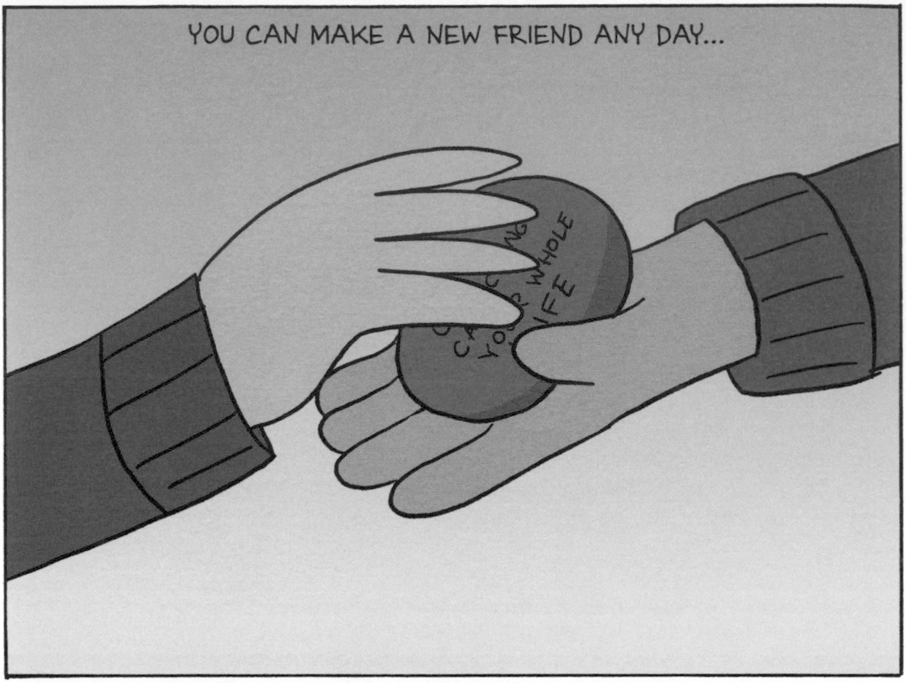
YOU CAN MAKE A NEW FRIEND ANY DAY...

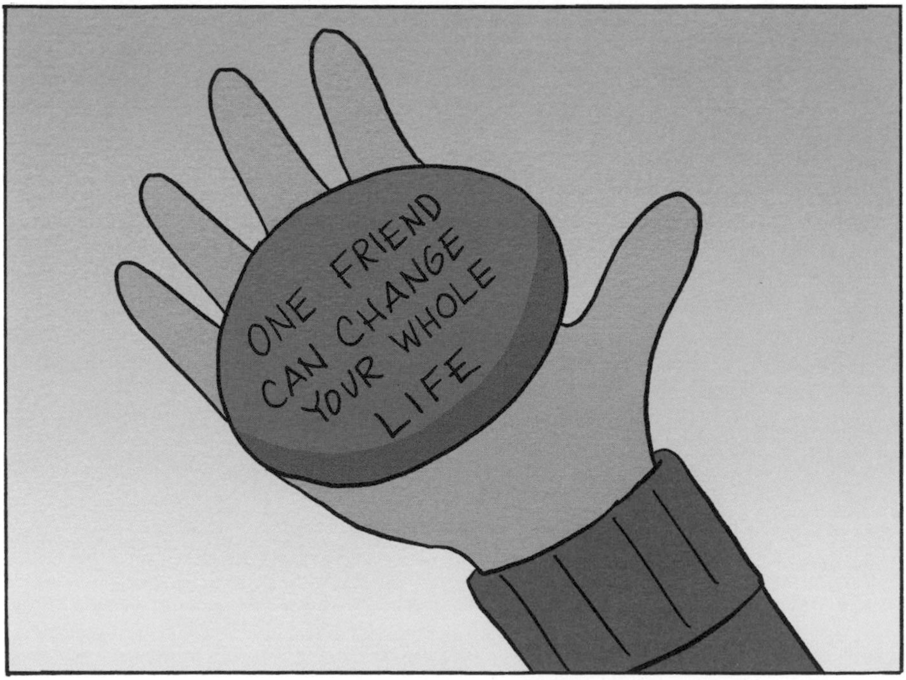
ONE FRIEND
CAN CHANGE
YOUR WHOLE
LIFE

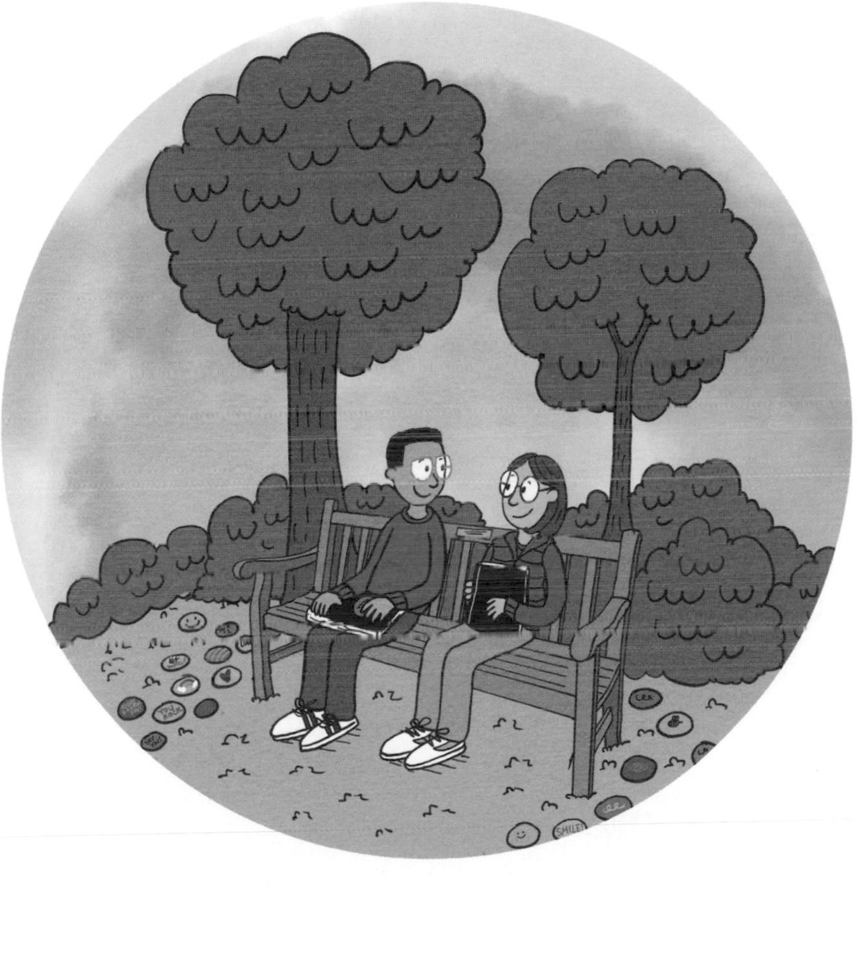
SMILE!

HOW TO DEAL WITH DOUBT GREMLINS

1. REALIZE THAT WHILE THEY MIGHT SHOW UP, THEY DON'T NEED TO RUN THE SHOW.

2. MEET YOUR GREMLINS. DRAW THEM, NAME THEM, WRITE WHAT THEY SAY. ONCE YOU GET TO KNOW THEM, THEY ARE MUCH MORE MANAGEABLE.

3. ONCE YOU'VE INTRODUCED YOURSELF, KINDLY ASK THEM TO TAKE A SEAT. YOU HAVE WORK TO DO. GIVE THEM SOME BOOKS OR PUZZLES TO KEEP THEM BUSY. THEY MAY NEVER GO AWAY ENTIRELY, BUT OVER TIME YOU'LL RECOGNIZE THE SOUND OF THEIR FOOTSTEPS, AND YOU CAN GENTLY MOVE THEM OUT OF YOUR WAY.

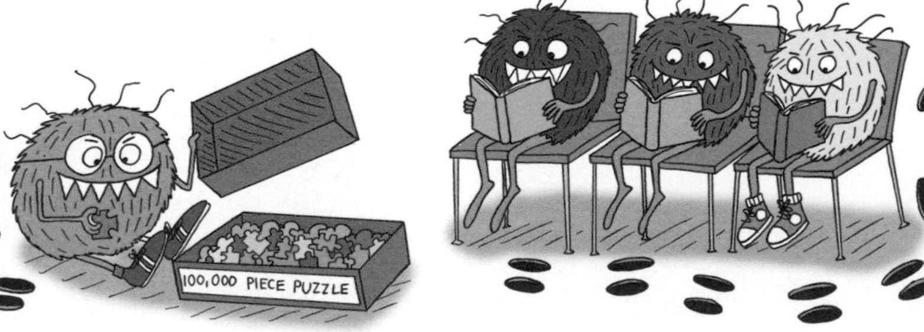
100,000 PIECE PUZZLE

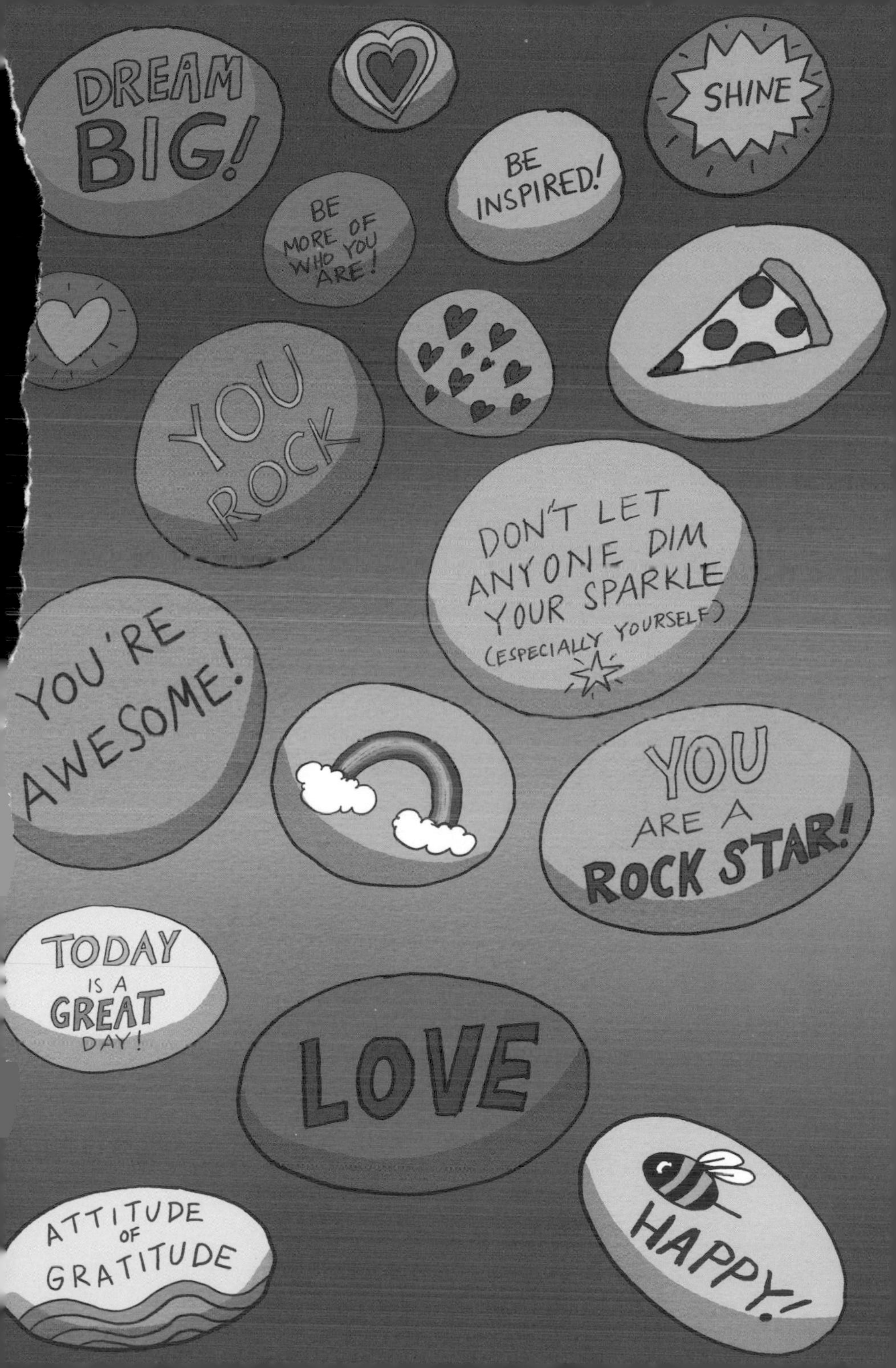
DREAM BIG!
SHINE
BE INSPIRED!
BE MORE OF WHO YOU ARE!
YOU ROCK
DON'T LET ANYONE DIM YOUR SPARKLE (ESPECIALLY YOURSELF)
YOU'RE AWESOME!
YOU ARE A ROCK STAR!
TODAY IS A GREAT DAY!
LOVE
ATTITUDE OF GRATITUDE
HAPPY!

Photo credit: Don Hamerman

MARIA SCRIVAN is a *New York Times* bestselling author, award-winning syndicated cartoonist, and speaker based in Greenwich, Connecticut. Her laugh-out-loud comic, *Half Full*, appears daily in newspapers nationwide and on gocomics.com. Maria licenses her work for greeting cards, and her cartoons have appeared in *MAD Magazine*, *Parade*, and many other publications. *Nat Enough*, her debut graphic novel, was an instant *New York Times* bestseller, and the follow-ups, *Forget Me Nat* and *Absolutely Nat*, also released to great acclaim. Learn more about Maria at mariascrivan.com.